Deputy Keeper of Public Records in   Ireland

Deputy Keeper of Public Records in Ireland

sixteenth report

Deputy Keeper of Public Records in Ireland

Deputy Keeper of Public Records in Ireland
sixteenth report

ISBN/EAN: 9783742812346

Manufactured in Europe, USA, Canada, Australia, Japa

Cover: Foto ©Andreas Hilbeck / pixelio.de

Manufactured and distributed by brebook publishing software
(www.brebook.com)

Deputy Keeper of Public Records in   Ireland

Deputy Keeper of Public Records in Ireland

CONTENTS.

THE SIXTEENTH REPORT

DEPUTY KEEPER OF THE PUBLIC RECORDS

IN IRELAND.

TO THE RIGHT HONORABLE JOHN POYNTZ,
EARL SPENCER, K.G.,

LORD LIEUTENANT-GENERAL AND GENERAL GOVERNOR OF IRELAND.

MAY IT PLEASE YOUR EXCELLENCY,

1. There were received into this department, during the year 1883, from the Record and Writ Office of the Chancery Division of the High Court :

Record and Writ Office, Chancery.

Records.	Vols.	Bdls.	Dates.
Orders Lodged,	16	—	1862
Masters' Orders,	11	—	1862
Rule Books,	12	—	1879–1882
Receiver' Accounts,	10	—	1883
Deed Rolls,	.	6	1830–1883
Patent Rolls,	—	3	1806–1882
Petitions,	8	—	1862
Reports,	6	—	1867
Chancery General Hearing Books,	8	—	1864–1867
Petitions of Appeal and Answers,	2	—	1862
Landed Estates Court Certificates,	1	—	1860–1882
Court of Appeal Hearing Book,	1	—	1867–1884
Rolls Motion Book,	1	—	1862–1882
Rolls Petition Hearing Book,	1	—	1862–1882
Rolls Hearing Book,	1	—	1862–1882
Draft Books,	9	—	—
Caveats,	9	—	1860–1882
Side Bar Orders,	3	—	1862–1882
Cross Depositions, Sandford v. O'Connor,	—	1	1718
Plea now Examinations,	—	8	1851–1881

A 2

Record and Writ Office, Chancery—continued.

Records.	Vols.	Bdls.	Date.
Interrogatories,	—	9	1655–1656
Depositions,	—	4	1660–1669
Commissions,	—	2	1645–1646
Exhibits,	—	1	1651–1652
Decrees,	6	—	1647–1660
Decrees, Enrolled,	2	—	{ 1544–1561 / 1564–1600 }
Affidavit Books,	75	—	1630–1642
Rolls Affidavits,	16	—	1646–1652
Cause Petitions,	16	—	1656–1658
Memorandum Books,	2	—	1651–1657
Appearance Books,	6	—	1616–1657
Cause Petition Entry Books,	3	—	1649–1652
Common Notices,	40	—	1600–1652
Motion Book,	1	—	1637–1640
Day Books,	16	—	1625–1643
Common Notice Entry Book,	4	—	1633–1646
Notices of Motion,	9	—	1600–1602
Recognizance Rolls,	—	9	1640–1603
Orders to Vacate Recognizances,	—	1	1650–1662
Masters' Certificates and Bank Certificates,	1	—	1651–1653
Exceptions,	1	—	1640–1643
Attachments,	1	—	1601–1643

2. From the Lunacy Office there were received:

Records.	Vol.	Bdls.	Date.
Petitions and Affidavits,	—	44	prior to 1843
Bonds,	—	2	—
Affidavits,	96	—	1713–1843
Accounts,	7	—	1843–1848
Reports and Accounts,	15	—	1594–1653
Petitions and Reports,	7	—	1643–1650
Petitions,	18	—	1660–1653
Miscellaneous,	—	9	—

3. From the Common Pleas Division.

Records.	Vols.	Bdls.	Date.
Plaint Books,	8	—	1600–1600
Returned Writ Book,	1	—	1640–1642
Affidavit Books,	9	—	1600–1641
Judgment Books,	3	—	1600–1602
Judgment Summaries,	44	—	1600–1642
Memorial Rolls,	—	6	1600–1642

From the Common Pleas Division—*continued*.

Records.	Vols.	Rolls.	Date.
Memorials, ...	3	—	1840–1843
Warrants to Satisfy Judgments, . . .	5	—	1840–1882
Cess Judgment Rolls, ...	—	13	1790–1847
Debt Judgment Rolls, ...	—	8	1840–1847
Cognovits, ...	5	—	1840–1847
Warrants of Attorney, ...	8	—	1840–1881
Certificates of Acknowledgments by Married			
Women, ... : . .	6	—	1840–1881
Do. do. do.	1	—	1847–1881
Affidavits, ...	71	—	1840–1881
Defeasances, ...	19	—	1840–1847
Fiats, ...	10	—	1840–1853
Returned, ...	6	—	1840–1853
Mortgage Affidavits, ...	7	—	1840–1863
Postea, ...	1	—	1840–1847
Postea Book, ...	1	—	1840–1849
Abstracts, ...	5	—	1840–1863
Interlocutory Judgments, ...	9	—	1840–1853
Interlocutory Judgment Rolls, . . .	—	2	1840–1847

4. From the Exchequer Division.

Records.	Vols.	B.D.'s.	Date.
Debt Judgment Rolls, ...	—	3	1840–1844
Cess Judgment Rolls, ...	—	10	1840–1844
Memorial Roll, ...	—	1	1840–1843
Judgment Books, ...	4	—	1840–1844
Summons and Plaint Books, . . .	4	—	1840–1843
Affidavit Books, ...	6	—	1840–1844
Affidavits, ...	27	—	1840–1843
Warrants, ...	6	—	1840–1843
Sheriffs' Oaths, ...	2	—	1840–1843
Satisfactions, ...	4	—	1840–1843
Memorials, ...	2	—	1840–1843
Abstracts, ...	6	—	1840–1843
Cognovits, ...	1	—	1841–1845
Cognovits, ...	4	—	1840–1846
Returned Writs, ...	6	—	1840–1843
Defeasances, ...	6	—	1840–1843
Plaints, ...	21	—	1840–1843
Judgment Pleadings, ...	44	—	1840–1843
Postea, ...	—	1	1844–1881
Revivors, ...	—	2	1840–1849

Land Judges' Court.

5. From the Chancery Division, Land Judges' Court, were received 114 Copy Rentals for 1881 and 1882.

6. The continuing operations of the Board of Works in the re-arrangement of offices, during the autumn, in the absence of the Right Honorable the Master of the Rolls, made it necessary to remove the Exchequer Records without warrant; but their transfer has since been duly validated as in former cases of the like kind.

15th Report, s. 6.

Record Tower.

7. From the Record Tower, Dublin Castle, there have been received 8 bundles of miscellaneous documents connected with the Four Courts Marshalsea Prison, and 23 volumes of King's Letters, mainly on military affairs extending from 1714 to 1824. I beg to refer to the interesting Report of the Keeper of the State Papers in reference to the recent acquisition of additional historical material, the ultimate destination of which will be here.

Appendix I.

Duke of Leinster

8. His Grace the Duke of Leinster has been good enough to present to this office the Records following, brought in under permit of the Right Honorable the Master of the Rolls, under 30 & 31 Vic. c. 70, s. 16.

Records.	Vols.	Bdls.	Dates.
Rolls of Oaths and Affirmations taken before the Commissioners of Array, Co. Kildare,			1784
Rolls of Oaths of Burgesses, &c. of Athy and Harristown,	-	1	{ 1725-7, 1765-79
Returns of Members of Parliament, Athy and Harristown,			1763, 1776 .
List of 40 Shilling Freeholders, Co. Kildare, .			1746-1760

Intern.

Concreting. Fourteenth Report, s. 11.

9. The floors of six further Bays in the basement of the Record Treasury have been concreted, and it is expected that this necessary protection against damp will be completed during the current year.

Iron fittings.

10. The replacement of wooden by iron shelving and re-adjustment of fittings so as to secure the maximum of light have been continued through eight additional Bays of the upper Treasury; the usual diagram of which is annexed, showing in red ink the changes made in the deposits and the new work done during the year.

Re-arrangement of Records. Common Pleas

11. The Records of the Court of Common Pleas in Bay 3 U which had remained in loose order from the time of their reception have been flattened, cleansed, paper covered, and re-deposited in their former order.

Hanaper Office.

12. The Records from the Hanaper Office, also in loose bundles as originally brought in, have been put through a like process.

13. The series of copies of Money Orders for the years 1784-1880 transferred from the Accountant General's Office of the Chancery Division has been flattened and arranged in order of date.

14. The Marriage Licence and Administration Bonds of the Diocese of Ossory have been flattened and arranged in their letters in order of date.

15. The arrangement of the Prerogative Cause Papers has been carried forward to letter P.

16. The stamping of the Cause Papers transferred from the offices of the late Master Murphy, has been completed ; also the stamping of the like series brought from the Receiver Master's Department.

Indexing and Calendaring.

17. The Index to the Prerogative Wills (1811-1858) has been proceeded with up to the letter L.

18. The collation of the Draft Index to the printed calendar of the Patent Rolls of James I. has been completed ; and the Index Locorum for the letter A has been arranged in its final order and is ready for press.

19. The Index formed to the catalogue of Fiants of Charles I. has been engrossed to page 73.

20. An Index has been made and engrossed to the Administration Bonds of the Diocese of Cashel and Emly.

21. The papers removed from the Lunacy Office, Chancery, which prior to April, 1843, are unbound, have been arranged in dictionary order and indexed.

22. The unbound Chancery Petitions previous to April, 1843, have been indexed to letter E. This will be a large work, the letters A, B, and C (1667-1843) alone forming one large volume.

23. A draft index has been made to the following volumes of the Grant Books of the Dublin Consistorial Court, viz., 1038-1057, 1065-1706, 1749-1757, 1757-1764, 1764-1771, 1771-1781, with the intention of framing a General Index to the entire collection on the plan of that made by the late Record Commissioners to the Grant Books of the Court of Prerogative.

24. The supplemental index to the Landed Estates unbound Rentals presented to this Department by Mr. Octavius O'Brien, has been completed to the year 1860 ; and, in addition, an index to each bound volume of the series has been placed in front of it.

25. The detailed index to miscellaneous small collections has been continued to page 255.

26. The calendar to the Fiants of Queen Elizabeth has been continued from Fiant No. 4935 to Fiant No. 5908, printed in the Appendix to this Report. This portion contains the bulk of the

Grants made upon the pacification of Munster and the settling of the county of Monaghan.

27. The collection deposited here in 1872 by the Dean and Chapter of Christ Church Cathedral, consisting of Ancient Bulls, Grants, Leases, and other muniments, has been put in order, and a Calendar nearly completed to all the pieces comprised in it.

28. The calendaring of the Disentailing Deed Roll has been advanced from Deed No. 4,461, enrolled 2nd March, 1864, to Deed No. 4,530, enrolled 8th December, 1864.

29. In the Bookbinding and Repairing Department 36 volumes of Parochial Registers, 40 volumes of Equity Exchequer Note and Rule Books, 6 volumes of Licences and Assignments of Patents for Inventions, and 30 Miscellaneous volumes have been bound, and 76 Membranes of Plea Rolls, 6 Wills, 6 Inquisitions, and various other Records have been repaired.

30. Referring to the Indexing work done since the establishment of the office, it has been thought desirable that the Public should be made acquainted in a compendious form with the new means of reference so placed at its disposal in addition to the Indexes brought in from the former repositories of the several classes of Records.

LIST of ADDITIONAL INDEXES accessible to SEARCHERS at the PUBLIC RECORD OFFICE of IRELAND.

	Vols. and Portfolios	Place Reference.
CHANCERY—		
Bill Books (1840-7, 1857-76),	7	Strong Room.
Cause Papers, Master Brooke,	1	Search Room, Press M.
„ „ Master Litton,	1	„ „ „ o
„ „ Master Murphy,	1	„ „ „ f
„ „ Rotulcer Master,	1	„ „ „ f
Decrees (1843-1845),	1	„ „ „ o
Deed Boxes (Masters Brooke, Litton, Murphy, and Rotulcer Master),	1	„ „ „ R.
Deeds (Masters Brooke and Litton),	1	„ „ „ b
„ Ecclesiastical,	1	„ „ „ b
Drainage Acts—Enrolments of Awards,	1	
Fiants—Henry VIII.,	—	Printed in 5th Report.
„ Edward VI.,	—	„ 5th „
„ Philip and Mary,	—	„ 5th „
„ Charles I. (catalogues),	—	Search Room.
Livery—Writs, Inquisitions, &c.,	1	„ Press M.
Parochial Endowments and Perpetual Curacies (Geo. III.),	1	„ „ „ „
Patent Rolls (James I.), Calendar,	1	„ „ „ „
Perambulations—Writs, Commissions, Returns, and Maps,	1	„ „ „ R.
Petition Rule Books (1496-1577),	7	Bay L. M.
Recognizances (1547-1641),	1	Search Room, Press R.

LIST OF ADDITIONAL INDEXES.—*continued.*

	Vols. and Port-folios.	Place Reference.
Reports (1567—19 April, 1843), ...	2	Search Room, Press M.
Shannon Commission—Enrolments of Inquisitions, Awards, and Conveyances, . . .	1	„ „ N.
Ulster Railway Company—Warrants for Inquisitions and Sheriff's Judgments, . . .	1	„ „ „
Usher's Collection, ...	1	„ „ M.
Charte Privilegia, &c., ...	1	„ „ N.
Common Pleas—Original Deeds, . . .	1	„ „ „
Exchequer (Equity) — Maps connected with Awards, ...	1	„ „ „
Exchequer (Equity) Cause Papers, . . .	1	„ „ „
„ Decrees (1624—1850), . .	2	„ „ M.
Exchequer (Law)—Calendar of Communia Rolls	1	Bay 6 F.
„ Calendar of Mem. Rolls, James I. and Charles I.	1	„ „
Landed Estates Court Rentals, . . . (at end of Volumes).	30	Bay 1 E.
Liber Munerum Publicorum Hiberniae, . .	—	Printed in 9th Report.
TESTAMENTARY AND CONSISTORIAL—		
Administration Bonds, Armagh Diocese, .	1	Search Room, Press S.
„ Cashel and Emly Diocese,	1	„ „ „
Caote Papers, Dublin Diocese, ...	1	„ „ M.
Grant Book (1744—9), Dublin Diocese, . .	1	Bay 1 F.
Marriage Licence Book, Ardfert and Aghadoe (1782—1832), ...	1	„ „
Will Books (Armagh Diocese), 1817—1823, 1834, 1844, ...	6	„ „
Wills, Original—Ardagh Diocese, . . .	1	Search Room, Press S.
„ Ardfert and Aghadoe Diocese,	1	„ „ „
„ Armagh „ .	2	„ „ „
„ Cashel and Emly „	1	„ „ „
„ Clogher „ .	1	„ „ „
„ Clonfert, „ .	1	„ „ „
„ Cloyne „ .	1	„ „ „
„ Connor „ .	2	„ „ „
„ Cork and Ross „ .	1	„ „ „
„ Derry „ .	1	„ „ „
„ Down „ .	1	„ „ „
„ Drogheda Sub-Registry, .	—	With Armagh.
„ Dromore Diocese, . . .	1	Search Room, Press S.
„ Dublin „ . .	9	„ „ R.
„ Elphin „ . .	1	„ „ S.
„ Ferns „ . .	1	„ „ „
„ Kildare „ . .	—	With Dublin.
„ Killala and Achonry Diocese,	1	Search Room, Press S.
„ Killaloe and Kilfenora „	1	„ „ „
„ Kilmore „ .	1	„ „ „
„ Leighlin „ .	1	„ „ „
„ Limerick „ .	1	„ „ „
„ Meath „ .	1	„ „ „

LIST OF ADDITIONAL INDEXES—*continued.*

	Vols. and Parts filled.	Place Reference.
WILLS, Original—Newry and Mourne, except Jan.,	1	Search Room, Press 2.
„ Ossory Diocese,	1	„ „ „
„ Raphoe „	1	„ „ „
„ Tuam „	1	„ „ „
„ Waterford & Lismore Diocese,	1	„ „ „
WILLS, Unproved—Prerogative Court,	1	„ „ R.
TIPPERARY—Palatinate of—		
Fines and Recoveries,	1	„ „ W.
Pleadings, 1642–1830,	-	Printed in 6th Report.
Rolls of Chancery of,	-	„ „

Proceedings under the Parochial Records Acts, 38 & 39 *Vic.,* c. 59, *and* 39 & 40 *Vic.,* c. 58.

Custodians' Returns. 31. The Returns from Custodians under Retention Orders show that the Parochial Records kept in safes under their charge have been to some extent affected by damp. Twenty-one Reports forwarded during 1883–4, refer to damp, and the necessity of airing the Records. The safes in all those cases, save three, are in the Vestry rooms of country Churches.

Continuing inconvenience of divided deposit. 32. Continuing inconvenience attends the necessary dispersion of those Records in various and fluctuating places of deposit. In Appendixes to my 12th, 13th, and 14th Reports, tables were given of their then three-fold distribution at each of these periods. In my 15th Report the table was not published in extenso, but an Appendix was given setting forth the changes caused by receipts on Incumbencies becoming vacant under 38 & 39 Vic., c. 59, s. 6, and by remittances on safes being provided in the country under **Appendix III.** 39 & 40 Vic., c. 58, s. 5, during the year 1882. A like table continued to the present is given in an Appendix to this Report, from which and the list published in the Appendix to my 14th Report, an inquirer may know in which of the three possible Repositories provided by the Acts the Parochial Record sought for may be found, subject to such further changes as may arise during the current year.

Records return on safes provided. 33. During last year, safes were provided in seven parishes, the Records of which, previously placed here, were returned to their respective Incumbents under Retention Orders.

Records retained ditto. 34. Safes were provided in eleven parishes the Records of which had not yet become attachable owing to the continuance in their former duties of those who were Incumbents in 1870, and these Records remain in the country under other Retention Orders.

Records brought up. 35. Twenty-five parishes which became attachable, did not provide safes, and their Records have been brought up and

lodged in this custody, subject to return on safes being provided.
A summary of the present distribution of the collection is here
given:—

	Parishes and Chapelries.	
	1882–3	1883–4
In this custody, ...	661	479
In the Country under Retention Orders, . . .	668	764
Remaining unattached, ...	633	667

36. The fees to 31st December, 1883, amount to £633 6s. 6d.,
the smallest income from that source for several years past.

Fourteenth Report, s. 62.

TABLE OF FEES, 1883.

Date.	Inspections.	Tracts.	Attendances	Folios at 1s.	Folios at 6d.	Total.
1883. January, . . .	177	9	Fees remitted, £2	114	1s. 1888	£ s. d. 61 16 0
February, . . .	144	1	1	170	2083	68 15 0
March, . . .	146	3	—	887	1776	62 0 0
April, . . .	185	2	Fees remitted, £4 17s.	200	1443	49 15 0
May, . . .	190	—	—	144	7254	70 7 0
June, . . .	182	1	Fees remitted, 15s. 1	85	1290	47 8 0
July, . . .	165	—	Fees remitted, £1. —	9	1804	55 15 0
August, . . .	118	8	Fees remitted, 2s. 6d. —	60	1882	89 17 0
September, .	80	8	—	14	884	29 4 0
October, . .	140	1	—	81	1914	44 6 0
November, . .	130	—	Fees remitted, 8s. 9	124	1875	44 13 0
December, . .	105	—	—	115	1784	41 16 0
Total, .	1880	14	4	1844	19878	£633 6 0

37. The renewed thanks of this department are due to William
F. Littledale, Esq., solicitor, a donor of former additions to our
collections, who has lately made a further present to this office
of a set of Dublin Almanacks and Directories from 1784 and 1760
respectively, in 123 volumes. The collection is perfect, and is
believed to be unique. I had been unable to accept a former offer
of Mr. Littledale to deposit it here subject to recall, but have
willingly received it on the only terms Mr. Littledale now im-
poses, namely that it shall be accessible to the Public. Mr. Littledale has further presented this office with a Manuscript Index to
Incumbered and Landed Estates Court Sales, 1850–1875. P.
M'Keuna, Esq., Londonderry, has presented a manuscript volume

Donations from private individuals, Mr. Littledale, &c.

Mr. M'Kenna. of " Monthly Returns of the Army and Militia in Ireland," 1803
to 1806 ; and J. F. Fuller, Esq., has been the means of placing a
Mr. Fuller. volume of the Register of Drakestown Parish, which had been
out of the proper custody, amongst the Parochial Records
here.

Official dona- 38. Thanks are also offered for donations of 12 volumes of
tions. Record Publications sent to this office by the direction of the
Right Honorable the Master of the Rolls in England, and of 2
such volumes sent by direction of the Lord Clerk Register of
Scotland.

Literary 39. The literary searches during the year have included an
searches. extended examination of the Records and documents illustrative
Rule regulating of the Cromwellian period. Under the Rule regulating the table
Table of Fees. of fees, the Deputy Keeper is at liberty to dispense with fees on
searches for exclusively literary subjects. In construing the
Rule I have held it to apply only to cases of intended publication,
or of compilations such as, if published, would be of some general
interest or utility.

All which is humbly submitted to your Excellency.

Dated at the Public Record Office,
Four Courts, Dublin, this 12th
day of March, 1884.

SAMUEL FERGUSON,
Deputy Keeper of the Public Records in Ireland.

I humbly certify to your Excellency that this Report is made
by the Deputy Keeper of the Public Records in Ireland, under
my direction, pursuant to the statute.

A. M. PORTER,
Master of the Rolls.

APPENDIX.

APPENDIX I.

To THE RIGHT HONORABLE THE MASTER OF THE ROLLS.—THE
SIXTEENTH REPORT OF SIR BERNARD BURKE, C.B., Ulster,
Keeper of the State Papers in the Record Tower, Dublin Castle,
dated 1st February, 1884.

SIR,—It is gratifying to me to be able, in my first report to your
Honour, to inform you of the acquisition by this department of a valu-
able contribution to our Records. In the course of last summer, the
Hon. Spencer Ponsonby-Fane, C.B., presented to the Irish Government
the Correspondence of John, Earl of Westmorland, K.G., Lord Lieutenant of Ireland from 5th January, 1790, to 4th January, 1795. At
the Earl's death, this series of documents passed to his daughter, the
late Lady Georgiana Fane, and from that lady to Mr. Ponsonby-Fane her
nephew, and Lord Westmorland's grandson, by whose liberality and
public spirit it now forms part of the State Papers of Ireland, and will
henceforth, in remembrance not only of Lord Westmorland but also
of the donor, be known as "The Fane Collection." The gift was thus
made :—

> " Lord Chamberlain's Office,
> "St. James's Palace, S.W.,
> " 2 July, 1883.

" MY DEAR SIR BERNARD,

" I came into possession, at the death of my aunt, Lady Georgiana Fane, of a
bundle of letters, &c. of Lord Westmorland's when Lord Lieutenant of Ireland.
I lent them to Mr. Lecky with reference to the History which he is writing,
and he tells me they are of great interest, and that there are many which are
not to be found amongst your Records.

" I think I cannot do better than to send them to you to look over, and I shall
have pleasure in placing at your disposal for the Record Office which you have
so admirably arranged any you deem worthy preserving. Let me know if this
will be agreeable to you and to the 'Authorities that be,' and I will at once
forward them to you.

> " Yours very sincerely,
>
> " S. PONSONBY-FANE,

" To Sir Bernard Burke, C.B."

I communicated this offer to the Lord Lieutenant, and His Excellency,
with a full sense of the importance of the documents, directed me to
accept the gift in his name and to thank Mr. Ponsonby-Fane most cor-
dially for his liberality.

On receipt of the papers, I went carefully through their contents and
perceived at once how important they were and especially how interesting was the correspondence between Mr. Pitt and Lord Westmorland.
Their letters, as well as those of Henry Dundas, enter confidentially
and largely into the political questions of the time, the Catholic claims,
and the state of Ireland generally, touching now and then on the aspect
of events occurring in Europe. The period was one of much excitement

in Ireland consequent on the French Revolution. One of Pitt's letters, dated 18th November, 1792, shows that the writer already, even at that date, contemplated a Legislative Union.

The collection includes, besides, letters from Grenville, FitzGibbon (afterwards Earl of Clare), Hobart, Mornington (afterwards Marquess Wellesley), Sir John Parnell, John Beresford, Edward Cooke, the Bishop of Cloyne, John Pollock, Arthur Wolfe (afterwards Viscount Kilwarden), John Toler (afterwards Earl of Norbury), the Archbishop of Cashel, Earl Fitzwilliam, Lord Kenmare, &c.

A good many of the letters describing the advent of Lord Fitzwilliam as Westmorland's successor, exhibit in strong relief the consternation of the office-holders at the sudden change, and finally refer to His Lordship's recall after his brief Viceroyalty of not quite three months.

To explain the position of the various writers in the correspondence, I subjoin their names and offices :—

THE EARL OF WESTMORLAND, Lord Lieutenant, 5 January, 1790, to 4 January, 1795.

THE EARL FITZWILLIAM, Lord Lieutenant from 4 January, 1795, to 25 March, 1795.

RIGHT HON. WILLIAM PITT, Prime Minister.

RIGHT HON. HENRY DUNDAS, Home Secretary, 8 June, 1791, to 11 July, 1794 : afterwards Viscount Melville.

LORD FITZGIBBON, Lord Chancellor of Ireland (afterwards Earl of Clare), 1789 to 1802.

ROBERT HOBART, Chief Secretary, 1789 to 1794 (afterwards Lord Hobart, and Earl of Buckinghamshire).

LORD MILTON, Chief Secretary, 1795 (afterwards Earl of Dorchester).

EARL OF MORNINGTON, Chief Remembrancer of the Exchequer (afterwards Marquess Wellesley).

SIR JOHN PARNELL, Bart., Chancellor of the Exchequer in Ireland, 1785 to 1799.

THE BISHOP OF CLOYNE (Charles M. Warburton, D.D.)

RIGHT HON. JOHN BERESFORD, Commissioner of the Revenue.

THE ARCHBISHOP OF CASHEL (Charles Agar, D.D.)

JOHN POLLOCK, Crown Solicitor.

ARTHUR WOLFE, Attorney-General (afterwards Chief Justice and Viscount Kilwarden).

JOHN TOLER, Solicitor-General (afterwards Earl of Norbury).

EDWARD COOKE, Under Secretary, 1796 to 1801.

&c.,   &c.,   &c.

This Fane collection is now deposited in the Record Tower. I have arranged it in strict chronological order, and have made a comprehensive calendar, as well as an Index Nominum, thus rendering a reference easy to each individual person mentioned in the letters. The correspondence concludes with the departure of Lord Fitzwilliam.

There is another collection formerly contained in two large boxes in a room in the Tower (opened in the year 1876), a collection of vast interest, continuing to some extent the Fane correspondence. The latter ends in 1795 ; the papers of the two boxes commence about that year and carry down the course of events to 1809. They comprise Letters from Lords Cornwallis, Camden, Castlereagh, and Sligo, Charles James Fox, Duke of Portland, Lord Auckland, Sir Jonah Barrington, Right Hon. Thomas Pelham, Earl of Donoughmore, Right Hon. Henry

Dundas, Lord Edward FitzGerald, Earl of Hardwicke, Colonel Little-hales, Lord Norbury, Wolfe, John Pollock, Sir John Parnell, Right Hon. William Wickham, Edward Cooke, Lord Redesdale, Lord Longueville, Arthur O'Connor, and very many others.

The last two months I have devoted to the minute examination of these papers, and am preparing to make a comprehensive Calendar and Index of them.

The current business of the year 1882 to 1883 shows the progress made. References from the Chief Secretary's Office for the production of documents have been numerous, and have occupied considerable time. The classification in cartons, already affected, of the MISCELLANEOUS PAPERS of each year has infinitely facilitated these inquiries. This classification and indexing have extended to the year 1872 with the exception of the years 1844 to 1856 now in course of similar arrangement. I look forward to the speedy completion of this classification with anxiety, as it will, when once finished, lessen to a great extent the labour of the searches so constantly required to be made in this Department.

The following Summary will explain the work done and in progress :—

1. An INDEX NOMINUM to a vol. of EXCISE ACCOUNTS, 1 May, 1658, to 24 June, 1660, and 24 June, 1660, to 24 June, 1652. This book, marked A is one of those belonging to the Council Office.

$$\frac{A}{18}$$

2. An INDEX OF NAMES OF PERSONS AND PORTS to a vol. of PASSES OF SHIPS, 1677 $\left(\frac{A}{76}\right)$. This also belonged to the Council Office.

3. An INDEX NOMINUM to a vol. containing AFFIDAVITS of SERVICE of ORDERS of COUNCIL, 1682-1688 $\left(\frac{A}{107}\right)$. This also belonged to the Council Office.

4. An INDEX to a vol. containing WOOL LICENCES, 1699.

5. An INDEX commenced to a book entitled "KILKENNY CONFEDERATE—ORDERS OF PROCESS, 1644-1649" $\left(\frac{A}{54}\right)$. This also belonged to the Council Office.

6. An INDEX to 23 volumes of KING'S LETTERS, MILITARY (original), 1714 to 1824. These books together with an index volume have, during the past year, been transferred to the Public Record Office.

7. An INDEX in Slips to the MISCELLANEOUS UNREGISTERED Papers of the years 1857, 1858, 1859, and 1860. The papers occupy 22 cartons.

8. The slips for the INDEX to the PETITIONS and other papers connected therewith proceeded with from 4635 to 5255.

9. The PAPERS of the years 1869, 1870, 1871, and 1872, received this year, arranged in 139 cartons and a carton catalogue made to them.

10. A CATALOGUE of the BOOKS, PAPERS, &c., contained in the Record Tower made.

RECEPTION OF PAPERS.

1. The CURRENT PAPERS of the years 1869, 1870, 1871, and 1872, received 26 February, 1883, from the Chief Secretary's Office.

2. Twelve bundles of Papers belonging to the Constabulary Office received from the Chief Secretary's Office.

3. The Westmorland Correspondence, 1790 to 1795, already referred to, and now indexed under the name of "the Fane Collection."

TRANSFER OF STATE PAPERS.

The following Documents with an Index prepared in this Department have been transferred to the Public Record Office during the past year.

King's Letters, Military.

Vol. 1,	1714–1720.		Vol. 13,	1781–1782.
„ 2,	1727–1733.		„ 14,	1783–1784.
„ 3,	1734–1740.		„ 15,	1785–1786.
„ 4,	1748–1752.		„ 16,	1787–1788.
„ 5,	1753–1757.		„ 17,	1791–1792.
„ 6,	1763–1764.		„ 18,	1793–1794.
„ 7,	1767–1768.		„ 19,	1795–1796.
„ 8,	1769–1770.		„ 20,	1797–1799.
„ 9,	1773–1774.		„ 21,	1818–1819.
„ 10,	1775–1776.		„ 22,	1819–1820.
„ 11,	1777–1778.		„ 23,	1821–1824.
„ 12,	1779–1780.		1 Vol. Index.	

The twelve bundles of Papers belonging to the Constabulary Office, received from the Chief Secretary's Office, have been by direction of the Government transferred to the Constabulary Office, on 5 April, 1883.

I have the honour to be, sir,

Your very obedient servant,

J. Bernard Burke, Ulster,

Keeper of the State Papers.

Record Tower, Dublin Castle,
    1st February, 1884.

APPENDIX II.

FIANTS OF THE REIGN OF QUEEN ELIZABETH—(CONTINUED).

1586.

4935 (4073.) Pardon to Rich. m'Brian M'Shee, of }
Rich. Conden m'Shoodou, of Coakebegg, genk, Maurice Poore, of Ballycoonghan, and Shane Poore, of Ballyronoghan, horseman, Con O·Calnen [   ], of Yushiquyne, horseboy, Shane m'Dermout Evghanell, of Yushiquyne, cowhard, Dermou m'Knowgher Emolen, of Shanegarle. Provided that they shall appear and submit themselves at sessions, and give security to keep the peace and answer at sessions. The pardon shall not extend to any in prison, or under bail to appear; nor include intrusion into crown lands, or debts to the crown; nor persons who have received any pardon, or committed any offence worthy of death in the time of the government of the then deputy (Perrot).—28 [   ] (Of record with fiants of the twenty-eighth year.)

4937 (4077.) Pardon to Peirs Butler fitz Walter, of Pallice, gent., Durbin O Dowyr, of Clowin Iborra, and Cahir fitz John glasse O Mulrian, of Gortkelly, gentlemen, Edm. Butler fitz Walter, of Seannahalidull, husbandman, John carragh Brenagh, of Swineoyn, Wm. fitz Serwyne Bourke, of Bwolanaheury, Walter Stackepole, of Ardquilly, horseman, Donell O Kenedie, of Brittes, Teig moell O Hasedy, of Castlemcell, husb, Peirs fitz John Butler, of Pinnoc, Gilladuf O Mulrian, of Sennabothe, and Philip O Kenedie, of Balysnlogha, no. Tipperary. Provisions as in 4935. The first three persons excepted in the last provision.—[   ] (Of record with fiants of the twenty-eighth year.)

4938 (4166.) Pardon to Gerald m'Mortogh oge Cavanagha, of Garchill, gent, Johanna ani Mortogh, his wife, Sawe ani Mortogh, her sister, David m'Garrot M'Shane, of Rahingeroge, kern, Thady M'Gilpatrick, of Mishall, Edm. M'Shertu, of Glard, husbandmen, Thady M'Donoghe, of same, leach, Carowle M'William, of Srowle, husb., Pair. M'Mortogh, of Donhryan, horseboy, Bran M'Cahill, of Srowle, and Donogh M'Mortogh, of same, husbandmen; co. Catherlogh. Provisions as in 4936. Provided also that this pardon shall extend only to those who are willing to submit and fulfil such articles as the lord deputy shall ordain concerning the lands which any of them had, in use or possession, at the time when any of their treasons or felonies were committed, whether the lands have been found by inquisition or not. (Sawe ani Mortogha excepted in proviso excluding those in prison or on bail.)—18 Nov. xxix.

4939 (6079.) Lease (under queen's letter, 12 April, xxvi.) to sir Thomas Lestrange, knt.; of three islands in co. Galway, called Arramoore, Innyahmanye, and Innyeharrye, possessions of the religious houses of Fynbenra, Annaghcoyne, Kyleenny, and Cornumroe, (recites No. 3953). To hold for 50 years in reversion. Rent £6 (part in corn). Maintaining 30 English footmen. Provided that he shall not alien, without license under the great

B

1586.   FIANTS.—ELIZABETH.

seal, to any except they be of English nation both by father and
mother, or born in the English Pale. He shall not levy coyne
or livery or other unlawful impositions, or permit any other to
do so, whereby her Majesty's lands by colour of custom might be
chargeable with the same hereafter. The lease to be enrolled in
the Auditor General's Office within four months.—[21 Nov., xxix.]
(*Auditor General's Patent Book* 20 p. 8.)

4940 (4034.) Lease (under commission, 17 Jan., xxvi.) to John
Rawson, soldier; of the castle (not fully built) and lands of Ballynecourte, co. Galway, parcel of the lands of John Walle, late of
Ballynecourte in the barony of Athenrye, attainted. To hold for
21 years. Rent 16s 9d. Provisions as in 1989.—24 Nov.,
xxix.

4941 (6658.) Lease (under commission, 17 Jan., xxvi.) to John
Rawson, soldier; of the market place of Athlone, being 20 yards
long by 15 yards, and a stonewall adjoining for the foundation
of a market house; in consideration of his building forthwith a
timber market house on this foundation; leaving room for two
carts to the High street and one cartway round the markethouse.
To hold with the customs of the market for 21 years. Rent 6s,
English. Provided that he shall not allen, without license under
the great seal, to any except they be of English nation both by
father and mother, or born in the English Pale. The lease
to be enrolled in the Auditor General's Office within four
months.—[24 Nov., xxix.] (*Auditor General's Patent Book* 17,
p. 70.)

4942 (6514.) Grant (under queen's letter, 1 Aug., xxviii.) to Elinor,
countess of Desmond; of a pension of £100, for life.—25 Nov.,
xxix.

4943 (4165.) Pardon to Gerald m'Mortagh Cavanagh, and Sawe
eny Moriogh Cavanagh, widow, co. Carlow. Provided that he
(Gerald) shall appear and submit before the justices at assizes in
that county at the next sessions, and be sufficiently bound with
sureties to keep the peace and answer at sessions, when summoned,
the just demands of all subjects.—26 Nov., xxix.

4944 (4157.) Pardon to Colle M'Dowle, of Clonfree, Thady
M'Tomolto, of same, Bryan M'One, of same, Feardorgh m'Shane
carragh Brenan, of Tronogrewe, Hugh duf m'Shane carragh,
of same, Hugh m'Hebart M'Brenan, of Tronsvalegan, Hugh
m'Shane M'Brenan, of same, Thady m'Edm. boy M'Brenan, of
Slowshane, Fardorghe m'Connor M'Brenan, of Tolev[   ]
Cale reogh, of Ballyduf, Connor M'Gaule, of same, Thady m'Cale
balle, of Longsford, Owin roe O Moghan, of Kilarights, Oak
m'Donogh reogh, of same, Rory keghl M'Brenan, of Clonecrowe,
Rory [   ] O Brenan, of same, Rory O Nary, of Clonellyn-
lagh, Hugh Byrne, of Clonelyan, Gittenenowe M'Naryne, of
Ballykiogs, Laghlen M'Naryn, of Lysroyne, Connor kyle O Byrne,
of Clouchy, Dermot M'Naryn, of Clonflynlagh, Dermot duf
M'Connor, of Corkarigh, Shan O Hoyn, of Ballyduf, Symon
M'Kegan, of Kiltrustan, Tho. M'Ullick, of Ballyduf, Donogh
O Flaughe, of Kiltrustan, Connor Qwyn, of same, Dermot duf
M'Cayle, of same, Owin O Connally, of Boblinge, shoemaker, Edm.
O Donnoghe, of Balladuf, Hubert m'Rory m Tomeltagh O Brenan,
of Lavally, Dermot M'Gilbride, of Kiltrustan, Thady M'Dermot,

     FIANTS.—ELIZABETH.

of Donarde, Shily ny Auly, of Ballaghboyge, Bryan M'Dowle, of same, Wm. Hallon, of Lavalles, Cormock O Coman, of Garrough, Wm. duf O Conan, of same, Hugh O Conan, of same, Hugh m'One boy, of Lecarrowe, Owin m'Rory O Moran, of Clonebranan, Oale re m'Shane O Moran, of Bealaoghter, Laghlen duff m'Teige M'Kego, Thady m'Donell O Dowim, of Belfadds, Donogh ne Cloise, of Cloughare, Dowaltagh m'Bren O Connor, of Clonebryne, Hugh m'Tyriagh mor, of Anagh, Bren M'Moran, of Clenykenn, Hugh O Colla, of Clonebrenan, Donnogh O Connalle, of Lavalle, Oale moyle O Connalle, of Garrogh, Tonoltagh moile O Hone, of Balleduf, Rory O Moylen, of same, Laghlen M'Brenan, of Clonaffynlagh, Morgh O Fyne, of Ballyne, Hugh O Moran, of Clonebrman, Rory O Corckeran, of same, Bren duf O Geblan, of Lysroyn, Thady m'Donogh Fiangha, of same, Gerald M'Rory, of Bealenemcile, Dermot m'Donell O Fleugh, of Kiltrustan, Laghlen roe, of Kilaright, Owin M'Key, of Lisdoyn, Cormock M'Key, of same, Rory O Hane, of Clonebrekan, Tyriagh M'Doill, of Ballaghboyge, Donogh O Kelly, of Skryne, Dermot dergh O Hanly, of Garoreeghe, Rory keigh O Hanly, of same, Laghlen glasse O Hanle, of same, Shan M'Rory, of Tonem'ranyll, Donell ballagh O Hanle, of Knockness, Hugh m'Shane O Hanly, of Cowlshaghten, Laghlen O Hanlon, of Clonecammill, Gilloinf M'Richarde, of Clonebrenan, John (   ), of Clonaffynlagh, Bryan M'Edmonds, of Bealenemcile, and David O Nary, of same; co. Roscommon. Provisions as in 4938. Fine 6s. 8d. each.—30 Nov., xxix. *Endorsed* "Pardon for 79 pure labourers in co. Roscommon."

4945 (4163.) Pardon to Tho. Masterson, of Fernes, co. Wexford, gent., Richard, Nicholas, John, and Henry Masterson, Owen duff M'Hugh, Garralt m'William boy, Philip M'Edmond, Morough M'Edmond, of Fernes, Patr. Roche, of Newcastle, same co., Rich. Roch, Redmund Roche, of same, Terrelagh m'Ene M'Vadaghe, of Fernes, Tarrelagh O Kelly, Our. Uztace, Donogh m'Morrish M'Dowlinge, of same, Henry Roche, of Ballyhane, same co., Wm. M'Ollendrick, of Ballyolough, Nich. duff O Belgie, of Fernes, James m'Elfadry M'Faller, of same, Art m'Donell m'Shane oge, of Cloughleaken, same co., Lich. M'Ener, of Fernes, Lymkh M'Ener, and David M'Fallon, of same. Provision for security as in 4943. The pardon shall not include any fine of alimation due, intrusion into crown lands, or debts to the crown, nor extend to persons who have had any pardon during the time of the present deputy (Perrot).—6 Dec., xxix.

4946 (4170.) Pardon to Tho. m'Donogh O Morohowe, of Kilcree, horseman, Shan m'Morikiartagh O Morohowe, of same, kern, Thady roe O Mahown, of Ballytardine, hush, Dermot m'Connor Croige O Mahownie, of same, kern, Wm. O Hiallhie, of Donnagh more, kern, Awlyve m'Mahown O Leyne, of Balentobrede, horseman, Mahown oge O Leyne, of same, yeoman, Daniel m'Owen M'Swyne, of Moamnglas, gent., Malronis M'Ydiain, of Dunnshiade, kern, Thady m'Dermod O Scanell, of Kilahie, yeoman, Philip O'Dowgnine, of Moamnglas, Shan m'Edm. O Conis, and Marc m'Oene M'Comgains, of same, gallaglasses, Donnogh O Riordane, of Mocromptny, Daniel m'Donogh O Riordan, of same, and Daniel m'Dermot O Callighane, of Aghedagh, horseman, Donogh m'Conogher O Mahowny, of Aglisse, Thady

B 2

1586.   FIANTS.—ELIZABETH.

m'Connoghor O Mahowny, of same, Conoghor m'Dermot O Riordan, of Clontalio, and Conoghor m'Dermot O Moroghowe, of Kilvanains, kerns, Donogh O Lary, of Carrigmogilagh, yeoman, Daniel m'Teige oge O Oronyne, of Carrignosary, Shan m'Donell O Oronyn, of Clohina, Donogh leattagh O Moroghowe, of Carriginmock, and Shan m'Donogh Y Moroghow, of Kilkea, kerns. Security as in 4943 in co. Cork. Provided that none of the parties were present at the slaying of Jasper Wager, lately slain; that they submit to the orders of the lord deputy concerning their lands, and that pardon shall not include intrusion into crown lands, or debts to the crown.—8 Dec., xxix.

4947 (4318.) License to Tho. Williams, esq., clerk of the cheque; to be absent in England for four months,—16 Dec., xxix.

4948 (4158.) Pardon to Cormac Malaghlen, of Rathashige, co. Westmeath; found by an inquest before Peter Ledwich, of Laken, one of the coroners of co. Westmeath, 25 March, xxv., to have slain in self defence Hugh O Ferrall, of Barne, co. Longford, kern. Security as in 4943.—16 Dec., xxix.

4949 (4133.) Grant to Rich. Bacon, esq.; of the office of the queen's principal attorney in Munster. To hold during pleasure, with such fees as Rob. Rodier had.—17 Dec., xxix.

4950 (4164.) Pardon to Edm. M'Jonyne, of Tubberkeagh, Jonyne M'Jonyne, John O Malone, Gillaspeak M'Lenne, Tho. Stacke, Wm. M'Brenan, of same, Edm. roe m'Edmund roe Ballagh, of Ballindery, Ullick M'Jonyne, of Culleconna, Redmund M'Jonyne, of same, Cahir M'Donell, of Athilliarde, Rory M'Donell, of same, Tho. m'Davie vine, of Kilkeran, Rich. M'Jonyne, of Killslenan, James Wall, of Ballsheade, and Cahir m'Alliester roe M'Donell, of Molealaghe. Security as in 4943. The pardon not to include intrusion into crown lands, or debts to the crown. Excluding those who shall not pay double the value of the goods which they shall be proved to have unlawfully taken. 20 Dec., xxix.

4951 (5613.) Grant (under queen's letter, 24 July, xxviii.) to George Thornton, gent.; of a pension of 8s. a day, for life, in augmentation of one of 4s. In consideration of his 20 years service.—11 Dec., xxix.

1586-7.

4952 (4319.) License to John, archbishop of Armagh; to be absent in England for four months.—3 Jan., xxix.

4953 (6050.) Lease (under queen's letter, 24 July, 1586), to John Lye [of Clonagbe, co. Kildare, gent.]; of the lands of Rathebride, (with common of pasture on the Curragh of Kildare), Marrytownobiller, and Crottianstown, co. Kildare, lands of David Sutton, attainted. To hold for 60 years. Rent £26 4s. Provisions as in 4939.—9 Jan., xxix.

4954 (6005.) Surrender by Richard Paulfreiman, assignee of Edward Burne, gent.; of the tithes of much and little Derieke, co. Meath, held under lease, 2982.—Dated 11 Jan., xxix.

4955 (4141.) Commission to Francis Lovell, esq., sheriff of co. Kilkenny; to execute martial law in that county, as in 218.—14 Jan., xxix.

4956 (4327.) Lease (under commission, 17 Jan., xxvi.) to Gerald Flemynge, gent.; of the rectories of Kyllyn, Knockebride,

1586-7.   FIANTS.—ELIZABETH.

Castleraghan, Templeporte, and Crodraghe, co. Cavan, possessions of the abbey of Kellos, co. Meath, waste and not leased to any since the suppression. To hold for 21 years. Rent £13 13s. 4d. Provisions as in 4939.—14 Jan., xxix.

4957 (4331.) Grant (under queen's letter, 1 Aug., xxviii.), to Nich. Taffe; reciting as in 4737; that he may retain the rents of 50s., £11 8s. 8d., and the moiety of £3 7s. 4d., severally reserved under recited previous demises of the lands granted to him in 4737, and forming part of the rent of £15 16s. 8d., therein reserved, during the continuance of those interests. The grant 4737 is recited as made to Nich. Taffe, of Athcolare, co. Louth, and Johanna Eustace, his wife.—18 Jan., xxix.

4958 (5517.) Grant (under queen's letter, 1 Aug., xxviii.), to Anthony Ferris, gent.; of a pension of 20d. sterling, a day, in succession to George Hunte, late pensioner.—19 Jan., xxix.

4959 (5900.) Grant to Richard Dansye, gent.; of the wardship and marriage of Christopher son and heir of Thomas Nugente, late of Moyrathe, co. Meath. Fine £5.—19 Jan., xxix.

4960 (4152.) Pardon to Shane m'Brian, of Belfaste, co. Antrim, Con O Neale, his brother, Dwalto M'Gie, Owen m'Quine M'Hugh, Brian oge m'Brian ballogh, Owen M'Gye, Owen boy M'Gye, Fellome modder M'Gye, Manus M'Towle, Fellom duffe m'Art oge, Owen modder M'Anallo, James duffe M'Anallo, and Fardoragh O Dornall, of the same place. Security as in 4943. The pardon not to include intrusion into crown lands or debts to the crown. (Murder also excluded by the usual clause excepting treason against the queen's person and coining).—30 Jan., xxix.

4961 (5904.) Grant to Anthony Biskoretothe, gent.; of the wardship and marriage of John, son and heir of William Farres, late of Killessell, King's co.; and custody of his lands, during minority. Rent 30s., and retaining 20s. for support of the minor. Fine 20s.—26 Jan., xxix.

4962 (4138.) Commission to Tho. FitzGerald, sheriff of Kildare; to execute martial law in that county, as in 218.—1 Feb., xxix.

4963 (4139.) Commission to Pierce Butler fitz Edm., sheriff of Tipperary; to execute martial law in that county; as in 218.— 1 Feb., xxix.

4964 (4328.) Livery to Edward, son and heir of George Fitz Gerralde, late of Tsigeroghane, co. Meath, esq. Fine, £13.—4 Feb., xxix.

4965 (4159.) Pardon to Alexander Fyttow, of Beotie, gent., Rich. Bedlowe, of Bedlowston, Walter Evers, Thady duf M'Bryan, footman, Walter Clynton, servingman, Tho. Fitz John, of Fyanston, James Fitz John, of same, horseman, Rich. Plunket, of Wylkenston, Alexander Plunket, of same, Hubert Tyrrell, of Donmore, Andrew Corbett, horseboy, Nich. Freman, servingman, Nich. Haworeth, servingman, Turlagh M'Cagane, of Tybbere, and Wm. M'Cogan, of same, footmen, Murgh O Hennia, Callogh M'Mahownde, of Raffyne, Bryan M'Comyne, Tho. Veldon, of Knoghe, Bryan O Gowen, of Moaretan, Nich. O Shill, of Newe Castle, James Daffe, footman, Rich. Plunket, of Moyagha, horseman, Tho. Gybnay, of same, footman, Rory M'Gillaley, of Kilcowen, Owin O Teige, of Killinay, Sherin M'Ricarde, of Garrand, Dermot O Kenney, of Bagarrand, and Mortagh Tagan, of Pomexton, co. Meath. Security as in 4943. The pardon not to include

1586-7.   **FIANTS.—ELIZABETH.**

murder, nor intrusion into crown lands, or debts to the crown.
—4 Feb., xxix.

4966 (4160.) Pardon to Walter Deverox, of Courthele, co. Wexford,
gent., and Katherine ny Brene Cavanagh, his wife. Proviso for
security as in 4945. The pardon shall not include intrusion
into crown lands or debts to the crown.—6 Feb., xxix.

4967 (4140.) Commission to sir Pierce fitz James, knt., sheriff of
co. Catherlagh ; to execute martial law in that county, as in 218.
—6 Feb., xxix.

4968 (4155.) Pardon to George Isaac, of Brianston, co. Wexford,
gent., John Power fitz Peirs, John Power fitz Edm., of same,
horsemen, Garrett m'Shane boge, of St. Molings, Edm. Butler
fitz Rich., of Glanballiculonan, and Shane m'Thomas gnaraghe,
of Brianston, kerns, Edm. roe m'Thomas Eglan, labourer, Andrew
Hazellwoode, servingman, Tho. Peirc m'Shane, kern, of the
same, Dermond m'Morrish Cavanagh, of the Knockancrogh,
Moriertagh m'Moriah Cavanagh, Morrough m'Moriah, and Brian
m'Moriah, of same, gentlemen, James m'Shane Enose, of Cloph-
nogarogh, gunner, Edm. keagh Forstall, of same, kern, Philip
Obo, of the Old Towne, Edm. O Moro, of the Bolls, husbandman,
Edm. Hoare, of Harperston, Gerrott Sutton, of Ballikeynoke,
and James Prenderorest, of Ballifarnoke, gentleman, Moriah
Prendrecost, and Philip Keytinge fitz James, of same, kerns, Patr.
Prenderecost, of Ballconiek, horseman, Patr. Furlouge, of Bally-
widder, gent., Morough m'Edm. M'Iffe, of Ballyvonyne, Philip
Ketinge fitz Peirs, of Dunganiston, husbandmen, Marcus Fitz
Harryes, of Ballentelley, gent., Gerrott Taillor, of same, kern,
Nich. Furlouge, of the Horetownes, and Rich. Myler, of Cul-
nayhan, horseman, in co. Wexford. Provisions as in 4966.—
7 Feb., xxix.

4969 (5903.) Grant to Rice Thomas, gent. ; of the wardship and
marriage of James, son and heir of Patrick. Fexe, late of the
city of Limerick, merchant ; and custody of the lands, during
minority; Rent, £3 16s. 8d., and retaining £3 for support of the
minor. Fine, £3.—6 Feb., xxix.

4970 (4326.) Livery to Paul, son and heir of James Sherlocke, late
of Illanbobuck, co. Waterford, gent. Fine £11.—8 Feb., xxix.

4971 (4161.) Pardon to Morgan m'Bryan m'Cahir Cavanagh, Sow-
nyn Elyne, his grandmother, Gerald m'Art rowe Cavanagh, of
Typerany, horseboy, Edm. duf M'Colletan, of Ballourungan,
horseboy, Gerald m'Shane boge, of S. Molings, footman, and
Edm. M'Donell, of Barnewdane. Provisions as in 4965.—16 Feb.,
xxix.

4972 (4323.) Livery to John, son and heir of Maurice Roche, late
of Cork, gent. Fine 5 marks.—13 Feb., xxix.

4973 (4316.) License to Edw. Finbazon, esq., one of the privy
council ; to be absent in England for one year, unless bidden to
return by the queen or the council in England.—13 Feb., xxix.

4974 (4324.) Livery to Alexander, son and heir of Francis Cosby,
late of Stabally, Queen's co., esq. Fine £10.—25 Feb., xxix.

4975 (4191.) Pardon to Connor O Mulrian, of Enaghowney, co.
Limerick, gent. Anis ny Brene, his wife, John O Mulrian, of
Tirrellagh, co. Tipperary, Edm. fitz John O Mulrian, of Ballicho-
regan, Connor m'Tho. O Mulrian, of Beachenchaltie, Thady fitz
Doniel O Mulrian, of Tirrellaghe, Donell and Henry m'Edm.

O Mulrian, of Curaghduf, Thady fitz Connor O Mulrian, Wm.
m'Henry O Mulrian, of same, Donogh m'Teige O Mulrian, of
Rossary, Rowry m'Donnogh O Mulrian, of same, Donogh
O Mulrowne, of Eneghowney, co. Limerick, Taige m'Donnall
O Mulrian, of Clonealnell, Kilm. fitz James O Mulrian, of Shally,
Dermot m'Morogh O Kalle, of Ballichahan, co. Tipperary, Donell
m'Teige O Mulrian, of Caronchala, Rory fitz Mahowne O Mulrian,
of Clonboany, Donell in'Kenedie O Mulrian, of Cowlewocke,
Shane m'Hee O Mulrian, of Clonconner, Thady m'Owen O Mulrian,
of same, Hugh boy in'Connor O Mulrian, of Shisicre, Mahown
m'Donnall O Mulrian, of Ballichalan, Philip m'Dermot O Mulrian, of same, Donall M'Glanchie, of Grange, co. Limerick,
Dermot m'Owen O Mulrian, of Tomin, Donell m'Connor
m'Henry O Mulrian, (of) Cortentronan, Thady m'Rory O Mulrian,
of Henaglantane, Roryer ro, of Ballenchlohe, hensebuy, Hewney
m'Rory O Mulrian, of Beallaghommocke, Morogh m'Melaughlin
O Mulrian, of Kilnelage, Dermot leigh m'Donnogh O Mulrian,
of Clonkine, Laughlin O Hee m'Moriartagh, of Cortnehabe,
Mahown O Chohere, kern, Cahire roe m'Donell O Mulrian, of
the Skully, Donell m'Dermodie O Mulrian, of Coroncharef,
Mahown m'Melaghlin O Mulrian, Kenedie leigh O Glienane,
of Frugh, Philip O Kenedie, of Lanuregh, Rich. fitz Thomas,
yeoman, Donall fitz Derby O Mulrian, Connell m'Shane
O Mulrian, David Powre fitz Rob., Edw. Cowerton fitz Patr., and
Thady fitz Donogh, of Ballitshire. Provisions as in 4985. The
pardon not to extend to any who received any pardon in the
time of the present deputy (Perrot); nor to any indicted or
condemned of any treason, robbery, or other felony, or who are
in prison or on bail to appear.—26 Feb., xxix.

4976 (4137.) Grant to Chr. Carleyle, esq.; of the office of seneschal
&c. of the whole country of Clandeboye, the Diffrene, and Kilultagh,
in the province of Ulster, surrendered by Nial. Dawtrye (see
4207). To hold during good behaviour, with authority as in
3077. As provided by queen's letter of 11 March, 1582, he
shall not be removed except for abuse of his office proved before
the lord deputy and council of Ireland, by them certified to the
council in England, and by them adjudged sufficient cause for
his removal.—8 March, xxix.

4977 (3042.) Surrender by William Bourk, of Loughmaek alias
Ballyloughemaek, co. Mayo, esq.; of the manor of Loughmaek,
&c., as in succeeding grant; with the intention of their being
regranted to him, his heirs and assigns. Signed, W. Bourk.
Dated 15 March, xxix.

4978 (4330.) Grant (under commission, 7 Dec., xxviii.), to Wm.
Bourk, of Loughmaek alias Ballyloughmaek, co. Mayo, esq., son
and heir of Rich. Bourk, knt. called M'William Ewghtry,
deceased; of the castle or manor of Loughmaek alias Ballyloughmaek, and 12 quarters of land belonging and adjoining to it in
the barony of Kilmean, co. Mayo, a rent of 3s. 4d. ster., from
each quarter of 15 towns of the lands of free tenants in the
barony of Kilmean, that is from the lands of the Bourkes, Jonnyns,
Clanonoiles, and Slight vic Tibbot, near the said castle, in all
60 quarters, making £10 ster. a year; the castle of Newton and
10 quarters belonging and adjoining to it in the barony of Moyn
alias Tyrawley, a rent of 5s. ster. from each of 80 quarters of

1366-7.   FIANTS.—ELIZABETH.

the lands of free tenants in the same barony, that is from the
lands of the Garretts, Bourkes, Lynotes, Clancpadyn, Carrows,
and Clancdonylles, near the said castle, which rents be receive
in satisfaction of all customs or exactions taken from the free
tenants by him or his ancestors. Also half of the goods of
persons attainted of felony, and half of other casualties within
the premises. To hold for ever, free of the composition, so that
he shall maintain so many armed horsemen and footmen, as by
the queen's commissioners shall be appointed for the defence
of the province, and shall answer all hostings without the
province as other chief lords there are bound to do. To hold as
of the castle of Stands in the same county, by the service of a
twentieth part of a knight's fee, and by the service of rendering
yearly on S. John Baptist's day to the lord deputy, a fair chief
horse, with these words inscribed in gold or silver gilt "unde
veni redeo." He may twice a year hold court baron and court
leet or view of frank pledge in the manor of Loughmask before
his seneschal. This grant shall not prejudice the rights of any
of the queen's subjects, except any claiming as M'William
Eughtry or tanist, which names are abolished. Provided that
if it be found that the queen is entitled to the lands otherwise
than by the surrender of the grantee, this grant shall be void.
Recites his surrender of the premises, 4977.—16 March, xxix.

4979 (3787.) Pardon to Wm. Archer, of Callan, co. Kilkenny,
gent., Wm. Arthur, of same, Philip Arthur, of same, Nich.
Owen, of Maylardeston, Tho. Rawghter, of Kilkenny, Gibbon
Maddoge, of Killaha, and David Howlen, of Kiltry. Not to include
murder, homicide, rebellion, arson, or rape; other provisions as in
4968, also excluding any in prison or on bail.—17 March, xxix.

4980 (4184.) Pardon to Irriall O Ferrall, of Mornyn, co. Longford,
esq., James m'Wm. O Farrell, of Barnelaughtykieve, Nich.
M'Cormick, of Clonekiy, and Donnogh m'Carthy O Farrell, of
Mornyn, horsemen, Brian roe M'Shane, of same, Gillipatrick
M'Kygo, Hugh M'Kygoe, Laghlin M'Kygoe, Connor O Hanly,
Connor M'Cormock, Tyrelagh M'Morghe, of same, and Gilli-
patrick bane M'Cormock, of Ardagh, yeomen, Daniel boy
O Farroll, of same, gent., Farriegh O Byrne, of Partynay,
Fardorgh O Byrne, and Gillernew oge O Byrne, of same, gentle-
men, Cormock oge M'Mortagh, of Kilmachanry, horsemen,
Bryan reogh M'Moragh, of same, gent., Owin O Kally, of
Ballyvrannagan, yeoman, Ferrall boy O Molloy, of Ballym'gille-
marry, gent., Daniel M'ne Kally, of Cloneagh, yeoman, Dermot
M'ne Kally, of same, yeoman, Oliver fitz Edward, of Fyne,
gent., Wm. oge O Flannagan, of Drishighan, Hugh O Flannagan,
of Clonykarran, Rory kiegh M'Dermot, of Croghan, and Owin
O Flannegan, of Rathroe, gentlemen, Sorrough ny Flannegan,
of Clonyvranan, widow, Thady M'ne Croghan, of same, yeoman,
Dermot reogh M'Tornolty, of Cloneffry, Owin O Morran, of Bally-
mollaghan, yeoman, Rory O Morran, of same, and Shane roe
O Mulchonry, of Graghabe, yeoman, Shane m'Edm. O Farrell,
of Clonemoran, Tomeltagh M'Owen, of Clonaffry, Edm.
m'Shanely M'Shanely, of Dromela, Edm. oge M'Shanely,
Rory M'Shanley, Thady balla M'Shanley, of the same, and
Orhill m'Hebbert O Farrall, of Clonnanny, gentlemen, Connor
m'En M'Geffrey, of Pallis, horsman, Donnogh M'Phelim, of

1586-7. FIANTS.—ELIZABETH.

Kilglasse, gent., Donell M'Phelym, of same, yeoman, Cecil Byrne, of Ballycomyn, widow, Donogh O Byrne, of Dangin, Garbiy O Byrne, of Clonychutkin, Lysagh M'Morogh, of Clonoghra, Wm. M'Kedagh, of Garvagh, Tho. m'Rich. m'Edmund duf, of Cregy, and Shane grana M'Richard, of same, gentlemen, and Rory O Corekran, of Clonybrenan, yeoman ; co. Longford. Provisions as in 4966. Excluding from pardon any guilty of murder or riot, or any in prison or on bail.—17 March, xxix.

4981 (4163.) Pardon to Francis Brannan, Humphrey Elliot, Tho. Wedde, Tho. Banes, Tho. Layes, Tho. Wryt, Rich. Taylor, John Wilkinson, and Randolph Flessey. Provided they conduct themselves well in future ; the pardon not to extend to treason or murder, nor to treason, robbery, or other felony committed in England, nor to release any debts to the crown.—22 March, xxix.

4982 (4166.) Pardon to Neil oge O Neale, Daniel O Neile, Shane O Neale, Manus M'Gilconnell, Edm. M'Gilconhell, Edm. m'Donell M'Gilconhell, Donogh O Mellane, Henry boy O Nellaghe and Patr. carragh O Cassy. Security as in 4942.—23 March, xxix.

4983 (4155.) Grant to Rob. Caddell, gent.; of the office of chief sergeant of the counties of Wexford and Wicklow. To hold during good behaviour, with the accustomed fees. He is not to be removed, as in 4970.—23 March, xxix. Endorsed "John Wilkinson his fiant."

4984 (5961.) Surrender by Con m'Neale oge, knt. ; of the lordship of Castlereaghe, co. Down. "Sr. Con his marke." Dated 24 March, xxix.

1587.

4985 (4333.) Grant (under queen's letter, 20 Jan., xxvii.) to Con m'Neale oge, of Castlereaghe, knt. ; of the manor or lordship of Castlereaghe, co. Down, and all lands and hereditaments belonging to it, surrendered by him by his deed, 4984, the lands of suppressed abbeys excepted. To hold for life, remainder to Hugh O Neale, his reputed son, in tail male, remainder to the heirs male of the body of Con for ever. To hold by the service of one knight's fee. Rendering yearly 250 beeves at the Newrye. He shall answer all hostings with 60 kern and 12 horsemen, armed, with victual for 40 days. If required he shall find and maintain 60 soldiers instead of the payment of beeves. He shall have a moiety of the goods of felons, and of amerciaments, waifs and strays, within the premises. He shall be free of all other composition and exactions (saving the queen's prerogative). He shall not alien for longer term than life or 21 years on pain of forfeiture.—30 March, xxix.

4986 (4192.) Pardon to Wm. Qwyne, of Crossardyrry, James Qwyne, of same, Barnaby Qwyne, son of said William, Edm. Lassy, of Lisandullone, Murughow Magonnowrey, of same, Cormac Magonnowrey, of same, and Hubert Qwyn, of same, in co. Westmeath. Provisions as in 4966.—[ ] March, xxix.

4987 (5949.) Surrender by Conill O Moloy, of Balle in the country of Fercalle, gent., chief and captain of his nation ; of the castle of Balle, and the great wood in the country of Fercalle, and all his manors and lands in that country, with the intention of their

1587.   PLANTS.—ELIZABETH

being regranted to him. "Conyll O Molloy is marke." *Dated* 31 March, xxix.

4988 (4336.) Grant (under commission, 7 Dec., xxviii.) to Conyll O Molloy, of Raly, in the country of Farrall in King's co., gent., chief and captain of his nation; of the manor, lordship, and castle of Raly with 3½ carucates of land belonging, and the great wood in Farrall, and all other lands and hereditaments which belonged to him as captain of the country of Farrall; surrendered by him by his deed (4987); also a moiety of the goods of felons, and of waifs and strays, within the country. To hold to him and the heirs male of his body for ever, by the service of the twentieth part of a knight's fee. Rent, £40 English. He shall maintain 4 horsemen, and 12 footmen for defence of the premises and to answer hostings. He may twice a year hold court baron and court leet or view of frank pledge before his seneschal. This grant shall not prejudice the rights of any of the queen's subjects, except those arising from the name O Molloy and tanist, which titles are abolished. If it should appear that the crown has title to the premises otherwise than by surrender of grantee the grant to be void. He may impose on the inhabitants of the country military service, socage, or other tenures of English law. Conyll shall during his good behaviour, according to the custom of his predecessors, be standard bearer in every general hosting.—[11 April, xxix.] (*Auditor General's Patent Book* 9, *p.* 33.)

4989 (3389.) Surrender by Rosse M'Mahowne alias Fitz Urysley, of Manachan in Ioriell alias Oriell, in the province of Ulster, knt., chief of his name; of all manors and lands in Manachan, Loghtia, Trough, Dartry, Oughnaghtia, Ballynalurgan, Tullaghegallegan, Clancarwill, and elsewhere in the cantred and lordship of Oriell, with the intention of their being regranted to him.— *Dated* 12 Ap., xxix.

4990 (3594.) License to Francis Lany, gent., to alienate the lands of Ballyowen, Kings co. to Robert Byrne, of Dublin, gent.; for the purpose of a family settlement on the marriage of John Lany, son of Richard, nephew of said Francis, with a daughter of Byrne. Julyan Grene is named as wife of Francis.—30 Ap., xxix.

4991 (4335.) Grant (under queen's letter, 20 Jan., xxvii.) to Rosse M'Mahowne alias Fitz Urysley, of Manachan in Ioriell alias Oryell in Ulster, knt.; of all manors, castles, lands, and hereditaments in Mannachan, Loughry, Troughbe, Oughmalty, Ballynalargan, Tullagh Gallagan, and Clancarwill, and all others that he has within the lordship and territory of Oryell; which he surrendered by his deed (4989); lands of religious houses excepted; also a moiety of the goods of felons, and of amerciaments, waifs, and strays. To hold in tail male, remainder to Hugh his brother in tail male, remainder to Bryan oge his brother and the heirs male of his body for ever. To hold by the service of one knight's fee. Rendering to the lord deputy yearly at Easter "a hackney;" rendering also yearly at Dondalke 400 fat beeves, 100 of which will be forgiven during good behaviour. He shall answer to all hostings with 60 kern and 24 horsemen, armed, with victual for 40 days. If required he shall find and maintain 70 soldiers with 14 allowances for officers, instead of the payment of beeves. He may twice a year hold court baron and court leet or view of frank pledge before his seneschal. He shall be free of composition and other exactions (saving the queen's prerogative). This grant shall not prejudice the rights of any of the queen's subjects, except any arising from the title of M'Mahowns or tanist which names are abolished. He shall not allow for longer than life or 21 years; or make war against the queen on pain of forfeiture.—1 May, xxix.

4992 (4148.) Pardon to Theobald Dillon, of Killenure, co. Westmeath, gent. Provisions as in 4965.—3 May, xxix.

4993 (4178.) Pardon to Walter Walshe, of Castlehowell, esq., late sheriff of co. Kilkenny, Edm. Walshe fitz Rob., of Garridufe, gent., Patr. Shortall, of Cloghmantagh, clerk, Rich. Forstall fitz Edm., of Callan, yeoman, Rich. Walshe fitz James, of Knockmoylan, James Graunto, of Ballynchohe, John Walshe fitz Wm., of the Ardery, gent., Wm. Brenagh fitz Rice, of Mallaghmore, yeoman, James Walshe fitz Oliver, of Liscrolin, gent., Tho. Mac Keylkey, of Tampullorum, husbandman, David Henebery, of Ballitresell, yeoman, Adam Grace, of Kilrindoine, Wm. Walshe fitz John, of Ballynere, Walter Butler fitz Edm., of Ballaraged, gent., John Comerford fitz Peirs, of Clone, John glass fitz William, of Ballihowell, Peter Walsh fitz John, of Ardery, Oliver Swetman, of Castellife, and Gerald fitz Lewes Brian, of Whiteswall, yeoman, Nich. Artore, of Callan, clerk, Wm. Butler fitz David, of Kereboll, gent., Oliver Walsh fitz John, of Ballyneowley, Peter M'Coddie, of Monero, Eny Kavanagh, of Castlehowell, and Walter Butler fitz Theobald, of Kildromy, yeomen, Walter Daton, of Clonecony, and Walter Butler fitz Piers, of the Annaghes, gentlemen, John Butler fitz Theobald, of Kildromy, Rich. Brenagh fitz Oliver, of Kiltockeghand, and Nich. Oroke, of Tampullorum, yeomen, James Dullany alias Britt, of Kilkeny, husb., Charles fitz Lewes Brian, of Whites wall, and John Butler fitz James, of Ballydavid, yeomen, Rice Brenagh fitz James, of Kilmanshin, husb., Arland Graunte, of Ballyneholy, John Walshe fitz Oliver, of Knockmoylan, Philip Walsh fitz Walter, of Ballogrike, John O Brohie, of Kilorwhe, Rich. Walshe fitz Wm., of Ballylosky, and Wm. Walsh fitz Wm., of same, yeomen, and Margaret Tobyn fitz Tho., of Moyhall, widow. Provisions as in 4965. The pardon not to include the killing of Cahir Eglanna.—4 May, xxix.

4994 (4190.) Pardon to Rich. Sals, of Saleston, co. Meath, yeoman. Provisions as in 4966.—5 May, xxix.

4995 (4189.) Pardon to Patr. Bath, of Trynleston, co. Meath, yeoman, John Barnewall, gent., Tho. Dardyz, yeoman, and Owny Magohegan, kern, of the same; for the slaying of Bryen roo O Manynge. Recites that a writ from the Exchequer, and a special warrant from Rich. Bingham, knt., principal commissioner of Connaght, directed Tho. Morton, sheriff of Galway, to deliver seisin of the castle of Molagh, co. Galway, to Teige oge O Kelley m'Enah. The sheriff gave the writ to his brother Hugh Morton, who authorised the above parties with many others to execute it, who being resisted had to use force, when the said Bryen was killed by said Patrick. Security as in 4943. The pardon shall not include murder.—12 May, xxix.

4996 (4329.) Grant (under queen's letter, 9 Feb., xxix.) to Wm. Parris; of the rent of £17 3s. 4d. reserved in 280. To hold

1587.   FIANTS.—ELIZABETH.

to him his heirs and assigns.   Reciter No. 217, Ph. and Mary
and 380 Eliz.—12 May, xxix.

4997 (4185.) Pardon to Donogh m'Dermot duff m'Donall oge,
yeoman, Maurice M'Thomas, of Kleryonrihle, ploughman,
Fynnen [   ] Dresmolla, yeoman, Margaret Horley, John
m'Donogh m'Shane O Holloghan, yeoman, Dermot O Regan,
Wm. m'Dermot oge Vige, Auliffe oge O Holloghan, Connogher
rowe O Lennan, and Thady m'Dermody O Hogain, yeoman,
Nich. Conrasy, clerk, Katherine uy Monyghan, widow, Ellis
Waster, Dermot m'Donnogh M'Fynnen, yeoman, Melaghlan
O Lyon, Thady [   ] M'Donnogh, yeoman, Thady m'Dermed
M'Kahlie, and David Connell, yeoman, Dermot row M'Mahowny,
Fynen m'Owen M'Dermady, gent., Philip m'Wm. O Hownyghan,
yeoman, Donogh fitz Wm. O Marayne, Donell m'Dermedy
I Regaine, yeoman, Dermot m'Teige m'Auliffe I Cralle, yeoman,
James fitz Philip Roche, merchant, Rob. fitz Wm. Barrett, and
Donogh m'Dermedy Lyneny, yeoman, Patr. fitz John Goule,
merchant, John Moore, Edw. Gosse, and Reyry m'Manns
M'Shihie, yeoman, Maurice m'Teige I Connoghor, Edm. m'Donogh
I Marroghowe, yeoman, Owin m'Auliffe I Swylyvan, Tho.
m'Teige I Murroghow, Thady m'Beige I Swyleven, Philip
m'Shirahie I Connell, James fitz [   ] Roche, Donogh
O Mahownigh, Fynen m'Donogh M'Auliff, and Murriertagh
O Shaine, yeoman, Nich. Barry alias m'Shlemla, gent., Rob. Lacy
fitz Rob., Donogh m'Dermedy I Hirine, Gerald fitz John Fitz
Edmond, Maurice fitz Davy Connyll, Maurice fitz Tho. Fitz
Nicholas, and Oyan m'Owen M'Oyan, yeoman, Shan oge
O Byrren, Donogh m'Donell Horley, yeoman, Ranall Hoorley,
junior, gent., Thady m'Donogh O Harraghan, Ellin ny Owen
uy Agherin, Dermot O Morroghow, yeoman, Gillis ny Morie
M'Wllam, Edm. Brydy, yeoman, Muroghow m'Teige I Agherin,
John Leyn, John oge M'Shane, Thady M'Kennealla, and Dermot
m'Donnoge oge O Daly, yeoman, Elline ny Donnogh I Mahowny,
Dermot m'Fynen raigh, Thady O Flwyn, Thady m'Donogh
M'Fynen, yeoman, Ellin Conden, and Andrew m'Dermot
O Daley; co. Cork.   Provision as in 1995. Provided that they
submit to any orders touching their lands as in 4936.—17 (?)
May, xxix.

4998 (4136.) Pardon to James Meagh, of Kynsale, co. Cork, merchant, by reason of letters of Walter Rawley, knt., to the lord
deputy, dated 12 August, 1586.   Provisions as in 1988.—
17 May, xxix.

4999 (5593.) License to Thomas Morys, to alienate to any of
English birth and a dutiful subject, the lands of Latey, Drenkny
alias Morishton, and Newton, King's co.   Held under grant
3471.—18 May, xxix.

5000 (5908.) Grant to John Morgane, gent.; of the wardship and
marriage of Anthony, son and heir of Richard Delabide, late of
Loghabanan, co. Dublin, gent.; and custody of his lands during
minority.   Rent, £3 6s. 8d., and retaining 33s. 4d. for support
of the minor. Fine, £5.—18 May, xxix.

5001 (4131.) Grant to George Plessanton; of the office of porter
of the fortress of Marryborough, Queen's co.   To hold during
good behaviour, as Rich. Fawcett held it.—20 May, xxix.

5002 (4188.) Pardon to Morragh M'Tyrlagh, of Clontrige, Oliver fits James, of Tomdoilyn, Manns oge M'Shee, of Ballisgine, Thady M'Murtagh, of Ballynealy, Manis m'Edm. M'Shee, of Bally-allyn, Philip oge M'Philip, of Castleton, Donogh O Dologher, of Yoynes, Morogh O Dologhar, Thady O Dologher, of same, Dermot M'Kenraghta, of Kilnaghtan, John O Callan, of Argell, John O Barry, of Ballistin, Thady M'Thomas, John M'Ea, of same, Maurice m'Teige O Drehitt, of Keary, Moriertagh M'Teige, of Carrygerry, Mahown M'Kennedy, of Ororanghan, Donogh m'Dermot M'Mahown, of Laffaly, Edm. Fitz Gerald, of Lessorell, Redm. Stackoldton fits Edm., of Fertramay, Daniel Kelly, of Ballitarsane, and Donogh O Kelly; on Limerick. Provisions as in 4997.—25 May, xxix.

5003 (4335.) Lease (under commission, 17 Jan., xxvi.) to John English Dongan, gent., second remembrancer of the Exchequer; of the rectory of Moyneal, co. Meath, parcel of the possessions of the priory of Moliagar, and the tithes of corn belonging to it in Moyned, Kiltride, Fylleston, Clonaffan, Strowan, and Robartis-ton, and one portion of the altarages. To hold for 21 years llant, £13 6s. 8d. Provisions as in 4039. Fine, £18 6s. 8d.— 20 May, xxix.

5004 (5005.) Grant to Edward Milles or Mylles; of the wardship and marriage of Nicholas, son and heir of John, son of Peter Poar, late of Ballalaghnyo, co. Waterford; and custody of his lands, during minority. Rent, 10s., and retaining 6s. for support of the minor. Fine, 16s.—20 May, xxix.

5005 (4167.) Pardon to Geoffrey Fitz Patricke, horseman, Wm. Moore M'Donell, Philip M'Hewgh, Neall duffe O Brenan, Shane M'Mulrian, and Teig M'Mullrone, kerns, James Britt, husband-man, Lym M'Arte, kern, Cahir m'Dallo O Brian, horseman, Donell owre O Lalor, kern, Dermond owre O Hanis, horseman, Shery M'Melaughlin, stokagh, Gill Patrisk M'Melaughlin, Tir-langh O Birne, James M'William, stokaghs, Dermond M'Shane, of Ballytarmey, horseman, sir Denny O Rowhan, priest; Queen's co. Provisions as in 4965.—1 June, xxix.

5006 (4314.) Pardon to Darmot O Brian, of Poblebryan, gent. Tho. oge O Haraghtan, Owin m'Donogh Mac Carty, husband-men, Edm. m'Roh Peirce, Moriertagh m'Dermot M'Bryen, of Poblegreny, Dermot owar mac Phillip Mac Conogher, of same, Teig rowe m'Wm. M'Shane, of same, and Malaghlyn rowe m'Donell O Haynyn, footman, Gobyrie O Donyall, of Balynay-bwrranche, husb., Dermot rowe mac Mahowny O Ryaky, of Cahirelly, laborer, Teige mac Brian ballagh O Brian, of Toogh-engrey, footman, Rory O Hee, of same, husb., Dermot cron O Moghytaughlan, of Clangibbons, Conogher m'Donogho M'Dar-nedy, of same, and Dermot m'Edm. O Klaghery, of same, footman, Donogh m'Shano moell MacCraith, of Galbally, Tho. mac Walter Browne, John fits Walter Browne, and John fits David Loppf }, of same, labourers, Philip Mac David, of same, husb., Donogho O Klocassy, and John m'Conogher O Mulcahy, of same, labourers, Donell O Hallynan, of same, footman, Donogh m'Teige M'Brian, of same, Donell oge O Glynan, of Balle Igry, and Donell roo M'Donogho, of Beallaghysymon, husbandmen, John fits Edm. fits Walter, of same, gent., John fits David M'Thomas, of Ballenlogban, husb., Charney O Hif-

1587.   FIANTS.—ELIZABETH.

ferman, of same, Donell M'Grath, of Garrenbon, yeoman, Walter Englishe, of Solkoidbegg, Mahowne O Hiffernane, of Latten, yeoman, Edm. fitz Patrick M'Reall, of same, labourer, Ullig m'Wm. Derry[   ] Bourke, of Clonmollen, horseman, Donnogh geankagh O Dhoygin, of Sroneil, Rory oge m'Donogho O Ree, in eo. Limerick, Tibbot Bourke, of Ballevadige, yeoman, John Breagagh M'Thomas, of Connollagh, Rich. oge White, of Logaill, husbandman, Cormoiok m'Ricoard Oher, of Pallyahegnay, yeoman, Rich. nvkoyily Brenagh, of Castelton O Coningh, and Donell m'Morrogho O Dwirky, of Myleton, footman, Mahowne reogh m'Morrogho O Dwirky, of same, yeoman, Donell m'Mahowny O Dwyrky, of same, Gilladuff m'Tho. O Hee, of Carrickogouagh, husbandman, Donell m'Dermot O Moiresh, of Owney, stockagh, Rish. Laas, of Toollaobhin, footman, Teig O Loyasaey, of Ballybrickyn, co. Limerick, hush. Owner roo m'Mahowny M'Brien, of Ballyvongne, Brian m'Owny M'Brian, of the Knockgar, footman, John O Hogaine, of Kwylhygan, Owin O Hiffernaine, of Bayttcarratho, husbandman, Ullig m'Ricoard Bourke, of Barranston, footman, Conall m'Et O Donall, of Carragh, Ellen Hesketh fits Wm., of Milliston, widow, Conoghor m'Owin M'Dermot, Mahowne O Hovrigaine, of Ballybrickyn, labourer, Donell boy M'Owen, Teig m'Rory oge, of Cahirkenlis, co. Limerick, smith, Phillip Hurty fits Edm., of Knorlagh, Donogho M'Teig, of same, kern, Tho. O Krighan, of same, kern, John O Dolane, of Newcastell, Riccard mac Ullig M'Mellary, of Knyllyhenaine, John m'Thomas Vernaygh, of Keanry, co. Limerick, John m'Edm. M'Shane, of same, and Edm. m'Shane oge, of the Pallish, footman, John O Kerynakyn, of Ballynygearde, hush., Donell m'Teige ra'ny Gilladuffe O Brian, John oge m'Shane M'Gervald, hush., and Gerald leigh Peiroe; co. Limerick and Tipperary. Provisions as in 1538.— Also excluding murder.—1 J[une], xxix.

5007 (4151.) Commission to Roh. Fowle, provost marshal **of the** xallis. province of Connaght; to execute martial law in the province of Connaght and Thomcunde, as in 218.—1 June, xxix.

5008 (4152.) Commission to Walter Nangle, sheriff of Downe; Pagew. to execute martial law in that county, as in 213.—6 June, xxix.

5009 (4187.) Pardon to Dermot O'Connor, of Ballynebeilly, co. Roscommon, gent., Tyriongh O'Conner, of same, gent., David O. Nary, of same, horseman, Dluryn ny Vyra, of same, Katherine ny Vym, of Portyreany, gentlewomen, Wm. m'Thomas Etlavry, of Casteltogher, gent., Bryen O Hedlan, of Tryennecrevea, Cormock fyn O Byrne, of Ballenaboyllie, Edm. O Flanegan, of Ballevoghter, husbandman, Melaghlin O Teige, of same, cottier, Shane O Flanegan, of same, Shane M'Gilgowlye, of Baare, husbandman, Teige O Feaghy, of Ballenebeilly, cottier, Feien O Flanegan, of Ballevoghter; hush, Edm. m'Donogho amagh, of Clombayonagh, cottier; Hubert m'Donogho narragh, of same, cottier; Direvorgill ny Connally, of Lovally, Kedagh O Connor, of Ballenebeilly, gent., Gerrott M'Gerald, of Clane, gent., Brien ballagh O Connor, of same, gent., Donagh M'Donell, and Garrott m'Rocry O Farvall, of same, kerns, Shane O Shaughnessa, of same, yeoman, Brien m'Edm. M'Breuan, of same, hush., Rory O Hallowcan, of Clara, Mahowne O Lavnan, Conchor M'Thomas, of same, cottiers, Shane M'Riccard, Rickard M'Hugh, and Hugh

O Syden, of same, kerne, Rich. Goldinge, of Lisduf, yeoman, Roger Tailun, of Clanbegury, Donell O Beolan, of Barnwicke, Gilpatrick m'Shane M'Coyne, of Dromsanis, Diermot m'Edm. M'Coyne, of same, cottiers, Melaughlen reogh O Donelan, of Ballydowelan, gent., Gillecreest O Donelan, of same, husb., Wonie O Loghlin, of Ballnamsan, and Rosse O Laughlen, of Corbally more, kerne, Wm. fyne O Donelan, of Ballydonelan, Rory M'Eynaghan, of Moate, Brien M'Maghn, of Garves, and Rickard oge M'Grovye, of Byanars, husbandmen, Rory oge m'Mosimury M'Dowda, of Corougy, gent., Owen m'Brien M'Gilmartin, of same, Manus m'Teige M'Gwen, of same, Henry m'Manus O Naighten, of Ardkynata, Diermot M'Dowill, of Loghsillyarn, Shane O Brollan m'Moriertagh duf, of same, Malnoghlin M'Downy, of Rathmore, Tho. O Mayn, of Gilragh, and Shane O Grady, of Garts, kerne, Robart oge M'Redmond, of Castleboy, husb., Hubbert boy M'Redmond, of Castleton, gent., Edm. O Hurm, of Fay, husb., Gilleduf M'Rickard, of Moy, kern, Diermott reogh M'Callo, of Killosse, husb., Donogh O Connor, of Clongary, and Collo M'Dowill, of Ballaneboylly, cottiers, Nich. Howet, of Kilcranaght, yeoman, and Shane M'Garrett, of Ballakanny, gent., co. Roscommon. Provisions as in 4065.—9 June, xxix.

5010 (4521.) Grant (under queen's letter, 1 Aug., xxviii.) to Tho. Challonur, gent.; of a messuage with a garden in the High street of Dublin, parcel of the lands of David Sutton, attainted, lying between the tenement late of John Burnall towards the east, and the land of Chr. Sedgrawe to the west, and between the High street on the south and the said garden on the north; also a vacant piece of land, 60 feet in length by 25 in breadth, in S. Patrick's street in the suburbs of Dublin, by the land of Chr. Hollywood, parcel of the lands of David Sutton, attainted. To hold for ever, in free soccage. Rent £5 16s. 4d.—13 June, xxix.

5011 (4334.) Grant (under queen's letter, 1 Aug., xxviii.) to Tho. Challoner, gent.; of a castle, 12 messuages with gardens, and a water mill in the town of Nass, co. Kildare, possessions of Tho. Eustace, attainted. To hold for ever, by the service of a fortieth part of a knight's fee. Rent £3 16s. 8d.—13 June, xxix.

5012 (4338.) Grant (under queen's letter, 1 Aug., xxviii.) to Tho. Challoner, gent.; of a castle in decay with gardens and a grove of ashes, 18 cottages with the customs of the tenants, and the lands of Carlistown or Cardiffstown, co. Kildare, with common of pasture on the moor there, parcel of the lands of Tho. Eustace, attainted; messuages and lands in Ballemadden alias Maddensten, co. Kildare, with liberty of making turf on the moor there, parcel of the lands of James Eustace, late viscount of Baltinglas, attainted. To hold for ever, by the service of a fortieth part of a knight's fee. Rent £10 for Cardiffstown, and £16 13s. 4d. for Ballymadden.—13 June, xxix.

5013 (4134.) Grant to Turlogh lenaghe (under queen's letter, 10 May, xxix.) for his life; of the captainry of the whole country of Tyrone in Ulster, with its jurisdictions, privileges, and hereditaments, except such parcels as he had demised to the earl of Tyrone at an annual rent of 1,000 marks English. This rent is to be paid to him by the queen's treasurer out of the same to be paid for by the earl for the pay and support of 50 horsemen. Should the same not prove sufficient, the lord deputy shall cause

1587.   FIANTS.—ELIZABETH.

the earl to give security to satisfy Tirlogh. Tirlogh may also exercise his superiority over Maguyer and O Chan and their countries, as under his first composition with the earl of Essex he might.—18 June, xxix.

5014 (4184.) Lease (under commission, 17 Jan., xxvi.) to Stephen Segar, gent., constable of the castle of Dublin; of a parcel of land within the precinct of the castle of Dublin, containing half an acre, lying against the east and south of the castle, where there have been fish ponds or weirs, another parcel of land against the walls of the castle towards the north, containing 100 feet in length by 100 feet in breadth, also a mill place where the king's mill sometime stood within the precinct aforesaid, with the water course, being part of the ditch of the castle, and running from Powll mill downwards along the south side thereof, all parcel of the queen's ancient inheritance. To hold for 31 years, rent for the land 20d., and for the mill place £5 6s. 8d. The lessee shall within two years, build a mill on or near the site of the king's mill. He shall not allen, except to English, without license. He shall enroll the lease in the Auditor General's office within 6 months.—16 June, xxix.

5015 (4182.) Pardon to Phelim Shennagh, Couconnsugh M'Kernan, Teig oge Mac Kernan, Phelim boy M'Kernan, John oge Mac Kernan, Patr. O Brenan, Ferrall M'Fengh, kern, Brian ogo m'Breno Ferroll, Wm. O Donnell, and Wm. M'Melanghlen, kerns, John O Multally, idleman, Donogh O Galligan, Wm. Frtigan, and Tho. Haiks; co. Westmenth. Provisions as in 4966.—1 July, xxix.

5016 (5906.) Grant to Thomas Thwaytu, gent.; of the wardship and marriage of Richard, brother and heir of John Nugent, late of Clonenakenan, co. Waterford, gent.; and custody of his lands, during minority. Rent 90s., and retaining 30s. for support of the minor. Fine 20s. English.—3 July, xxix.

5017 (5515.) Grant (under queen's letter, 4 Ap., xxix.) to Katharine Carew of a pension of 12d. sterling a day, for life. Her husband Peter Carew, one of the pensioners, and constable of the castle of Donluce, had been betrayed by his man and slain in the castle by the Scots, leaving his widow with five small children.—4 July, xxix.

5018 (4337.) Grant (under queen's letter, 1 Aug., xxviii.) to Tho. Challoner, gent.; of lands in Newtown of Clane, and a grove of ash there, co. Kildare, parcel of the lands of Edm. Eustace, attainted. To hold for ever, by the service of a fortieth part of a knight's fee. Rent £3 10s.—5 July, xxix.

5019 (5909.) Grant to Nicholas St. Laurence, of Obreston, esq.; of the wardship and marriage of Walter, son and heir of John Goldinge, late of Pairstonlaundy, co. Meath, gent.; and custody of his lands, during minority. No rent, on account of the charges for the children of Walter Goldinge, father of John. Fine 40s. —11 July, xxix.

5020 (5910.) Grant to Jonatan Quarlesse and John Walford, gentlemen; of. the wardship and marriage of Robert, son and heir of James Preston, late of Balmadon, gent.; and the custody of his lands and of those which shall fall in by the death of Jane Howthe, mother of James, and Eleanor Talbot alias Preston, his widow, during minority. Rent of £5 16s. 8d., and retaining £5 16s. 8d. for support of the minor. Fine £11 13s. 4d.—13 July, xxix.

5021 (4146.) Commission to Adam, archbishop of Dublin, lord chancellor, Tho. earl of Ormond, lord treasurer, John, archb. of Armagh, Wm. archb. of Tuam, Henry, earl of Kildare, Ullick, earl of Clanricard, Donagh, earl of Thomond, Tho. bishop of Meath, John, bishop of Kilmore, Stephen, bishop of Clonfert, John, bishop of Elfyn, Edm. lord Bernigham, H. Wallop, knt., vice treasurer, N. Bagnoll, knt., marshal, chief justices Gardiner and Dillon, chief baron Dillon, N. White, knt., master of the rolls, Tho. Le Strange, knt., chief commissioner in the province of Connaught, Henry Colley, knt., Edw. Watirhouse, knt., Geoffrey Fenton, esq., and Edw. Brabazon, esq., members of the privy council, Tho. Dillon, chief justice of the province, Edw. Fitz Symon, serjeant at law, Charles Calthorp, attorney general, Roger Wilbraham, principal solicitor, Anthony Brabazon, George Byngham, Nathaniel Smyth, Francis Barkley, Rob. Fowle, esquires, and the mayor of Galvey; to be commissioners in the province of Connaght, to take musters and array of the inhabitants, and assess them, according to their lands and goods, in horses, arms, horsemen, and footmen; to raise and distribute men for defence of the country; to punish, fine and imprison disobedient persons and rebels; to treat with enemies and rebels, granting safe conducts for that purpose, and conclude terms at discretion; to levy forces for the prosecution of rebels, and chasties them with fire and sword, (Le Strange to be general of the forces in the field); and to execute the instructions of the lord deputy, of 14 July, xxix.—13 July, xxix. "Commission for marshall affaires in Conaght."

5022 (4313.) Commission to Adam, archbishop of Dublin, lord chancellor, and others in preceding commission, with the addition of Tirlangh O Brien, knt.; to be justices and commissioners in the province of Conaght, for the civil government of the province, with power to hear and determine all suits, and to take recognizances.—12 July, xxix.

5023 (4145.) Commission to sir Tho. Le Strange, knt., chief commissioner of the province of Connaght and Thomond; to execute martial law in the province, as in 318.—13 July, xxix.

5024 (4183.) Pardon to Teig O Mahowne alias Teig ne Beligy, of Kilpatrick, co. Cork, gent., Gerott m'Wm. reagh Roch, of the Sheghan, Wm. and Owen m'Teg M'Morish, of Kilmahonnock; accused of the robbery, or of abetting the robbery, of cows of David oge O Culan and his tenants. Security as in 4943. They are to make restitution.—18 July, xxix.

5025 (4181.) Pardon to Wm. Goughe, husbandman, in co. Waterford. Provisions as in 4968.—25 July, xxix.

5026 (4180.) Pardon to Teige oge O Harte, of Doncoore, Teig O Harte, of the Grandg, Owin, Hugh, Brian, and Mullaghlin O Harts, of the same, Donell crone O Connor, of Taghtample, Teig buy O Connor, and Hugh buy O Connor, of same, horsemen, Maw ny Connor, daughter of Cahill og, of Sligo, gent., Owan bantagh O Harte, of Castlelonghdeargan, horseman, Kendagh M'Dowany, of Sligo, husb., Sawerly O Harte, of Sligo, horseman, Finghrae O Dowds, of Inishgrewin, gent., Brian M'Donoghey,

c

1587.   FIANTS.—ELIZABETH.

of Ballinaghan, Cahill oge M'Donoghey, and Hugh M'Donoghey, horseman, Walter M'Johain, of the Longford, husb., Shane oge O Harra, of Balliharaa, horseman, Gille Oullam O Higgin, of Moytaugh, Brian O Higgin, Wm. O Higgen, of same, and Shane O Cahan, of Sligo, husbandmen, Redmond M'Gwyre, Bryen oge M'Gwyre, of same, horseman, Cahill M'Hugh, of Ballindowne, and Owen M'Nymye, of Emalaghyshill, husbandmen, Rory O Harta, of Brakeaallen, Kradagh O Harta, Phelim O Harta, Donogh oge O Harta, and Connor O Harte alias M'Swyine, of same, horsemen ; co. Sligo. Provisions as in 4938. Also excepting murder. Teig oge O Harte excepted from the provisions excluding any in prison, or who have committed offences worthy of death. Fine 20s, for Teig oge O Harte, and 5s. for each of the others.—27 July, xxix.

5027 (4143.) Commission to sir Coohonaght Magwyre, knt., to execute martial law in the county of Inyahkillye, as in 216.— 18 Aug., xxix.

5028 (4179.) Pardon to Geralt m'Brien Cavanaghe, of Tynerann, co. Carlow, gent., Morish and Turlangh m'Cahir Cavanagh, Donell m'Brian m'Dowlin Cavanaughe, Edm. m'Art m'Dowlin Cavanaghe, Chriffin m'Morish m'Dowlin Cavanaghe, of the same, Chriffin M'Donnell, of Ballocormoke, co. Wexford, yeoman, Adam O Currin, Teige carrough O Currin, James duffe O Currin, Teige ne monne, Teige and Davie m'William Carde, Turlaugh ballow M'Morrough, Donall O Neill, Art m'Hugh O Neill, Owen m'Donnell O Neill, Edm. duffe M'Colletan, Mortagh moill O Neill, Donnell duffe M'Colletan, Shane M'Conoghor, Dermot m'Shane O Molinge, Shane m'Teige igh Counie, Hugh m'Edm. O Neill, Shane booy O Kannedia, Dermot m'Morough m'Morish Cavanaughe, James m'Richard ballowe, Henry carrough M'Donnogh, Geralt m'Donnell M'Arte, Morough m'Cahir O Donell, Donnogh roe O Fogertie boye, Dermott O Fogertie, Donell m'Shane leagh boye, Edm. m'Teige ower boye, Edw. O Cleare, of Ballarill, co. Wexford, Shorany O Mullconnor, of Culrowe, co. Kilkenny, Owen M'Braine, of Ballicannie, co. Wexford, Katherine ny Kahir Cavanaghe, Katherine nyne Owen O Donell, Donell roogh m'Morrogh backeugh Cavanagh, freeholder, Dermot ower m'Morough baokagh, of Knockin, freeholder, Edm. ower M'Donnell, of Ballihanry, freeholder, Donnogh duffe m'Morough O Ryna, of S. Molinge, husbandman, Edm. m'Donnell M'Garralt, of Ballecronagan, and Morogh m'Donnell M'Garalt, of same, freeholders, Donogh m'Dermot M'Gillpatrick, of Okunimerigh, Morogh carrogh m'Shane glame, of Lasmullion, Donnell m'Shane O Ryan, of Oollahan, Emonds M'Redmonde, of S. Molinge, Gilledaffe O Currin, of same, Morogh more O Currin, of Ballian, Donnogh rowe m'Donnogh Duell, and Edm. duffe m'Morogh O Donell, husbandmen, Turlagh duffe m'Morrogh O Rian, Arte m'Dermott Cavanaghe, of Tinanrigh, freeholder, Edm. m'Morogh M'Mortagh, of Killegasy, co. Wexford, freeholder, Wm. O Folligh, of same, husb., Teige m'Mortagh moill, of Mungart, co. Wexford, husb., Davie Lade alias O Laoye, of Tomgaddy, in co. Wexford. Provided that they appear and submit before the justices of assize next after the succeeding Michaelmas, and be bound with sureties to keep the peace. (The remainder of this clause as in 4943 was struck

1587.   PLANTS.—ELIZABETH.

out by the lord deputy.) The pardon not to include intrusion into crown lands or debts to the crown.—18 Aug., xxix.

5029 (6103.) Pardon to Gerald Comway, lord baron of Courcey; for alienating to Florence M'Carty, the manor of Ringroone, containing 1 carucate, both Killokyrans ½ car., Ballycantyns 1 car., Cortnyerusaye 1 car., and Ballyvisradmonde 1 quarter; to Patrick Meaghe, the Castle of Parke with 1½ car.; to Owen M'Carty, knt., the manor of Downe-M'Patricke alias the Oldahedd of Kynsale 1 car., Lyswadigge 1 car., Kylemore 1 car., Cortnyerusaye 1 car., Cortnyperusaye 1 car., Manemore ½ car.; to Shena ny Kayntye, widow, Ralyns ½ car., and Kyleboge ½ car.; to Donagh oge O Kullane, Curryhwo and Ballyhander ½ car., Dromedoghar 1 car., Cowreytahilley ½ car.; to John m'Teige Y Murhillye, Ballenedowney ½ car., Carigwilyne ½ car., Ballyroe ½ car., and Dromduoghbegge ½ car.; to Thomas m'Moryce Y Maddigane, Banynyscartye; (to Philip Roche fitz John, Ballynetwolye 1 car., Arikyllye 1 car., Glawencytewhrey ½ car., Bally-vicdaridegge 1 quarter, Ardywarigge 1 quarter, struck out); to Richard Roche fitz Phillippe, Eanaghan 1 car., and Downemuckeane ½ car.; (to Christopher Galwaye, Toonmogyha 1 car. struck out); to Donald m'Conoghor boye, Ballynagarteghe 1 car., Rookeston 1 car. in occupation of Dermot m'Donyll M'Cartyn, and Killsodman 1 car. Fine £19 10s.—26 Aug., xxix.

5030 (4126.) Grant to John Ball, gent.; of the offices of serjeant-at-arms of Ireland, and marshal of the four courts. To hold during good behaviour, with such fees as Hugh Payne, or any other had. Not to be removed, as in 1476.—27 Aug., xxix.

5031 (4415.) Commission to chief justices Gardener and Dillon, chief baron Dillon, N. Whit, master of the rolls, Geoffrey Fenton, secretary of Ireland, and Charles Calthrop, attorney-general, according to queen's letter of (   ) May,   , and indentures with Hugh, earl of Tereone, of 13 May last; to view and set out, by oath of a jury, the bounds and contents of the manors and lands in the country of Tereone granted to the said Hugh, and also all other manors and lands in the same country held by Neill, late father of Turlaghe leinaghe, or any other person, by rents or services to Con, late earl of Tereone, and also the amount of such rents and services as were answered to the said Con after he was created an earl.—1 Sep., xxix.

5032 (6550.) Grant to Sir Edward Fytun, knt.; of the barony, manor, castle, and borough town, of Awney, containing in demesne 4 ploughlands, the lands of Kilkellan, Caima, the castle and lands of Ballynemonymoore and Ballynemonybeg, the castle and lands of Knockmonye, the castle and lands of Fitown, 6 ploughlands; the lands of Banoge, Cloghdolordy and Balintawvishy, Tirvowe, the castle and lands of Cloughbrettin, 3½ pl.; the lands of Rahan, Bawhunda, Rowre, and Glenamore, 1½ pl.; the castle and lands of Cromwell; the castle and lands of Karrykettle, the house called the Carbe, and late house and lands called Killilie, near Karrykettle, 1½ pl.; a stone house and a thatched house in Kilnalloch, lately occupied by George Meagh fitz Richard; the castle and lands of Coullanaghgrough, in the counties of Limerick and Tipperary, 4 pl.; the castle and lands of [   ]Jardan, with the Tough, 3 pl.; the castles and lands of Balynecourty, Clonbeg

and Dungrott, in Aharlow, 1 ploughland ; the reversion and rent
of 13s. 4d., Irish, out of a house in Waterford, occupied by
(   ) Thewe ; the manor, castle, and lands of Kylmanchin, co.
Waterford containing in demesne 3 pl. ; and all appurtenances of
the premises in the counties of Limerick, Tipperary, and Waterford, amounting in all to 26½ ploughlands, and rated to 11,515
acres of English measure at the rate of 16½ feet to the perch ;
also the rents and services of the free tenants within the said
barony and manors, viz.:—the yearly rent of £6 "halface" and
other customs from James Foxe for Ballygidden and his freeholds,
£4 halface and all other customs of Richard Doundowne for
Balyhuarde, 20s. halface and all other customs of Philip Suppell
for Balinonl[   ], £4 12s. 0d. halface and all other customs of
James Rowley for Ballynrowley, £4 halface and all other customs
of Edmund Boggott of Boggottstowne for his freehold, 24s. halface
and all other customs of Mahone MacTego of Ballynsholly for
his freehold, 24s. halface and all other customs of Wm. Richford
for Ballyhubbard his freehold, 20s. halface and all other customs of
Wm. Nugent for Kilfrust his freehold, 10s. halface and all
other customs of William Marshall for Cloughvillair his freehold, 5s. halface and the services of the inheritors of the lands
called the [   ], £5 and all the customs of the burgages of
the said borough town of Awney, and all other rents and services
of the free tenants of the barony and manor of Awney ; the
fairs and markets in Awney with their customs and tolls ; and a
rent of 20s. Irish and all services out of the lands of Russells-
towne, Kilronan, and Banfin, belonging to the said manor of
Kilmanchin, 20s. Irish, and all services out of Conaughe, Sylyhin,
Welches garden, Balevicalebry, to the said manor, 20s. Irish and
all services out of Courtersw[   ], Ballygewer, and Rallyrogan, to the
said manor, 12s. Irish and all services out of Ballimachoe to the
said manor, and all rents and services of all the free and other
tenants within the manor of Kilmanchin. To hold for ever by
the name of the seignory of Goldesworth, in fee farm in free and
common socage. Rent £98 19s. 2½d. English, from Michaelmas
1594 (half that sum for the preceding three years) and also
£41 18s. 4d. starling for the rents and services of free tenants.
This grant is under queen's letter, 27 June, xxviii. for the repeo-
pling of Munster with loyal subjects, and is subject to the following
conditions. There must be paid on the death or alienation of
the tenant or owner of the principal residence and demesne, the
best beast as a heriot ; relief must be paid on the death of grantee
his heirs and assigns according to the usage in England between
common persons ; if within seven years the value of any of the
lands is found to have been concealed, and that at any former
time anyone paid a larger rent, such rent shall become payable
under this grant ; if the commissioners of Survey in Munster
return that the premises contain more than 11,515 acres at the
rate of 16½ feet to the perch, the rent shall be increased at the
rate of 2½d. for each additional acre in co. Limerick, 1½d. for
each acre in co. Tipperary and Waterford ; grantee and assigns
may export to England and Wales, corn, grain and other victuals
whatsoever grown upon the premises free of custom poundage or
other duty ; they may enclose and impark 600 acres or less, for
horses and deer, with liberty of free warren and park for ever ;

1587.   FIANTS.—ELIZABETH.

grantee and inhabitants are discharged from all rents, charges,
incumbrances, cesses, customs, and impositions whatsoever
except those named in this grant, or which shall be imposed
by parliament after 1594, or which are required by the articles
of the plantation; grantee shall erect houses for 87 families,
one of which to be for the principal residence of him and his
assigns, 6 others for freeholders having each at least 300 acres,
6 others for farmers having each at least 400 acres, 38 others
for copyholders or others of baser tenures having each at least 100
acres, and to each of the remainder either 50, 25 or 10 acres at
the pleasure of the grantee; if any of these houses be unbuilt
by Michaelmas, 1594, the crown may enter a corresponding
portion of the land and retain it until the houses be built; if
after that date any of the houses remain uninhabited for 60 days
in one year, notice shall be given by an officer of the crown, and
they remaining unoccupied for 6 months may with the lands belonging be entered by the crown, grantee receiving no abatement
of rent but being able to recover them on providing occupants;
grantee and his assigns may alien any part of the lands, the
capital messuage and demesne excepted, to any person willing to
take the same, to be held of him for ever; provided that if any
alienation of any part of the premises be made by grantee or
his assigns to any being mere Irish not descended of an original
English ancestor of name and blood, and be not redeemed within
a year, the premises so alienated shall be forfeited, but the full
rent to be payable from the remaining lands; if any portion of
the lands be lawfully recovered from grantee, a proportionate
allowance to be made from his rent. 2 membranes.—9 Sept.,
xxix.

5033 (6546.) Grant to Thomas Fleetwood, esq., son and heir of
John Fleetwood, of Caldwich, Staffordshire, esq., and Marma-
duke Redmayne, of Thornston, Yorkshire, esq.; of the lands of
Cloghlyeh, containing by estimation 1 ploughland, Glanmore
alias Glancure and Ballenokarigry 1½ pl., Kyllordy 2 pl., Kari-
ginotan and Muckroby ½ pl., Ballenohowe alias Ballendrawyn
1 pl., Bearne ne fowly alias Barnafallogh ½ pl., Glanshoakin 1 pl.,
Kilolohy alias Kikslagher 1 pl., Ballegart alias Ballenaglass and
Glanegurtine 1 pl., Oarrongowld alias Garrencovle, Sloghnachara
and Kiloorane 2½ pl., Kilbug 4 pl., Ballymthonick and Kilwalermoy
6 pl., Kilnecarriggye 1 pl., Ballensanchory, Ballenloare, and
Curryhynemoght 1 pl., Cromho ½ pl., and Morenilloge 4 pl.,
co. Waterford, amounting in all by estimation to 12667 English
acres, as parcels of two seigniories one of 12000 acres allotted to
Fleetwood, and one of 8000 acres allotted to Redmayne. To
hold, by the name of Colonye Fleetwood, for ever, in fee farm,
by fealty in common socage. Rent, £71 2s. 6½d. English, from
1594 (half for 8 years preceding). If the lands are found to contain
more than the estimated number of acres, grantee shall pay 1¼d.
for each additional English acre. Grantee to erect houses for
95 families, of which one to be for themselves, 8 for freeholders,
6 for farmers, and 42 for copyholders. Other conditions usual
in grants for planting the undertakers in Munster as in 5032.
2 membranes.—3 Sept., xxix.

*The following remark appears in the volume in the Auditor-
General's collection entitled :—"Schedule of lands in Munster*

1587.   FIANTS—ELIZABETH

passed to undertakers," 1599. "Memorandum that the patentee would never get possession of the premysses; and therfore to be considered of."

5034 (4172.) Grant to Arland Uscher, gent.; of the office of sole registrar of appeals or provocations spiritual, made to the queen in the Chancery of England, or to the deputy in the Chancery of Ireland, as Roland Cowick held it. To hold during good behaviour, with the accustomed fees. He shall not be removed except as in 4976.—7 Sept., xxix. (Col. P. R. p. 115.)

5035 (4177.), Pardon to Boyne Forborne, of Outrarda, co. Kildare, and Ricard Woods. Provisions as in 4965.—8 Sept., xxix.

5036 (4129.) Grant to sir Tho. Perrot, knt.; of the office of master of the ordinance, Jaques Wingfilde, esq., being dead. To hold during pleasure, with the usual fees, and with the leading of 30 horsemen.—11 Sept., xxix. (Cal P. R., p. 115.)

5037 (4180.) Grant to Henry Parkins, gent.; of the office of clerk of the ordinance. To hold during good behaviour, with the usual fees as Henry Fisher, John Leake, and Rich. Shepheard had— 12 Sept., xxix.

5038 (4142.) Commission to those named in 5021, *omitting Stephen bishop of Clonfert, and Edw. Brabazon, and adding Rich. Bingham, knt.,* as principal commissioner of Connaght and Thomond. George Bingham is described as deputy to his brother Richard in the government of Connaght, and Thos. Le Strange, knt., is without further designation. To be commissioners in the province of Connaght as in 5021. Geo. Bingham is confirmed in the government of the province in the absence of his brother, and is to execute the instructions of the deputy dated 11 Sept.— 12 Sept., xxix.

5039 (4150.) Commission to George Bingham, esq., deputed in the government of Connaght and Thomounde in the absence of sir Rich. Bingham, his brother; to execute martial law in that province and country, as in 218.—12 Sept., xxix.

5040 (4820.) Lease (under commission, 17 Jan., xxvi.) to Charles Howarde, lord Howarde of Effingham, high admiral of England; of the whole river of the Banne in the north of Ireland in the province of Ulster, and the fishing for salmon and other fish there. To hold for 21 years. Rent £10, and £40 for every year in which he shall quietly enjoy the fishing. Provisions as in 4941. 14 Sept., xxix.

5041 (5050.) Surrender by Oghe O Hanlon, gent, chief and captain of his nation; of the countries called the upper and nether Orrier in the province of Ulster; with the intention of their being regranted to him. "Ohanlons marke."—*Dated* at Drogheda 20 Sept., xxix.

5042 (4332.) Lease (under commission, 17 Jan., xxvi.) to Henry Duke, gent.; of the site of the monastary of Clonyes in the Dartrye in M'Mahowne's country, and 22 small parcels of land called taythes of land, each tayth containing 10 acres, viz: four taythes called the Channons quarter, the taithes of Clonvoriall and Anowghegillye, the four taithes of the two Granges, the taythes or taithes of Rathogewlyn, Capoghe, Tullamoure, Knockoryn, Intemple, Mollansoppan, Killoleman, Killeksroughe, Bhanetallogbe, Clonscownbar, Clonagalgynecannoughe, and Lyadrowmno in Fermanogh, and the tithes of the same, the

FIANTS.—ELIZABETH.

rectories of Clonyes, Monoohan, Tullumbidd, Clontibored, and
Dromullys in the Dartrye in M'Mahownes country; also the
great church of Clonyes, and 28 taythes of land belonging to it,
viz.: the taithes of Mowlite, Lyssegarian, Clonakana, Clonakirkall,
Clonaynahe, Carrowewghter, Mowllaghmagherenever, Awghin,
Drowmeranye, Lymerowarte, Lymettanvallya, Craghe, Aghnaoloy,
Lysmacallye, Edenforan, Lattycallan, Bolgybran, Ternemoroghe,
Droumboo, Tankillye, Dromullohe, Lyserano, Tattigarran,
Lymaroughe, Loghtameutan, Loghowne, Kilgrome, Churuhe
Angbye, and the tithes of the same, possessions of the said monas-
tery. To hold for 21 years. Rent £4 10s. Maintaining a ward
of 8 Englishmen to guard the premises. Provisions as in 4939.
—23 Sept. xxix.

5043 (6539.) Grant to Edward Denny, esq.; of the lordship of
English Dennyvalle alias Traly, co. Karry, the castle and lands of Tau-
laght, Knookenaghe, the castle and lands of Lestrym, [Kermor],
Kerbagg, Ballym'kuegog, Kahsrard, parcels of the inheritance
of Garrett, late earl of Desmond, the castle and lands of [Lysse-
hane], late of John oge m'John M'Thomas, attainted, all which
are together bounded on the south by the great bay called the
bay of Traly, on the north beginning towards the east by a little
brook separating them from the lands of Browduff, on the middle
of that side by the lands of Ty[boranamolte], on the northwest
by the lands of Rathowyny being the bishop of Kerry's lands,
on the east side by the burgage lands of Traly called Ballynallorr,
and so thence westward to the island and land of Feyanyd, and
to the main sea; the house and site of the abbey of Traly, the
castle and lands called Ballanemridan, the town and lands of
Newmaner, the castle and lands of Castelmore, of the attainted
earl's inheritance, which are together bounded on the east by the
lands of Ballygowen, on the west by the lands of Ballygaulys,
on the north by the lands of Faringullah, and on the south by
the great mountain called Slyevemiahe; the town and lands of
Glannegalty and Kilbally lahyrs, together bounded upon the
west by a small brook, on the east by the lands of Ballemahave,
on the south by the mountain Slievaletrough, and on the north
by the main sea; the lands of Derrymore late the earl's, the lands
of Kyllelty late of Morris m'Owen M'Taig, together bounded on
the east by a brook and land called Bracklone, on the
west by a brook called Buneg[undell], on the south by the
mountain Slavemiahe, and on the north by the bay of Traly; the
castle and lands of Carignefyly, late of John m'Ullig M'Thomas,
[Boallnane]keartye, late of James m'Edmund Gerald, together
bounded on the south by the mountain Slievemiah, on the north
by the mountain Slyevelophnle, on the east by the lands of
Ballyhegrele[gh], Ballyheg, [Nalagh, and Monemle], and on the
west by a small brook which separates them from Rathma-
gunogh, Tolwyraina, and Ballynolabyne; a small parcel of wood
growing on the west of Slevelogbrye, called Glannegyntie; the
friary, with a little piece of land belonging thereto, in Arda[re];
all amounting by estimation to 6000 English acres, besides
much bog and waste as are thought good to be allowed for
common, together with free pasturage of the mountains of
Slyevemiah and Slevelogbrys, co. Kerry; and the rents and
services of the free tenants, viz.:—£160, halface, amounting

1687.   FIANTS.—ELIZABETH.

to £213 6s. 8d., sterling, and 120 cows yearly out of the barony
or country of Clanmorish, due to Garrett, late earl of Desmond,
attainted ; 100 marks, halface, amounting in sterling to
£142 4s. 8d. and 80 cows yearly, due to the late attainted earl
out of the hundred or trughland of O Farrabwy Browne and
Oontlone, and also the chief rent due to the earl out of the
half hundred called OFarrabwy, that is, 9d. halface out of
Bally[nadrenagh], 4s. out of Cahirvimily, 5s. out of Liskena,
10s. out of Loghertoaman, 8s. out of Ballymowlort, 10s. out of
Knockynagh, 8s. 8d. out of Ballyaboggan, 4s. out of Thomas
Towne, 4s. out of Ballyboodyrry, 6d. out of Ballymbellagott,
6s. 8d. out of Lamharcahold, 10s. out of Ballem'[eutarjruddry,
10s. out of Killfalay, 8s. 8d. out of Clonaclough, 8s. 8d. out of
Killo[line, 4s.] out of Rath[kud]dery, 13s. 4d. out of Oowlaonghe,
10s. out of Annagh in Boddery, 6s. 8d. out of Dromal[can]bogg,
2s. out of Gorigiasse, 5s. out of Killmamy, 10s. out of Ballo-
moyler, 26s. out of Keonoegyily, which being £8 9s. 11d.
halface, makes £11 6s. 8d. sterling ; and £10 halface, amounting
to £13 4s. 8d. sterling, out of the lands of Traly, due to the
late earl, and 7 marks halface, amounting to £6 18s. 4d.
sterling, out of all the chargeable lands and freeholders in as
much of the hundred of Trughnacry as is contained from Ballo-
tobin on the east, to Ballanallort on the west, and from
Slaveloghry on the north, to Slavemish on the south, containing by estimation the quantity of an accustomed knight's fee in
that country, and also 5 cows or beeves out of the said part of
Trughnacry. To hold, by the name of the seigniory of Den-
nyvale, for ever, in fee-farm, by fealty in common soccage.
Rent, £100 English, from 1594 (half rent for preceding 3
years); and for every acre of waste reclaimed ¼d. ; and for the
rents of freetenants £373 11s. 2d. English, and 195 cows ;
30 marks star. and 10 kine being deducted, because Lyakahane,
Clanegeaŀt, Hilbalyiahive, Derrymore, Carrignsphily, Behalla-
hmakaartey, and parcel of Clanegynty, are escheated and granted
to Denny, in demesne. (These rents were afterwards compounded
for, see " Schedule of lands passed to undertakers.") Conditions
usual in grants to the undertakers in Munster, as in 5032.
3 membranes. Much defaced.—[27 Sept., xxix.] (Auditor-General's Patent Book, James and Charles I., 7 B., p. 245.)

5044 (4147.) Commission to sir Hugh Magennys, knt. ; to execute
martial law, jointly with the sheriff of Down ; in his country
of Iveagh, as in 213.—28 Sept., xxix.

5045 (6740.) Patent of grant to Stephen Segar, gent. ; of the office
of constable of the castle of Dublin. To hold during good
behaviour, with a fee of £36 13s. 4d. yearly.—9 October, xxix.

5046 (5060.) Grant (under queen's letter, last Feb., xxix.), to sir
Walter Raloghe, knt. ; of the barony, castle, and lands of
Inchequyn in Imokilly, with appurtenances, the castle and lands
of Shrone Cally alias Strongeally, the castle and lands of
Balluntra, the castle and lands of Killnntora, and the lands
lying upon the rivers of Broadewater and Bryde, late the lands
of David m'Sheane Roche and others, with the decayed town of
Tollowe, and the castle and lands of Lisfyny, the castle and lands
of Mogilla, the castle and lands of Killmacowo, the castle and

1587.   FIANTS.—ELIZABETH.

lands of Sheane, and all other lands already measured for sir
Walter "as by a plot thereof lately taken more plainly appeareth,"
and as these lands do not make up the intended amount of 3½
seignories each of 12,000 acres of tenantable land, which he was
to receive of the land forfeited by the earl of Desmond and other
rebels as near the town of Youghall as convenient, there is
further granted : the castle and lands of Mocollop, and the castle
and lands of Temple Mighell with appurtenances, and the lands
of Ahavenna alias Whitte Island with appurtenances, all in
counties Cork and Waterford. The lord deputy is to issue
commissions for the measuring of these additional lands and of
such of the lands late escheated of Patrick Condon adjoining the
Sheane, and of the lands in Imokilly adjoining Ahavenna, or
adjoining any other of the lands granted as shall make up the 3½
seignories. To hold for ever, in fee farm, in free socage. Rent
100 marks sterling. According to the articles for the inhabitation
of the escheated lands, in queen's letter of 27 June, xxviii. Also
under queen's letter, 2 July, 1587, grant of the possessions of the
late abbey of Molannass alias Molana, and of the late priory of
the observant friars or black friars near Youghall in the occupation
of the widow Thickepenny, with all their appurtenances. To
hold for ever in feefarm in socage. Rent £12 19s. 6d. Irish.
*This grant does not set out the conditions imposed on the
Munster undertakers.*—16 Oct., xxix. (Cal. P. R., p. 323).

5047 (4339.) Grant (under queen's letter, 25 May, xxix.) to Rob.
Pyggotte, gent., son and heir of John Pyggotte, late of Dysart,
deceased (see 496); of the lands of Dysarte alias Dysarte,
Derrye alias Ramaspoke and Ballecloydra, Colkey alias Colenaghra,
Mollenaknawor, Rabynnake, Carricknepairke, Kilteeloghe, Balle-
kurrold or Ballecarrolde, and Cowlarne, Queen's co. To hold for
ever, by the service of the fourth part of a knights fee. Rent
£9 11s. 6d. Conditions as in 474 substituting Maryborough
for Philipstown. The prohibition of alienation is omitted.—16
Oct., xxix.

5048 (4144.) Commission to Alexander Briener, mayor of Waterford,
and Geoffrey Fenton, esq., secretary of Ireland. Forasmuch as
foreign invasion may be doubted from beyond seas, and if any
such happen their landing-place likely to be at the haven of
Waterford ; the commissioners are to view and muster the able
men in the city of Waterford, and the suburbs, and such as are
upon the river from the city to the tower and so upwards to the
town of Rosse, from the age of 16 to 60, to see that they be well
provided with armour and weapon, and trained under captains
whom the commissioners shall appoint ; they shall cause fortifications to be erected in fit places ; they shall muster the great fleet
of fishermen accustomed to be in that haven at this time of year,
and if need be press them into the queen's service ; and further
to execute the instructions of the deputy. They may execute
martial law, as in 218.—16 Oct., xxix.

5049 (4172.) Pardon to Rich. Platterer, of Waterford, Rich. Jeanes,
and Wm. Jones, of same ; for all felonies and piracies committed
on the high sea or between the flux and reflux of the same.—
26 Oct., xxix.

5050 (5907.) Grant to Edward Goore ; of the wardship and marriage
of Edmund O Ferrell, son and heir of Tirlaghe mˈWilliam reighe

1587.   PLANTA.—ELIZABETH.

in co. Longford, gent., and custody of his lands, during minority.
Rent £6 sterling; of which he may retain £3 for support of the
minor. Fine £4.—28 Oct., xxix.

5051 (4332.) Grant (under queen's letter, 1 Aug., xxviii.) to Tho.
Challoner, gent.; of the lands of Ernhill, Bortlew, and Kilcoke,
co. Kildare, the castle of Ernhill, and common of pasture upon
the King's moor alias the Heath moor, co. Kildare, possessions
of James Eustace, late viscount of Baltinglas, attainted. To hold
for ever, in free socage. Rent 36s. 8d.—1 Nov., xxix.

5052 (6356.) Grant to George Thornton, esq.; of the castle and
English lands of Ballyrastan alias Downamanna, containing 1½ ploughlands, half of Urgarre ½ pl., Ballinevolline, Karrowreoghe and
Ballinxtonybegg 0 great acres, Ballyustonymure ½ pl., Ard-
kryllymerty 4 great acres, and the castle and lands of Ballynourry
½ pl., co. Limerick, possessions of John Lacy fitz William containing 8½ ploughlands, which, at the rate of 9½ pl to a seignory
of 4,000 acres, makes 1,500 acres. To hold by the name of
Mylott for ever, in fee-farm, by fealty, in common socage. Rent
£15 12s. 6d. English, from 1594 (half for the preceding three
years), and ½d. for each acre of waste land reclaimed. If the
lands are found to contain more than the estimated number of
acres, grantee shall pay 2½d. for each additional English acre.
Grantee to erect houses for 12 families, one for himself, 2 for
freeholders, 1 for a farmer, and 2 for copyholders, with other
provisions usual in grants to undertakers in Munster, as in 5032.
3 membranes. Dated at Dublin, 2 Nov., xxix. (Cal. P. R., p. 112.)

5053 (4149.) Pardon (under queen's letter, 30 August, xxix.) to
Brian M'Goghagan, gent., and Coulagh M'Goghagan, his brother.
—2 Nov., xxix.

5054 (4173.) Pardon to Hugh m'Tirlagh roo, of Clonahirne, and
George fitz Peter Nugent, of Oyoloo, in co. Roscommon. Provisions as in 4966.—2 Nov., xxix.

5055 (4174.) Pardon to Rob. fitz Peter Newgent, of Ballinegilla,
co. Roscommon. Provisions as in 4966.—2 Nov., xxix.

5056 (4171.) Pardon to Garrott M'James alias Garrott bracke, late
of Mucolpe, Melanghlen O Leyne, of Blaryne, Donogh oge O Cul-
laine, of Caroncam, Redmond m'James, of Hamorockstown,
Moleyn O Twohy, of Graineaghe, Fynin merigagh M'Cartie, of Kil-
kivan, David fitz Rob. fitz Richard, of Ballscaulthy, Edm. m'Shane
M'Kenedy, late of Clanbibbon, Edm. m'Philip Roche, late of
Drumfynin, Morogh m'Brian M'Swyny, late of Oahir, Cown
m'Conogho Yquife, late of Kilcanny, Shane O Dalie, late of
Carcker, Hellane Pooer, late of Inzie, Wm. O Morosie, late of
Inzie, Wm. m'Edm. M'Robistowne, late of Malliomany, Tho.
m'James Fitz Garrott alias Thomas bracke, late of Macolop,
James fitz Edm. fitz John, late of Ballinyoor, Edm. fitz Rich.
Barry, of Ballenvony, James fitz Rich. Barry, of Ballenvoy,
Eliah ny Shane Y Morrogho, of Knockivilly, Shane m'Tho.
M'Nicholas, late of Templenycarrigh, Tho. fitz Morrice fitz Wm.
Aghlern, late of Abicarne. Security as in 4943 to be given to
Tho. Norris, vice-president of Munster. Other provisions as in
4965. Excluding also any in prison or on bail.—3 Nov., xxix.

5057 (4169.) Pardon to Rich. Hovedon, gent., and Maud Hovedon,
his wife; co. Louth. Provisions as in 4966.—4 Nov., xxix.

1887. FIANTS.—ELIZABETH.

5058 (4176.) Pardon to Walter Bourke, of Belick, Oliver Bork, of
Yanicake, Wm. Borke, of Ardmore, Ulick Borke, Rich. Borke,
of Belicke, Edm. boy m'Tho. Bocke, of Cloghare, Wm. Borke
m'Tho., and Walter Borke in Tho., of Cloghare, Edm. roo m'Tho.
M'William, Shane m'Davie duffe, David oge m'Davie duffe,
Edm. boy m'Riccard m'Edm. boy Bourke, Ulick Carran, Shane
O Higgin, Cormock O Higgin, Wm. crone m'Shane tallagh,
Conall oge m'Conell M'Donell, Ulick Borke, of Enaghe, Rich.
Borke m'Rich. m'Davie bane, Hubbart krone Lynott, of Karne,
Gilbracke M'Kigane, of Castle Lake, Cahir and Enos m'Keda
M'Donell, Ulick Lynott, of Karne, Oonoghar oge O Chaam,
Rich. m'Walter Gelin, Donell O Kellie m'Laghlin, and Bicoard
m'Ulick m'Davie bane. Provisions as in 4965.—4 Nov., xxix.

5059 (5516.) Grant (under queen's letter, 28 August, xxix.), to
Owhny m'Shane O More, gent.; of a pension of 20d. a day, for
life—4 Nov., xxix.

5060 (4168.) Pardon to Francis Lovell, gent., sheriff of co. Kilkenny, (Wm. Newman, sub-sheriff struck out), Tho. Howthe,
gent., Tho. Brian, horseman, Geoffrey Graunte, Rich. Graunte,
gent., Nich. Howlinge, James Howlinge, John m'Dermot
O Downy, Rob. Goer, and Rich. roo Ivranagh, yeoman, Rich.
fitz Edm. Butler, Wm. Tewe, Edm. Hardinge Maurice Kelly,
shot, John bege O Phelan, and Philip roo O Rian, grooms.
Security as in 4943 in co. Kilkenny, Lovell excepted. The
pardon not to include intrusion in crown lands or debts to the
crown.—5 Nov., xxix.

5061 (6102.) Pardon to Thomas Johnes, bishop of Meath; of all
intrusions into the bishopric of Meath, the deanery of S. Patrick,
Dublin, the rectories of Loughsewdy and the Nobber annexed to
the bishopric, and the prebend of Tassagard. Fine 5s. English.
—5 Nov., xxix.

5062 (5947.) Surrender by William O Ferall Bane, chief and captain
of his nation; of the manors and lands of Longford, Liser-
dowly, Onockenacha, Fernaght, Ballym'carmicke, Cowlfeny, Clonconway, Liniargaill, Clyvri, Camckmaghe, Olacky, Lyanny,
Leymagh, Ballevorise, Rathmowe, Levanny, Ardachullan, Lis-
tran, Cartronsillagh, Cartronglanagh, Prulsan, Droymlove,
Bornahorn, Liscon, Clonard, Aghakillamore, Aghecorredrenan,
Ballengall, Correboy, Ballenoy, Lindaf, Cartron var, Racranan,
Tivmore, Cartron ne faive, Killenawon, Mota, Montergeran,
Clanhue, Moytra, half of Montergelgan, Sliswarbry, Clangiller-
newe, and Clantean, co. Longford; with the intention of their
being regranted. (See 5107.) Signed, Willm. offerall als
Offerall bane. Dated 7 Nov., xxix.

5063 (5948.) Surrender by Foghna O Ferrall Boy, chief and captain
of his nation; of the manors and lands of Longford, Carrigbegge,
Rath-hlalmen, Clonconboy, Rathaghe, Ardenragh, and Clonmore,
Moybruvany, Clanawly, Clangillarnewe, Moyntergelgan, and the
Callow, co. Longford; with the intention of their being re-
granted to him. Dated 19 Nov., xxix.

5064 (4817.) License to Ambrose Forth, LL.D., one of the masters
of Chancery; to be absent in England for one year.—13 Nov.,
xxix.

5065 (4170.) Pardon to Dermot oge Onellan, of Killeneboy, co.
Clare, Brian m'Mahowne M'Moroghe, of Moygow, Mahown

1587.   PLANT.—ELIZABETH.

M'Brian, of Cahirpolla, Donnogh oge M'Considen, of Rynire, Donell M'Considen, of Ballharraghan, Gillepatrick roo O Hogan, of Ballicnnellan, Teig m Tirlagh O Brian, of Carneonngowle, Hugh m'Borie M'Gillekelly, of same, Donogho O Quyne, of Killinoboy, Teig O Howe, of Ballyharraghalna, Mortagh lieth O Kerrin, of Ballyohasane, all in co. Clare, Brian m Tumoltagh M'Shane, tailor, Hugh boy O Heine, of Oaherrillan, co. Galway Donell O Quyne, of Rosscahan, co. Clare, Donogho m'Donogh M'Rorie, of Inahiqwyne, in said co., Donogh O Nellan, of same, Simon Fowle, of Rinaha, tailor, Teig oge m'Davis oge Miniter, of Inabiqnyne, Rich. Miniter, of same, Solla M'Davie, of Denis, in said co., Tirlagh O Heine, of Desarts, in said co., Teig M'Considen, of Cahirhlaine, in said co., Donill M'Considen, of same, Shane O Nellan, of Ballimaokaywill, in said co., Laughlin oge M'Considen, of Cahirblany, Gillereogh alias Donogh O Hamine, harper, Shane ne meane M'Lomenation, of Illand Arren, Conoghor O Hirnan, of same, Moyler M'Ullicke, of An Waile, co. Galway, Felime M'Loghlin, of Nosnagh, co. Clare, Rosse m'Owin M'Rorie, of Keappagh, Dermot duffe M'Moriartagh, of Illand Arren, Moyler endowne, of same, Teig O Donowan, of same, David O Cloghertie, of Ballinegleragh, co. Clare, Donell Clancey, of Killaman, in said co., David Nellane, of Killaspocklonan, in said co., Rory boy, of Tomultaly, in said co., Edm. m'Thomas roo, in co. Galway, and Shane O Kanvan, of same. Provisions as in 4968. Excluding from pardon any who do not produce sufficient security before some one of the council in the province of Connaught; and any in prison or on bail.—13 Nov., xxix.

5066 (6546.) Grant to Hugh Cuffe, esq.; of the castle of Kylbolaus with the appurtenances, late possessions of Thomas Neakarye, attainted, co. Cork, the lands of Dalegan bogg and Downye, Abalnake and Kyntyre, Nemoyne, Carrigholagh, Tierwhirrye, Meanes, and Farrenwater, the castle and lands of Castle Nekylly with appurtenances, Tyvynyc, Arlagha, Clonolowra, Schahadenure, Caragh, Clonnybro, Kyldonadaravy and Dromyna, Oraghgan, Cloynlagha, Ballynrtybrod, Ballinekylly, Glancampan, Garrony glynnyc, Lynyhollana, the abbey of Kylbra, with the appurtenances, the moiety of Ballynygronon alias Garrynygronan, Ballychangurogh, and Kylbally Valltiahey, the castle and lands of Cloghemora, late of Thomas Neakarty, attainted, the lands of Shanedrome, the castle and lands of Bellenowran, with the appurtenances, Kulcam, Nygarron, Kullynagh, Kyltaveny, Nefeddane, Arglan, Kyllyearthlane, Boylearel, Nomoygo, Kylbryde, Kyppane, Kylcolman, Ballyillagh, Kilmagoragh, and Cloinemore, and the two villages called Cowlin and Ballintredin, with all other lands called Kylmore alias the Great Woode, co. Cork, late the lands of David incorig; all which lying together are bounded on the south-west by a small brook called Awglann shanacourta, on the north-west by the river Maye, south by the river Awiacky, and east by the river Awbogg, and amount by estimation to 11,020 acres; also the castle and lands of Rathgogan, late David encorig alias M'Gibbon's lands, Nagraga and Bahaiample, late the earl of Desmond's, bounded on the west by the lands of Brooghill, east by Ballybola, north by Croaghane, south by Garrinogrenagh, amounting to 900 acres; a little broken castle called Doon castle, in the town and parish of Ballyha, containing 80 a. ; all the lands amounting by estimation to 12,000 English acres, in co. Cork; also 6s. 8d. halface out of Ballinvollin, 3 marks halface out of Dalligmore, and 20s. halface out of Ballynegarrogh, making in all £4 8s. 10½d. English, being the rents of the free and other tenants within the limits. To hold, by the name of Cuffs wood, for ever, in fee farm, by fealty in common socage. Rent, £06 13s. 4d. English, from 1594 (half for the preceding 3 years), and £4 8s. 10½d. English for the rents of free tenants ; and also ½d. for each acre of waste land reclaimed. If the lands are proved on measurement to contain more than the estimated number of acres, grantee shall pay 1½d. for each additional English acre. Grantee to erect houses for 91 families, of which one to be for the grantee, 6 for freeholders, 6 for farmers, and 42 for copyholders, with other conditions usual in grants for planting the undertakers in Munster, as in 5032. 2 membranes. —14 Nov., xxix.

5067 (4132.) Grant to Ralph Hamon, gent. ; of the office of usher attending on the president, or gentleman porter of the province of Munster. To hold during good behaviour as Patr. Grantee had it.—16 Nov., xxix.

5068 (5041.) Surrender by Hubert Bourk, of Glink, co. Galway, knt., alias M'Davod, of Clanchonow, chief and captain of the country of Clanchonow ; of all his castles and lands of Glink, Downsmaine, Cloghnekillebegg, Castelreogh, Lyucrissaghan, Kearowkillanlagg, Ballenegrack, Ballengarwie, Ballyearnan, Ballidengintarry, Ballyloughlange, Kearow Clancaghin, Kearowrossmidan, Ballien, Clonoahe, Ballielonocmiake, Balletonragey, Creggan, Gilongh, Cornemoolagh, Tawos, Dyrovaid, Kyllebagge, Tonaghryme, Leotorry, Ballynorgher, Beallaghm'ibboct, Lyryca, Kearowreogh, Kearowkillemore, Kearow Kilraghnabby, Kearowcrantagher, Kearowmoghar, Lynanchonghor, Laryn, Boarisdobber, Ardchloae, Feranntenode, Kyltawny, Bealaghderogh, Ballistamaghan, Kaggall, Keappanagh, Clonmore, Kearownyny, Cregbyll, Kearowrow na dawolon and Kearowrow Lynaahonn, in co. Galway, Aclare, Farraragh, Ballemeakahy, Kyltultoga, Ballymickurylly, Raakyntly, Ardloaghin, Lyalonakeghan, Kearowduff, Ballentarly, Ballenew, Kearewrinbackan, Crefe, Ymalaghabegge, Ymalaghnegry, Ballimorgan, Balligowly, Ballim'fedran, Ballichlonenhalgan, Corballa, Ballelevure, Kyllenraght, Ballyscaghar, Rathmawe and Coirestown, co. Roscommon. This surrender is made that the lands may be regranted by patent to him and his heirs for ever. He also renounces the name M'Daved and all Irish customs incident to it.—Dated 30 Nov., xxx.

5069 (2912.) Pardon to Tho. m'Brian O Karnis, of Kiltilly, co. Limerick, Wm. duff O Grogaine, of Ballicmlanie, same co., labourer, Conogher ny Ouolly m'Fiakrath O Oahisie, of Pobulbrien, labourer, Donall m'Teige M'Shane, of Bronkie, husbandman, Wm. oge England, of Ballivcakoge, labourer, Rery m'Donoghe m'Casane M'Shihie, of Grange, yeoman, Reynat ny Koyne I Vokane, of Casteltonogonaghe, Theobald roe fits Theobald M'Reynat, of Ballingahessie, labourer, Donell merrigagh O Mulkainy, of Pobulbrien, husbandman, Sheife inyne Art Kevanaghe, in co. Cork, widow, Terrelagh ricogh m'Mahoway boy, of Callleghe, yeoman, Kenady buy M'Mahowny, of Cullogha, labourer, Reiry m'Morrogho ballufe M'Shehie, of Grange, husbandman, Donall

1587.   FIANTS.—ELIZABETH.

duffe O Clie, of Carrigonill, husbandman, John M'Laghlen, of
Karanody, carpenter, Dermot m'Donogho O Brien, of same
labourer, Edm. O Riordane, of Ballishoa, tailor, John fitz Tho.
M'Craghe, yeoman, John m'Richard Meiler, of Castelorkine,
husbandman, Edm. roe M'Teig, of Boburnygragie, husbandman,
Owen m'Cormock oge O Hallinaine, of Pobulbrien, husbandman,
Wm. llth boy M'Conoghor, of Rosse, gent., Mahowne m'Wm.
M'Donill, of Clanbrien, labourer, Owny m'Ricward, of Clan-
b[ri]en, gent., Donill m'Edm. Inkwane M'Swyny, of Allin-
vallaine, husb., Marrogho m'Brien duffe M'Swyny, of same,
labourer, Conoghor roe O Daniell, of Rosodilo, husb., Donogho
O Cronine, of Nahae, gent., Philip O Cronine, labourer, Theobald
more m'Wm. Bourke, of Ossellaghis, husb., Henry duffe m'Wm.
oge Booroke, of Coline, labourer, Walter fitz Wm. Power, of
Naize, yeoman, Edm. fitz Wm. Power, of same, yeoman, Philip
O Daa, of Dromoheir, husb., Edm. fitz Tho. Wale, of Clon-
garrie, labourer, Tho. fitz Pierce Purcell, of same, gent., Ellin
inion Tho. Wale, of same, Garrat m'Edm. M'Shane, of Ard-
camerie, husb., Donogho m'Brien dowinagh M'Sheahie, labourer,
Terrelagh m'Brian dowiagh, gent., Morrice fitz John Wale, of
Karranbeg, labourer, Rich. buy Rolley, of Oahircornie, labourer,
Morrice fitz David M'Phillipp, of Corry, husbandman, Donogho
m'Shane oge Barehie, of Carrigenvatdill, gent., James m'tagh
m'Morrice M'William, husb., Gubbon duffe M'Thomas, of Kosse,
labourer, Edm. ni'Shane Carraghe, of Ballingaddy, husbandman,
John roe m'Donogho bane, of Ballyboy, yeoman, David Brenaghe
m'Shiarone, of Kilmahina, labourer, Edm. m'Morrice M'Donogho,
of Ballihiokie, Patr. fitz Piers Purcell, of Ballaniarrigie, yeoman,
Morrice fitz Edm. M'Gibbone, of Oullaina, labourer, Teige m'Morrogho M'Riccard, of Currehe, husbandman, Wm. M'Owny, of
Aberloe, labourer, Nich. O Riordane, of Ciahina, husb., Marrogho
m'Brian bullagho O Brien, of Pallis, yeoman, Wm. llth English,
of Salloghodbog, labourer, Wm. m'Ewstace English, of Bahicy-
garran, husb., Wm. O Hogaine, of Garriestowne, husb., John
m'Tho. O Meaghir, of Glanveaghe, John m'Philip O Dwire, of
Downoghaile, John m'Brian O Kenedy, of Cuis Rosse, and
Donogho m'Nicoll O Haine, of Cahirkenliahe, labourers, Rich.
roe Keating, of Ballindowny, gent., Tho. m'Edmund, of Mal-
gorroun, gent., Edm. m'Henry Hubbert, of Ballivokane, labourer,
David m'Morrice Hubbert, labourer, Onorie ny Morrice, of
Norrey, Johan ny Morris, of same, Rowland fitz Rich. roe
Bourke, of Ballivaggie, gent., Donell m'Incomy M'Clanghie, of
Bowaine, labourer, Walter fitz John English of Rashine, labourer,
Moolemory M'Shane, husb., Donell meole O Kenedy, labourer,
Shiefe innine William inine Teige, of Ballimorry,'Matthew Gilam,
of Allen roliana, husb., John Dilleo fitz James, of Dowles, husb.,
John fitz Morrice fitz William, of Yademor, labourer, John
kinghe Dilleo, of Dowles, labourer, James m'Da Dilhasie, of
Kilmakery, yeoman, John O Hingerdell, of Monarter de
Beantry, gent., Edm. fitz David Bourcke, of Ballaniarrigie,
husb., Donell M'Craghe, of Downaman, labourer, Walter
M'Unack, of Ardartie, labourer, Garrat M'Ellistrom, of
Traly, labourer, David O' Dowinaghane, of Ardartie,
yeoman, Morrish Howraine, of Ballinoaslane, clerk, James m'Tho
Piares, of Aghymory, yeoman, Art O Lery, alias O Lery, of

Carrignigillagh, co. Cork, gent., Conoghor m'Conoghor O Larye, of same, yeoman, Donogho m'Conoghor O Larye, labourer, Owni m'Donill M'Cartie, of Kilmartery, Conoghor and Dermod m'Teig m'Donoghe O Laris, husbandmen, Awliffe m'Donill O Swillivan, of same, gent., Awliffe m'Dermod O Swillivan, gent., Conoghor m'Teig O Henrighaine, of Glan Crona, gent., John m'Mahowny O Riordaine, of Cahirkeghaine, husb.; Conoghor O Mahowny, labourer, Dermod m'Teig O Riordaine, of Culnidaine, husb., Teig m'Mlaolen O Riordaine, of Oallagaine, and Conoghor O Garry, of Castell m'Awliff, labourers, Teig m'Morrietagh O Riordaine, of Cullindaine, gent., Donill m'Donill m'Teige O Lary, of Ymullary, labourer, Dermod m'Donogho M'Cartie, of Fiarlighaine, co. Limerick, and Gerrott m'Wm. M'Thomas, of Kilmkae, gentlemen, Edm. Wale, of Garreistowne, yeoman, Walter fitz William, of New Castell, labourer, Ellinor fitz Morris Dowlly, of same, Ellinor Browne, of Knockmunihle, Rary m'Gully Patrick O Mulrian, in co. Limerick, Edm. fitz Wm. Hurley, labourer, Owin M'Awliffe, of Gurtintubbered, labourer, Donill oge O Sheghaine, Dermod M'Donill, and Teig ro m'Shane M'Awliffe, husbandmen, Brian ro O Conoghor, of Earitt, labourer, Dermod m'Donill O Skanllan, and Donogho boy M'Morritagh, husbandmen, Conoghor m'Donogh Oley, David og m'David M'Owin, and Conoghor m'Cragh O Skanisine alias Cragh, labourers, Teig m'Rory O Skanleine, husb., Philip M'Canraught and Callough M'Canraught, labourers, Finolly ny Conoghor, widow, Ellinor Bourke inyne Ulick, Brien ro M'Tirrelagh, husb., Tirrelagh m'Shane ny Corck, husb., Conoghor og m'Conoghor O Drien, labourer, Walter Breth, husb., Brien og m'Tirrelagh M'Brien, labourer, Conoghor m'Wm. M'Brien, and Teig m'Dermod M'Brien, husbandmen, Donogho m'Teig alias Gully Duff O Moryne, husb., Nich. m'Morris O Riordaine, labourer, Reyrie M'Cragh, of Cullimpishe, gent., Teig m'Malolen reugh, and Edm. roe m'Teig O Dwier, husbandmen, Shane m'Conoghor oge, labourer, John m'Philip O Dwier, in co. Tipperary, husb., Rayry m'Donogho O Dwier, labourer, Donoghe boy, of Creg, shoemaker, Wm. m'Teig Y Mulrian, labourer, Shane m'Rery Y Mulrian, husb., Rary m'Conoghor Y Mulrian, John m'Donill M'Shane, and Donogho m'Donill M'Shane, labourers, Owin m'Rory O Mulrian, Boellagh m'Brien M'Byrry-haggerey, and Donill m'Brien M'Birryhaggery, husbandmen, Teig m'Philip m'Hae O Kenide, and Wm. m'Morrogh O Kally, labourers, Fynollie nyne Edmund ynyne Teig, Conoghor m'Donill O Mulrian, labourer, Teig m'Dermod O Mulrian, and Donill m'Mlaghlen O Mulrian, yeomen, Shane m'Conoghor O Hiaknie, husb., Morish melagh fitz Tho. Fitz Morris, husb., Kowkingill O Dally, of Dromore, co. Cork, and Donogho m'Teig M'Cartie, of Corroghnody, labourers, Teig m'Donill M'Owni, of Ballyinadle, husb., Mahownam'Morragho O Mulrian, of Torbin, co. Tipperary, and Gully Duffe m'Teig O Mulrian, of Salagune, labourers, Roger Lucas, of Cloaneshare, co. Limerick, gent., Edm. Wale, husb., Teig M'Morris and Rich. M'Morris, labourers, John Fitz Garrot fitz James, of Cloane Larye, husb., Patr. Tirrel fitz Frauncis, of Cork, gent. Security as in 4943. The pardon not to include intrusion into crown lands, or remit crown debts. It shall also exclude any person not born in Munster,

1567.   FIANTS.—ELIZABETH.

any person who has committed murder, any convicted or in
prison at the time of granting the pardon, or any who will not
submit to the orders to be made by the deputy concerning their
lands. Each must give security by recognizance in the sum of
£200 English to abide by such order concerning the disposition
of their lands.—21 Nov., xxx. (?).

5070 (6594.) Lease (under queen's letter, 26 May, xxv.) to Andrew
Poppard, gent.; of the priory of the Holy Trinity in
M'Dermoyde's country alias Moylarge, within the isle of the
Holy Trinity in Loughkee, co. Roscommon, with its possession,
as in 1794. To hold for 80 years from the determination of
the interest in No. 1724. Rent, 50s. English. Maintaining
one footman. Provisions as in 4939.—21 Nov., xxx.

5071 (6596.) Lease to Rice ap Hughe, esq.; of all the customs
and subsidies of merchandise brought into or shipped out of the
haven of Dundalke, and all creeks belonging to the same, and
all cockets, bills, certificates, entries of ingate and outgate of all
merchandise, wines excepted. To hold for 21 years. Rent, £5.
Not to let to any not English, except by license of the lord
deputy. Power of surrender at pleasure.—22 Nov., xxx.

5072 (4199.) Grant (under letter of the council in England, 6 Sept.,
xxix.) to John Vicars, gent.; of the office of usher of the fort
of Phillippeston, in King's co., after the death or other vacation
of it by Tho. Fearman. Recites 4325. To hold during good
behaviour, with a fee of 20d. a day. In consideration of his
service in the wars.—22 Nov., xxx.

5073 (4206.) Grant (under letter of the council in England, 20 Sept.,
xxviii) to John Williams, gent.; of the office of keeper of the
gaol of Gallwey. To hold for life, with the usual fees.—23 Nov.,
xxx.

5074 (5918.) Grant (under commission, 17 Jan., xxvi.) to James
Morgan, gent.; of the wardship and marriage of Robert, son and
heir of Nicholas Bourober, late of Ballyconnicks, co. Wexford,
gent., and custody of his lands, during minority. Rent, 50s.,
and retaining 50s. for support of the minor. Fine, 40s.—25 Nov.,
xxx.

5075 (6692.) Pardon to Wm. Borke, alias the Blynd Abbot, Rich.
Borke fitz Wm., Katharine Borke fitz Walter, Tho. and David
Borke fitz Wm., Edm. Bork fitz Richard ewaren, Walter Bork
fitz Richard ensren, David Bork m'Tho. duffe, John and
Richard Borke m'Daved m'Tho. duffe, Theobald Borke
m'Tho. duffe, Edm. Bork m'Shane, Tho. and Theobald Bork
m'Rich. glare, Swaf Bork ny Walter oge, Meiler oge Borke
m'Walter fadde, Onor Bork fitz Edm., Walter oge Bork
m'Walter fadde, John Bork m'Richard ensren, Reward,
Walter, Ulog, David duffe, Roland, and Tho. Bork m'Hebard,
Rich. Bork m'Rich. m'Meiler, Ricard Bork m'Rich. m'Reard
m'Meiler, Una Bork ny Hebard, John Bork fitz Wm., Ricard
Bork, of Clonskere, Miaghling M'Teige, of same, Walter oge
m'Walter m'Ulog Bork, Heard m'Walter oge m'Walter
m'Ulloge Bork, David Bork m'Edm. m'Oliver, David M'Gibbon,
of the Olston, Redmund M'Gibon, of Marsk, Edm. and Walter
m'Meiler m'Theobald M'Gibon, Meiler oge, Theobald, and Gilleduffe oge m'Gilleduffe m'Theobald M'Gibbon, John and Richard
m'Shane ne gowne M'Gibbon, Tho. m'Wm. ne gowne M'Gibbon,

1587.

Rich. chone m'Wm. ne gume M'Gibbon, Gilledaiffe m'Shonick M'Gibbon, John, Rocard, Mailer, and Wm. m'Gilledaff m'Shonick M'Gibbon, Geoffrey m'Shonick M'Gibbon, Rocard m'Sharon m'Shonick M'Gibbon, Edmund, Shane, Walter, and Tho. m'Rich. m'Shonick M'Gibbon, David m'Wm. m'Shonick M'Gibbon, Wm. crone m'Hebard m'Shonick M'Gibbon, John m'Mailer M'Gibbon, Theobald, John, and Rocard m'Shane m'Mailer M'Gibbon, Wm. m'Mailer M'Gibbon, Meiler oge, Wm. oge, and Rocard m'Wm. m'Mailer M'Gibbon, Tho. m'Edm. m'Meiler M'Gibbon, Wm. crone m'Edm. m'Meiler M'Gibbon, Mailer m'Sharon duffe m'Mailer M'Gibbon, Recard oge m'Recard M'Gibbon, David, Richard, and Tho. m'Recard oge M'Gibbon, Theobald m'Ricard M'Gibbon, Theobald oge m'Theobald M'Gibbon, Gilleduffe and Shonick m'Theobald m'Ricard M'Gibbon, Shane m'Recard M'Gibbon, Theobald grane m'Shane m'Recard M'Gibbon, David m'Shane m'Recard M'Gibbon, Shane is oge m'Shane m'Recard M'Gibbon, William, Recard, Henry oge, and Theobald m'Walter m'Henry M'Gibbon, Mailer oge m'Mailer m'Sharon M'Gibbon, Callogh m'Mailer oge m'Mailer M'Gibbon, Redmund m'Gilleduff M'Gibbon, Shane ne gowne M'Gibbon, Rocard cogge M'Gibbon, Recard oge m'Recard cogge M'Gibbon, Malere merre m'Recard cogge M'Oybbon, Theobald m'Henry M'Gibbon, Edm. grane m'Tybald M'Gibbon, Farregh m'Turlagh roe M'Donill, Marcus roe m'Turlagh roe M'Donill, Rory oge, Marcus, Malemorre, and Colle m'Ranell M'Donill, Oshier m'Felym m'Enese M'Donill, Feylem and Alexander m'Hew buy M'Donill, Rory oge m'Horle M'Donill, Urten M'Donill, Rory, Hewe buy, and Marcus m'Brene buy m'Marcus roe M'Donill, Dodarre O Maly, Thomas, Teyg, Dermot, Awen, and Hugh m'Dodarre O Maly, Thomas and Darby m'Hew O Maly, Donill crone m'Tuhelle cogge O Maly, Ullog m'Walter more M'Enaheran, Henry m'Ulloge m'Walter M'Enaheran, David and Mailer m'Henry reough M'Enaheran, Owen m'Owen M'Shieh, Wm. oge, Walter oge, Ullog, Edmund, Richard, and Theobald m'Wm. M'Richard, Wm. m'Rory M'Tohell, Tho. oge M'Ewarde, Teig buy m'Tha. M'Evadde, Ullog M'Hugin, Walter oge and Ullog buy m'Walter M'Shane, Brene reough m'Gilleorist M'Evadde, Cormock and David O Holeghane, Bryan m'Walter M'Eviles, Edm. oge m'Edm. M'Eviles, David buy O Royle, Evire Stanton, Tho. Stanton, Derby Nagten, Teig oge Kally, Ullog oge Borke, Recard m'Shane m'Wm. M'Philibbene, Edm. fits Theobald buy, David oge m'David m'Walter buy, Rich. oge m'Rich. buy, Edm. duffe m'Rich. buy, Harbard m'Tho. m'Walter buy, Wm. m'David m'Walter buy, Walter buy M'Edmund, Recard oge M'Tumyn, Henry, Callogh, Mayr, Brene, and Rob. M'Tumyn, Hew m'Brene Ivrogan, Hew buy m'Alen dnff, Hew m'Jane m'Riccard more, Shane oge m'Shane M'Breene, Wm. duffe m'Wm. M'Rory, Kneeghor, Doele, and Wm. oge, m'Wm. dnffe m'Wm. M'Rory, Henry m'Rdm. M'Beeard, Callogh m'Tho. M'Recard, Faniarogh m'Wm. O Hugin, Carbare m'Cocoggerie O Hugin, Edm. Fitz Phillibene, John Kecough m'Rich. roe, Wm. etotan m'Farrele I Canevant, Wm. and Recard m'Daved I yane, Rory duffe and Mlaghling m'Owen O Fyn, Donill O Reyle, Tho. m'Daved O Rayle, Hebard oge m'Eharon M'Enaheran, Edm. oge m'Edm. Doele, John buy O Leyne, Recard and Rory m'Tho. m'Recard M'Shordane, Darby m'Edm. M'Thomas, Tho. m'Teyge m'Wm. M'Mahon, Edm.

1587.   PLANTS.—ELIZABETH.

Brynegan, Hew M'Kegan, Donell grane O Malans, Farikcagh
M'Daaltagh, Rich. m'Walter M'Philibbena, Edm. buy m'Walter
M'Philibbens, David roe m'William Emaheren, Edm. O Hue
m'Wm. luy M'Ennheren, Herberd oge M'Hugin, Ricoard m'Wm.
m'Walter Stanton, Walter reogh m'Wm. Stanton, Wm. oge
m'Wm. m'Walter Stanton, Breen m'Owen I Knoughor, Edm.
m'Rich. m'Shane M'eRuddere, Tho. m'Edm. M'Philubbene,
Lyshagh m'Daved keagh M'Philaldione, Ricoard ne kille
m'Rich. m'Shane Clanerickera, Shane m'Tuige O Kynneddy,
Melare, m'Wm. keegh m'Tho. buy, Edm. O Hue m'Tho. buy,
Edm. and Riccard m'Daved m'Tho. buy, Gilledufh m'Theobald
m'Henry M'Philibbene, Thomas oge and Walter m'Theobald
m'Henry m'Tho. buy, Walter M'Loeghling, Gilladuf m'Edm.
m'Rich. M'Theobald, Owen dwfe O Leyglenayne, of Ballymkery,
co. Roscommon, husbandman, Mahowne m'Shane M'Donagh,
of Cwllyshoig, co. Clare, kern, James oge m'James Lynsigh, of
Cragroaty, co. Galway, gent., Tuig backagh O Higgan, of Downe-
kallagh, co. Galway, hush, Teig O'Mackoge, of Kwyllyn, co.
Mayo, hush, Molaghlen m'Tho. O Brwodar, of Carrowntralla,
co. Galway, gent., Farikeragh m'William karegh, of Lesskin,
Markys M'Walter, of the Lettere, and James Dalton fits
Garrett Dalton. Provision for submission as in 1543. The
pardon not to include any who are not in and of the province of
Connaught, or who do not give security for their conduct before
one of the council there; and shall not pardon intrusion into
crown lands or debts to the crown.—23 Nov., xxx.

5076 (6618.) Lease to Owen Elyot, gent.; of the customs of the
English town and haven of Knockfergus in Ulster. To hold for 21
years. Rent £10. Not to assign without license, except to
English.—24 Nov., xxx.

5077 (5914.) Grant (under commission, 17 Jan., xxvi.), to John
Gwynne, gent.; of the wardship and marriage of James, son
and heir of Donnell O Farrill, of the co. Longford, gent., and the
custody of his lands, during minority. Rent, £5 17s. 6d.
English, retaining £3 out of the rent for support of the minor.
Fine 40s.—25 Nov., xxx.

5078 (4216.) Grant to Wm. Trenchard, esq.; of the castle and
English lands of Corgraige, Ballyneeragy, and Moynagronoge, the castle
and lands of higher Shanyd, the castle and lands of lower
Shanyd, Balylonne, Ballyphenon, Cloinegarey, Shanegowlly,
Ballyhahell, Craig m'Twige, Clonoclohor, Clonegaddigane, Fenee,
Nelagh, Cappa, and Ballyoormuck, Bally Robert, Fican, Kilcor-
grane, and the church and lands of Knockpatrick, lying together
and bounded on the north by the river Shanan, and with Bally-
nash and Knocknobwolly, on the west by the river Lawghill,
on the south by Monemilkana, and Dunmoylyne, Wales lands,
Knockbradren, and Lisheghan, and on the east by Ballystyne,
Cruffe, Desert and Craige, and parcel of the Mulregane, in all
containing 9268 acres; the castle and island of Fuyne and
the island of Dorrynis, containing 385 a.; the castle and
lands of Ballyneclohy bounded on the north by Ballystinane,
on the west by Craige, on the south by Levan, and on the
east by Lisin Kary; containing 327 a.; the castle and
lands of Ballyegasmore and Ballyegnebege, Corgraigelagg,
Dendane, Lisbeghane, and Ballylysan, Lysanckilly, Garrane,
Dorf Jagage, Ballyhaury, Dillie, Lisnigaddy, Corkapeghe,

Arlaine, Kilcran, and Rathruwgh, bounded on the north by
Ballylaidall, Rahanane, Kilcran, Bally[ ]ety, Ostranbegg, and
Kilcolman, on the south west by Ballywohane, on the south by
Knockane in Voddy, on the east by Ballylynye, containing in
all 2100 acres. All the lands are in Conolagh in co. Limerick,
and amount to 12000 acres, besides 2100 acres of bog and waste
land allowed for common. To hold by the name of Mount
Treachard, for ever, in fee-farm, by fealty, in common socage. Rent
£150 English from 1604 (half this rent for the preceding 3 years);
also ½d. yearly for each acre of bog or waste enclosed or tilled.
If found on measurement to contain more than the estimated
number of acres, grantee shall pay 3d. rent for each English acre
in excess. Grantee to erect houses for 95 families, of which
one for himself, 6 for freeholders, 6 for farmers, 42 for copyholders. Other conditions usual in grants to undertakers in
Munster, as in 5032. 2 membranes.—26 Nov., XXX.

5079 (4217.) Grant (under queen's letter, 22 March, XXIX.) to Henry
Harington, knt. ; of the lands of Kilpoole and Kilrothery, and
the tithes of Kilpoole, co. Dublin. Recites 2305 and 2286. To
hold for ever, in common socage. Rent £8 4s. 8d. for Kilrothery,
and £4 9s. 4d. for Kilpoole. Maintaining two English footmen.
—26 Nov., XXX.

5080 (4220.) Grant (under queen's letter, 22 March, XXIX.) to
Henry Harington, knt. ; of the preceptory, manor, or lordship
of Kilhologan, the town of the Hooks, Tampiton, and the parish
of the same town of Tampiton, the rectory of Hooks, the rectory
of Tampiton, the tithes of Ballichillan, Whytchurch, and Kilbrid,
the rectory of S. Michael in Wexford, and the late hospital of S.
John by Wexford, with diverse messuages in the town of
Wexford. Recites 3697. To hold for ever, by the service of a
fortieth part of a knight's fee. Rent £35 16s. 8d. Maintaining
one English horseman. This grant not to affect the parcels of
the preceptory granted to the earl of Ormond nor the rectory of
Doncornock.—26 Nov., XXX.

5081 (4227.) Grant (under queen's letter, 22 March, XXIX.) to
Henry Harington, knt., of the site of the monastery of Baltin-
glas, the lands of Kilmoory, Ladistowne, Shalstonestone alias
Ballyhalton, Slarothie, Newegraange, Oargin, Teighnoran, Col-
lyns, and Broganeston, Ranghan, and Brananghaston, Boranston,
Knockoricke, Grangexon, Newshouse alias Ballymure, Balli-
griffen alias Griffenston, Ballibooke alias Hokeston, Ballivilla,
Drynlne, Mileston, and Billestone, parcel of Rathbran, Maanger
Tirrelaghe alias Tronell, Roadstowne, Ballinaroghe (Roadstown
alias Ballinecroghe in recital), Tuckmill, Killmanaghe alias
Mounkeswood, Ballilog, and Kilhaleneguwn, co. Dublin, Newo-
hets or Newohayes, and Wasterton, co. Kildare ; and the lands
of Frainston, co. Dublin. To hold for ever, by the service of a
fortieth part of a knight's fee. Rent £9 7s. for the possessions
of Baltinglas, and 59s. for Frainston. Maintaining three
English horsemen. Recites 3746.—20 November, XXX.

5082 (6606.) Lease to Thomas Parrott, of Dublin, gent. ; of the
tithe lambs and tithe fish of the rectory of Portrane, co. Dublin,
of the possessions of the house of nuns of Gracedewe ; also the
castle of Lynksameane with 4 quarters of land, co. Galway, in
the occupation of Jonnar Lynche fitz Williams, of Galway, of the

1587.   FIANTS.—ELIZABETH.

possessions of Theobald Bourcke called Tibbott lieghe, of Lyskeamane, attainted. To hold, for 21 years. Rent 30s. Irish for the tithes and 40s. English for Lyskeameane, besides the composition. Provisions as in 4961.—26 Nov., xxx.

5083 (6734.) Pardon to M'Con O Clere, of Donsallagh, Teig O Clero, of Clondoverne, Dermot O Clere, of Ballegunan, Toole O Clero, of same, John M'Quyne, of same, Donogh M'Quyne, and Loghlin M'Quyn, of same, Connor O Heer, of Ballin, Egi Obeer, of same, Donogh boy M'Clancie, of Ballelanott, Moriegh M'Bridey, of Anagh, Teig O Beolin, of Ynche, Donell m'Tirlogh ne Prechan, of Cnapport, Donell oge O Slattra, of Ballakatra, Theobald M'Huberte, of Craghbrenye, Wm. M'Shane, of Cloghballenore, Robert Hamlen, of Clonrawud, Tirlagh m'Donell roe, of Balle Irille, Duhegh O Clere, of Ballegunan, Rorie M'Morroghe, of Killele, Moore enl One, of Roberston, Garrott m'Shane ballagh, Teig O Courren, Cahir roe M'Donell, Shane M'Clone, of Oriva, and Banycoe O Boolan, of Barnentacke, in the province of Connaght. Provision for security for good conduct to be given before the council of Connaght. The pardon not to extend to any in prison, or who have committed murder, or who have been pardoned previously under the present lord deputy, nor shall it include intrusion into crown lands or debts to the crown.—27 Nov., xxx.

5084 (6707.) Pardon to Nicholas St. Lawrence, esq., George Stokes, Patrick Stokes, gent., John Elles, of the Grallagh, and Patrick Morcho alias Melaghlen. Provisions as in 4965.—28 Nov., xxx.

5085. (6716.) Pardon to Richard Keatinge, of Nicholstan, co. Tipperary, gent. Edmund Keatinge, of same, and Rory O Hifernan, of Sroell, yeomen, Donnogh indmffree O Hiffernan, of Ballinecleraghe, Melaghlen fitz Teige en Coule O Hiffernan, Derby O Tyarny, of Ilsaghe, and Edmund melaghe O Muldaya, of Cames, husbandman, Dermot O Duir, of Clone Ithorp, gent., Daniel or Donill O Keinde, of Knockillegenan, gent., Thady M'Moroghe alias M'Morihle, of Aharla, Matthew fitz Wm. M'Brene, Philip Lopin, of same, John Kilroaght O Dwull, yeoman, Thomas O Dwire, of Ballinemone, gent., Dermot O Hiffernan, of Gorttroden, husbandman, John O Dwire, of Donoghle, gent., Thady Enaghe O Keinde, of Belanlogh, Thady fitz Rory O Mulryan, of Cowlin, John O Mulrian, his son, and Wothney fitz Richard I Bruine, of Aharla, yeoman, Ulick alias Hugh fitz Wm. Bourk, of Belankisle, gent., Edm. Bourko, of Dericlone, husbandman, John roe O Dwir, of Rathkena, Dermot glasse O Mulryan, of Moneynealegh, and Wm. fitz Hue O Magher, of same, yeomen, Thomas fitz Wm. Bourk, of Dericlone, husbandman, Tyriagh duffe M'Connygan, horseboy, Gilduffe O Fahie, of Ardamale, Rich. more fitz Davie Bourke, of Pallia, and Matthew fitz Hughe fitz Connor O Mulryan, husbandmen, Donagh en Collin fitz Teige ny Corky, of Ely, yeoman, Thady O Clery, of Balliaghe, husbandman, and Wm. m'Wothney M'Breine, yeoman. Provision for security as in 4943, in co. Tipperary. Pardon not to include intrusion into crown lands or debts to the crown. They are to abide any order by the lord deputy affecting their lands, and any who have been in actual rebellion to find £200 English, security to obey such orders.—28 Nov., xxx.

1587.   FIANTS.—ELIZABETH.

5086 (6587.) Licence to Edward Waterhouse, knt., one of the Privy Council; to be absent in England for 6 months.—28 Nov., xxx.

5087 (6589.) Licence to Charles Calthrop, esq., attorney-general, to be absent for 4 months in England; provided he be not absent in term time.—28 Nov., xxx.

5088 (6710.) Pardon to Nicholas Tate, of Drogheda, merchant, indicted for killing Nicholas Monfeilde, of same, merchant, on inquisition taken before John Lemvicke and Richard Porter, coroners of Drogheda. Richard Belings is mentioned as clerk of the town. Security as in 4943.—30 Nov., xxx.

5089 (6568.) Livery to John, son and heir of Peirs Power, late of Carrige phillipp, co. Waterford, gent. Fine 10s. sterling.—1 Dec., xxx.

5090 (4238.) Grant to Oghie O Hanlon, knt.; of all the manors, castles, lands, and services, in the countries of the Orrye alias Upper Orier and Nether Orryar, surrendered by him, also half the goods of felons, of the profits of waifs and strays, and of fines in the territory. To hold for life, remainder to Oghie oge O Hanlon in tail male, remainder to the heirs male of said Oghie O Hanlon, knt., remainders severally in tail male to Tirelagh, Shane, and Bryan O Hanlon, reputed sons of said Oghie O Hanlon, knt., also to Patrick, Molaghlen, Shane oge, and Felomie O Hanlon, brothers of said Oghie O Hanlon, knt., for ever; by the service of half a knight's fee. Rent £60 English. He shall attend the deputy or the governor of the province of Ulster, with 12 kerne and 8 horsemen armed, with victual for 40 days, at all hostings. He may twice a year hold court baron and view of frank pledge before his seneschal. This grant shall not bar the rights of any subject not of the sept of O Hanlon. Provided that no person shall have any title claiming as O Hanlon or tanist, which titles are abolished. If grantee alien, or levy war against the crown, this grant to be void.—[1 Dec., xxx.]—(Torn.) (Auditor General's Patent Book 9, p. 51.)

5091 (4237.) Grant (under commission, 7 Dec., xxviii) to Faghna O Ferrall of the [Pallice] alias lord O Ferrall Boy, chief of his name; of all castles, manors, lands, and services, in the countries of Moybraven, Clanswly, Clandillernew, Mootargolgan, and Callow, and the lands of Longford, Corrybegga, Saybalmon alias Rathybalmon, Clonassboy, Rathashghe, Ardanraghe, and Clonmore, co. Longford; which he had surrendered by his deed 5063; also half of the goods of persons attainted of felony. To hold for ever, by the service of a fourth part of a knight's fee. Rent 14s. 4d. This grant shall not alter any rents or services reserved in the composition made between Henry Sydney, knt., late lord deputy and said Faghna, nor shall pass any possessions vested in the crown otherwise than by the surrender of Faghna. He may hold court baron and view of frank pledge four times a year before his seneschal. This grant shall not prejudice the rights of the heirs of N. Malby, knt., or any of the queen's subjects, except such as are conferred by the titles, tanist, captain, or O Ferrall Boy, which titles are abolished.—2 Dec., xxx.

5092 (6577.) Livery to Thomas, son and heir of Patrick Gernon late of Killencowle, esq. Fine £9.—2 Dec., xxx.

1587.   FIANTS.—ELIZABETH.

5093 (6576.) Livery to John, son and heir of Henry Draycott, late of Marinerstone alias Marlingstone, esq. Fine £66 10s. 0½d.— 4 Dec., xxx.

5094 (5912.) Grant (under commission, 17 Jan., xxvi.) to Nicholas Bagnall, knt.; of the wardship and marriage of Nicholas, son and heir of Dudley Bagnall, late of Laughlanbridge, co. Carlow, gent., and custody of his lands during minority. Rent £8 18s. 0d. Fine £8 18s. 0d.—4 Dec., xxx.

5095 (6720.) Pardon to Richard Harding, gent., Tho. M'Cragh, of Castellcomagh, gent., Tho. O Phelan, of Kilbalikiltie, yeoman, Edm. fitz Peirce Power, gent., Tho. fitz Dermot m'Teig Cragh, of the Graunge, Connor og M'Conigan, John Launder, Donogh M'Clanoghie, of Dromania, gent., Morice fitz Tho. M'Donoghe, gent., David fitz William, Richard Comyne, Morilagh O Spollan, clerk, Tho. Moell, and Jeffrie boy Power, yeomen, John fitz Dermot m'Teig Craghe, of the Graung, Dermot m'Teig Cragh, of same, Walter Monnsfeilde fitz Edm., of Clashmore, gent., Edm. Mannsfeilde fitz Water, of same, gent., Shane m'Owin M'Cragh, John Allen, Donogh O Kanidye, Philip Nogio, Philip Brennagh, Wm. fitz Edmond Garoldine, of Kilnenon, Tho. fitz Wm. Garoldine, of Corohan, and Rich. fitz Wm. Power, of Tenychorie, co. Waterford, gent. The pardon not to include intrusion into crown lands, debts to the crown, and (excepting Harding) any persons who do not give security as in 4943, or any who are in prison or on bail, or have committed murder.—4 Dec., xxx.

5096 (4234.) Grant (under queen's letter, 12 May, xxix.) to Nich. Walshe, esq., one of the privy councll ; of the site of the abbey of Mawre alias de Fonte Vivo, co. Cork ; and land and a fishing, of the demesne, lands in Lislivan, Curraghevrin, Lenaghe alias Lehanaghe, Gradie alias Grange, the Garrans, the Curranghes, Ardgohan alias Ardgahan, Limevarrin alias Limevarrie, Oregan, Aughephaine alias Aughephoire, Kahernemansghe, and Mawre, and lands in Redharries country in Lislivan, Curagher[rin], and Gradie, co. Cork, the cell called Manister an Inuhorie alias Manister na srohurro, and the rectories of Mawre or Mawe alias Mawns, and Lislie, co. Cork. To hold for ever. Rent £23 7s. 6d. 5 Dec., xxx.

5097 (6610.) Lease to Arthur Bostocke, gent.; of the site of the religious house of the College of S. Brandon in the town of Annaghcoine, in the occupation of Clement Skirret and Thady M'Imylle, priests, a common pasture there, the tithes of 23 quarters of land appertaining to the College, viz.: Annaghcoine, Cahirmoriabe, Balirahoge, Killetaile, Ballinccowlle, Dromgriffe, and Clonclone, co. Galway, in the occupation of the same. To hold for 21 years. Rent £4 6s. 8d. Provisions as in 4932.— 6 Dec., xxx.

5098 (4204.) Grant to Bryan O Farall, of Tulloo in Clantane, in co. Longford ; of the office of vice-seneschal of Clautane heretofore called the tanyst. To hold during pleasure, with such lawful customs and profits as have been taken by the tanyst.—7 Dec., xxx.

5099 (6726.) Pardon to Langhlin m'Owny O More, Owny m'Shane O More, gent., Donell m'Owny O More, Donell m'Nelle Doran, David m'Gilpatrick O Lalor, and Donell m'Gilpatrick O More, kerns, Molrony m'Dermot M'Ewy, farmer, Thomas m'Molrony

1587.   FIANTS.—ELIZABETH.

M'Ewy, stokagh, Donagh O Doran, kern, Laughlin m'Shane
O. More, Patrick m'Firr O Doran, David M'Fighnis, Shane
m'Mortigh O More, Mortigh m'Davie M'Ewy, Taig m'Davis
M'Ewy, kern, Taige fin O Doran, Robert M'Ewy, boys, Edmund
caragh O Demmey, Donall oge M'Calten, kern, Richard Lalor,
and Richard Nevell, of co. Kildare, labourers, Gerald Dillon, of
Killenure, co. Westmeath, gent., Margery Enos, of Levidston,
widow, in co. Kildare, Redmund Keatinge, Geoffry Keatinge,
Edmund O Doran, Taige m'Donogh O Brenan, Patrick m'Owin
O Brenan, Ferdorough Keatinge, Taige m'Robert O Casy,
Pairce Keatinge, Brian m'Cahir glasse, and Nicholas Keatinge.
Security in Queen's co.   Provision as in 4966.—7 Dec., xxx.

5100 (6690.) Pardon to John Macoghlan, knt, Edward Herbert,
esq., James O Mclaghlan, of 'Rossyn, gent, Faroghe M'Hughe,
of Rosfarchan, kern, Maurice Shaghan, Brian reoghe M'William,
Rory O Mulchlohie, of Carrigcarrell, serjeant, Cahir begg
M'Owin, Cormac M'Morche, Feardorgh O Kelly, of Aghrim,
gent., Ambrose O Madden, of Clonfeaghe, gent., Theobald
M'Cahir, of Kilorna, kern, Peter Leynaghe, Thomas Dalton, of
Kilcomyn, kern, Theobald M'Fahy, Gerald Dalamare, Mortaghe
duf M'Rory, Owin M'Shane, of Ballynekilly, Thomas M'Owen,
of the same, Gillisy O Daly, Edmund O Daly, Donogh O Kelly,
Tyrlagh M'Kena, Mortagh m'Moroghe reaghe, Gilleduffe O Fahie,
kern, Wm. Comyn, and Feardorghe M'Edmond, of Levanaghan,
stokagho.   Security as in 4943.   The pardon not to extend
to intrusion into crown lands nor debts to the crown, nor to any
person in prison or bail (except John Macoghlan and Edw.
Herbart), nor to murder (with the same exception.)—8 Dec.,
xxx.

5101 (6691.) Pardon to Charles O Carroll, knt, Owny O Carrall, gent.,
Eyan duffe m'Donnell O Carroll, gent., Wm. Duna, of Tallagh,
gent., Donogh O Daloghantine, of Clenurkin, freeholder, Donill
M'Gilpholie, of Sinrowne, Brian m'Taig leagh, of Cynaghan, and
Edm. m'Teige leagh, of same, gentleman, Mulrony m'Taig, of
same, Tirlagh m'Rory, gent., Owni M'Gilpholie, of Cinron,
freeholder, Daniel m'Mulrony og O Carroll, of Tullaghe, freeholder, Taig m'Taig O Carroll, of Culishall, gent., Taig owne
m'Teigh leagh O Carroll, of Knighan, Daniel O Banan, of
Ballylybie, Lhagh m'Edmunde oge, of Dromoile, Florence
m'Owin M'Coghlan, of Garrybally, Wm. m'Donoghe ny Kelly,
of Ballingloghie, and John m'Wm. og M'Mortagh, of Broghny,
freeholders, Shane M'Murraghe, of Broghinis, Neale M'Limagh,
of Dromellagh, Donogh m'Collin m'Taig ne Carrigy, in Queen's
co., gent.   Provisions as in 4066, Charles O Carroll excepted
from requirement for security.—8 Dec., xxx.

5102 (6725.) Pardon to Walter Archer, of Kilkenny, Redmund
Everarde, of Fytherd, co. Tipperary, Oliver Shartall, of Aghe, co.
Kilkenny, Tho. m'Donogh roe O Corran, of Borredestowne, co.
Tip., gent., Rob. Hussey, James Britt, of Fytherd, yoomen, John
son of Thomas O Corran, of Borredeston, Cornelius or Knoghor
oge m'Knoghor O Corran, of same, Kedagh O Kelly m'Tho., of
Kiltoynan, same co., Shane m'Tho. O Magher, of same, Rich.,
son of John O Shee, of Killetle, same co., and Rob. Hacket, son
of Peter, of Rashmackarty, same co., yeomen, Katherine
O Corran, of Durrenlowacen, widow.   The pardon not to include

1587.   FIANTS.—ELIZABETH.

murder, hearing of mass, and (with exception of Archer and
Everards) the other provisions in 4945, and not including any
in prison or on bail.—15 Dec., xxx

5103 (6567.) Grant to Walter Harpoll, clerk; of the deanery of
Laghlin, vacant by the resignation of Rich. Foall.—15 Dec., xxx.

5104 (4215.) Grant (under queen's letter, 14 June, xxix.), to
Owin O Swillivan, of Donboy, co. Cork, knt. ; of a rent of £30
more or less, payable out of his lands to the late earl of Desmond,
attainted. To hold for ever, without account.—16 Dec., xxx.

5105 (4329.) Grant (under commission, 7 Dec., xxviii.) to Hubert
Bourke, of [Glinsk], co. Galway, knt., alias M'David, of Clan-
chonowe, chief of his nation ; of all castles, manors, lands, and
services, in Glinskie, Downamaine, Cloghnikillebigg, Castellreough,
Lystrimaghan, Carowekillenlegg, Ballenagreagge, Ballingarwis,
Balligarnan or Ballykearnan. Ballydengintorry, Ballyloghlong,
Carowelonfeghnsy, Karowe Rosmylan, half of five quarters in
Ballien, half a quarter in Clonshae, Ballycloncomiske, Ballyton-
regy, Cregan, Gylkagh, Cornemoklagh, Temou, Dirrevode, half
Killibegg, Tamaghrim or Tomecharin, Leotory, Ballinorghar,
Beallagh-m'Tibbot, Lyaryoss, Carowe reough, Carowkilmore,
Carrow, Kalragh ne behy, Carow Crantagher, Carow Clanmaghar,
Lymichonocrbor, Laryne, Bonnedobber, Ardchlone, Fezintemode,
Kiltownsy, Bellagh Dorogh, Balliatemeghan, Kaggale, Kaap-
anagh, Clonmore, Karowamyny, Croghill, Karow roe ne Daw-
olone, and Karow roe Lynhnasham, in co. Galway, Achlare,
Farmagh or Falragh, Ballinakeahyn, Kiltultoke, Ballem'kirilis,
Bakynylla, Arlaghin, Lialonakeaghan, Carowduff, Ballintaris,
Dallenowe, Karowrenmakan or Carowerintakan, three quarters
of land of Cryve or Crieve or Krief, Ymelaghbegg, Ymelagh-
nygry, Ballivorgan, Ballyghowley, Ballem'feran, Ballychlory-
cholgan, Korbally, Dallclovois, Killemrughts, Ballyakaghar,
Itanewe, and Coroatowne, co. Roscommon, in M'Walten
country. Recites his surrender of the premises by deed, 3062.
To hold for ever, by the service of one knight's fee, as of the
castle of Athlone. Rendering yearly one goshawk. This grant
not to affect the rents and services reserved by the composition.
He shall not extort from the inhabitants any rents or services
except those assigned by the composition, without their assent.
He may twice a year hold a court leet and four times a year a
court baron in the country of Clanchonowe, at Glinskie, co.
Galway, and Curbally, co. Roscommon, before his seneschal.
This grant not to prejudice the claims of any subject, except
such as may be conferred by the titles M'Davy, captain, and
tanist, which are abolished.—16 Dec., xxx.

5106 (6604.) Lease to Thomas Yorcke, gent. ; of houses in the Naas
                in the occupation severally of John Lattinge, Bartholomew White,
Nicholas Walshe, Nich. Aishe, Walter Lewen, James Robyns,
Henry Walker, James Aishe, Patrick Kellye, the widow of
Thomas Duffe, Robert Aishe, Tho. Rafter, the widow of Ritcheban
Bane, Tho. Edwards, Wm. Browne, Chr. Sutton, Donell Scullyn,
David Sutton, More Mores' daughter, Wm. Walsh, and (   )
Sampson, land in the Mawdelenes, co. Kildare, in the tenure of
Nich. Walker, land called Girgarstone in the tenure of James
Sherlocke, land in the Naasse in the tenure of Philip Grante,
land in the tenure of John Lattryne, of Rob. Dowlan, and of the

1587.   FIANTS.—ELIZABETH.

executor of Edw. Allen, lying in the Naas, co. Kildare, long
concealed from the queen, To hold for 21 years. Rent £7
16s. 7d. Provisions as in 4939.—17 Dec., xxx.

5107 (4323.) Grant (under commission, 7 Dec., xxviii.) to Wm.
O Ferrall Bane, chief and captain of his nation; of the castles,
manors, and lands, in Longford, Lisardowly, Onockeoacha, Fer-
naght, Ballym'carmicke, Oowllony, Clonearwoy, Lisiargaill,
Clyvri, Carnakmagh, Clacky, Lyenny, Leymaghe, Ballevorise,
Rathmowe, Lovonny, Ardaghullen, Lisurem, Cartromaillagh,
Cartron Glanagh, half cartron in Pralaan, Cartron Droymlous,
Cartron Bornehorn, Cartron Liscon, two cartrons in Clonard,
Cartron Aghakillemore, Cartron Agheanrredrinan, Cartron
Rallengall, Cartron Correboy, Cartron Ballenoy, Carcron Lisduf,
Cartron var, Carcron Ratrenan, Cartron Twnore, Cartron ne fewe,
and Cartron Killenawe, Mota, Montargeran, Clanhue, Moytra,
half of Montergalgan, Silewcarhey, Clangillernews, and Clantean,
in co. Longford; surrendered by him by his deed, 5062. To hold
for ever, by the service of a twentieth part of a knight's fee.
Rendering yearly one goshawk. This grant shall not alter any
rents or services reserved in the composition made between the
late lord deputy Sydney and said Wm. O Ferrall. Grantee may
once a quarter hold a court baron and view of frank pledge before
his seneschal or subseneschal. This grant shall not prejudice the
claims which the heirs of Nich. Malby, knt., or any other subject
may have to the premises. The titles, tanist, captain, and
O Ferrall, are abolished.—18 Dec., xxx.

5108 (6917.) Grant (under commission, 17 Jan., xxvi.) to Edward
Keyes, gent.; of the wardship and marriage of John, son and heir
of John Apprice, late of Dallinrath, King's co., and custody of
his lands, during minority. Rent £3. Retaining 30s. of the
rent for support of the minor. Fine £3.—13 Dec., xxx.

5109 (6605 bis) Commission to sir Henry Wallop, knt., to execute
martial law in the counties of Wexford, Kilkenny, Catherlagh,
and Waterford, as in 218.—18 Dec., xxx.

5110 (6717.) Pardon to Moritogh m'Edm. O Birne, of Moyne,
Morghe, Melaghlen, and Dermot m'Edm. M'Hughe, of same,
Donald M'Geralt, of same, Arte M'Hughe, of Ballihade, Shane
m'Ferganamhin Earreall, of Duffer, Dermot M'Enirre, of Oollitory,
Mulmurry m'Toell M'Geighoe, of same, Rob. Handlon, of Moyne,
Brian O Howgin, of same, James M'Shane, of same, Geralt
M'Dawllowe, of same, Donogh M'Dallowe, of same, Morgho
M'William, of same, Donnogh O Turrelan, of same, and Gerot
M'Moritogh. Provisions as in 5095. Excluding also any who
have been pardoned in the time of the present deputy (Perrot).
—18 Dec., xxx.

5111 (6721) Pardon to Walter reogh fitz Morice, of Glasshelie, co.
Kildare, gent., Margery O Birne, his wife, Grane O Birne, of
Coultowre in Shilealoghe, Kedangh O Toole, of Killmecloine in
Emale, gent., Dermod O Toole, of same, gent., James Nolan, of
Ballitarme, co. Carlow, Turlowgh more M'Dermod, of Brittas in
Emale, Turlogh ro M'Edmonde, of same, Henry O Corrin, of
Corraghmore, co. Carlow, and Geralt Nolan, of Kulln, same co.,
freeholders, Hugh duffe M'Murrogh, of Ballinlan in Shilealogh,
Donnogh M'Shane, of Knockederris in Emale, Geralt M'Gil-
patricke, of Spinan in Emale, freeholders, John Kinselaogh, of

1587.   FIANTS.—ELIZABETH.

Kinshelaughe, yeoman, Rosse M'Conne, of Killmoge, Queen's co.,
yeoman, James more M'Morghe, of Fernes, co. Wexford, gent.,
Donell M'Dalloughe, of Aghrin in Birne's country, Hugh
M'Mulshaghlin, of Ballinskillagh, co. Carlow, Dermod M'Conor,
of Brittas in Shilealogh, John Wolf, of Newton, co. Kildare,
Patrick Nolan, of Ballitarene, co. Carlow, and Arte O Doell, of
Corranourne in Shilealogh, freeholders, Donill O Doell, of same,
gent., and Brian M'Donogh, of Ballinlougher, co. Carlow, gent.
Not extend to any person in prison, or to include intrusion into
crown lands, or debts to the crown.—18 Dec., xxx.

5112 (6716.) Pardon to Hubbert Bourk, knt., Tomaltagh oge
M'Dermot, of Croghan, Molaghlin M'Thomas, of Ballinkilly,
Donald M'Tomaltaghe, of Borlare, Tirlagh or Terence O Connor,
of Ballintobber, Gilleboy O Flanegan, of same, Thady M'Gilvarin,
of same, Molaghlin O Berne, of Porkarin, Fernighe and Fardorghe
O Birne, of same, Hubbert M'Ullicke, of the Kregg, Hubbert
boy M'Edmunde, of the Mote, Walter M'Ullick, of Mainde,
Richard White, of same, Redmund m'Shane garrowe, of Castell-
reogh, Wm. m'Shane garrowe, of same, Thady oge O Kelly, of
Dengirerick, Hugh O Higgin, of same, Thomas Croyne
O Chanchanin, of Feddan, Hugh O Conohanine, of same, Thomas
m'Shane oge, of Clonastragh, Redmund O Lyne, of Dengiarick,
Gilledaffe Altanaghe, of Castell Connor, and Donnald M'Donill.
The pardon not to include intrusion into crown lands, or debts to
the crown, and, excepting Hubert Bourk, the other provisions in
5110.—10 Dec., xxx.

5113 (6727.) Pardon to Garrott m'Mortogh og Cavannagh, gent.,
Donogh m'Mortogh og Cavannagh, gent., Brian, Arte, and Tir-
lough, his sons, Morto m'Morto og Cavannagh, gent., Brian
M'Connley, Dermott m'Shane O Berne, Morogh m'Shane O Berne,
David and Shane m'Garrott O Berne, Brian m'Shane O Berne,
Garrett Carran, Shane oge O Connoe, Donogh m'Teige O Curren,
Donogh m'Brian O Corran, Edmund O Curren, Wm. m'Donogh
O Curran, Mourrogh M'Quine, Tege O Lagh, Raney Cavannagh
and Dermott m'Arte Cavannagh, kerns, Kahir ro m'Donill
Cavannagh, horseman, Morishe M'Codie, kern, Turlough O Neele,
stolkough, Gilpatrick O More, Morough O Morohuigh, Fardinand
M'Morogh, stolkoghe, Edmund m'Deermod Cavannagh, Kahir
O Berne, Patigine O Conowe, Thomas O Nele, and Morrogh
m'Morto Cavannagh, boys, Davie m'Cullan O Berne, Fullim
m'Cahir O Nolane, Garrott m'Edmund O Berne, Shane m'Cormock
M'Conglanie, Wm. m'Cormack M'Conglane, and Wm. m'Morishe
M'Canrick, kerns, Shane beg O Conoye, and Donogh M'Mahowne,
boys. Provisions as in 5095.—20 Dec., xxx.

5114 (4219.) Grant (under queen's letter, 22 March, xxix.) to Henry
Harington, knt.; of the rectory of Balmadown, co. Dublin.
Recites 2697. To hold for ever in common socage. Rent £15 6s. 8d.
and rendering yearly 20 pecks of corn, half wheat and bere malt
and half oat malt, for which 36s. 8d. will be deducted from the
rent.—20 Dec., xxx.

5115 (6602.) Lease to Henry Wallop, knt., treasurer at wars; of
the rectories of Salaker and S. Tullocks in Wexford, S. Peters
and S. Tullocks, Carricke, Killian, Killmocry, Isartmon, S. Ivories,
S. Margaretts, Ballylonnane, Kiltran, Ballynealane, Takillen,
Castlerwye, Kilmollocke, Killusky, S. Nicholas, Ballyvaldin,

1587.   FIANTS.—ELIZABETH.

Ardcolme, Ardkevan, Killile, and the Shrine, co. Wexford,
possessions of the late abbey of Selsker, co. Wexford. To hold
for 21 years. Rent £101 13s. 4d. Not to alien except to English,
without license.—20 Dec., xxx.

5116 (6601.) Lease (under queen's letter, 12 May, xxix.) to Robert
English Collam, of Dublin, gent, of the site of the house of friars of the
Trinity, of Adare, co. Limerick, called the house of friars of the
redemption of captives, cottages and land in the Burgage of
Adare, land in Adare, Castell Robert, Kilcoyle alias Kilkryle;
the tithes of the rectory of Adare collected in the towns of Adare,
Ballynfinter, Chore, Cloghrane, Twoth, Curraghe, Kilnage, Roer,
Kilorill, Ballyrobert, Ballyfanninge, and half Balligale, the altarages and two couples of corn to the curate serving in the church
excepted. Also a weir or fishing for salmons upon the river
Maye in said co., of the possessions of the late house of friars
preachers of Adare; the site of the house of friars of the
order of S. Augustin of Adare, land in Adare, and land in the
said parish called Moddulflie] alias Madologhie with the tithes,
and a weir or fishing for salmons on the river Maye; the
site of the abbey of Nenagh, co. Limerick, with all appurtenances;
and the monastery of S. Katherine alias the monastery of Kay-
laghe alias Negaylaghe with all appurtenances, now held by sir
Henry Wallop under lease, 4757. Also the site of the house of
friars minors of the order of S. Francis of Adare, with a mill, a
weir for eels and salmon on the river Maye and all other appurtenances, held by sir H. Wallop under lease, 4756. To
hold for 50 years (after the determination of any existing leases).
Rent £26 17s. 8d. Maintaining 2 English horsemen. Provisions
as in 4939.—24 Dec., xxx.

5117 (6666 bis) Commission to sir Thomas Williams, knt., to ex-
English ecute martial law in the counties of Wexford and Catherlagh, as
in 218.—28 Dec., xxx.

5118 (5521.) Grant (under queen's letter, 30 Aug., xxix.) to Brian
Magroghegan, gent.; of a pension of 6s. sterling a day, for life,
in 2s. of which he succeeds George Hunte, pensioner, deceased.—
31 Dec., xxx.

5119 (6583.) License to sir Thomas Williams, knt., muster master
English and clerk of the cheque, to be absent in England for 4 months.
—31 Dec., xxx.

1587-8.

5120 (5945.) Surrender by Moragh nedoe O Flahertie, knt.; of all
his manors and lands in the barony of Mocollen, on Galway,
Aghnanewer, Fowagh, Oberia, Imie m'Coyne, Mocollen,
Cloynmuffe, Ballenmortagh, Kalroe, Bothcowna, Balleycourke,
Corcollen, and Ballennonagh, in the barony of Rosse on Maio,
Ballendowne, Kerrahey, Ballenahinnie, Ballemoylleu, Ballesell-
herne, Moydollan, Moybilloy, Moyarde, Mongg, and Ardegh,
Emelye, Kar Morvey, Cornevoyagh, in the barony of Ballanc-
hinnie, co. Galway; with the intention of their being regranted
by patent to him his heirs and assigns. He also renounces the
name and title O Flahertie and all Irish customs incident to
it. "Morghe ne Doe is mark."—Dated 10 Jan., xxx.

5121 (4230.) Grant (under commission, 7 Dec., xxviii.) to Moragh
ne doe O Flahertie, knt.; of all manors, castles, lands, and

1587-8.   PLANTS.—ELIZABETH.

services in the castle of Aghnanewer, containing 4 quarters of
land, castle of Fowagh, 4 quarters, castle of O Horie, 4, Innio
M'Coyne, 2, castle of Mocollen (the eighth part excepted), 3½,
Cloyn naffe, 3, Ballenaforbagh, 1, Kellroe, 1, Bothoowna, 1,
Balleycoowrk, 1½, and Corcollan, 1, in the barony of Mocollen,
co. Galway, the castle of Ballennonagh, in the barony of Ross,
co. Maio, 18 quarters, the castle of Dallendown, 4, Ballenchinie,
1, Ballsmoyllen, 8 cartrons, Ballesellhern., 4 quarters, Moydollan, 2, Moybilley, 2, Moyarde, 2, Mongg and Ardagh, 1,
Emolye, ½, Ker' Morvey, 1, and Corneveyagh, 1, in the barony
of Ballenchinie, co. Galwey, which premises are in the country
of O Flahertie, in the baronies of Moycollen, Ballenshinie, and
Ross, in co. Galwey and Maio, called Ther Connaght, and
known by the names of Guomore, Guobegg, Connomarra, and
the Joyes country. Also half the goods of persons attainted of
felony, and half the fines arising in the country. Recites his
surrender of the premises, 5120. To hold for ever, by the service
of a twentieth part of a knight's fee, as of the manor of Arkin in
in the great island of Arin. Conditions as in 5106; the courts
to be held at Aghnanewer, Ballendown, Karvahey, and Ballennonagh. 2 membranes.—12 Jan., xxx.

5122 (6661 bis) Commission to Tho., bishop of Meath, John,
    bishop of Kilmore, Chr., visc. Gormanston, Tho., baron of Slane,
    Peter, baron of Trymletston, Rob. Dillon, knt., Lucas Dillon,
    knt., Chr. Plunket, sheriff of Meath, Pat. Barnewell, knt, Wm.
    Flamynge and Mich. Cusake ; to take the muster and array of
    the people of co. Meath.—16 Jan., xxx.

5123 (6664 bis) Commission to John Norreys, knt., lord president
    of Munster, and in his absence, Tho. Norreis, vice-president, and
    the others of the council there ; to take the muster and array of
    the inhabitants of each county in the province.—16 Jan., xxx.

5124 (6667 bis) Commission to Robert Harpole, sheriff of co.
    Catherlogh, Edm. Butler, knt., Wm. Harpole, gent., Joana
    Mynce, and James Grace, of Ravillie, gent. ; to take the muster
    and array of the inhabitants of co. Catherlogh.—16 Jan., xxx.

5125 (6668 bis) Commission to Ol., baron of Lowth, Nich. Bagnall,
    knt., Henry More, sheriff of Louth, John Bedlowe, knt., Geo.
    Plunket, of Rowley, Francis Stafford, Rob. Taaffe, of Cookeston,
    Nich. Taaffe, of Athclare, and Rice ap Hugh; to take the
    muster and array of the inhabitants of co. Louth.—16 Jan., xxx.

5126 (6669.) Commission to Geo. Bowrchier, knt., Hen. Warren,
    sheriff of King's co., Edw. Harlard, Geo. Cowley, Tho. Wakley,
    and Tho. Moore, esquires ; to take the muster and array of the
    inhabitants of King's co.—16 Jan., xxx.

5127 (6670.) Commission to Lisson, bishop of Ardagh, Lisene
    O Ferrall, sheriff of Longford, Faghue O Ferrall alias O Ferrall
    Boy, Wm. O Ferrall alias O Ferrall Bane, Irial O Ferrall, and
    Fergutius O Ferrall, esq. ; to take the muster and array of the
    inhabitants of co. Longford.—16 Jan., xxx.

5128 (6671.) Commission to Daniel, bishop of Kildare, Nich.
    Whyte, master of the rolls, Wm. Eustace, sheriff of Kildare,
    Peter fitz James Fitz Gerald, knt., Wm. Sarsfeild, knt., John
    Allen, Gerald Aylmer, esq., and Wm. Sutton, of Tipper, gent. ;
    to take the muster and array of the inhabitants of co. Kildare.—
    16 Jan., xxx.

1587-8. FIANTS.—ELIZABETH.

5129 (6672.) Commission to Richard Byngham, knt, chief commissioner of Connaught and Thomond, and in his absence Geo. Byngham, his deputy, Wm. archb. of Tuam, Donat, earl of Thomond, Ulick, earl of Clanricard, John, bishop of Elphin, Edm., lord Brymyngham, Tho. le Strange, knt., John Blake, mayor of Galway, Tho. Dillon, ch. justice of the province, Terence O Brian, knt.; Anthony Brabazon, Francis Barkeley, Nathanael Smyth, Rob. Fowle, and Francis Shane, esq. ; to take the muster and array of the inhabitants of the province of Connaught and Thomond.—16 Jan., XXX.

5130 (6673.) Commission to Henry Duke, sheriff of Cavan, John O Rallie, knt., Edm. O Reylie, esq., and Tho. Bearagh, gent. ; to take the muster and array of the inhabitants of the county Cavan. —16 Jan., XXX.

5131 (6674.) Commission to Lucas Dillon, knt., Tho. Strange, knt., Tho. Dillon, sheriff of Westmeath, John Tirell, knt., Wm. Tute, esq. and Edw. Nugent, gent ; to take the muster and array of the inhabitants of co. Westmeath.—16 Jan., XXX.

5132 (6675.) Commission to Warham St. Leger, Alexander Coshle, sheriff of Queen's co., Geo. Harvie, John Barnes, and Tho. Lambin, esquires; to take the muster and army of the inhabitants of Queen's co.—16 Jan., XXX.

5133 (6676.) Commission to Edm., viscount Mountgarret, Hugh, bishop of Ferns, Henry Wallop, knt., Tho. Williams, knt., Tho. Masterson, Tho.Colclough, Nich. Devorex, and Rich. Synnot, esq.; to take the muster and array of the inhabitants of the co. Wexford.—16 Jan., XXX.

5134 (6685.) Commission to Adam, archb. of Dublin, chancellor, Chr. lord of Howth, Rob. Gardiner, ch. justice, Geoffry Fenton, Henry Harrington, knt., Tho. Fitzwilliams, knt., Edw. Fitzsymons, serjeant at laws, Robert Pypho, and Richard Netterville; to take the muster and array of the inhabitants of the county of Dublin.—16 Jan., XXX.

5135 (6614.) Lease to Richard Paulfreman, of Dublin, gent.; of *English* the tithe corn and hay of Mueh and Little Derricke, co. Meath, containing 3 copies of corn, parcel of rectory of Dounshaghlen, of the possessions of the monastery of Thomascourt. To hold for 21 years. Rent £3. Provisions as in 4941.—16 Jan., XXX.

5136 (6712.) Pardon to Randulph m'Nease M'Chonall, Sorle m'micNease M'Chonall, Donagh grome m'Chole M'Alester, Rorie og M'Uilin, Owen M'Caragh, Donagh M'Cloister, Guillasbege M'Murry, Hugh M'Neale, Donill M'Neale, Guillasbeg M'Chaghen, Nise roe M'Tliegane, Guillasbeg M'Guillemoyall, Guillas'M'Chay, Gilpatrick M'Enargidagh, Cormock roe M'Brian, Donogh M'Chalertim, Owen og M'Enanne, and Randulph og M'Chalest. The pardon not to include intrusion in crown lands or debts to the crown.—32 Jan., XXX.

5137 (5522.) Grant (under queen's letter, 5 Aug., last) to captain *English* Nicholas Marryman; of a pension of 4s. (Irish) a day, while he does not hold any office.—25 Jan., XXX.

5138 (6710.) Pardon to Thomas Mostian, of Ballehowghter, co. Roscommon, esq., Donill O Moloy, of Ballhowghter, husbandman, Thomas Magroirke, of same, kern, Dowaltagh m'Felim boy O Connor, of same, Felim og m'Felim boy O Connor, Rory and Donogh m'Felim boy O Connor, Garret Newgent, and Edmund m'Tomul-

1587-8.   FIANTS.—ELIZABETH.

tagh M'Dermot, of Ardesms, gentlemen, Derby Owlingh, soldier, Donill moyell O Mauyn, husbandman, Shane m'Melaghlin O Flanagan, Donogh O Connor, of Knockdowe, Morogh M'Rory, Moriah M'Rory, Rosse m'Connor O Ferroll, James m'Teig O Ferrall, Fally m'Feagh O Ferrall, Teig O Kellie, of Mott, Melaghlin O Kelly, and Turlogh reogh M'Swine, of Monaduff, co. Galway, gentlemen, Teig m'Tomultagh M'Dermod of Kilean, Edmund douch O Kellie, of Callowe, gent., Riccard Brennagh, of Cloynigne, husbandman, Thomas Powell, gent, Donill M'Jonine, of Durdoragh, husbandman, Teig M'Egane, of Kiltober, co. Westmeath, Art O Brinan, of Adamstowne, gent., James M'Garrot, of Bushopstowne, Dermod O Brinan, of Kilnvaly, Carbery M'Egane, of Logacory, and Edmund O Relie, of Cloyntege, gentlemen, Melaghlen Magranell, of Lowged, co. Leitrim, and Hubbert M'Granell, gent. Provisions as in 4936; excluding also murder. (Mortian excepted from the requirement of security.)—28 Jan., xxx.

5139 (5911.) Grant (under commission, 17 Jan., xxvi.) to Patrick Crosbey, gent. ; of the wardship and marriage of Thomas, son and heir of William Board, late of Calte, Queen's co., and the custody of his lands, during minority ; free of rent, retaining 30s. a year, the value of the lands, for support of the minor. No fine. —9 Feb., xxx.

5140 (4235.) Grant (under queen's letter, 12 May, xxix.) to Nich. Walshe, esq., one of the privy council ; of the castle and manor of Great Ballikerocke and Balligleaman, co. Waterford, and appurtenances, as held by Rich. Fitz Thomas, alias M'Thomas, of the Pallis, co. Limerick, gent., attainted, or by Matthew Kinge or said Nich. Walshe, as farmers. To hold for ever. Rent, £3 6s 8d—16 Feb., xxx.

5141 (4240.) Grant to Gerald Dillon, of Dryname, gent. ; of the offices of clerk of the peace, clerk of the pleas of the crown, and clerk of the assizes, in the counties of Kildare, King's, Queen's, and Oatherlagh. To hold during good behaviour, with the usual fees.—16 Feb., xxx.

5142 (6715.) Pardon to Tirlogh duff O Ferrall, of Lorne, co. Longford, gent, Shane m'Ferral M'Enlen, of Krinagh, husbandman, Bryne O Ferrall, of Dromillou, gent, Morgh M'Edmond, of Knockanban, stokagh, Maloghlin M'Edmond, of Grenard, stokagh, Phelim M'Enganna, of Kilnecreke, Teig Emologhere, of Insanegrane, kern, Connor M'Enganne, of the Newcastell, stokagh, Tirlogh m'Roris O Ferrall, of Clonsoit, gent., James high m'Owin O Ferrall, of same, gent., Shane O Solloghan, of Aghakillmore, husbandman, Edmund roe M'Evaister, of same, horseman, Gerrot m'Teig O Ferrall, of the Newtowne, gent., Conchonogh m'Wm. O Siredane, (of) Slewarbry, Nicholas m'Wm. O Siredane, of same, husbandmen, Teig m'Donogh O Ferrall, of Clonrayet, gent., Tirlogh M'Evaister, of Grenard, kern, Rosse m'Cormock Magmore, of Montergrean, husbandman, Lisagh M'Garrot, of Lisnegaynim, gent.; Shane O Morogbe, of Kelcore, husbandman, Nicholas m'Wm. O Siredane, of Slewarbry, husbandman, Shane boy M'Felim, of Grenard, kern, Teig m'Gerrott O Ferrall, of same, kern, Cochonoght O Caine, of St. Michaell's, husbandman, Edmund m'Owin O Ferrall, of Bal-

1587-8. FIANTS.—ELIZABETH.

linkerowe, gent., Howin m'Rory O Ferroll, Farraigh O Farall, and Wm. O Ferrall, of same, gentlemen. Provisions as in 4965. Excepting also any in prison or on bail.—20 Feb., XXX.

5143 (6715.) Pardon to Thomas Dahon, of Orans, Garot Dalton, of same, Richard O Brene, of same, Cnogher O Callenane, of Rossman, Nicholas Ledwiche, of same, Teig riag M'Biancotie, of Eris, husbandman, Owin m'Donogh reogh, of same, Morteph M'J Crowghan, of the Slewin, Gillednffe M'Hacket, of Iland m'Hacket, John and Thomas M'Hacket, of same, James Newgent, of Farenemanagh, Jesper Broune fitz Wm., of Athenry, Jesper Broune fitz Richard, of same, Stephen Broune, of same, Cnogher M'Callenan, of Dere m'Laghny, Jouick M'Kwick, of Laokfin, stokagh, Shane roe O Molghan, John Colman, of Logh Bengh, Tirlagh O Gowen, of Coralia, co. Cavan, Richard More, of Corduff, "horacoser," in co. Dublin, and Cahill m'Tirlagh M'Echie, horseman. Provision for security in co. Galway, Roscommon, Dublin, or Cavan, and other provisions as in 5138.—25 Feb., XXX.

5144 (6701.) Pardon to Rowland Baron, of Coppenagh, co. Kilkenny, husbandman, Robert O Brohie, of Kilcowle, same co., Peter Shortall, Wm. fitz Rich. Brenagh, of Maighmore, yeoman, Moriertagh M'Evie, of Killagh, husbandman, Oliver Weton, of Growe, yeoman, John Sweetman, of Eriston, gent., Rich. duff O Clerie, of Gurtina, yeoman, Philip Quemerford, of Pottlorath, Ellen fitz Rich. O Shea, of Cronn, co. Tipperary, Tho. Fanninge fitz Wm., of Ballingarry, yeoman, John Cantwell, of Lisvicky, gent., Mahowne O Carran, of Kilteynan, yeoman, Mahowns duff O Hermody, of Athashall, John O Line, of same, husbandman, George Forstall, of Kilcowle, Gogh O Fogartie m'Cnogbor ne Sore, of Ballifairicken, Tho. boy Bourke, of Ballithomasin, Wm. m'Donagh O Magher, of Temple more, Philip m'Donagh O Magher, of same, Wm. fitz Edm. English, of Solohoyed, and Wm. m'Shane og. of Ballenard, co. Limerick, gent. Provisions as in 4965.—27 Feb., XXX.

5145 (6711.) Pardon to John Tirrell, knt., James Tirrell, of Castellos, Henry Travers, of Canersto, John Tirrell, of Clonemoile, Donogh Macgoghegan m'Owny, of Graffogh, Nale Magoghegan, of Lohertane, and James Magoghegan, of Castellos, gentlemen, Rich. duffe Tirrell, and Dowlin O Birne, of same, footmen, Redmond Tirrell, of Pace, gent, Wm. Morrell, of same, Donill oge O Connor, of same, Richard Tirrell, of same, James Walshe, of Canerston, footmen, Feltim O Mulloye, of Brohelle, gent., Wm. O Gromaganns, of Kilganvane, husbandmen, Dermod O Gradie, of Newcastell, horseboy, Chahill O Gawen, of Rosse, footman, Donill Magmore, of Pace, footboy, Moriah O Shanechan, Sawe ny Donllane, of Ballevicallen, and Wm. Tirrell, of same, co. Westmeath. Provision for security (John Tirrell, knt., excepted.) Other provisions as in 4965.—28 Feb., XXX.

5146 (6612.) Lease to Robert Bico, of Dublin, gent. ; of the rectorial tithes of the parish church of Dirpartrick, the grange of Tullameathen, and the Olde parish, co. Meath, and all appurtenances of the said rectories, and a house and garden in S. James' parish in the suburbs of Dublin, possessions of the late monastery of S. Thomas the Martyr, Dublin. To hold for 21 years. Rent, £8 13s. 4d. for the tithes, and 8s. for the house. Provisions as in 4939.—4 March, XXX.

1587-8.   FIANTS.—ELIZABETH.

5147 (6558.) Lease to John Baskerfield, gent.; of the lands of
English. Ballicaalan Omoy, Kilcrosa, Cownebegg, and Ballifinnan alias
Cloneonnan, Queen's co., formerly granted to John Bernyes in
tail male (No. 1697), who died without male issue. To hold for
21 years. Rent, 40s. Provisions usual in leases, as in 4939.
Also those to which the grantees in King's and Queen's
co. were subject, as in 474, omitting the clauses referring to
dower and jointure, and those covered by the ordinary lease provisions. He shall maintain one English horseman.—9 March,
xxx.

5148 (6565.) Grant to James Ware, gent., of the place of footman
in Dublin Castle, held formerly by Thomas Tailor and by Patrick
Colley. To hold during pleasure with a fee of 8d. English a
day.—8 March, xxx.

5149 (4200.) Grant to Michael Apsoley, gent., of the office of clerk
of the court, prothonotary, (keeper) of the writs and records,
clerk of the crown and peace, and clerk of the peace and of
assizes, in the province of Munster. To hold during good
behaviour, with such fees as Bartholomew Russell or Walter
Archer had. Not to be removed, as in 4976.—9 March, xxx.

5150 (6581.) Lease to Hugh m'Tireloghe ro, gent.; of the ruinous
English. castle of Clonybirne in the country of O Connor Roe, ½ quarter
of land adjoining the castle, 2 quarters called Cormockcowen,
Corballie 1 qr., Cearrowekewic 1 qr., Cearroweraglewe 1 qr.,
Ballefraghan ⅓ qr., Cuartronnetorre 1 cartron or ⅓ of a quarter,
Cartron an Lougharte 1 cart., Dromliahemore in the country of
Tiravu woughtar 1 cart., Silawnaugh and Leightearrows 3 cart.,
Tully ½ quarter, Cearrowaarode 1 qr., Cearrowe Cloonycallaghe
1 qr., Menturaghe and Cargenden ½ qr., Leigh Cearrow wardaghe
½ qr., and Leigh Cearrowe arreraglie ⅓ qr., and Cartron Drismaghe
1 cart., in all 12 quarters and 1 cartron, possessions of Hugh
son of Terence rufus O Connor, called Hugh m'Tireloghe ro
O Connor, in co. Roscommon, attainted. To hold for 21 years.
Rent, £12 5s. 0d., besides any composition payable out of the
lands. Provisions as in 4939.—12 March, xxx.

5151 (6598.) Lease to Rich. Kindlamarshe; of the lands of Lagh-
English. tasks and Killadowne in O Connor Roes country, co. Roscommon
1½ quarter, with their tithes, of the possessions of the late house
of canons of Inchevicokrine in Loghkie, co. Roscommon; the cell
or house of friars called [Toemonia in the country of] O Connor
Dun, and one quarter of land with the tithes adjoining; the cell
or house of friars called Knockvicoarie in the barony of Boyle,
same co., with ½ quarter of land adjoining, and ½ quarter called
Clonevans in the parish of Ardkearne with their tithes; the cell
or chapel of friars called Clonrowghan in O Connor Roe's country,
with ½ quarter of land adjoining, in same co.; the monastery of
the order of S. Dominic in Elphine, and the ¼ of a quarter of
land adjoining with the tithes, in the occupation of John Lynche,
bishop of Elphine, and ½ qr. called Kilvegoone in O Flannigane's
country, with the tithes, also in the occupation of the bishop;
the house of friars called the monastery of Courts, bar. of Leyny,
co. Sligo, and two quarters of land adjoining, viz., Cearrowardowne
and Cearowen Tawny; the house of canons called the priory of
Ackeris, bar. Tirerragh, co. Sligo, and a quarter of land adjoining,
the vicarage of Aghumlie, bar. Carbrie, with one quarter of glebe

1587-8. PLANTS.—ELIZABETH.

land, and one little island in the sea there in co. Sligo ; the chapel
or cell called [Ballindowne], bar. Tirreragh, co. Sligo, and a
quarter of land with the tithes there ; the chapel or cell called
Clonemenaghan, bar. Corran, co. Sligo, and a quarter of land called
Ronyroge with the tithes ; all which religious possessions were
long time concealed. To hold for 21 years. Rent, £7 18s. 3½d.
Provisions as in 4939. (Partly defaced, see Auditor General's
Patent Book, 18. p. 21.)—12 March, xxx.

. " There was none of the parcells within mentioned formerly in
charge."

5152 (6611.) Lease to Thomas Cheyny, gent. ; of the castle of Clon-
down, two quarters of land called Clandowan and Carrowe
m'Shaen duffe, the site of the castle of Monyoppan and two
quarters of land, the castle of Kilkedy and lands of Carrowe en
Poole roe, and Carrowe Gillcife de Killeyn, the lands of Kil-
ohroohan, Dromodymona, Carrowe Dowene, Kawlveria, Clonell-
bonyre, and the island of Manahowe, co. Clare, the rectory of
Killowlanohye, and a third of the tithes of Morye and Carrowe
in Goule, and all other tithes belonging to the rectory, in co.
Clare, of the possessions of Matthew or Mahown O Breyn m'en
Aspugge, slain in rebellion. To hold for 21 years. Rent, £5,
and paying the composition due, amounting to £5 English,
belonging to the barony of Inchequin. Provisions as in 4939.
—12 March, xxx.

5153 (6590.) License to Richard Meredith, clerk, dean of S. Patrick's,
to be absent in England for 4 months.—16 March, xxx.

5154 (4208.) Grant to Wm. James, gent. ; of the offices of controller
of the great and small customs, and of searcher and gauger, of
Dublin and Drogheda. To hold during good behaviour, with
such fees as Tho. Plunkett or any other had. Not to be removed,
as in 4975.—18 March, xxx.

5155 (6706.) Pardon to Edw. Brymingham, of Milton, co. Galway,
gent., Jordan m'Thomas duff, of Tomore, Callagh m'Thomas
duff M'Jordan, Edm. m'Tho. M'Jordan, Hugh O Malohly, Wm.
M'Morrisbe, Conor og O Hirly, Moyler M'Ooisht, Edmund
m'Moyler og M'Morrishe, Redmund boy Prindergast, Rob.
O Maly, of Oacelan, Robanet Purcell, of Curhilles, Wm. oge
Brymingham, Patrick Ronowe, Edm. Gromly, of Couraghston,
Peter Baron, Philip Thobbin fitz Water, Theobald Bourke fitz
Blob., of Ballimadaghe, Cahir m'Epriour O Rely and Tho. fitz
Nich. Asbold. The pardon not to include murder, intrusion on
crown lands, or debts to the crown, and (except Edward
Brymingham) the other provisions in 5110.—18 March, xxx.

5156 (4205.) Grant to John Kernan, gent. ; of the office of
seneschal of the territory of Upper Talconchoe alias M'Kear-
nans country in co. Cavan. To hold during good behaviour,
with all accustomed profits. With power to raise the inhabitants,
and command them for defence of the territory, the public weal
of the inhabitants, and the punishment of malefactors ; to
prosecute, banish, and punish by all means malefactors, rebels,
vagabonds, rymors, Irish harpers, bards, bentules, carrowes,
idle men and women, and those who assist such ; and twice a
year within a month after Easter and Michaelmas respectively to
hold a court and law day. He shall not take any unlawful
Irish exactions from the inhabitants, as to cess them with kern,

E

1567–8.　　　　FIANTS.—ELIZABETH.

  · ·nor impose cesey or lyvery, without direction of the lord·deputy.
    —20 March, xxx.

5157 (6613.) Lease to Henry Duke, of Castleyordane, co. Meath,
English gent.; of the rectories of Ballibogan and Castleycirdan, co.
Meath; Killedery, King's co., Kilbride, co. Westmeath, and
Orenckedaghe, in Offallye, and the tithes arising from the lands
of Ballibogan, Harienstone, Killenkellinge, Knockcawoarde, Kilyne,
Doboraghe, Balliskistie, Cardlstone, Castleyoirdane, Ballan-
brockill, Ballebochepe, Killodadorie, Doyne, Longhtone, the
moiety of Ballyowan, Castlewarnaghe, Moilehoughe, Lough-
lakinge, Tibberdaloghe, Kilbryd, Grenckedaghe, Ballkurbitt,
Temastone, Dowyn, Olonam, Killimaghe, Kilbride, Carrowgon,
Killena, and Cloocmore, spiritual possessions of the late monastery
of Ballibogan. To hold for 21 years. Rent, £20 for the first
11½ years and £36 afterwards, and paying £4 yearly for proxies.
Provisions as in 1941. Fine 20 marks.—20 March, xxx.

5158 (6615.) Lease to James Dillon, gent.; of the tithes of the
English rectory of Beakyn, co. Westmeath, of the possessions of the late
monastery of St. Peter of the Newetowne by Trym. To hold
for 21 years. Rent 40s. Provisions as in 1941.—23 March,
xxx.

1568.

5159 (4302.) Grant to Ralph Haman, gent.; of the office of usher
attending the president of Munster, or gentleman porter of the
province. To hold during good behaviour, with all fees as Patz.
Grannte had. Not to be removed, as in 1576.—26 March, xxx.

5160 (6633.) Lease (under queen's letter, 17 Nov., xxv.) to Robert
English Nangle, gent.; of the lands of Hoare alias Rupe, co. Tipperary,
and the rectories of Lammaltin and Boylaston, parcel of the late
abbey of Rupe alias Hoare abbey (recites 2968); the rectories of
Ballingill and Garvock, co. Kildare, in the tenure of sir Wm.
Sarsfield, parcel of the late hospital of St. John of Jerusalem;
lands of Ballivilly, co. Longford, late of Gerald m'Hobbert boy
O Ferrel, attainted; the rectory of Shrowell alias Urre, co.
Longford, of the possessions of the monastery of the B. V. M. of
Shrowell in O Ferrall Boy's country, in the possession of sir
Wm. Collier; the rectory of Timoghe, co. Kildare, of the
possessions of St. John of Jerusalem, in the tenure of Sir Wm.
Sarsfield. To hold for 40 years from the determination of any
existing interest. Rent £19 6s. Provisions as in 1639.—27
March, xxx.

5161 (6574.) Livery to Edmund Barrett fitz William, kinsman and
heir of James fitz Richard Barrett, of Rathnemiall, co. Cork,
gent., who held in socage, by the payment of one rose yearly,
the manors and lands of Rathemnyell, one carucat, Garrany-
viarige 1 car., Knockmemaruffe 1 car., Farrenstunugwole 1 car.,
Lackenthonan 1 car., Ballyhanlok ½ car., Ballyvickowe and
Ballykonen ½ car., and 32s. chief rent out of Clane m'donell.
Fine 18s.—28 March, xxx.

5162 (6566.) Pardon of alienation to sir Thomas Williams, knt.,
English and dame Clare, his wife, executrix of sir Anthony Coldloughe,
of Tinterne, knt.; and license to alienate to any English persons
the premises leased in 1269.—29 March, xxx.

1588. FIANTS.—ELIZABETH.

5163 (6714.) Pardon to Rewigh M'Gynnas, knt. Not to include murder, intrusion into crown lands, or debts to the crown.— 30 March, xxx.

5164 (6705.) Pardon to Hugh M'Eavore, Ferdoragho M'Evore, of Dondrom, Robert Trewman, Francis Piggott, Edmund M'Prior, Con m'Arte m'Brian M'Arte, of Dondrom, Philip duffe m'Edmunde m'Shane, Patrick m'Phelim m'Manus M'Kartan, Phelim duffe m'Edmunde m'Shane M'Kartan, Patrick m'Edmonde m'Shane M'Kartan, George FitzSymons, of Dublin, and Thomas Rogers, of Downe, co. Down. Provisions as in 1585.—4 April, xxx.

5165 (6605.) Lease (under queen's letter, 3 Sept, 1587) to John Talbot, esq.; of the land called the Tayte near the bridge of Knockmylla, co. Louth, the Graunge near Myleton, 2 pounds of wax of chief rent out of Rathdown, Clinkerwill, Lative, and Lowthe, the temporal possessions of the late abbey of Knock, co. Louth, and now in the occupation of Nicholas Taithe, of Rathcaker, gent.; the rectory of Waspailleston, co. Dublin, including the tithes, 12 copies of corn at 13s. 4d. the copie, the altaragos, 20s., and the glebe, possessions of the house of nuns of Gracedew, in the occupation of Thomas Finglas; a castle, land, and common of pasture, in Cromlin, co. Dublin, of the possessions of David Sutton, attainted, and in the occupation of John Talbot, of Cromlin, gent. To hold for 50 years from the determination of existing interests, at rents of £8 10s. 4d. for Knock, £9 for the rectory, and £8 for Cromlin. Provisions as in 4939.—10 April, xxx.

5166 (4201.) Grant to John boy Roche, of Kilfynan, co. Limerick, gent.; of the office of chief and general cessor or collector of the county Lymerick. To hold during good behaviour, with the accustomed fees. Not to be removed, as in 4976.—29 April, xxx.

5167 (6591.) License to Michael Apsley, gent., clerk of the crown of the province of Munster, Ralph Hamon, gent., gentleman porter of the province, Anthony Stowghton, gent., clerk of the castle chamber, and Thomas Keare, marshal of the court of castle chamber; to be absent in England for 12 months.—29 April, xxx.

5168 (6728.) Lease to John Talbot, esq.; of ½ acre of land within the precinct of the castle of Dublin, against the east and south sides of the castle, where there have been fish ponds or weirs, another parcel against the castle walls towards the north, 100 feet by 100 feet, also the king's mill newly builded by Stephen Segare within the said precinct, with the watercourse being part of the castle ditch, from the l'owell mill down, along the south side (recites 5014); the tithes of recuries of Clonakroe and Kilcowan, with glebe lands, &c., co. Wexford (recites 2977); the tithes of Athade extending to Athad and Caricke nahane, and land in Adristine, co. Carlow, (recites 1370). To hold for 50 years from the determination of existing interests. Rent £13 3s. 8d. Provisions as in 4939.—30 April, xxx.

5169 (4310.) Grant (under queen's letter, 12 Dec., xxx.) to Tho. Springe, gent.; of the office of constable of the castle of Castelmaigne in Munster, with a fee of 3s. a day, and with 4 horsemen at 9d., and 18 footman at 8d. a day. To hold during good behaviour, as John Savadge or any other held it. The horsemen

1586.

and footmen are to be of English or Walsh race, except John
Plonket and James Farrall who are respectively to be a horseman, and a footman.—2 May, xxx.

5170 (6913.) Grant to John Gilbert and Lewis Jurdan, gent.; of
the wardship and marriage of John, kinsman and heir of John
Tuite, late of Cloughran, co. Westmeath, gent.; and custody of
his lands, during minority. Rent £3, and retaining £4 "parcel
of the said £3," for maintenance of minor. Fine 53s.—2 May,
xxx.

5171 (6542.) Grant to Henry Billingsleye, esq.; of the castle and
lands of Killmacow, late of John Supple, attainted, the lands of
Killanloghe, Ballybullogge, Grenaughe, Gortenaughe, Bally-
grenan, Gragemorte, Leudcan, Killature, Gragehurro, Ballycho-
neall, and Ballyknockan, late John Supple's, the castle and lands
of Kyllfynen, with Gortnegaraghe, and Ballynckille, late of
Garret M'Thomas, attainted, Ballenahaghe, late of Nicholas
Fitz Williams, attainted, the castle and lands of Larvoto, Bally-
hoboll, Girtnefoihegh, late of Richard m'Thomas reoghe, attainted,
Ballimoroho, Ballyellana, Ballymary, and Farantanaklyn, late
the earl of Desmond's, the abbey of Killahane, with a small
parcel of land, all which lands lying together are bounded on
the east by the bishop's lands called Diserte, Dologhe, the earl
of Kildare's, Killm'anarrie, Bornsane, Ballylyne, Killmoare,
Templeshanaboy, and Corruns, on the south by Capnehane,
Oragnekerill, Dorocloghe, and Ballygurry, on the west by Ballygurry, on the north by Purrellstowne, [   ], Ballyfollyn,
the bishop's lands called Teutarenaghe, and Downamcane, and
contain 5365 acres; the castle and lands of Drumarde, with the
castle and lands of Castlemetraske and Court Mutris, late of
Nicholas Fitz Williams, attainted, the castle and lands of
Rannsere, with 90a. called Farrentegin, late the earl of
Desmond's, Kilmonaghe, belonging to the abbey of Kilbaghe,
the castle and lands of Amogan, late of Edmund m'Morryt
Sarcell and Clane Nicholas Duffe, attainted, Ballywilliam, Innish-
couahe, late of Patrick Woulfe, the castle and lands of Clohoco-
tared, late of Richard Wale, attainted, the abbey and all the
lands in the town of Rakelye, escheated to her majesty, the
castle and lands of Callowghe, with Balligarin, Dohell, and Bally-
feracka, late of Richard de London, attainted, the castle and
lands of Clohonoralte, late of Davis Encorig, attainted, which
lying together in one continent, are bounded on the north by
Ballyvackoge, north-east by Capneghe, Purselstowne, and Bally-
garry, south-east by Ballingarry, Ballinroge, and Dunlerne,
south by Balline, south-east (sic) by Knockederry, Lislagastaghe,
Ballyaldenan, and Ballinlinn, north-west by Olohocotared boys,
Ardgoulaghe, Ballindigan, and Curreen, and contain 6043 acres;
also the half ploughland called Borbradaghe, with the moiety of
Killchaven, late of John Supple, attainted, containing 392 acres,
bounded east by Ballysediter, south by Ballyraghoghe, west by
Purealstowne and Killchaneate, north by Garranboye; the
lands of Clonaberebege, late the earl of Desmond's, 100a. bounded
on the east by Rowremore, south by Garrenallan and Carran-
boye, west by Clonenhirstemple and Gorkegraver, north by
Ooraghs and Toughs; amounting in all to 11800 English acres,
To hold, by the name of Knockbyllingalye, for ever, in fee-farm,

1588.   FIANTS.—ELIZABETH.

by fealty, in common socage. Rent, £147 10s. from 1594
(£74 5s. for the preceding three years). If the lands are found
by measurement to contain more than the estimated number of
acres, grantee shall pay 3d. for each additional English acre.
Grantee to erect houses [   ] 43
for copyholders, with other conditions usual in grants for planting the undertakers in Munster, as in 6032. 2 membranes.—
[2] May, xxx.

5172 (6599.) Lease (under queen's letter, 12 Dec., xxx.) to Thomas
Springe; of the site of the abbey of Killaha, alias our Lady Abbey
de Bello Loco, co. Kerry, land in Callynyflirry, Killderroy,
Balloughtraghe, Clownamore, Brackill, Kiltalaghe, Killny-
fynin, Ballynymonye, Kilremyn, Incha, and a piece of land in
the Dingill, the rectory of Killaha, a moiety of the rectories of
Kiltalaghe and Garriniondrya, the rectories of Dingill, Killori-
glyno, Kilmacollock Ocestar, a moiety of the rectories of Kean-
narey, Templenoce alias Nowenhurche, Kilcrokano, Dromada,
Kilmouane, Kilmore, Cahirbegg, Rincaharraghe, Glenbehie,
and Kilvonane, co. Kerry. (Recites 4319.) To hold for 21
years from the determination of the previous lease. Rent,
£17 1s. 9d. Maintaining 2 English horsemen. The abbey
to be strongly rebuilt "castlewise." Provisions as in 4039.—
3 May, xxx.

5173 (6700.) Pardon to Grany ny Maly, Shawe Bourke enl Davy
Burk, widow, Tibbott Bourk m'Richarde enarau, gent.,
Margaret O Flahartie, daughter of Grany, Morroghe O Flahatie
m'Donill a coggie, Shane, Brian, and Taige M'Furilve, Edm. og
M'Furrive, Donill and Dermot M'One, Edmund M'Gibbon
m'Ullick M'Gibbon, Redmund and Tibbot m'Ulick M'Gibbone,
Tibbot m'Thomas etotan M'Gibbon, Walter doffe ni'Fibbin owry,
Shane m'Fibbin owry, Brian reogh O Moran, of Kilera, Shane
O Moran, of Killera, Hugh M'Laghlan, of Killera, Taige M'Tohill,
of Rnistrick, Thomas, Cormack, and Connor M'Tohill, of same,
Richard M'Walter, of Cahir m'Emilly, Shane Bourk m'Mayler,
Wm. Burk m'Shane, of Bealanelobo, Shane og m'Shane Burk,
Shaghnes O Moran, of Kilera, Donogh O Moran, of same, Edmund
og M'Edmunde, of Hakill, Hubbert M'Mayler, of Kilmaglashir,
Shane Burke m'Hubbert, Thomas Bourk, his son, Oliver Bourk
m'Shane, Ulick Bourke m'Mayler, Edmund m'Ullick, Mayler
m'Ullick, Shane m'Brian O Mallia, Thomas m'Bryen O Mally,
Thomas M'Edmonde, of Moyore, and Tuige og M'Taige roe
O Mally. Provisions as in 4965.—4 May, xxx.

5174 (6708.) Pardon to Taige m'Kilpatricke O Connor, of Cappen-
onrrowe, gent., Brasill m'Dermot O Connor, of same, gent.,
Feallim m'Owny O Connor, of Killenmore, kern, Cahir m'Carte
O Connor, of same, horseboy, Morrish M'Gennan, of same, cottier,
Braine m'Dermot O Connor, of same, horseboy, Shane m'Cahir
O Connor, of same, horseboy, Walter O molone O toaffe, cottier,
Richard O Collogan, of Cappen Corrowe, horseboy. The pardon
not to extend to any in prison or on bail, or to include murder,
intrusion into crown lands or debts to the crown.—4 May,
xxx.

5175 (6600.) Lease to Isabell Fallowes, widow of Robert Fallowes,
of Dublin, girdler; of a little house place and shop place where
lately a house and shop covered with boards stood, sometime in

the occupation of Thomas Pynnocke, with two little backsides lying within the precinct of the queen's castle ditch of Dublin, and all land from the bridge of the castle westward to the city walls, and from the castle against the west and north side; the water and watercourse of the castle ditch 24 feet broad excepted. Recites as consideration the surrender of a previous lease for 5 years, the pulling up of certain fruit trees and the reducement of the backsides in enlarging and scouring the ditch. To hold for 21 years. Rent, 13s. 4d. Lessee may not assign to any but English, without license, and must not erect any building without license, nor do anything to the nuisance or stopping of the ditch.—8 May, xxx.

5176 (4212.) Grant (under queen's letter, 20 Sept., xxix.) to sir Tho. Williams, knt.; of the office of muster master and clerk of the cheque, with the leading of 10 horsemen at 9d. English a day each, and with a fee of 4s. English a day for himself. To hold for life. Recites 4606 and its surrender. Not to be removed, as in 4976.—9 May, xxx.

5177 (6609.) Lease to sir Edward Denney, knt.; of the church of Lislaghty, co. Kerry, and the circuit of the house of Franciscan friars of Lislaghtie in Iraught I Knoghor's country, the fishing of the creek there, part of the great river of the Shennon, and land in Lislaghty belonging to the said house. To hold for 21 years. Rent, £3 2s. 2½d. Provisions as in 4939.—10 May, xxx.

5178 (6709.) Pardon to John M'Gerald, Nicholas M'Gerald, Teig, Donill, and Art m'Dermod O Lery, Donill m'Donogh O Swillivan, Donill m'Moriertagh Y Gunny, Donogh m'Dermod Inn, Dermod m'Conochor O Swillivan, Pabike O Brenyne, Owin m'Donogh M'Carmock, Richard M'Heligoide, Donill m'Da I Moichaa, Teig O Falben, James (son of) William Barruits O Ma'ba ganagh, Conell m'Teig O Connell, and Dionisa O Hilay; coa. Kerry and Desmond. Provisions as in 4905. Excluding also any in prison or on bail to appear; and any who do not submit to orders as to their lands as in 4938.—11 May, xxx.

5179 (6628.) Grant to Richard and Alexander Phitton; of the castle and lands of Balligibbone and Ardnegillinagh, Ballenavally, Ballewyrrny, Coch, Ballencurry, Ellanbwy, Bowly, Ballystephen, Ballinchinoby, Grangpaden, Rasa, and Ardpatrick, containing 4½ plowlands and 26 acres, Ballenvisiallenadowne and Glanebagelshy, containing 2 plowlands, the castle and lands of Cloghtackea, ½ plowland; in all 7 plowlands and 26 acres, which after the rate of 28 plowlands to a seignory of 12,000 acres, amount to 3,026 acres. To hold for ever by the name of Phitton's Fortune in fee-farm by fealty in common socage. Rent, £31 10s. 6d. from 1594 (half for preceding three years), and 2½d. an acre for every acre by which on measurement the lands may be found to exceed the estimate. Grantees must erect houses for 23 families, 2 of which for the grantees, 2 for freeholders of 300a., 1 for a farmer of 400a., 10 for copyholders of 100a., with other conditions as in 5032.—14 May, xxx. (Much defaced. There is an entry of this grant in Auditor-General's Patent Book, James and Charles I., vol 11 B., p. 239).

5160 (6603.) Lease to Hugh m'Tirrelaughe roe; of the lands of Casciltane, Poolecry, Carrowenstrowan, Carrowbannenagh, Leigh Cearrowangeraghe, and Leigh Cearrowaniarbe, being five quarters, the lands of Hugh, son of Terence rufe O Connor alias

1888. FIANTS.—ELIZABETH.

Hugh m'Tirrelaughe roe O Connor, in the county Roscommon, attainted. To hold for 21 years. Rent, £5 English. Provisions as in 4989. Reserving to Captain Thomas Woodhowse power to prove his claim to the lands within two years.—16 May, xxx.

5181 (5915.) Grant to Oliver Skiddmore, gent.; of the wardship and marriage of Gerald, son and heir of Nicholas Rossell, late of Russellerton, co. Westmeath, gent., in the queen's hands by reason of the minority of George, son and heir of Christopher Darcy; and custody of the lands, during minority. Rent, £4 16s., retaining out of the rent 55s. for support of the minor. Fine £3 6s. 8d.—20 May, xxx.

5182 (5697.) Pardon to Robert Murphe, of the Passage, co. Waterford, sailor. Provision as in 4965.—20 May, xxx.

5183 (4214.) Livery to Katherine, daughter and heir of James Barrett, late of Ballincollo, co. Cork, gent., of his lands in Cloghm'ullig, Cwilroe, Great Island, Cwilvridogy, Minyfuigh, Gerryvaghe, Carrignavine, Arolaman, Ardroune, and Inyakarry, Cwrrylioghe and Carrigfowky, Cwilgoyn and Cwilnahaby, Farryngwole, Girtinaghiloe, Ballysly and Cwirtyonllanain, Ballyenisy and Monlvanesir, Kallybeggy and Knockaallighane, Knockanthynedory, the Hwany, a water mill there, Lywynyallisy, Knocknybwrdownaghe, Corryvallimore, Magellin, Ballinvordownaybege, Cwillnetwbberrid, Cwilvane and other hamlets adjoining, Castlenyhinshy, and Castlemore. Fine £5 16s. 2d.—21 May, xxx.

5184 (6698.) Pardon to Morise fitz James Fitz Morice, of Cloghananinan, kern, Connor M'Tirlogh, of Ballikelly, kern, Thomas m'Edmunde M'Ullick, of Lissicurringe, kern, Morice Fitz Thomas, of Dromkenie, karn, Donill og O Morrhie, of Ballykoaly, Edmund Guer, John M'Conry, Malmory M'William, Morrice M'William, of same, husbandmen, Margaret Fitz Edmonde, of same, Gerald m'Shane Biondon, of same, labourer, Connor O Marrho, of Ardarth, and David O Redy, of same, husbandmen, Gerrot m'Wm. Browne, of Arda, Wm. oge, of same, Mortogh O Gillhinan, of Ardarth, labourer, John m'Tho. Stack, of Glandalen, and Robert m'Edm. M'Ullick, of Lissicurrige, kerns, Ellice eni Tane Fitz Thomas, of Tyreckihie, Robert fitz Wm. Fitz Peirce, of Ardath, labourer, Philip m'Rich. Stack, of Ardarth, and Gerrot m'Edm. M'Shane, of Ballikeoly; kerns, Shane m'Melaghlan O Dogan, of Laharte, yeoman, James Browne, Donogh m'Donill O Solevan, of Bondoglassye, Dermod m'Boogh O Swillivan, of Cahir, John M'Murtogh, of Kilkrine, Connor oge O Mtnyghan, Teige roe M'Fynan, of Dunymarke, Donenha og M'Conry, of Ballikellye, husbandman, co. Kerry. Provisions as in 4938. Excluding also any person who has committed murder.—22 May, xxx.

5185 (6669 bis.) License to John Garland, gent.; to export 25 tons English of wheat or other grain to any country in amity with the queen. "Inasmuche as (thanks be unto allmightie God) the plentie and store of corne is suche, within this oure Realme of Irelande, as our subiectes heare may well spare some convenient quantetie thereof to be transported els where into anny other Cuntris in amytie with us, and there converted and retorned hither againe in some other commoditie more acharse and needefull within this our Realme."—28 May, xxx.

1588.   FIANTS.—ELIZABETH.

5186 (4207.) Grant to John Ball, gent. ; of the office of serjeant-at-
arms, and the office of marshal of the four courts. To hold
during good behaviour, with the usual fees as Hugh Payne or
any other had. Not to be removed, as in 4976.—1 June, xxx.

5187 (3642.) Pardon to Patrick M'Henry, Tirloghe boye M'Henry,
Arte m'Neale boy M'Hugh, Patrick mudder M'Henry, Richard
m'Gorrey boy M'Henrye, Donill m'Nell boy M'Hughe, and
Daltinus M'Henry. . Not to extend to any intrusion in crown
land, debts to the crown, or murder.—4 June, xxx.

5188 (6573.) Livery to Charles or Cahill O Kelly, son and heir of
Ever rufus O Kelly, late of Rathaspicke, Queen's co. No fine.
—7 June, xxx.

5189 (4233.) Grant (under queen's letter, 3 Feb., xxx.), to Edm.
fitz Thomas, gent, heir of his grandfather Thomas fitz Thomas,
late Knight of the Valley, attainted ; of the manor of Glancorbary
with the demesne lands, in the parish of Kilfaririe in the country
of Connelo in the great co. of Limerick, containing 10½ quarters
or carucates of land which are called Farrenie Ruddarye of the
Glan alias the Knight's free land in Glancorbary, the castle
and land of Cloghlan within Togha of Glancorberie, containing
1½ quarter or carucate, Skartinn, 1 quarter, Killoballagh, 1 qr.,
Knockdulloboy in the parish of Kilfarisie, 1 qr., Philliane in
same parish, Cromiglan in same parish, Clonsellagh in same
parish, with a mountain or parcel of land called Killyentaigdowry,
1 quarter, Tullaghleighe in same parish, 1 quarter, Rahanna in
same parish, 1 qr., Curragbagaddy in same parish, 1 qr., which
amount to 10½ quarters within Togha of Glancorbary, which
are called Farrenior Huddary, and are in the country of Connelo
in the great county of Limerick ; also the lands of Towlogiasse,
1 quarter, Keynard, 1 qr., Ballicollan, 1 qr., Ballicoughlan, 1
qr., Meanes alias Meanis, 2 qr., Tannacort, 1 qr., Ballynammodagh,
1 qr., Ballynegalt, 1 qr., Ballinagonnoho, 1 qr., which amount
to 10 quarters, in the Togh of Glancorbary, in the parish of
Kilfarisie same country and county, and are called the earl of
Desmond's chargeable lands, and sometime in the possession of
Thomas M'Ruddary alias the Knight of the Valley. To hold
to him and the heirs male of his body for ever ; by the service
of a fourth part of a knight's fee. Rent for each quarter 20r.
English, immediately after they come to his possession, making in
all £20 10s. ster. Recites 3277.—13 June, xxx.

5190 (5953.) Surrender by John O Dockertie or O Dogherrye,
knt, chief or captain of his name ; of the manors and lands of
Ilighe, Coulemoar, New castle, Insie, Bartie, Faine, and diverse
others in the country of Inisioeqine ; with the intention of their
being regranted. See 5207.—Dated 15 June, xxx.

5191 (6570.) Livery to John, son and heir of Thomas Tute, late of
Sonaghe, co. Westmeath, gent. Fine £66 0s. 4d.—18 June,
xxx.

5192 (6571.) Livery to John, son and heir of Nicholas Ewstace,
late of Confynn, co. Kildare, gent. Fine £7.—18 June, xxx.

5193 (6575) Livery to John, son and heir of Simon Barnewall,
late of Kiltrus, esq. Fine £30.—18 June, xxx.

5194 (5991.) Surrender by Richard Striche, of Limerick, merchant,
assignee of Gamaliel Crace, gent ; of two water mills called the
royal mills on the bank of the Shenyn in Limerick, between

1588.   FIANTS.—ELIZABETH.

Cordowes on the west and the manor of the chanter of the
cathedral, of the queen's ancient inheritance. Revise lease
4852. *Signed,* R. Streiche.—*Dated* 19 June, xxx.

5195 (6608.) Lease (under letter of the English Privy Council, 16
Oct., xxix.), to Richard Stricha, of Limerick, gent.; of the two
water mills called the Kinges mills in the city of Limerick, upon
the Rook of the Shennyn between Cardowes on the west and the
manor of the chantor of the church, parcel of the queen's ancient
inheritance. (Recites a lease to Gamaliel Croca, gent., 4852,
surrendered.) To hold for 60 years. Rent £4 13s. 4d. Not to
alien except to English without license.—20 June, xxx.

5196 (6663 *bis.*) License to Luke Fitz Symon, gent.; to export 20
tons of wheat to any place in amity with the queen, the dominions
of the king of Spain excepted.—20 June, xxx.

5197 (6209.) Grant to Anthony and John Stoughton, gent.; of
the wardship and marriage of Katharine, daughter and heir of
Nich. Power, late of Kilballykilty, co. Waterford, gent., and
custody of the lands, during minority. Rent 20s. Fine 40s.—
[21 June, xxv.] (*Date from the patent remaining in Rolls
Office collection.*)

5198 (4194.) Grant to Arland Usther, gent.; of the office of
register or clerk in Chancery for faculties. To hold during
good behaviour, with the fee appertaining.—22 June, xxx.

5199 (4239.) Grant (under commission, 7 Dec., xxviii.) to Giller-
newe O Faghny or m'Faghny, of Rathdyne, co. Longford, esq.,
captain and chief of the territory of Callce same co.; of all
manors, castles, lands, and services, in Rathklen, Forkill, Drom-
harfe, Aghadain, Aghloughan, Cooletaggell, and Farrinegiragh
or Ferrenakragh, and elsewhere within the territory of Callo,
surrendered by his deed of 20 May, xxx.; also half the goods of
fugitives and persons attainted of treason or felony, and all goods
of waifs and strays, and fines within the territory. To hold for
ever, by the service of a twentieth part of a knight's fee. This
grant not to alter any rent or service reserved by composition,
nor shall it pass any possessions vested in the crown otherwise than
by the surrender of Gillernew. He may once in each
quarter hold a court baron, and twice a year a court of view of frank
pledge at Rathklen, or elsewhere within the premises, before his
seneschal. This grant shall not prejudice the rights of the heirs
of N. Malby, knt. or any other of the queen's subjects, except to
the title of captain or chief of the Callo, which title is abolished.
—22 June, xxx.

5200 (6686.) License to Nicholas White, knt., master of the rolls,
to be absent in England for 6 months.—22 June, xxx.

5201 (6677.) Grant to William Donne, gent.; of the office of
interpreter for the state, to attend on the lord deputy. To hold
during good behaviour, with the stipend of 18d. a day, as formerly
allowed him. Not to be removed, as in 4976.—22 June, xxx.

5202 (6292.) Patent in pursuance of the foregoing fiant.—At
Dublin, 22 June, xxx.

5203 (6702.) Pardon to Richard Fitz Geralde alias Baron, of Burn-
churche, co. Kilkenny, Rich. fitz John Power, of same, Tho.
m'Shane Brenagh, of Kilcregan, Wm. Brenagh, of Millagbe,
Redmund Archdecon, of Granagh, Rich. Archdecon, of
same, Nich. fitz Tho. Geraldine, of Gurtines, Walter fitz

1568.   FIANTS.—ELIZABETH.

Tho. Geraldine, of same, Patrick Archdeacon fitz Edm.
of Knocktofer, James Archdeacon fitz Edm., of same, David
Hennebres, of Bradlstone, Walter Daton, of Gragnoe, Walter
Daton, of Cloncunny, Redmund Baron, of Kilcregan, James
Walshe fitz Oliver, of Lisdrolin, John Grace fitz Redmond, of
Garryhigin, Richard Walshe alias Brenagh, of Lisdrolin, James
Cantwell, of Clone, Patrick Archdccon, of Cowlcassin, Henry
O Clony, of Fowkesrate, Rob. Clantwell fitz Pairce, of Moigts-
shane, Peirce Sweteman fitz Edm., of Castellife, and Edm. fitz
Pairs Butler, of Cowlrve, co. Kilkennyn. Provisions as in 1965.
—22 June, xxx.

5204 (6663 bis.) License to Thomas Clynton, gent., to export 25
English tons of wheat or other grain, as in 5185.—24 June, xxx.

5205 (5523.) Grant (under queen's letter, 13 Jan. last) to Patrick
Clinch ; of a pension of 6d. English, a day, for life. In consider-
tion of his wounds.—26 June, xxx.

5206 (6113.) Pardon to Johanna Hussey, widow of Laurence
Delahide, of Moclare, esq., and all seised to her use ; of all alienations and intrusions in the manor of Moyclare, and the lands of
Brynston, Gillianston, Toolegrye, Harriston, Killan, Aishewolle,
the Newton of Moyagh, Porterston, Isynaghton, Ballegortaghs,
the Kemmons, the Barrocke, the Newton of Rathgwrinlagilgrelga,
Baldongell, Myclue Moygadde, little Moygadde called the Barrock
in the tenure of John Rochford, little Moygadd in the tenure of
Thomas Talbott of Dardeston, Butlerston, and Gallo, belonging
to the said manor. Not to extend to pardoning the fine on livery.
Fine £30 English.—27 June, xxx.

5207 (4228.) Grant (under queen's letter, 20 Jan. xxvii.) to John
O Dockertie, knt., chief of his name ; of all manors, castles, lands,
and services, in Ilighs, Conlemore, Newcastle, Insia, Bartia, and
Faine, in the country called Inisioeqine, and wheresoever in the
said-country or in O Dockerties country ; which he had surrendered (5190), also half of all goods of felons, and of waifs and
strays, and fines, within the country ; reserving to the crown the
possessions of abbeys. To hold for ever, by the service of one
knight's fee. Rendering yearly 30 good fat beeves at Newry.
He shall attend hostings with 20 kern and 6 horsemen victualled
for 40 days. He may twice yearly hold a court baron and court
leet or view of frank pledge, before his seneschal. This grant not
to prejudice the rights of any subject not of the sept of O Dockertie. The titles O Dockerdie and tanist are abolished.—28 June,
xxx.

5208 (4225.) Grant (under queen's letter, 24 Aug., xxix.) to Edw.
Fitz Gerald, gent., son of Maurice Fitz Gerald, of Leakagh, knt,
deceased ; of the manor of Kildroght alias Castlestone Kildroght
(recites 3971 and 4181), Kilmacredock (recites 4911), and the
mill of Kildroght (recites 4180), with their appurtenances, co.
Kildare, in the queen's hands by the attainder of David Sutton.
To hold for ever, by the service of a fortieth part of a knight's
fee. Provided that this grant shall not convey any lands
not parcel of said manor or that exceed the annual value of
£28 13s. 4d. In consideration that the premises were shown to
be the ancient right of Thomas Fitz Gerald, brother of said
Edward, whose estate he has.' Provided that this grant shall
not convey the lands of Kildrought of which Maurice, the father

of said Thomas, released his right by feoffment of 31 Oct., 1570.—
28 June, xxx.

5209 (6592.) Lease to Robert Myles, gent.; of the lands of Kilma-
kanocke, Clancormocke, Kiloughe, Cowlamore, and Glanmore, in
Glancap, co. Dublin, possessions of Dermott fitz Edmonde Toole,
attainted. To hold for 21 years. Rent, 20s. English. Provisions
as in 4939.—28 June, xxx.

5210 (6660 bis.) License to Nicholas Walshe, second justice of the
Chief Place; to export 260 barrels of his own wheat from Waterford to any country in amity with the queen. Recites the plenty
of corn (as in 5185) especially in counties Waterford and Kilkenny.
At Dublin, 8 May, 1588.—28 June, xxx.

5211 (6704.) Pardon to James Butler, of Carinles, Peirce Butler,
of same, Wm. Bourke, of Cowlamoggie, Walter Bourke, of Balle-
[   ], John Butler, of Colline, Elm. Butler, of Wodington,
Edm. Bourck, of Killardry, Cornelius O Carran, of Dirreoloney,
Tibbot m'Rich. Bourke, of Cowlemoghie, Ellice St. [John],
of Soulaxton, Derby roe O Carran, of Rathgowls, James Butler
fitz Theobald, of Jordanston, Wm. fitz Rich. Butler, of Oughter
Rath, Shane m'Art O Brenan, W[   ] O Fogartie, of Carrinlea,
James Purcell fitz Rich., of Loghmo, Ullick Burke, of Balliwaire,
David O Carran, of Dirrleakane, Donill Hickey, of the Garrane,
James fitz Edm. Butler, of Baronston, Wm. ro O Fowlant, of
Drangane, David Hickey, of Knockgraffan, Tirrelogh O Brin, of
Kaltoynan, Donill O Meagher, of Glanbehigh, John Bourke, of
Lismakan, Wm. Boi[rke], of same, James Ewstace fitz Water, of
Bollycollin, Edw. Walsh, of Griffonston, Wm. St. John, of Lisa-
moynan, James O Rian, of Ballicleim, John O Carroll, of Lagh-
ardan, Philip m'Theobald Purcell, Donell moyle O Kallye, Oohe
O Fogartie, of Moen Roe, Rob. Shortall, of Ballenabronagh, Wm.
O Meagher, of Carinlea, and Wm. fitz Thomas O Meagher, of
Littlegraunge; co. of Cross of Tipperary and Queen's co. Pro-
visions as in 4938 (except James and Peirce Butler, of Carinlea).
They shall submit to such orders as the lord deputy may make
concerning their lands.—28 June, xxx.

5212 (6695.) Pardon to John Ball, Wm. Mortian, junior, of the
Downs, co. Galway, John Parker, Edw. Muckley, Henry Good,
Wm. Clattero, and Rich. Woodd. Not to extend to murder,
intrusion into crown lands or debts to the crown.—29 June, xxx.

5213 (6696.) Pardon to Tirelogh lenagh O Noyle, chief of his name,
Anne Cambell, his wife, Arte O Neale, his son, knt., Neall
O Neill, of the race of Art ogg, Cormack O Neal, son of said
Tirlogh, Ferdorcha O Neall, of Baile an Tackan, and Henry
Dowgan, gentlemen, Rory M'Conny, of Mounter Lonygh, Seaan
M'Conny and Art domylagh M'Conny, of Mounter Lonigh,
horseman, Salomon Fernan, of Ardaratha, clerk, Doughs M'Rory,
horseman, Brian duffe M'Hewe, and Rory ballagh O Doghartie.
The pardon not to bar the rights of the earl of Tyrone or any
other subject.—29 June, xxx.

5214 (6703.) Pardon to Edmund duff O Moloy, Moriah Tallon,
Wony O Morishe, Shane ballagh m'Rory O Moloy, John [   ],
Arte O Brenan, Carbery M'Kegan, of the Leahan, Rorie more
O Kenane, Onory ny Morish, Donill oge m'Borie O Moloy, of
Balanegilsie, Teig m'William moile, and Ramsitt O[   ];
King's co. Provisions as in 5110.—29 June, xxx.

1588.   FIANTS.—ELIZABETH.

5215 (4195.) Grant to Christopher Ussher, gent.; to be king of arms and principal herald of Ireland with the name Ulvester, surrendered by Nich. Narbon alias Ulvester, esq. To hold during good behaviour, with all accustomed profits, and with a fee of 40 marks English a year. He shall not be removed, as in 4976.—30 June, xxx.

5216 (6562.) Livery to Gerald Fay, grandson and heir of Gerald Faye, late of Derrenegarraughe, co. Westmeath, gent. Fine £10 sterling.—30 June, xxx.

5217 (6075.) Grant (under queen's letter, 20 May, xxvi.) to Nicholas Wogan, son of William Wogan, attainted; of a sixth part of the demesne lands and a mill in the manor of Rathcoffie, co. Kildare, lands of Belgarde, Portagloriam, Cloneferte, Clane, Castalkile, and Oldtowne of Donowre, and sixth part of Carnalwey, forfeited by the attainder of Thomas Eustace, of Kerdiffestan, who was seized jointly with Peter Boyx, James Flatisburie, Chr. Flatisburie, Wm. Sutton, and Wm. Bermynghame, to the use of Wm. Wogan, of Rathcoffie; also the lands of Gragfootall, Gragoddre, and Kilcock, same co., which will come to the queen's hands immediately after the death of Catherine FitzGerolde, widow, by the attainder of said Wm. Wogan; also 10s. chief rent in Richardston, 16s. in Farnanton, 12d. in Cloncfart, 13s. 4d. in Boyeston, 2s. 0d. in Byrtenballagh, 6s. 8d. in Garveston, 5s. in Clangerston, 9s. in Halvoyenton, 7d. in Burretanton, 12d. in Landanston, and 34s. in Clane, in the queen's hands by the attainder of the said Wm. Wogan. To hold for ever, by the two hundredth part of a knight's fee. On petition of Henry Burnell on the part of said Nicholas.—*Not dated.*[*]

5218 (6557.) Grant to Arthur Robins; of the castle of Policurry alias Polykirry, co. Cork, containing 600 acres, the lands of Noghevally, Glangaila, Dungarren alias Dongarrott, Rennes, and Treddynes, 1,000s.; the butt of an old castle and lands of Burdenston with a grist mill, ½ a ploughland, and of English measure 200s., co. Cork; a rent of 19 marks halface, due to the late earl of Desmond out of Barretts country, and a rent of 6 marks and 1d. halface due to the same earl out of Courseis country, making together £15 4s. 5½d. English, all the lands containing by estimation 1800 English acres. To hold for ever by the name of Robins Bocke, in fee farm, by fealty, in common socage. Rent £10 English from 1594 (half only for the preceding three years), and for the said rents and services of free tenants £15 4s. 5½d. and ½d. for each acre of waste land which shall be utilised for pasture and tillage. If found by measurement to contain more than the estimated number of acres he shall pay 1½d. for each English acre as in excess. Power to impark 100s. Grantee to erect houses for 14 families, of which one to be for himself, 2 for freeholders, 2 for farmers, and 2 for copyholders. Other conditions usual in grants for planting the undertakers in Munster, as in 5032.—2 membranes.—*Not dated.*

5219 (6562.) Grant to Thomas Norreys; of castles and lands in co. Cork, viz. [Moallo, Callinferriakerrie alias] the Ould towne, [Ballingwrald] alias Geraldstowne, Ballthough alias Loaghin[eston, the Old towne within the Erles]wood, Farrenkoraghe ne soudrye alias [the Shoemakers towne, [the Shortcastle] alias Castle[garr,

1588.   FIANTS.—ELIZABETH.

Curniguere] alias Sheepa[twiter], Curabeg[ ], and Cloghlaces,
amounting in the whole to 6,000 English acres. To hold, by the
name of [   ] alias Moallo, for ever in fee farm, by
fealty, in common socage. Rent £33 6s. 8d., from [1594], (half
for preceding three years), and for every acre of waste land
enclosed [¼d.]. If the lands are certified to contain more than
6,000 English acres, grantee shall pay 1½d. for each acre in
excess. Grantee shall erect houses for 45 families, of which one
to be for himself, 3 for freeholders, 3 for farmers, and 21 for
copyholders.   Other conditions usual in grants to undertakers
in Munster as in 5082. (Some of the names of lands supplied
from a later grant Pat. Roll x. James I., part 4.—Date defaced.

5220 (6553). Grant to Arthur Hyde. (Granting clause, tenure, and
rent, defaced. Portions of two or three names traceable appear to be
those of lands included in the subsequent grant to Arthur Hyde,
5291.) Grantee to erect houses for 95 families, one for himself,
8 for freeholders, 6 for farmers, and [   ] for copyholders; with
other conditions usual in grants to the undertakers in Munster
as in 5032.—Date defaced.

5221 (6634.) Commission to Ambrose Forthe, LL.D., master in
Chancery, Henry Usher, archdeacon of Dublin, [
          ] rector of the church of S. John, Dublin,
Thomas Spensfeld and Nicholas Hally, learned in the law, as
delegates ; to hear an appeal from Robert Conwey, LL.D., vicar-
general of Dublin, in a cause between Thomas Weshile, gent.,
farmer of the vicarage of Ballyburley, King's co., and Henry
Warren, farmer of the rectory of the same.

5222 (6363.) Commission to John, archbishop of Armagh, Thomas,
earl of Ormonde, John, lord president of Moanster, sir Richard
Bingham, knt., Edward Fitz Symons, serjeant at laws, Charles
Calthroppe, attorney general, James Smithes, queen's solicitor,
and Richard Meridith, bachelor of divinity; to be commissioners
adjoined to the high commission of 10 Ap., xxiii. (3698), and the
commission of adjuncts of 7 Ap., xxv. (4138.)—Date destroyed.

5223 (6353.) Grant (under commission, 17 Jan., XXVII.) to Thomas
Wyseman, gent. ; of the wardship and marriage of Christopher,
son and heir of Thomas Cusack, late of Geraldston, co. Meath,
gent. ; and custody of his lands, during minority.   Rent,
£13 6s. 8d. English, and retaining £6 13s. 4d. Irish for maintenance of the minor. Fine £3 6s. 8d. English.—Not dated.

5224 (6314.) Pardon to William Nugent, of Clanyn, co. Westmeath,
esq., and Janet Marward, his wife ; reciting that he with others
had rebelled at Robenston, co. Westmeath, on the 20 March,
xxiii.—No date.

5225 (6342.) Pardon to Gerrott Stacke alias Gerrott oge roe, of
Lishtohill, co. Kerry, gent., Thomas M'Shane, of Koyselly, gent.,
John m'Morrishe Stacke, of Lishtohill, Moriabe oge Stacke, of
the same, Rob. m'Rickard duf Stacke, of Byall, and Edm.
m'Robert Stacke, of the same, horsemen, John O Skanlan, of
Lishtohill, Edm. fitz Robert duf Stacke, Rob. oge Stacke, Edm.
fitz Wm. Stacke, Conoghor O Skanlan, James fitz Rickarde
Stacke, and Conoghor m'Shane menla I Connor, of the same
place, kerns, Moroghe O Ryada, of Ballymvoneany, smith,
Donald O Leyne, of Licksnawe, surgeon, Thomas howy O San-
pighan, of the same, shot, John Stacke m'Garrott, of Lishtohill,

student, Thomas O Moholahane, of Carrignyfalle, freeholder, Conoghor m'Shane M'Thomas, of Kearhune, shot, Wm. m'Teig M'Shane, of Dromokyna, and Richard M'Donill, of Rathmoen, kerns, Oyne O Linsie, of Ardarta, clerk, John m'Gerald M'Robert, horseman, Gerrott m'Morriah Stacko, of Rathtough, keru, John m'Thomas M'Shane, of Lishtohill, kern, and John m'Roberts Stacke, of the same, kern, in co. Kerry. Provision for submission as in 1943.—*Not dated.*

5226 (6364.) Pardon to Donogh M'Carlie [   ] Clancear, Philip O Swyllayan, of Ardoe, Owin O Sheyne m'Connoghor, of Toughor, Donogh m'[De]rmot O Swylevan, John O [   ] m'Meloghlen, of same, Thady m'Corke Fallif, of Castlalonghe, Auley O Falif, of Moycrum, Thady oge M'Curty, of Lyscray, Thady m'Cornick M'Carty, of the same, Thady m'Fynin M'Dermot, of Ryngrahne, Maurice orone O'Connell, Mortagh m'Ea I Conell, Donogh roe, David grany, of Dinglecuishe, Conoghor O Naghten, Richard Moore, of Moorestown, Edmund M'Shane, of Rathonyn, Maurice m'Thomas M'Moriah, Conoghor m'Teige M'Donogh, Moriertagh [Lonran, of Mago, Maurice m'Owen m'Teige M'Moriercy, Gerald M'Nicholas, Conoghor m'Dermot M'Donogh, John O'Brack, Edmund oge Yglanwe, Edmund M'Shane, Owen m'Mortagh M'Teige, of Fawney, John m'Conoghor I Dowdey, Ferris M'Teige, Daniel moile m'Donogh oge O Swylevane, Daniel Y Channaghna, Thady m'Conoghor O Deley, John Champion, [   ] O Hungrall, of Valencia, Edmund m'Shane oge, of the same, Charles Wall, Edmund Wall, Donogh Keagh, of the same. *Other names obliterated or torn away.* Security in co. Kerry or Desmond, and provisions as in 1938. Donogh M'Cartie excepted from clauses excluding any in prison, or already pardoned.—*Date destroyed.*

5227 (6365.) Pardon to Brian m'Tirrelagh Magowan, of Dartry, kern, Owen O Harry, of Cowlese, horseman, Owen M'Gillawred, of Loughwayltagher, gent, Fenlagh M'Katye, of the same, horseman, Arte og M'Gillebride, of Ranegromanaghe, Neile M'Gillebride, and Dermot O Duffe, of the same, husbandman, Tirrelagh Magawran, of Cargin, gent, Donogh, Fergananim, Gillenemevo, Cahill, Gillspatrick, and Brian Magawran, of the same place, gentlemen, Andrew Magawran, of the same, vicar, Edmund Magawran, of the same, clerk, Connoghor, Shane, and William M'Keaven, of the same, kerns, Phelim O Rwirke, of Garre, priest, Laughlen M'Owen, of [Don]oghmore, chief of his name, Brian, Cahill, Ferdorogh, Donnogh, Donnogh oge, Donell, Cormack, Mannae, and Tearnan M'Morre, of the same, horsemen, Moriah Ultaghe of Offane, surgeon, Shane Ultaghe, of the same, surgeon, Donell Ultaghe, of the same, surgeon, Gerald M'Tiernan, of Lisapple, horseman, Edmund, Donogh, Hue, Tiernan, Fenlim, and Woony M'Tiernan, of the same, horsemen, Hue m'Meleughlin M'Tiernan, of the same, husbandman, Brian M'Laughlin, of Ballem'laghlan, chief of his name, William, Dwaltagh, Towle, Tirrelagh, and Laughlin M'Laughlin, William M'Loughlen, Thomas crone M'Loughlen, and Brian oge M'Loughlin, of the same place, horsemen, Woony M'Loughlen, Danill M'Loughlin, Towell m'Wony M'Laughlin, Richard m'Connor M'Laughlin, and Teige m'Connor M'Laughlin, of the same, kerns, Connor m'Oen ballagh M'Loughlin, of the same, Donogh grana m'Oen ballagh M'Loughlin, Owen M'Loughlin,

1588.　　　　　　FIANTS—ELIZABETH.

of the same, kern, Donell M'Gillewy, of the same, and Gerald m'Edmond boy M'Loughlin, kerns, in co Leitrim. Provision for submission as in 4943.—The pardon not to include any who are not followers of Brian O Rwirke, but (Offences before 4 Dec., xxviii. only, pardoned.)—Date torn.

5228 (6366.) Pardon to [　　　] O Madden, of Ballinabrainagh, co. Galway, gent., Collo m'Teig m'Collo, of Lisbeg, gent., Shane m'Teig m'Collo, gent., Mellaghlen M'Woltaghan, of Addergowill, kern, Rich. Hea m'Tho. m'Richard, of Clogbstolin, kern, [　　] Helyarrowe, kern, Shane M'Brian, of Ballacurra, kern, Morrbo m'Shane M'Farry, of Cappysollagh, kern, Brian reiogh m'Shane m'Brian Gillekeylly, of Clogvallevor, gent., Wm. m'Shane m'Brian, of the same, gent, Fla[　　] Wony m'Shane m'Brien, gent., Edm. doghom Edm. boy M'Gillekelly kern, Morritagh m'Dermod lea M'Gillekelly, husbandman, Flan m'Hugh M'Gillekelly, kern, Thomas m'Farriagh M'Gillekelly, kern, Collo m'Edmund [　　], Edm. m'Owin mantagh O Heyn, gent., Owin mantagh O Heyn, of Downgowcry, gent., Rory m'Donogho M'Sy, of Illannykarragh, husbandman, Morritagh O Ferrall, of Kilboght, clerk, Edm. O Kelly m'Hugh, of Clogher, gent., [　　] Moeltully, labourer, Hugh M'Moeltully, labourer, Shane m'Rory og O Fahy, of Poblewintarfahy, Morritagh O Fahy m'Ricoard, Edm. M'Gillagblen, of Cortally, Ulick Bourke m'William [　　] and Rich. Bourke, of the same, gentlemen. Donill O Beollan, of Kilchoan, and Rory M'Oragh, of Illan m'Cragh, husbandman, Donill M'Shconyn, of Lirtar, cottier, Conchor ni'Manus O Naghten, Mellaghlen ni'Manus O [　] m'Rory og Joys, of Tirnakilla, gent., Donill m'Rory O Flahertie, of Ovare, Teig og O Flahertie, of Aghamare, Moyler m'Theobald boy, of Tiroby, Rowland Bourke, of Blanor, and Edm. O [　　], of Clonbrock, gentlemen, Teig carn M'Grevy, Donill M'Nemarra, of Bynnor, and Edm. M'Brian, kerns, Cormock O Donelan, of Balledonelan, and Donogho O Donelan, gentlemen, Edm. sallagh O Flaher[　　], Mallaghlen O Brodar, of Kyarrowmeylagh, gent., Conchor grany M'Conegry, of Blewahan0owo, Dermod O Kallaghan, of Illanogunnnagh, Wm. O Henym, of Crovreohan, Cahill M'Dermod, of Ynchedromenillar, Edm. [　　], of Ballegias, Hubbart Fox, of Downe, gent., Dermod O Sherman, of Clonyn, gent., Shane m'Thomulagh M'Dermod, Gilledony M'Keane, cottier, Edm. m'Ullick Wale, of Droght, gent., Teig M'Enyny, of Arde[　　], Mortagh M'Owin, of Ardarragh, kern, Mellaghlen O Birne, of Porlyrryny, husbandman, Shane M'Owin, of Bunnahowne, cottier, Tirlogh reogh M'Swyne, of Sylamchy, kern. Provisions as in 5065, and excepting any already pardoned by the deputy Perrot. (Offences before 20 Nov., xxx. only, pardoned).—Date torn.

5229 (5518.) Grant (under queen's letter) to Bryan Fits Wllllam, Engllsh esq.; of a pension of 5s. sterling a day, for life, in succession to Hugh O Donill, gent., deceased, (who held it under queen's letter 8 March, 1586).—2 July, xxx.

5230 (6679.) Commission to John Maplesden, gent.; to take up English within the counties of Dublin, Kildare, Meath, Westmeath, Louth, Catharlogh, and Wexford, as much hay as may be required for the queen's horses at Kilmaingeham, paying the usual prices ; also to impress mowers and other labourers, paying 2s. sterling

1588.   FIANTS.—ELIZABETH.

for every acre cut and made into hay, as has been accustomed;
also to impress carts, horses, boats, and mariners, for carriage of
the hay.—4 July, xxx.

5231 (3966.) Surrender by Edward Waterhous, knt.; of the office
of surveyor and keeper of the whole river of the Shenin (granted
by 3641). With the intention of its being regranted for life.
Signed Ed. Waterhous.—Dated 6 July, xxx.

5232 (2866.) Grant (under queen's instructions, 8 March, 1587) to
Edw. Waterhous, knt., one of the privy council; of the office of
overseer, water bailiff, and keeper of the river Shenin. To hold
for life, with a fee of 2s. English a day for two masters of galleys,
and 8d. a day each for 30 other men. He shall maintain four
galleys, for the transport of soldiers, munition, and victuals across
the river to the countries of O Rwarke, O Farrele Boie, O Farrole
Dane, O Melaughlen, M'Coghlane, the M'Egane, O Carroll,
Ormund, the three races of O Kanides, M'brian Arra, the
O Mulriana, M'brien Ogownaughe, Ricardmor of Glanwilliam,
on the east side, and also to the countries of M'Dermot, O Brien,
O Conor Roe, O Conor Doin, the O Kellies on the east of the
river Suck, the O Kellies on the west of that river, O Madden,
Ricardmor, the O Gradies, M'Namarra, and the Brines, on the
west of the Shenin. He is empowered to remove weirs which
impede the navigation, those belonging to the manor and abbeys
of Athlone excepted. Anyone having a boat need for transport-
ing goods to the disobedient Irish or rebels to be bound by recognizance. Recites the surrender 5261.—[7 July, xxx.] (*Auditor-
General's patent book* 9, p. 39.)

5233 (6682.) Commission to Adam, archb. of Dublin, chancellor,
Tho. earl of Ormond and Osory, treasurer, the primate, Wm.
archb. of Tuam, Hon., earl of Kildare, Donogh, earl of Thomond,
Ullick, earl of Clanricard, Tho., bishop of Meath, Stephen
bishop of Clonfert, John, bishop of Elphin, Edm., lord Brimigham,
H. Wallop, vice-treasurer, N. Bagnall, marshal, R. Gardener,
ch. justice, R. Dillon, ch. justice of the Common Bench, L.
Dillon, ch. baron, N. White, master of the rolls, Richard Bingham,
knt., chief commissioner of the province of Connaught, Geo.
Bourchier, Edw. Waterhous, Tho. le Strange, knights, and
Geoffrey Fenton, members of the privy council, Tho. Dillon, ch.
justice of the province, Edw. Fitzsimons, serjeant at law,
Charles Calthrop, attorney general, Roger Wilbraham, principal
solicitor, the mayor of Galway, Tirlogh O Brien, knt., Anth.
Brabazon, Geo. Bingham, Gerald Quemerford, Robert Fowle,
John Bingham, John Crofton, Nathaniel Smith, Nicholas
Mordant, and John Marbury, esquires; to be commissioners in
the province of Connaught, as in 5021 (Richard Bingham to be
general of the forces in the field in the absence of the lord
deputy), to execute the instructions of the lord deputy, dated
11 July, and do all other things for the good government of the
province.—11 July, xxx.

5234 (6678.) Commission to sir Richard Bingham, knt., chief
English commissioner of Connaught and Thomond; to execute martial
law in his province, as in 218—11 July, xxx.

5235 (4313.) Grant (under letter of the council in England, 31
English March last) to Rob. Fowle, gent.; of the office of provost marshal
of Connaught and Thomond. To hold during good behaviour

1688.   FIANTS.—ELIZABETH.

with such fees as Barnaby Gouge or Francis Barckley or any other had, the ordinary fee of £40 star. a year heretofore allowed excepted; with diet at the board of the chief commissioner, a fee of 4s. 6d. ster. a day, and the leading of 10 horsemen, to be Englishmen or Englishmen's sons. Not to be removed, as in 4976. Recites the surrender of his previous interest in the office.—22 July, xxx.

5236 (5051.) Surrender by Hugh boy O'Heyne, son and heir of One Heyne, of Leidigan, co. Galway; of the name and title of O Heyne, and 33s. 4d. sterling English, chief rent, out of Crannaghe, Clonahie, Oaher, Culrecarne, Cromy, and Rahasana, same co., 33s. 4d., out of Simoleidgan, Twellegon, Corevaighe, Kinticrlevaighe, and Dungoerie, 63s. 4d. out of Caberkillyno, Caherglasanuc, Kcapaghbeg, Cahermadoriabe, Powlanevaighe, and Rahalben, 33s. 4d. out of Ballebaige, Lawghee[ure], Killtwyne, and Clherenkarlyo, 41s. 4d. out of Ballevanagran, Mancaoribe, the May, Fuchenbeg, Keapaghmore, and Clogher, 25s. 8d. out of [Knockgan], Gortwallailo, Dromyn, Trelick, Powahanmore, [Rewa], Dowrea, Towranghe, Lynsindwffe, Agard, Ballykra, Killyly, and Clonaston, same co., in all £10 English; with the intention of the rents being regranted to him. See 5237.—Dated 22 July, xxx.

5237 (4236.) Grant to Hugh boy O'Heine, son and heir of One O'Heyne, of Leidigan, co. Galway; of chief rents of £10 English surrendered by him. To hold for ever, by the service of a twentieth part of a knight's fee. Rendering all rents and profits due to the queen, and any composition payable. Saving the rights of all subjects. Recites his surrender 5236.—24 July, xxx.

5238 (5680.) Commission to Christopher Carleill, esq., governor of *Engsh.* upper and lower Clandeboy, Duffren, Kilnltogh, the Rout, and the Glynnes; to execute martial law in those countries, as in 218.—24 July, xxx.

5239 (4905.) Appointment of capt. Chr. Carleill, esq.; as governor *Engsh.* of the upper and lower Clandeboye, the Diffren, Kihultagh, the Rowte, and the Glinnes, with the direction of the queen's forces and the inhabitants there. The Scots, being enemies, and other traitors, he shall prosecute and kill with fire and sword to the utmost of his power. He may call to his assistance the queen's forces remaining in Torsane or other part of Ulster. He shall do all things tending to the preservation of peace and good government in the district.—26 July, xxx.

5240 (4208.) Grant to Chr. Carleyle, esq.; of the office of constable of the palace or storehouse or of the late dissolved monastery of Knockfargous in Ulster, with a fee of 2s. 8d. a day, and with 20 armed footmen at 8d. a day each. To hold during good behaviour. Not to be removed, as in 4976.—20 July, xxx.

5241 (5694.) Pardon to Richard Buttler, of Powleslowne, co. Kilkenny, gent., Nicholas Shortall, of Clarecagh, same co., gent., Oliver Sartall, of Aghagh, horseman, John Sartall fitz Richard, yeoman, John Butler fitz Richard carragh, horseman, Patrick and Nicholas Sartall fitz James, Dermod O Corryn, Edmund Ballegie, and Owen m'Donagho Yvryne, yeoman. Provisions as in 4965. Excluding also burglary and burning of houses or corn.—27 July, xxx.

F

1583.   FIANTS—ELIZABETH.

5242 (4282.) Grant (under queen's letter, 6 March, xxx.) to Oliver Stephenson, of Don Millne; of the manor of Donmilline, co. Limerick, parcel of the possessions of Ullick de Wale alias the Faltagh, of Donmilline, 16s. 10½d. issuing out of Ballloghan, Ballinakery, Kwileman, Belliwicrnallia, Ballegan, and Tonpill, to the manor belonging, and all other possessions of the manor. To hold for ever, in free socage. Rent £5 12s. 2½d. Maintaining one English horseman. Recites 387l.—[28 July], xxx. (Auditor-General's Patent Book 8, p. 43.)

5243 (6582.) Lease to George Goodman, gent; of the site of the monastery of S. John Baptist by Loughris in Omany in Connaughts, 6 waste cottages in the town of S. Johns, one quarter of land called Knockoskohana, Iancure alias Nure one quarter, Nomaddrys 1 qr., Renagane 1 qr., Glanne 1 qr., Galcheg and Leigh-carros 1 qr., and Cloghs alias Kilclogh[er] ½ qr., all being within the town and fields of S. Johns, a castle and 2 quarters of land called Skagin and Krevoquyne near the same in Omany, 16 quarters in Taghtample in O'Connor Sligoes country and other waste towns there; a third of the tithes and altarages of the vicarage of S. Johns extending to the said lands in Omany, and the rectory and tithes of Teaghtample. Recites 3241. To hold for 31 years from the determination of his existing interest. Rent £6 1s. 8d. Maintaining one English archer. Provisions as in 4939.—31 July, xxx.

5244 (6683.) Pardon to Teig O Nollan, of Ballinwherey, co. Kilkenny, Far m'Donneghe O Brenan, of Conafelly, and Walter Purcell, of Diralogh, same co., kerns. Provision for security, as in 4943. Pardon not to include murder, burglary, burning of houses or corn; nor intrusion into crown lands, nor debts to the crown, nor any persons who have lands outside the counties Tipperary or Kilkenny.—1 Aug., xxx.

5245 (6296.) Patent in pursuance of the foregoing fiant.—At Dublin, 1 Aug, xxx.

5246 (6684.) Pardon to Thomas Sartall fitz Peirce, of Ballinvalla, co. Kilkenny, kern, James Sartall fitz John, of Kilboy, co. Tipperary, kern, Richard Tobin, of Poolecaple, same co., kern, and John Butler, of the Grannge, same co., gent. Provisions as in 5244.—1 Aug, xxx.

5247 (6687.) Pardon to Johan' Ny en goen, of the Grannge, co. Tipperary, Edmund Purcall, of Aghalle, same co., kern, James Butler, of the Nenaugh, same co., and Geoffry O Rian fitz Davie, in co. Carlow, karns. Provisions as in 5244.—1 Aug., xxx.

5248 (6693.) Pardon to Redmund Blanchfield fitz Richard, of Bathgarran, co. Kilkenny, horseman, Mortagh O Blen fitz Edm., of B[   ], Wm. Butler fitz The., of Shenskill, same co., horseman, and Rob. Purcall fitz Edm., of Dunynge, same co., kern. Provisions as in 5244.—1 Aug., xxx.

5249 (4215.) Grant (under queen's letter, 6 Aug., xxix.) to Wm. Phillipps, gent.; of the office of clerk of the hanaper, in reversion after Lancelot Alford, who held for life under a grant of 31 March, lv. To hold for life, with such fees as Nich. Stanyhurst or Tho. Allen, or Lancelot Alford had.—1 Aug., xxx.

5250 (6580.) Lease (under queen's letter, 12 Aug, xxvii.) to sir Patrick Barnewell, of Gratiadei, co. Dublin, knt.; of the tithes of the parish church of Kilcok, co. Kildare, extending to Brangunston, Cortarton, Cowtane, Cloncosto, Portagiorle,' Lawrangh, and Goddergraunge, amounting in the whole to 13 coples of corn at 13s. 4d. the cople; the tithes of the parish church of Clane, same on., extending to Clane, Ballcappo, Betanghston and little Newton, amounting to 19 coples. To hold for 31 years from the determination of a lease by John Rawson, knt., late prior of S. John of Jerusalem, to David Sutton. Rent £21 6s. 8d. Also the late monastery of Cloutowakirtie in O Kellie's country, in co. Roscommon, that is to say, the site of the house of canons of Clontowakyrtie ni Sinna in O Kellie's country, lands of Clontowakirtle, the tithes of the rectory, extending to Clontowakirtle, Balligonnollen, Lykyuny, Kyllanerowake, Ballevis, the Blyes, Kyllvrny, Crustatna, Cultmark, Clonekaine, Ballidaghie, Carraghdowe, Cloghguoell, Brancowe, Cowlommregan, Aghrims, Monahicknane, Garrolie, Garrowria, Mackny, Duncardie, Gartenemartny, and Carrie, in O Kellie's country; the site of the monastery of Kylmore near the Shynnen in the country called Ivire, co. Roscommon, the lands and rectory of Kylmore; (leased by 4885; recited as of 18 May, xxvii). Also the tithes of the parish church of Clonshambo, 8 coples, co. Kildare (besides the tithes of Balgard, land in Hoggiston, and the altarages), possessions of S. John of Jerusalem. The site of the friary of Roswricke, co. Mayo, with 2 quartars of land; the site of the friary of Strade, co. Mayo, with 2 quartars of land, which 2 friaries are leased by 3368. To hold for 40 years from the determination of the present interests. Rent £20 1s. 4d. viz.:—Clontowakirt £7 19s. 8d., Kylmore 70s., Clonshambo £4, Roswricke 40s. 8d., Strade 45s.—[9] August, xxx.

5251 (6681.) Commission to sir John Norris, knt., lord president of Munster, Tho. Norris, vice-president, sir H. Wallopp, vicetreasurer, sir Valentine Browne, knt., Jesse Smythes, chief justice of the province, Roger Wilbraham, general solicitor, and James Gowle, gent.; to call before them all who pretend title to the lands lately escheated by the attainder of the earl of Desmond and others, to receive their claims in writing and thereof to make a register; to consider how the claims may be answered, and thereof to make another book, to be ready for other commissioners who shall after visit the province; as it is expected that the proofs to be tendered by the lords and freeholders of the province will consist chiefly of depositions of witnesses, the commissioners are to appoint a wise person to take the depositions on oath, and to digest them into good form for the information of the future commission. They are also to consider disputes between undertakers relative to the bounds of seignories and other matters, and if they cannot determine them to refer them to the lord deputy and council; also to make inquisition what seignories, rents, and other profits are due to the queen within the province, upon whom they are due, and who has received such rents since the attainder of the earl, and thereof to make a perfect book or register.—22 Aug., xxx.

5252 (4195.) Grant to Conoke m'Kedaghe O Farrall, gent.; of the office of seneschal of the country of Sleightwilliam, in co. Longford. To hold during good behaviour, with all usual profits, as in 2190. —23 Aug., xxx.

5253 (6572.) Livery to Richard, son and heir of Walter Evanster,

F 2

1588.   FIANTS.—ELIZABETH

late of Tamhagarde, co. Wexford, gent. Fine, £5 16s. 2d.—
23 Aug. xxx.

5254 (6689.) Pardon to Charles O Carroll, knt., and others as in
5101; also Maurice m'Edmond Sarsalagh, of Amagan. Provision
for security, as in 4943 (Charles O'Carroll, knt., excepted). The
pardon shall not include murder, burning of houses or corn,
debts due to the crown, or intrusion into crown lands.—23 Aug.,
xxx.

5255 (6679.) Lease to Brian Fitzwilliams, esq. ; of the site of
house of nuns of Innishmean, in the island of Loghmeaka, co.
Mayo, and 4½ quarters of land with their tithes in Joyce
country, on the west side of the water of Loughmeaka, viz.—
Dromselling, one quarter, Farnaigbe, one cartron, otherwise
the fourth part of a quarter, Downrice, 1 cart, in Grogill
1 cart, Sanencharron, 1 cart., Tonemaony, ½ qr. Leiter-
lageighe, ½ qr., Bean, ½ qr., Dristan, ½ qr., Ballanebol ½, ½ qr.
The chapel or cell of the order of S. Francis, called Annaghe, with
two half quarters of land called Leghkearrow Inarry, and Leigh-
kearrow Clondowre, with their tithes, co. Mayo ; a ruinous
chapel called Kilcrawe, near Ballinrobbe, in the barony of Kilmean, with half a quarter of land and the tithes. The queen's
castle of Castlebarr, in the barony of Carr, with ten quarters
of land appertaining, viz. :—6 quarters adjoining the castle,
1 qr. called Claggur, and 3 qr. in Slew Invray ; 4 other quarters
in Ballinrobbe, in the barony of Kilmean ; the collecting of an
annual rent of £91 6s. 8d. out of the country called Cloncoan,
co. Mayo ; all which are possessions of Edmund Bourk, late
of Castellmarry, in said county, attainted ; the chapel or cell
of Killmaroy, co. Roscommon, with one quarter of land and
the tithes belonging, late in the tenure of Milles Cavenaghs ;
the small chapel of Mullaghnedoce alias Ballintobarr, in the
barony of Ballintobarr with ½ quarter of land and the tithes,
co. Roscommon ; the chapel and town of Ballanehober, in the
barony of Ballintobber, with 4 quarters of land and the tithes,
co. Roscommon, parcel of the possessions of the late monastery
of Knckmoy, co. Galway ; the chapel or cell of Tobborelley, in the
Maghery alias O Connor Don's country, with one quarter of
land and the tithes, co. Roscommon ; one quarter of land called
Monnymucke, in O Connor Roe's country, co. Roscommon,
of the possessions of Calloughe m'Tirrelaughe, late of Clonmaroy,
attainted ; 2 quarters in Moyden, one called Loughballymoyden
and the other Garrymaroghe, in O Connor Roe's country, same
co., of the possessions of Rory grana m'Phelim boye O Connor,
late of Innishe Annaghe, same co., attainted ; one quarter
called Clonestrene, in O Connor Roe's country, same co.,
of the possessions of Dermot m'Carberey keighe O Connor, late
of Clonestrene, attainted ; one quarter called Kewlanecalrey in
Oughterbarey, same co., of the possessions of Cahill m'Tirrelaughe
M'Dermot, attainted ; ½ quarter called Linmeleagh in the barony
of Ballintobber, same co., of the possessions of Thomas O Flyn,
late of Mylsaghe, attainted ; the third part of a castle and ½
quarter in Cowlega[rr]y in O Kelley's country, of the possessions
of Conor m'Teig oge O Kelly, attainted. To hold for 21 years.
Rent, £43 15s. 7d. Maintaining (   ) English horse

men. Provisions as in 4939.—26 Aug., xxx. "There was none
of the parcels within mentioned formerly in charge."

5256 (6595.) Lease to Bryan Fitzwilliams, esq.; of the lands of
Rahanlon, half a cartron, in the barony of Down Kellen, [co.
Galway], of the possessions of Ferrogho O'Kelly, late of Rahanlon,
attainted; Ballenocreggy, one cartron, barony Kiltaragh, co.
[Galway], of the possessions of Thomas O Donelaghe, of that
place, attainted; Rahalban and Moynore, 2 half cartrons, same
co., of the possessions of [Ferrogh O Heyne], of Rahalban,
attainted; Cappenyleby, one cartron, barony Kiltaraghe, co.
Galway, of the possessions of Cugollo O Hayne, attainted; Ballymore, one quarter, in O Madden's country, same co., of the possessions of Forogh Kiltagh, of Boluak, attainted; Kilbeg ½ of ½
quarter, barony of Clare, same co., of the possessions of Gillidell
O Heny, of that place, attainted; a third part of the castle of
Galvally, a third of the [castle of Be]nemore, with a third of 6
quarters of land to the said castle adjoining, a third of the castle
of Lowym with a third of 6 quarters of land belonging, same co.
possessions of Theobald Bourk, of Byumore, attainted; a third
of Macknelonny, one quarter, bar. Loughart, same co., a third of
Ennysherick, one cartron, same bar. and co., a sixth of Kiloran,
same bar. and co., lands of Awle oge O Madden, of Kiloran,
[attainted]; the church of Alternan, bar. Tirraraghe, co. Sligo,
with one quarter of land belonging, possessions of the late abbey
of [Knockmoyo in Imany] co. Galway; Kmrownikippy, one
quarter, and 7 quarters called Knocktan, Dromeon, Lyrnechc,
[Clonaghourra], Ranny, Sko, and Sharra, in the country of Luyu,
co. Sligo, possessions of O Harvey, of Kmrownikippy, [attainted];
the site of priory of Ballyassadara alias Astnrey, co. Sligo, 3 small
quarters of land and the tithes of the town of Asnadara, [land
called] Truncballis, bar. of Leyns, a third of the tithes of the
rectory of Ballyassadara called Templmore, with a third of
tithes belonging to the same from the towns called Ternaelas, the
vicarage of Evenaghe in the country of Tirrerall, the vicarage of
Drumratt, bar. of Corron, the vicarage of Kilnegarven in M'Jorden's
country, possessions of the said priory; Moyntwer with Carrick
I naghton, one quarter, and Cregan, oneqr., in O Naghton's country,
co. Roscommon, in the occupation of Conogher O'Naghton, late
the lands of Shaen O'Naghton, of Carrick I naghton, attainted.
To hold for 21 years. Rent, £11 18s. 0½d. Maintaining one
English horseman. Provisions as in 4939.—26 [Aug.], xxx.
(Torn, see Auditor General's Patent Book 16, p. 95).

5257 (6607.) Lease to Brian FitzWilliams, esq.; of the lands of
Oldtowns, co. Kildare, Johnston pingret, Roulandston, Lynams-
gardinge, Merriwall, Rocheston, the site of the manor and town
of Kilcullen, lands of Knoktotan, Kilgons, Killenan, Uske,
Ballyzaxe with common of pasture on the curragh of Kildare,
co. Kildare, possessions of James Eustace, viscount Baltinglass,
attainted; also lands in the Nas, co. Kildare, of the possessions
of Thomas Eustace, of Cardanton, attainted. To hold for 21
years. Rent, £59 13s. 4d. Maintaining one English horseman.
Provisions as in 4039.—26 Aug., xxx.

5258 (6564.) Lease to Eustace Harte, gent.; of a ruinous castle,
and land of Billiet, co. Kildare, with a liberty of common of
pasture on the Curragh of Kildare, the land of Bralisaan, meadow

1588.   PLANTS.—ELIZABETH.

called Inanegrey, Inusnelcher, and Shenolons, land called Collartlands in the Greyfriars of Kildare, also lands being parcel of the lands belonging to the late White friars of Kildare with a liberty of common of pasture upon the Curraghe of Kildare, and the lands of Tippenan, containing 40 acres of great measure being 120 of standard measure, co. Kildare, all possessions of David Sutton, attainted. To hold for 21 years. Rent, £26 12s. Maintaining one English horseman. Provisions as in 4930.—22 Aug. (3), xxx.

5259 (4197.) Grant to Tho. Cahill; to be interpreter of the Irish language to the lord deputy. To hold during pleasure with such fees as Wm. Deyn had.—30 Aug., xxx.

5260 (6675.) Lease to Katherine Vaghan, widow; of the castle and lands of Rawlagh, co. Dublin, possessions of lord Baltinglas, attainted, and held under a lease from him to John Bathe; lands in Sarwaldestoun, Rahoakes, and Morganston, co. Kildare, possessions of Thomas Eustace, attainted; the castle and lands of Newcastle, and land in Agos, co. Dublin, possessions of David Sutton, attainted, and held by John Ball under a lease from Sutton to Anthony Enos; land in Sheltonston near Mitcheston called Shallonslnide, co. Kildare, of the possessions of Christopher Eustace, attainted, leased by 1154; and a moiety of the lands of Ballybahricke, co. Louth, of the possessions of John Bussell, attainted, already leased to Katherine Braudon, widow. To hold for 50 years these already under lease from the determination of the several interests. Rent £31 6s. 8d. Provisions as in 4939.—10 Sept., xxx.

5261 (4193.) Grant to Rich. Chichester, gent.; of the office of constable of the castle of Lymerick, and the Kings Island, the fishing weirs and all other appurtenances. To hold during good behaviour, with a fee of £10 sterling and all other profits as said Chichester or as John Blacke had. Not to be removed, as in 4976.—16 Sept. xxx.

5262 (4241.) Grant (under queen's letter, 3 March, xxx.) to Robm Fitzwilliams, esq.; of the lands of Culceonian, co. Meath, parcel of the possessions of James Fitz Geralde, gent., attainted (recites No. 1542); and Mableston alias Mapeston, co. Dublin, parcel of the possessions of David Sutton, attainted (recites a lease from Sutton to Rich. Bussell, for a term still in being). To hold for ever, in free socage. Rent 30s. for Coulecoonan, and for Mableston £5, besides £3 6s. 8d. chief rent to the dean and chapter of Holy Trinity, Dublin.—16 Sept., xxx.

5263 (6655.) Pardon to John Greife, of Killnomoove, co. Clare, gent., Ursula Greife, of same, Thady Greife, of same, Robert Hamlyn, of Clonrahan, same co., gent. The pardon not to include intrusion in crown lands, or debts to the crown. Provision for security, as in 4943, before commissioners in co. Ennys.—16 Sept. xxx.

5264 (6656.) Livery to Patrick Savadge, lord Savadge of the little Ardes, co. Down, son and heir of Rowland Savadge, late lord Savadge; of his lands of Balliporteferrye, Ballyburde, Ballyhenrye, Ballybodye, Ballym'kinyabe, Ballicorrugge, Ballikirrye, Ballinan, Ballyrussell, Balliblacke, Ballitollemerewe, Ballyknockmoller, Ballynaskee, Ballyzoner, Ballyinwraghe, Ballytuadbye,

1588.   FIANTS.—ELIZABETH.

Ballycomton, BallyIdogge, Balligarviger, Ballynckerter, Bally-tollynecarton, Ballyfurneraghe, Ballytruxigan, Ballydanyvill, Ballytolleborde, and Ballynicholl, on Down, held by the service of supplying 4 horsemen and 14 footmen for the wars in Ulster. Fine £50 English.—28 Sept. xxx.

5265 (4721.) Grant (under queen's letter, 1 Feb., xxx.) to Doball O Moriertie and Owen O Moriertie, sons to Donell O Moriertie, of Casteldromy; of two several moieties of a rent of £15 1s. 1½d. called strahenmarts, payable out of his lands by their father to the traitor Gerald, late earl of Desmond. To hold severally in tail male. Recites that Donell the father held Castelldromy contain-ing 4 ploughlands, Killemardunak 3 pl., Ballegarveighe and Ballemaldwenick 2 pl., and 6 acres in Ambroealands called Enohmamhrosick, co. Kerry, of the earl, by the rent and services of 22s. 4½d. ster., and one beef now valued at 18s. 4d. ster. out of each ploughland, amounting in all to £15 1s. 1½d. In consider-ation of their good service against the earl.—28 Sept., xxx.

5266 (6630.) Grant to Phane Beecher, of London, gent.; of the castle of O Mahowny alias O Mahowns castle, and a moiety of the country and cantred of Kilnalmachi alias Kinalmechi, which lies on both sides of the river of Bandon and adjoins the country of Carbry on the south, and Muskery on the north, in co. Cork; and to Hugh Worth, of Somerton, Somersetshire, gent.; of the other moiety of Kinalmechi; the country containing in all 28,000 acres. To hold for ever, in fee farm and common soccage. Rent from each, from 1594, £66 13s. 4d. (half only for the preceding three years) and ½d. for each acre of waste land brought into til-lage. If the lands are found by measurement, within 10 years, to contain more than the estimated number of acres, they shall pay 1½d. (one penny farthing and the third of a farthing) for each English acre so in excess. Each of the grantees is subject to the conditions imposed on the undertakers in Munster as in 5032. 2 membranes.—30 Sept., xxx.

5267 (6833.) Commission to Nich. White, master of the rolls, Rob. Dillon, chief justice, Rich. Bealing, Chr. Flattesburye, gent., Henry Usher, archdeacon of Dublin, and Michael Fitzsimons, LL.B., as delegates; to hear an appeal from Ambrose Forthe, LL.D., surrogate of the archbishop of Dublin the master of the court of Prerogative, in a cause between Richard and Maurice Ewstace, and James FitzGarrolde, of Walterston, concerning the will of Margaret Ewstace, of Walterston, diocese of Kildare.—No date. (The will was proved 7 Oct., 1588. Prerogative Will Book, sol. i.)

5268 (6004.) Surrender by Bryan Fytzwyllyam, esq.; of a pension of 5s. sterling a day. (See 5269.) With the intention of receiv-ing one of 10s. which William Collier, knt., had. (Signed) Bryan Fytzwyllyam.—Dated 10 Oct., xxx.

5269 (5524.) Grant (under queen's letter, 8 March, xxx.) to Bryan FitzWilliam, esq.; of a pension of 10s. sterling a day, for life, in succession to sir Wm. Collier, knt., deceased. He surrendering a previous pension (5268).—10 Oct., xxx.

5270 (6616.) Lease to Thomas Bee, esq.; of the castle and lands of Galmorestown, with liberty of a common moor to cut turffs (turf), on Kildare, of the possessions of James Ewstace, viscount of Baltinglas, attainted. To hold for 21 years. Rent, £16 13s. 4d. Provisions as in 4939.—10 Oct., xxx.

1588.   FIANTS.—ELIZABETH.

5271 (4193.) Grant to James Ryan, of Dublin, gent., one of the
officers of Chancery ; of the liberty of not being put on assizes,
juries, &c., and of not being made mayor, sheriff, coroner, alderman, justice, escheator, bailiff, keeper of the peace, collector of subsidies, or other officer, against his will, during his life.—19 Oct., XXX.

5272 (6723.) Pardon to Thomas Leigh, of the Queen's co.   Not to
include arson or debts to the crown.—19 Oct., XXX.

5278 (5813.) Commission to Daniel, bishop of Kildare, Roger
Wylframe, queen's solicitor, Richard Thompson, treasurer of St.
Patrick's, Dublin, Henry Ussher, archdeacon of Dublin, and
Robert Richardson, precentor of the Holy Trinity, Dublin ; to
hear an appeal from a decree of Miler, archbishop of Cashel and
bishop commendatory of Lismore and Waterford, made on appeal
from a decision of Donat pro archdeacon of Lismore, in a matrimonial cause between John, son of Gerald Butler, of Boolye
in dlaert, diocese of Lismore, and John Brennagh alias Walsh.—
21 Oct., XXX.

5274 (6541.) Grant to Edmund Mannering, of the Springe,
English. Cheshire, esq.; of all the barony of Fendymore with
the appurtenances, viz: the castle and lands of Ballyea
containing 1 ploughland, Kyllfendymore ½ pl., the old castle
of Fendymore ½ pl., Toallyck 1 pl., Fannyngstowne and
Garry Ellen 2 pl., Killdyrry ½ pl., Lackengranan ½ pl.,
Bowrone and Kilkerrydloy ½ pl., Bally Bronay ½ pl., and Killvoy
alias Killbuy ½ pl., co. Limerick, possessions of the late earl of
Desmond, attainted ; the castle and lands of Dunkypp with
appurtenances, viz. : Ballynall, Dallynowgun, Farren in Pur-
dialige, and Ballin Doule, 1 pl. and 5 acres, of the lands of
Walter La, attainted, co. Limerick ; the whole amounting to 8½
ploughlands and 5 acres, making id English measure 3747 acres;
also the rents and services of the free tenants in the said barony
of Fendymore, viz. : John Struiche for the two Skulls 23s. 4d.
halfsoc, the heir of Carnon 2s. 11d. halfsoc, the heir of Roche
for Ballinrossy alias Rochey 6s. 8d. halfsoc, making in halfsoc
money 32s. 11d., amounting to 44s. 11d. starling.   To hold
for ever in fee farm by fealty in common socage.   Rent £36
0s. 7½d. English from 1594 (half for the previous 3 years), and
for the rents 44s. 11d. English.   Grantee to erect houses for 26
families, of which one to be for himself, 2 for freeholders, 2 for
farmers, and 12 for copyholders ; with other conditions usual in
grants for planting the undertakers in Munster, as in 3032.   2
membranes.—24 Oct., XXX.

5275 (4226) Grant (under queen's letter, 1 Sept., XLIV.) to the master,
brethren, and poor of the hospital of the Holy Trinity of New
Home ; of two chapels, called the chapel of S. Saviour and the
chapel of S. Michael, and 11 messuages and 5 gardens in the town,
called the land of S. Saviour.   To hold for ever, in free alms,
without account.   Recites that the hospital was founded by Tho.
Gregory, of New Rosse, merchant, and lately incorporated by the
queen, that the corporation of the town are prepared to transfer
their claim to the premises, valued at 31s. yearly, to the hospital,
and that this grant is made at the request of Patr. Walshe, knt.
—26 Oct., XXX.   (See Cal. P. R. pp. 165-7.)

5276 (4242.) Grant (under queen's letter, 16 Jan., XXX.) to Maurice,
lord Roch, viscount Fermoye ; of the lands of Johnston and

Downanaghin, co. Cork, parcel of the possessions of the monastery of Ardmoy alias Fermoy alias Iermoy, in same co. To hold in tail male in common socage. Rent £16 13s. 4d.—26 Oct, xxx.

5277 (6636.) Grant to sir Valentine Browne, knt. and Nicholas Browne, his son; of the country of Cosmange, in the countries or counties of Kerry and Desmond, the manor, castle, and lands of Malaheif, the castle called Molans, with the lands belonging called Malaheif and Kilmalaheif, containing by estimation 8 quarters, Kilcumyn Et la alias Etly, 4 quarters, with Togbe, and the town of Kilcumyn alias Kilchonine yeley, 8 quarters, Knockan Eralty 2 quarters, three towns called the Clonamoylans, 2 quarters, late in the occupation of Teige m'Dermoda M'Curmack of the nation of the Clancarties, containing in all by estimation 24 quarters or ploughlands at the rate of 40 acres the quarter; the town of Nedloyre in the said countries, late of Owni m'Fynen ega, 8 quarters; the country of Onaght alias Onaght O Donogho moore, in the county of Desmond in the old county of Kerry, that is to say, the manor and site of the castle of Rosse I Donogho in that country, with the demesne lands 2 quarters, a church and town called Killarmeye, with small islands called Loughline, Innisfallen, and Mockerush, and sundry other islands whose names were unknown, late in the tenure of Rory O Donogho alias O Dono moore, all which country of Onaght contains 50 quarters; with certain fishings to the said manor of Rosse I Donogho, in the several islands, appertaining; the whole containing 6560 acres besides the fishing. To hold for ever, in fee farm, by fealty, in common socage, from the determination of the estate tail of Donald, earl of Clancarre, under grants of 18 April and 28 June, xxx, by conveyance from whom the grantees already hold the premises. Rent from 4 years after the death of the earl without heir of his body, £59 13s. 4d., and after 7 years from his death £113 6s. 8d. Grantees must erect houses for 40 families, of which one to be for themselves, 4 for freeholders, 8 for farmers, and 23 for copyholders. If found by measurement to contain more than the above estimated number of acres, grantees to pay 4d. for each English acre so in excess. Other conditions usual in grants from the commissioners for planting the undertakers in Munster, as in 5032. 8 membranes.—26 Oct., xxx.

5278 (4223.) Grant (under queen's letter, 29 July, xxix.) to Florence M'Artie, esq.; of an annual rent of 67½ cows out of the barony of Carbry, lately payable to the earl of Desmond, attainted, with power of distraint in the barony. To hold for ever. Rent £5 English.—20 Oct. xxx.

5279 (5520.) Indenture with Manus Shihle or M'Shehy, gent, under queen's letter, 29 June, 1588. In consideration that the queen owes him £401 10s. 0d. for his entertainment at 2s. a day, and for 40 kern and their boys at £1 a day, for a year. Manus agrees to accept half the sum, with a pension of 30d. sterling a day, till he is better provided for.—31 Oct., xxx.

5280 (6593.) Lease to Robert Harpole and his son William; of the manor of Catherlanghe, and other premises as in No. 1600. (Athais written here Athcoa.) To hold for 21 years, subject to the same rent and conditions as in 1600.—31 Oct., xxx.

5281 (6722.) Pardon to Edm. Waynman, late of Yoghall, gent., James Askerwill, of same, gent, John Sadler, Wm. Webb, George

1588.   FIANTS.—ELIZABETH.

Flowre and John Pyne, of the same, and John Bostocke, gent.
Not to include any intrusion into crown lands or debts to the
crown.—31 Oct., xxx.

5282 (6543.) Grant to sir George Bowrchier, knt., lieutenant of
English the fort of Phillipstowne, King's co.; of the castle of Loughgirr
with the lough there, and the houses and lands belonging, containing 4 ploughlands, the castle and lands of Glanogre with land
called the Creana 4½ pl., Dromebegg ½ pl., the third part of
Clarenny, in the parish of Corokamore ½ pl., the castle and village
of Ballyregan, in the occupation of Thomas Durgett, in the country
of Poblebrian, in the parish of Ballycahell, 1 pl., Ballybousty
called the Countesse land beside the town of Killmallocke 2 pl.,
Ballyrologg, par. of Corokamore, 1½ pl., the castle and lands of
Morrynett, par. Morrynett, beside the bishop's lands called Morrynett de Temple, 3 pl., Ballyloughs alias Ballyrokenenoghe, late in
the occupation of John Browne, 3 pl., parcels of the possessions
of Gerald, earl of Desmond, attainted, being 19½ ploughlands;
also possessions of divers other rebels, attainted, viz.: the castle
and lands of Rahyne ½ pl., the third part of a ploughland in
Clonnaney, containing 40a., lying in Cosunye, late possessions
of John O Kahynney, attainted, together ½ pl. and 40a.; the
country or lands called Boalruhyn in Owny alias Onhy O Mulrian,
late the possession of Teige O Mulrian, slain in rebellion, 3 pl.;
the townshippe called Caherduffe, late of Brian rowe, attainted,
½ pl.; Castlenygarde 1 pl., Ballymacvery ½ pl., Rathbrannoghe
½ pl., Ballymonie of the pills ½ pl., Carroughamore ½ pl.,
Flanghmony ½ pl., and Ballintaider, which last seven parcels
being of divers possessions and concealed contain together 3½
ploughlards; the castle of Cregan with appurtenances 1½ pl.,
Ballyneugollo ½ pl., and the castle of Ballincollo with appurtenances ½ pl., which 3 last parcels, lying in Cosmaye, were possessions
of John Suppell, attainted, which said 14 parcels of the possessions of divers rebels contain 10½ ploughlands; all the premises
are in the great and small counties of Limerick and amount to 30
ploughlands, which at the rate of 428 English acres to the ploughland make 12880 acres; also the rents of the free tenants, viz.:
6s. 8d. sterling out of 2 tenements and a garden in Sainct Johns-
streete near the town of Killmallock, late of William Meagh
executed for murder, as in the right of the late earl of Desmond,
10s. sterling out of a decayed watermill, parcel of the manor of
Glanoger, and 53s. 4d. ster. English, out of 3 tenements in Killmallock, in the tenure of Dermott M'Donell and others, with the
gardens and 18a. of land appertaining. To hold for ever, in fee
farm, by fealty, in common soccage. Rent, £134 8s. 4d. English
from 1594 (half for the preceding three years), and for the rents of
free tenants £3 10s. 0d. English. If within 10 years the lands are
found by measurement to contain more than the above estimated
number of acres, grantee shall pay 2½d. for each English acre so in
excess. Grantee must erect houses for 84 families, of which one
to be for himself, 7 for farmers, 8 for freeholders, and 48 for copyholders. With other conditions usual in grants for planting the undertakers in Munster, as in 5033. 3 membranes.—2 Nov., xxx.

5283 (6519.) Grant :(under queen's letter, 13 Dec., 1585) to John
English Gillson, gentleman; of a pension of 3s. 4d. sterling, a day, for
life, in lieu of one of 2s.—4 Nov. xxx

1588.   FIANTS.—ELIZABETH.

5284 (4234.) Grant (under queen's letter, 8 March, xxx.) to Brian Fitzwilliams, esq.; of the lands of Boubns, co. Kildare, parcel of the lands of David Sutton, of Castleton of Kildrought, attainted. To hold for ever, in common socage. Rent £4.—4 Nov., xxx.

5285 (6597.) Lease to Brian Fitz Williams, esq.; of the castle and lands of Harestown, co. Kildare, with a water mill, in the tenure of Wm. Bowan, late of the possessions of James Eustace, viscount Baltinglas, attainted. To hold for 21 years. Rent £17 12s. 0d. Maintaining [   ] English horsemen. Provisions as in 1939.—5 Nov., xxx.

5286 (6617.) Lease to Henry Brouckard, esq.; of the customs and imposts on all wines imported during five years following the preceding Michaelmas. To hold for 5 years. Rent £2,000 English. Provided that if war shall arise with France or Spain so as to interrupt the wine trade, lessee shall not be accountable for this rent but only for so much as he shall account for on his oath in the Exchequer. The lease not to be delivered until lessee give securities in £3,000 English for payment of the rent.—[   ] xxx. 1588.

5287 (6692.) Pardon to Walter O Rian fitz Edm., of the Pollogh, co. Kilkenny, horseman, James Butler fitz Theobald, of Jordanstowne, same co., yeoman, [   ] fitz Edmond of Clasgiany, same co., kern, James Sartall fitz Pierce, of Kilkerall, same co., horseboy, and Oliver Fannynge fitz Davie, of Farranrerie, co. Tipperary. Provisions as in 5244.—1 [   ] xxx.

1588-9.

5288 (4260.) Grant to Wm. Fitzwilliam, gent.; of the office of principal registrar of the high commissioners for ecclesiastical causes, and clerk of the recognizances taken before them. To hold during good behaviour, with such fees as John Byrd, or Paul Maylard, had. Not to be removed, as in 4976.—6 Jan., xxxi.

5289 (4279.) Commission to captain Tho. Henshawe, in the absence of capt. Chr. Carliell, seneschal of Clandeboy and governor of the Rowte, the Glynes, Killultagh, and the Duffery, now being in England; to execute martial law in those countries, as in 218.—16 Jan., xxxi.

5290 (4284.) Commission to Rob. fitz Peter Nugent, sheriff of the co. Leitrym; to execute martial law in that county, as in 218.—20 Jan., xxxi.

5291 (6535.) Grant to Arthur Hyde, esq., second son of William Hyde, of Hyde, in the parish of Denchworth, Berkshire, esq.; of the castle and lands of Carigg in edye alias Temple Logan, Cloghs Lowe, Kill   ], the castle and lands of Carrigebrick, Ballyvoda, Ardy, Lyancalla, Shanacloine, Crogh Surdan, Bally In Nyne, Skart Ehole, and Downcrider, the castle and lands of Granaganaghe, Farranaclere, Caherhowe Jordayne, and Knocknagaple, the castle and lands of Ballynahawo, Bally Arthur, Ballym'ahanckyn, Ballyaduck, and Gurtinahouaane, the castle and lands of Cregg, Ballym'lowacase, and Ballym'ehallen, the castle and lands of Ballyclohee, the castle and lands of Manoge alias Manning in Condons country, the castle and lands of Chahergraine, the castle and lands of Dyrrewyllane, Farrensperine, and Ouirehowbegg, the castle and lands of Agh Crosse, the castle and lands of Ballymariscall alias Marshallstowne, with Ballym'Phillipp and

1588-9.   FIANTS.—ELIZABETH.

Cowlemooke, the castle and lands of Ballytana, Kaslane-Roddery, Ballyenchan, Skart Valle Vehagan, and Ballyvertala, co. Cork, amounting by estimation to 11,760 English acres. To hold for ever, in fee farm, in common socage. Rent, £66 3s. 10d. English from 1694 (half only for preceding three years). If found by measurement to contain more than the above estimated number of acres, grantee shall pay 1½d. for each additional English acre. With other conditions usual in grants to the undertakers in Munster, as in 5092.—30 Jan., xxxi.

5292 (4294.) Commission to Rich. Sheo, esq., sheriff of co. Kilkenny ; to execute martial law in that county, as in 218.— 3 Feb., xxxi.

5293 (4285.) Commission to Wm. Edwards, esq., sheriff of the co. Waterford ; to execute martial law in that county, as in 218.— 6 Feb., xxxi.

5294 (4251.) Livery to Gerald, brother and heir of Rich. Breminghame, late of Greunge, co. Kildare, and of Ballicomen, King's co., gent. Fine £4 0s. 8d., also 40s. for pardon of alienation.—6 Feb., xxxi.

5295 (5521.) Grant (under queen's letter, 17 Sept. xxix.) to Barnaby Riche, gent. ; of a pension of 2s. 6d. ster. a day, for life—6 Feb., xxxi.

5296 (4268.) Grant (under queen's letter, 8 March, xxx.) to Brian Fitz Williams, esq. ; of the lands of Wuntotowne, co. Meath, parcel of the lands of John Burnell, attainted. To hold for ever, by the service of a fortieth part of a knight's fee. Rent £4 11s. 4d.—8 Feb., xxxi.

5297 (4280.) Commission to sir Tho. Norrice, knt., vice president of Mounster, Nich. Walshe, second justice of the Queen's Bench, Jesse Smythes, chief justice of Mounster, Rich. Bocon, queen's attorney in Mounster, Walter Dowrishe, esq., Arthur Robins and Francis Jobson, gentlemen ; to enquire and set out so much of the 3½ seigniories, not already measured and set out, granted to sir Walter Raleghe, of the escheated lands in co. Cork and Waterford, near the town of Youghell, and of the escheated lands, late Patr. Condon's, and those in Imokillie adjoining Aghavena alias Whites Island, and others adjoining the same.—8 Feb., xxxi.

5298 (4250.) Livery (under commission, 17 Feb., xxx.) to Walter Whitt, son and heir of Wm. White, late of Angevileston, co. Meath, gent. Fine 10s.—10 Feb., xxxi.

5299 (4293.) Pardon to Peirce Nangle, of the Clonghan, farmer, Cormock M'Gillpatterick, of same, Nich. Hikie, of Ballincany, Walter Dawlton, of Dashopston, Neill M'Gochegan, of the Pallace, and Ferdorgh, his brother, Chaell m'Shane O Maddy, of same, Cahall O Fannan, of the Greunge, Melaughlen O Horan, of the Darris, Donell Oregay, of the Feddane, Wm. O Dowll, of Knocktocher, husbandman, David O Dowll, of same, Edm. Walshe, of same, Peter Nangle, of Kelenbregh, and Theobald Dawlton, of Drolauston, co. Galway. Security as in 4943, at Mollangar, co. Westmeath. Other provisions as in 4906.—10 Feb., xxxi.

5300 (4259.) Grant to Francis Capstock, gent. ; of the office of chief engraver of the Exchequer. To hold during good behaviour, with a fee of £10, and such other profits as Mich. Kestlewell or any other had. Not to be removed, as in 1976.—11 Feb., xxxi.

1588-9.   FIANTS—ELIZABETH.

5301 (4289.) Pardon to Donnell O Donnell, gent., sheriff of co. Donnygall, Teig oge O Boyle, gent., and Donnagh M'Swynne banny, in same co. Provisions as in 4966.—12 Feb., xxxi.

5302 (4301.) Grant (under queen's letter, 31 May, xxx.) to Rich. Power, son and heir of lord baron Power, lord baron of Coroghmore ; of the reversion of the lands of Odder and Callaghton by Skryne, co. Meath, leased with others in 306 and 2235, and the rents incident to the reversion amounting to £19 5s. To hold for ever. Rent £19 5s. To hold by fealty and the said rent — 17 Feb., xxxi.

5303 (4246.) Grant to Peter Fimber, gent. ; of the wardship and marriage of Justinian Brit, son and heir of John Brit, late of Turrogh, co. Roscommon, gent. ; and the custody of his lands. To hold during minority. Rent 4 marks, of which he may retain 10s. for maintenance of the minor. Fine £3.—17 Feb., xxxi.

5304 (4254.) Livery to Dermot m'Owen, son and heir of Owen M'Donoughe alias M'Donoghe, late of Keanturke, co. Cork, gent. Fine £6.—18 Feb., xxxi.

5305 (4278.) Lease (under commission, 17 Feb., xxx.) to Henry English. Stanley, of Crosso Hall, co. Lancaster, esq. ; of the rectories of the B. V. M. of Trym, and Kildalkia, and two parts of the tithes and alterages of the rectory of Clonarde, co. Meath, possessions of the late abbey of the B. V. M. of Trym. To hold for 21 years. Rent £73 0s. 0½d., part in corn. Provision as is 4941. Fine £20 English.—19 Feb., xxxi.

5306 (4307.) Lease (under queen's letter, 29 June, xxx.) to John English. Champon, gent. ; of the site of the abbey of Odorney alias our lady abbey of Kyryleison, lands in Clonseanroirke, Dromycomygunyn, Ackrie, and Ballyusin, Boher Roe, Leckinmore, Lackybege, and Clonenymetanghe, and Ballibromaine, also the rectory of Odorney, extending to Clonseanroirke, Dromycomygunyn, Ackry, Rallliusyn alias Balliusur, Boher Ro, Leakimore, Laokibege, and Clonanymentaugh, also the rectory of Mallahiffe, co. Kerry, (recites 3759) ; the site of the abbey of Bathstowe alias Arragaxia, order of S. Augustin, lands in Addergewill, Tirrilanghaghis, and Ardcullen, half the rectories of Lisaltin and Gallie, the other half belonging to the vicar there, and a fourth part of the rectory of Aghabanally, co. Kerry, (recites 3758) ; the tithes of the rectories of Ballimarter, Iteshocke, Corbo, Castrocar, and Balliamaine, with the chapel and tithes of S. Nicholas in the suburbs of Cork, co. Cork, (recites 4374) ; the chapel of Kilmurry, in Two M'Walter, in the barony of Bealeamo, with land in Kilmurry and Lismobege, co. Galway, (recites 4843) ; the parcel of land called Monasteris Evan alias Kearnett, lying by the town of Higgens, in the barony of Roscoman, (recites 4930). To hold for 40 years, from the end of the interests in being. Rent £20 3s. Maintaining 2 English horseman. Provisions as in 4939. 2 membranes.—[22 Feb.], xxxi. (Auditor General's Patent Book 21, p. 17.)

5307 (4299.) Lease (under queen's letter, 29 June, xxx.) to John English. Champon, gent. ; of the site of the house of friars of Timolage, and appurtenances, co. Cork, (recites 3940) ; the site of the house of friars of the B. V. M. of Kinsale, with appurtenances, co. Cork, (recites 4021) ; and the site of the house of friars of

1588-9.   FIANTS.—ELIZABETH.

Castellaughan alias Castellian, with appurtenances, co. Cork, (recites 3278). To hold for 40 years from the end of the term in being. Rent £4 10s. 2d. Provisions as in 4939.—22 Feb, xxxi.

5308 (6540.) Grant to George Stone and John Champen alias English. Champion, gentlemen; of the village and butt end of a castle with appurtenances late Ballym'Donnells, lands of M'Edmonds, the lands of Donnkyne and Ballyneighe beside Smeerewicke, Menarde, late of Shane m'Edmond M'Ullicke, Farren Edyllhe near Lemache, the two Clonduffe, Glangertarkorrane, and Bally-nscorly, late of Moriah m'Shane Hussee, the park, a mill (which is to pay to the queen as it shall be valued by the survey), certain lands and tenaments in and near Dinglecushe, viz : one house within the town, sometime in the tenure of David Bromghes, 6s. 8d. a year, a house with appurtenances there called Ballibra-doughe 13s. 4d. a year, a house between the lands of Stephen Rice, on the north and east and of Thomas M'Gerrot on the south 6s. 8d. a year, which houses belonged to the said earl in his letting at will, a house and garden in Dingle, late of David duffe Gerrald, attainted, 3s. 4d. a year, a house with land there, late of John Hussie, slain in rebellion, 10s. a year, a burgage and garden late of James Russell, 15s. a year, two burgages. with a garden there, late of Dominick Fitz Moriahe, 10s. a year, a tenement there, late of Thomas fitz William ne Boy 5s. a year, together with Ballybe, and all other lands eschouted within the trokahld of Corkoneyny, co. Kerry. To hold for ever in fee farm, by fealty, in common socage. Rent, 4d. sterling for each English acre which the lands, when surveyed, shall be found to contain, from 1594 (half for preceding 3 years); besides the above named rents in Dingle. Grantees to build houses for 90 families, of which 9 must be for the grantees, 6 for freeholders, 6 for farmers, and 42 for copyholders. With other conditions usual in grants for planting the undertakers in Munster, as in 5032. Two membranes. —23 Feb, xxxi.

5309 (4256.) Grant to Tho. Vryn; of the office of one of the English pursuivants or chief messenger to the high commissioners for causes ecclesiastical. To hold during good behaviour, with the fee of £10 English, and her majesty's coat as other pursuivants have. Recites that the great number of causes depending before the commissioners makes it necessary for some one to attend them for serving writs, &c.—4 March, xxxi.

5310 (5525.) Grant (under queen's letter, 1 Aug., 1586) to Patrick Cullan; of a pension of 12d. ster. a day, for life, instead of his previous pension of 6d.—4 March, xxxi.

5311 (4269.) Lease (under queen's letter, 4 July, xxx.) to John English. Balinge, gent. ; of lands in Dewockeston and Skrine, parcel of the temporal possessions of the late abbey of Odder, co. Meath (recites 306); the rectory of S. Brigid of Odder, and the tithes of Callianghton near Shallon alias Shalton and a parcel of land there, parcel of the spiritual possessions of the said abbey (recites 2236). To hold for 40 years from the end of the interests in being. Rent, 42s. for temporalities and £8 6s. 8d. for spiritualities, part in corn. Provisions as in 4932. Also that lessee shall within two months put in, in the chief Remem-

1568-9.   FLANTS.—ELIZABETH.

brancer's office sufficient security for the payment of rent and fulfilling the conditions.—6 March, xxxi.

5312 (6547.) Grant to sir William Herberts, knt.; of the English castle of the Ilands with the lands belonging, late the earl of Desmond's, co. Kerry, the lands of Coggeriskerry, late the earl's, the castle of Ballin'Addam and the lands belonging, the township of Deserts with the lands, late Prouvells, same county, the castle of Ardnegraughs with the lands belonging, late of Thomas fits Davy Gerulde, with the castle of Kilcostenlo and the lands belonging, and certain woods and lands of the said Thomas, called Drumleggughe, the township of Balli[marrishell] with appurtenances, late the earl's, and the castle and lands of Ballinroddery, escheated or concealed, in counties of Kerry and Desmonds. To hold by the name of the [signiory of Mountdagle Loiall], for ever, in fee farm, by fealty, in common soccage. Rent, 4d English for every English acre which the land shall be found on survey to contain; this rent payable from 1594 (half for the preceding three years). (*The "Schedule of lands," see 5038, gives the acreage at 13,270, and the rent £391 5s. 0d. ster.*) Grantee must erect houses for [ ] families, one of which to be for himself, 6 for freeholders, 6 for farmers, and 42 for copyholders. With other conditions usual in grants for planting the undertakers in Munster as in 5032. 2 membranes.—6 [March], xxxi. In part obliterated, see *Cal Carew MSS.*, 1575-1588, p. 454, also "*Schedule of lands passed to Undertakers.*"

5313 (6557.) Grant to Charles Herbert, esq.; of the castle and lands English of Lemericknell with the advowson, Fearan makillikill, Ralynalashen, and Balynottinis, all the Knights' lands in Maglas, viz., Balincambulike, Ballnathsy, Cleyntarls, and Balinantrick, the castle and lands of Cournes, Minnes, Tardaron, Fearnavergan, Orbogile, Knookanlechim, Carraghamore, with the advowsons and fishings, the lands of Gortaicale with the appurtenances, 4 quarters of the Cross, late M'Shane's lands, Fernoantoinke, the lands of Knoppook, the castle and lands of Balino, the manor and chief house called Bramagh with its lands lying on the mountain of Slevlogher, the lands of Ballinclonesige, Kilvalsagh alias Kilvalslahife, in the counties of Kerry and Desmond. To hold, by the name of Gwlade Herbert or Lemerycahill, for ever, in fee farm, by fealty, in common soccage. Rent, 4d. English for each English acre which the commissioners shall return that the lands contain; this rent payable from 1594 (half for preceding three years). *The "Schedule of lands" (see 5033) gives the acreage as 3,708, and the rent £69 16s.* Grantee to erect houses for 90 families, one for himself, [6] for freeholders, 6 for farmers, and 42 others for copyholders. Other conditions usual in grants to undertakers in Munster, as in 5032. 2 membranes.—6 March, xxxi.

5314 (4255.) Grant to John Maplasden, gent.; of the office of constable of the castle of Dublin. To hold from 16 Jan.;last, when Stephen Sedgree, gent., relinquished the office, during good behaviour; with a fee of £26 13s. 4d. and all other profits as Wm. Denham, Jaques Wynokafielde, Silvester Cooley, or S. Sedgree, had in the office. Not to be removed, *as in 4976*.—14 March, xxxi.

5315 (6101.) Grant (under queen's letter, 8 March, 1587) to Brian Fitzwilliams; of the lands of Hollaneston and Arronan, co.

1588-9.   PLANTA.—ELIZABETH.

Meath, possessions of Christopher Eustace, attainted (recites
2454), (Rent 61s.); a moiety of a house and a castle in Naas
with two gardens, a moiety of a messuage and garden late in
the tenure of Philomena M'Gormley, of another messuage and
garden of Patrick Colgen, of another messuage and garden of
Patrick Keunett, and a moiety of certain land in Naas, possessions
of Christopher Ewstace, attainted, co. Kildare (recites 1430 and
2611), (33s. 8d.); a messuage on the north side of the
High street of Dublin, in the tenure of Patrick Dixon, merchant,
late in the occupation of Nicholas Fitz Simond, of Dublin, alderman, parcel of the possessions of John Burnall, attainted (recites
2331 and 2542), (40s.); the lands of Kilologlas, a moiety of
parcels of land called Ballicloughan and Tully, and a sixth part
of a parcel called Ballinalower which Colman O Malaughlin gave
in exchange for so much in Clonedaffe, of the lands of the said
Colman, attainted, co. Westmeath (recites 4809), (23s. 8d.); the
site of the castle or manor of Olde Castleton and its appurtenances
in the lands of Castleton (20s.), the site of the castle or manor
of Michellaston and the town of Kilcoghlau, and there belongs
to the manor a carucate and a half of land, late in the tenure of
Ellinora Fitz Desmonds late wife of John og fitz John Gibbon
Gerald, possessions of the said John oge, attainted, co. Cork
(43s. 4d.), (recites a lease to James boy Iloahe, see 3046, also
3583 and 3736); the site of Newcastle, ruined, to which belongs
the lands of Glannaghonanghe and Nugurtiny (36s 8d), the
site of the manor of Balliloy, ruinous, with its appurtenances
(10s.), of the possessions of the said John og fitz John Gibbon
Gerrald, attainted, co. Tipperary (recites 3583 and 4390); the
lands of Loughton and Blobloiston alias Blobiiston, parcel of the
manor of Ragarlande, of David Nevenle, attainted, co. Wexford
(45s.), (recites 910 and 4091); a moiety of the lands of Crott
alias Crott, Mellaughecrosse, and Knockan, escheated by the
death of John Till without male heirs (recites 520) in the occupation of Thomas Moore, esq., King's co. (23s. 3d.).   To hold
for ever, in common socage except the lands in King's co. which
are held in capite by the twentieth part of a knight's fee.
Rent, £15 10s. 7d., distributed as above.—14 March, xxxi.

5316 (4270.) Lease (under commission, 17 Feb, xxx.) to Ellyn
Butler alias Sherlocke, widow of John Sherlocke, gent., son and
heir to Patr. Sherlocke, late of S. Katharyne's, gent.; of the site
of the abbey of S. Katharine, co. Waterford, and all its possessions,
the Grange called S. Kathaeryn's Graunge only excepted, being
already passed to Daniel Kellyn.   To hold for 21 years.   Rent,
£117 5s. 8d.   Provisions as in 4939.   She shall give security to
Rich. Aylwards, and James Sherlocke, gent., executors of said
Patr. Sherlocke, to abide by an order made by the lord deputy
concerning them.   Recites 2938, forfeited by the nonpayment of
the rent.   2 membranes.—[17 March], xxxi.   (Auditor General's
Patent Book 21, p. 12.)

5317 (4272.) Grant (under queen's letter, 31 May, xxx.) to Rich.
Power, esq., son and heir of John Power, lord Power; of the lands of
Newtone of Kilmainham, with the tithes, co. Dublin, parcel of the
possessions of the late hospital of S. John of Jerusalem in Ireland.
To hold for ever, in common socage.   Rent, £6 13s. 4d.   Recites
Nos. 1438, 2525, and 4923.—20 March, xxxi.

1588-9.   FIANTS.—ELIZABETH.

5318 (4300.) Grant (under queen's letter, 31 May, xxx.) to Richard,
son and heir of John Power, lord Power; of the lands of Termonfeighan, (rent 113s. 4d.) (recites 2608); 3 messuages within
the walls of Drogheda on the side of Ulster, upon the quay, and
a curtilage without the walls and gate of S. Laurence of that
town (20s. 8d.), (recites No. 1537, also a lease in reversion for
40 years to the earl of Ormond, 22 June, xvii.); a chamber
with a cellar, and a little garden, on the north side of the church
of S. Olave alias S. Tullock, 13s. 2½d. (recites 2435 giving date
as 1 December); a messuage on the Woodkey, Dublin, parcel of
the rectory of S. Olave, late in the tenure of Patr. Dowdall, of
Dublin, alderman, deceased, and parcel of the possessions of the
monastery of S. Augustin by Bristoll (26s. 8d.), (recites 3354);
a garden in S. Francis-street, parcel of the possessions of the
hospital of S. John the Baptist without the New Gate, (16d.),
(recites 3354); half of a messuage in the High-street of Dublin,
on the north side, late in the tenure of Wm Nowman, now of
Nich. Ball, alderman, which lies in length between the land of
S. Michael's and that formerly of Rob. Dowdall, knt., late
justice, towards the west, the land of the said Robert towards
the east and north, and the High street towards the south,
parcel of the lands of the late monastery of the B. V. M. by
Dublin, (8s. 4d.). To hold for ever in common socage. Rent
£9 4s. 6½d., as above.—20 March, xxxi.

5319 (6009.) Ecclesiastical commission. *Concluding membrane*
English only. *None of the commissioners' names appear. So far as it
remains it is in the same terms as the similar commission, 5831
post.—[   ] 1588 (?).

1589.

5320 (4367.) Grant (under queen's letter, 11 Jan., xxxi.) to Rich.
Meredith, dean of S. Patrick's, Dublin; constituting him bishop
of Laughlin; with license to hold the deanery of S. Patrick's,
in commendam, in consideration of the poverty of the see
through the depredations of the Moores and Cavanaghs.—13
April, xxxi.

5321 (4358.) Livery to Gerald, son and heir of James FitzGerralde,
late of Dromany, co. Waterford, knt. Fine £50 and £7 for
pardon of alienation.—16 April, xxxi.

5322 (4275.) Lease (under queen's letter, 9 Aug., xxiv.) to Emarye
English. Lye, gent.; of the site of the abbey of the B. V. M., of Kil-
beggan, containing, with other buildings, a small church belonging
to the parishioners of the monastery, lands in Kilbegan, a mill
there on the small river Brosnagh, two eel weirs there, lands
in Skeanagh and Clonoglyne, Ballendirre, Ballym'morish, Bally-
hoban alias Loghnecore, with the grange of Kilbegan, Bally-
moyre, Ballenskarvan, and Kilmonyn, temporal possessions of the
said abbey, the rectory and tithes of Kilbegan, Skeanagh, Ballendirre, Ballem'morish, Ballehoban, the grange of Kilbegan, Balle-
moyre, Thuyre, Balletrastne, Balleakarvan, Loghnecore, Balle-
hickan, Killaloran, Moyldruym, Swyren, the grange of Kiltob
ber, Kilmonyn, Ballensowder, Clonoglyne, Gwynemanagh,
Cowla, Aghnemanagh, Homow, and Ballyno, which are gathered
                                                                    G

1589.   FIANTS.—ELIZABETH.

by 16 copies of corn, besides the altarages and 2 copies of corn
for the curate, all are in Magooghegan's country, in co. Westmeath. To hold for 40 years, from the end of No. 1391. Rent
£18 5s. 10d. Maintaining one English horseman. Not to
charge coyne. He shall enroll in Auditor-General's office, and
give security for rent to chief remembrancer within 8 months.
—17 April, xxxi.

5323 (6529.) Grant to Thomas Saye; of the castle and lands of
English. Carriglemlery, co. Cork, 13 plough lands or 5776 acres. To
hold for ever, of the castle of Carriggrohan, by fealty, in common
socage. Rent £31 18s. 8d. English from 1584 (half only for the
preceding 3 years.) Grantee must erect houses for 90 families, of
which 1 is for himself, 6 for freeholders of 300 acres 6 for farmers
of 400a. and 42 for copyholders of 100a. Other conditions as in
5032.—21 April, xxxi.

5324 (5527.) Grant (under queen's letter, 15 Oct., 1588) to Thadeus
Nolan, gent.; of a pension of. 16d. (Irish) a day, for life—22
April, xxxi.

5325 (4298.) Lease (under queen's letter, 4 July, xxx.), to John
English. Boalinge, gent.; of the prioral chamber, manor or preceptory of
Kilbog, with the rectory of Kilbeg and the lands and tithes of
Kilbeg, co. Kildare (recites a lease from the hospital of S. John
of Jerusalem to Nich. Stanihurste for 41 years from 1555, of
the premises as fully as Gerald Suton, of Richardstown, held
them; also 2258 to James, son of said Nicholas), To hold
for 40 years from the end of the terms in being. Rent £12.
Provisions as in 5311.—24 April, xxxi.

5326 (6336.) Livery to Philip Roche, son and heir of John Roche,
late of Kinsale, co. Cork, merchant. Fine £10 11s. 9d.—
27 April, 1589.

5327 (4274.) Lease (under queen's letter, 31 March, xxvii.) to
English. Rob. Hamons, of Trime, gent.; of the manors of Tryme and
Moygare, co. Meath, as in 922, (*Malyvondrisshe is here written*
Maryvondrishe, *Corbragh*e as Cabraghe, *Galleston* as Daleston,
Dowgerstowns at Dowgerston.) Exemption as in 923. Recites
No. 1568. To hold for 40 years, from the end of the interests
he now hath. Rent £63 6s. 8d., part in corn. Not to charge
coyne or livery.—[28 April, xxxi.] (*Auditor-General's Patent
Book* 21, p. 14).

5328 (4273.) Lease (under queen's letter, 3 Sept., xxix.), to John
English. Talbot, esq.; of the house, with a wine cellar, called Tailor's
hall, in the parish of S. John, Dublin, parcel of the possessions
of Thomascourt, (reciting 2306); the lands of Gabrocston,
co. Dublin, in the tenure of Walter Scadgrave, mayor of Dublin,
parcel of the possessions of the monastery of B. V. M., Dublin
(reciting 2675.) To hold for 50 years from the end of the
terms in being. Rent £13 18s. 1d. Provisions as in 5311.—
1 May, xxxi.

5329 (4287.) Pardon to Rich. Welshe fitz Rob., James Madden
fitz John, Edw. Madden fitz John, James Harrold, James
Fagan fitz Wm., Alex. Leonard, John Power, James White,
John Magner, Rich. Renan, Daniel Canylyn, Wm. Barry,

Jasper Lombard, Wm. Donogho, David Roche, James Walshe, Rich. Nogle, and Patr. Mortle; for the slaying of Edm. Symson, gent. (under the conduct of capt. Markam), and any other offences. Security as in 1943, in co. Waterford. The pardon not to include treason, burglary, arson, intrusion on crown lands, or debts to the crown.—1 May, xxxi.

5330 (5960.) Surrender by Cormac Carty fitz Darby alias Cormac m'Diermod m'Teig M'Carty, of the Blarny, co. Cork; of the manor of Blarny, Twohasblarny, and the whole country of Muskry, co. Cork, the territories of Ivelearia, Twonedromen, Ifanlow, Twmerouskaghe, Clanncoughor, and Clanfynnine; the manors of Blarny, Kilkrea, Macrowny, Castlemore by Movidda, Carricknamock, Castlenyhensie, Carrickydrohidd, Downyne, and Iniskeane; and the lands of Blarny, Kilkrea, Macrowny, Castlemore by Movidda, Carricknamock, Carrickdrohidd, Downyne, Castle ny hynssie, Grinaghe, Glanawne, Rathduff, Inishnane, Kilmahonny, Kilwylie, Knockivillia, Ballyrantane, Ballyworoughowe, Garranwaterig, Garrihislie, Balle[   ], Knockigogalne, Ballihullin, Balligarvan, Kilanemarterie, Downdearyke, Carrignegeillaghe, Carricknacurry, Anaghalis, Kilemorihin, Mothey, Tavir, Ballincrany, Garmndaragh, Downaghmore, Ballivourny, Kanwy, Aghibollick, Currikupane, Curriworoughowe, Karrigrowghanbegg, Kowle, Itanywally, Olohinoe, Kilmibile, Kiltary, Kilahensian, Cloghda, Ballanoe, Inshaali, Aggles, Mohallaghe in Rwe, Knockardo Blenghane, Knockahanvois, Knockogronyne, Cloghroe, Knockikhireill, Owilfuighe, Kilnanrackie, and Kilmor, and the patronage of the churches of Knockivillie, Kilvenane, Moviddy, Aghinaghe, Macrowny, Clonedrohid, Kilcolman, and Kilcorny, same co.; with the intention of their being regranted. Signed con. CARTY.—Dated, 2 May, xxxi.

5331 (4309.) Grant (under queen's letter, 22 May, xxx.), to Edw. Smythe, gent.; of a pension of 2s. 6d. English a day. To hold for life.—4 May, xxxi.

5332 (4288.) Pardon to Peter Butler fitz Tho., of Old Abbey, co. Kilkenny, gent., James Howlinge, of same, yeoman, Nich. m'Tho. Byrne alias M'Eclagaly, of same, footman, David fitz Edm. galde M'Cody, of Monyne, Rich. fitz Edm. M'Cody, of Old Graunge, and John fitz Edm. M'Cody, of Collamkille, farmers, Walter Forstall, of Kilbride, gent., Edm. Forstall, his son, yeoman, Peter Dobben, of Jenkinston, gent., Wm. Bolger, of Cowlero, Nich. Fannings, of same, Nich. More m'David, of Balliogan, Peter Dalton fitz Edm. of Cnockmoan, and Donogh Morfis M'Dermead, husbandmen, co. Kilkenny. Provision for submission and security as in 4943. This grant shall not pardon any murder or homicide of malice aforethought, burning of houses or corn, nor intrusion in crown lands or debts to the crown.—6 May, xxxi.

5333 (4302.) Grant (under queen's letter, 13 Jan., xxx.) to Cormac Carty fitz Darby alias Cormac m'Dermode m'Teige M'Carty, of the Blarny, co Cork; of the manor of Blarny, Twhonsblarny, and the whole country of Muskry, and the territories of Ivelearis, Twhonedromen, Ifanlowe, Twhonerouskeagh, Clanncomochor, and Clanfynine, in said co., the manors of Blarny, Kilkrea, Macrowny, Castalmore by Moviddy, Carricknamocke, Castelnehensie, Carrickydrohidd, Downyn, and Iniskeane, and

1589.   PLANTS—ELIZABETH

all lands, rents, and services, in Blarny, Kilcrea, Mocrowny,
Castelmore by Moviddy, Carricknemocke, Carrick Idrohidd,
Downyn, Castelnyhenzie, Granaghe, Glancawne, Rathduffe,
Iniskean, Killynahomny, Kilewyle, Knocknsville, Ballyvantana,
Ballyworoughowe, Garranwaterig, Garryhissie, Ballea, Knock-
lgogane, Ballyhullina, Balligarvane, Kilnemartine, Downedericke,
Karricknegilaghe, Carrignecurry, Annaghally, Kilenorehina,
Mothey, Tawir, Ballincrany, Garrandaragh, Donnaghmore,
Ballyvourny, Kanwy, Aghibollicke, Carricknapan, Carry-
woroughowe, Karigroughanbegg, Kowle, Ibanywally, Clahins,
Kimikile, Kilbery, Kilahoandian, Clogda, Ballenoe, Inaheale,
Aggles, Mohallaghe in Rvo, Knockarde, Braaghbane, Knock-
shansvoie, Knockrogronyne, Cloghro, Knockikhirinll, Owilalnighe,
Kilnawracke, and Kilmore, and the patronage of the churches
of Knock Iville, Kilvenane, Moviddy, Aghinaghe, Mocrowny,
Clondrohidd, Kilcrony, and Kilcolinan, co. Cork; all which the
grantee had surrendered by his deed 5330; also half of the
goods of felons and outlaws, of all fines, and of waifs and strays
within the premises. To hold for ever, by the service of a
twentieth part of a knight's fee. Rent, £5 13s. 4d. Having
the possessions of religious houses, and the rights of all the
queen's subjects. Also grant of the lands of Carricknevar,
co. Cork. To hold for ever, in common socage. Rent, 10s.
He may hold, once a quarter, a court baron and view of frank
pledge.—[0 May, xxxi.] (Auditor-General's Patent Book 9,
p. 56.)

5334 (4310.) Charter to the sovereign and commons of the town of
Kinsale (under queen's letter, 13 Jan., xxx.) Recites and con-
firms a charter of xxii. Edw. IV., exemplifying the statute
confirming a previous charter of vii. Edw. IV. The corporation
to enjoy all privileges heretofore granted, and the lands and hereditaments belonging to or to be acquired by them or their parish
church, not exceeding in yearly value £30 English. The bounds
of the franchises by water having been from Bolman rock and
Whitebay (Whitebayne in recital) to Ineshonane in the harbour
of the sea, to the middle of the water as well salt as fresh,
within which the sovereign was eschentor, justice of the peace,
and admiral, these limits are extended one mile in every direction. The bounds by land hitherto undefined shall extend 1½
miles from the walls, viz., to the north part of Colkaren
and Glanknocknegoole towards the north, to the Old Court,
Glantanellice, and Courthurtyne, beyond the water and ferry
of Kinsale towards the south, and from Beallgoollie and
Phreghane on the east, to the church of Downderowe
and the water of Glaslen, towards the west. All the lands and
people living within these limits to be under the government of
the sovereign and officers of the town, as if they were within the
walls. The sovereign to be sole eschentor, justice of the peace,
admiral, and clerk of the market, within the franchises. The
corporation to perambulate the bounds when they please; to receive the profits and forfeitures arising from the offices of clerk
of the market, eschentor, and admiral, for the use of the town;
and to exercise the offices of searcher and gauger, half the forfeitures to go to the queen, the other half with the other profits
to be for the use of the town. The corporation to elect annually

a customer and collector of customs and subsidies within the
ports and creeks between the old head of Kinsale and the island
of Dorsees, who shall also be searcher and ganger, and shall
account in the Exchequer. The sovereign and recorder, with
two senior burgesses associated with them, to be justices of the
peace and justices for gaol delivery (treasons under 25 Edw. III.
excepted) within the franchises. The corporation to have a gaol.
The serjeants of the town to return juries, inquisitions, and
attachments of the justices as a sheriff would. The corporation
to have a market on Wednesdays and Saturdays, and a fair on
the feast of S. Bartholomew and three days after. The sovereign
to be clerk and governor of the market and fair, with power to
hold court of pie powder. Also grant to the town of the custom
or coquet of hides being 8d. from each dicker exported from the
port, also a rent of £3 6s. 8d. from the Courcies country called
Oriobourein, near the town, which rent had come to the queen's
hands by the attainder of the earl of Desmond; to hold the said
coquet and rent for 31 years, to be expended on the fortifi-
cation of the town.—10 May, xxxi.

5335 (4248.) Grant to Nich. Champion, gent.; of the wardship and
marriage of Shane m'Tirrelagh O Farall, son and heir of Tirelagh
O Farall, son and heir of Tirelagh m'Breyn, of Ballinlagh, co.
Longford, gent.; and custody of his lands. To hold during
minority. Rent £3 5s.: of which he may retain £3 for maintenance of the minor. Fine 15s.—14 May, xxxi.

5336 (4244.) Grant to Nich. Champion, gent.; of the wardship and
marriage of Gerald O Farall, son and heir of Teige oge O Farall,
late of Tully, co. Longford, gent.; and the custody of his lands.
To hold during minority. Rent £4 5s., of which he may retain
£4 for maintenance of the minor. Fine 40s. "The extent of the
lands of Teig og amounts to £0 11s. 8d., whereof the town of
Tully and eight cartrons, valued at £4 ster., belong to the tanist
of Clonysbaio for the time being. And his wife, Catherine ny
Farrall, hath 2 cartrons in dower."—14 May, xxxi.

5337 (4305.) Grant (under queen's instructions, 1 Aug., xxviii.) to
James Fitz John, of Knockmoane, co. Waterford, and Johanna,
his mother; of two carucates of land called Kilmalow and Kil-
gabriell. To hold for ever, in free socage, as of the manor of
Dongarran. Rent 30s. English.—16 May, xxxi.

5338 (4247.) Grant to John Hoye, gent.; of the wardship and
marriage of Walter, son and heir of Edm. Tuite, late of Mollauly,
co. Westmeath, gent.; and the custody of his lands. To hold
during minority. Rent 5s. He may retain £4 4s. 10d. residue
of the extent of the possessions for maintenance of the minor.
Fine 5s.—18 May, xxxi.

5339 (4290.) Pardon to Edm. Pursell, of Ballimlagh, co. Kilkenny,
gent. Provisions as in 5332.—28 May, xxxi.

5340 (4281.) Grant to Tho. Lisle (endorsed Lislie), gent.; of the
office of marshal or gaoler of the high court ecclesiastical. To
hold during good behaviour, with all fees appertaining.—31 May,
xxxi.

5341 (4266.) Grant to Wm. Phillips, of Dublin, gent.; of the office
of clerk of the crown in Chancery, which Edw. Fitz Symon, of
Dublin, gent., lately held. To hold during pleasure, with the
usual fees. Not to be removed, as in 4976.—2 June, xxxi.

5342 (4282.) Commission to Adam, archbishop of Dublin, lord chancellor, Tho., earl of Ormond and Ossory, lord treasurer, John, archbishop of Armagh, Henry, earl of Kildare, Chr. viscount Gormanstown, Tho., bishop of Meath, Tho., baron of Slane, Chr., baron of Howth, Chr., baron of Delvin, Peter, baron of Trimletston, Oliver, baron of Louth, Henry Wallop, knt., vice-treasurer, N. Bagnoll, knt., marshal, chief justices Gardener and Dillon, chief baron Dillon, N. White, knt., master of the rolls, N. Walsh, second justice of the Chief Place, Rich. Bingham, Edw. Waterhouse, Tho. Le Strange, Geo. Bourchier, Geoffrey Fenton, knights, and Edw. Brabazon, esq., members of the privy council; to be justices, commissioners, and keepers of the peace in the counties of Dublin, Meath, Westmeath, Kildare, Wexford, Kilkenny, Louth, Queen's, King's, and Catherlagh, during the absence of the lord deputy, Sir W. Fitzwylliam, in Connaught and other northern parts; with powers as in 2445. One or two of the temporal lords or others, to be nominated by the lord chancellor, to act as general of the forces when called out.—2 June, xxxi.

5343 (4277.) Lease (under commission, 17 Feb., xxx.) to Wm. Monynges, gent.; of the tithe corn of the rectory of Moiaclare gathered in Moiaclare, Kilgregen and Bultarstone, Porterstown, Kynnan and Parrocks, Baldogen and Aghole, great Moygarde and little Moygarde, and Killan, co. Meath, parcel of the possessions of the monastery of S. Thomas court, the tithes and alterages due to the vicar and curate excepted. To hold for 21 years. Rent during first 18 years £4 13s. 4d., being that reserved under *No.* 1027, which had been forfeited for non-payment of rent; and during the remaining 3 years, £18 18s. 8d. He shall not alien without license except to persons English by both parents or born in the Pale, and shall enroll in Auditor-General's office within 4 months, and shall within three months put in sufficient security in the Chief Remembrancer's office for payment of the rent.—3 June, xxxi.

English.

5344 (4308.) Grant (under queen's letter, 8 March, xxx.) to Brian Fitzwilliam, esq.; of a moiety of a messuage and lands of Kilcloighe alias Cloghes lands in Baltrigen, co. Dublin, parcel of the lands of John Burnell, attainted (rent 43s. 4d.); four tenements or shops with another tenement newly built on what was a vacant space in the city of Waterford, parcel of the lands of James Fitzgeralde, attainted (26s. 8d.); five carucates of land or martlands, each containing 40 acres arable, and 80 acres pasture, wood, and mountain, viz.: in Ballishean Carragh ½ a carucate, Balliperis ½, Kildonan ½, Ballyvaltrym ½, Clonigall 1, Cowlemalagh ½, Ballikeamicke ½, Garrihistie ½, and Babon ½, in the country of Ferren O'Neyle and Leverocks, co. Carlow, Cowlerowe ½ a carucate, lying in the territory of Cowlrowe, same co., seven carucates or martlands, viz. in Tenehencie and Teneran or Tenaran alias Cowlen Ilan 1 mart, and Ballyhenrie 6 marts, in the barony of Symolyn near the Barrow, possessions of Maurice Cavenaghe, called Morrough leighe m'Cahir Cavenaghe, of Tenehencie, attainted (£15); a castle and 4 quarters of land in Liskeanan, co. Galway, parcel of the lands of Theobald leighe Bourke, late of Liskeanan, attainted (53s. 4d.). To hold for ever, in common socage. Rent £21 5s. 4d., as above. Main-

1589.   FIANTS.—ELIZABETH.

taining one English horseman on the lands in co. Carlow ; and
rendering the usual composition for the lands in Connaught.—
12 June, xxxi.

5345 (4258.) Grant to John Heath, gent., register of the prerogative
court ; of the office of collector and receiver of all fines imposed
by the commissioners for Ecclesiastical Causes or by the Prerogative Court, and sums due by recognizance or bond acknowledged
before the same. To hold as long as commissions for those
courts continue. Fee £40 English, in consideration of costs in
maintaining messengers and clerks. He shall be bound with
sureties in 1,000 marks.—16 June, xxxi.

5346 (4311.) Grant to sir Chr. Hatton, knt., lord chancellor of
England ; of the castle of Knockmoane, and the demesne lands
adjoining and belonging thereto, containing ¼ a ploughland,
Cayent 1 ploughland, Ballyloman 2, Carrigro ¼, Ballyntullane ¼,
Ballyncarroole [1], Glannyvaddon 1, Cowleorompy 1, Templegall
¼, Larraghe 1, Carrigleigh ¼, Killyshell ¼, Ballekennedy ¼,
Kcoroohe ¼, Ballimackillmore 1, Dunbrockly ¼, and Ardramony
1, being demesne lands of the castle of Knockmoane, late the
lands of Rich. fitz John Fitz Morice, of Knockmoane, attainted,
and containing, by measure, 3,482 acres of tenantable land ; also
the lands of Ballynccourtie alias Courtstown, containing 500
acres, Kypaghe Coyne and Saltabarett 415 acres, Cappaghlynrays
1,191 acres, Aghameane 1,472 acres, Ballym'mawghe and Bally-
gwyn 400 acres, lands of Garrett, earl of Desmond, attainted ;
the lands of Moynarett, Kilgowghe, Ballikmockagh, and Kilgat-
tanitt, in the barony of Conaroghe or adjoining it, containing by
estimation 500 acres, parcel of the lands of Brien m'Donnogh
m Terralogh I Brien, attainted, the lands of Graige, Kiloumane,
and Mogallege, parcel of the lands of [   ] oge m'Thomas, of
the Sept of the Garaldines, containing two ploughlands and rated
at 800 acres, the lands of Glamtullchans, Kiltigane, and Castle-
lanalane rated at two ploughlands and to be eight [hundred]
acres, and Kilkypp alias Killyhyppe, containing one ploughland
rated at 400 acres, of the lands of Maurice m'Thomas M'Edmund,
traitor ; all in co. Waterford and containing 10,910 acres, English
measure. To hold for ever, in fee farm, in free and common
socage. Rent £60 7s. 9d., English, from 1594 (£30 3s. 9d. for
preceding three years), and ¼d. for each acre of bog or waste
which he may reclaim ; also 1¼d. for each acre certified by the
commissioners of survey that the lands exceed the number stated
in this grant. He may empark 550 acres. He must erect houses
for 82 families, of which one for himself, 5 for freeholders, 5 for
farmers, and 36 for copyholders. Other conditions usual in
grants for planting the undertakers in Munster, as in 5032.—18
June, xxxi.

5347 (4296.) Lease (under queens letter, 27 (?) Dec., xxvi.), to
Edw. Apalye, Marie Apalye, and Joan Apalye, children of
capt. Wm. Appalie, deceased ; of the commandery or manor of
Aneo, and all its appurtenances in Aneo, Ballencloghe, Limrick,
Kilmalloke, Adare, Croghe, Askeine, Rathakilly, Ardanghe,
Casahill, Carricke, Ardartry, and Dengle ; also the rectaries
of Aneo, Loynge, Kilfrusee, Kayruoray, Meynarde, Karrefusuok,
Kilcullane, Moretown, Owlys, Browe, Garyuskan, Garynowsy
or Carewownde, Rochestown, Ardare, Newtan near Ardare,

1589.   FIANTS.—ELIZABETH.

Narlaghe, Kilwilla, Killens, Killyno, Killane, Killon, Bathroman, Kilbaran, Areffynan alias Ardfynan, Mortlaston, Knockgraffon, and Carrintobber, cos. Limerick, Kerry, Tipperary, and Clare, and all other possessions of the commandery. To hold for 40 years from the determination of 3250. Rent £47 7s. 6½d. Maintaining one English horseman. Provisions as in 5311. 2 membranes.—23 June, xxxi.

5348 (6112.) Grant to John Hoye, gent.; of all fines arising from certain concealed alienations discovered by him, of the lands of Monaley, Garrenrye, Brittas, Droynmore, Droynbegge, Coylanmore, Coylanbegge, Blackastle, Brockaghe, Balrobbyn, Loghgarbegge, Mayston, and Cartelone, in the baronies of Moyashell and Corkerye, and lands and weirs, in Tuterathe alias Farrentonrathe in the Newetowne by Trym, or elsewhere in cos. Meath and Westmeath, conveyed by Andrew Tute, of Monaley, gent., 19 Oct. iv., to James Dowdall, of Knock, esq., Peter Wellealy, of Blackehall, gent., and others; Blackcastle of Ballnegall, same co., with half the wood of Carge, conveyed by John Tute, of Balnegall, gent., Rich. and Wm. Nangle, 1 Ap. viii., to Theobald Dalamare and Wm. Tirrell, gent., and others; Monaley, Garryarye, Brittas, Droynmore, Droynhogge, Callanmore, Kilbride, Robynston, Cullambegge, Corcartlan, Tutarathe alias Farramourathe, 27s. chief rent out of Foxes lands, and the fishing of Callanmore, conveyed by James Dowdall, second justice of the Chief Place, and Peter Wolkelye, gent., 10 May, 1581, to Oliver Nugent and Anne Cusacke, his wife; Brockaghe, co. Westmeath, conveyed by John Tute, of Blackastle, Edw. Cusacke, of Loomullen, and others, 23 June, xxiv., to Hugh Onaye.—[10?], July, xxxi.

5349 (4276.) Lease (under queens letter, 20 Sept., xxx.), to Chr. Nugent, lord of Dalvin; of the site and possessions of the priory of Fowre, co. Westmeath, and the monastery of Inchemore in the Annallie O Ferrallie Baue, as in 1089, (Fayron is in one place written Fayreton, and the last name appears here as Ballenmollen). To hold for 30 years, from the end of the interest in being. Rent and conditions as in 1089. He shall not alien without license; other provisions as in 5311.—20 July, xxxi.

5350 (4263.) Grant to Tho. Cahill, gent.; of the office of interpreter of the Irish tongue before the deputy and council. To hold during good behaviour, with such fees as Wm. Don had.— 26 July, xxxi.

5351 (4307.) Grant (under queens letter, 13 Oct., 1586), to Anne Thickepannye, formerly widow, now married to Rich. Hardinge, gent.; of the lands of Batonghton, co. Meath, parcel of the lands of David Sutton, attainted. To hold for ever, in free socage. Rent £5 6s. 8d. Recites that the lands were leased 10 March, iv. and v. Philip and Mary, by Gerald, earl of Kildare to Bartholomew Russell, gent., for 61 years, and that the earl subsequently transferred his interest to Sutton.—26 July, xxxi.

5352 (4245.) Grant to John Browne and Josias Belknappe, gentlemen; of the wardship and marriage of Donell O Kelly, son and heir of Donell reoghe O Kelly, late of Downe, co. Galway, gent. To hold during minority. Rent 71s. 8d., of which he may

1589.   FIANTS.—ELIZABETH.

retain 40s. for maintenance of the minor. Fine 20s.—29 July, xxxi.

5353 (4281.) Commission to the same persons and to the same effect as 5342. The lord chancellor or one or two others named by him to act as general of the forces when called out.—3 Aug., xxxi.

5354 (8741.) Patent of grant to Walter Harpoll, clerk; of the deanery of the cathedral church of Leighlin.—5 Aug., xxxi.

5355 (4271.) Lease (under commission, 17 Feb., xxx.) to Daniel Neylande, bishop of Kildare; of the lands of Sillot with liberty of common on the Curraghe of Kildare, Braliman, Imsegrey, Insenaloher and Shenclone, Colioreland in the Greytreers of Kildare, lands pertaining to the late Whitefriars of Kildare, with a liberty of common on the Curragh of Kildare, and Tippenan, all in co. Kildare, possessions of David Sutton, attainted, lately re-entered for non-payment of rent. To hold for 21 years. Rent £25 12s. Maintaining one English horseman. Provisions as in 4999.—9 Aug., xxxi.

5356 (4308.) Grant (under queen's letter, 5 Aug., xxix.) to George Sherlocke, gent.; of the rectory of Whitchurche, co. Kilkenny, and all tithes of Whitchurche, Castleton, Graigno, and Killenerro, same co., parcel of the monastery of Enystyogge, now in the tenure of James and Edmund, sons of John Oaffe, deceased, and concealed from the queen. To hold for ever, in free socage. Rent 20s.—9 Aug., xxxi.

5357 (6294.) Patent of commission to Nicholas Walshe, second justice of the Chief Place, Jasse Smithes chief justice of Munster, the mayor of Waterford, Tho. Wadinge, Rich. Aylwarde, and John Terrell constable of Dungarvan; to take inquisition post mortem of Robert Power, of Killmedan, gent., and John Power, late of Ballolanyn, gent.—At Dublin, 23 Aug., xxxi.

5358 (4308.) Grant (under queen's letter, 8 March, xxx.) to Brian Fitzwilliam; of lands in Keppoge and Dengan, and Ballonakeppaghe, co. Kildare, parcel of the lands of Edmund Eustace, brother of James, late viscount of Balltinglas, attainted. To hold for ever, in common socage. Rent 50s.—29 Aug., xxxi.

5359 (4248.) Grant to Rob. Byrne, of Dublin, gent.; of the wardship and marriage of Walter Dowdall, of Droughede, son and heir of George Dowdall, of same, merchant; and the custody of his lands. To hold during minority; without account, because it appears by the certificate of George Byrnhall, deputy eschentor general, that all the lands are charged with jointures and dowers. Fine 5s.—31 Aug., xxxi.

5360 (4349.) Livery to Bartholomew, son and heir of Nicholas Dillon, late of Keppock, co. Dublin, gent. Fine £6 13s. 4d.— 2 Sept., xxxi.

5361 (4283.) Commission to Edw. Harbert, esq., sheriff of the co. Cavan; to execute martial law in that county, as in 218.—8 Sept., xxxi.

5362 (4256.) Grant to James Gold, esq.; of the office of second justice in the province of Munster. To hold during good behaviour, with a fee of 100 marks ster., as John Miagh had. Not to be removed, as in 4976.—20 Oct., xxxi.

5363 (6534.) Grant to Robert Ansley, esq.; of the castle and lands of Bathurd 2 ploughlands, the castle and lands of Corbally ½ pl., the Dominican friary in Lymericke containing 24a., land called Courthrack ½ pl., land called Corlishe in Labmaghe, 1 pl., land

1589.   PLANTS.—ELIZABETH.

called Kayerocray, and three parts of Rolliston, 1 pl., and Frevrion alias Ballenobrehle in Toghoreyn, ½ pl., making 6 ploughlands and 34a., which after the rate of 28 ploughlands to a seigniory of 12,000a. make 2,599a., co. Limerick. To hold for ever, by the name of Analoes lot, in feefarm, by fealty, in common socage. Rent £27 1s. 6½d. English from 1594 (half only for preceding three years). If found on survey to contain more than the estimated number of acres grantee shall pay an increased rent of 2½d. for each English acre in excess. Power to impark 100a. Grantee to erect houses for 18 families, of which one to be for himself, 2 for 300a. freeholders, 2 for 400a. farmers, and 6 for 100a. copyholders. Other conditions as in 5032.—22 Oct., xxxi.

5364 (5995.) Surrender by Edward Waterhouse, knt.; of the office of chancellor of the Exchequer, granted by 4931. (Signed; Ed. Waterhouse).—Dated 24 Oct., xxxi.

5365 (4364.) Grant to George Clive, knt.; of the office of chancellor of the court of Exchequer, surrendered by Edw. Waterhouse, knt. To hold during good behaviour, with the usual fees.—25 Oct., xxxi.

5366 (2811.) Grant to Morogh m'Tege O Farrell, gent.; of the office of seneschal of the country of Clonecwlie, co. Longford. To hold during pleasure. With power to assemble the freeholders and inhabitants and command them for defence of the country, the public weal of the inhabitants, and the punishment of malefactors; to punish by all means malefactors and their followers which shall be malefactors, rebels, vagabonds, rymors, Irish harpers, idle men and women, and all such unprofitable members; and to hold a court baron.—28 Oct., xxxi.

5367 (4291.) Pardon to Shane M'Craghe, kern, Shane m'Teig O Follan, horseman, Tirlagh Fynine, Torne m'Morish O Mulchonery, Edm. m'Loghlen M'Geoffrey, Convery m'Morish O Mulchonery, Redmond M'Codo, farmer, Murtagh m'Dermot M'Eboy, farmer, Wm. m'Donogho O Follan, and Donogh m'Teighe O Follan, stokagh, and James Fitz Jones, gent., Queen's co. Provision for security as in 4943. The pardon not to include murder, burglary, or arson, nor intrusion into the queen's lands, nor debts to the crown.—29 Oct., xxxi.

5368 (4295.) Lease (under commission, 17 Feb., xxx.) to sir Rich. Shea, knt., upon surrender; of the rectories of Gallmoye and Glasmare, co. Kilkenny, parcel of the possessions of the late hospital of S. John of Jerusalem in Ireland. To hold for 21 years. Rent, £17 6s. He shall not alien without license, except to English, and shall give security in the chief remembrancer's office within four months to answer the conditions.— 2 Nov., xxxi.

5369 (4252.) Livery to Nicholas, son and heir of Robert Powr, late of Kilmedan, co. Waterford, esq. Fine, £80.—9 Nov., xxxi.

5870 (4366.) Pardon to Tho. O Dowles, of Aghoure, Philip Birth, of Kildrroe, Teig O Rian, of the Gurtins, Peirce leigh Brensgh, of Castellowne, Malaghlin O Harny, James Grace, of Graighissie, Philip O Boe, of Corrivtowne, Donnell O Lonnan, of same, John Poer fitz Rich., of Irishtown, James Archer, of same, Tho. Grace fitz Redmond, Rob. Shortall, Patr. Shortall m'Firr, John Shortall fitz Roh., Wm. Liales, of Ballym'Cloghne, Wm. fitz Tho. Butler, late of Shaniakell, James Forstall, of Kilferagh, and

1589.   FIANTS.—ELIZABETH.

Gerald M'Codye ; co. Kilkenny. Provisions as in 5367.—4 Nov., xxxi.

5371 (4267.) Grant (under queen's letter, 11 Jan., xxxi.) to captain Tho. Woodhouse ; of a monopoly of the making of glass for glazing, drinking, and all other uses. To hold for 8 years. Paying such customs as heretofore are paid by any merchant for glass imported into England from beyond sea. Grantee shall compound with unlicensed makers, so that they be not endamaged in their possessions. Recites that all manner of glass may be made in Ireland at as small rates as the like made in foreign parts. In consideration of his service in the wars.—8 Nov., xxxi.

5372 (4262.) Grant (under queen's letter, 1 Feb., 1587, and letter of English council, 1 July last) to George Carewe, knt., one of the gentlemen pensioners ; of the office of master of the ordnance. To hold for life, with a fee of 6s. 8d. sterling a day. He shall have the conduct of 30 horsemen, with a lieutenant or vice-captain, and a standard bearer or guydon. Recites that Wm. Standley, knt., had been granted the office by English patent, 6 March, xxv., in reversion after Jaques Wingefilde ; that Wingefilde was dead, but that Standley had absented himself in foreign parts, and had been outlawed for treason. (See *Liber Munerum Hibernia*, part 2, p. 102).—7 Nov., xxxi.

5373 (4304.) Grant (under queen's letter, 13 Oct., xxviii.) to Anne Thickpeny, widow (at date of queen's letter, now married to Rich. Hardinge, gent. ; of lands in the town or preceptory of Killure, co. Waterford (rent, 53s. 4d.), parcel of the lands of the late hospital of S. John of Jerusalem in Ireland, a messuage in Tryme called the Frankhouse (4s.) parcel of the possessions of the same, in co. Meath, a water mill called the stone mill near Ladiscastell (30s.), messuages and lands in Belraine, and land in the north part of Painerston (20s.), parcel of the possessions of David Sutton, of Castelton of Kildrought, attainted. To hold for ever, in common socage. Rent, £5 7s. 4d as above.—8 Nov., xxxi.

5374 (4293.) Pardon to James Fitz Symons, of the Carne, John Fitz Symons, of Tullemalle, Oliver Fitz Symons, of same, Keadaghe m'Shane O Farroll, of the Carr, Shane duffe M'Gillechrist, of same, Fergus O Farroll, of Killsam, Rich. O Farroll, of same, Turlagh O Farroll, of Kinckhullie, Karbere M'Gillechrist, of the Carr, and Edw. Fytz Gerrald, of the Nurne ; co. Westmeath. Provisions as in 5332.—15 Nov., xxxi.

5375 (4425.) Grant to James Gallwale, of Limerick, merchant ; of the wardship and marriage of Michael, son and heir of James Water, late of Limerick ; and the custody of his lands. To hold during minority. Rent 40s. Retaining 15s. for maintenance of the minor. Fine 40s.—20 Nov., xxxii.

5376 (4363.) Pardon to Brian reogh m'Wm. O More, Fergananan m'Donell O Carroll, Mulronie m'Shahien Itley O Carroll, John M'Robert, kerns, Dermod O Lawler, boy, Wm. m'Donagh O Kennedie, of Braham, Tho. M'Cillfalle, Teig O Kinge, kern, Ghr. O Haverin, and Ownye O Murryon ; King's co. Provisions as in 5332.—21 Nov., xxxii.

5377 (4350.) Pardon to Ullick Burcke, of Ballmanenan, co. Galway, condemned for the murder of Patr. O Dowle. Security as in 4943. The pardon not to include arson, intrusion in crown lands or debts to the crown.—22 Nov., xxxii.

1589.   FIANTS.—ELIZABETH.

5378 (4369.) Pardon to Wm. O Felane, of Mogorye, co. of Cross of
Tipperary, James Tobin fitz Rich., of Jamestowne, Oliver
Fannyrge, of Scadenrtan, James Comen fitz Redmond, of Kil-
konell, Rich. Comen fitz Tho., of Kilbraghe, Rich. Fannyrge, of
Farrenrorye, David Bourke fitz Tho., of Ballyhostia, Edm.
O Donell, of Dyrreluscan, Wm. Bourke fitz Tho., of Ballyhostie,
Tavance Kally, of Ballacarryune, Edm. Foer, of same, John
Hackett, of Dowell, Edm. O Cahill, of Cowilchoils, John Hayden,
of Croghan, Tho. fitz Edward, of Knockgraffin, Kadogh O Kelile,
of Kilcaste, Tho. Comen, of Danogston, husbandman, James
Comen, of same, and Tho. Dongan, of Corroghtarme; co. of Cross
of Tipperary. ‡ Provisions as in 5367, (the exception of murder
not to include Wm. O Felane.)—28 Nov., xxxii.

5379 (4420.) Grant (under letter of the English privy council,
English. 29 Sept. xxxi.) to George Thornston; upon his surrender; of the
office of provost marshal in Mounster. To hold during good
behaviour, with a fee of 2s. ster. a day, and the leading of 12
horsemen at 12d. ster. a day each; also diet at the board of the
lord president of Mounster, and such other profits as Warham
St. Leger had. Not to be removed, as in 4976.—28 Nov.,
xxxii.

5380 (4349.) Safe conduct and protection for sir Brian Owrark,
English. knt., chief of his name, and his servants and followers who shall
attend him, to come to the lord deputy and return to his country
of Brenyowrark alias the county of Letrim.—29 Nov., xxxii.

5381 (4342.) Lease (under commission, 17 Feb., xxx.) to Tho.
English. Lambyn, gent.; of the tithe corn of the rectory of Rathmore, the
tithe corn of the rectory of Johnestone with the altarages, the
tithe corn of the parish of Cardeston with the altarages, the
tithe corn of Tippar and Oradockeston, co. Kildare, possessions
of the late hospital of S. John of Jerusalem in Ireland; the lands
of Nicholeston, co. Kildare, parcel of the possessions of Tho.
Ewstace, late of Oardeston, attainted; the site of the house of
friars called the Newe Abbey, co Kildare; 15 ruinous messuages
with gardens in the town of Mollingar, co. Westmeath, a park
called the Feighe nigh the high way called Barter Sedgres, a
meadow called Garrynell alias Lenaghmore, a parcel of land
lying towards the Spittall House of Mollingar, and to the water
of Rathonell nigh the king's way, parcel of the possessions of the
priory of Mollingar. To hold for 21 years. Rent £80 6s. 8d.,
part in corn. Provisions as in 5311.—1 Dec., xxxii.

5382 (4370.) Pardon to Art Ochoin Cavinagh, Mortogh m'Chaire
O Berns, Garralt m'James O Berns, Garralt m'Edm. O Berns,
Donaill m'Cahire Cavinagh, Orean m'Cahire Cavinagh, Morrogh
m'Dermott Cavinagh, Garralt Caron, Patr. riagh m'Loyzagh
O Brine, Donnogh ballogh m'Loyzagh, Edm. O Currin, Donell
and Cahire m'Hugh O Currin, Patr. m'Shane Tomyne, Tirlagh
m'Shane O'Berne, Fergonandus M'Mortoghe, John Harpper,
and Tirlagh M'Rorie; co. Carlow. Security as in 4943. Intrusion into crown lands, and debts to the crown excepted.—4 Dec.,
xxxii.

5383 (4879.) Pardon to Redmund O Fallon, of Mylton, co. Roscommon,
gent.; and Brian begg Magierreght, of same, yeoman. Provisions
as in 5382.—10 Dec., xxxii.

1589.   FIANTS.—ELIZABETH.

5384 (5528.) Grant (under queen's letter, 21 Sept., 1589) to Donagh, earl of Thomond; of a pension of £200 ster. out of the revenues of the province of Connaught and Thomond, for life.—11 Dec., xxxii.

5385 (4378.) Appointment (under queen's letter, 20 Nov. last) of sir Rich. Bingham, knt., chief commissioner of Connaught and Thomond; as chief leader of the army in that province; with power to punish rebels with fire and sword, to raise and lead the queen's subjects and soldiers, and take victual and forage at the queen's usual rates, to treat with rebels and grant protections, receiving all who submit.—12 Dec., xxxii.

5386 (4415.) Grant (under queen's letter, 23 Sept., xxxi.) to Mary Travers, now wife of Gerald Aylmer, esq., and commonly called viscountess of Baltinglass; of the preceptory of Killarge, co. Carlow, lying in the towns of Frirton, Court Killardga, Russellstown, Tullaghphall, and half Noynanne, the tithes of the rectory of Killargie, Frirton, Courts of Killargan, Russellston, Bussardston, Ardinlinathe, and Ballinrabin, co. Carlow, parcel of the possessions of the late hospital of S. John of Jerusalem in Ireland. Also the right of redemption of the premises out of the hands of Owin O Gormogan or any other. To hold far ever, by the service of a twentieth part of a knight's fee. Rent 46s. 9d.—13 Dec., xxxii.

5387 (4373.) Commission to Adam, archb. of Dublin, chancellor, Tho., earl of Ormond, lord treasurer, John, archb. of Armagh, Henry, earl of Kildare, Chr., viscount Gormanston, Tho. bishop of Meath, Tho. baron of Slane, Nich., baron of Howth, Chr., baron of Delvin, Peter, baron of Trimletiston, Oliver, baron of Louth, Henry Wallopp, knt., vice-treasurer, Nich. Bagnoll, knt., marshal of the army, chief justices Gardyner and Dillon, chief baron Dillon, N. White, master of the rolls, Nich. Walsh, second justice of the chief place, Rich. Byngham, Edw. Waterhouse, Tho. Le Strange, George Bourchier, knights, members of the privy council, Geoffrey Fenton, knt., principal secretary, and Edw. Brabazon, esq., also of the council; to be justices, commissioners, and keepers of the peace, in the counties of Dublin, Meath, Westmeath, Kildare, Wexford, Kilkenny, Louth, Queen's, King's, and Catherlagh, during the absence of the lord deputy in Connaught and other northern parts, as in 5342.—16 Dec., xxxii.

5388 (4444.) Grant (under queen's letter, 6 March, xxx.) to Brian Fits Williams, esq.; of the castle and lands of Flemington, co. Kildare, parcel of the lands of James Eustace, viscount Baltinglass, attainted, (rent £6), (recites 4691); the lands of Clegnanston alias Clergnanston, same co., parcel of the lands of Edm. Eustace, brother of said viscount, (13s. 4d.); land in Ellwardston alias Ellverston, co. Dublin, parcel of the lands of Tho. Eustace, of Cardifston, attainted (10s). To hold for ever, in common socage. Rent £7 8s. 4d. as above.—18 Dec., xxxii.

5389 (4348.) Lease (under queen's letters, 7 Oct., xix., in favour Connoghor, then earl of Thomonde, and 21 Sept., xxxi.) to Donagh, earl of Thomond; of a moiety of the site of the abbey of canons of Clare in Thomonde, and its demesne lands, a moiety of the rectories of Kilcriste, Kilmoile, Kilmacedovan, and Killsoveraghe, Ballimackragan, Ballsloghbrains and Ballelogwfadd, and

1589.   PLANTS.—ELIZABETH.

the chapel of Killowe, co. Clare; the site of the house of grey
friars of Inche Clonramatu, a mill and eel weir on the river
Fergus, and messuages and gardens in Inche, co. Clare (leased by
4738). To hold for 21 years, from the end of the interests in
being. Rent £3 15s. Maintaining one English shot. Provisions as in 5311. Reserving right to hold assizes and sessions
in the friary of Inche.—25 Dec., xxxii.

1589-90.

5390 (4882.) Pardon to Hugh O Hanleyne alias Hanley, late of
Powerskourt, co. Dublin, yeoman. Provision as in 5882.—2 Jan.,
xxxii.

5391 (4345.) Lease (under commission, 17 Feb., xxx.), to Edw. Fitz
Eagles Bymun, of the grange of Baldoile, co. Dublin, esq., serjeant at
law; of the rectory of Dullardstone, co. Kildare, as in 2689,
which leases had surrendered by deed of 28 May preceding To
hold for 21 years. Rent £10, part in corn. Provisions as in
4939.—8 Jan., xxxii.

5392 (4449.) Lease (under commission, 17 Feb., xxx.), to Francis
Eagles Capstock, of Dublin, gent.; of the tithes of the rectory of Ball-
rath alias Balraine, co. Kildare, amounting to 10½ copies of
corn, besides the tithes of Baltarnye, Painston, and part of the
Grange of Wittocke, and the altarages, belonging to the vicarage;
the tithes of the rectory of Maynam alias Mayno, co. Kildare,
amounting to 10 copies of corn, besides the tithes of Ballrenat
and Ballinbrill, and the altarages, belonging to the vicarage,
possessions of late hospital of S. John of Jerusalem. To hold
for 21 years. Rent £13 6s. 8d. part in corn. He shall not
alien without license under great seal, nor let to any but English
Lease to be enrolled in the Auditor General's Office within 4
months.—1 Feb., xxxii.

5393 (4366.) Commission to sir Rich. Shea, knt.; to execute
Eagles martial law in co. Kilkenny, as in 218.—13 Feb., xxxii.

5394 (4381.) Pardon to Rich. Shea, knt., late sheriff of co. Kilkenny,
Nich. Swetsman, late sub-sheriff, Edw. Ragged, of Kilkenny, and
Patr. Shortall, of Fowlkrath, gentleman, Wm. Davis, of Kilkenny,
Rich. Launte, Hugh Coyn, Redmund Raron, John Moclere, Tho.
m'Shane O Birne, and John Cantwall, of same, yeoman, David
m'Donogh O Daly, serjeant, James Shortall, of Prickyshryes,
gent., Rich. Nayshe, of Frenyston, yeoman, Rob. O Coyne, of
Suttonrath, Hugh roe O Birne, serjeants, Garrot Archdescon fitz
Nich., John Archer fitz Walter, of Kilkenny, and Edm. Shortall,
of High Rath, gentleman, Ody m'Shane leynagh M'Cody, kern,
Jasper Shea, serjeant, Peter M'Cody alias Archdescon, bailiff
arand, Rob. O Broby, kern, Philip O Shea, horseboy, Oliver
Blanchfeild, of Coyrkeston, Tho. Ballagh, groom, Edm. Blanch-
vill, of Mocolly, Dermot O Daly or O Dowly, of Frenaston,
Robinet Purcell, of Glanballifoile, gent., Redm. M'Cody alias
Archdescon, of Grannagh, gent., Rich. M'Cody alias Archdescon,
of same, Peter Heydon, husb., and Donald O Lahy, husb.
Intrusion into crown lands and debts to the crown excepted.—
13 Feb., xxxii.

5395 (4485.) Livery to Limgh m'Mortogh oge O Moore, son and
heir of Mortogh oge alias Mortogh Moore, late of Raynduffe,
Queen's co., gent. Fine 18s.—20 Feb., xxxii.

1589-90.   Fiants.—Elizabeth.

5396 (4442.) Livery to Martin Lynte alias Skelton, son and heir of Matthew Skelton, late of Sleyty alias Skeltons rathe, Queen's co. Fine 40s.—20 Feb., xxxii.

5397 (4371.) Commission to sir Henry Bagnall, knt.; to execute martial law throughout Ireland, as in 918. Also to conclude good orders with rebels who come to him.—24 Feb., xxxii.

5398 (4380.) Pardon to Tho. Dillon, of Canorston, co. Westmeath, esq., John Talbott, of Canorston, gent., Patr. Ellis, Donell O Ferrall, Conolagh M'Ullemst and Ellis Griffin, of same, yeomen, Edm. Dillon, of the Corr, gent., Redmund m'Nicholas, of same, gent., Donoghe M'Gwire, late of Ballymore, yeoman, Wm. Caron, of Tibberclare, gent., Edm. m'James, of Waterston, gent., Cahill M'Rory, of Tolghan, horsekeeper, Gerald M'Faghney, of Tang, Hebett M'Geffrey, of same, husbandman, Henry m'Hebett, of Bonowne, gent., Edm. M'Tymolty, of Kilkenny, husb., Dermot M'Guill, late of Kilkenny, yeoman, Rob. Dillon, of Bawne, gent., Maurice M'Geffrey, of Tolchan, gent., Sydey O Noble, Rob. Dillon, of Lysmode, gent., Edm. O Quin, of Corr, horsekeeper, Enos Albanaghe, of Bawne, husb., Tirlagh O Gowne, of Canorston, horsekeeper, Garrett Fraine, of same, husb., Wm. M'Guiffe, late of Kilkenny, yeoman, Wm. O Kelly, of Felesson, labourer. Security as in 4943 (Tho. Dillon excepted). Excluding murder, burglary, and arson (with same exception). Excluding also intrusion in crown lands or debts to the crown. —29(so) Feb., xxxii.

5399 (4419.) Grant to John Eliot, esq.; of the office of third baron of the Exchequer. To hold during good behaviour with such fees as Michael Cusacke had.—11 March, xxxii.

5400 (4443.) Grant (under queen's letter, 29 Jan., xxx.) to Patr. Grante, gent.; of one messuage or tenement in the town of Marlborowghe, in Queen's co., and 12 acres arable, and 4 acres pasture, in Clonroske within the liberties of the town, in the tenure and occupation of Rich. Chapman, another messuage there, with like land in Clonroske, in the tenure of Rich. Fox, another, with land in Donnore, lately in tenure of John Demevet, now of John Starelinge, another, with land in Donmoconghe, late in tenure of Tho. Morgan, now of John Starelinge, another messuage late in tenure of Tho. Parsons, another in tenure of Michael Marshall, another in tenure of Tho. Reynolds, another in tenure of Katherine Woodward, another in tenure of John Starling, with a meadow in tenure of Arnold Cosby, other messuages in tenure respectively of Walter Lawrence, Rob. Aire, John Bortall, Wm. Aire or Donat Whyte, and Wm. Drote, and a garden in tenure of Isaac White, another messuage in tenure of Nich. Harman, another in tenure of Roger Joynor, and a croft or garden in occupation of John Paynter, other messuages in the tenure respectively of John Whitney, Dermicins Dowley, Henry Good, John Barington, John Starlinge, Elizabeth Cosbie, Edw. Parsons, Walter Lawrence, and Rob. Harpole, two others late in tenure of Joshua George, others in tenure respectively of George Pleasanton, Rob. Bowen, Randolph Holland, Rice Appowall, and John Casey, and all commons of pasture to the said town of Marlborowgh belonging. To hold for ever, in common soccage. Rent 45s.—21 March, xxxii.

1588–90.   FIANTS.—ELIZABETH.

5401 (4377.) Pardon to Mahowne M'Donoghe, of Kilkish, gent., Maghowne M'Inerinn, of Ballesolloghe, gent., Teige in'Donough M'Shane, of Balledudf nore, Rory m'Magoghe O Flanor, of Kiltailais, David m'Dermot oge, of Laghardan, Dermot roe M'Clanchie, of Balle m'Oonell, Tege m'Shane O Molowneis, of Slontallon, Melaughlan O Meaohan, of Ardakeaghe, Donnogh O Grady, of Mylick, Teige m'Rory M'Tsook, of Gortemalrom, Donell boy O Hickye, of Balle M'Connell, Turlagh M'Donell, of Balle-Arallye, Doanell m'Teige O Molowny, of Glaxdis, Shane O Halloran, of Killensny, Morogh M'Donell, of Tormon O Grady, Shane m'Davis O Molowny, Dermot M'Okarmodie, of Moyarta, Donogh O Kermody, of same, Shane ne Gurion, of the Knock, Langhlin oge O Kowtie, of same, Brian M'Maghowny, of Derricrossan, John M'Donel, of Kilkys, Teige O Cahan, of same, Donnough M'Kinrata, of Ballehoila, Donell O Nealan, of Nealanstowne, Gildof O Hoare, Edm. roe M'Tege, of Monagmaghe, Sids m'Donill M'Hugh, of Cloantrae, Morogh M'Clowna, of Ballem'towne, Langhlin M'Clowne, of same, Hugh O Conell, of Dingembraak, Donogh O Myre, of Dromo Cleva, Hugh roe M'Clanchie, of Ballesallaughe, Nich. Nealan, of Killinohalli, in co. Clare, Feraghe m'Conoghor O Madden, of Killevny, Ferlagh M'Donoghe, of Coppagbsollaughe, Edm. Owine M'Redmond, of BalleConnell, Teige oge M'Evairde, of Cloonpole, Donnough m'Shane M'Farrie, of Kill-tornar, Carbrie M'Kagan, of Downcrie, and Hugh roe Oakott, of Kilfaughtoono, in co. Galway. Provisions as in 5367.—23 March, xxxii.

5402 (4428.) Grant to Rich. Chichestre, gent.; of the wardship and marriage of Edward, son and heir of Donatus alias Donnell O Moloy, late of Ilane Kilttobert, King's co., gent.; and custody of his lands. To hold during minority. Rent 46s. 8d.; of which 26s. 8d. may be retained for maintenance of the minor. Fine 46s. 8d.—24 March, xxxii.

1590.

5403 (4376.) Pardon to Garald m'Mortagh oge Cavanagh, Mortagh oge, his brother, Garret m'Shane O Birne, David m'Garrott O Birne, Shane m'Garrott O Birne, Brien m'Shane O Birne, Donogh m'Foreis O Birne, Brien m'Conleigh O Birne, Morogh m'Shane O Birne, Donell m'Turlaghe oge, Donogh m'Teige O Owen, Wm. O Coren, Henry m'James O Ooren, Wm. m'John, Shane O Henyll, Cahier m'Rory O Birne, Patr. M'Morvartagh, of Downtrin, Morogh M'Coyne, Darmod O Towle, Keddos O Towle, Morris M'Richard, Tibbott M'Richard, and Garrott M'Gilpatrick; co. Carlow. Provisions as in 5367.—25 March, xxxii.

5404 (4446.) Grant (under queen's letter, 4 July, xxx.), to Terence or Tyriagh O Byrne; of a third part of a cartron of land in Moylteny in' Olonoawile by Monasterdirge, co. Longford (rent 3s.), 2 cartrons in Lisrinogy and Syllynamaago (5s.), 2 cartrons in Kyllynboy, 9 in Rathmallagh, and 2½ in Tulloman, co. Longford (26s.), possessions of the abbey of Strowill, in said co.; the rectory of Kylbryd (15s.), and the lands of Kyllsainblawrence with a mill (15s.), belonging to the preceptory of Kyllure, co. Waterford, possessions of the priory of S. John of Jerusalem in Ireland; the islands of Lucheboffyne, Lnohetowvrky, Ilane Rloige, Illannagowne, and Illanagany, upon the river of Loghry, in co. Longford (4s.); half a cartron of land in Dorrolg belonging to Carbry m'Lysagh O Ferrall, attainted (2s.); ½ cartron in Killevahan belonging to Donagh m'Edm. O Ferrall, attainted (12d.); a cartron in Dromloone belonging to Rory m'Donogh O Ferrall, attainted (4s.); a cartron in Curowroe belonging to Shane m'Donogh O Forrall, attainted (12d.); ½ cartrou by Dallibege belonging to Tirlagh m'Owen O Ferrall, attainted (6d.); a cartron in the Newton by Moote belonging to Rich. M'Brenn, attainted (0d.); a cartron in Lystoist, belonging to Onin O Ferrall and Mortagh O Ferrall, attainted, in co. Longford (12d.); lands in Rahenekeraghfyne, co. Wexford, belonging to Gerald M'Ener, attainted (5s.); and Moynarte, same co., belonging to Hugh oge, of Moynarte, slain in rebellion (7s. 6d.); two messuages and lands in the Burren alias Burgage, co. Carlow, belonging severally to Tyrlagh m'Tirlagh O Rian, Melaghlin m'Henry O Rian, Dermot O Rian fitz James, and Thady m'Redmond O Rian, attainted (12d.); messuages and lands in Ballyclowe, same co., belonging severally to Mellaghlin O Rian fitz John, Tirlagh m'Mortogh O Rian, Donald m'Dermond O Rian, Henry roe O Rian, and Thady O Rian fitz Walter, attainted (2s.); two messuages and land in Ballynegreene, same co., belonging to Donald m'Morogh Kynselagh, attainted (12d.); messuages and land in Ballyuenllogge (9d.), Ballynegrane (9d.), and Olonegore (9d.), same co., belonging to Tirlagh m'Cahir m'Gerald Cavenagh, attainted; land in Ballyngharryo or Ballenegarry, same co., belonging to Dermot m'Geoffray O Rian, attainted (2d.); land in Ballyheighlegh or Ballinteighlaighe, same co., belonging to David roe O Rian, attainted (2d.); a garden in Fyddown called Garryborleginge, co. Kilkenny, belonging to John ro Brenagh, attainted (4d.); land in Aghilltane, same co., belonging to Dermot m'Gyllpatrick O Rian, attainted (6d.); land in Gurtyne, same co., belonging severally to Malaghlin moell O Rian fitz John, (1d.), Terence m'Mortagh O Rian (1d.), Donald owro O Rian (3d.), Cahir O Rian (2d.), Owen m'Malaghlin alias O Rian (4d.), and Henry m'Edm. O Rian (4d.), attainted; land in Ballyculrus, co. Kilkenny, belonging to Forgananin fitz Walter O Ryan, attainted (16d.); land in Stacule belonging to Peter fitz Henry O Rian, attainted (2d.); land in Dongarvan, same co., belonging to James Archdeacon, attainted (2d.); land in Gurtyne, aforesaid, belonging to Thady fitz Walter, attainted (0d.); two parts of Ballychlanie, same co., belonging to Robonot Purcell, attainted (2s.); land in Curraghlaban, same co., belonging to Arte m'Arte O Rian (3d.), and to James m'Mortagh O Rian (3d. ?), attainted; land in Glansaintsaviours, in same co., parcel of the chapel of Saintsaviors in New Rosse, in the occupation of George Conway (3s.) To hold for ever, in common socage.   Rent £5 6s. 9d., as above.—11 April, xxxii.

5405 (4376.) Pardon to Thady m'Donoghoe Cassie, of Killmalyne, co. Cork, yeoman, Tho. m'Owen Cassie, of same, David fyrno Brennaghe, of Garrynebolonkie, same co., Gerald fitz John Gibbon, of Ballinighams, same co., gent., Shane sharroffe Brenaghe fitz Tho., of Gortroae, co. Tipperary, Wm. fitz The. Connoghor, of Kyllicharomy, same co., John oge fitz John Connoghor, alias Shane Saladie, of same, Donogho fitz Edm. Conarye, of same co., Symon fitz Morishe Conary, of same, Tho. fitz Rich. Neahe, of Michelstowne, co. Cork, Gerald M'Liahie,

H

1590.   FIANTS.—ELIZABETH.

of Ballynlondre, co. Limerick, Wm. fitz Tho. O Breyen, Tho. fitz
Gerot Gibon, John fitz Gerot Gibon, Edm. fitz John oge Gibon,
of same, Tho. M'Gibon Gerot, of Ballinloghie, same co., Rehmund
Brenaghe fitz Geoffroy, of Kilgiss, same co., Jerotte fitz John
fitz William, of Kilcoane; John m'Gullyeduffo O Moholane, of
Ballinlondrie, Tho. roe Brenaghe fitz Roh. (of) Achliske, co. Cork,
Dermond m'Tho. Iseyn, of the Logherte, same co., Dermoi
m'Donell Cartie, of same, Donell roaghe m'Donell Solevane, of
same, and Mahowne m'Shane I Hollohan, of same. Provisions
as in 5367.—14 April, xxxii.

. **5406** (4387.) Pardon to Donogh m'Donell J Wooroghoe, Dermoni
m'Donagh I Rebellis, John m'Dermod I Solevane, Philip m'Shane
I Conell, Kealaghen m'Teige m'Fynine Carte, Thady m'Edm.
I Moroghoe, Donald m'Donoghoe M'Awhe, of the Logharde,
Teralagh reaghe m'Molowyne M'Kanedie, of Kalogh, co. Limerick,
yeoman, Bryan m'Mahowne M'Kanedie, of same, Donogh carragh
m'Teralagh M'Conoghor, of Craighbeg, same co., yeoman, Owen
O Halynane, of Cloughketyne, same co., and Shane M'Hebert,
of Carrygoginill, same co., yeomen, Margaret Coddie, of Pillowne,
co. Wexford, Thady O Day, of Carrigoginill, co. Limerick,
husbandman, Tho. Hurly fitz Wm., of Knockangie, same co.,
Tho. O Marroghoe, of Ballencbruher, same co., yeoman, James
fitz Tho. Roohe, of Aheghayrayn, co. Cork, Henry Houghe, of
Faningstown, same co., yeoman, Uwin m'Donoghoe roe,
Conoghor O Hogane, Joan Lacie, of Bruris, Wm. Whelan, of
Waterford, and Katherine Whelan, of same. Provisions as in
5367.—14 April, xxxii.

5407 (4418.) Grant (under queen's letter, 21 March, xxxi.) to John
Bleeke, gent.; of the office of constable and keeper of the walls
of Limerick. To hold during good behaviour, with the usual
fees as Andrew Wyse, Rich. Chichester, Hercules Rayneforde,
or Rob. Longe had. Not to be removed as in 4976.—14 April,
xxxii.

5408 (4344.) Lease (under commission, 4 July, xxx.) to Rich.
Netterviald, esq.; of the rectories of Holicke, Clonings, Rathcoule,
Ballinelackin, Mogowrn alias Mougaure, Colmane, Drongane,
Fethard, Athfaghe, Railerston, Pepperton, Skaddanston, Crampston,
Cowlagh, and Ballinure, co. Tipperary; parcels of land in
Cowlaghe, Pepperton, Moyganre, Drongane, Cloninge, Crampston,
Rathcowrthe alias Rathcoule, Fetherd, Colman, Kilconnell,
and Ballinna alias Ballinure, co. Tipperary; glebe land and
tithes of the rectory of Straffan, and 30s. yearly to be paid by
the vicar as a portion of the altarages, co. Kildare, 8s. yearly
out of a house in Cock-street, in Dublin, a house with appurtenances
in Navan, co. Meath, and land in Almoneston, co.
Louth, possessions of the late hospital of S. John the Baptist
without the Newgate of Dublin. To hold for 21 years. Rent,
£55 12s. 11d. Provided that he shall not alien his interest
without license under the great seal, nor let to any except they
be of English nation both by father and mother, and shall not
levy coyne or livery.—15 April, xxxii.

5409 (4413.) Lease (under queen's letter, 1 July, xxxi.) to Henry
Sheffyelde, gent.; of the market place in Athlone as in 4941
(rent, 6s.); the tithe lambs and fish of the rectory of Portravon
(leased in 5082) (30s.); land in Inchemacoudder, and Tymollinbegg.

co. Kildare (leased in 3377) (8s.); the lands of Newcastle and Rathtowe alias Rathcoon, co. Wexford, (leased in 916) (40s.); the globe and tithes of the rectory of Straffan, as leased in 5408 (£11 5s. 4d.); the house of friars preachers of Glannoure, co. Cork with appurtenances (leased in 3319) (15s.); lands of Corkaghe, and tithes of Corkaghe and Stablerstoun in the parish of Balloygho, and the tithe corn of Horigeston in the parish of Tymoghoe, co. Kildare (leased in 3206) (£4); the rectory of Ennaskoye, co. Westmeath, (leased to Elis Jans, 10 Feb., 1583) (rent, £9 6s. 8d.); the globe of the rectory of Ardrollicke, with the tithe corn of Moyfine alias Moyane (leased in 3168) (18s.); lands in Moygaddie, co. Meath, (leased in 3323) (2s. 8d.); a messuage two cottages and a garden in Granok, co. Meath, late in the tenure of John Mannaghan, deceased (leased in No. 1794), (13s. 4d.). To hold for 31 years from the end of the several recited interests, at the rents above noted. Provisions as in 4939.—17 April, xxxii.

5410 (4437.) Grant (under letter of English privy council, 23 Jan., 1589) to Rich. Kinwellmershe, of Dublin, gent.; of the office of clerk of the market throughout Ireland. To hold during good behaviour. With power to enquire by the oaths of good and lawful men, of all artificers and tradesmen who falsely exercise their trade by using false weights and measures or other deceptive means, or who forestall or regrate contrary to the statute against grey merchants or otherwise; and to commit them to gaol until they pay the fines imposed by him; certifying the names of the delinquents, and the fine, to the Exchequer. Annual fee, £10 English. The Exchequer to make him allowance for his expenses.—22 April, xxxii.

5411 (4391.) Pardon to Hugh O Lallore, of Tenahencie, in the barony of Symolins, co. Katerlagh, husbandman, and John or Shane O Canoran, of (   ) in Queen's co. Provisions as in 5382.—24 April, xxxii.

5412 (4392.) Pardon to Morrogh m'Turlogh M'Soine alias na martt, Donell m'Rory O Donoghowe, Shane m'Moriertagh I Moroghowe, Baholagh m'Carbary M'Egan, Owen m'Shane Iline, Rory oge O Donoghowe, Donogh m'Dermide I Howllvan, Fenyn m'Donogh M'Awley, Donogh m'Fenyn M'Awley, Teige m'Fenin M'Awley, Dermot m'Donogh I Dowgan, Darmot m'Melaghlin I Dowgan, Owen m'Moriertagh M'Enoghemer, Donell m'Shane I Riverdan, Owen m'Donogh M'Owen, Cnoghour m'Rory I Donoghawe, Shane m'Dermot I Howllvan, Taig m'Dermot I Hollvan. Security as in 4943, in co. Cork and Limerick.—28 April, xxxii.

5413 (4421.) Grant to Wm. Dongan, gent.; of the office of clerk of the first fruits or remembrancer and receiver of the first fruits, tithes, and twentieth parts of spiritual benefices; with an annual fee of £10. To hold during good behaviour, as John Clerk or any other held. Not to be removed, as in 4976.—28 April, xxxii.

5414 (4422.) Grant to Philip Williams; of the office of clerk of the market throughout Ireland. To hold during good behaviour, as in 5410.—28 April, xxxii.

5415 (4364.) Pardon to Edw. Everson; for the robbery of 20 sheep. Security as in 4943, in King's co.—4 May, xxxii.

H 2

1590.   FIANTS.—ELIZABETH.

5416 (4412.) Lease (under commission, 17 Feb., xxx.) to Rice
Ap Hughe, esq.; of the tithes of Riagheston, Clintonrathe,
Cardenston, Tullaghakillie, and Moreton, the tithes of the
Newetone, and Rathe beside Termonfeighen, the tithes of
Tollogborde, Miletone beside Termonfeighen, and Galrothistone,
the tithes of Karristone, Priorton, and Newehouse, the tithes
of Thomastone, Gilbertestone, Dromeleke, the Miltons, Nysely-
rath, Tollaghes, Aghclints, Stephenstone, and Gibbeston Palmer,
possessions of the monastery of Louth, co. Louth. To hold for
21 years. Rent, £33 6s. 8d. Provisions as in 5343.—4 May,
xxxii.

5417 (4341.) Lease (under queen's letter, 5 Aug., xxxi.) to George
Greame, gent.; of the site of the hospital of S. John of the
Nass, co. Kildare, and its possessions as in No. 1354, also
land in Tristeldermot. Recites 1354. To hold for 30 years
from the end of the interests in being. Rent, £40 5s. 6d.
Maintaining two English horsemen, or paying yearly at Evan,
co. Kildare, 40 pecks of corn, which, at 2s. a peck, will be allowed
for in the rent. Provisions as in 5311. In consideration of
his good service in the realm for 27 years.—6 May, xxxii.

5418 (4365.) Pardon to Manus m'Edm. oge M'Shahie alias Manus
Neglegan, Manus oge m'Morogh m'Edm. M'Shihie, Wm. m'Owen
M'Shihie, Wm. m'Donnogh M'Shihie, Wm. m'Shane M'Shihie,
Dermott m'Wm. M'Shihie, Morrogh m'Morirtagh M'Shihie,
Molmory m'Colloy M'Shihie, Roris m'Cahill M'Shihie, Rory
m'Manus oge M'Shihie, Morrogh duff m'Wm. M'Shihie, Shane
O Conor alias Gillilaff m'Donell, Morrish m'Richard Maune,
Wm. fitz Nich. Maune, Morrish ne Puttoge O Toughill,
Moritagh m'Tho. M'Kenraght, Shane m'Rory more O Toughill,
Mahowne og M'Kenrathe, Shane m'Patrick Voulfe, Stephen
fitz Nicholas Sarfiell, Gerrod og m'Garrod lea M'Gibbon, Maw-
howne m'Donnoll Eine Iwaddigan, Mahowne m'Donnell M'Kil-
larce alias Gillarce, Connor m'Philip m'Connor m'Shane Cleiry
M'Kenney, Tho. m'Philip m'Connor m'Shane Clarry M'Kenny
Dermond O Duney m'Shane O Connor, Connor m'Morirtagh
Ieghie alias Iffhinghe, Owen boy M'Kyllycollom, Donnell boy
O Calhan, Morirtagh m'Donnell M'Gillerogh alias Gillerieveigh,
Wm. m'Donnogh O Hannanne, Donnogh roe O Griffen, Don-
nogh duff O Quine, Manus m'Moroghowe m'Shane M'Conry,
Rich. m'Edm. Carron alias Carewe, Gerrod m'Rich. m'Rob.
M'Morrishe, Donnell Tlevy U'Connor, Gerrod m'Tho. M'Nicholas,
Shane Tlevy m'Brien O Roddir, Tho. mantagh M'Eanraght,
Tirrelogh m'Donnell O Quynegan, Edm. m'Philip Eoullen
M'Gibbon, Teig m'Shane Magwier, Rory O Buyll, Philip m'Edm.
Magwyer, Dermond O Canenan alias Taylar Fian, and Evan
m'Wm. O Quynggan. Security as in 4043, in co. Limerick.—
9 May, xxxii.

5419 (4372.) Pardon to Matthew Crosse, and Connor Crosse, of
Adamstone, co. Westmeath, husbandmen. Provisions as in
5382.—10 May, xxxii.

5420 (4389.) Pardon to Connor M'Donnough, of Ballindowne,
Carbaris M'Donnough, Tumulltagh M'Donnoghe, of same, Teige
O Hegen, of Dowgherne, Shane M'Donnogh, of Cowlan, Mc-
laughlan M'Donnough, of Cowronye, Moraugh M'Donnough,
Deurmonde M'Donnough, of same, Dermond O Dowde (of)

1590. FIANTS.—ELIZABETH.

Downslin, Shane glass M'Donnough, of Cowlrony, Hugh M'Donnogh, of Castleloughdargan, Teige oge M'Donnough, of Cowles, Ferdorsugh, Fergananym, Rory, and Brian M'Donnoghe, of same, Rory O Dowde, of Downeslin, Feraugh, Donell, Shane glasse, Connor, and Dahie O Dowde, of same, Ferall O Kyvan, Connor O Corrhan, of same, Donell m'Shane boy, of Ballomererenoghe, Shane oge O Harie, Rory keaghe O Harie, of same, Owen O Connor, of Dowrecho-lue, Teige boie O Connor, of Totample, Connor meroghe O Con-nor, Donnell aroone O Connor, of same, Brian O Dowde, of Yskerowen, Donnough O Dowde, Shane glasse O Dowde, of same, Shane oge O Garie, of Knockmare, Brian oge O Gary, Dualtaugh O Garie, Connor oge O Garie, of same, Manus M'Rorie, of Bonenaldon, Cormack M'Rorie, Shane M'Skreldsn, Hugh boye O Corvolan, of same, Cahill M'Hugh, of Ballin-downe, Cahill oge m'Cahill, of same, Tumaltagh m'Owen duff, of Gortanomery, Teige boy, Owen duff, and Donnall m Tumul-tagh, of same, Tirlagh M'Keally, of Cowlen, Rorie O Hellie, of same, Carberrie O Hellie, of same, Donnough m Teige O Hary, of Girannge, Gyllochriste keaghe O Harie, Owen and Molrony O Harie, of same, Ferall M'Rorie, of Bonenaldon, Wm. Toth, of same, Wm. granie O Harie, of Downislie, Donnough oge O Harie, Shane O Harie, of same, Phelim O Connor, of Skardon, Shane O Connor, Rory O Connorda, Owen O Connor, of same, Cormack M'Donnoghe, of Loghnogowye, Cahill M'Donnough, of same, Edm. M'Dearmonde roe, of Dirremore, and Tumultagh M'Der-monde roe, of same, in co. Sligaughe. Provisions as in 5382.—27 May, xxxii.

5421 (4388.) Pardon to Shane O Kally, of Mollaghe, Feagh O Kelly, of Mallaghmore, Wm. M'Brian, of Craguin, Shane M'William, of Carroulene, Melaughlan oge, Conhour M'Shane, Gillernow M'Thomas, Toige M'Connell, of same, Gyllernow boys, of Lis-karye, Teige M'Keigan, of Cloncomuske, Brian M'Keagan, of same, Hugh O Kankaroine, of Kiltollaughe, Edm. oge, of Islande, Teige oge O Kellie, of Daggaine, Tho. cron O Kenkovelne, of Faddan, Connor O Callen, of Moltaghe, Shane O Raghter, of same, Donnough O Manin, of Lyamolle, Gilleduff M'Cahill, of Liskarie, Cahell M'Connor, of same, Brynn O Kellys m'Connor oge, Teige O Kellye m'Connor oge, Rory caraghe O Fihelie, late of Athenrye, and Shane O Molconrie, of Mallaghamore, in co. Galway. Pro-visions as in 6382.—1 June xxxii.

5422 (5595.) License to William Bath, of Athcarne, second justice English of the Common Pleas, assignee of John Parker, esq.; to alienate to any, being English by both parents, the site of the priory of Duleeke, Arborbusuh, Langanan, Westerparke, the common green of Duleake, Castalcott, the Cowepark, a culverhouse, Boglas, the Smythes meadow, pasture by the town of Langford, land on the east of the Neweton, and on the south of Caranston, cottages and land in Dulaka, the College yard, the Culverhouse park, land on the north of the church of Duleke, the Foxe parke, a field full of ashes 32 years growing. Atkins acre, pasture on the south of Smyth's meadow, in Duleke, and the Mandlyn meadow in Duleke, parcel of the possessions of the priory of Lanthony in England, held under lease 622.—3 June, xxxii.

5423 (4368.) Pardon to Doghdaly O Kelly, of Belaghmartoregh, Margaret Kelly, Tho. M'Glyn, Wm. douff M'Glyne, Morertagh

1580.   FIANTS.—ELIZABETH.

O Hanyn, Grany ny Hanyn, of same, Edm. oge M'Edmond, of
Lesnamnamahy, Melaghlin M'Brasell, Wm. M'Brasell, of same,
Phelyn oge Dowle, Connor O Naghten, of Moynare, Hugh
O Naghten, of Kreoghane, Teig m'Hugh O Naghten, of same,
Donyle karregh O Naghten, of Ardkeyvane, Connor m'Manyse
O Naghten, Mylaghlin m'Manyse, Teig m'Teig O Naghten, of
same, Teig m'Shane M'Edmond, of Darrowkey, Moryah M'James,
of Ballykreggan, Donagh O Naghten, of Clonnake, Connor m'Edm.
O Kelly, of Kowlgarie, Donaltegh M'Kelkanye, of Kowlekaldryn,
Brien M'Dowle, of Corsegey, Phynan M'Moltaller, of Carow-
darree, Edm. M'Downey, of Kerrowkeylen, Farraigh O Ryrn, of
Porterrin, Gilpatrick kyogh M'Kerryla, Irell M'Moltally, of
Benwycke, Hugh O Morishe, of Kregan grogoy, Shane boy
M'Brian, of the Kayloghe, Donell M'Melaghlin, of Belashanvoy,
Koliye M'Keogh, of Ardmolan, Owen grane M'Enelle, of Down-
garr, Donyle, Fardoregh, and Shane M'Enellee, of same, Oray
Morvarnegh, of same, Donegh m'Hobart oge, of Molackan, James
Fitz Jeffrey, of Ballym'Moregh, Donegh m'Donyll O Kelly, of
Clonloyn, Rory karrogh M'Phylye, carpenter, and Shane O Laghan,
of Cloghan keyrye.   Security as in 4043, in co. Roscommon.—4
June, xxxii.

5424 (4343.) Lease (under queen's letter, [5 Oct.], xxx.) to Edw.
English. Button; of the reversion of tolls of the market of Trime, as
leased by 3376; three small parks in Kilmainhame, co. Dublin
(leased by 3323); Ballicaslane Omoye and other lands in Queen's
co. (leased by 5147); the tithe corn of Downings and Karangh,
co. Kildare, possessions of the late hospital of S. John of Jerusalem
in Ireland (leased by Oswald Massingberde, knt., prior, 17 Jan.
1559, to Edm. Devenishe, of Dublin, merchant), the site and
possessions of the house of friars of Inche of Clonramate, co.
Clare (leased by 4738); the site and possessions of the priory of
"S. Thomas" (recte the priory of Thome) in co. Tipperary
(leased by 3355); the lands of Tobberrogane, parcel of the lands
of James Eustace, viscount Baltinglas, attainted; a messuage and
garden in the parish of S. Nicholas in the church of S. Patrick,
in the suburbs of Dublin (leased by 3552).   To hold for 60 years
from the end of the interests in being.   Rent £30 6s. 8d.—6
June, xxxii.

5425 (4429.) Grant to John Abbott, gent.; of the wardship and
marriage of Deanos, son and heir of Patrick Conwaye; and
custody of his lands.   To hold during minority.   Rent 5s., of
which 1s. may be retained for maintenance of the minor.   Fine
5s.—[10 June, xxxii.]   (*Record Commissioners' Catalogue.*)

5426 (4448.) Lease (under queen's letter, 12 Aug., xxxii.) to sir
English. Patr. Barnewall, of Grneedewe, co. Dublin, knt.; of the town
and rectory of Marterye, co. Meath, parcel of the possessions of
the late house of S. John of Jerusalem in Ireland.   To hold for
40 years from the expiration of a lease to Wm. Hill (see 3296).
Rent, £15 4s. 8d.   Also 15 ruinous messuages with gardens in
the town of Molingaro, a park called a faigh, near the king's
highway called Bater Sagre, a meadow called Garnell alias
Lannaghmore, a parcel of land lying from the Spitle house of
Molingare to the water of Rathonell, near the king's highway,
possessions of the late prior of Molingare, co. Westmeath.   The
island of Inchemore, in the Loghrie and in parts of the river
Shennon, the islands of Inchahigen, Incheloughrene, Calannishe

alias Inchecalla, Inchenenagh, and Inchekerbeg Dermid, in the Loghrie, possessions of the monastery of Inchemore alias Incheloughren, co. Roscommon. The lands of Ardnefadle alias Ardnaffaddan, co. Galway, Graunge Neaghrie Rannagh, and Aghrime, with a chapel called Moore Aghrime, Cosballie and Tawnaghe, Uranbeg, the Graunge of Cowleraghe, Knocknemanagh in Clanricarde, Cowloortin in the barony of Teaqeane, Drishaghan, Doffish beside Gallwaye, co. Galway, Ballyworrie alias Ballymurrie, Clonsallie and Clonknawa, co. Roscommon, with portion of their tithes as in 1219, possessions of the monastery of Collis Victorie alias Knockmoy. To hold for 60 years from the end of any existing lease. Rent, £33 2s. 7½d. Provisions as in 4939.—11 June, xxxii.

5427 (4367.) Pardon to Donell O Hanlye, gent., Rory boie O Hanlie, Gillernow O Hanlie, Fergananim O Hanlie, Teige m'Wm. O Hanlie, Hugh m'Owen O Hanlie, Uin keagh O Hanlie, Melaughlen modder O Hanlie, and his brother, Gillernow m'Langhlen carragh O Hanlie, Duoltagh m'Laughlen O Hanlie, Dermot dorragh m'Laughlen carraugh O Hanlie, Teige, Fergananim, and Hugh m'Laughlen bane O Hanlie, and Rory boie m'Ferriaghe O Hanlie, gentlemen, Dermond duf O Hanlie m'Edm. knighe m'Gillealin, Odne m'Ego M'Grime, Dermond m'Dunlaghe O Hanlie, gent., Fergananim m'Duoltagh O Hanlie, Teige and Fergananim m'Edm. duf O Hanlie, Teige, Dermonid, and Shane M'Ganleie, gentlemen, Ferrall M'Egoe, Connor M'Ego, Hugh M'Egoe, Melaughlen glass M'Egoe, Gille Duff and Melaughlen m'Tho. carrie M'Ego, Donnell M'Skallie, Manus M'Kelleguile, of Clon lragh, Hugh, Ferdorragh, and Shane M'Kelloguille, Laughlen duff M'Bellan, Teige, Donnagh, and Manus M'Bellan, Donnongh M'Neile, Hugh O Heveryne, Ferahdie O Morrey, Geoffrey m'Edm. M'Brian, of same, Connor boy M'Brenan, of Inmagallaghe, Hugh m'Connor boy, of same, Brian m'Conn M'Brenan, of Triell, Jeffrey m'Edm. duff M'Annonny, of Kellennenan, Wm. m'Edm. duff M'Annonany, Melaughlen M'Annonany, of same, Brian m'Une M'Brenan, of Clonfrere, Cahelle m'Une, of same, Donnogh m'Teige M'Edmond, of Lishew, Connor m'Laughlen m'Teige M'Edmond, of same, Ferall, Melaughlen, and Patrick M'Grain, Dermot O Sharvan, Gilleduff M'Geline, Enoxu, Donnell, and Teige m'Rorsie O Hanleie, Rich. fitz Christopher, and James M'Keadie, of Caconvilleie, in co. Roscommon. Provisions as in 5332.—17 June, xxxii.

5428 (4574.) Appointment of sir John Norrels, knt., president of [English:] Mounster; as general of the army, especially in the province of Mounster, in the absence of the lord deputy. With power to punish with fire and sword all enemies and rebels; to raise the queen's subjects, to form the ablest people of Mounster into bands, appoint officers, and arm them from the queen's munition, to complete the fortifications in that province. To execute martial law, and treat with and pardon rebels. To take victual and forage at usual rates. Recites the prevalence of rumours of an invasion by foreign enemies.—23 June, xxxii.

5429 (4449.) Livery to James O Ferrall, son and heir of Donald or Donell Evnugherie O Ferrall, late of Granarde, co. Longford, gent. Fine, £6 17s. 6d. sterling.—25 June, xxxii.

1590.   FIANTS.—ELIZABETH.

5430 (4384.) Pardon to Lawghlin O Birne, of Kilmore, Rory
    boy M'Gillerdoger, Brian hane O Faroll, Laughlin garrowe
    M'Mewlecke, Shan ro M'Mealcnke, Wm. grane M'Mealecke,
    Owen M'Mealecke, Moris ro M'Mealcke, Brien carragh
    M'Gillerdoger, Skmely ny Birne, Katherine ny Birne, Brasell
    M'Donell, of Cregan sallaghin, and Shane Cloghan, of Cloghan.
    Security as in 4948, in co. Roscoman.—30 June, xxxii.
5431 (4425.) Grant to Henry Piers, gent.; of the office of seneschal
    of the Daltons' country in Westmeath. To hold during good
    behaviour. With power to assemble the inhabitants for defence,
    to punish malefactors according as the common laws allow, and
    to parl with traitors and malefactors. He shall receive the
    following duties yearly under the name of seneschal's fee:—
    From each ploughland, not being free, 6s. 8d., at Lammas, or in
    default a cow; from the sept of Sleight Morish, that is to say,
    on Ballinragh and Conrey and Croghold, and the rest of their
    lands, 10s.; from the sept of Henry Dalton, of Pierston, 10s.;
    from O Daly, two beeves; from Ballinlogher, 6s. 8d.; from
    Ballintine (not in the country), 6s. 8d.; from the Clancowers, two
    beeves; also the lands of Moyveroo, two ploughlands, which be-
    longed to the captainship, and for every bloodshed or fray, 6s. 8d.;
    these duties being almost identical with those formerly paid to
    the captain. See No. 1618 (where the words in brackets may be
    supplied as two meals). He shall hold a court baron.—1 July,
    xxxii.
5432 (4388.) Pardon to Brian O Flannegan m'Edm. O Flanagan,
    of Ballarrevy, Allyne M'Dowyle m'Moyllmury M'Dowyle, of
    Ballyning, Alexander, Tarlagh, and Phelim M'Dowyle, of same,
    Kollye M'Dowla, Teig m'Allyne M'Dowylo, Saverly M'Koanne,
    Teig Ettnavio m'Rory boy, Teig M'Koanne, Edm. M'Koanne,
    Moylle M'Gillyelo, Koaune m'Connor boy, of same, Hulbart
    M'Owen, (of) Killtrustan, Connor m'Hubart M'Owen, of same,
    Hugh m'Tierlagh fonre, of Aughe, Shane M'Gillokolle, of
    Ballyny, Sawe M'Kiggan, of Lyahyughta, Terrelagh ogo
    M'Terlagho, of Anagh, Konue m'Kallagho O Connor, of
    Clouvisory, Dermod O Jimdagnu, of Ballyany, Mollrouny
    m'Tomoltagh M'Owen, of Clounfry, Moyllaghlin boy
    M'Eughigny, of Clonybiruo, Loghlin Naknrlly, of Skavage,
    Hugh O Narie m'Nieh., of Kelltyntawyne, Doaltagh m'Brian
    O Connor, of Nalarehie, Cormock m'Trige Mngauly, of Clona-
    kahna, Hawe m'Cormock Mugonly, of same, Mewo nyne
    Phelino roe, of Nalanehio, Edm. m'Edm. M'Chahell, of
    Towmackranell, Teig ogo O Flannegan, of Cortmohau, Malaghlin
    O Flanegan, of Clouylaywan, Wm. ogo O Flannegan, of Dry-
    sigham, Hewe O Flanuegan, of Clonekeran, Teig m'Teig O Flane-
    gan, of Gortmighan, Doultagh O Flannegan, of Clonybriman,
    Connor O Flanegan, Donell O Moran, Owin O Moran m'Rory,
    of same, Sheary M'Countolly, of Clonykaran, Donagh O Mor-
    aghan, of Clonybrinan, Shano O Connor, of Clouybye, James
    O Narie, of Killockine, Wm. m'Tirlagh O Flannegan, of
    Bellalotar, Ferginamynne O Flannegan, Edm. m'Tarlagh
    O Flannegan, of same, Teig m'Cosmy O Flannegan, of Garyduf,
    Hewe m'Cosmy O Flannegan, of same, Cahell O Moran, of
    Bellacrivy, Shane Etomyne, of same, Shane m'Melaghlin bane,
    of Hany, Owen O Moran m'Hewe, of Bellacrivio, Doultagh

m'Philim boy, of Annaghe, Phelim oge m'Phelim boy, Rory
m'Phelim boy, of same, Mannea keaghe M'Eneriny, of
Lishione, Donell M'Eneriny, of same, Brian O Flannagan
m'Brian, of Garriduf, Owen oge M'Dowyle, of Lishtallinardan,
Terlagh M'Dowyle, Gilleduf M'Dowyle, Cahell ogo O Fyny,
Taig O Finy, Taig roe M'Gillekole, of same, Taig roe O Birne,
(of) Kenalenn, Brian m'Teig roe, Tomeltagh m'Teig roe, of
same, Hugh duf m'Rory boy, of Lishtallinardan, Cormock
carrogh O Bradigan, of same, Connor O Hanley, of Gortmighan,
Connor m'Teig bore, of Anaugh, Fallim carrogh m'Connor
O Connor, of same, Edm. O Narie m'Nish., Cormock Brian
Gilleguly, Shane grane M'Bronan, Owen boy M'Bronan, Farrall
Makarrill, Connor M'Gillemardine, Taig oge O Moran, Darmought
reagh m'Terlagh boy, Coughe O Maddyn, in co. Galway, gent.,
Morogh reagh O Maddyn, of Clare, Donagh M'Awloy, of
Clonylohean, Toig kewgh O Kelly, of Clonbrock, Donnell
O Kelly, his son, Brian O Kellie m'Connor oge, Taig
O Kellie m'Connor oge, Laughlin bane O Molullye, Hubbert
Browne m'Edm., Wm. M'Laughline, Cawea reagh ne Mary, of
Ardlovinge, in co. Clare, Furginanyme M'Ne marie, of Kilcornan,
Teig M'Ne marie, of Ballalinshen, Shyde Neill M'Ne mary, and
Shane m'Teige M'Ne marie.   Security as in 4943, in coa. Ros-
common, Galway, Clare, Mayo, or Sligo.—1 July, xxxii.

5483 (4350.) Pardon to Manows m'Shane O Roirke, of Tullie,
Phellim O Roirke, of Cloncorireke, Chaier O Roirke, Loughlin
O Roirke, Hugh M'Kiggan, Cormock M'Courrin, of same,
Wm. oge M'Courrin, of Droumbreaniahe, Brian M'Connor, of
Droumbillough, Donnell M'Courrin, of Aughemoroo, Dermovate
M'Courrin, Gilpatrick M'Connor, of same, Conn O Roirke, of
Tullie, Owen M'Curin, Melaughlin duff M'Curin, of same,
Chaiell M'Curin, of Droumgoillia, Shane M'Curin, of same,
Parras M'Kiggan, of Monlledarough, Hew, Manows, and Ferrell
M'Kiggan, of same, Brian M'Owen, of Dooroo, Dermovate
M'Ourine, of Behahie, Manows duffe M'Ourine, Owen O Hiselan,
of same, Malaughlin M'Kiggan, of Tullie, Cormock M'Kiggan,
of Beahie, Teig M'Curin, of Aughmoroo, Shane reavagh, of
Tullie, Dernovate M'Kiggan, of same, Brian roe M'Ourine, of
Droumbranlishe, Brinn O Roirke, of Tullie, Tornan O Roirke,
of Cloncoorieke, Cormonak M'Curin, of Tullie, Farrall M'Lisse,
of Ardmoynen, and Moulmourre boy M'Shea.   Provisions as in
5382.—2 July, xxxii.

5484 (4385.) Pardon to Errill O Garye, of Moy, chief of his name,
Fergonaynim O Garye, Toige O Garrie, Rory O Garrie, Brian
O Garrie, Brian dorough m'Donogh grany, Tho. duffe, of same,
Hugh O Hart, of Bradsollie, Hugh oge O Hart, Phellim, Rory,
and Donogh m'Hugh O Harte, Ambrose Kharee, Donogh grauy
O Harte, Neile O Harte. Connor O Hart, Phelim revagh
O Harte, of same, Taige O Harte, of Grandge, Teige oge O Harte,
of Downfoure, Phellim O Harte, of same, Rorie ballagh O Harte,
of Ardstermon, Wm. O Harte, of same, Parlan O Scannill, Teigu
oge O Connor, of Craigravagha, Hugh M'Swine, of Bonneyn,
Deirmot O Harie, of Moynleagh, Taige M'Donogh, of Bohi,
Teige O Banoehan, of same, Teige O Harie, of Fullinefanoghe,
Donogh O Harie, of Claonyn, Dowalltagh M'Swine, of Ardno-
glasse, Henry O Oreran, of Sligoe, Sowerly O Harte, of same,

1590.   FIANTS.—ELIZABETH.

Dermot M'Enanhie, of Balleddaraewon, Shane glasse M'Donogh, of Ballenogbegg, Alexander M'Swyne, of Dromgrania, Cahill oge M'Donogh, of Ballinoashell, Tomolltagh M'Donogh, of same, Donnell O Connor, of Larraeke, Cahill M'Enyllie, of Ymlagh. faddie, Connor M'Enyllie, of same, Manus revagh m Taige boy, of. Killtofaddie, Telgo O Gronogan, of Bonnenaddan, Arhille O Griffe, Tho. Bonrke, Cormuck O Banochan, of Clonomahiu, Dowalltagh O Banochan, Hugh O Banochan, of same, Hugh M'Donogh, of Killtofaddie, Taige, Tumolltagh, and Brian M'Donogh, of same, Tumolltagh morree M'Donogh, of Cowles, Cormuck O Coman, of Tullye, Tha. O Say, Moihmorrye M'Der-moddie, Brian O Higan, Wm. O Gigan, of same, Kedagh M'Gilleghamharoe, of Tamplavunyn, Donnoll O Flim, of Dromgrania, Cahill O Flim, of same, Manus m'Brien revagh, of Bonemaidan, Deirmot m'Brien revagh, Shane M'Brchewna, of same, Erovan M'Swyne, of Ballenspurr, Mollmory M'Swyn, of Clonbamagh. Wm. O Ohorrhan, of Coorte, and Hugh O Corrhan, of same, Wm. O Harie, of Castlecarragh, Shane grany O Harie, of Braydoollym, Fardorarough O Harie, of Downfware, Teig O Griffe, of same; co. Sligo. Provisions as in 5382.—2 July, xxxii.

5435 (4386.) Pardon to Edm. Kelly fitz Hugh, of the Cloghar, co Galway, Feagh, Teig, and William O Kelly fitz Hugh, of same, Shane M'Moultally, Hugh M'Multally, Donnell m'Rory O Donnellan, of same, Donnogh m'Brien M'Donnogh, of Carnagh, Edw. M'Collei, of Coumbeigin, Donnogh M'Koghow, of Rakell, Markius M'Cownen, of Castellnove, Conkorey m'Hngh oge, in co. Roscoman, Edm. moyle M'Tiege, Rosse M'Mallaghlin, of Balleihaghan, co. Clare, Owen carragh m'Gillyduff M'Donnogh, of Kilbride, co. Galway, and Wm. oge m'Hugh oge, in co. Roscoman. Security as in 4043.—7 July, xxxii.

5436 (4438.) Livery to Robert O Naghten, grandson and heir of John or Shane O Naghten, late of Mynure in the country called the Fass, co. Roscommon, gent. Fine 38s. 4d.—8 July, xxxii.

5437 (4348.) Pardon to Donnall M'Farroy, of Bure, co. Roscommon, gent., Sheane ley O Dolau, husbandman, Kearrowle O Daley, tailor, Nich. O Harreghdane, shoemaker, Donnell O Gallvan, labourer, Gillerniwe M'Gay, carpenter, Shean O Galvane, and Donnall O Dolane, labourers, all of same place. Security as in 4943.—9 July, xxxii.

5438 (4360.) Pardon to Connor og O Kellia, of Cowilnegeyor, co. Roscommon, gent., Durryny Viodonnall, his wife, Collo m'Walter bane M'Dowill, of same, Alexander m'Donogho M'Dowill, of Ballynaregan, Donogho og m'Donogho M'Cormooke, of Cowillaegeyr, Owin M'Lenagh, of same, Mollaghlin m'Wm. M'Moriartagh, of Castle Brade, Wm. carragh m'Donogho M'Dowill, of Knonkerrosbary, and Dermot O Maynine, of Cowilnegeir, karns, Oliver Burke, of same, gent, Tho. reongh O Leyna, of Ballmobanabe, cottingar, Nich. O Kennovan, of same, husbandman, Jamag m'Waltar roe, of Ballilin, kern, Owen O Fahye, of Karowchyrn, yeoman, Dowaltagh m'Dermot roy, of Loghan-ovama, Brian m'Dowaltagh M'Diermot, Owin m'Dowaltagh M'Dermot, of same, Manus m'Edm. m'Diermot roya, of Fernan, Teg reogh m'Diermot grana, of Mollaghnacronaighta, and Tomaltagh M'Conchor, of Corderre, gentleman, Brien keagh m'Thomas og.

1590.   FIANTS.—ELIZABETH.

of Dromennealette, kern, Shane m'Geoffrey M'Tiernan, of Logh-rodda, gent., Teig m'Donogho O Cowan, of Ardklern, husb., Carbre O Birne, of Dowgan, Connor O Birne, and Gillidaff O Birne, of same, gentlemen, Donogho M'Phelim, of Row, and Shane m'Melaghlin glas, of Cartron, yeomen, Rory M'Dowill, of Grang, husb., Benvy M'Conchor, of Bowhie, Rory carragh M'Farrill, of same, carpenter, Donnell M'Melaghlin alias M'Moriertie, of Kilkachell, husb., Cormock O Hikia, of Glanne-gaillagh, gent., Donell bane O Haigan, of Balledowana, labourer, Any duff ny M'Evroone, of Owylnagere, Onora ny Cowill, of Knockbryangarrowe, Donogh oge O Naghtyne, cf Kiarrownlk eny, Melaghlin O Kelly, of Clonbrick, in co. Galway, and Egnehan O Kelly, of same. Security as in 1913, in co. Roscommon.—9 July, xxxii.

5438 (6301.) Pardon to Donnell O Rourke, of Loghdoncorre, Rorie M'Cabba, of Laghnecou, Tirlanghe M'Cabba, Melaughlen M'Cabba, Cahier M'Caba, and Alexardar M'Caba, of same, Colle M'Caba, of Loghdoncorrey, Hugh M'Cabba, Melaughlen M'Cabba, of same, Brian M'Gillekyne, of Killmyne, Malanghlin and Teige M'Gille-kyne, of same, Shane M'Gillekyne, of Kilfegh, Donnell M'Gille-kennle, of same, Donnough M'Cabba, of Loghdoncorre, Donnough m'Jeames M'Cabla, Fale M'Cabba, of same, Connor O Rourk, of Dromeheure, Farrell O Rourke, Melaughlen O Rourke, of same, Tirelaugh O Rourk, of Drominchan, Con and Oaell O Rourke, of same, Brian O Rourk, of Lawchell, Conghe and Laughlen O Rourk, of same, Laughlen bane O Rourke, of Killenemarne, Owen O Rourke, of Corglasse, Shane O Rourke, of same, Shane O Rourke, of Aghnill, Cahier O Rourk, of same, Owen O Rourke, of Cloghbaghe, Melaughlen O Rourke, of same, Fardorragh O Rourke, of Erocroese, Teige and Shane O Rourke, of same, Laughlen M'Carnick, of Malkester, Teige M'Cormick, of same, Conaugh M'Caggan, of Dromile, Fergus M'Caggan, of same, Oaell M'Caggan, of Corglass, James M'Morrese, of Dromile, Teige O Rourke, of Cawlohie, Carberric M'ne Gawne, of same, Connor M'ne Gawne, of Lowche, Doghe dallcy O Rourke, of Cowlohie, Shane and Fardorraghe M'Hoyne, of Mannenne, Gilpatrick M'Hoine, of Loghen, Owen O Rourke, of Loghnoofe, Geoffrey O Rourk, of Lishnolfo, Laughlen O Rourke, of Aughtowne, Shane O Rourke, of Loughnecoufe, Owen O Rourk, of same, Teige O Rourke, of Kildamne, Brien O Rourke, of Dromrean, Arte O Rourke, of Kilgirre, Ternan O Rourk, of Lexhnetollaghie, Hugh O Rourke, of Aghtowne, Conghe O Rourke, of Mayo, Brian, Teige, and Geoffrey O Rourke, of same, Donnell go O Rourke, Pharragh O Rourke, of Leetawne, Owlerighte O Rourke, of Leacolfo, Pharragh M'Gillemichell, of Cashelrage, Teige oge and Donnough M'Gillemichell, of same, Melaughlen M'Gillemichell, of Camaghe, Owen oreone M'Gillemichell, of same, Owen roe M'Gillemichell', of Castelrage, Teige O Rourke, of Loghnecoufe, Ternan O Rourke, of Killomoda, Wm. M'Ternan, of same, Phelim M'Ternan, of Loughnecoufe, Phelim M'Ternan, of Laghard, Teige M'Ternan, of Killeanne, Moyleabaghlen M'Ternan, of Lorgin, Pharell M'Etiese, of Ardmoyne, Donnough M'More, of Loghdoncho, Gilleduff M'Ecorbe, of Dromirrall, Tirlaugh O Molmochore, of same, Donnall, Manus, Garrott, and John O Molmochore, of same, Donnough O Molchorre, of same, Flave M'Kiggan,

1590.   PLANTS.—ELIZABETH

of Carrick, Fyne M'Kiggan, Manus M'Kiggan, of same,
Ollisho m'O Molomnare, of Gortaslogha, Melanguilen, Flarin,
Turne, and Fedll O Molconnere, of same, Farfame O Molconnere,
of Ballokillecomin, Moriah O Molmochore, of Ballaneglenaghe,
John, Tirlangh, Gerrott, James, and Caell O Molmochore, of
same, Manus and Gillernow M'Boylin, of same, Margaret
O Molmochori, Ellen O Molmochore, Brian O Moltolle, of
Dromerrell, Edm. O Meltolle, of Fenaugha, Teige O Fline, of
Balleneglenaghe, Gilpatrick m'Mortagh O Fline, Gilpatrick
m'Hugh O Fline, Cahell, Donnough, and Melaughlen O Fline,
of same, Nicholas, Manus, and Hugh O Molmochore, of same,
Gillegruome O Fline, of same, Melaughlen, Caell, and Gilpatrick
M'Boylin, of same, Gillernow O Fline, of same, Kirrewo
m'Nymo O Downegan, of Killerro, Kirrowe and Dowls
O Downegan, of Carrick, Dalvay O Dowgenan, of same,
Cogogrie O Dowgenan, of Dromecalpe, Farfame, Toell,
Richard, Fartasse, Moylamorro, Kirrew, Dalvay, and Donnogh
O Dowgenan, of same, Cahell ro O Dowgenan, of Dromcalpe,
Congho O Dowgenan, of same, James M'Cahreaghe, of Dorre,
Caell M'Calle, of Korrenarre, Dermond boy M'Hoine, (of)
Castellior, Donnell and James M'Haine, of same, Pharrell
ballagh M'Laughlen, of Loghrire, Owen M'Laughlen, of
same, Pherrell O Dowgenan, of Gowell, Teige M'Gorch, of
Dromeranan, Tirlaugh M'Gorch, of Loughnacoule, Melaughlen
M'Gorcha, of same, Tirlaghe O Rourke, of Laghard, Melaughlen
M'Etreste, of Armoynin, Teig O Doelan, of Loughnecoule,
Donel M'Nema, of Dromeraan, Teig M'Ternan, of Killemodan,
Dermonde M'Ternan, of Lissolfa, Brian M'Nema, of Logh-
kirrell, Edm. O Dowgho, of Dromearde, Wm. M'Kiggan, of
Argourin, Tirlaugh M'Owen, of Dromgo, Donnell m'Edm.
M'Rainell, of Croadrom, Olisse O Clare, of Stukie, Hugh
M'Kiggan, of Gowell, Owen M'Gillehole, of Killaghah,
Pharrell M'Gillehole, of Tillegorte, Teige M'Gillehole, Parrell
M'Piarce, Donnell M'Gynnau, of same, Caell M'Sharre, of
Tirmanervin, Melaughlen M'Share, of same, Connor M'Der-
monde, of Dronowise, Donnell O Dowgenan, of Corrobart,
Pharragh O Baicke, Nich. M'Gillehole, of Killehorte, and
Pharrell M'Parrholan, of Kilgirre, in co. Leotrim. Provisions
as in 5382.—10 July, xxxii.

5440 (4362.) Pardon to Hugh oge Owrourke, of Luchinilerie, Shane
Owrourke, his brother, Brian M'Anleyne, of Carnacloghela,
Dnalltagh M'Anleoyne, of same, Tirlaugh M'Anleoyne, of
Dromerevruie, Alasterayne M'Anleoyne, of same, Teige
M'Anleoyne, of Droymallemeis, James M'Anleoyne, of same,
Fbelim M'Anleoyno, of same, Brian m'Rory M'Anleoyne, of
Inchinillerrye, Gillernow M'Auleone, of Correnghe, Owen
M'Ternan, of same, Teige keagh M'Antegnerte, of same,
Gilleahrise M'Kellye, of Molderaughe, Donnell Guff M'Gowffer,
of same, Hugh M'Anleone, of same, Allesterrise m'Melaughlen
M'Cabboy, of Tulley, Edm. M'Cabby, Allesterrise m'Rorie
M'Cabby, and Sheano M'Cabby, of same, Melaughlen M'Cabby,
Owen M'Cabby, Chahire and James M'Cabby, of same,
Melaughlen m'Edm. M'Cabby, of same, Hugh roe m'Edm.
M'Cabby, of same, Rorie M'Annovoie, of Cornacowreie, Hugh
M'Annovoie; Teige m'Rorie M'Annovoy, Kedangh, Connaghta,

1590.   FIANTS.—ELIZABETH.

and Cahill M'Anovoy, of same, Wm. M'Parlon, of Carrye, Cahill oge M'Parlon, Donnell M'Parlon, Phelim Balle M'Parlon, Brian boy M'Parlon, of same, Teige m'Hughe, of Dromeanlassu, Donnell O Donayne, of same, Donnell O Donnell, of Inchinillorrie, Brian bowaghe M'Angawnery, Donnell M'Anleyous, Millomoreie M'Anloyne, of same, Ternan M'Ternan, of Glassvoyre, Geoffrey, Shane, and Edmund keaghe M'Ferrall, of same, Cahier, Con, and Donnough M'Ternan, of same, Hugh M'Ternan, of Loghe Reddy, Rory, Sheane, and Fergananim M'Ternan, of same, Tirlaugh m'Brian keaghe, of Storkay, Une roe M'Ternan, of Glasdrone, Une O Collian, of Droymorarie, Tirlaugh O Coillaghe, Ferrell O Collian, of same, Brian M'Anhard, of Inchsnillerry, Owen reoghe O Mallmoghrie, of Agaghkallemorry, Sheane begg M'Anaboy, (of) Greaghnashvine, Donnogh reoghe M'Parlon, of same, Teige M'Kelly, of Lesgormaise, Mary and Sawe ne Rowrk, daughters of Brian O Rowrke, Brian M'Manose, of Dromarlee, Owne ne Rowrk, daughter of Brian O Rowrk, Connor M'Malmoghory, of Dromaries, Gilpatrick M'Molmogherye, of same, Carberry O Trevoire, of Killargaie, Owen, Ternan, Donnough, and Arte boy O Trevoire, of same, Dermoghte M'Carberrie, of Templemohie, Gilpatrick M'Angawney, of same, Hugh O Rourk, of Derrye, Gilpatrick M'Anclary, of Conkeyle, Teige m'Tirlaghe M'Anclery, of same, Cale m'Edm. M'Anaboye, of Cornaoorye, Gilpatrick keaghe Triatill, of same, Donltangh M'Ternan, and Shane M'Ternan, in co. Leitrim. Provisions as in 5382.—11 July, xxxii.

5441 (4358.) Pardon to Tirlagh M'Rannell, of Dromarde, Gerald and Ono M'Rannell, of same, Donald M'Rannell, of Cloncalrie, Melaghlin, Brian, Fairill, and Thady M'Rannell, of same, Connor M'Rannell, of Conclawe, Owen and Melaghane M'Rannell, of same, Gillogrume and Bryan M'Rannell, of Correkrayne, Wm. M'Rannell, of Tomiske, Melaghlin and Iree M'Rannell, of the Rine, Dermond M'Rannell, of Incercak, Melaghan, Conner, and Edm. M'Rannell, of same, Morroghe m'Phellame M'Rannell, Fallim M'Rannell, of Coraocalogh, Morrogh M'Rannell, of Dumbradda, Rosse M'Rannell, of Moybill, Folim and Melaghlin M'Rannell, of same, Cahill M'Rannell, of Iisteshnan, Bryan and James M'Rannell, of same, Edm. M'Shanloy, of Droimed, Edm. oge M'Shanley, of Dromd, Cormock and Tuady M'Shanley, of same, Morrogh M'Shanley, of Dirregrascon, Carbary M'Shanloy, of same, Gilloduffe M'Shanley, of Dirrocarud, Patrick and Connor M'Shanley, of the Carricke, Thady M'Rannell Aglire, Morrogh M'Shanley, of the Dirre, Hugh and Bryan M'Garre, of Claneghe, Bryen and Geoffrey M'Garr, of Dromard, Thady banne M'Garr, Gerald M'Rannell, of Laghom, Owen M'Rannell, of same, Roris M'Gillebride, of Killime, Tirlagh, Bryan, Dooltagb, Edm., and Shane M'Gillebride, of same, Connor M'Moree, of Treen, Dermond M'Moores, of same, Bryan M'Moore, of Roose, Thady M'Hugh, of the Carkine, Melaghan, Edm., and Dermond M'Hugh, of same, Moriah and Thady O Mulmochore, of Dromarde, Golpatrick M'Come, of Dromarde, Cormock M'Kian, of Cloon, Tirlagh M'Kian, Tho., Mortagh, and Fardaragh M'Kyan, of same, Wm. M'Mahown, of Cloon, Bryan M'Conway, of same, Thady M'Garr, of Conoalge, Dermond, Morrogh, Cahill, and Conor M'Garr, of same, Garragh O Donell, of Laghan, Roris O Donell, of same,

1590.   FIANTS.—ELIZABETH.

Nich. M'Kyan, of Clain, Gillernow M'Kyan, of Cloon, Con and Bryan M'Ranall, of Ballogortologe, Donald M'Owen, of Dromard, and Shane O Donell, of Laghan. Security as in 4343, in co. Leitrim.—11 July, xxxii.

5442 (4390.) Pardon to Cahill M'Ranell, of Inchmory, Edm. M'Ranell, of same, Ferdorogh and Connor M'Ranell, of Carrig, Teig M'Ranell, of the Droudarragh, Hugh og M'Ranell, of same, Morogh M'Ranell, of Clongowran, Fauganunym, of same, Hubert M'Ranell, of Drowdarragh, Melaghlen M'Ranell, of Muckfachan, Teig M'Ranell, of Goutenbum, Wm. M'Ranell, of same, Irre M'Ranell, of Taese, Morish O Helly, of Lishnegar, John O Helley, of Dramoreye, Owin O Helly, of Lishnegar, Mortagh O Helley, of Dromoray, Cahill M'Gillachrist, of Dristenan, Dearmot duf M'Gillacrist, of same, Gillagra, Gilladuf, and Owin M'Gillacrist, of same, Melaghlen MacRanall, of Leatrym, Edm. M'Ranell, of Grottawne, Morogh M'Teig, of Clondagagh, Fergananym M'Ranell, of Carrig, Tirlough M'Ranell, of Clonahe, Mulrony M'Ranell, of Barnagh, Connor M'Ranell, of same, Gerald M'Ranall, of Bonronan, Cahill M'Ranell, of Clondagagh, Melaghlen M'Ranell, of same, Rory og O Moran, of Ayttezarie, Conor O Moran, of same, Cahill O Moran, of Cram, Carbry O Moran, of Dromgoall, Dermot and Brian O Moran, of same, Dermot m'Cahill O Moran, of Caryn, Cormock O Moran, of Dromroisk, Donogh and Towhill O Moran, of same, Brian M'William, of Aghmoynagh, Hugh O Moran, of same, Edm. O Moran, of Aghrarigh, Owin O Birryn, of Ballynnoy, Brian and Tirlagh O Birrin, of same, Cormock M'Ranell, of Dogheerrick, Donogh MacRanell, of Stokerry, Rory M'Ranell, of Cornegeaunge, Morogh M'Ranell, of same, Katherine ny Ranell, of Stutery, Pharrall and James M'Ranell, of Dughearrick, Owin M'Ranell, of Carrick ne mahan, John boye M'Ranell, of Dirrinhooe, Tirolagh M'Ranell, of Tanoorrick, Edmund and Brian M'Ranell, of Dirrintowne, Cahill M'Ranell, of Cornekeeragh, Conn M'Ranell, of Ayheroinen, Manus M'Ranell, of Carrickniclawen, Donnogh O Flaunigan, of Dromkirrin, Tho. O Flanygan, Edm. O Flanigan, of same, Connor M'Ranall, of Aghclogher, Manus M'Ranell, of same, Hugh M'Gillaholly, of Doghearrick, Parshee M'Gillaholly, of Stickerry, Wm. and Morrish M'Ranell, of Dromkirve, Cormock M'Ranell of Stuckery, Iray m'Donell M'Ranell, of Dologh, Tirrelogh M'Ranell, of Loghconwaye, Teig MacRanall, of Edenmore, Rory and Owen M'Ranell, of Dologh, Owen M'Ranell, of Loghoor, Tirlagh M'Ranell, of Clonly, Irey Morrogh, of Carrick, Owin M'Ranell, of Cloona, Mortagh O Fynnan, of Aghacor, Donell, Teig. Owin, and Gilladuf O Fynan, of same, Gillerno O Flyn, of Drynagh, John M'Ranell, of Annaghkyn, Connor and Gormell M'Ranell, of same, Phelim M'Morrise, (of) Edumore, Hugh M'Morogh, of same, Tirelagh M'Morogh, Owen and John M'Cormock, of same, Jeffry M'Ranell, of Lismakagan, Cormock M'Ranell, of Leghcoll-Dafeagh, Tirrelagh M'Owine, of Laghaine, Manus M'Owen, of Corbachill, Teig M'Owin, of Halkon, Hugh M'Owen, of same, Gillaballagh M'Owin, of Laksin, Molmary M'Owen, of Bynnaghinare, Brian M'Owen, of Creighan, Ferrall O Behan, of Drumkerry, Cahill O Behan, Manus O Bohen, of same, Brian

M'Hugh, of Dromlagh, Farrill Hugh, of Lorgin, Tirlagh O Mul-
line, of Loghinclie orive, Teig O Mullme, of Mogherey, Teig
O Mulme, of Dromed, Rory O Mulme, of Mogherey, Brian
O Mulme, of same, Edm. M'Ranell, of Loghooldafeagh, Farrill
M'Ranell, of same, Edm. M'Ranell, of Nathrum, Dermond
M'Rannall, of Liskelsroan, Brian roe O Mulme, of Carrick, John
O Mulmee, of same, Caholl O Redeghan, of Loghinchcreive,
Farrell O Roedeghan, of same, John M'Gillshoke, of Cordirry,
Cahill O Mulme, of Aghcashill, Gerald O Mulme, of Aghtuskerban,
Cahill M'Ranell, of Stuckory, Wm. and Gerrot M'Ranell, of
Clonshellagh, Tirelagh M'Ranell, of Loghooldsfeagh, Cahill
MacRanell, of the Clogher, and Phelam M'Ranell, of Nathrum.
Security as in 4948, in co. Leitrim.—11 July, xxxii.

5443 (4417.) Appointment of Nelanus m'Brian ferto O Neale; to
be captain of the country of the Upper Clandeboy in Ulster.—
16 July, xxxii.

5444 (6544.) Grant to George Beston and Lancelot Bostocke,
esquires, two of the queen's gentleman pensioners; of the seigniory
or lordship of Castletowne containing 3 ploughlands, the castle
and lands of Bohagh 8 pl., Ardlynan, 2 pl., Kilbryddy, 2 pl.,
Cloghrane, 2 pl., Fay, ½ pl., Ballynawge, ¼ pl., Dromloghane, 1 pl.,
the castle and lands of Court[Rothery], near Kilmalloche, ½ pl.,
Ballynhaght, 2 pl., Garragho, ¼ pl; in all 17 ploughlands which
at the rate of 28 ploughlands to a seigniory of 12,000 acres
make 7,285½ acres in Kenry and Oonway, co. Limerick; also the
rents of the free tenants of the seigniory of Castletowne, viz:
10s. sterling out of Kylly, of Edmund M'David of Bellegel-
leghane, 10s. out of a ploughland of Shane M'Morrish of Bally-
nemory, 15s. out of a ploughland in Degretty, of Morris M'Gerald,
out of Shanevallymore, 30s. out of Ballynegoell, of said Morris
M'Gerald, 10s. out of Ballycahane, of Morris m'Shane oge, 10s.
out of Ballynaknockbane, of Edmund m'Thomas M'Richard, 10s.
out of Ballenoe, of Garrett M'Morrys, 17s. 9d. out of Ballyne-
kerrigry, 13s. 4d. out of Ballylyein, 22s. 2½d. out of Drombegge,
22s. 2½d. out of Ballengarren, and 22s. 2½d. out of Lyraneahyrye,
in all £9 3s. 8½d. sterling. To hold, by the name of the seigniory
of Castletowne, for ever, in feefarm, by fealty, in common soccage.
Rent £75 17s. and a farthing ¼ sterling, from 1594 (£37 18s. 6½d
for the previous 3 years), and for the rents of the free tenants
£9 8s. 9½d. sterling, and ½d. for each acre of waste land enclosed.
If the lands are found by the survey to contain more than the
estimated number of acres, grantee shall pay 2½d. for each English
acre so in excess. Grantees to erect houses for 54 families, of
which one to be for themselves, 4 for freeholders, 3 for farmers,
and 25 for copyholders. Other conditions usual in grants for
planting the undertakers in Munster as in 5082. 2 membranes.
—20 July, xxxii.

5445 (4393.) Pardon to Worrish fitz Thomas, of Ballemony, Boris
boy O Corban, Walter Cullen, Jennet Storie, Edm. Boggod,
Jevan yny ison O Duire, Dermot M'Connell, Wm. m'Edm.
O Ryan, Pierce fitz Pierce, of Garrenlashie, Moriertagh Brian,
of Garri[]onie, Donell O Twigher, Taige O Dwigher, Shaine
Twighari, wife (of?) Pierce St. Jhon, of Roane, and Teige O Trahi,
of Ballecarne, in cos. Limerick and Tipperary. Provisions as
in 5832. Fine, 6s. 8d. each.—6 Aug., xxxii.

1500.   FIANTS.—ELIZABETH.

5446 (4394.) Pardon to Myles Bourk, of Feartagh, Owenye Bryan,
of Corrighie, Wm. Edmond Oahan, Wm. reogh O Twirlie, Boris
O Kellie, Morrough M'Clonnye, Edm. m'Morriah Browne, Teige
m'Manghonnio O Gradie, John m'Donnough M'William, Rob.
m'fitz Moriah Browne, in co. Limerick, also Rowland Poore, of
Branau, co. Waterford, gent., Shane m'Owen M'Cragh, of
Mountaine Castle, co. Cork, Gerrot in'Shane M'Rudderin, Rob.
Lambart, of Dublin, yeoman. Provisions as in 5339. Fine,
6s. 8d. each.—6 Aug., xxxii.

5447 (4395.) Pardon to Tomaltagh oge M'Dermody, of Croghane,
gent, Brian m'Mulrony M'Dermody, Mulrony in'Mulrony
M'Dermody, Tomultagh m'Mulrony, Rory reogh m'Teige
m'Tamultagh, Cahill m'Teige m'Tumultagh, and Tomultagh
Murray in Tomultagh, of same, gentlemen, Nich. O Colly, of
Killewkine, clerk, Wm. Trustaue, of Russeny, husbandman,
Teige oge in'Teige M'Dermody roe, of Kuockydowe, Tomultagh
M'VinDermody, of same, Moriertagh M'VicDermody, of
Kilvickurrell, Cahill m'Fergananym M'Dermody roe, of
Clopeboy, horsemen, Cahill m'Oonoghor oge, of Drumtreak,
Rory keogh m'Conoghor oge, of sane, Owen grany m'Cormock
m'Manus keogh, of Scormore, Cormock oge m'Cormock m'Manus
keogh, of same, Manus oge m'Cormock m'Keogh, of same, Rory
and Mulrony m'Brian M'Dermody, of Dowagarr, and Owen
grany M'Inilly, of Teoghboyhin, gentlemen, Fardarragh
M'Inilly, of same, Edm. dorragh m'Donogh grany, of Ballin-
killin, Conoghor oge m'Teige M'Brien, of Krivia, horsemen,
Teige O Coan, of Ardearne, and Hugh O Coan, of same, clerks,
Shane O Brin, of Ballinkillin, husbandman, Dowaltagh m'Donogh
M'Farrill, of Belanegarr, gent., Brian m'Donogh grany, of
Ballincallin, horseman, Rory m'Owen M'Swiny, of Ballintober,
galloglas, in co. Roscommon, Edm. Burk, of Downcauan, Rich.
Burk, of the Island, and Tho. Bnrck, gentlemen, sons of Hubert
Burk, knight, Rich. duffe M'Moyler, of the Cartrone, gent,
Wm. grany M'Moylar, of same, Henry M'Davy, of Osse, gent,
Rich. reogh, of Ballyfoill, Gillernew O Donelan, of Lyottony,
kern, Walter M'Click, of Liaroe, and Shane m'Ulick oge, of
same, gentlemen, Shane oge m'Shane bwoy O Shaghnea, of
Gertinegory, Moiler M'Feyrick, of Eddergowla, horseman,
Towill O Donelane, of Barnenbllegh, Brian O Kelly, of Ballagh-
duffe, gent, Slany nyne Loghlin, his wife, Tho. O Regan, of
Carrowentober, husbandman, Garmaly ny Leyua, his wife,
Conoghor O Regan, of same, Donell M'Drian, of Lisccarrie,
Shane M'Ernan, of Ballaghduffe, husbandman, Wm. reogh
M'Conoghor, of Gallagh, Teige M'Donell, of Newcastle, Hugh
M'Donell, of Clandawnper, and Donogh M'Graly, of Ballagh-
duffe, kerns, Donell O Hallowran, of the Killin, Moriertagh
m'Hugh boye O Heyne, of the Lidegans, gent, Nich. Owen,
of the Killin, yeoman, Conoghor m'Owen O Mulranis, of same,
Towill O Donelane m'Tho., of Leatanye, gent, Bahillagh
M'Kagan, of the Organ, gent, Tho. M'Kevy, of Killbegg,
Tho. oge O Hurrely, of Rosmnelan, James Comin, of Ballin-
garry, gent, Donell M'Teige, of the Feddan, Tho. O Higgen,
of Kilclony, Donell oge O Higgen, Brian O Higgen, and
Towhill O Higgen, of same, gentlemen, and Donell O Donnowly, of
Ballindarry, co. Galway. Provisions as in 5389.—10 Aug., xxxii.

5448 (4396.) Pardon to Henry m'Davie M'Henry, of Ballaghowly, Rob. M'Davie, Rich. M'Ouog, Moolro m'Rondagh M'Hovish, of same, Shane boye M'Cahir, of the Corballis, Ulick M'Shane, Rory M'Shane, Wm. M'Robert, of same, Moilro oge M'Richard, of Breacklone, Shane O Doghwyne, of Ballinsmale, Oghy m'Connor M'Griffen, of Ballaghowly, Rich. M'Adam, Hugh M'Ebrehowne, Shane M'Jordan, of same, in co. Mayo, John oge O Skynin, of Killvegintie, clerk, Hugh O Mannin, of Kakerglasse, gent., Moriartagh oge O Kanewane, of Killtullagh, labourer, Edm. M'De, of Kilswoher, gent., Wm. O Hisrely, of Cionberne, husbandman, Teige m'Shane cneaugh O Kelly, of Monevane, Melaghlin m'William begge, of Pollwickgranaye, Wm. m'Tho. oge, of Barinboy, Fengh O Kelly, of the monastery of Oncokmoy, gent., Shane oge O Kelly, of same, gent., Tho. m'Brien M'Rory, of Anaghbegge, Owin O Birne, of Anaghmore, Edm. reogh m'Henry Crone, of same, Dominick White, of Beggarry, gent., Dermot m'Melaghlin M'Owly, of Cionslahin, Edm. m'Melaghlin, of Carowlany, gent., in co. Galway, Hugh O Connigane, of Castletane, priest, Sily wodiry ny Connoghor, of Clonnybirne, Brian O Connoghor m'Rory, of Clonecanny, in co. Roscommon, Onora uy Da wicke Edmund, of Gortindive, Sirvrehagh Folain, of Moiris, gent., Nehamiah Folain, of Moyris, Rostius Folain, Naokragh Folain, Farnand Folain, and Connor M'Seraly, of same, Rory O Hallowran, of Barna, Edm. O Towhill, of Immoehina, Farnand O Towhill, of same, and Hugh boy m'Edmund oge, of Lettermelane, gentlemen, in co. Galway, Rory m'Donogh m'Rory m'Confinne M'Nemarre, of Ballydoneghan, Shane and Donogh m'Rory, of same, and Edm. fits Theobald Butler, of Downymalmilhills, in co. Clare. Provisions as in 5382.—10 Aug., xxxii.

5449 (4362a.) Pardon to Rich. boye M'Hoste, of Gortiwargye, Richard, Farris, Edmund doroghe, and Hubert oge M'Hostie, of same, Moylar m'Ricard M'Hostie, of same, Rickard duffe Plemen, Donogh ro Plemen, Wm. duffe Plemen, of same, Tho. Brimicham, of Conoghor, Edm. Brimicham, of Downstally, Wm. Brimicham, of Meltons, Tho. oge Brimicham, of Torlavaghar, Redmund m'Moyler og Brimicham, of same, Brien ro M'Donall, of same, Brien M'Hostie, of Kelkenslive, Brien M'Cassarie, of Limeline, Moyler kyagh, of same, Wm. M'Hostie, of same, Edm. duffe M'Hostie, of Cungilte, Walter m'Wm. granny M'Hostie, Hubert m'Edm. oge M'Hostie, Walter m'Hubert M'Hostie, Rickard reogh M'Hostie, Edmund and Sarowne m'Faris M'Hostie, and Hobert reogh M'Hostie, of same, James duffe M'Hostie, of Curaghkin, Teig m'Radmond M'Hostie, of same, Edm. m'Brien oge, of Dunmore, Donnell Carragh, of same, Donnall M'Koge, of Clownagh, Carbery O Lowrowe, Hugh O M'akoge, Shane O Finne, of same, Hubert duffe M'Johniake, of Killm'nillowe, Gerald M'Johnick, David Brannagh, of same, Donogh O Horan, of Dery, Domscowne O Higen, of Kellbegg, Connor M'Downey, of Deryhowne, Redmund M'Ullick, of Clunmore, Ferragh m'Hugh O Kallye, co. Roscoman, Edm. O Dowland, of same, Edm. M'Knogher, Hugh M'Brasnill, Tirlagh M'Farrill, Tirlagh M'Owen, Flatter M'Laughlin, Donogh M'Laughlin, Donnell O Doland, and Moylrey M'Hostie, of same, in co. Galway. Provisions as in 5382.—11 Aug., xxxii.

I

5450 (4424.) Grant to Rich. Maisterson, of Ferns, esq.; of the office of seneschal of the manors and lands in co. Wexford, and of the liberty of Wexford; with a fee of £30. Also the office of constable of the castle of Wexford, with a fee of £5. To hold during good behaviour as in 4076.—14 Aug., xxxii.

5451 (4402.) Pardon to Edm. Boork, of Cong, co. Mayo, Soroghany Flaartie, of same, Shane and Ricoard M'Morles, of Eyldnvwagh, Tho. Borke m'Edm., of Athoork, Sawe Boorke, of same, Walter Boorke m'Edm., of Cong, Ullick Borrke m'Edm., of same, Felim M'Moyler, of Neale, Theobald m'James M'Moyler, Wm. m'Jonick M'Moyler, Hooge and Ullick m Henry M'Moyler, Feagh m'Rich. M'Moyler, Ullick m'Rich. reogh M'Moyler, Theobald m'Rich. reogh M'Myler, Moyler m'Walter M'Moyler, Ullick and Moyler m'Davie M'Moyler, and Wm. m'Feagh M'Moyler, of same, Sheonyne m'Wm. M'Jonne, of Kellmadra, Moyler and Gilladniffe m'Wm. M'Jonino, and Moyler m'Gilledniffe M'Jonine, of same, Walter reogh m'Gilleduffe M'Jonine, Ullick M'Shane, of Ballym'gibbow, Wm. M'Walter, Shane M'William, Ricoard, Feagha, and Shane M'Thomas, Felim and Caher m'Tirlagh M'Connell, Moyler M'Richard, and Moyler kyttagh M'Hubert, of same, Redmond and Moyler m'Wm. M'Jonine, of Croste, Shane m'Hage M'Jonine, of Killyllynane, Walter m'Redmund m'Ullick M'Jonine, of Toryne, Tho. and Shane m'Theobald reogh M'Jonine, of Ballenogasmagh, Shane m'Hubbert M'Jonine, of Dora, Shane boy m'Ricoard M'Jonine, of Elisranaghe, Ricoard roe and Theobald m'Ricoard M'Jonine, Tho. and David m'Walter M'Jonine, of same, Conla m'Shane Ykeanevaine, of Kyllmeane, Connoghor m'Teige M'Faltagh, of Turloghnighane, in co. Galway, Redmund M'Jonine, of Clonmore, same co., Donald O Lanama, of Toame, same co., Ambrose Kirowan, of Galway, Nehemus Folone, of Newtown, same co., Maurus O Brien, of Cong, Conoghor O Brien, Ricard Morrick, of same, in co. Mayo, Tirlagh m'Donell M'Dwyle, of Ballonnmill, Walter M'Riddery, of Castlerof Jie, Felim Rilldry, Wm. keoghe m'Felim, of same, Owen M'Donellane, of Killvmnie, Moyler orons m'Tho. M'Walter, of Carriduffe, Ricoard m'Shane fyne M'Adam, of Clonoonnor, Shane O Henigane, of Crosboboine, priest (sasardos), Shanowne M'Coiste, of Killakowaghe, Wm. O Marroghe, of same, Wm. and David m'Tirlagh M'Riddrie, of Downm'kyrne, David m'Wm. hallogh M'Mories, of Ballekinknave, Wm. M'inbrahone, of Belynclurehone, Moyler bane and Wm. m'Davis oge M'Costellow, of Redhdagen, Edm. m'Davis oge M'Costalo, of same, James M'Maries, of Gormedin, Henry M'Mories, of Barrill, Oliver Boorke, of Inishkine, Ullick Carrone, Mayo m'Moylny M'Andrew, of same, Ricoard m'Henry M'Tamultagh, of Inishkwoe, Ricard M'Robug, of Bolle flleame, Dermot M'Walter, of Neddnycorrn, Ricard roe M'Walter, of Turlagmoghame, and Philip m'Hugh M'Walter, of Sennycorrn, in co. Galway. Security as in 4043.—27 Aug., xxxii.

5452 (4403.) Pardon to Walter Burke, of Cloyngnshall, gent., Margaret O Flahartie, Walter m'Ricoard Burke, of same, Walter oge M'Feaghe, of Clongolein, Iulicke duffe m'Shane m'Ricoard, of same, Gilleduffe m'Teig O Conor, of Cloingnshall, Shane M'Jonyn, of Killeleman, Rich. m'Riccard Jonnyn, of same,

1590.   FIANTS.—ELIZABETH.

Morogh m'Teige, of Cloyngashall, Edm. aslagh m'Riccard
M'Jonyn, Faagh m'Riccard M'Jonyn, Riccard M'Hubert, of
Cloingashall, Edm. M'Walter, of Liskelin, Rich. M'Edmond, of
same, Edm. M'Hules, Tho. oge M'Morris, Brien Eterrup, Tho.
M'Tibbold, of Creingh, Tho. oge M'Tibbolds, of same, Shane
m'Tho. M'Tibbalds, Moyler m'Shane M'Richard, Davi oge
M'Nales, of Lebbale, James reogh M'Davy, Riccard boy M'Davy,
of same, Walter M'Edmond, of Crofine, Marcus m'Nabs
M'Conill, of the Togher, Kahier, Phelim oge, knoas, and Caiell
m'Marcus, of same, Gilliduffe Maloye, Riccard M'Gibbon, of
same, David m'Tho. Kevaghe M'Jonyn, of Skelooan, Tebalde
boy m'Tho. M'Jonnyn, Jonyn m'Ulick m'Edm. boy M'Jonnyn,
of same, Wm. Burke m'Sheane Tarmayn, of Clonkerry, Moyler
m'Tibbot Keogh Burke, of same, Edm. Burke m'Davy, of
Cloynegashall, Tho. Burke m'Davy, of same, Jonyn m'Redmond
M'Jonyn, of Killcoyre, Edm. boy M'Jonyn, of same, Wm. une
m'Davie M'Jonyn, Riccard m'Edm. boy M'Jonyn, Hubbert
m'Edm. boy M'Jonyn, Tho. oge Burke m'Tho., of Newcastell,
Wm. O Higgen, of Clonerin, Caher m'Bryen boy M'Donill,
Tirlagh m'Bryau boy M'Donill, Shoan M'Koogan, of Ballinraba,
and Gilleduffe m'Shoane M'Tiobald, of the Togher, all in co.
Mayo. Security as in 1043.—27 Aug., xxxii.

5453 (4404.) Pardon to Riccard Burke, of Darneenlashney alias
Derry m'Laghney, Taig O Donally, of Ballinlary, Wm.
M'Donell, of Kyllneknock, Edm. M'Melaghlin, of the Ilan, and
Riue O Donnolly, of Ballinlary. Security as in 4943.—27
Aug., xxxii.

5454 (4447.) Lease (under queen's letter, 12 April, xxi.) to Edm.
[italic marginal] O Fallon, of Athlone; of a mill in Clonkille, and mills and other
premises in Athlone, as leased in 3447, also premises in Athlone,
and the friary of Beallanony, as leased in 3402. To hold for
30 years from the end of the recited leases. Rent, 45s. 7d.
He shall not alien without license under the great seal. Other
provisions as in 5811. Subject also to the special provisions in
3402.—28 Aug., xxxii.

5455 (4430.) Grant to James Moaghe, of Clenliahe, gent.; of the
wardship and marriage of Maurice m'Thomas, son and heir of
Tho. Cawne fitz John de Gerraldynes, late of Gortnetubberadd,
co. Limerick, gent.; and custody of his lands. To hold during
minority. Rent £6, English; of which 40s. Irish may be retained for maintenance of the minor. Fine £6 ster.—39 Aug.,
xxxii.

5456 (4400.) Pardon to Fining m'Dermot O Drisanll, of Downegall,
Donogh M'Malmogby, of Kinalmoke, Dermot m'Donnell
M'Cormack, of Balligunoaig, Patr. Garland, of Shiprspoole, Shane
lader O Mahowne, of Kinalmocke, Teig m'Shane O Mahowne, of
same, Donnogh O Mahowne alias Donnogh glassolagh, Fining
m'Donnell M'Carti, of Dromlegaghe, Shane O Kerne, of Ardten-
nams, Wm. Thomas, of Kersalls, David Roobe, Rich. Nogell, of
same, Dermot m'Fininge M'Cartie, (of) Karlgnasse, Wm. m'Edm.
M'Shiche, of Castletowne, Donnell oge m'Donnell M'Rannall,
of Cartie, Enans keaghe O Daly, of Moyntervarye, Fininge
M'Donoghor, of Ballinmore, Dermot m'Oon M'Faghey, of same,
Donnoge Ogulloghoe, of Mashanglasse, Tho. m'Morish m'William
O Hagiren, of Conahe, Teig M'Cangellyo, Wm. Shane O Cangolly,

1590.   FIANTS.—ELIZABETH.

of same, Dermot m'David O Kelly, of Magillis, Donell ror
m'Shane M'Shiche, of same, Shane O Con, of Machanoglasse, and
Patr. Martell, of Kensall, co. Cork. Provisions as in 5367.—
81 Aug., xxxii.

5457 (4401.) Pardon to Garred fits Redmond Stack, of Achamrhy,
co. Kerry, Morrice fits Redmond Stack, of same, John fits James
Stack, of Achanycrannye, John m'Richard duffe Stack, Donald
roe Sullywayne, Dermot oge M'Nicoll, Edm. fits Gerald fits
Redmond, of Achanry, Wm. fitz Rich. fits John Stack, of
Achanicrannye, Wm. Showe, of Kilfickna, Wm. Sheyne, of
Likmawe, John and Tho. fits Edm. fitz John Fits Morice, Edm.
fits Tho. fits John Fitz Morice, Edm. fitz Patr. Fits Morice, Tho.
oge fits Tho. fitz Riccard oge Stack, Thady m'Connoghor ne
brooka, John ne broicke Stack, John Leylon alias Rod aclawdis,
Farcowertie O Layne, Philip fits Rich. fits John Stack, Riccard
Bonane, Eyllis M'Edmond, John m'Tho. oge fits Teige, John
Molaghan, Riccard Stack alias Totan, Edm. Birne, Maurice
Stack alias Morice aghoallowe, Tho. Browne, Dermot m'Owen
fits Teige fits Dermot, Tho. Stack fits Morice ne mansstragh
Stack, Tho. Stack fits Morice fits Riccard duffe Stack, Edm. fits
Morico fits Redmond Stack, Tho. oge fits Tho. fitz Riccard duffe
Stack, William Gerrald, of Enis more, Tho. garve Stack, Tho.
Marshall, Duald ne croughe, Gerrad roe fits Robard fits James
oge Stack, Tho. Stack fits Wm. Stack, Thomas Stack alias
Thomas achcalla, Conor Morre, Edm. fits Morice fits Gerald
Stack, Donogh O Dorchie, Edm. gancagh fitz Gerrad oge Stack,
Wm. Stack alias William negan, Patr. Horie, Rob. M'Kallgoide
alias Keill ne ferge, Wm. Kallgoide alias Fwobe ne boule, Rob.
fitz Gerrad fitz Gerralt Fitz Morice, John m'Donell ne croughe,
Riccard fits Morice roe fits Riccard Fits Morice, John snowlie,
Finen M'Owen fits Teige fits Dermot, Rob. fits Tho. Showe, John
fits Tho. Showe, Donald Cassie, and Maurice gancaghe Stack, in
co. Kerry. Security as in 4943.—1 Sept., xxxii.

5458 (4398.) Pardon to Henry kough M'Morris, of Ahena, Gerald
and Tho. M'Morris, of same, Wm. oge Flemings, of Corrantawe,
Ulick M'Sherowen, of Kinkeille, Gerald M'Sherowne, of same,
Teig cronagh O Higran, of Cloinnegrosse, Shane and Redmond
M'Ulick, of Kinkelly, Henry M'Bedmond, of Cnockycanoghor,
Tho. M'Eryderioy, of Donmacknain, Teig M'Eridery, and Walter
M'Eriderie, of same, Hubert M'Jonick, of Ahena, Redmund and
Jordan M'Jonick, of same, James boy m'Tho. M'James, of Ilandroe,
Rich. O Moroghowe alias Plockery, of Garlen Abbe, Wm.
M'Adam, of the Clogher, Garrott M'Adam, Moller M'Adam,
Rich. M'Addam, of same, Moller more m'Richard boy, of Ilandroe,
Henry oge O Moroghowe, of Loghnehdll, Phelim m'Ulick
duff, of Gurran Nabbe, Rich. boy m'Moyler more, of Iland Roe,
Hugh boy m'Alexander roe, of Kialloolla, Tho. Browne, of same,
David M'Heile, of Cloynbanowe, Heylis M'Heilie, of same,
Moyler m'Philip Keugh, of Ahena, Rich. O Morogh m'Donell
reogh, of Gormaden, Rich. m'Hanrie roo, of same, Edm.
M'Walter, of Ballikinknowe, Tho. m'Shane M'Gorrat, of Kilbe,
Tho. m'Walter reogh, of same, James m'Shane M'Gerrott, of
Kirbe, Tho. hallogh M'Enris, of Mayo, Walter og M'Addam, of
Ballio Addam, Gillidof M'Addam, of same, Gillidof O Moroghowe,
of Gortmaden, Shane glas m'Walter boy, of Ballinestampcragh,

1590.   FIANTS.—ELIZABETH.

Hobberd oge M'Eperson, of Donamony, and Redmund boy
m'Richard duf, of Ballikinknawe, in co. Mayo, Shane O Dowlin,
of Clonkin, Cowell O Donolan, Donogh O Donolan, Shane m'Edm.
roe M'Britin, of same, Flan m'Connor Corweyn O Heine, Dermond
reogh M'Malaughlin, Shane O Keggan, Shan oge m'Shane boy,
Teig m'Shane Iline, of the Gort, Shane m'Owen m'Donell kragh,
Rosse nyn Hiue, of Kiltormen, Edm. oge M'Cough, of Killindima,
Shane m Tho. M'Cough, of same, Shane keagh Wall, of Kellfadda,
Edm. m Brittin M'Morogh, of Castlebin,Flan m'Keugh M'Gille-
kelly, Owny M'Gillekelly, Conor O Manyn, and Shane m'Hugh
Onitayn, of Kellilgie, in co. Galway, Hugh ballogh O Fallon, of
Nidtowan, and Con O Fallon, of same, in co. Roscommon, and
Garret fits Thomas, of Raneraher, co. Limerick. Security as in
4943.—2 Sept., xxxii.

5459 (4399.) Pardon to David O Douda, of Kilglass, co. Sligo, gent.,
Thady boy O Douda, of Ballynhawen, and Molmory O Douda, of
Kilglash, gentlemen, Feniagh O Douda, of same, James M'Swyne,
of (written m') Ballicottle, gent., Mulmory, Owen oge, Collo,
Morgh, Donald, Owen, Edmund, Bryan, and Molmory more
M'Swyne, of same, gentlemen, Dermod O Douda, Ricard roe
M'Gerrald, Hugh O Kevan, of same, Hannos M'Nemy, of the
Collyn, Owen M'Nemy, of Kearowangonn, Flan M'Nemy,
Salomon alias Solon M'Nemy, of same, Morrish M'Nemy, of
Kill, Hubbart Allbanagh, of Rathelie, Alse, Henry, Edmund,
and Philip Albanagh, of same, Mullmory M'Donell, of Rosaly,
Cahill, Rori, Luder, Dowell, and Phelim M'Donell, Mulmory
m'Hanos M'Donell, and James M'Donell, of same, James
M'Oraxie, of Leackan, Dowaltagh, Bryen, and Ferissea M'Oraxie,
of same, Conoght M'Nemy, of Ballecottell, Dermod M'Oraxie, of
Leackan, Hugh, Filgorny, Mullmory, Karvoy, and Gillogias
M'Oraxie, of same, Gerald O Kevan, of Kanowanrodda, Caiher,
James, and Cormuck O Kevan, of same, and Bryen O Douda, of
Lianhim, gentlemen, Morriertagh O Douda, of same, Redmund
Albanagh, of same, gent., Shane Camman, of same, gent., Evelin
ne Douda, of Castellomnor, Moriertagh boy O Ferris, of Kilglass,
Owen O Farris, of same, gent., Owen O Beolan, Shane O Morry,
Wm. O Morry, of same, Thady reoghe O Flanhill, Donald
M'Eypany, Edm. M'Brady, Darmod crone O Flanhill, Mullmory
M'Eypany, and Rob. M'Eynpany, of same, gentleman, Neile
maile O Korrogan, of same, horseboy, Conchor M'Donhie, of
Dromrahine, gent., Ferfissea O Dougnan, of Ballindown, Tho.
M'Donghie, of Ballielaghabe, Carbery keagh M'Donchie, Dowal-
tagh crone M'Donchie, and Cahill carragh M'Donchie, of same,
gentlemen, Hugh O Helie, of Balli Ielly, Thady O Mulleven, of
Ballindown, Rori oge m'Moriertagh fean, of Bahie, and Cahill
reoghe M'Donchie, of Carbally, korns, Ferdorogh O Flanegan, of
Killglasse, and Cahill O Flanegan, of same, horsekeepers, Bryen
M'Swyne, of Ardneglasse, and Mulmory M'Swyne, of same,
gentleman, M'Mea M'Nemy, of Killglasse, Moriertagh duffe
O Farris, of Fuenyd, korn, and Forderagh M'Donell, of Rosaly,
gent., in co. Sligo. Security as in 4943.—2 Sept., xxxii.

5460 (4397.) Pardon to Roxie M'Swnye, Manus M'Swnye, Diermond
M'Carhie, Diermond M'Sulevan, Philip O Sulevan, Conacher
M'Fowlue, Anny alias Amihie M'Donell, Donell M'Carhie, Teig
O Fowlue, Diermond M'Donell, Connacher m'Donell revagh, Teig

1590.   FIANTS.—ELIZABETH.

M'Kanna, Teig O Monnechan, Donnchoe O Kallenan, Connchor O Donavan, Teige M'Donell, Donnell m'Connchor Iyegh, Donogh M'Diarmadie, Connchor O Dalye, Connchor m'Teig M'Rorie, Morrough M'Gillakirre, Donnell M'Keown alias Owen, Shane boy M'Diarmodie, Connchor M'Donoghe, and Donell grankaghe. Security as in 4943, in con. Cork or Desmond. Provided that they fulfil such orders as may be made by the lord deputy concerning the lands belonging to them.—6 Sept., xxxii.

5461 (4507) Pardon to Derby Donnor, of Myllton, Tho. fitz Teige O'Donnor, of Clogher, and Matthew fitz Owen Rian, of Gortenakaghe, in co. of the Cross of Tipperary. Provision as in 5332.—9 Sept., xxxii.

5462 (4405) Pardon to Brien m'Teige oge O Birne, Garret, Murrough, Edmund, Donough, Kallagh, and Cayber m'Teige oge O Birne, Barnaby O Toole, Phelim, Donald, Alexander, and Hugh O Toole, David Eustace, Callough m'Murrogh O Birne, James Walle, Murrogh O Farrall, and Rob. Lambert, yeoman, in co. Dublin. Security as in 4943.—10 Sept., xxxii.

5463 (4426) Grant to Zachary Paires, gent. ; of the wardship and marriage of Redmund, son and heir of Tho. Fitz Gerralds, late of Clonbolge, King's co. ; and custody of his lands. To hold during minority. Rent £5 ; 50s. of which may be retained for maintenance of the minor. Fine 10s.—16 Sept., xxxii.

5464 (4441) License to Rob. Richardson, chanter of the cathedral . of the Blessed Trinity, Dublin, to be absent in England for 12 months.—21 Sept., xxxii.

5465 (4432) Livery to William, son and heir of John Bathe, late of Drownanrathe, co. Dublin. Fine £37 8s. 4d. Part of the lands had been conveyed to the use of Jennets Finglass, the widow of John Bathe.—24 Sept., xxxii.

5466 (4409) Pardon to Geoffrey son of John Iraill, from Solan Darra, Wm. Jordan son of Cognosus from Villa Templi (Ballintemple), Unerus Jordan son of Wm., from anno, Hugh Jordan son of John, from Duum faolan, Barnard Jordan son of John, from Doum faolan, Thady son of Fergal raffus Mocmaigister (from) Salacmough, Donald Jordan son of Edmund from Deire Aghne, Cognosius son of Donald magrus Meicighsernan (from) Soothoran, Owen m'Tugh O Reli, Shane m'Brian bane O Donchow, Edm. m'Rich. Ovaillie, Tho. O Donchowe m'Tirlaghe, Tho. bane m'Killepatrick O Shiridan, Brien O Douffon, Tirlagh boye O Haran, Philip O Haran, Cormac son of Donatus Meicighearnaim, from Spart Aniobhaire, Fallanas flavus son of Malachy Meicighearnaim, from Tigh Congras, Wm. O Clervan, John son of Follim Meicighearnaim, from Gurtin an tairbhe, Carbriaius son of Folom Meicighernaim, from Gurtin an tarbha, Terence son of Fergal albus I Siridae, from Rosse, Maginimus rufus M'Maighister son of Fergal rufus, from Saluche nighinghe, Bernard rufus son of John, from Rosse, Odo son of Malachy Ibbecithim, Malachias Siridens son of Nialsrus, from Tabunighbeg, Colla M'Cabe son of John, from Achodghe ancann, Thady M'Dobhmill son of Malierus, Malanghlen M'Karvan, Fergall juvenis son of Bernard Iraghillagh, from Mount Carbre, John, son of Barnard Iraghillaghe, from Mount Carbre, Carallus son of Bernard Iragbillaghe, from Mount

1500.   FIANTS—ELIZABETH.

Carbre, Cornelius Jordan son of the dean, from Ecclesia Magna (*Kilmore*), Cognisius Siridens son of Thomas, from same, Unerus Siridens son of Patrick, Edmund Siridens son of Unerus, Hugh Siridens son of Unerus, and Bernard Siridens son of Terence, from same place, Unerus Siridens son of Terence from Gorte na nabhall, Wm. Siridens' son of Donatus from Drumaalache Cormac son of Padin Siridantus an lothhaill, Hugh Siridens son of Golredus, from Mount Carbre, Cognosius Siridens son of Wm., from Villa Templi (*Ballintempls*), Nich. Siridens son of Wm., from same, Eugeneus albus son of Thady Siridanns, from Tochar, Tho. Siridens son of Felem, from Cluain liagan, Bernard son of Hugh Iraghelighe, from Belaghamori, Patr. O Danco son of Malachie, from Ballagillisbearte, Cognosius O Danco son of Wm., from Colli Ornobhach, Bernard O Donco son of Wm., Edm. O Doncho son of Wm., Bernard O Donahoe son of Arterus, Odo O Donoho son of Arterus, Malachy O Donohoe son of John, Patr. O Donoho son of John, John O Donohoe son of Wm., Patr. O Doncho son of Wm., of same place, Fergall O Relly son of Donald, from Collis Doncha, Bernard Siridens son of Tho., from Tabninug oroir, Carall Siridens son of Tho., John Siridens son of Cornell, Edm. Siridens son of Edm., Donald O Donohoe son of Patr., Caiell O Relly m'Cahill m'Hugh, of Cororave, Teige m'Gerrott boys m'Swyne O Farroll, Hugh m'Shane O Relly, Dermott m'William alias Clandonell, Donell m'Dermott, and Grany Nollan, in co. Cavan. Provisions as in 5382—29 Sept., xxxii.

5487 (4416) Grant to Henry Burnall, esq.; of the office of third justice of the Chief Place. To hold for this Michaelmas term only, with such fees as Bartholomew Russell had.—15 Oct., xxxii.

5488 (4406) Pardon to Hugh m'Owen grane, of Lemgeare, Owin og m'Owen grane, Tirlaugh lennagh m'Owen grane, Mellaughlan don m'Owen grane, Teig m'Edmond Evagbery, Nich. Trostane, of same, Owin og m'Brien m'Owen, of Loakane, Teig O Donogher, of Ardboy, Hugh O Donogher, Donell O Donogher, of same, Dualtagh m'Tieg M'Rory, of Cornevegh, Kedaugh and Brien m'Owen M'Dermot roe, of Knocknemoonaoks, Hugh O Gornayle, of Lemgare, Shane O Clabby, of Skarmore, More uy Mallaghlen don, of same, Brian og O Malchonany, of Cloyn-baban, Hugh O Moran; of Ardboy, Brien Eveale m'Owen m'Connor giash, of Bahnahooe, Iriell m'Cahill duff O Moeltalye, of Kankall, Dermot M'Gagher, of Ballenaden, Shane m'Teig ne holy, of Ballehoghtar, Mulmory m'Donnough M'Dwyla, (of) Cnockroghery, Hugh O Brien, of Portenyn, Donall O Dohartye, of Ardaarne, Donogh boy O Beiru, of Porterin, Teig O Coan, Fearaboy O Bragane, Teig O Fuathane, of same, Dwaltagh m'Tieg M'Farrill, of Ballinvila, Irgas M'Gebenay, of Ardaarne, Edm. m'Malaghlen O Kaddy, Morugh O Birne, of Ardaarne, Shane Santagh O Kelly, of Monymore, Brien mak Shane O Kelly, of same, Cormock O Gormaly, of Moybedden, Donogh O Coan, Hugh O Coan, Teig O Coan, Donogh O Marry, of the Corry, Rich. O Gormooly, of Moybedden, Fardorogh O Birne, of Porterin, Malaghlen O Birne, of same, Brien m'Dwaltagh m'Donogh duff, Tieg m'Hugh balle, of Ballenehoe, Donnall M'Gownake, of the Corry, Rory keagh m'Hugh balle, of Balla-

1590.   FIANTS.—ELIZABETH.

nehooe, Tomullagh O Birne, of the Erilegh, Hugh M'Brien, of
the Kelloges, Connor oge m'Tieg m'Brian M'Dermody roe,
Dwaltagh M'Chllowe, Cahill roe m'Dwaltagh m'Cahill roe, Dermot M'Dermody roe, of Neay Clonvard, Brien m'Dermot reogh
m'Cahall M'Hugh, Ferdorogh m'Hugh M'Dermot roe, Owin
m'Dwaltagh m'Donnogh duff, Brian m'Rory M'Dermot roe,
Cahill m'James M'Dermot roe, Owin na Kelly, of Cloinbroke,
Riccard M'Hubbert, Henry boy M'Hubbert, David boy M'Riccard,
and Jonick M'Riocard, of CasHekyla, and Philip M'Morris, of
Castle M'Gerall. Security as in 4948, in co. Roscommin, Galway or Mayo.—16 Oct., xxxii.

5469 (6549) Grant to Francis Barckley, esq.; of the lands of
Mohinerly containing 6 quarters, Kilrahenagh 1 quarter, Ballymore 2 quarters, Leheshiraghin lacy ¼ ploughland, Bwollygiame
and Inaberwork 1½ quarter, Kapp[   ] and Ardnegawne
¼ quarter, the castle and lands of Ballynaaby ¼ quarter, Bally-
homine ¼ quarter, Ballyonorky ¼ quarter, Gortahighan ¼ quarter,
Ballinekilly ¼ quarter, Clonaeloghye ¼ quarter, Clonansbrakir
alias Abbyland 10 acres, the castle and lands of Tomagwelly 4½
quarters, Laghvane 1 quarter, the castle and lands of Lymy-
kerry ¼ quarter, Tullagh 1½ quarter, Ina[   ] 1½ quarter,
Oowdtomins 1¼ quarter, Ballanloghan ¼ quarter, Bally Iaon 1½
quarter, Rathnaghane in mortgage with Emery Lye for 5 marks
halfnoe, Ballinridiallye 2 quarters, Farrenecarragh 8 acres, also
all the lands and tenements in the town of Aaketon, excepting
the castle with 40 acres adjoining reserved to the crown, co.
Limerick, amounting in all to 7250 English acres. To hold, by
the name of Rock Barkley, for ever, in fee farm, by fealty, in
common socage Rent, £37 10s. English, from 1594 (half for
preceding 3 years). Also ¼d. for each acre of waste enclosed.
If the lands are found by the survey to contain more than the
estimated number of acres grantee shall pay 8d. for each English
acre so in excess. Grantee to erect houses for 56 families, one
to be for himself, 4 for freeholders, 3 for farmers, and 46 for
copyholders. Other conditions usual in grants for planting the undertakers in Munster, as in 5032. 2 membranes.—18 Oct., xxxii.

5470 (4431.) Grant to Tho. Molinex, esq.; of the office of chancellor
of the Exchequer, vacant by the death of George Clyve, knt To
hold during good behaviour.—19 Oct., xxxii.

5471 (4414.) Grant to Patr. Grannt, gent.; [of the office of marshal
of the queen's courts and gaols in the province of Munster. To
hold during pleasure, with the fees pertaining to the office.—
23 Oct., xxxii.

5472 (4340.) Lease (under commission, 17 Feb., xxx.) to Tho.
Lambyn, gent.; of the site of the house of canons of Lurgho, or
Living Spring of Lurgho, in Ormounde, co. Tipperary; the
town of Lurgho, containing 12 cottages, built after the Irish
manner, within great ditches, lands in Lurgho called Baalacogho,
and other land there, a chapel and lands in Raihenakenanagho,
two parts of the tithes of Ballebrene, parcel of the rectory of
Lurgho belonging to the archdeaconry of the cathedral of Killaloe,
which tithes amount on the average to two copies of corn, a third
part of the tithes and altarages of the vicarage of Lorgho, the
vicarage of Durroghoe, extending to Dorrogho and Balledogho,
amounting on the average to 6 copies of corn, and altarages and

1590.   FIANTS.—ELIZABETH.

the tithes of the glebe land, the third part belonging to the priory, and two parts to the parson being in the gift of the bishop of Killaloe, the vicarages of Bonoghan, Killeroghe, and half the waste town, extending on the average to 8 copies of corn, with a third part of the alterages, which corn and alterages are allowed for the stipend of a curate there, possessions of the said monastery. The site of the house of Dominican friars of Lurghoe, land in Lurgho, and Bathenakynar, and the tithes of the lands belonging to the house; all which were leased by 5273, and re-entered by the crown for non-payment of rent. Land called Ferranemanaghe, near Limerick, leased by 2903, and re-entered for non-payment of rent. To hold for 21 years. Rent, £5 12s. Provisions as in 5311.—[26 Oct., xxxii.] (Auditor-General's Patent Book 21, p. 34.)

5473 (6536.) Grant to Edmund Spenser, gentleman; of the manor, castle, and lands of Kylcolman, co. Cork, containing one plough-land, Kylnevalley, one pl., Lyssemucky 1 pl., Ard Adam 1 pl., [   ] Ould Rossack alias Croskack 1 pl., Carrigyne, 1 pl., Bally Ellis, 1 pl., Kyllmack Ennes, ½ pl., and Ardambane, ½ pl., co. Cork, amounting by measure to 3028 English acres; also a rent of 26s. 8d. due to the late lord of [   ] out of Ballynaeg[   ] and a rent of 6s. 8d., payable to the late traitor, sir John of Desmond, out of Ballynloynigh, co. Cork. To hold for ever, in fee farm, by the name of "Hap Hazard," by fealty, in common soccage. Rent, £17 7s. 6½d. from 1594 (half only for the previous three years), and 33s. 4d. for the services of the free tenants. Also ½d. for each acre of waste land enclosed. If the lands are found by the survey to contain more than the estimated number of acres, grantee shall pay 1½d. for each English acre in excess. Power to impark 151 acres. Grantee to build houses for 24 families, of which one to be for himself, 2 for freeholders of 300A., 2 for farmers of 400A., and 11 for copyholders of 100A. Other conditions usual in the grants to the undertakers in Munster, as in 5032. (In part defaced).—26 [Oct.] xxxii, 1590.

5474 (4407) Pardon to Mulronye M'Crowe, of the Drum, co. Roscommon, Brian O Kinslane, Teige O Kinslane, Owin grane m'Teige roe, of same, Tege carrogh m'Mulronye boye, Mulronye oge m'Mulronye boy, Roris glas m'Wm. M'Malaghlin, Owen and Ferrall m'Donogh reogh, of Oris, Edm. O Kellie fitz Hugh, of the Clogher, Hugh O Kenmey, Murtagh O Kennye, Feagh O Kennye, Tege O Kelly, Wm. O Kelly, Farry O Kenny Wm. O Multully, Hugh O Multally, Wm. reogh O Multully John Wale, of Drought, in co. Galway, Donogh oge O Kenny, Tege m'Donogh oge O Kenny, Shane m'Doniell O Kenny, Murtagh m'Donell O Kennye, Murius Mac Multally, of Aughrime, Tege moyle M'William, Tirlagh m'Hugh O Kennye, Doniell O Dolan, Cawla M'Donogh, Thomas roe, Donnogh mac Thomas, Laughlin M'Manus, Brian O Gannan, James O Haraghton, and Cormack M'Donnogh. Security as in 4943.—27 Oct., xxxii.

5475 (4408) Pardon to Brian O Conor, of the Grange, co. Sligo, James M'Swyne, of Sesincaman, Donill, Owin, and Edmund M'Swyne, Owin oge m'Rorie keagh, Morrogh m'Rorie keagh, of same, Mulmorry M'Collo, of the Mollan, Collo oge M'Collo, of same, Cormock m'Kean O Hara, of Colanie, Cahill O Mynis,

1590.   FIANTS.—ELIZABETH.

Rorie O Boyell, Conor grana M'Gwyre, of same, Moriartagh M'Manus, of Cawnacrive, Owen keagh m'Cahill M'Mulronie, of same, Hugh boyo m'Connor atotan, of Tulleghugh, Donell roe O Gilan, of the Grange, Melaghlin m'Gillenbrick O Coman, of Culanie, and Gillodaf O Mynye, of Tullehugh. Security as in 4943.—27 Oct., xxxii.

5476 (4353) Pardon to Hugh M'Tiernan, of Loghroddy, Geoffrey oge M'Tyernan, Fergananim M'Tiernan, of same, Tirlagh m'Brien kooghe M'Tiernan, of Stocke, Farrall ballagh M'Loghlen, of Loghkirrill, James M'Tiernan, of Kilchoaagh, Farrian m'James M'Tiernan, Brian m'James M'Tiernan, Tiernan m'James M'Tiernan, of the same, Hugh roe m'Farroy O Roirke, of Aldderpile, Tirlagh m'Farrey O Rircke, Con roe m'Shane reogh O Roirke, Donnogh m'Tirrelagh m'Farrey O Roirke, Phelim m'Tirlagh m'Farrey O Roirke, of the same, Donnell M'Morrea, of Clonkoyn, Shane m'Carbarie M'Tiernan, of Glaseruaan, Wm. carragh O Faghy, of Cnoakroo, Con O Roirke, of Addergoyle, Hugh roe O Roirke, Phelim O Roirke, Dermot O Roirke, Donogho O Roirke, Fardorogh M'Morreo, Owin grana O Roirke, Gillspatrick crone M'Shorry, of the same, Mannus M'Morrea, of Donoghmore, Melaghlin M'Donill, of Newcastle, husbandman, Carbarie M'Kegan, of Kyarowvadyn, Owin M'Kegan, of same, and Gillepatrick M'Kegan, of Park, gentlemen, Redmund O Loyn, of Kealtraghdonan, Conoghor M'Collo, of Clonbigin, husbandman, Tirlagh M'Swine, of Clonepole, yeoman, Donell O Mulchirrill, of Clouskirrill, Rorie roe O Mulchirrill, of same, husb., Rose ny Mulchirrill, of same, Evelin ny Vickevurid, wife of said Rorie, Onora Bourk nine Riccard, late of Ballynnemaghe, Shane M'Davy, of Harownover, gent., Wm. carragh M'Downy, of Lymeponery, husb., Conoghor m'Edm. M'Brian, of Tryanvalgan, Conoghor oge, Fardorogh, and Dermod m'Conoghor m'Edm. M'Branan, of same, gentlemen, Shane Egeylagh M'Emarrow, of Ballemalronowe, Don O Monoge, of Cotten, Conoghor Kentagh M'Donoghoe, of Tyrovanen, John Bourk m'Tybbot, of Balle-vahen, Tho. leh M'Shedey, of Dromarroa, Wm. m'Shane O Moran, of Ballatorroh, Riccard m'Shane O Moran, of same, Shane ne caple m'Shane M'Nemarrow, of Mortallon, Dave M'Shedey, of Inyscaltreh, Donogho m'Shane moall M'Rorie, of Correb, Edm. m'Tho. M'Cowge, of Balloquow, gent., Rich. O Morroghe, of Garrenabbe, yeoman, Shane M'Hubart, of Kil-charownan, Edm. oge O Fahy, of Lyasedill, Wm. carragh O Fahy, of Cnookro, Dermot reogh O Madden, of Omaghoorbe, Caoll carragh O Madden, of Lesmore, Hugh M'Shane of Anagh, gentlemen, Callogh m'Allen M'Dowell, of Cariaken, Mullmory m'Donogho M'Dowell, of Cnookrochery, Tho. m'Shane oge, of Tullery, gent., Donoghoe O Fahy, of Ballinroan, yeoman, Tho. reogh O Loyn, of Clogher, husb., Brien carrogh m'Edm. Keogh, of Killernan, Gillarnowe O Hanly, and Rory M'Aulie, of May-mwe, gent. Security as in 4943, in counties Galway, Letrym, Mayo or Sligo.—30 Oct., xxxii.

5477 (4415) Grant (under queen's letter, 17 Jan., xxi.), to John Kearnan, gent., of the office of clerk of the pleas of the Exchequer. To hold during good behaviour with such fees as Rich. Edward had. Not to be removed, as in 4976.—30 Oct., xxxii.

1500.   FIANTS—ELIZABETH.

5478 (4410) Pardon to Owin M'Dermody, of Bracckleive, Tirlagh
m'Owen, Dermot m'Owen, Morish O Gawney, Cahill, Shane,
Dermot, Melaghlyn, and Connor O Gawney, of same, Teig
O Harte, of Dromklive, Rory ballagh O Hary, of Knockmore,
Dwaltagh O Scanlane, of Koonymy, Brien O Scanlane,
of Rosslyan, Art boy O Scanlane, Kellyagh O Scanlane,
of same, Tirlagh O Harte, of Braidoaly, Turlagh m'Brien
O Hart, of same, Brien O Dowdis, of Leoffynna, Rowry
O Dowda, of same, Edm. M'Swyna, of Cashelloghdargan,
James O Kevan, of Longaford, Edm. Kevan, Kahir Kevan, Brien
O Holie, of same, Nich. M'Elea, of Cowleofynne, Farrall M'Dermot
roe, of Buncmedan, Manns M'Donogh, of Rathmullan, Cale
M'Donogh, of Lissaconnows, Murtagh m'Mulrony fyan, of
Roonslaght, Dowaltagh O Connor, of the Balhy, Teig O Roirk,
of the Carry, Brien, Tiernan, Hugh, Turlagh, and Cormock
O Roirk, Donill M'Cormuck, Owen M'Laghlin, of same, Falym
M'Guolryeck, Cale M'Brien, of same, Brien m'Donell nawda,
Brien M'Kevyn, Gilpadrick M'Guolrieck, Donogh M'Donell,
Tiernan M'Phelym, and Owin O Mullaghtyn, of same.   Security
as in 4943, in co. Sligo and Mayo.—3 Nov., xxxii.

5479 (4411.) Pardon to Donogh M'Swyny, in co. Kerry, Tho.
m'Connor O Knoyrk, Callogh m'Keone M'Klaghlen, Brien
m'Neile M'Glaghlan, Thady m'Connor I Lyaris, Owen m'Donell
I Swivan, Owen m'Connor M'Glaghlan, Thady m'Donogh
M'Korhie, Thady m'Dermodie M'Karhie, Donell m'Donogh
O Swivan, and Donogh m'Donogh O Donill, in co. Kerry.
Security as in 4943.—4 Nov., xxxii.

5480 (4427.) Grant to Walter Sedgrave, of Dublin, alderman ; of
of the wardship and marriage of Patrick, son and heir of John
Barnewall, late of Kylbrue, gent. ; and custody of his lands.
To hold during minority.   Rent £10 ; £5 of which may be
retained for maintenance of the minor.   Fine £20.—5 Nov.,
xxxii.

5481 (4434.) Livery to Nicholas, son and heir of John Sankye,
late of Ballilaken, King's co., gent.   Fine £6.—5 Nov., xxxii.

5482 (4433.) Livery to Redmund, son and heir of Cognulus alias
Conghe O Fallon, late of Myletowne, co. Roscommon, gent.   Fine
£7 0s. 4d.   The widow, Benvy ne Conoghor, has a jointure.—7
Nov., xxxii.

5483 (4347.) Pardon to Donogh reogh m'Morintagh O Dowell, of
Ballinlinck, horseman, Rob. fitz Edmond, of Clanhenricke, and
James fitz Conoghor O Dowell, of Ballcaristell, husbandmen,
Tirlagh m'Owen O Moroghoe, of the Court, James m'Tirlagh, of
Ballenamone, Cahir m'Enir O Moroghoe, of the Court, Brien
m'Donoghe m'Art Cavenagh, of Ballinloghan, James m'Owen
O Dowell, horseboy, Wm. m'Moriahe alias Leam fyn, of Ballin-
teskrin, horseboy, Owen roe M'Donell, of Kildeynce, Melaghlin
O Harne, of Donmellan, Derby alias Dermot m'Effe O Rian, of
Ballean karre, and Morogh m'Edm. O Moroghoe, of Ballinvarre,
husbandmen, Dermot carragh m'Donall roe, of Tonnemaghtfire,
Edw. fitz Patr. Keatinge alias M'Negarred, Donogh m'Art
M'Dowlinge, of Ballsbane, freeholder, Rich. fitz Donall gangagh,
of Kildire, David Sutton alias Da begg, of Ballesop, Peirs Freine,
of the Skarke, ploughboy, Wm. fitz Philip O Coman, of Aghlarc,
husb., Morogh alias Morgan m'Edm. Cavenagh, of Balleloghan,

1590.   FIANTS.—ELIZABETH.

Art m'Morogh M'Moriartagh, freeholder, Gilpatrick m'Dermot more M'Fir, of Cowlstore, husbandman, James m'Donogh oge, of Tomeeure, Redmund m'Da O Rian, of Ballonmartin, Cahir m'Donell reagh Cavanagh, Owin m'Donogh M'Morrogh, of Clonhanragh, Edm. M'Burtick, of Rahinnehowan, and Donogh m'Teig M'Edmond; co. Carlow. Provision for security as in 4943. The pardon not to extend to any in prison or on bail, nor to pardon any riot or offence of which any of the parties stand accused in the Castle Chamber.—8 Nov., xxxii.

5484 (4351.) Pardon to Charles O Carroll, of Leamsvanan, knt., John Lye, of Rathbride, co. Kildare, Owney O Carroll and Teige O Carroll, brothers of said Charles. The pardon not to include intrusion into crown lands or debts to the crown.—10 Nov., xxxii.

5485 (4352.) Pardon to Mulronie dalenaghe m'Shane O Carrole, Hugin m'Tho. O Magher, Wm. laghin O Madden, Melaughlen more O Hogan, Lyahagh m'Edmond oge, Nelle m'Lisaghe m'Edmonds, Donnell fitz William Donne, alias Daniel Donne, Arte oge Donne fitz Arte, Chr. Woolele fitz Walter, Daniel m'Molronie oge, of Tullaghe, Donnough O Dullughoutie, of Glanurkyns. Security as in 4943. The pardon not to extend to any in prison or on bail, or include intrusion into crown lands or debts to the crown.—10 Nov., xxxii.

5486 (4354.) Pardon to Tirlagh M'Doyll, of Loohsallerym, co. Roscommon, Edm. oge M'Donill, Collo M'Doyll, Mullmury M'Doyll, Bryan M'Doyll, Unny ny Conill, Dermott m'Owen M'Fayly, Donald M'Aglyne, Donald M'agourke, Cormock O Flangan, of same place, Alyn m'Eallon M'Doyll, of the Imlaghe, Lynagh m'Kallow M'Doyll, Phelim m'Kallow M'Doyll, of same, Dermot oge M'Ela, of Carickbeg, Oahall and Edm. m'Owen M'Dermot roe, of same, Rory duffe M'Gellequinye, of Loohannebolne, Gilleduffe M'Gillequinye, of same, Walter M'Doyll, of Cornaghbey, Phelym m'Walter M'Doyll, of same, Conn O Mulloye, of Songhaghnenylaghe, Gilledoffe O Birne, Wm. O Birne, Thady O Birne, Cahall O Bradagane, Donell O Birne, and Edm. M'Hubart, of same, Sallo M'Gogane, of Ardearnaghe, Murroghe O Birne, Tirlagh fewore O Connor, of same, Hugh boy m'Hugh Cahall, of Droharlaghe, Thady m'Hugh M'Cahall, of same, Tomoltagh m'Teige M'Tirrlagh, of same, Ferdorogh m'Hugh M'Dermot roe, of the Glorina, Shane m'Tomoltagh M'Dermot, Dermot m'Shane M'Dermot roe, Cormock m'Mortagh M'Darmot roe, and Tomoltagh m'Quyne M'Dermot roe, of same, Ferryll boy m'Bryane M'Cormocke, of Claineine, Unnagh m'Fearill boy, Edm m'Teige oge, Ferdorghe m'Owen ballagh, Cahall and Manus m'Bryan m'Owen ballagh, Owen m'Thomas boy, Hugh and Rory m'Teige oge, Rory m'Fergananym M'Dermot roe, and Rory m'Cormock M'Owen, of same, Arte M'Cormocke, of Slafformuly, Edm. M'Cormooke, Fergananim m'Wm. M'Cormocke, Shane M'Cormock, and Rory m'Jeames M'Dermot roe, of same, Bryan m'Ferryll Irgan, of Komonne, Shane m'Bryan Irygan, of same, Rose nyclny, of Kenlgennenrule, Connor oge m'Donill M'Dermot roe, of the Meaye, Edm. m'Murtagh M'Dermot roe, Duwaltagh m'Cahall M'Dermot roe, and Hugh m'Bryan M'Dermot roe, of same, Dermot Maghynan, of the Clonyn, Hugh m'Donill O Kelly, of Gortnapourragh, Donagh bron O Birne, of Clonkalane, Melaghlin Balue, of same, Carbery Roaaghe, of Chartron, Neill O Brudagan, of Cartrongryaghe, Rory garnaghe m'Phelym boy, of Clonmore, Bryan M'Kallone, Tirlaghe carraghe m'Phelym m'Teige oge, of same, Wm. roe M'Enyarny, of Dunnyne, Alexander M'Doyll, of Towlynyry, Dermot reaghe m'Donnoghe M'Ferry, of same, Melaghlin O Falon, of Newtowne, Thady O Kelly Olaghan, Mannes oge M'Gerreghty, of same, Thady m'Fergananym M'Dermot, Mullroy, Tirlagh, and Fergananym m'Bryan m'Fergananym M'Dermot, Thady oge O Birne, of Donyne, Meaw ny Vyrne, Edmund boy, of same, Cormock carragh O Brodegan, of Cortnenreaghe, Donogh Maguyer, of Clonarty, Connor oge M'Tirnane, of same, Donogh O Biru, of Donnyn, Melaghlin O Bryaan, of the Dangan, Hugh boy O Shenecane, of same, Owen Grannes, of the Chartron, Owen M'Cahall, of Carykekelyne, Bryan and Donnagh M'Cahall, Dwoltagh O Birne, of same, Bryan m'Connor O Birne, of Moygiosse, Tirlagh Owen, of the Arris, Bryan m'Edm. O Fallan, of Bylaforme, Connor m'Ferrill M'Dermot roe, of Balamonre, Rory m'Muriah M'Dermot roe, Fergananym m'Muriah M'Dermot, and Owen grannagh m'Muriah M'Dermot roe, of same, Tirlagh m'Muriah M'Dermot roe, of Cnockglasse, Dermot O Higant, of Aghaynane, Shane O Bradagan, of Hudaghnenyla, Murrough O Connor, of Garrynemonre, Donnogh m'Owen M'Doyll, of Onockrnery, Collo M'Doyll, Owen oge M'Doyll, Bryan M'Doyll, of same, Shane M'Kaoygh, of the Corregha, Collo m'Donogh Keogh, of the Carriak, Lysagh m Lysagh O Connor, of the Clonyn, Rory granaghe O Mulranyn, of Ballaintober, Cahall Keoghe O Carmully, of same, Donald Trombutdar, of Kelinmulranye, George fitz Peter Nugent, of Arklose, Connor O Birne, Nich. Nugent, Bryan O Birne, of same, Manus O Loghe, of Dongara, Connor m'Manus Keogh, of Sekrmore, Bryan m'Dermot roogh, of Ballymore, Rory boy, of Carowwonyn, Wm. O Rime, of Aracllaghe, Nynyn duffe ny Arte, Lysagh m'Manus M'Doyll, of Seanbolne, Phelym m'Lysagh M'Doyll, of same, Hugh roe O Conor, of Arklone, Dermot Logha, Thady m'Fergananym M'Dermot, of same, Cahall O Rinne, of Lymagabraghe, Owen boy M'Kearly, of Clonmore, Rury m'Phelym ban, of Annaghe, Phelym oge m'Phelym boy, Keadagh m'Shane santagh O Kelly, of Moynaghmore, Anable ne Keoyghe, of the Correaghe, Uomy O Mulloy, of the Clonyn, Art O Conor, of Aghremale, co. Mayo, James M'Muriaha, Riccard oge M'Murise, Walter duffe M'Murise, of same, Moyler M'Murise, of Mornyne, Tomeltagh oge M'Higbane, of the Tarmore, Shan oge M'Christick, of the Cloubas, Riccard m'Walter oge M'Murise, of the Barrelle, Moyler oge m'Moyler M'Hubart, of Balenknave, Gilber m'Tho. M'Gilber, of Kellydane, Moylere m'Edmond roe, of Stangarde, Donogh O Boylan, of Drunmahey, co. Leitrim, Donald O Boylan, Owen O Boylan, Melaghlen O Boylane, Wm. Keoghe, Thady M'Donnogh, Uny Renagh, Hugh M'Donnogh, of same, Connor carragh, of Cnoakanconor, Patr. Dignam, of same, Edm. M'Murrogh, of Castlaben, Owen duffe O Rorike, of Drumnahyar, Donagh carragh m'Colle M'Dryan, of the Ballagh, co. Galway, Wm. Fehoe, of the Dirae, James Phillip, of Ballar[   ], Connor roe M'Bryan, of Garowe, Edm. O Kelly, of Clolnbrook, Irell m'Gillernyff M'Faghna, of the Callow, co. Longford, Connor M'Gillernyff, Donald M'Gillernyff, Fearyee M'Gillernyff, Edm. M'Thomas, Phelym M'Gillernyff, Bryan carragh m Thomas boy, of same, Connogher M'Thirrelagh, in Rahoen, in co. Clare, Donaghie M'Rossie alias Encawmnen, of Clane, Tirlagh M'Donchie, of same, and Thady Ottyn alias ne Karten, of Killcharahagly. Security as in 4943.—10 Nov., xxxii.

5487 (4855.) Pardon to Donnell m'Brien O Kelly, of the Behagh, Breassall m'Brien O Kelly, Benvon ny Viren O Kelly, Annigh m'Shane carragh O Kelly, Owen m'Shane O Kelly, Egneghan m'Shane O Kelly, Donogh m'Shane O'Kelly, of same, Brien duff m'Cormook O Kelly, of Cloynrelliagh, Laughlen m'Brien O Kelly, of same, Brien carragh O Kelly, of Aghneakie, Owen m'Brien carragh O Kelly, Brassill m'Brien carragh O Kelly, Dermot reogh m'Philip M'Ennise, Teige m'Dermot O Kelly, Shane m'Edm. O Kelly, of same, Owen roe M'Manus, of Cloynrolliagh, Rob. Long, of Tirandarriff, John og O Kelly, of Killin, Farren roe O Kelly, of Killeroen, Edm. kerogh O Kelly, Owin duf O Kelly, Donogh carragh O Kelly, of same, Owin m'Teig O Kelly, of Clonkyne, and Tho. M'Kyne, of th. Micheal. Security as in 4943, in co. Roscommon or Galway. The pardon not to include riot or unlawful assembly, nor intrusion into crown lands, or debts to the crown.—12 Nov., xxxii.

5488 (4356.) Pardon to Cahir Fitz Lewis, of White's wodd, Gerald Fitz Lewis, his brother, Ricard m'Rob. O Shee, of Shanrenagh, Tho. fitz James Toben, of Clomlanghe, Mortagh M'Esvoye, of Kalla, husbandman, and Nich. Blanchfielde, of Blanchfieldston, horseman, co. Kilkenny. Provisions as in 5362.—12 Nov., xxxii.

5489 (4514.) Pardon to Ferrall M'Gawran, of Breachlaghe, gent. Edm. M'Gawran, of Gortnckargee, gent., Phelim O Doylane, Mahon O Doylan, of same, husbandmen, James O Doylan, of Ownygalleise, horsekeeper, Edm. O Doylan, of Aghamoynaghe, cottier, Con O Doylane, of same, horsekeeper, Ferdorogh O Doylane, of same, husb., Brene O Doylane m'Rowry, of same, cottier, Patr. M'Echie, of same, horsekeeper, Patr. O Doylane, of Killecrynu, husb., Tiernan O Doylane, of Carrenmcngan, horsekeeper, Cahill O Doylane, of Tonyaneake, labourer, Philip roe O Doylane, of same, horsekeeper, and Gerald m'Shane O Reighlia, of Drumbrughus, husbandman. Security as in 4943, in co. Cavan. The pardon not to extend to any in prison or on bail to appear, nor to extend to riot, intrusion on crown lands, or debts to the crown.—12 Nov., xxxii.

5490 (4439.) Livery to Henry, son and hair of David Sumpter, late of Phillipston, King's co., gent. Fine, 20s. English.—12 Nov., xxxii.

5491 (4430.) Livery to Maurice O Bryan, baron of Inchequyne, son and heir of Maurice, late baron. Fine, £21 6s. 8d.—13 Nov., xxxii.

5492 (4357.) Pardon to Rob. Fowle, gent., provost marshal of Connanght, and Lawrence Esmond, his servant.—15 Nov., xxxii.

5493 (4513) Pardon to Edm. duffe Prendergast, of Gortillegh, co. Tipperary. Provisions as in 5382.—15 Nov., xxxii.

5494 (4610) Pardon to Alexander m'Hugh boy, of Rahleakane, co. Mayo, Rich. m'Edmond oge, of Portnehally, Wm. duffe O Murearie, of Cloynedoby, Rich. O Murearie, of same, Davy

1590.   PLANTS.—ELIZABETH.

oge White, of Bahlaakana, Hugh O Mureario, Ullyck roe
M'Qylikn, Edm. M'Davy, of same, Teige o Togher M'Qurakan,
of Carrowmore, and Rich. O Muloyne. Security as in 4943,
in co. Mayo. The pardon not to extend to any riot or offence
of which any of the parties is accused in the Castle Chamber,
Dublin.—16 Nov., xxxii.

5495 (4450) Grant to Rich. Power, [son and heir to lord Poer];
of the island of Inchemore in the Loughrye and in part of the
river Shynnan, [the islands of Inahchigen], Inaheloughrene,
containing certain stone walls of a monastery, [Callanishe] alias
Inchecalla, Inchemanagh, and [Incho]kerbeyclermid, in the
Loughrie, possessions of the late monastery of Inchemore alias
Inaheloughrene, co. Roscommon, (rent, 25s. 2d.); the manor of
Mileok, and the site of the manor or castle of Mileok in the
Yellow island in the river Shenan alias Shynnan, another island
near the Yellow island, the town and lands of Meleck, two other
islands in the Shenan, and three fishing weirs in the river, in co.
Galway, (£3 0s. 8d.); four carucates of land in Ballymore
Loughsowdy, half a carucate in Kilinboy, one carucate each in
Ballimakall, Skiffen, Ballihesker, Ballygallock, and Ballincor,
one quarter of land in Clonemangh, two carucates of land in
Ballmorren, half a carucate in each of Tobbercorrmook, Mododo,
Ballipaden, Ballimadrone, and Ballipersage, co. Westmeath,
lands of Oliver Fitz Gerald, attainted, (£11 10s.); lands, bog to
cut turf, and the ruins of a castle and houses in Baccourton and
R[ol]eston, (£6 8s.), Baccourath and Ballindirry, (50s.), and
Jordanston, (£5), co. Meath, lands of David Sutton, attainted;
land in Cullendrought, parcel of the lands of the monastery of
S. Peter of the Newtown by Trym, co. Meath, (4s. 8d.) To
hold for ever in common socage. Rents as above; the whole
rent given as £30 4s. 0d.—[16 Nov., xxxii.] In part obliterated
(see Auditor General's Patent Book, vol. 30, p. 1).

5496 (4518.) Grant to Rich. Chichester, gent.; of the office of
controller of the great and small customs in the port of Drogheda.
To hold during good behaviour, with a fee of £10, and such other
fees as Henry Purkins had.—21 Nov., xxxiii.

5497 (4513.) Pardon to Conor og M'Dermot, of Aghahare, Margaret
ny Knowghar, his wife, Coralie ny Rorke, Bannowne ny Dermott,
Cormock M'Dermott, brother of Conor, Tumultie M'Dermot, his
brother, Teig M'Owen. Brian m'Edm. Maghrie, Dermot M'Granye,
Easil M'Dermot rolde, of Roskna, Rory M'Dermot ro, of same,
Connor og M'Dermot ro, of the Smottrona, Keaddowgh m'Edm.
M'Dermot roe, Cormock M'Dermot roe, of Aghohare, Teig and
Owin M'Dermot ro, his brothers, Gilleduffe M'Dermot ro,
Edmund, his brother, Teig m'Quyne M'Dermot ro, Dowyltagh
M'Dermot roe, his brother, Dermot M'Dormot ro, Brian m'Edm.
M'Dermot ro, of Agohare, Mortagh m'Connor og M'Dermot ro,
Manus m'Edm. M'Dermot roe, of Kylmanroe, Knowghar
m'Teig M'Anabe, of Balladowne, Mourtagh O Mellenny, Brian
O Mellenny, Tierlagh O Mellony m'Morragh O Mellenny,
Cormack m'Shane boy O Mellenny, Owin grany O Mellenny
Rory O Mellenny, Wm. grany O Mellenny, Connor og O Mellenny
Mallony M'Gilleduffe, of Ballaworrill, Edm. reogh m'Owen boy,
Owin og m'Owen boy, Caiell reigh O Mellenny, Teig o Koggie
m'Shane oge, of Cloncarne, Dermot Balla, of Cowyllafyne,

1590.   FIANTS.—ELIZABETH.

Farrall m'Donnoghare Kame, Brian O Brian, Brian O Hally,
Dowaltagh m'Shane og, brother of said Teig o Koggie, Dermot
ballow M'Mallrony, Laughlen m'Mullronny Iyna, Nich.
Flannegan, Teig og M'Dermot roe, of Knocke Dreats, Teig
Koogh m'Dermot granie, Tho. O Ournyne, Towill O Boy, Edm.
m'Rory glas, Lauglen M'Cormock, of Slyweformile, Teig
M'Grannall, Hugh O Connellon, Caiell O Connellon, brother of
said Shane, Tumultie m'Rorie og, Langhlen m'Rory og, his
brother, Teig Ruddare O Connellon, Teig m Tha. bane
M'Connellon, Con O Donnall, Cormock O Gawin, Caiell, his
brother, Owin keagh M'Tey, Shane garron M'Tey, his brother,
Brian m'Manus boy, Dermot M'Laughlin, Hugh M'Gyllamooke,
Tieg reogh m'Rory oge O Connellan, Cormock m'Knowghare
M'Hew, Wm. keygh O Gawine, Farrell duff O Gawine, Tieg
m'Hugh M'Dermot, Hugh reogh m'Cormack oge, Caiell m'Rory
glame, and Cormock m'Carterry O Connellana. Security in co.
Sligo, Roscommon, or Galway, as in 4943.—23 Nov., xxxiii.

5498 (4515.) Pardon to Shane oge M'Donogh, of Tullagh, Mulrony
m'Shane oge, of same, Rorie M'Donogh, of Lysconaghs, [   ]
M'Donogh [   ] boy m'Mulrony fyn,
of Ranelaght, Dermott reogh m'Mulrony fyn, Hugh O Healie,
Moriertagh keugh M'Donogh, Owen [   ] m'Mulrony fyn, [   ]
hallogh m'Mulrony fyn, Teige M'Carley of same, Elm. reogh
m'Mulrony fyn, of Ardfart, Malaghlin m'Mulrony fin, of same,
Owen m'Teige [   ] of [   ] Iafoddy, Manus
M'Emelley, of same, Cormick roe M'Eleam, of same, Gille-
gromaie O Benahan, of Kyncrevyn, Tirralagh duffe O Davan, of
Fenlagh, [   ], Dermot O Healy, of Caselloghdargan,
Hugh M'Sharre, of same, Rory m'Cormick M'Donogh, of same,
Ferriall m'Tomultogh O Garie, of Shrowe, Teige boy O Gary, of
same, Edm. oge O Garie, of [   ] Brien m'James M'Swyne, of
Downlyn, Mulrony boy O Conellan, of Cowlas, Ferriall O Kelly,
Hugh O Kelly, Owen keugh M'Kegan, Dowaltagh M'Donagh,
Tirrelogh O Kelly, of same, Callogh O Connor, of the Graunge,
Hugh and Rory O Connor, of same, Mulrony O Dowgynan, of
Ballydowganan, Donogh grane m'Tomultagh [   ] ie, of Balli-
claria, Wm. O Harrie, Manus O Harie, of same, Dermott
O Comyn, Cormock O Comyn, Francis Ultagh, Owen boy
M'Gillamartiin, Brien [   ] O Brenan, Mulrony oge m'Mulrony
boy, Tirrelagh M'Tearnan, of Ballymrienan, Manus M'Donogh,
of Castle loghdergan, Teige boy M'Sharrie, of same, Murtaugh
O Gibleain, of same, Wm. Kelly, and Murtagh M'Malronyn, of
Lysconnogh, in co. Sligo. Provisions as in 5382.—25 Nov., xxxiii.

5499 (4552.) Lease (under queen's letter, 1 July xxxi.) to
Baglish. Henry Sheffield, gent.; of a piece of ground in the Castle
ditch of Dublin, as leased by 3377 (rent 2s.), the tithes
of certain lands which the heirs of Murrogh O Farrall lately
held in the co. Longford, the tithes of Magherygranard, co.
Longford, the tithes of the rectory of Strade, co. Westmeath,
the tithes of the parish church of Ballinkellan alias Ballivickie-
leny, in M'Kernan's country, co. Cavan (recites 3500)
(£17 13s. 4d.); the tithe fish of Mornanton alias Maryverion,
in the parish of Colpe, co. Meath (recites No. 1547) (40s.); the
lands of Little Grange, co. Kildare, parcel of the lands of Edm.
Ewstace, attainted, granted to John Travers, knt., by patent of

1590.   FIANTS.—ELIZABETH.

13 Nov., lii., now in the queen's hands by the attainder of
Ewstace (53s. 4d.) To hold for 31 years from the end of the
recited interests. Rent as above. Provisions as in 4939.—
25 Nov., xxxiii.

5500 (4460.) Pardon to Bartholomew Clynch, of Navan, co.
Meath, Edm. Kelly fitz Hugh, of the Clogher, Feagh, Teig, and
William O Kelly fitz Hugh, William and Hugh M'Moultully,
Donell m'Roris O Donnellan, of same, Donnogh m'Brian
M'Donnogh, of Carnaghe, Edm. M'Colloy, of Connlaigin,
Donnogh M'Koghowe, of Rakill, Marcus M'Comen, of Castell-
nove, Wm. oge m'Hugh oge, Edm. moyll M'Telge, Rosse
M'Mallaghlin, of Ballaiheaghtane, co. Clare, and Owin carragh
m'Gyllyduffe M'Donnogh, of Kilbride, co. Galway, and Con-
kerroy m'Hugh oge. Security as in 4943, in cos. Galway or
Roscommon. The pardon shall not extend to any riot or
offence of which any of the parties is accused in the Castle
Chamber, Dublin.—26 Nov., xxxiii.

5501 (4524.) Grant to Gerald Dyllon, gent., clerk of the crown in
the Chief Place; the office of third justice of the Chief Place.
To hold during pleasure, with such fees as Bartholomew Russell
had.—26 Nov., xxxiii.

5502 (6736) Surrender by Edmond Fitz Gibbon, gent.; of the
manor or castle of Balliboy, and other lands and chief rents held
under lease, 3583. See 5517. (Signed Edd. G[   ].—28
Nov., xxxiii.

5503 (4508.) Pardon to Rich. moore Burke alias m'Tomcok, of
Elis O Carroll, King's co. Provisions as in 5382.—30 Nov.
xxxiii.

5504 (4511.) Pardon to Tirlagh M'EmdyDalias Tirlagh M'Donogh,
of Cowlewynury, Mulmorry M'Brinon, of same, Phelim m'Shane
keoghe O Hart, of Eanagh, Donnogh m'Donell O Hart, Roris
m'Donell giasse O Hart, of same, Brian m'Ultagh O Connor,
of Downalley, Rory ballagh O Connor, of Eanaghe, Calwagh
O Connor, of Olonderrare, Hugh O Connor, of same, Dowgh-
dally O'Connor, of Loghane, Teige m'Fergananme O Connor,
Brian carragh O Connor, of same, Wm. grace O Hart, of Brad-
cully, Connor oge m'Wm. O Hart, of Ardiearmayn, Phelim
O Connor, of Formoyle, Tybbot M'Jonnin, of Longford, Rory
O Connor, of Sararden, Owin O Connor, of same, Brian oge
m'Brian oge O Hart, of Ballecara, Connor oge m'Teige keogh
O Hart, Connor oge M'Mulronyn, of Templebanne, and James
O Crean, of Sligo, gent.; co. Sligo. Security as in 4943. The
pardon not to include intrusion into crown lands or debts to
the crown, or any riot or offence of which any of the parties is
accused in the Castle Chamber in Dublin.—30 Nov., xxxiii.

5505 (4486.) Pardon to Peter Butler and James Butler, gentlemen,
and Tho. Cavenagh.—4 Dec., xxxiii.

5506 (4491.) Pardon to Teig duffe m'Donell M'Calighan, of Inshi-
legh, co. Cork, husbandman or farmer, Wm. O Chalighan, John
m'Wm. O Chalighan, of same, husbandmen, Onnora inis Quyne,
of Driahan, Elin nie Tane nie Gerrald, of Peake, Connor m'Dermot m'Philip M'Keaghan, of Oranagh, husb., Donogh m'Davie
Oring, of Iverling, husb., Aulivo m'Connor O Leye, of same,
farmer, Teig m'Donlle m'Donnogh duffe, of Muingarivhat, Cormak
m'Brien O Dale, of Duaghe, yeoman, Teigroe m'Donlle Y Comele,

                                        K

1590.   FIANTS—ELIZABETH.

of Tuenodronine, Donile m'Donell Y Conell, Donell m'Dermot
M'Cartie, and Morice m'Donell Y Conell, of same, husbandmen,
Ellen nie Donell M'Carte, of same, Shane m'Mahowne Y Conell
Teig m'Donell m'Dermot Y Connell, Brein m'Donnogh Y Connell,
and Teig m'Shyaghrie ni'David O Hierieghie, of same, and
David m'Mahowne O Ring, of Carignecorie, husbandmen, Donell
oge O Lerye, of same, yeoman, Shane m'Dermot O Ring, Connor
m'Shane O Cronyne, Donnell m'Dermot O Connell, Donnell
m'Teig O Sulivan, and Connor m'Shane O Connell, of same, husbandmen; co. Cork or Limerick. Provisions as in 5504. Provided that the pardon shall not avail for any who do not fulfil
such orders as may be made by the lord deputy, concerning the
lands which they hold when their crimes were committed.—4 Dec.,
xxxiii.

5507 (4482.) Pardon to Hugh m'Morgh M'Swyne, Wm. English,
of Scartine Kilcolman, Margaret Walsh, of Kilmyvine, Dermot
m'Mahiro I Combe, of Loberigyein, Philip m'Donell O'Moroghe,
of same, yeoman, Morertagh· m'Donell O Morgho, of saur,
yeoman, Art m'Killednffe O Morgho, of same, Nich. Blust
fitz Melchior, of Yoghell, Connor m'Donogho Regan, of Carbrn,
Connor m'Teig reogh O Mahand, of same, Tirlagh m'Shane
O Shirine, of same, Donell M'Moriertagh, of Kilneckine,
Morogh m'Tirlagh M'Briane, of Whitstown, Tho. m'Dermot
O Morine, of Temple bridan, Moriertagh m'Brien M'Teig, of
Tagh Clogyne, Phelin O Tohill, of Kilmacthomas, Edm. Power
fitz John, of same, Ellen inie Moris, of Castle ne henche,
widow, Elis nie Tane M'Thomas, of Inshilagh, Ricoard Barrod
m'Shane, of Carrick Roghan, Connor m'Richard O Mahoney,
Johanna nie James ne Garruld, of Whitstown, Elis ne James ne
Gorrald, of same, Donell m'Dermod Cartie, of Lohirte, Teig
m'Dermot Cartie, of Castle ne henrye, John Barrie, of Listarnlis,
and Peter Jellons, of Grastastle; oo. Cork and Limerick.
Provisions as in 5506.—4 Dec., xxxiii.

5508 (4493.) Pardon to Dermot m'Dermot O Sulivan, of Cargnecov,
husbandman, Fining m'Art, of Dunbolige, gent., Erevan m'Brene
M'Swyne, of Nadered, yeoman, John Follow, of Cork, tailor,
Edm. m'Teige O Morghow, of Drishan, yeoman, Teig m'
Molaghlen O Riordane, of Cnokvoikig, hush., Morgh m'Morie-
tagh M'Shie, of Listarnlie, Manus m'Moriertagh M'Shie, of same,
yeoman, Teig O Hangelen, Owin m'Eavoy O Riordawe, John
m'Conoghor O Riordane, and Conoghor m'Mahownd I Ourike,
of same, husbandman, Donell dorgh M'Cormok, of same,
yeoman, Donell m'Connor O Bren, of Tushe, and Donnogh
m'Donell O Bren, of same, gentleman, Shane m'Donell O Maghowne and Philip Malefant, of same, yeoman, David Burk, of
Polnesilagh, gent., Donell O Lehan, of Carrighloyne, and
Dermod O Cronyne, of same, husbandman, Anlone O Brene,
of Whitstown, gent., Owin O Moroghe, of Blarne, Teig m'Connor
O Mahowne, of Molde, Dermot oge beg O Mahowne, and Donnogh
m'Dermot oge O Mahowne, of same, yeoman; oo. Cork and
Limerick. Provisions as in 5506.—4 Dec., xxxiii.

5509 (4548.) Grant (under queen's letter, 8 March, xxx.) to Brian
Fitz Williams, esq.; of half of Abbottestane, parcel of the lands of
James Ewstace, attainted, in oo. Dublin (rent 53s.), four quarters
of land in Ballinrobbe, in the barony of Kilmean, oo. Mayo, parcel

of the lands of Edm. Bourke, late of Castelbarrye, attainted (£3 11s. 1½d.), (recites 4126 and 5255). To hold for ever, in free socage. Rent £6 4s. 1½d. as above.—6 Dec., xxxiii.

5510 (4554.) Lease (under commission, 17 Feb., xix.) to Bryan Fitz Williams, esq.; of three half quarters of land called respectively Leighcarrowebeggowghhall, Leighcarrowe knocktwo, and Leighcarrowe Carran Raighe, a parcel of land called Gorte Clonemore, on the west of the river of Lyskeynan, a parcel of land called Farren Dyen, nigh Laccagh, the lands of Theobald Bourke, of Lyskynan, co. Galway, attainted, excepting the castle of Lyskynan and four quarters of land adjoining. To hold for 21 years. Rent 15s. 9d. Provisions as in 5311. "There was none of the parcells formerly in charge."—6 Dec., xxxiii.

5511 (4505.) Pardon to Edm. duff M'Connell, of Rally, Rory oge M'Rory, of the Pallice, Moylery M'Moryertagh, of Ballen Kilmore, Peter Leynagbo, Cormok M'Shane, Flatro O Kenny, Tyriagh M'Coghlane, of Clomanna, in King's co., Auly M'Coghlane, of same, [Brian M'Coghlane, of Clcinelegan, King's co., Moylery M'Coghlane, of Bannan, James O Don, Shane boy Daltone, Calwagh M'Connell, of Skregan, Edm. M'Donnagh, of the Palice, Hubbart M'Edmund, and Edm. m'Donnogh carragh. Security as in 4943, in King's co. The pardon not to include murder, burglary, or arson.—7 Dec., xxxiii.

5512 (4502.) Pardon to John O Relie, knt., and Rich. Gall, of the Beglass, co. Dublin, Mulmory O Relie, of Cornegall, co. Cavan, esq., Donill Bradie, of Aghneglogh, Philip Bradie, and Barnaby Bradie, of same, gentlemen, Simon Brangan, of Stydalt, and Brian m'Edm. O Relie, of Killnecortt, gent.; co. Cavan. Provisions as in 5504.—8 Dec., xxxiii.

5513 (4544.) Commission to Nich. Kenny, esq., deputy auditor of Ireland, George Thorneton, esq., provost marshal of Mounster, Henry Billingsley and Tho. Springe, esquires, Roger Lucas and Wm. Farmer, gentlemen; to view, survey, and measure the number of acres in the lands held by Wm. Carter, gent., as administrator to his brother Arthur Carter, esq., in the country of Kannery and elsewhere in co. Limerick, parcel of the lands escheated by the attainder of Tho. FitzGerrald called the Knight of the Valley, as by demise to sir W. Drury, knt., deceased, may appear, except the castle of Glanne, and lands granted in fee farm to Edm. m'Thomas. With the intention of the lands being granted in reversion to Carter.—11 Dec., xxxiii.

5514 (4539.) License to Edw. Waterhous, knt., one of the privy council; to be absent in England for one year.—14 Dec., xxxiii.

5515 (4519.) Grant to Wm. Rilandes; the office of porter of the castle of Dublin, with a fee of 12d. a day, as Rob. Cooke had. To hold during good behaviour.—15 Dec., xxxiii.

5516 (4556.) Lease (under queen's letter, 14 Oct., xxi.) to Wm. Bathe, of Dromounrathe, gent.; of the rectory of Damore, the tithes and alterages of the parish church of Balloughbre, the tithes of 6 quarters of land in Balimanagbe in the Analie, the tithes of land of the lord M'Genure in the Aralie, of land in Montekarbary, and of four granges in Granard, the granges of Tonaghmore, Ryncoll, Goldanny, Clonecrall, and Deraghe, the tithes of the parish church of Dromloman, the tithes of the parish church of Ballmakewe, possessions of the monastery of Granarde, in the

K 2

1590.   FIANTS.—ELIZABETH.

counties of Longford and Meath (recites 9300); land and a great
mountain called Slewwood, in Ballimorry, co. Dublin, parcel of
the lands of Tho. Eustace, of Cardeston, attainted; (the tithes
due to the vicar of Demore, and any other vicar, excepted). To
hold for 21 years from the determination of the recited lease.
Rent £26 13s. 4d. Provisions as in 5311.—15 Dec., xxxiii.

5517 (6834.) Grant to Edmund Fitzgibbon, esq., called the White
Knight; of the lands of Ballirenan, Balliphillip, [Ballialey],
Killadirrye, and Kilmacullen, Kilclony, [possessions of John ogg]
fitz John Gibbon de Gerrald, White Knight, attainted, in the
co. Cork, belonging to the manor of Oldcastleton (rent, 58s. 4d.);
the lands of Balliancghan and the Scarte, same co. (£3); the
lands of Pollardestone, by Brigowns (3s. 4d.); Killiglasse
(13s. 4d.); 53s. 4d. ster. chief rent out of the manor of Ard-
skethe, in the tenure of John Fitz Gerralde, esq., [26s. 8d.] out
of Brigowns, in the tenure of William Fitz Thomas, 14s. 8d.
ster. out of the castle of Farrehie, in the tenure of Richard
Cumben, 40s. ster. of Garrandrolane, in the tenure of viscount
Iarmoye, 17s. 9d. ster. out of Mountenrobbin, in the tenure of
Richard Cumben, co. Cork (£12 2s. 10½d.); the lands of Balline-
greny and [Jamestons], co. Limerick (£5); Karrowgarrowe, by
Kilmallock (16s. 8d.); Raynewitagbe (20s.); 40s. ster. chief
rent out of Kilfynan, in the tenure of Shane boye Roche;
13s. 4d. out of the castle of Ballindromite, late in the tenure of
Gerald M'Richards, and now in the hands of William Teige;
13s. 4d. ster. out of Ballinakally, in the tenure of Gerald
M'Thomas; 13s. [4d.] ster. out of Downamowne, in the tenure
of John M'Shehie; 20s. ster. out of Ballenvoscolladon, in the
tenure of Conohor roe O Hernan; 20s. ster. out of Ballena-
akaddan; 26s. 8d. ster. out of Dallingaldie, in the tenure of
Peter Oreaghe; 40s. ster. out of Fountelande, in the tenure
of Fornte; 20s. ster. out of Dallinwranye, in the tenure of
Gerald M'Thomas; 20s. ster. out of Glanlare, in the tenure of
Gibbons Dirronte; 10s. ster. out of Stephenestone; 26s. 8d.
ster. out of Dirraghe, in the tenure of Shane boye Roche;
13s. 4d. ster. out of Ballieshanhoye, in the tenure of [M'Ehaine]
boye; 106s. 8d. ster. out of Cloghenodfoile, in the tenure of
John Laughan and other clerks of Ardpatrick; 40s. ster. out of
Dallinlondrie, in the tenure of Gerald M'Gibbon and [Edmund
M'Gibbon]; 26s. 8d. ster. out of Ballinehowe, in the tenure of
Richard Foxe, of Limric; 13s. 4d. ster. out of Ballenanonowe,
in the tenure of Shane boye Roche; 13s. 4d. ster. out of Balli-
alone; 33s. 4d. out of Caherolina, in the tenure of Donald
O Heyne and Teige O Heins, all belonging to the late White Knight,
in the co. Limerick (£34); also part of the castle of Balliboye,
which extends to the towns of Balliboye and Ballindamaher, co.
Tipperary; the lands of Kilcharrownaghe, Dirragharricke, and
Skianaughdan (£6); Coultellaghe, Naggarrame, and Balliechane
(33s. 4d.); 13s. 4d. chief rent out of Shanraughan, in the tenure
of Richard Keating, with the perquisites of the court there, co.
Tipperary (18s. 4d.); also the site of the castle of Co[art] Rad-
darye, near the town of Kilimallocke, surrounded with a stone wall,
the court being ruinous, the land belonging to it, a water mill, and
a third part of another upon the river of Killmallock, co. Limerick
(40s.), all possessions of the late John ogg fitz John Gibbon de

Gerrald, the White Knight, attainted. To hold in tail male, in
caplte by the service of [a twentieth part of a knight's fee].
Rent, £72 4s. 0½d., divided as above.—[15 Dec., xxxiii.] *Much
defaced.* (*Auditor-General's Patent Book 0, p. 71.*)

5518 (4500.) Pardon to Morgh ne doe O Flaertie, knt. The pardon
not to include Intrusion into crown lands or debts to the crown.—
16 Dec., xxxiii.

5519 (4501.) Pardon to Brian dorgh m'Edm. M'Nurtagh, Taige
M'Owen, of Aghnenswer, Roger Sheogh O Flaertie, Hugh duff
O Flaertie, Brion I Chowly O Flaertie, and Morrogh oge
O Flaertie, sons of Morgh ne do O Flaertie, knt., Conoghor oge
m'Conoghor more, of Cardowly, Cahill M'Morine, of Oughter-
ard, Walter m'Donell M'Brien, Hugh boy M'Murny, Conoghor
more M'Murny, Donnogh m'Teige ne glavo, of the Gleans, Morogh
m'Teige ne glavo, Morogh m'Edmund Revy, Hubberd m'Edmund
Revy, Hugh boy m'Redmund M'Key, Rich. Rewaghe m'Redmund
M'Key, Gilleduffe M'Dermott, Brien Ohie, of Moyestragha, Teige
O Hulleran, of Oharny, Moyler m'Dermot O Hulleran, Shane oge
m'Shane O Brien, of the Foughe, Moriertagh oge, Carberie oge
O Kenewine, Feighe m'Cormock more, Owen ni'Cormock more,
Moyler oge m'Moyler M'Morogh, of the Carriak, Conoghor og
m'Donogh M'Connoghor, of Killaina, Rich. reogh ni'Donogh
M'Conoghor, Edm. grane m'Donogh M'Conoghor, Taige m'Brien
reogh, Wm. m'Rich. M'Walter, Hugh boy m'Dermot M'Donogh,
Wm. oge M'Colly, of Glintrelge, Theobald M'Cally, Edm. M'Colly,
Henry og m'Henry boy, Shane m'Robert boy, Walter m'Tho.
M'Davie, Henry more m'Richard M'Ted, of Twamavy, Tho.
M'Richard, Rich. M'Alistran, Ricard og m'Ricard M'Moylere, of
Slewartry, Ricard m'Edmund duffe, of Macontramy, Redmund og
m'Redmund M'Davy, of Monteroine, Shane m'Edmund duffe,
Henry m'Henry buy, Rich. m'Walter more, Tibot m'Edmund
duffe, Tho. m'Shane M'William, of Ballenillagh, Moyler M'Aline,
of Kilbrealo, Rowry m'Donagh M'Shane, Ulick M'Donogh,
Moyler M'Hugh, Moyler m'Tibott M'Donagh, Edm. boy m'Tibot
M'Donagh, Wm. M'Richard, of the Carick, Rich. m'Shane
M'Walter, of Reulvilla, Moylere m'Tibot boy, Ullick oge
m'Ullick M'Edmund, Walter oge m'Shane M'Walter, Shane
m'Rich. M'Shana, Redmund m'Thomas Myorey, Feagh m'Davy
M'Redmund, of Kilmore, David and Henry m'Wm. M'Davy,
Rich. buy m'Feagh M'Davie, Rich. m'Edm. og, of Tierne-
kally, Rory m'Redmund M'Edmund, Uliak buy m'Redmund
M'Edmund, Taige M'Rory, of the Cleigin, Brian M'Conoghor,
Edm. O Toole, of Unnya, John roe O Higkin, of Conigy, Shane
O Grady, of Moyvally, yeoman, Taige O Grady, Owny O Farby,
of Limbrin, Shane O Cowhow, of Moyvaly, Fynally ny Prawill,
Fynollie ny Cohowe, Melaghlin M'Gindale, Moylere duffe
m'Wm. Davye, Shane Croan m'Wm. M'Davy, Tho. m'Richard
oge, Wm. m'Richard oge, Edm. m'Richard oge, and Walter
m'Richard oge, in co. Galway. Provisions *as in* 5382.—16 Dec.,
xxxiii.

5520 (4550.) Grant (under queen's letter, 18 July, xxxii., and a
letter of lord Burghley, lord high treasurer of England, 25 July,
xxxii.), to Thady m'Dermot M'Cartie, of Donemayneway, co.
Cork, gent. ; of the castle and lands of Donemayneway, co. Cork,
one quarter of land called the quarter of Kilwarrye, and one

1590.   FIANTS.—ELIZABETH.

quarter of land respectively in each of the following: Dromlynie, Inshie, Drowndrustell, Qaynrahe, Kiarow ny Wadirye, Togher, Tulhighe, Altaghe, two carucates of land in Balbhallcinge, one quarter in Mwhonnye, Kilronan, Lisbiallad, Drenaghe, letter Gorman, Viarlighan, two carucates of Clowne and Dowgan, half a carucate of Derynikarraghe, and half a carucate of Inynlghrery, in the cantred of Glannoryn, in said county; which lands extend from Cloghan Cowleshannaghe on the east, to Fenghe lieghtiry on the west, and from Carrige ny forrey on the south, to Cow-nighan on the north, and Shanelaraghe on the east, to Glashine yerraghe in Cwosane on the west, and were the lands of Cormack downe M'Cartie, late of Glancryne, in the cantred of Carbrye, attainted, lying in co. Cork. To hold in tall male, by the service of a twentieth part of a knight's fee. Rent 40s. English. Maintaining ten footmen when required for the queen's service.—18 Dec., xxxiii.

5521 (4494.) Pardon to Donogh m'Donell M'Carty, Gillyduffe m'Diermodie Y Knoghor, Owen M'Eagane, Dermod m'Finen M'Cryhew, of Lettyr, Diermod m'Shane M'Donell, of Rommy-carten, Owen and Conoghor m'Shane M'Donell, of same, Teige m'Shane Y Swlywane, of Kyleynana, Neill M'Leghilline, Donell m'Fellmy M'Carttie, Owen and Donell m'Conoghor M'Cartie, Conoghor O Shey, Donell m'Teige Y Swlivan, of the Cahir, Owen m'Donogho M'Cartie, of Killoyne, Finen M'Cormock, of same, Dermod m'Teige I Soliwane, Conoghor m'Shane Y Enolaghane, Owen M'Craghan, of Lettyr, Donogho m'Teige M'Craoyn, of same, Donogh m'Dermod Y Snlywane alias M'Gulluchud, Donogho oge O Huraghtine, of Garraneyarightane, and Anna M'Crulsan, of Lyttyr; in coa. Kerry or Desmond. Provision for security as in 4043. The pardon not to include intrusion into crown lands or debts to the crown. Provided that this pardon shall not be effective for any persons who will not obey such orders as may be made by the lord deputy concerning the land which they held when their offences were committed.—23 Dec., xxxiii.

5522 (4495.) Pardon to Donogho m'Wm. O Morowhwo, of the Pallis, Murryhirtagh O Ninaime, of same, Nich. oge Hannoroge, Donogho m'Onoghor M'Neale, Nich. M'Carroll, of Ballyduffe, Morris m'Owen I Wyrryhirtaghe, Donell y Knockane, Donell m'Awlywe I Laine, Dermod m'Wm. I Chamhey, of Ballyakealighe, John oge O Corkyrane, of Castlemor, Telge ny Kelly, Dermond m'Owen boy, Ullick oge M'Thomas, Dermond roe, Donell m'Shane I Riurdan, of Castlemore, Shane m'Teige I Morwghwo, Morris m'Dermond I Coronyn, Toige m'Donogh I Mowghne, Ellyn m'Mwrugh I Eagan, Owne m'Rorie m'Mui-wgh I Mulrian, Finine m'Dermod O Driscoll, of Downigall; and Dermod m'Mlaghlen m'Murghwe I Mulriane, coa. Kerry or Desmond. Provisions as in 5521.—23 Dec., xxxiii.

5523 (4503.) Pardon to Hugh Magenise, knt., Ivor Magenise, Mourtagh Magenise, Brian oge Magenise, John Magenise, Rorie m'Con Magenise, Art m'Rosse Magenise, Edm. oge m'Arte oge Magenise, Mourtagh m'Edm oge Magenise, Edm. oge m'Donnell m'Brian Magenise, Glassie and Brian m'Donnell m'Brian Magenise, Dermot oge M'Cowley; Brian m'Brian m'Shane carragh, Shane oge m'Brian m'Shane carragh, Patr. oge

1590.   FIANTS.—ELIZABETH.

and Hugh m'Brian m'Patr. M'Hugh, Brian modder M'Brian, Phelim M'Brian, Ferdorragh M'Gnamo m'Phelim M'Prior, Hugh m'Rosse Magenisse, Patr. m'Phelim duff M'Cartan, Hugh oge m'Phelim duff M'Cartan, Shane oge O Doran, Patr. oge O Doran m'Shane oge, Redmund O Doran, Phelim duff O Doran m'Redmund, Manus O Doran m'Redmund, Dwaltagh O Doran m'Patr. oge, Patr. oge M'Gilroie, Phelim buoy M'Gilroie, Gillegroome, Arte, Tirlagh, and Donnell M'Gilroie, Patr. roe O Collo, Murtagh Bartinangh O Collo, Tirlagh oge O Downylye, Aghowlie M'Crosman, Patr. more M'Quiggen, Phelim m'Mourtagh M'Quiggen, Arte m'Donnell carragh M'Quiggen, Patr. oge m'Patr. more M'Quiggen, Tirlagh m'Arte m'Donnell carragh M'Quiggen, Manus M'Quiggen, Owen M'Quiggen, Langhlim oge O Rorie, Rorie M'Conwall, Edm. m'Tirlagh M'Conwall, Gilduff M'Conwall, Hugh molle O Morgan, Cormock modder O Kellie, Owen carragh O Kellie, and Brian boye O Kellie, in co. Down. Provisions as in 5382.—( ) Dec., xxxiii.

1590-1.

5524 (4496.) Pardon to Melaghlin m'Teig M'Hugh, of the Skreine, Tho. oge and Edm. m'Teig M'Hugh, of same, Donagh glasse m'Manus M'Laghlin, Jue m'Manus M'Laughlin, of same, Hugh m'Tho. M'Glynn, Teige M'Tumultagh, of Clonfrie, Tumultagh M'Laghlin, of Corbelley, Brian M'Laghlin, of same, Hugh keoghe m'William carragh, of Moylytragh, Shane m'Hugh m'William currogh, of same, Rich. Dowhertie, of Rahanowe, John Stanton, Shane reogh M'Warde, of same, Walter M'Collie, of Ballynemore, Connor m'William carrogh, Shane roe M'Awarde, Edm. O Maghery m'Laughlin donne, of Lemger, More ny Laghlin donne, of same, Teige M'Dowltagh, of the Skreine, Wonas nyne Teige, of Ballynofadda, Rorie m'Hugh O Conor, Shane m'Hugh O Conor, of same, Tumultagh M'Deirmod, of Clonfrie, Deirmot m'Tumultagh M'Dermod, of same, Donogh m'Farell O Flanigan, of Ballinofadda, Lynagh oge m'Lisagh O Farill, of same, Keadagh m'Tirlagh O Conor, of Annagh, Tumultagh m'Owen M'Dermot, and Dermot M'Dermot, his son, in co. Roscommon. Provisions as in 5382.—2 Jan., xxxiii.

5525 (4557.) Lease (under queen's letter, 1 Aug., 1586), to Patr. Cullen ; of the lands of Christianston, co. Louth. To hold for 60 years from the determination of 4770. Rent £3. Provisions as in 4939. In consideration of his having built the bridge of Blackwater, and having surrendered his land there, now in possession of the constable of Blackwater.—2 Jan., xxxiii.

5526 (4534.) Livery to Farragh, son and heir of Turlogh M'Donell, late of Newcastle, Queen's co., galloglas. Fine 5s.—28 Jan., xxxiii.

5527 (4517.) Grant to James Ryan, of Dublin, gent. ; of the office of one of the masters of Chancery. To hold during good behaviour, with a fee of £20 English, and such other fees as John Ball had. With power to grant injunctions and other writs in the absence of the chancellor or keeper of the great seal, to take recognizances, examinations and appearances, assign days for pleading, punish for contempt, receive affidavits, and do all other things belonging to the office.—1 Feb., xxxiii.

1590-1.   FIANTS.—ELIZABETH.

5528 (4526.) Grant to Patr. M'Eagan, gent.; the office of seneschal English of Corrabeg alias Ballom'keagan, in the co. Longford. To hold during good behaviour with all profits belonging to the office. With power to call together the farmers and other inhabitants and command them for the defence of that town and lands, the public weal of the inhabitants, and the punishment of malefactors; he may prosecute and punish by all means malefactors, rebels, vagabonds, rymors, Irish harpers, idle men and women, and other unprofitable members.—12 Feb., xxxiii.

5529 (4525.) Grant to Wm. Jones; of the office of marshal or usher of the court of Castle Chamber in the castle of Dublin, vacant because Tho. Keares remained in England without license. To hold during good behaviour, with a fee of £13 6s. 8d. Not to be removed, as in 4976.—13 Feb., xxxiii.

5530 (4484.) Pardon to Murtagh oge m'Murtaghs oge Cavenaghe, Shane M'Garald, Donnell duffe O Birn, Art M'Urn, Donogh M'James, and Rory O Birn, in co. Carlow. Provisions as in 5382.—13 Feb., xxxiii.

5531 (4498.) Pardon to Rich. Branaughe fitz Tho., David Branaughe fitz Tho., Donagh fitz William Molaughlen, Katharine Breanaghe, Wm. Browne fitz John, Tho. m'Da m'Diermodie boye, Wm. Breanaghe fitz Nich., Teige m'Donough I Miloaghy, Teige m'Donnogh roe I Kellis, Tho. bane m'Shane O Fluyn, Dermot m'Tho. m'Teige Iaghie, Tho. m'Teige O Morishie, David Flaghevan, David Baron fitz Pierce, Wm. O Ooman, Donnough M'Shane, Pierce Butler fitz Walter, Dermott Redwarde alias Albanaughe, Wm. m'Shane O Fowlowe, Gerrott Fitz Morris alias Bowhedoblle, Rich. Redwardes alias Albaneghe, Cahell O Doine, Wm. O Lonin, Morice m'Tho. M'Geraldis, Philip O Morchewe, Morice Fitz Nicholas, Rob. Swetman fitz John, of Earlestowne, John Gall fitz Rob., Moriertagh oge M'Brian, Owen m'Teige m'Donnough I Callaghan, Rich. Albanegh, and Rowland Powre, in co. Waterford, Garrett Caron, of Johnstowne, David m'Garrett O Birne, of Ballebarr, and Cahier O Carron, of Knocklowe, in co. Carlow. Provisions as in 5506:—14 Feb., xxxiii.

5532 (4499.) Pardon to Wm. grany M'Remon, of Clogbynaire, Shane boy and David m'Wm. grany M'Ramon, and Ullick m'Walter M'Ramon, of same, gentleman, Conogher grany O Cloan, of same, kern, Riccard M'Maylery, of same, gent., Enahly ny Eyne, Donogho, Melmory, and Tirrolagh M'Swyny m'Owen, Shane Moynagh m'Murish, Rory O Kenny m'Ranyll, of the same, Shane M'Nemes, of Gallway, yeoman, Brian M'Kyroghan, of Tyaquyn, Donnell O Higgin, of Downbally, Walter kittagh M'Feyrick, of same, Riccard Bourke m'Shane, of Dirremacklaghny, gent., Onora Bourke nyne Riccarde, of same, Wm. M'Donnell, of Kilnocknock, horseman, Tho. Bourke m'Edm. meole, of same, Riccard M'William, of Bealena, gent., Hugh O Donowey, of Ballendirry, kern, Colly baccagh O Kelly, of Carowne, gent., Teige O Donowly, of Ballendirry, husbandman, Shane O Donowly, of same, kern, Edm. duffe O Kenady, of Clontume, and Rob. Cardyne, of the Killyn, yeoman, Shane oge O Harely, of Rosmelan, co. Galway, Owen O Faby, of Clanmeoge, Connor m'Conyn M'Donoghe, of Tarmonmackrethyn, Conogher m'Owen O Callynan, of Kilveryrane, Donogh m'Tirraly M'Teige, of Glaskyne, co. Clare, Maylery croane M'Phyllipine, of Carna, husbandman, Maylory Bourk, of Ballierlagh, Ricoard Bourk, and Wm. Bourk, of same, in co. Mayo, gentleman, Callogh m'Allyn M'Dowill, of Barnacullyn, co. Roscommon, Donogh M'Teige, Riccard reough M'Custny, Teige came M'Greo, late of Garvaleh, Donogh m'Hugh O Muldony, of Kilghary, husbandman, Riccard oge M'Greo, of Garvallagh, kern, Shane boy M'Cooge, of Ballscune, gent., Cahir oge M'Costile, of Caherdangan, Teige O Mongan, of Drominary, Donogh Omannar m'Melaghlen m'Teige m'Wm., of Iskerroo, James M'Tiernan, of Laghaarowards, co. Clare, Farries and Teirnan m'James M'Teirnan, Shane Ultagh M'Owen, Moriah Ultagh M'Cormock, of same, Wm. oge m'Wm. M'Loghlan, of Capnepestah, Edm. Bourke m'Rowland, of Dirramacloghney, Riccard Bourke m'Walter, John Bourk m'Roland, Redmund roe Bourke m'Ullig, of same, Rich. Hackett m'Myller, of Illand, Wm. Hackett m'Walter, Myller Hackett m'Willig, of same, Wm. Grane M'Redmond, of Annaghkyne, Edm. Illev M'Redmond, of Shaneballeghbaine, and John M'Kylleroy, of Abartte, in cos. Mayo, Galway, Clare, and Roscommon. Provisions as in 5504. The pardon shall not apply to any offence committed outside the province of Connaught and Thomond.—14 Feb., xxxiii.

5533 (4490.) Pardon to Conor M'Tirrelagh, of Rahyn, co. Clare, Donogh MacFarssey, Tirrelagh M'Donogh, Teig Otten, Scanlan m'Teige M'Gillefadrick, of Corcomro, co. Clare, Wm. O Donnovan, of same, Donogh Entleve athew, of Leydegure, co. Galway, Mylar O Halcran, Rob. Kendall, Donnogh O Mannyn, Wm. M'Donogh alias Ballogh, Edm. macBrien O Kelly, Ferdorgh m'Rickard O Kelly, Owny O Loghlin, of Corballinure, Rosse O Loghlen, of same, Rickard Bourk fitz Redmond, of Ballanenan, Edm. O Lean, of Clonluakere, Hugh moryagh O Maden, of Neantenan, Owen O Boylle, of same, Donell M'Hugh, of Beladonily, Cogela M'Edmond, of Caherserady, Mortagh O Kelly and his wife Margaret ny Krahe, of Enrosse, Mollmorry M'Swyne, Dermod O Kelly, John m'Edm. Hubbert, Coun O Mulshaghlen, of Kilmacshane, Phelim m'Donell M'Coghlan, of same, Donell O Mokeran, of Rahrenan, co. Roscoman, Edm. m'Melaghlen don, of Sonrmore, same co., Fergenanym M'Dermot, of Callone, co. Roscoman, Teige M'Dermot, of same, Cahell M'Hubbert, Edm. M'Cahell, Hubert M'Hugh, Teige M'Cahell, Brian MacDonogh, Shane M'Donogh, James M'Hubbert, Tho. Doyde, Muren M'Teige, Teige M'Gilla, Teige Maganye, Laghlen M'Donoghe, Connor M'Edmond, Brian M'Edmond, Terence M'Dermond, of Cargin, Rory M'Darmond, Wm. M'Geartayne, Donell M'Hubbert, Cornelius M'Hubbert, Cornelius O Gara, of Rathelan, John O Bagayn, Teige O Hiriall, Cahell M'Carbery, of Dirregawny, Teige M'Gwylly, of Callaghmore, Manus ogo O Mulreill, Connor M'Donell, Teige roo O Buyle, Donogh m'Rickard M'Kedagh, Johanna ny Kilconell, Rory boy M'Hubbert, Daniel O Kelly, of Kiltoghor, co. Galway, Roris carragh O Madden, of Clonlam, Gilleduff m'Shane m'Morogh oge, Owny duff O Horan, of Lismyfaddae, Shane boy m'Shane boy O Horan, of same, Caell beg M'Feary, of Corclogha, Owen O Rowrke m'Connor, of Caltaghimarren, and Daniel m'Geffrey Gareyll, of Lisensirure. Provisions as in 5532.—18 Feb., xxxiii.

5534 (4541.) Licence to George Carewe, knt., one of the privy

1590-1.   FIANTS.—ELIZABETH.

council and master of the ordnance; to be absent in England for three months.—19 Feb., xxxiii.

5535 (6643.) Grant (under letters patent of England, 28 Feb., xxxii.) to William Power fitz Peeter fitz Nicholas, of Kilmeadan, co. Waterford, gent., and Helena fitz Edmonde Gibbon, granddaughter and next heir of Thomas m'Shane m'Morris alias Thomas na Scarta, and wife of said William; of the castle and lands of Kylbullan alias Kilblane in Munster; and all lands late of the said Thomas, as found by an inquisition taken at Mcallo, 29 Jan., xxxiii. (Exch. Inq., Cork, Eliz., 41), to consist of Kilbullan alias Kilblane, containing land called the island of Kilbullan, and bounded on the west by Glancarran, being land of O Nownan, and Barnahollis on the east, Kilmoore and Gortinmeris on the north, the land of M'Insyria, and Daliggibege, land of O Nownan, on the south; also Cloanmore 1½ carucate, bounded by Glassinetoren, land of M'Insirye, on the north, Lyniconllan, parcel of Kyllmore, on the south, Cowleamultan, parcel of Kilholan on the west, and Ballidahin, parcel of Brohil, on the east; Agtram ½ car., bounded by Deliggis on the west and north, lands of Hugh M'Shane, and Kilballiworibie, called Knahilly, on the south, land of Thady M'Charte, and Darigvoan, parcel of Killmore, on the west; the castle of Cloghenorie, containing 15 acres, bounded by Balliuwollen, late of Moris M'Phillipp, on the south, and Freagho on the east and north, being common to the adjoining inhabitants, and Killmore on the west; Barneforirie, bounded by Killmore on the west, north, and east, and Cloghenorie on the south; Lysletrim ½ car., bounded by Feddans on the south, land of Garrett m'Shane M'Edmonde, and Ballinwollen on the north and east, and by Killmore on the west; Farren Wallter ffynne, bounded by Ballenlenige, land of Uligg O Keyve, on the east and north, and land of John Fitz Garrett, called Ballinagarraghe on the south and west; Killeollman 1 car., bounded by Garynegronoge, land of Gybban M'Thomas, on the west, and Balliaghie, land of viscount Fermoye, on the east, and by Killmore on the south and north; Ballemallaghe ½ car., bounded by Rathgoggan, the queen's land, on the west, Garunydirkye, land of the earl of Kildare, on the east, Farren Gilliwranrie on the south, Ballencollye, land of Philip Shuppall, on the north; another part called Kippan, 1 car., bounded by Garynegronoge on the north, Brohill on the north and east, and Killmore on the west; Cowleamultan 1½ car., bounded by Killmore on the west, Cloanmore on the east, Glassinetoren, land of M'Insiria, on the north, Garynegronoge on the south, and Killmore on the west; land called Henriea land, bounded by Cloanmore and Cowleamultian; also Lystrim by Ardartis, co. Kerry, 1 car.; also Agbalnake, Towayes, and Dalliggyaarraghe, bounded by Baringurtinevallick on the west, being lands of O Nownan, and by Kilbullan on the other sides; also a chief rent of 11s. 11½d., English, out of the lands of Rathnekally, and belonging to the castle of Kilbullan, £4 0s. 10½d., out of Mouacrinownan, from the north part Clighoamow, 18½d. out of Arddrubbuck, 11s. 1½d. out of Feddans, 58s. 4d. out of Dalliggmore, all belonging to the castle of Kilbullan. The premises were surrendered by Hugh Cuff, esq. To hold to them and the heirs of their bodies, remainder to the heirs of the body of Helena, remainder to the heirs of William

by any other woman of the race of Helena. To hold by the service
of one knight's fee.—20 Feb. [xxxiii.]—(*Slightly defaced, see
Auditor-General's Patent Book, vol. 22, p. 28, and vol. 9, p. 79.*)

5536 (6558.) Grant to Richard Beacon, esq.; of the manor and
lands of Dromswichen, Rendogan, [Dromynhanny, Dromalnnyrie,
Dromedonell], Lymynebarren, Nahaligh, Embaarlone, Drome on
Olobig, Glanehannowe, and Lytterfynyt, and all other hereditaments
sometime the possessions of Clandonell Booe, with the
appurtenances in Bantry, containing by estimation 4 ploughlands,
[the abbey of Bantry, the castle, lands, and manor of] Clanderaod
and Kylarmook, co. Cork, with appurtenances, 2 pl., the lands
of Torcragh alias the Woodshouse, Stradvalbegge, Conkenie,
Stradvally, Williamstowne alias Ballylchane, Carrignahae,
Ragherakellege, Iland Hubbook], Kildeglane, Garryduffo,
Dromloghane, Oraghtarcanye, Sleghbelly, Ballybegge, Ballen-
gowne, Ballenvallowny, Kylmaynneyona, Kylvarraghane,
Curryne London, and Ballyvonyne, 8 pl., in co. Waterford,
possessions of M'Thomas of the Pallyoe, co. Limerick, attainted,
amounting in all to 6,000 acres. To hold by the name of
Beacons fee farm, for ever, in fee farm, by fealty, in common
socage. Rent, £33 8s. 8d. from 1594 (half for proceeding 8
years), and ½d. for each acre of waste land which shall be
enclosed. If found by the survey that the lands contain more
than the estimated number of acres, grantee shall pay 1½d. for
each English acre in excess. Grantee to erect houses for
[47] families, one for himself, 4 for freeholders, 3 for farmers,
and 21 for copyholders, and other conditions usual in grants to
undertakers in Munster, as in 5032.—last Feb., xxxiii. (Cal.
P. R. p. 266.)

5537 (3997.) Surrender by John Bellinge, of Kyleoakan, co. Dublin,
and Arland Usshere, of Dublin, gentlemen; of the Fermorie,
with its dependent houses, the brewhouse, bakehouse, and gate-
house (of S. Mary's Abbey, Dublin), gardens near the river
Anilyffe, portion of the demesne lands, the Farm of S. Marie
Abais, and the land and mill of Clonlyffe, county Dublin, held
under lease 2 June, xxxi, to Bellinge, who assigned to Usshere.
Signed, John Belling, Arland Usshere.—*Dated*, 2 March, xxxiii.

5538 (4545.) Lease (under queen's letter, 6 July, xxxi.) to Rob.
Bertocke, gent.; a great house called the Farmory, within the
precinct of S. Mary's Abbey, a cloister and garden, a brewhouse,
a bakehouse, the porter's lodge, a messuage called the Castle
regge, another little house in another part of the Castle regge,
with demesne lands of the abbey, and lands of Clonaliefe (recites
4189). To hold for 31 years from the end of existing interests.
Rent £40 8s. Provisions as in 5311.—3 March, xxxiii.

5539 (4555.) Lease (under queen's letter, 4 July, xxx.) to John
Boalinge, gent.; of a castle, land, and common of pasture called
the Read mountain, in Tiperkevin, co. Dublin (recites 4925);
the site of the house of begging friars of Baltimore called the
monastery of Innistircan, co. Cork, with land appertaining
(recites 3203); the site of the Augustin friary of Killnemallaghe
alias Buttivante with appurtenances, co. Cork (recites 3278);
certain messuages in Clane, parcel of the rectory of Clane, co
Kildare (recites a lease from John Rawson, prior of the hospital
of S. John of Jerusalem in Ireland, xxxi. Hen. VIII.; to David

Sutton for 61 years, at a rent of 53s. 4d.); lands in Baltrasse, Ballihigan, Kilialorin, Moildrome, Swerin, the Grange of Kiltober, Ballisowder, Obwlaa, in M'Geoghegan's country, co. Westmeath (recites 3234); two tenements late of Rob. Damporta, in Athlone near the north gate beside the house of friars, containing in breadth 106 feet, and from the street to the walls of the town in length 160 feet, in co. Westmeath, parcel of the queen's ancient inheritance (recites 4220); a messuage in the town of Knockfergus with a parcel of land belonging, in co. Antrim, parcel of the queen's ancient inheritance (recites 3186); the site of the house of friars of Roserey with appurtenances in O Carroll's country (recites 3309); the house of friars called Tosmonia in the country of O Connor Dun, co. Roscommon, with one quarter of land and its tithes, possessions of the late house of friars of the third order of S. Francis in O Connor's country; the house of friars called Knockviocaris in the barony of Bolle, same co., with ½ quarter of land adjoining, and ½ quarter called Clonevan in the parish of Ardkearne, with their tithes, possessions of the house of friars of the third order of S. Francis called Knockviocaris; the cell of friars of the order of S. Francis called Clonrowghan in O Connor Roe's country, with ½ quarter of land adjoining; the monastery of S. Dominic in the city of Elphine, ½ of a quarter of land adjoining and ½ quarter called Kilvegunne in O Flannagan's country, with their tithes; the chapel or cell called Ballendowne in the barony of Tireraghe, in co. Sligo, ½ quarter of land there with the tithes, possessions of the late begging friars of S. Dominic's order beside Ballendowne (recites 5151); the castle of Ulondowan, and land of Clondovan and Cearew m'Shane duff, the site of the castle of Monicappen and lands, the castle of Kylkedy and lands of Cearowenpalroe, and Cearowgillae de Killen, lands of Kilchrochan, Dromedimon, Cearowdowme, Kewlovarin, Clonailhenrie, the island of Monahowo, co. Clare, possessions of Mahowne m'Enaspige O Brien, late of Clondowan, attainted; the rectory of Killowlanchie, and one part of the tithes of Moire and Cearowangowle, co. Clare, parcel of the possessions of the bishop of Elphine late in the occupation of said Mahowne O Brien m'Enaspigg (recites 5152). To hold for 40 years from the end of the recited lease. Rent £18 4s. 3½d.   Provisions as in 5311.—3 March, xxxiii.

5540 (3114.) License to Wm. Phillipps, esq., clerk of the hanaper and clerk of the crown in Chancery; to be absent in England for one year.—14 March, xxxiii.

5541 (4538.) License to Wm., bishop of Cork; to be absent in England for six months.—19 March, xxxiii.

5542 (4509.) Pardon to Donald m'Fergananim O Hanly, of Polnen, kern, in co. Roscommon, Thady m'Fergananim, of same, kern, Wm. boy m'Rory O Cayn, of same, hush., Conor m'Cormick Magenyne, of same, Cormack (m')Hugh boy Magrein; of same, Hugh boy m'Cormick Magrein, of same, Conor glasse m'Mulcony O Canally, of same, Dermott boy m'Edm. keagh O Hanly, Thady m'Dowltagh O Hanly, footman, Connor m'Dowltagh O Hanly, footman, Wm. Rory O Hanly, of Mullaghe, Mellaghlin O Hanly, of same, Gillegowin Maxally, of Clonmor, horseman, Thady m'Dermot M'Scally, of Rallymacolly, Shane M'Akolly, of same, husbandman, Donald m'Moragh Makolly,

1590-1.   FIANTS—ELIZABETH.

Gillepatrick m'Donell Makolly, of same, Hugh m'Brean Mage-
nill, of Cargin, Rori m'Teige M'Hugh, of Ballymoyton, Manname
m'Hugh Makolly, of Ballimakolly, Melaglyne duffe M'Kolly,
of same, Loughlin m'Breane Makolly, of same, Shaane M'Thomas,
of Moylaloghry, kern, Donald m'Donkaha Makigo, husbandman,
Fynyne M'Mutolly, of Clonwala, Edm. M'Evaisor, of Kelscrolis,
Conor M'Evaister, of same, Rory O Farroll, of Collarde,
Thady m'Fynine M'Multoly, of Cloncaneals, Donald m'Thomulty
O Byrn, of same, Dermot M'Kigo, of Kargine, kern, Thady
O Duffy, of Ballymollyn, husb., Rory carragh O Fyny, of Bally-
fyny, husb., Gerrot M'Teige, of Newtowne, Rorey m'Molaghlin
boy, of same, Wm. M'Evaister, of Ballliagh, Donald M'Hosry,
of Kellscrolly, Donald O Fyny, of Ballsfyny, husb., Tho.
O Fyny, of same, husb., Conor, Morragh, and Gillernowe
O Fyny, of same, Rory bane M'Kigo, of Dallym'kywacke,
Donald duffe M'Kigo, Cahill M'Kigo, of same, Rosy m'Faghna
m'Hobert Farroll, kern, Donagh M'Kigo, of same, Dermot
m'Farrall M'Kigo, Thady m'Sheane M'Kigo, of same, Phellym
M'Cahaille, of Anagaooy, husb., Rory O Farrall, of Newton,
Donald m'Phelym moyle M'Cahaille, Owan M'Kenor, of
Clonarda, Sheane M'Keefe, of Ballyfiny, Farrall m'Mortagh
Makolly, Wm. m'Hugh M'Kolly, of Ballymackolly, Dermot
m'Gilpatrick M'Girne, Gillernow m'Gilpatrick Magirne, Mo-
laglin M'Genor, of Ballenusa, Gillapatrick Magenor, of same,
Edm. Ferrall, of Cularde, Donald and Hugh m'Sheane
M'Manusa, of Ballefiny, Melaghline m'Donogh M'Killeclyna,
Cahill m'Leaghline Magillaclyne, Donowgh m'Gillernow M'Gille-
clyne, Sheane O Farrall, of Ballymacrusa, Dermot reogh
m'Donell O Hanly, Neyle M'Keagard, of Ballynollyna, Sheane
M'Greayne, of Ballenagrenyn, Edm. M'Kenry, of same, kern,
Keadagh O Farrall, of Liffiloughe, gent., Farrall boy m'Edmond
Keaghe, Edm. oge m'Ferraga boy, Wm. M'Evaister, of Kils-
croly, Carbery M'Evaster, Owen, Sheane, and Gillaaghe
M'Evaister, of same, Sheane m'Donell O Kargue, of Bally-
moylin, Hugh m'Donall O Hanly, of same, siokagh, Morragh
M'Donagh, of Lystosty, siokagh, Symon M'Gillowman, of
Enochall, Rory moyle m'Brean O Mullmihall, of Clacass, Brian
M'Sheane, of Corrynaleaghololo[ny], Donowghe m'Phelim James,
of Coulentry, Edm. m'Gerrot duffe, of Coulnory, Thady
O Boyle, of Lysduffe, Riccard m'Irrall O Farrall, of Kellyn,
Cahaill M'Anhogay, of Tully, kern, Donald moyle m'Thomas
Thaylor, Edm. m'Cahill M'Nagcogy, of sama, Melaglin
m'Gillernow M'Carmink, Wm. Bardan, of Teaghayny, Cattayene
O'Farrall, Onora, his daughter, Donald m'Rory m'Cahill Farrall,
of Cloaghankyng, Connor m'Owen Keagh M'Carmick, Caher
m'Tirriagh O Connor, Owen m'Connor M'Annany, of Lyapolle,
Sheane m'Connor M'Anenany, of same, Cormick m'Edm.
Mortaghe, Cormick M'Magoe, of Kalraohporteawer, Iheane
M'James, of Corrynaleagholony, kern, Hubbert m'Shanya
O'Farrall, of Ballraghe, gent., Hugh M'Scully, of Teaghayny,
husb., Bryan m'Edm. Mirlaght, Wm. m'Geffry Farrall, of
Colcory, Gillernow O Birne, of Porsrny, Thady O'Brean, of
Kilcolman, gent., Donowgh O Connowe, of same, James
Ferrall, of Killscroly, gent., Caher m'Tirlagh Rely, gent.,
Molaglin m'Edm. M'Bronan, of Cloncleave, kern, Dowltagh

1590–1   FIANTS.—ELIZABETH.

m'Cormick M'Bronan, of same, kern, Thady m'Rory M'Bronan, of same, kern, and Bren roe M'Tirrlagh, kern. Security as in 4943, in co. Roscommon.—[   ] 1590.

1591.

5543 (4452.) Pardon to Owen O Mulrian, of Fymon, in co. of Cross of Tipperary, and William his son. Provisions as in 5504.—30 March, xxxiii.

5544 (4522.) Grant to Lewis Phillips; of the office of porter septa of the castle of Carrickfergus in Ulster. To hold during pleasure, with such fees as Andrew Flemings had.—31 March, xxxiii.

5545 (8078.) Grant (under queen's letter, 1 July, xxxi.) to Edmund Barrette, gent.; of the Carbrye one carucate or cartron, Ballinrodde ½ car., co. Longford, now or late in the tenure of Keddaghe m'Shane O Ferrall, (rent 0s. 8d.), Cowlaiorte 1 car., Killenaviehe ½ car., same co., of the lands of Moroughe m'Convicke O Ferrall, late of Ballinrodde, attainted, (6s. 8d.); Corrobehie 1 car., Lyssomins 1 car., Cartrone Reaghe ½ car. (13s. 4d.), Cartrone Aghenecrose 1 car. (6s. 8d.), same co., of the lands of Gerald m'Rosse O Ferrall, of Lissomins, attainted; land in Killnemoddaghs, same co., of Owin roe m'Edmond O'Ferrall and Moylaghiyn moyle O'Ferrall, both of Killenmoddagh, attainted (16d. and 16d.); Lyssadanan 2 car., Cowlbane 1 car., Tolcbebeadam 2 car., Keapaghs 1 car., Garlfadd 1 car., and Drowsychsoys 1 car., possessions of the late monastery of Moghill, same co. (26s. 8d.); Aghegor ½ car., same co., and the weir of Snawowlls on the river Shenan, late possessions of Roris M'Aulye, late of Aghnegor, attainted (8s.); Oroghillen ½ carucate or cartron, same co., forfeited by the attainder of Morroghe m'Convicke O Ferrall of Croghillen (4s.); a ruined castle, and land in Grange by Molingar, co. Westmeath, with bog called Moninhegge ne Granngie (13s.), a gallon called 8 Mary gallon from each house where ale is brewed in Mollingar (6s. 8d.), possessions of the late monastery of the B. V. M. of Mullingar; the site of the monastery of Cavan, co. Cavan (3s. 4d.); Aghlsare in the barony of Castleraghyn, co. Cavan, two polls or cartrons, forfeited by the attainder of Brian O Relye (2s.) All which were found by inquisitions to have been long concealed. To hold for ever, in free socage. Total rent £4 19s. 8d., distributed as above.—7 April, xxxiii. (Cal. P. R. p. 219.)

5546 (4520.) Grant to Rob. Painture or Paynter, of Dublin; the saglet office of master gunner of Ireland. To hold during pleasure, with a stipend of 20d. sterling a day—13d. for himself, and 8d. for a man to attend him.—12 April, xxxiii.

5547 (4211.) Commission to Miler, archbishop of Cashel, Daniel, bishop of Kildare, Rob. Dillon, knt., chief justice of the Common Pleas, Ambrose Forthe, doctor of laws, Henry Usher, archdeacon of Dublin, Riah. Tompson, treasurer of S. Patricks, Dublin, and Chr. Usher, bachelor of laws; to hear an appeal by Nich. Allen, of Knockmark, co. Meath, gent., from a sentence, given in a matrimonial cause, by Rob. Conwaye, LL.D., pro vicar general and official principal of the archbishop of Dublin, in favour of Eglentina Dallahyde and of Michael Fitzsimons, interveniant.—21 April, xxxiii.

1591.   PLANTS.—ELIZABETH.

5548 (6551.) Grant to Thomas, earl of Ormond and Ossory; of the castle and lands of [Swyffin] with its members Kiltane and Caharvar, in Clanewilliam, in the co. and liberty of Tipperary, parcel of the land of John Bourck fitz Wm.; Gortrodan, in Clanewilliam, Balnamhin, in Clanewilliam, [Lyacibbon, Slan]haggard, Loghbegg, half Sowrlockstowne, and half Kylnecaste, the castle and lands of [Ballin]oggan, Ballynenairinghe alias Masterstowne, and Dirredonye, in Clanwilliam, the castle and half the lands of Brannagh and all the lands of Clonepacha, late lands of John Bourck fitz William, in Clanewilliam; Barrostan alias Ballenvarrowne.; Balleng[ortye], late of John Bourck fitz Walter; Ballyamery with the members thereof, viz., Bathone and Rathfismynge, the lands of Edmund H[edon]; Laghvalla the lands of Edmund ballagh Bourck; Cappagh [in Muskryquirk] co. Tipperary, late of Walter Bourck fitz Johns; Grelaghmore [in Muskryquyrck, lands of said Walter]; half of Drongano, late [lands of John Bourk fitz Walter]; Bally[hummyne], late the lands of said John; [Bealbadrebid and] Killardry, in the cross of co. Tipperary, late lands of Garrett, late earl of Desmond, containing 1,000 acres; Bally[nemonyokircke lands of Walter Kirck]; Ballen Willen alias Mille[towne] in the said cross of Tipperary, [lands of Melaghlin roe O'Ca]rron; a house in S. [Nicholas] street in Cashell; amounting in the whole to 3,000 English acres. To hold for ever, by the name of Mownt Ormonde, in fee farm; by fealty, in common socage. Rent, £16 13s. 4d. English, from 1594 (half only for the preceding 3 years). Also paying ½d. for each acre of waste land enclosed. Should the lands be found by the survey to contain more than the estimated number of acres, grantee shall pay 1½d. for each English acre In excess. Grantee to erect houses for [25 ?] families, of which one to be for himself, 2 for freeholders, 2 for farmers, and 11 for copyholders. Other conditions usual in grants to undertakers in Munster, as in 5082.—26 April xxxiii. 2 membranes. (Much obliterated). See Auditor-General's Patent Book 30, p. 135.

5549 (4465.) Pardon to Rich. Dillon, late sheriff of co. Westmeath, James m'Turlagh O Melaghlin, Brien m'Edm. M'Oghlan, and Molaghlin m'Brian O Dowlin, co. Westmeath. Provisions as in 5382.—1 May, xxxiii.

5550 (4537.) License to George Carewe, knt., one of the privy council, and master of the ordnance; to be absent in England, for four months.—11 May, xxxiii.

5551 (4477.) Pardon to Teige owr m'Teige leagh, Brien Evally m'Teige leaghe, Edm. m'Teige leaghe, Wm. Donne m'Moulronye oge, Daniel m'Teige m'Moulronye oge, Sheane O Dulloughantye, Mourtagh m'Morraugh reaughe, Mourtaugh m'Turlaugh O Doyne, Moulrony m'Donnogh oge, Moulrony m'William Donne, Cormack oge M'Coghlane, Teige m'Kallaugh of (O) Byrne, Hugh O Flanagan, shot, Bryan O Counell, shott, Moulrony M'Sheane, Chr. Bryan, gent., Moulrony m'Teige leaghe, John Meny, shot, Connell O Farrell, Pierce Leynaghe, Shean O Trighen gragaghe, Moulrony m'Wm. O Carroull, Donnogha O Boghan, and Mullaughlen M'Hugh, of Raghebegg, in Elie Ocarroull, King's co. Provisions as in 5382.—13 May, xxxiii.

5552 (5714.) Commission to sir Henry Bagnall, knt., marshal of the army; to be chief commissioner and ruler throughout the province of Ulster, the county of Louth excepted; with power to perform the functions of justices of assize and of gaol delivery, and of commissioners of oyer and terminer, and to treat and grant protections to any persons, in which case he shall at least every three months certify to the deputy that he has done so. The following are named assistant commissioners—the chief justices of the Queen's Bench and Common Pleas for the time being, Wm. Bath, esq., second justice of the Common Pleas, the serjeant at laws, attorney and solicitor general, seneschal of Clandeboy, and the mayor of Cragefergus, each for the time being, Rice Ap Hugh, provost marshal, Wm. Moore, of Bearmeath, gent., Matthew Smyth, Roger Gernon, of Stabanan, and Patrick Creely, of the Nury, gent.—18 May, xxxiii.

5553 (4460.) Pardon to John O Hogan, of Rahagall, Tho. O Hogan, of Killarney, Rob. Oondan, of Clonmell, Edm. Grate fitz Water, of Shart, Nich. O Shee, of Glanakaghe, and Rob. Ragged, of Kilkenny; co. Kilkenny. Provisions as in 5382.—20 May, xxxiii.

5554 (4472.) Pardon to Fergus O Forrall, of Tenslick, Hubert, William, and Connell m'Fergus O Ferrall, of same, Donnell duffe M'Cormock, of Ballevickahan, horseman, Garrett m'Moriatagh O Ferrall, of Leaghore, gent., Owen m'Hughe, of Clancawell, kern, Rory m'Cormock O Ferrall, of Kailte, gent., Donnall duffe M'Glawnyo, of Balletobber, Teige m'Gillegroome O Hallye, of Clonaheare, gent., Chaell M'Gonogey, of Tulle, and Murtagh M'Felim, of Tenslick, in co. Longford Security as in 4943, Fergus O Ferrall excepted, and provisions as in 5504.—2 June, xxxiii.

5555 (4475.) Pardon to Barnaby m'Florence FitzPatrick, Wm. m'Florence Fitz Patrick, Donogh m Dowrey, Conoghor O Bolane, of Karagine ne Veigh, Peter Dugin, of the Rahine, Rory Dulgin, of Ballycragh, Melaghlen m'Teigh meoll, of Keylcrrun, Callogh M'Tuige, of same, Donogh O Phelane, stokagh, Lysagh M'Rowry, of Keylncaare, Shane M'Rwory, of same, Shane Callegh, of Archerrowne, Wm. Phelne, yeoman, Callegh M'Tuige, of Lyaduff, Murtagh meoll O'Felane, Melaghlen O Helane, of Granntstown, Edm. M'Kalleb, of Ballynoe, Gilpatrick og, of the Rosse, Phillip M'Gillenboile, Hugh O Glhaine, Wm. roe O Phelane, of Kilbride, Shane Englishe, Donell Groome, of Ballywoyve, Donogh oge, of Aghemacart, Dermot M'Donnell, Brien eveally Fitz Patrick, and Shane m'Carrell M'Teige. Provisions as in 5382.—10 June, xxxiii.

5556 (4527.) Grant to Rob. Newcomen, gent.; the office of general surveyor of the victuals of the soldiers. To hold during pleasure, with a fee of 10s. English a day, and such other fees as George Beverlie or any other had.—14 June, xxxiii.

5557 (4521.) License to Petre Graunt, of Waterford, merchant; to erect a tan house at the Magdelens near the city of Waterford, and to use it during his life. The statute of 11 Eliz. notwithstanding.—18 June, xxxiii.

5558 (4474.) Pardon to Edm. Fitz Walter, of Ballynegarry, co. Limerick, David M'Henry, of the Parke, Thady m'Donoghe m'Cormock Conyck, Reiry carraigh Makonygham, John m'Carrell I Daly, of the Grange, co. Cork, Davi m'Redmund Barry, of Abaglaslyne, Owen m'Rery I Ryordane, of Dirry Roe, Walter Bishford, of Richfordstowne, Arte m'Teige O Lary, of Bally-

1591.　　　　　　　PLANTS.—ELIZABETH.

nowen, Owen m'Brien M'Swiney, of Shanafoyle, Shane O Too-
hicke, of same, Dermot oge beg O Mahowne, of Killworhy,
Shane m'Wm. I Morrogho alias Baddy, of Killoreghe, Donell
m'Dermond m'Shane I Callaghen, of Gortincarrall, Dermod
m'Connoghor M'Callaghane, of Killymll, Shane O Keyfe, of
Ballyagrowncugh, and Tho. m'Shane mor Garrald; cos. Cork and
Limerick. Provisions as in 5521. The pardon shall not include
any riot or offence of which any of these persons stand accused
in the Castle Chamber, nor shall it pardon any of them who are
in prison or on bail to appear.—19 June, xxxiii.

5559 (4470.) Pardon to John Lyons, of Rosse, Hugh O Driscoll,
of Ricoliakin, Dermod m'Conochor M'Conn, of Kilgarleightaigh,
Darby m'Fynyn m'Dermot oge, of the Cales, Fynin m'Conogher
m'Das O Mahowne, of Lemeonne, Derby oge m'Darby M'Ma-
houna, of Killwilliam, Fynyn m'Dermot M'Donell, of Gortne-
hortne, Donogho m'Moylmoe O Mahowne, of Kilm'Rodderie,
Donell m'Donogho I Holly, of Bantry, Margaret en Terralaigh,
Donogho m'Dermody I Mahowney, of Ballengronyghe, Maurice
O Gerigh, of same, Fynyn m'Donogho O Mahowne, of Dro-
maannas, Philip roe Roch, John Roch, Donnell O Beggly, of
Collogh roe, and Donnell O Hegerdall, of Oronkahaven. Security
as in 4948, on Cork and Limerick. Other provisions as in 5558.
—19 June, xxxiii.

5560 (4478.) Pardon to John m'Patr. oge O Carrolan, of the
Nobber, Edw. Walshe, of Garmanston, gent., Tho. Duffe,
Dionysius Doin, of same, Shane m'Teig O Carrolan, of Nobber,
Bryan duffe m'Tho. O Carrolan, Hugh m'Cahill O Carrolan, of
same, Wm. ban O Carrolan, of Garmanaghe, Henry and Thomas
m'Wm. daffe O Carrolan, of the Nobber, Wm. M'Nemarge, of
same, Murtagh M'Gargan, Donyl O Reily, of Ournasake, James
Duffe m'Henry more, of Rouske, Tho. Dufle, of same, Fayle Duffe,
of Dromoarraghe, Chr. Veldon, of Raffin, Wm. Veldon, Patr.
Erwarde, of same, Chr. Plunckett, of Braghvule, Ferrall oge
Gowe, of Ardnaghbreige, Edw. Plunckett, Donyll Gowe, Terlagh
boy Gowe, of same, Rory m'Cowconaghtae duffe O Carrolan, of
Nubber, Shane m'Tho. O Carrolan, Cahill oge m'Cahill O Carrolan, of same, Collo M'Mahon, of Legan, Rich. m'Cahill
M'Ekey, of Cormy, Henry m'Bryen ne Mointe M'Ekey, of
same, and Alexander Plunckett, of Ardnaghbreige. Security
in cos. Meath and Cavan, as in 4948. Not to pardon murder,
burglary, or arson, except to Chr. Plunkett, Edward Walshe, Tho.
Duffe, Dionysius Doin, Donill O Reily, James Duffe, Faile Duffe,
Tho. Duffe, of Rouskie, Shane grane m'Teig O Carolan, Collo
M'Mahon, and Patr. Erward, for the slaying of Cahire bane
m'Henry oge M'Ekey, Rob. roe Cruse, Moillmore mollo
O Reily, Tho. anannter M'Gilsanan, Edm. beddie M'Gilsanan,
and Shane Eiotan M'Ekey. Excluding also offences of which
they may stand charged in Castle Chamber, intrusion in crown
land and debts to the crown, and any person in prison or on
bail.—19 June, xxxiii.

5561 (6388.) Commission (under queen's letter, 6 March last) to sir
Thomas Norryes, knt., vice president of the province of Munster,
Jessey Smithes, the chief justice, and Richard Beacon, queen's
attorney of that province, Arthur Currey, esq., learned in the laws,
and John Fitz Edmond, esq.; with the intention of removing diffi-

L

1591.   PIANTS.—ELIZABETH.

calties in the way of the undertakers; to hear controversies arising between sir Warham Saintleger, knt., and sir Richard Greenefield, knt., with any others concerning the queen's title to the "chargeable lands" in the co. Cork; to establish Saintleger as patentee in such of them as are found to belong to the queen; and to appoint at the expense of Saintleger a skilful man to measure the number of English acres, at the rate of 16½ feet to the perch, they contain, in order that they may be passed to him by plot set down, under the great seal of England.—At Dublin, 21 June, xxxiii.

5562 (4464.) Pardon to Shane O Kenelly, Gully patrick O Hogan, James O Hogan, Philip O Hogan, Art m'Donough I Quife, Cormuck m'Shane I Grogan, Edm. m'Tho. M'Richard, Dermond O Hickes, of Renany, David bny O Carnell, Wm. fitz Edm. Fitz Robert, John fitz James reeogh, Donough m'Martegh M'Rory, Wm. m'Teige O Carrin, Oonocher m'Donogh Imane, Donogh m'Diermod Innane, Dermod m'Eo I Gradie, Mourist oge m'Moriah Mustart, Rory O Morisha, Conogher O Caman, Edm. buy M'Thomas, Peiroe Fitz James, Rob. Shoe, Conogher m'Loghlen I Barrie, Olpher Fitz James, Patr. Creagh, of Corbalie, Foy O Fariell, Morish m'Tho. M'Garditie, Walter roe Richford, Philip O Comen, Rorie O Comen alias Rory begg, Teig m'Dermode rowe, Morish Bernaght, Morish Fitz Richard, Redmund fitz John Wayle, John O Fornan, Edm. O Fornan, Moriah Mawin fitz William, Kenedie M'Tarrelly, David M'Garilte, Teig and Connogher m'Donogh gnnckngh O Brien, Conogher O Nellane, John Neallane, Murriertaght m'Donell M'Brien, Teig M'Rorie, Donogh M'Millaghalen, Teag O Dea, Bethgallagh M'Clanchie, Teag O Mungarie, Rorie oge M'Nete, Oulligias O Hownyn, Brien O Loghin, John M'Donnogh, Owin M'Swine, Muriertalgh M'Rory, Mahon M'llory, Brien m'Teig M'Brien, John Berry, Redmund Pursell, Owne O Hoheir, John Realy, of Askontten, and Donnell O Nellan. Security in con. Limerick, Clare, or Kerry; and other provisions as in 5558.—23 June, xxxiii.

5563 (4549.) Grant (under queen's letter, 11 Feb., xxv.) to Tho. Coppinger, gent.; of the lands of the Grannge of S. Katherine, by the city of Waterford, parcel of the lands of the abbey of S. Katherine there, (rent 54s. 4d.), (recites a lease, 3 April, 1 and 2 Th. and Mary, to Patr. Sherlock, also 4926); two messuages with land and certain customs in Brownestone, co. Meath, parcel of the possessions of the abbey of the B. V. M. by Dublin, (24s. 4d.), (recites 2718). To hold for ever, in free socage, by fealty only. Rent £3 18s. 8d. as above.—23 June, xxxiii.

5564 (4546.) Grant (under queen's letter, 1 July, xxxi.) to Edm. Barrett, gent.; of a toft and small croft with land in Kilmore Brennaghe, co. Kildare, the possessions of Peter Walshe, late of Clonniffe, attainted, and concealed from the queen, (rent 16d.); another toft with land in the same, the possessions of Robert and Maurice Walshe, gent., late of Tecroghane, co. Meath, attainted, (16d.); the lands of Killenscariggin, co. Waterford, parcel of the lands of Edm. roe Power, of that place, attainted, concealed from the queen, (5s.). To hold for ever, by fealty, and in free socage. Rent 7s. 8d. as above.—26 June, xxxiii.

1591.   FIANTS.—ELIZABETH.

5565 (4561.) Grant (under queen's letter, 5 Aug., xxix.) to George
Shearlocke; of the town of Ballivorishe, co. Tipperary, (rent 3s.),
Ballibghin, in same co. (3s.), lands of Walter Bourke fitz John,
of Cappaghe, same co., attainted; the fourth part of Garrydnffe,
Ballioctereghan, Ballihoe, and Tamplamahorney, same co., lands
of Rich. Bourke fitz Tho., late of Garyduffs, attainted, (3s.);
the fourth part of Tanganaghe, same co., lands of Ricard
Bourke, late of Tanganaghe, and Edm. offallce Bourke, his
brother, attainted, (12d.); Ballimackeades and Killnemakes,
same co., lands of Geoffrey bwy Bourke, late of Ballimackeades,
attainted, (6s.); Ballinvy, (20d.), and Ballinomoght, (20d.), same
co., lands of John Bourke fitz Wm., late of Swyfns, attainted;
land in Kilnaory, in the cantred of Kilnemanagh, same co., lands
of Edm. Evony alias Edm. O Dowyre, late of Kilnaory, attainted, (12d.); the fourth part of Ballinlyntee, lands of Rich.
Bourke fitz Ricard, late of Ballinlyntes, attainted (16d.); land
in Aralemau, (2s.), Knockebully Loghanny, Inchanagonine, Lis-
senogowny, and Corraghcarbrye or Claraghcarbry, (6s. 8d.), same
co., lands of Walter Bourk, attainted; Clonmoylan, lands of
Ullig m'Wm. dunranagh Bourke, late of Clonmoylan, attainted,
in said co. (15d.); Lismackhee in Mouskerie Quirke, (7s. 4d.),
Olde Cappaghe, Ballihanckarde, Gralaughbegge, and Knockurty-
niall, (7s.), same co., lands of Walter Bourke fitz John, late of
Cappaghe, co. Tipperary, attainted; the third part of Cowlee,
lands of Tho. Bourke, late of Cowlee, attainted, (2s.); Clequill
and Corroga, lands of Tho. Bourke fitz Rich., of Clequill,
attainted, (5s.); half of Bremahighe, lands of Theobald Bourke fitz
Redmund, late of Bremahighe, attainted, (6s.); a messuage and
four gardens in the town and burgage of Clonmell, of which one
garden lies at Loughgate, in the east part of Barior, two others
in the west part of Loughgate and Barior, and another extends
from the land of Walter Wale on the west to the highway on the
east, a parcel of land in Richardes park in the burgage of Clonmell, Priors park in the said burgage, land in the north part of
Boliske called Bowyn, and land by the way called Friherdes
boother in the west, in the said burgage, in the tenure of Ballina
alias Beale Whitt, and Victor Whitt fitz James, parcel of the
lands of the priory of S. Edmund the martyr, of Athashell, co.
Tipperary, (52s. 6d.); the lands of the Graunge by the priory of
Athashell, also parcel of its possessions, (8s.); the New mill in
the franchises of Callan, co. Kilkenny, with a parcel of land near
it called the Inche, (2s. 8d.), a parcel of land called Cortnam-
rahor, within the said burgage or franchies, (4d.), parcel of the
possessions of the house of Augustin friars of Callan; all which
had been concealed from the crown. To hold for ever, by the
service of a fortieth part of a knight's fee. Rent £5 13s. 7d.,
divided as above. In consideration of the good service of Peter
Shearlocke, gent., deceased, father of the grantee.—26 June,
xxxiii.

5566 (5315.) Grant (under queen's letter, 7 March, xxxiii.) to Rich.
Grensvile, knt.; of the site of the late monastery of Farmoy alias
Iarmoy, containing with other buildings the stone walls of a
church which was the parish church, a parcel of land about the
monastery called Garrinle, Ardevalligg, Aghavanister, Kilcroige,
Cowlevalintervanosige, Kilvallentervanosige, Foroghmore, Down-

L 2

1591.   FIANTS.—ELIZABETH.

bahoane, Kilconnan, lying on the south side of the river Blackwater, Ballimabone, Grancaheaghe, Ballinegehia, Carrowhardan,
Carrigginchroughere, and Glassiganiahe (recites 4252); the
site of the monastery de Antro of S. Finbar alias Gilley,
with the buildings, gardens, closes, and water mill, two weirs for
taking salmon called Corringraghina and Corinckowpoge, a fourth
part of which belong to the monastery (rent £4), land called
Balligagin (20s.), Kilmoney in the country of Kerry Curhis
(£4 2s.), Killynecananaughe lying on the north side of the water
of Cork (£4 10s.), certain land in Innishloughe in the country of
Muskery (23s.), land called Farranduffe, the island of Innshquyny
(5s. 6d.), and a chief rent out of the island of Croghanle (3s.),
(recites a lease dated 30 Aug., xxiv. to Warham St. Leger, esq.
See 4026.) To hold in tail male, after the end of the interests
in being, by the service of one knight's fee. Rent for Fermoy
£16 18s. 4d., and for Gilley £16 3s. 0d.   He shall maintain five
armed horsemen at Fermoy.—26 June, xxxiii.   (Cal. P. R., p.
201.).

5567 (4543.) Lease (under queen's letter, 7 March, xxxiii.) to sir
Rich. Greynsvile, knt.; of the spiritualties of the abbey of Ardmoye alias Iarmoye, viz.: the tithes of the rectory of Fermoye
and of the demesne lands of the abbey, and the tithes of Cowlenaghe, Curraghahurdan, Gortokoishe, Culmuke, Cloghloe, Ballyarture, Johnston, Ballishoane, and Farrolehesserne, the greatest
part whereof is now waste (rent £7), the tithes of the rectories
of Downanaghan (£6), and Ballishan (20s.), the vicarage of
Templeogan, to which belongs a moiety of the tithes of Templeogan, Templencmegge, Carrickanadia, Monycreoghe, Garranmore,
Garranbeg, Knockmecuple, Ballegowdia, Ballioduffo, Dunredyn,
and Kilvanaion (23s.), the vicarage of Kilcromper, to which
belongs the moiety of the tithes of Kilcromper, Ballehomden,
Ballinecargie, Ballanegawlesci, Ballydirriawne, Ballegawdio,
Templenequillan, Kylvynitio, Ballinrushe, Lismefallaghe, Garranemaronic, Downanaghe, and Marreeroghe (26s. 8d.), the vicarage
of Mocrenaghe, to which belongs the moiety of the tithes of
Mocrenaghe and Downaquillau (10s.), (recites 4252); also the
spiritualties of the monastery of Antro S. Fynibar alias Gilley, co.
Cork, viz.: the rectories of Kyllynycananaghe (40s.), Kilmonye
(40s.), Barnyhalis (30s.), Kilpatrick (60s.), Ballynabowe (£6),
Kilmarrye (£6), Inchegainlaghe (20s.), Killmichall (30s.), and
Kilcornocke (£9), and the vicarage of Durrushe (6s. 8d.), co.
Cork (recites a lease of 30 Aug., xxiv. to Warham St. Leger, and
4020, also one of (   ), xxxii. to Henry Davells).   To hold
for 40 years from the end of the recited interests.   Rent £53 6s. 4d.,
part in corn.   Also paying as a fine one year's rent at the end of
every 21st year.   Provisions as in 5311.—26 June, xxxiii.

5568 (4528.) Grant to Hubert Foxe, gent.; of the office of seneschal
of Forus country called Mointerragun, in the King's co.   To
hold during good behaviour, with all profits appertaining.
Powers as in 5366.—26 June, xxxiii.

5569 (4466.) Pardon to John Stephenson, and Evelin ny Conell,
his wife.   Proviso as in 5518.—1 July, 1591.

5570 (4468.) Pardon to Robuck French, Shane M'Egerkie, Nich
Linch fitz Stephen, of Galwale, alderman, Edm. French fitz
Robuck, of same, merchant, Robuck Martin, Robuck Kirwan,

1591. FIANTS.—ELIZABETH.

Robuck Linch fitz Nich., Tho. French fitz Valantine, Chr. Linch fitz George, Marcus Linch fitz Stephen, Peter French fitz Valantine, Peirs Kirwan fitz Edm., Chr. Skerret, of Galwale, merchant, Donogh O Curin, of Liskenanan, husbandman, and Shane duff O Morochowe, of same. The pardon not to include intrusion in crown lands or debts to the crown.—1 July, xxxiii.

5571 (4535.) Livery to Richard, son and heir of Peter Dillon, late of Skryne, gent. Fine £7 14s.—4 July, xxxiii.

5572 (4523.) Grant to Ralph Brereton, of Killanlaghe, co. Down, gent. ; of the office of sheriff of co. Down. To hold during pleasure.—5 July, xxxiii.

5573 (4469.) Pardon to Shane m'Brian O Neile, Neale m'Brian O Neile, Neale m'Hugh m'Mortagh O Neile, Owen m'Quyn m'Hugh O Neill, Brian oge m'Brian ballogh O Naill, Owin m'Donall O Naill, Con m'Brian ballogh O Naill, Ivar m'James og M'Ynully, Phelym duffe m'Art oge M'Ynully, Manus m'Toole M'Ynully, Owin m'en abbe M'Ynully, Rory m'Art M'Ynully, Ferdorogh m'Donell M'Gye, Toole M'Can, Edm. M'Can, Owin moddary M'Ynully, Phelim duff Neill m'Hugh, Phelim duff m'Neill m'Hugh O Neill, Neill O Neill m'Phelym duffe, Henry groome M'Ynully, Hugh ballogh O Mulballan, Phelim m'Bory O Neill, Con m'Brian O Naill, and Toole roe M'Ynully; co. Antrim. Provisions as in 5382.—9 July, xxxiii.

5574 (4470.) Pardon to Edm. Bourke m'Davie, of Clonegashell, Wm. Bourke m'Shane in tormone, of Clonoerie, Tho. and Shane Bourke m'Davie, of Clonegashell, Moyler and Richard Bourk m'Tibbald reogh, of Clonoery, Moyler M'Walter, of Clonegashell, Falliagh M'Walter, Mellaighim roe M'Cone, of same, Conell m'Marcus M'Donell, of the Dogher, Moylmory M'Donell, of the Clonyne, Allyne M'Donell, of Clonyne, Cully M'Donell, of the Clonyne, Eneah M'Donell, of same, Donogh M'Donell, of Tonaght, Umon M'Donell, Edm. ballaigh M'Donell, of same, Shane M'Johnyne, of Killkore, Rich. M'Nevadae, of the Clonyne, Brian O Boyell, Henry Stanckard, of same, Walter Bourk m'Davie, (of) Beallanaluhe, Badmund Bourk m'Davie, of same, and Moyler M'Richard, of same. Security in co. Mayo. Provisions as in 5532—9 July, xxxiii.

5575 (5755.) Commission to John, lord primate of Ardmagh, Thomas, baron of Slane, sir Henry Bagnall, knt., marshal of the army, sir Robert Dillon, knt., chief justice of the Common Pleas, sir John Bedloe, knt., and Rice Ap Hugh, esq., provost marshal of the army ; to be commissioners under the statute 11 Eliz., in the province of Ulster, to enquire of all countries not shire ground, or doubtful to what shire they belong, and to divide them into as many counties, shires, and hundreds as they think fit.—10 July, xxxiii. This commission and the return are printed in "Repertory of the Inquisitions of the Chancery of Ireland," Vol. II., Ulster, published by Record Commission, pp. xix.-xx.

5576 (4531.) Grant to Iriall m'Wm. O Ferall, gent. ; of the office of seneschal of the country of Clanconnor, in co. Longford. To hold during pleasure, with the profits appertaining. Powers as in 5366.—7 Aug., xxxiii.

5577 (4540.) License to Nathaniel Dillon, esq., principal clerk of the council, to be absent in England for three months. Rob.

1591.   •   FIANTS—ELIZABETH.

Mylles, gent., his servant, is authorised to act as his deputy.—
11 Aug., xxxiii.

5578 (4469). Pardon to Maurice Stack fitz Moris fitz Gerrots
oge Stake, of Killenea, oo. Kerry, Tho. Stacke, Edm. Bren-
hagh fitz Geoffrey, Brien O Hanraghane, Tho. fitz Wm. Stack,
Wm. beg Stack, Tho. fitz John Stack, John fitz Teige fitz John,
James duff Stacke, Bartholomew fitz Dominick, Onora nyn
Teige Fitz Mahowne, Wm. duff M'Nicholl, Wm. Oasy, Tho.
Fitz Richard, of Polhalullia, husbandman, Wm. O Ryeddy, and
Philip Lynch, all in said county.   Provisions as in 5382.—22
Aug., xxxiii.

5579 (4533.) Commission to sir Tho. Norries, knt., vice president
English. of Mounster, Jesse Smithes, esq., chief justice there, James
Gold, second justice, Arthur Hide, sheriff of oo. Cork, George
Thorneton, esq., provost marshal of the province, John Vardon,
George Robinson, and Jaspar Meeagh, gentlemen ; to enquire
by the oaths of jurors or otherwise, what castles, lands, rents, and
services belong to Donogh m'Cormock, in oo. Cork, and what
rights the queen or any subjects may have in them. Recites
that Donogh desired to surrender his possessions in order to
their being regranted, and that in such grants formerly, injustice
had been done in regranting lands to persons who had not a
right to surrender them.—23 Aug., xxxiii.

5580 (6739.) Surrender by Edw. Goghe, of Clonmell, esq. ; of the
site and possessions of the late monastery of Innyslawnaght,
as regranted in 5591.—Signed Edward Goeghe.—27 Aug.,
xxxiii.

5581 (4536.) License to George Carewe, knt., one of the privy
council, and master of the ordnance ; to be absent in England for
four months.—28 Aug., xxxiii.

5582 (6720) Commission (under queen's letter, 20 Jan., xxxiii.) to
English. Thomas, lord bishop of Meath, Thomas, lord baron of Slane, sir
Henry Bagnoll, knt., marshal of Ireland, sir George Bowrchier,
knt., one of the privy council, John Ellott, esq., third baron of
the Exchequer, Roger Wilbraham, esq., queen's solicitor, Henry
Burnell, esq., and John Oonolan, parson of Moynaltia. Reciting
that the lands forfeited by the attainder of Hugh M'Mahowne,
having been assured by patent to the chief gentlemen of the
county Monaghan ; it was desired that the inferior inhabitants
should live out of thraldom, and depend only on the crown.
The commissioners are directed to assign freeholds to such of
the inhabitants as they think fit, each rendering fixed rents
and services to their superior lord. Provided that the whole
forfeited lands yield to the crown not less than £400 sterling a
year.   The new freeholders to be confirmed by patents.—10
Sept., xxxiii.

*The return to this commission is preserved among the Rolls
Office Miscellaneous Records (No. 22).   It sets out the names of
all those to whom freeholds were to be assigned with the lands
allotted to each.   It is printed at length in the "Repertory of the
Inquisitions of the Chancery of Ireland," Vol. II.—Ulster, pp.
xxi.-xxxi.   The grants made in pursuance of this allotment appear
below 5621 to 5630.*

5583 (4529.) Grant to Gerald Comerford, esq. ; of the office of queen's
attorney at laws for the province of Connaught.   To hold during

1591.   FIANTS.—ELIZABETH.

good behaviour, with a fee of £20 English. Not to be removed, as in 4976.—14 Sept., xxxiii.

5584 (6630.) Grant (under queen's letter, 9 Jan., 1683), to Gerald Comerford, of Callan, co. Kilkenny, esq.; of a pension of £20 English, till he receive a grant in tail of forfeited lands in Munster.—14 Sept., xxxiii.

5585 (6629.) Grant (under queen's letter, 26 July, xxxiii.) to Hugh O'Moloy; of a pension of 20d. (Irish) a day, during pleasure.—15 Sept., xxxiii.

5586 (6631.) Grant to sir William Courtenay, of Powderhame, co. Devon, knt; of the castle and lands of Castlenoa alias New-castle in the parish of Moneaghdare, containing the following parcels, Kintogher, par. Killidy, Ballyregan, par. Moneaghdare, Gortmoynan, and Ballyowen, par. Killidy, Ballyguyle, par. Moneaghdare, Rahanogh, Ballyshane, Ballyourk, Gort-comykyn, Ballynahawn, Ballyconnowe, Ballyulowan, Bally-m'ywo, Ballyra'Ranyll, Trean, and Culynoughe, in the parishes of Moneaghdare, Killidy, and Castellnoa, containing together 4 ploughlands; the town and castle of Portrynard in the parishes of Templedley and of the monastery of [Nephelough], containing 4 ploughlands; Lyskarryo and Clonebrowne, in the parish of Killakannell, containing one quarter; Clonoghwyllen and Kearrough beg molloghe, in the parish of Kilakannell, containing 8 ploughlands and 20 acres; Templatly, including Templetle, Corbally, Ouillnaluila, Lyahrwo, Glannygorte, Aghaduan, Gormagrosa, Ourraghduffe, Sroanonan, and Muna-gor[n], containing together 4 ploughlands, and lying in the parish of Raronan; Glanughwym in the parish of Moneaghdare, containing 5 pl.; Templeglen ten in Slelogher in the parish of Moneaghdare containing 7 pl., Kilrndane containing 4 pl., in all 32 ploughlands and 20 acres; Killahine in the parish of Kilsannall, containing 1 pl., late the lands of Thomas Cam; Lysoorden in the parish of Raronan, containing 1 pl., late the lands of Morryoe m'[Shane Walle]; of Ballynuaky; Ballylond-rigge, par. Raronan 1 pl., late the lands of David Eucharige; Orannoghe, including Buskoighmore, Ruskeighbegg, Droome M'Terrelaghe, and Downegonewylly, in the parish of Castle-noa, Ballyinge and Ballyloghan, in the parish of [Arda]ghe, containing 4 pl., late the land of Morroghe M'Bryan, lord of Grannogh alias M'Turrelagh; Mohuagranahy, late the land of Donnogho M'Bryan, of Dyrry; Doakatten in the parish of Castlenoa, containing half a quarter, land of Donell M'N[eyle]; Garrankyvan, par. of Castlenoa, ½ quarter, land of James Walle, of Clonealereen; Ardnocrogh, par. Moneaghdare 1 pl. late of Morrogho m'Edmond oge; [Rathkeale,] par. Moneaghdare, 1 pl., late of Ger[rat M'Donnogh and Edm. Gancagh]; Ballynetubberta, par. Moneaghdare, 1 pl. late of Garrott Fitz Thomas and Edmund Gancagh, of Kylfynney, co. Limerick; amounting in the whole to 43 ploughlands and a half and 20 acres, or 10,560 English acres. To hold by the name of Newcastle (?) for ever in fee-farm. Rent £131 5s. from 1594 (half only for first three years.) Also paying ½d. for each acre of waste land enclosed. Should the lands be found by the survey to contain more than the estimated number of acres, grantee shall pay 3d. for each English acre in

1591.   PLANTS.—ELIZABETH.

cross. Grantee to build houses for 80 families. Other conditions usual in grants to undertakers in Munster as in 5032. Much defaced. (See Auditor-General's Patent Book 30, p. 134.)—23 Sept., xxxiii.

5587 (4461.) Pardon to Charles Egerton, gent., constable of the castle of Carigfergus. Provisions as in 5504 (except the requirement of security).—4 Oct., xxxiii.

5588 (4454.) Pardon to captain Tho. Lee, esq., Francis Drurie, Rich. Mannering, and Tho. Lee, junior, gentlemen, Alexander Ewstace, James Wale, David O Doren, Wm. Grom, sen., Wm. Grom, jun., Nich. Bagot, Darie Dempsy, Connor oge Crowell, Wm. roe, Mortagh Dempsy, Matthew Scotte, Daniel m'Moroghoo Nowlane, Tho. Rochforth, Teig m'Donell O Dowlin, Patr. Browne, John Taylor, Clement Lane, Callowgho O Dowle, Dermot reaghe, John Stephenson, Dertie M'Davie, of Galmorerton, James Cantwell, of Ballenay, and Wm. m'Mellaghlen O Lawlare. Not to pardon intrusion into crown lands or debts to the crown.—19 Oct., xxxiii.

5589 (4648.) Pardon to John Dallaway, ensign of the footmen under the command of Henry Wallop, knt. Not to include intrusion on crown lands or debts to the crown, or any riot or offence of which he is accused in the Castle Chamber.—21 Oct., xxxiii.

5590 (4459.) Pardon to Rowland Savadge, of Lisbane, horseman, Henry Savadge, of Castleboy, in the Little Ardes, James Hadsor, and Gillodul M'Ne Marry, of same, horsemen; co. Down. Provisions as in 5504. Also excluding murder.—25 Oct., xxxiii.

5591 (4547.) Grant (under queen's letter, 31 May, xxxiii.) to Edw. Goghe, of Clonmell, co. Tipperary, esq., and Mary Goghe alias Wodhowse, his wife; the site of the abbey of Innyslawnaght alias Eunislawnaghe alias Inuyslanaghe, co. Tipperary, the town of Innyslawnaght, in cos. Tipperary and Waterford, the church of the abbey, the demesne lands in Innyslawnaght, 1,000 acres of mountain and common pasture in co. Waterford of the demesne lands, also messuages, land, two mills, three eel weirs and one salmon weir, and one little island, belonging to the abbey, the lands of Grange of Innyslawnaght, Ballyorcley alias Ballyorley, Kilmalashe, Loghkeraghe alias Loghtikearaghe, Grangeherwye, in co. Tipperary, Kilmaveighe alias Kilmavie, and its tithes, a messuage and garden at the west gate of Clonmell, the rectory of Innyslawnaght, and the tithes of grain and hay of Innislawnaght, Grangehervie, the Grange of Innislawnaght, Ballyorcley, Kilmalashe, and Loghkearaghe, the manor of Kilmack, co. Waterford, and the lands of Kilmack alias Kilnemack, the rectory and tithes of Glanwydan, co. Waterford, all castles and lands in Curraghnemanagh, Groman, Insemore, Kilmoghome, Muicke, Kanan, Dromcure, Knokmecarragh, marsh land and weir of Glanbane, and all lands between the bounds of Kilmanhyne on the west and the bounds of the burgage of the town of Clonmell on the east, the mill field, the dean's field, the high field, and the field of Clonmell, and the mill of Tipperheny, Lemlismolleran alias Kilmereran alias Kilvereran, in cos. Waterford and Tipperary, and all other hereditaments of the abbey, in Innislawnaght, Ballyorley, S. Patrick's, Monkestown, and Kilmereran, or other the premises

1591. FIANTS—ELIZABETH.

Recites surrender 5580. To hold to them and the heirs male of the body of Edward, in common socage. Rent £24.—25 Oct., xxxiii.

5592 (6111.) Pardon to Elias Shee, of Kilkenny, gent.; for an alienation made to him by Christopher, bishop of Ossory, of a parcel of the river Noer, and a piece of land covered with water upon which to construct a mill; also by Thomas Wale, treasurer of S. Canice, of a small thatched house with a passage to the Noer, and a parcel of land adjoining the river to form the site of a mill, being in and near the town of Kilkenny. Fine 20s.—27 Oct., xxxiii.

5593 (4551.) Lease (under queen's letter, 17 April, xxxiii.) to Ambrose Forth, esq., one of the masters of Chancery, and judge of the Admiralty; of the site of the hospital of S. John by Kells, co. Meath, and its possessions as in 868, the lands of Ballinogrango and Ballinelaye, possessions of the monastery of the B. V. M. of Trym, co. Meath, (recites 3652); the lands of Clongorman, co. Meath, possessions of Rich. Walshe, attainted, (recites 4094); the rectory of Trevett, co. Meath, and its tithes amounting to 18 copies of corn, besides the glebe and 5 copies reserved to the vicar, (recites 4200); the tithe corn, hay, and furze of Killrowe, co. Meath, (recites 4094). To hold for 30 years, from the expiration of the terms in being. Rent £47 1s. 10d., part in corn. Provisions as in 5311.—(1 Nov., xxxiii.) (Auditor General's Patent Book, 22, p. 36.)

5594 (4542.) Livery to Richard, son and heir of James Aylmer, late of Dullarston, co. Meath, esq. Fine £28 14s., reduced to one half by order of the court of Exchequer, 22 Feb., 1590. Also for pardon of alienations, £27 6s. 8d.—3 Nov., xxxiii.

5595 (4530.) Grant (under letter of the English council, 12 Sept., 1591), to Gerald Comerford, esq.; of the office of queen's attorney at laws in the province of Connaught and Thomond. To hold for life, if he shall so long behave himself well in the office, with the fee of £20 English. Not to be removed, as in 4976.—4 Nov., xxxiii.

5596 (5722) Commission (under queen's letter, 10 July, xxxiii.) to the seneschal and the sheriff of the co. Wexford for the time being, Lodewick Briskett, esq., James Synot fitz Richard, gent., Robert Codd, gent., learned in the laws, and Robert Roch, gent.; to enquire what lands and customs belong to Dermot m'Moris Cavenagh, of Knockangarrowe, co. Wexford, and his freeholders, and to accept a surrender from him and them. Recites the purpose of granting the lands by patent to him, with provision that he confirm the freeholders in their rights.—11 Nov., xxxiii.

5597 (4456) Pardon to Donell O Boylane, of the Beahy, Dermott O Boylane, Oyn O Boylane, Donell O Conor, Teig O Connor, Rory O Harte, and Morys m'Rory O Connor, of same, Connor m'Melaghlen M'Donogh, of Ballodowne, Casbry M'Donogh, Gillyne O Haly, Moris grany, Farrill O Higgen, Loghlen O Higgen, and Donogh O Higgen, of same, Manus M'Donogh, of Cloynemahine, Brien O Banachane, of same, Dermot M'Evrehon, of Lisnegeale, Donell O Connor, of the Gartine, Brian M'Awly, of Cowlela, Owin Ultagh, of Grangbegg, Dermot Ultagh, of Ardinoglasse, Hugh O Marine, of Killnelassy, Cormack M'Gilleconill, of Cashill loghdeargane, Dermot O Haly, Brian Keogh, of same,

1591.   FIANTS.—ELIZABETH.

Tyrlagh M'Donogh, of Coolvony, Molmury m'Brien Doyn, of
same, Brian O Charry, of Loghford, Brien M'Nenollen, Melaghlen
O Fearry, of same, Owin M'Swyne, of Downedyn, Feigh M'Gilleboy, of Ardtarman, Tho. O Leen, of Roananedana, Tho. M'Coagh,
of the Beahy, Owin reogh O Mullmechory, of same, Rich. Lynch,
of Tawnagh, Teig M'e Clery, Carbery O Haly, Rory O Haly, of
same, Forgananyn M'Donogh, of Cowls, Donogh O Horiske, of the
Beahy, Wm. M'Shearry, of same, Callough O Connor, of the
Grange, Brian darogh O Connor, of same, and Shane M'Donogh,
of Cowlas. Security in co. Sligo, as in 4943. The pardon shall
not extend to any in prison or on bail, or any offence committed
outside the province of Connaught, or any person not now living
in that province, and shall not pardon intrusion into crown lands
or debts to the crown.—15 Nov., xxxiii.

5598 (4647.) Pardon to Peter fitz James Fitz Gerald, of Ballysonan,
co. Kildare, knt, Wm. Smith, of Athie, yeoman, Rich. Fitz
Gerald, of Strollans, horseman, James Fitz Gerald, of Grange
Myllou, gent, Art m'Donell Cavenagh, of Grange Myllon, kern,
Rich. m'Nich. Bremingham, of Ballysonan, horseman, James
O Magawie, of Ballysonan, Art m'Hugh O Neile, of Ballyomeek,
Donill m'Shane O Neile, of Clonigall, Serevrehagh O Shiell, of
Cloghnogan, Shane m'Morys Bremigham, and Owin duf O Neile,
of same, kerns, Owin m'Fir O Birn, of Ballybare, Tirlagh
m'Fir O Birne, of Grange ne spedak, and Kahire m'Dallagh
O Birn, of Ballynlengart, horsemen, Shane m'Morogh O Rime,
of Ballislina, stokagh, and Mortagh m'Cahire O Birne, of
Knockloy, horseman. Security in coa. Kildare and Carlow
(except Peter fitz James). Excluding, with the same exception,
any in prison or on bail; also intrusions on crown lands, and
debts to the crown.—16 Nov., xxxiii.

5599 (4516.) Grant to Dermot Magennure, gent.; of the office of
somehsal of Magennure's country called Monteygarran in co.
Longford. To hold during pleasure, in as ample manner as any
of his predecessors had as chief of that name. Powers as in
5366. Provided that this grant be not prejudicial to any former
grant.—* Not dated.

5600 (4451.) Pardon to Brian M'Dermot, of the Carrick, Brian
m'Rory M'Dermot, of [   ] Brian M'Dermot,
Dermot reogh m'Cartie m'Rory glasse, of Ballynaclogher, Conor
oge M'Tiernan, Shane M'Tie[   ] O Mullany, of the
Longeford, Manus m'Shane M'Dermot roy, Edm. m'Tumultagh
M'Dermot roe, Brian mac Tumaltagh MacDo[   ]
Tumultagh m'Brian m'Donogh reogh, of Ballymore, Wm. oge
Maganay, Owen oge m'Brien O Myhiden, Mulrony m'Cormock
[   ], of the Longurt, Teige M'Kevan, of
same, Edm. O Lavin, of Knocke Idowe, Brian O Lavin, of same,
Cahell m'Tho. MacDermot roe, Edm. oge [   ]ahary,
Owen O Carcaide, of Kilvryn, Melaghlen dune M'Buybry, of
Canboe, Ferdorgh M'Cormock, of same, Melaghlin O Mulconary,
of same, Rory boy M'Carbry, of Driniahduyve, Edm. Keogh
MacCarbery, of same, Hugh O Durvin, of Canboe, and Teige

---

* This and 20 following fiants, without dates, are of record among the fiants of the
thirty-third year.

carrogh MacBrian, of same. Security in co. Roscommon. Other
provisions as in 5532.—[   ].

5601 (4453.) Pardon to Terence O Dempsie, esq., late sheriff of
King's co., Hugh Dempsi, of Clonemore, alias Furdarogh, Lisagh
M'Brian, of Ards, Brian M'Phelim, of Hariston, Edm. M'Eboye,
of Clonin, Owin m'Donnough M'James, of Ramore, George
Comen, of Ballebrittas, Tirlagh O Kellye, of same, Wm. O Duff,
of Beherie, Donnell O Kellye, of Kilnecourte, Theobald
M'Edmond, of Ballinteggarte, Con m'Teige M'Caltin, of Ballebrittas, and Phelim Dempsie, of same, in King's and Queen's
counties.   Provisions as in 5504.—[   ].

5602 (4455.) Pardon to Hugh [   ], of
Maghary boy, gent., [   ] Magwire
[   ], Charles Magwire, gent., [
            ] M'Caffry, horseman, Rory Magwire, gent.,
[   ] Duoll O Flanigagan, gent.,
[   ] O Flanigagan, gent., Hugh
O Flannagagan, gent., [   ] Rory M'Cable,
horseman, [   ], Ogha O Hagassa, of
Balyogahsa, freeholder, Kithrin O Hogassa, of same, [   ],
Thady M'Caffry, of Iniskelly, horseman, Edm. and Wm.
M'Caffry, of same, horsemen, Hugh M'Caffria, of same, [
        ] M'Caffrie, of Toughraby, John, Felmeus, and Philip
M'Caffrie, of same, horsemen, James Mag[   ], gent.,
Terense, Roger flavus, Donagh, John, Philip, Malachy, and
Eugenius M'Caffrie, horsemen, James juvenis Magwire, gent.,
Terence O Willdane, priest, of same, John Magwire, of Tougharye,
James juvenis Magwire, Barnard Magwire, of same, gentlemen,
Hugh O Corcran, of same, stud., Mi[   ] O Corcran, of same, stud.,
Hugh Magwire, and Philip Magwire, gentlemen, Duall M'Cabie,
horseman, Donagh juvenis Magwire, Rory (son of) Patrick
Magwire, and Rory juvenis Magwire, gentlemen, of same place,
Maurice O Skanlahu, of Inchekillin, husbandman, Katherine
ny Mokellie, of same, Barnard Magwire, of Ferranareaghta,
gent., Redmund and Donagh M'Caffrie, of same, horsemen,
Cornelius O Corcran, stud., Roger O Corcran, stud., of same,
Edm. Maguire, of Owill, Donagh juvenis, Rory, Felmeen, and
Terence Magwire, of same, gentlemen, Felmeus, Hugh, and
Terence M'Caffry, of same, horsemen, Barnard O Hogassa, of
Balliogassa, freeholder, Barnard O Corcran, of Fearran amuny,
stud., John O Corcran, stud., Wm. O Corcran, stud., of same,
Obscurus O Hogain, of Carrick, Rich. O Hogan, of same, horse-
men, Cornelius Magwire, of Maghary Skaffanagh, gent., Philip
Magwire, of same, gent., Edmund, Niger, Terence, and Eugenius
M'Brian, of same, horsemen, Donald, John, and Donald (son of)
Bernard, Magwire, of same, gentlemen, Geoffrey M'Gillurno, of
same, Geoffrey (son of) Eugenius M'Gillurno, horseman, Niger
Dacani Magwire, of same, student, James Magwire, and Charles
O Morvughe, of same, priests, Magonius O Houlltughan, of same,
stud., Arthur Magwire, of Cloyen Kellwae, Patrick, Terence,
and Redmund Magwire, of same, John juvenis Coghalanus,
of Owill, Donagh an Cwoyn, of Ballinaclohi, (   )
M'Donnell (of) Cloonin Keelow, Poricius M'Doaill, Obscurus
M'Donnill, Barnard M'Donnyll, of same, and Marincus Carrall,
of Legin, gentlemen, John Magrath, priest, Hugh Magwire, of

Gwinancrir, John Meaghair, of Glann benhagh, and Felmum
Magwire, of Gwylnancrir, gentlemen, Bernard Magwire, of
same, Terence Magwire, of same, gent., Eugene Magwire, of
same, and Hugh Magwire, of same, gentleman, Thady O'Thouher,
of Killgoughy, husbandman, Sceihina Hinayn, of same, Donald
O Toughari, of same, hush., Honorea Carrell, of Dehalidonogh,
gent., Dermot Gwyrk, hush., John Flannaggan, of Inchekellyn,
horseman, Gilliduffe Tierney, of Gortmoide, hush., Philip Meary,
of Cnockaglas, hush., Barnard Magwire, of Onoak, Eugenius and
Terence Magwire, of same, gentleman, M'Goffrie, of same, chief
of his name, Barnard and Terence Magwire, of same, gentlemen,
Patrick M'Moenya, of Ballim'amennya, and Theobald Brian, of
Bawn Owly, gentlemen, Matthew Rian, of Owlenylly, husband-
man, Alexander Grace, of Bures, and Hugh O Donnall, of Rath-
nalltayn, gentlemen, Donald Keaddofaa, of Ballinguny, hush.,
Donagh M'Moenua, of Balin m'moenna, Comatius M'Meenua, and
Cornelius M'Moenua, of same, gentlemen, Cornelius (son of)
Thomas M'Meenua, of same, Cormac M'Meenua, of same, and
James (son of) Patrick M'Meenua, horsemen, Miler O Hogan,
of Balligan, freeholder, Thady (son of) Thady I Carroll, of
Owyl Iall, gent., Barnard (son of) Cornelius M'Meenua, of
Ballinnoya, and Magenius M'Moenasa, of same, horsemen,
Donald Teigeua, of Balnaire, student, Feargananym duff Carroll,
of Ballinglogha, Caffir O Donnill, of Rathmanlltayn, and Ma-
genius O Donill, of same, gentlemen, Roger Johes Rian, priest,
Mariola ny Omahor, of Rathmalltayn, John M'Neile, yeoman,
of Iniskellin, James maury Kenedy, of Killvaim, Cormac Ma-
gwire, of Clodyn owly, and Barnard and James Magwire, of
same, gentlemen, John m'Ile alias M'Hugh, Thady M'Hugh,
Cormac juvenis, Nyallan M'Hugh, Cormac corragh M'Hugh,
Edm. juvenis M'Hugh, Charles M'Hugh, Barnard juvenis
M'Hugh, Niallan M'Hugh, Eugenius M'Hugh, and Hugh
M'Hugh, of same, horsemen, Donagh William Leighe, of Bally-
[layed, hush., Eugenius Awlltagh, of Balimghayr, stud.,
Eugenius flavus O Gallohair, of Rathmaltan, and Donagh juvenis
Magwire, of Mayntir faodaghin, gentlemen, John O Skalyn, of
same, horseman, Donald O Donnyll, of Rathmalltayn, and Cona-
tius O Donnyll, of same, gentlemen, Malachy O Scalayn, of Main-
tirfaodaghin, Cormac O Schalain, Donagh O Scalain, and Niallan
M'Caffrie, of same, horsemen, Eugenius M'Skolog, and Charles
O Mihain, of same, priests, Barnard M'Gaurayn, of Le ragga,
Patrick M'Gaurayn, Donagh hallagh Maguarayn, Gillimamis
Magaurayn, and Charles Magaurian, of same, gentlemen, Barnard
M'Caffrey, of Mintairfaodaghin, horseman, Cormac (son of) Bar-
nard Magwire, of same, gent., Cormac M'Caffrie, Malachy, Fel-
meus, Barnard, and Roger M'Caby, of same, horsemen, Donald
Caffredy, of Rathmaltin, gent., Cornelius O Camedie, of Ballo-
camedie, Malachy Magrath, of Moyncaffrin, and Daniel Magrath,
of same, husbandman, Terence Maugenrin, of Learga, gent.,
James liath Grace, of Bures, hush., John O Doclayn, of Learga,
Terence O Doclaine, Charles O Doclayn, of same, Rob. Grace, of
Bures, and Charles (son of) Felmeus I Domlain, of Larga, horseman, Patrick Purcell, of Lickely, gent., Patr. Starbould, of Bal-
lihuby, Cornelius O Mulriagn, of Corbally, Thady O Mulrigan, of
Balinamonabeg, and John O Mulroni, of same, husbandmen,

1591.   FIANTS.—ELIZABETH.

Soeybina William Teige, of same, Tho. oge M'Coaguyr, of Tire-
kennada, horseman, Patr. Magwire and Obscurus Magwire, of
sumo, gentlemen, Collwe Magwire, of Coaillcw, Roger, Malachy,
Edmund, Barnard juvenis, and Lawrence Magwire, of same,
gentlemen, Hugh alias Ulleg m'Ca[yn] Borake, of Cnockyursata,
gent., Onoria Doyn Bourck, of same, Glicorin ny Rucirck, of
Balinos, Eugene (son of) Cormac I Gallchamy, of Rathmallton,
horseman, Egnighan O Donnell, of same, gent., Malachy M'Gillucoskill, of Donrybromi, and Barnard M'Gillucoskill, of same,
husbandmen, Acerbus M'Gillucoskill, of same, priest, Peter
Magwire, of Cloenya, gent., James O Loinyn, of Dowymullin,
and Edm. Magwire, of same, priests, James, Redmund and
Thomas Magwire, of same, gentlemen, Charles Magwire, of Lis-
chowill, Philip, John, and Hugh Magwire, of same, gentlemen,
Nilan O Durnyn, of Ineskillin, horseman, John M'Gillculeathayn,
of same, yeoman, Moenus moddarby O Ournyn, horseman,
Cahill O Treasan, of same, priest, John O Hogan, of Iniscwin,
Thady and James O Hogan, of same, Edm. O Hogan, of Cawins,
horsemen, Malachy O Cororan, of same, stud., Patr. O Cororan,
of same, stud., Falmeus O Corgan, of sams, stud., Theobald (son
of) Walter Bourk, of Culralle, gent., Dermot Lyssin, of Burse,
James O Brislcayn, of Dosyry aulan, husbandmen, Cornelius
O Corruran, of Ferran an muillyn, priest, Philip O Meagharia, of
Aillballin, Thady Odoins Megabir, of same, husb., Terence
M'Araghayn, of Bessih, husb., and Marnan Carrall, of Mothu-
gwir, horseman.—{   }

5609 (4457.) Pardon to Brien m'Hugh oge M'Mahoune, of Ruska,
Rori m'Hugh oge M'Mahowne, of Dromgowly, Edm. oge
M'Mahoune, of Derynmeylia, Shane M'Mahowne, of Dromca-
hell, Brien m'Redmond roe M'Mahoune, of Currin, Tuohill
m'Brien M'Mahoune, Rory m'Rosse m'Coin M'Mahoune, Colla
m'Tuohill boy M'Mahoune, of same, Con and Owin m'Hugh
m'Owen M'Mahoune, of Dromavane, Owin m'Gillepatrick
m'Rory M'Mahoune, of Crullincortan, Patr. glasse M'Donell, of
Anaghmore, Gillopatrick m'Philip oge M'Mahoune, of Corna-
porny, Gillepatrick m'Brien oge M'Mahoune, of Lishheagh,
Brian ne deantagh M'Mahoune, of Corcloghyrow, Tho. M'Mahowne, Patr. m'Art more M'Mahoune, of same, Shane duffe
M'Mahoune, of Dromchany, Laighlan M'Mahoune, of same,
Twohill boy M'Mahoune, of Tunnagh, Brien beddy M'Twohill
boy M'Mahoune, of Karowglasse, Rosse and Colla m'Tuohill boy
M'Mahoune, of Corlicke, Coochonaght O Gownaght, of Carrad-
dirdalosse, Farrall O Neily, of Droynstloisr, Shane O Neily, of
same, Ferrall O Shariddaue, of Corretobber, Phelim O Roddy,
Tirlagh M'Guirck, of Ruska, Brien m'Cormack O Duffe, of
same, Rosse m'Manus M'Mahowne, of Dromboanchur, Rory,
Hugh, and Patr. m'Rosse M'Mahoune, Art oge m'Coin m'Manus
M'Mahoune, Redmund m'Rosse M'Mahoune, and Patr. m'Coin
m'Manus M'Mahoune, of same, Aghy and Brien m'Hugh roe
M'Mahoune, of Darnamoyly, Shane m'Hugh m'Manus M'Mahoune, of Dengen, Brien boy M'Mahoune, Brien reogh M'Mahoune, of same, Loghlen M'Mahoune, of Dromgowly, Hugh
bane M'Mahoune, of Dengen, Patrick m'Colla M'Mahoune, of
same, Hugh bane m'Colla M'Mahowne, of Corrusy, Brien bane
and Rosse duffe m'Colla M'Mahoune, Colla m'Hugh bane

1591.   FIANTS.—ELIZABETH.

M'Mahonne, Leghlen m'Brien bane M'Mahonne, and Patr.
O Connolay, of same, Patr. m'Morogh M'Phillipp, of Lewally,
Patr. oge m'Patr. M'Phillipp, Nele m'Feraile M'Phillip,
Donell and Coochonaght m'Donogh more M'Phillip, Edmund,
Cahir, and Neile m'Coochonaght M'Phillip, of same, Donell oge
Obleige, of Coyltmore, Patr. beddy O Gowne, of same, Mahy
M'en Tye, of Lewally, Patr. O Troowire, of Ruske, Phelym M'Cale,
of Drommacheannan, Phelym O Roylie, of Dromchassisy, Mol-
more O Reyle, of Inismore, Rory O Reyle, of the Parrinhagh,
Phalim O Heyly, of Oreghane, Awe O Kyna, of Ballykyna,
Gillabride O Kina, of same, Hugh O Cadane, of Mullaghiradan,
Oyne M'Kwoly alias M'Kwolyne, of Clowneis, Patrick, son of
the said M'Kwolyne, Philip M'Kwolin, Patr. m'Tirrelagh
M'Kwolins, Coochonnagirt roe M'Kwoline, Cahill M'Kwoline,
Nicoll m'Art M'Colein, Brian reogh m'Owen boy M'Colein, Owin
boy M'Colein, Henry m'Owen boy M'Colein, Magnes og M'Ma-
houne, chaplain, James m'Person M'Mahoune, of the same, Donell
M'Crolin, late of same, Patr. m'Donogh M'Person, of Clones,
Magnes and Philip m'Brion M'Mahoune, Donogh reogh m'Brien
M'Mahoune, Leighlen m'Gillepatrick oge M'Mahoune, Patr.
m'Brien M'Mahoune, Patr. m'Manus M'Mahoune, of same,
Leighlen M'Feraile, of Dowhaile, Art M'Enony, of Clones,
James Fleming, of Cnockechappell, Cormack oge Brady, of
Derryhine, Donell M'Brady, Owin, Patr. bane, Nich., and Wm.
M'Enany, of same, Patr. boy m'Wm. M'Eneny, James M'Enany,
of same, James and Brien m'Manus M'Mahoune, Patr. m'James
M'Persomon, Owin m'Donell M'Donell, of Anaghmor, Gillgrony
m'Donell M'Donell, of Erynagh, Brian O Neile, of Ruske,
Phalim oge O Neile, of same, Brien and Shane M'Cwlin, of
Clowneis, Philip m'Leighlin Deyll M'Mahoune, of Dromynany,
Patr. m'Leighlin, of same, Patr. beddy O Connolly, of Corrynay,
Rosse duffe M'Mahoune, of same, Rory and Brien m'Con
M'Mahoune, of Coyltmore, Ardell m'Oyne Connally, of Ruske,
Art m'Ardell O Connalley, Teige m'Ardell M'Connally, Phelym
and Cahill m'Oyno O Connally, of same, Hugh O Klerkane, of
Franstowne, Brien kegh M'Cabe, Alexander m'Patr. M'Cabe,
Henry m'Owen M'Cabe, and Rosse duffe M'Cabe, of same,
Connor M'Cabe, of Dengen, Rosse m'Colla M'Cabe, of Carri-
backan, Patr. m'Colla M'Cabe, of Rurk, Patr. m'Owen M'Cabe,
Faly M'Cabe, Aghy roe O Connollay, and Connor O Molgeirge,
of same, Phalim M'Mahoune m'Patrick, of Dromgonnar, Donogh
oge Bradie, of Aghederriplus, Connor M'Cabe, of Lissoigy,
Cormack Bradie, Patr. m'Aghy roe O Connolay, Cahill and Brien
m'Aghy roe O Connallay, of same, Brien m'Rory m'Art moyle
M'Mahoune, of Kelly kerran, Patr. m'Tho. O Connalle, of Rusk,
Owin m'Alexander M'Donell, of Cloncowly, Shane roe m'Oyne
M'Donell, of Clonkeilane, Donogh gilla M'Donell, of same, Cormak
boy M'Donell, of Cloinkoraioke, Magnes M'Colein, of Clones,
Brian and Owin m'Magnes M'Colein, Phelem m'Magnes M'Col-
lein, and Philip O Lonyne, of same, Phelem m'Connor O Connolls,
of Coilingan, Patr. m'Phelem O Connallay, of same, Art beddy
O Connollay, of Corrygholter, Tirlagh m'Art beddy O Connallay,
of same, Owin O Connally, of Franston, Arowaill M'Eward, of
Dromgowly, Brien m'Arowill M'Award, Twoell M'Gilleahry, and
Cormac m'Gillean M'Brade, of same, Terlagh O Keally, of Clow-

1591.   FIANTS.—ELIZABETH.

neis, Magnes O Bwylane, of Aghydrumkyne, Shane M'Nemye,
Magnes duff M'Nemye, of same, Rory O Lonyne, of Dowaite,
Donnogh O Lonyne, of Coyllmore, Patr. M'Ardall, of Tydawned,
Patr. m'Rosse oge M'Mahoune, of Killiclonaghe, Con and Ardell
m'Gillepatriuk M'Mahoune, of same, Owin m'Brien m'Donogh'
M'Mahoune, of Dongovin, Shane m'Colla M'Mahoune, of Tawnagh duluik, Rory m'Twoill M'Mahoune, of Lissobwick, Patr.
m'Philip M'Mahoune, of Kwohin, Cormac and Brien M'Entye,
of Rusk, Phellim skippy M'Mahoune, of Dengan, Brian m'Rory
m'Toole M'Mahoune, of Caillnelong, Rosse and Con m'Rorie
m'Toole M'Mahoune, of same, Edm. M'Donell alias M'Donill, of
Loghnegalkrin, Patrick, Owin, James, Ferdorogh, Cormac, and
Brian M'Donill, of same, Hugh and Edmund m'Colla M'Donill,
of same, Coochonaght m'Hugh roe M'Donill, of Clowngalghy,
Colla M'Donell, Donogh m'Hugh roe M'Donill, of same,
Henry M'Phillipp, of Taghreogh, Patr. m'Hugh bane M'Philip,
of Corretrane, Laghlen and Edmund m'Shane molle M'Donill,
of Kornoe, Patr. M'Donell, of same, Patr. oge m'Magnes
O Connallay, of Rusk, Brian m'Magnes O Connallay, Magnes,
Edm., and Ardill m'Farr. oge O Connally, Tirlagh and Patr.
m'Brien O Connaly, Cahill evally O Connally, Patr. m'Cahill
evall O Connally, Phelem roe and Twoill m'Cormack O Connally,
Con m'Artt m'Edm. O Connally, Edm. m'Rory O Connally, Brian
reogh O Connally, Twoell m'Rory O Connally, Owin m'Phelem
O Connally, Patr. backagh O Connally, Edm. roe O Connally,
and Brien m'Edm. roe, of same, Donall O Nary, One O Rodane,
of Rousk, Una ny Roirke, of Corryne, Coochonaght oge M'Cowlyn,
Gillanenowe O Mollinochory, Shomine O Myane, of same, Rosse
M'Mahoune m'Gilduf, of Corleghroe, Rory M'One, of Leaghteohros-
mane, Coochonaught and Colla m'Brien M'Donill, of Oirynagh,
Patr. M'Donill, of Cowlsmell, James oge O Donnylly, of Grauinge,
Patr. O Donnylly, Hugh O Donnylle, Brien m'Philip M'Morogh,
of Lehrally, Art M'Philip, Hugh M'Philip, and Henry m'Morogh
M'Philip, of same, Philip Magraghrane, of Dromlane, Connor
m'Tirlagh M'Philip, of same, Twoill O Bwy, of Koylmore, Brian
O Coegly, of Cloyntarryim, Gilbride and Donogh O Coegly, of
same, Edm. M'Donell, of Cloyninsy, Art boy M'Donell, of same,
Brian M'Donell, Nele O Prontye, of Rusk, Patr. m'Cowlyn
M'Donill, Katherine ny Keally, of Rousk, Brien and Nele
m'Edm. boy O Connally, of same, Gillym M'Cowlin, of Clainase,
Philip O Molpatrick, of Ballyneglogh, Donill O Fryertane, of
same, Mellaghlen O Gowne, of Baby, Mellaghlein M'Keally, of
Rouske, Hugh M'Keally, Donill M'Keally, and Hugh reogh
O Kenedy, of same, Brien M'Cahill, of Crossay, Donnogh
O Connelane, of Coyllnehaltoragh, Patr. M'Diarmot, Edm.
O Dermot, Cale O Dermot, Coochonnaght M'Keaghry, Melaghlen
M'Donall, Moriertagh M'Donall, Donill M'Donill, Brien
M'Keaghry, Par duff M'Keaghry, Donogh O Gowne, of same,
Gillecoym M'e driwe, of Cloynse, Patr. reogh M'e drwe, Hugh
carragh M'Gillakierny, Teig reogh M'Gilleklerny, and Patr.
M'Gillakierny, of same, Oen O Coeglie, of Cloynturrin, One
O Coeglie, of same, Hugh ne kelly M'Donell, of Cloyninshy,
Edm. M'Donell, senior, Colla boy, of same, One reogh M'Donell,
Donall m'Arcwill M'Eward, of Dromgawly, Hugh grome

1591.   PLANTS.—ELIZABETH.

O Mullahallane, of Ruske, and Donogh reogh M'Morogh, of
Ballynaglogh.—[   ]

5604 (4458.) Pardon to Patr. M'Kena, chief of his name, esq; Art
M'Kena, Edm. M'Kena m'Shane, Donslewe M'Kena, Donslewe
oge M'Kena, Owen M'Collave, Coochonaght M'James, Patr.
Poninge M'Gillegrooms, Gillegrooms m'Owen oge, Owin M'Gille-
grooms, Patr. m'Gillegroms M'Neile, Toole m'Brian M'Glassy,
Gilleduffe M'Brien, Patr. m'Nele M'Gillepatrick, Tirlagh duffe
M'Kena, Patrick Poninge M'Shane, Brien m'Edmond oge,
Phelom carragh M'Kena, Brien carragh M'Kena, Nele M'Kena
m'Gillepatrick, Brian M'Kena m'Coochonaght, Donslewe M'Kena
m'Owen, Tooall boy M'Kena, James M'Phelyme, Mony M'Kena
m'Hugh duffe, Mony m'Manus rooe, Donn M'Kena, Patrick
Poninge m'Owen carragh, Ardell M'Kena m'Farrill, Art O Leane,
Rosse boy m'Brien M'Alexander, Dwaltagh M'Manus, Brien
M'Grwonyne, Hugh carragh O Kannahans, Donogh m'Hugh
m'Shane moile, Hugh m'Shane moile, Shane boddy M'Kena,
Jovane ny horpe, Patr. m'Toole M'Coochonaght, Tooall M'Coo-
chonaght, Melaghlen m'Rosse boy M'Kena, Melaghlen M'Gille-
grome, Edm. m'Aghy M'Kena, Patr. boy m'Aghy, Gilleduffe
m'Aghy, Conoghor m'Aghy, Patr., Coochrouaght, and Twohill
M'Kena m'Shane, Brien ballagh M'Kena m'Neill, Patr. m'Phillip
M'Cremer, Patr. m'Edmond M'Shane, Shane duffe M'Kena,
Phelem m'Gilleduffe M'Manus, Faly m'Art M'Kena, Patr. boddy
M'Melaghlen, James m'Edmond oge, Hugh m'Gillepatrick
M'Shane, Mony m'Brian oge, Toohill m'Brian oge, Moris
m'Cremer M'Manus, Cormake M'Kena m'Hugh carragh, and
James m'Gillepatrick boy M'Kena.   Security in co. Monaghan.
The pardon shall not take effect for any one not born and residing
in co. Monaghan.—[   ]

5605 (4463.) Pardon to Garalt m'Bryan m'Cahir, of Ballanfbrenagh,
Edm. m'Brian, of same, Elizabeth ne Brian Kavanaigh, of Haris-
town, Dowling m'Moriah m'Moriah, of Ballin Colaigh, Dermot
m'Morgh m'Morish, Donough m'Chrifen m'Chalar, Taig roe
m'Dermod O Rian, Morish m'Tirallaigh m'Chaiber, of same,
Shane oge O Conway, of Ballynebranigh, Tho. O Conwale, Owney
m'Donell O Rian, James ballow m'Sheron O Rian, of same,
Walter boy m'Edm. O Rian, of the Pollagh, Donell mor O Rian,
of Collahan, James and Moriah m'Richard ballaigh, of the Boeard,
Edm. m'Tirillaigh M'William, Farginanyn m'Conocor M'Donell,
Owin m'Dermod M'Owen, Henry m'James O Corin, Taig
m'William oarde, of Ballinghaylor, Donnagh roe m'Donogh
O Murley, Dermod leigh, of Gertie, Donnough roe, William more,
of same, Donall fyne m'Shane laigh, Garalt m'Terilaigh O Dowell,
Dallaigh m'Dermod O Haurike, Edm. m'Arte M'Dullinge, of
Ballihan, Taig m'Moriah leigh, of Killtsly, Teig more m'Kill-
patarick O Dowell, Dermod m'Melaighlein M'Donough, husbandman, Garalt m'Chaihar M'Murtaigh, Donogh m'Moriah
M'Dowlinge, and Richard alias Ristin Lalea, of Ballvraighy,
husbandman; co. Carlow.   Provisions as in 5604.   Excluding
also murder, burglary, or arson, or any person in prison or on
bail.—Not dated.

5606 (4465.) Pardon to Tho. m'Tomultagh M'Donogh, of Daghclowne, Owin m'Tomultagh M'Donogh [   ] Cowlafyne,

1591.　　　　　　　FIANTS.—ELIZABETH.

Shane boy and Bryen oge m'Owen Mac Rory, Teige and Bryen
O Spallane, of same, [　　　　　　　　], Tho. oge Mac Rorye,
Philip O Gormull, Gillegrome mac Dermot mac Bryen reogh,
of Clonsolagh, Tomoltagh mac [　　　　　　　] Tomoltogh
Mac Connell, of Tawnytragh, Melaghlyn moddar, of Clonsolagh,
Cahill duf O Harye, of Kiltelayny, Bryen mac Dermot Mac
Rory, of [　　　　　　] Dermot Mac Rory, Donell O Coman, of
Ballynehown, Loghlin m'Melaghlin O Coman, of Benady,
Morrice Mac Shane, of same, Morrish keogh [
Clonymaighyn, Ferriagh O Dowde, of Iskerowan, Wm. O Kelley,
Edm. Fuere, of same, Brian O Harte, of the Graig, Hugh oge
O Harte, of same, Cormock [　　　　] Wm. granagh O Harte,
Owin O Harte, Felym M'Brien, of Bonemadan, Teig roe
M'Kevyn, of same, Telge O Kervoll, of Tullaghneglog,
Wm. M'[　　　　], of same, Shane M'Egarky, Wm. Mac
Costeloe, of Tulghane, Cormock O Dowde, of Iskerowan, Mul-
morry M'Kevyn, of same, Edm. M'Farriall, of Grangemore, co.
Sligo, Matthew Fitz Patrick, of Iland Igenanan, co. Clare,
Fearrall O Skingin, of Ardcarnagh, co. Roscommon, James
O Skingin, James Carrowne, and Rowry reogh Omleny, of
same, husbandmen, Tirlagh M'Twohill, of Clonakeyle, and
Twohell M'Kodagh, of same, gentlemen, Anahla ny Kelly, of
Lackan, Fynyn M'Elen, of Oallon, husb., Neile roe M'Crowane,
of the Clonin, and Ferdorgho O Bradagan, of Legne, husband-
man, Diermot O Branyll, of Tonelegy, Kodagh O Kelly, of the
Clone, gent., Iriell O Higgyn, of the Clonyn, Melaghlyn
M'Hugh, of Lackan, Tirlagh M'Teig, of Corrybaghty, gent.,
Teige m'Rory O Connor, of Mollaghgollane, Hugh M'Conell,
of the Imlagh, Alvagh ny Connell, of same, Hugh m'Rory
M'Teig, of Skryne, Teige m'Shane granagh, of same, Teig
M'Ternane, of the Funahonagh, Rory m'Teig O Kelly, of the
Moate, Phealym m'Donell m'Teige oge, of Corrymore, gent.,
Dwaltogh m'Brian O Connor, of Nathnevey, Cahell og m'Fergon-
anlm, of Cowlnakellry, gentlemen, Brian m'Cahell M'Dowill,
of Imlaghe, and Brian mac Calowe O Connor, of Cloonagh.
Provisions as in 5582.—[　　　　　　　]

5607 (4467.) Pardon to Theobald Burke, of Beallyoke, co. Mayo,
gent., Edm. Burke m'Ullick m'Thomas, Ennys m'Marcus
M'an Abbe, Enys O Higgene, Sheane O Higgene, Ferryagh
m'Enys oge M'Donell, Owen O Fyrye, Dwaltagh m'Richard
duffe, Ferdorghe O Durayne, Rich. crone m'Dwalteghe m'Richard
duffe, Wm. duffe m'Sheane grane M'Robert, Donell m'Rich.
oge M'Robert, Moyler m'Ricard oge M'Robert, Tirlagh O'Firrie,
David M'Agoyle, Niell O Donnyll, Mayowe an Cotty
M'Andrew, Ricard crone m'Mayow m'Cotty M'Andrew,
Charles, Shane, Wm., Robert more, and James m'Dwaltegh
Keogh M'Andrew, Rob. Barrett m'Tho. ny giwlie, Wm.
Barrett m'Tho. ny gywle, Artor Barett fitz John, Edm.
Barrett m'Mayowe, Riocard ryaghe, Donnagh M'Gwyvir,
Donnell reaghe m'Donnogh M'Gwivir, Wm. O Moghane fitz
Cormock, Riocard Merick fitz Hobart, Diermott O Clery, Edm.
crone O Clery, Mollmoris O Clery, Ferryagh m'Tirrelagh roe
M'Donell, Tho. m'Wm. M'Thomas, Mayow m'Tho. riaghe
M'Robert, Moyler M'Haly, Ennys m'Bryen boy M'Donell,
Brian Avely M'Donnell, Mary ny Donnell, Sawe Burke, Tho.

M

1591.   FIANTS.—ELIZABETH.

Barrett m'Rich., Rob. roe m'Tho. Barrett, Moyler Barrett
m'Tho., Ricard Henry Barrett fitz Rich., Ullick Barrett fitz
Mayowe, Davi M'Tibbott, Moyler keogh fitz Walter fitz
Moyler, Walter Acoggy fitz Moyler keghe, Moyhmovria
M'Phillipp, Tho. Lyvott fitz Ullick bwy, Hubert crusa
Lynott, Ullick boy fitz Tho. Lyvott, Philbunke Livott fitz Tho.,
Tho. roe Livott fitz Tho., Cahall O Birne, Moryurtagh duff,
O.Garry, James M'Phillipp, Brian boy m'Dwaltagh M'Donell,
Ricard O Illanane, Kowconnaght M'Korckrane, of Rossmen,
and Moyler Barrett m'Tho. ny gzwlis, in aforesaid county. Pro-
visions as in 5532.—[   ]

5608 (4471.) Pardon to Florence, baron of Upper Ossory, Teig
and John m'Florence Fitz Patrick, Donogh M'Kynyne, gallogla,
Teige oge M'Kynyne and Shane M'Kynyne, kerns, Dermot
Evenle, horseman, [   ], Wm. M'Maghowne, Patr.
M'Maghowne, Conoghor M'Maghowne, Donogh m'Teige
M'William, Wm. m'Rory M'Donell, Donogh oge m'Donogh
M'William, Patr. Hackett, of Doell, Wm. m'Donogh m'[
         ] Fynine m'Dermott M'Fynine, John Burk, of Bally-
neclohy, Gillepatrick M'Rowry, Teig m'Dermot M'Teige, Wm.
m'Donogh M'Art, Dermott O Dooly, Rich. Britt, of Lys-
moriertagh, Donogh [   ] O Phelane, Moriertagh
M'Kenane, Wm. M'Costogine.   Security as in 4943, the
baron excepted. Excluding intrusion into crown lands and debts
to the crown.—[   ]

5609 (4473.) Pardon to Shane roe m'Conoghor m'Philip I Hinder-
gell, of Bantry, Philip m'Conoghor oge m'Conoghor m'Rory
[   ] I Hindergell, Onora ny Ed. Gerald, of Carduffe, Rory
m'Conoghor oge, Wm. Yonge, Donnell Morley, of Cariglyre, Ea
alias Hugh Morley, of same, Shane m'Gerald Yagherin, of
Bally[   ] Donogho m'Dermod m'Teig M'Connylligho alias
Donnough glasse, Gullyorist m'Donell M'Gullyoriste, of Bally-
warnsy, Donoll m'Ea M'Connogher, of Ashigarde, Walter
Graunte, of Downedanyre, Jaffrey Corr, of co. Waterford,
Kenedie m'Teaig m'Donell bwye, of Arlagh,. John Berrye,
of Castellmayngo, and Brian m'Teig M'Bryen, of Conaghe.
Security in co. Cork or Kerry; other provisions as in 5532.
[   ]

5610 (443L) Pardon to [the beginning of this fiant is destroyed; the
following names remain] John Camye, [   ] O Flavane, Brian
duff M'Connor, Redmund Breanhagh, Gerrott fitz John Fitz
Peirs, Tirlaugh roe O Connor, Edmund fitz Thomas ne buelly,
Hugh oge O Shanlane, husbandman, Dave m'Owen O Stanlane,
of Ackrum, husb., Hugh m'Reyry I Connoghor, of Assdey, and
Tho. boy m'Bryan I Connoghor, of Tullohynelt, yeoman, James
fitz Edmond Diermott m'Tirrelagh I Connor, of Kilbeagh, husb.,
Owen m'Tirrelagh I Connoghor, of same, Ricard Lyatowne,
of Kyllcanell, husb., Donall m'Nelle M'Gillevartin, of Two-
heaghtyne, husb., John Byrne, [   ] I Volguirine,
of Kilnnure, husb., Tho. fitz Tho. England, of Englandstowne,
husb., John Ofyn Donell m'Shane I Kelly, of Cullevarge, husb.,
Donell m'Owen I Vaddegane, labourer, Moris Stacok, Diermott O Langan, labourer, Dave Breanhagh, of Ballygellighane,
[   ] m'Tho. I Mullguinm, of Killmurre, John m'Dermott

1591. FIANTS.—ELIZABETH.

I Connoghor, of Cnogkhavade, labourer, and Morogh m'Dyerody M'Keghane, of Cloynlahard. Security in co. Kerry or Limerick; other provisions *as in* 5500.—[   ]

5611 (4482.) Pardon to Taige boy O Connor, gent., Dermot O Connor, Donnogh O Connor, Tirlagh roe O Connor, Tirrelagh m'Kedagh O Connor, Tirrelagh m'Calwagh O Connor, [   ] O Narye, William roe O Nary, Dwaltagh, Hugh, Cormack, and Dermott O'Nary, Rory oge M'Carrelly, Owin M'Calhedooker, Mclaughlan M'en Crokane, Teig M'en Crokane, [   ], Brien O Hedeane, Dwaltagh O Flanegane, Cormak fyn O Byrne, Brien O Morane, Rory O Howen, Katharine nyn Edm. O Farrall, Sawe ny Connor, Owin oge M'Dwile, Brien dorghe m'[   ] M'Branane, Brien m'Edm. M'Branane, Connor O Larryne, Hugh O Duffye, More reeghe, Cormack O Bradegane, Owin O Bradegane, Wm. O Flanigane, Connor m'Melaghlan O Flanigane, Teig oge m'Teig O Flanigane, Con. m'Hugh M'Branane, Una ny Henley, Grane ny Cahane, Rob. fitz Peter Nugent, Hugh M'eOheeny, Dermot O Morane, Carbry O Morane, Garrat m'Rory duff, Donnell O Kelly, Melaghlen og O Kelly, Teige O Kelly, Onora ny Kedagh O Farrill, Onora ny Lyanagh O.Farrill, Dermot Magoron, Garrot m'Lyaeagh, Malaughlen callagh O Hare, Donnogh O Kelly, Hugh O Kelly, Callo O Fein, Owin M'Dowill, Teige boy O Hely, Henry Kaven, James Dugen, Owin M'Eorey, Donogh O Carhe, James M'Erydarry, Walter Fay, John Comrell, Morogh boy, Philip Gowe, Hubart M'Ferdaeogh, Connoghor m'Tirlagh ballagh, Teig boy m'Connor M'William, Redmund kittagh M'Coog, Wm. Lynch fitz Pyera, Owin carragh M'Gilladuff, Shane Enyllane O Maddin, Rich. O Fahy of Gort, Malaughlen m'Teige O Horane, Colla O Flin, and Feariagh O Flin. Security in co. Roscommon and Clare, *as in* 4943. Not to. include intrusion in crown lands or debts to the crown, or any treason or crime committed outside the province of Connaught.—[   ].

5612 (4483.) Pardon to [   ] Connogher M'Dermody, Teige m'Donnell Y Connowe, Hugh m'Donnell [   ] Neale M'Donall, of the Corraghe, Edm. m'Shane Carrig. Wm. fitz Ullick Bourke, [   ] m'Kanedie m'Moriertagh Y Brien, Wm. m'Wony M'Rickard, Morice fitz John fitz Redmund Roche, Rich. Condon alias M'Mawige, John m'Walter [   ] James O Hurioke, Dermott M'Laghlin, John and Donogh m'Rory m'Convey M'Conyn, Wm. O Casy, Owen m'Awly O [   ], John O Longan, of Ardpatrick, Philip m'Gybon M'William, John O Hinky, Morogh O Hinky, Donnell m'Mary alias Donnell roe M'Cragh, Owen m'Teige O Coe[   ], Redmund oge M'Walter, Tho. Marice, Donnell molls, of Bearehaven, Connor O Brian, Dermott crone O Kinely, husb., Mahowne m'Dermod m'Shane Barra [   ], James Barrett m'Ullick, Edm. fitz John Barry, yeoman, Donell m'Teige Y Hownan, Garrett M'Coddoe, Connoghor m'Donogh Y Brian, Garrett m'David M'Gibbon, [   ] of Lanhagelsey, husbandman, Peirs Lacy m'Edm., gent., Walter

1591.   FIANTS.—ELIZABETH.

Condon m'James, Shane Condon m'Davy, John Hankard,
of Knockanamonelagh, husb., Riccard [   ]
m'Ullick Barrett, Wm. m'Donnell I Sulvaine, Nich. Fitz Red-
mond, of Balhacard, Teige m'Shane Derige, James fitz John
Poers, Owen m'Morgho M'Shehy, Rory m'Morogh M'Shehy,
[   ] Gerald fitz Tho. Gerrald, John fitz James
Gerald, Brien m'Morgho M'Shehy, gent., Tho. m'Philip
M'Nicholas, Rory m'Brien M'Gillescommull, Edm. m'Donnell
m'Morierta[   ], Gerald M'Redmond, yeoman, Brien
O Nolan, John Allyne, of Ballyhindle, Teige O Kelaghe, of
Shane cloane, Edm. m'Walter Condon, Morice M'Patrick, yeo-
man, Donogh O Dasam [   ], David Tobin, of Gortny-
skaghy, husb., Brien M'Donoll, Katherine ny Kye, of Carrig-
nowaroe, Donnell duffe O Lye, of Tyrbuy, John Conden fitz
Rich., of Carrygnownary, John M'Pattrick, of Dowgwilliam,
Owen m'Morrice O Connary, Connoghor m'Awliffe M'Clyny-
cane, Teige m'Awliffe M'Clynnycane, James Freinde, of Miltowne, Tho. moile O Leighe, Donnell m'Teige M'Donnogh, Rory
m'Donell m'Teige, his son, Donogh m'Thomas alias Donogh
Negrowre, Dermot oge O Crompe, Redm. M'Gerald, of Geirtyn
in Kryanagho, Donogh m'Edm. Y Connary, and Tho. Pursell fitz
Philip, in cos. Cork, Limerick, and Tipperary. Provisions as in
5532; also excluding murder.—[   ]

5613 (4479.) Pardon to Conogor Negarrogh O Kelly, of Gallagh,
gent., Sowe ne Kelly, of same, Donell O Kelly m'Melaighlan
cayn, of Killicloghir, Wm. M'Edmond, of Killywoggy, Shane
reogh m'Shane m'William oge, Rory m'Da m'Edward, of same,
Rory meole O Manyn m'Tho., of Ballane Crossynye, Oghy
M'Coagh, of Derrylesaigh, Ullick roe m'Ramon M'Henry, of
Ballenduff, Bedmund M'Richard, of Ardnasaddell, Edm.
M'Hugh, of Moylis, Fargannayn M'Kegan, of the Parke, Teig
oge M'Kegan, of same, Wm. Maglyn, of Leting, Ferdorgh
O Donelan, of Letalve, Donell carvaigh O Manyn, of Cloncarryn,
Dermot begg O Conygane, of Carrowlayny, Donogh duff O Cony-
gan, of same, Wm. O Kenny, of Liaro, Melaighlan M'Kegin, of
Cnockana, Ross ny Donelano, of same, Walter reugh m'Moyler
M'Click, of Clonmore, Shane duff m'Mollery M'Ulick, of same,
Redmund M'Jolnyn, of Clonmore, Wm. roe m'Ramon M'Ullick,
of the Camer, Donogh m'Inilly M'Shane, of Rakeryn, and Brian
m'Donnell M'Brian, of Croggan, co. Galway, Donogh m'Ross
m'Brian O Loghlein, of Anygalowane, Lisagh m'Donogh M'Lis-
aigh, of Cnockancoowakore, co. Clare, and Wm. M'Kegyn, of
Knockana, co. Galway. Security in cos. Galway or Clare,
with other provisions as in 5532.—[   ]

5614 (4487.) Pardon to Gerald fitz Tho. Dillon, of Manyn, Rory
M'Myle, Wm. Mac Myle, Philip m'Hobert M'Henry, Tirlagh
m'Hugh boy [   ] ne Caple M'Donell,
Owen MacDonell, Fargananym M'Donell, Keadagh m'Owen
M'Donell, Edmund and Choolao m'Oen M'Donnell, [   ]
[   ] M'Dounell, Allyn M'Donnell, Bannyll
M'Donyll, Nele M'Morogh, Donnogh roe Mac Mortagh, Aly mac
Edmond ballogh, Rickard M'Moriah, of the Mornyn, Honner oge
ny Onougher, Edm. M'Adam, Tho. Stangford, James Dockrd,
Lenagh O Melaghlan, James roe Mac Jurdan, Philip M'Philip,
Walter more M'Rorie, Gillaspicke M'Edonaltagh, Feragh M'Gil-

1591. FIANTS.—ELIZABETH.

laspick, Molmorie M'Alexander, Phelim m'Conill M'Donell,
Gooree dufe M'Kahir, Owstian m'Ranyl M'Donell, Neale boy
m'Dowle M'Donell, David m'Thomas MacCostello, Cormook ugo
M'Henrie, Walter m'Cormok M'Henrie, Ferdorgh m'Walter boy,
Molmory O Coffie, Edm. Morvornagh, Rorie Morvornagh, Wm.
oge m'Wm. duffe Morvornagh, Feragh Morvornagh, Kale
O Konylan, Melrony O Konyllan, Dermot M'Gawran, Melaghlyn
O Mulridie, Edm. M'Owyny, Rich. O Grady, Moylor m'Rickard
O Grady, Moylor, Jurdan, and Dermot m'Donogh O Grady, Edm.
m'Moylor O Grady, Hugh m'Henry oge O Grady, James duff and
Jordan m'Henry O Gradie, Rickard duffe M'Evasseller, Dualtagh
grany MacPhillip, Philip M'eCullogh, Rich. revagh O Moryly,
Con mac Moyleahaghlin O Melaghlin, Melaghlin and Henry
m'Manus O Naghten, Tho. M'Morie, Rich. M'Tenn, Conocher
O Dalie, of Killmymore, Laughlin M'Teige, of Bealagad, John
M'Edmond, of Lishrough, Hugh Mac Brian, of the Kallaooges,
and Gilleduffe m'Conor more. Security in cos. Galway or Roscommon; with other provisions as in 5532.—[   ]

5615 (4488) Pardon to Thady M'Dermot gale, Keadagh
M'Dermot gale, Rowri M'Dermot gale, Cahell ogo M'Mol-
rony, Donald O Garey, Ferrall m'Hugh M'Dermott, Thady
boy O Laven, Maurish O Mullany, Shanu O Laven,
Dualtagh and Fergananim M'Morishey, Cormock oge O Kerny,
Thomas m'Moriah M'Melaghlen, Shane M'Dermot gale,
Wm. Renogh, of the Carne, Knougher grany O Flene, Shane
M'Dermott, Thady m'Morishey M'Connor, Melaghlen oge
M'Morishey, Manus m'Dermot boy, Cahell O Connor, Owen
keogh O Connor, Henis Morvornaghe, Brone reogh Morvorny,
Gillecollen Morvornagh, Owen O Connor, of Bealanegare, Der-
mot carragh, of same, Gilleduffe M'Glene, of same, Wm. oge
M'William, Owen grany m'Cahell M'Nely, Fardoragh M'Nele,
Donall m'Cahell M'Nely, Grany Vervornagh, Caher m'Thomas
duffe, Henry M'Cowni, Philip m'William oge, Wm. M'Branan,
Thady M'Morrogh, Benmowne ny Connellan, Cone m'Teige
Bower, Owen m'Dowaltagh M'Morishey, Henry duffe m'James
Dillon, Rory O Garey, Owen O Garey, Shane M'Costello, of
Castlemore, Tibbot fitz Tho. Dillon, Owen M'Growrick, of same,
Walter m'Parie M'Donell, Walter whoeffe M'Myle, Chaler
m'Walter M'Donell, Jurdan M'Myle, Edm. M'Myle, Wm.
M'Myle, Dwaltagh M'Ullick, Ullick and Rickard M'Dwaltagh,
Cone M'Cowne, Moriah m'Hobart duffe, Tho. m'Moyler roe, Thady
oge M'Rory, Moyler boy m'Walter Keoghe, Wm. m'Edmond roe,
Henry Keoghe m'Moriah roe, Ricokard boy M'Shane, Colla roo
M'Jurdan, Ricoard boy M'Henry, Rowry M'Coyne, Edm. dor-
ragh M'Shane, Shane me kiltie m'Walter more, Dwaltagh keiogh
M'Costello, Moriah oge M'Henry, Dwaltagh m'Moriah roe, Ferdoragh M'Dualtagh, Connor grany m'Mannyahe M'Morishey,
and Rob. M'Coyne. Security in cos. Galway or Roscommon,
with other provisions as in 5532.—[   ]

5616 (4489) Pardon to Hugh O Connor, of Ballintobber, co. Ros-
comman, gent., Brien m'Donall M'Swyne [
             ] Rob. O Flynne, of Clwoynakroos, Brien
m'Moylmury M'Swyne, of Rathafryne, Connor grane O Connor,
of [   ] Brien m'vailla

1591.   PLANTS.—ELIZABETH.

m'Morogh M'Swyne, of Knockelaghta, Dwaltagh m'Dermot
M'Bryen, of Arrym, Cahyre M'Owen, of [
                ], of Cloynfadda, Bryen M'Gillakayre,
of Ballintobber, Thady O Connaghtane, Shane m'Owen boy, of
same, Moyler M'Jordan, of Cloya[
                ], Donell O Taige, Moriertagh m'Owen
boy, of Cloynynaklion, Tho. m'Moriertagh m'Owen boy, of same,
Owen m'Rary M'Owen, of Cloynakyne, [
                ] M'Fynyn, of Ballyntobber, Callowe
m'Freghra O Flyne, of Ballynlagha, Tomoltagh m'Rory O Flyne,
of Kenghyre, Tho. m'Hugh M'Connor, [
                ], Donell M'Tirlagh, of Cloukyne,
Callough O Flynne, of Mongeigh, Owen O Lavin, of Ballintobber,
Phellam M'Terlagh, of Kloynkyne, Thady O Connor [
                ] M'Keherne, of Cloynadicke, Connor,
Tomoltagh, Jordan kewgh, and Shane grana M'Keherne,
of same, Tho. reowgh [   ] Ferriagh
m'Bryen M'Owen, of Cloynnaklion, Edm. roe M'Keherne, of
Cloynarwka, Wm. roe M'Keharne, of same, Brien O Taige,
of Balliglasse, Thady ogo O Hnunyreagh [   ],
Hugh O Blye, of Keagher, Wm. O Gownane, of Coynkyne,
Molaghlen O Lavyne, of Ballintobber, Donald m'Gilleboy
O Flin, of Mongagh, Edm. boy m'William boy, of Ballyn-
tobber, [   ] Gillaruaffe, of Cloynroghan, Tho.
M'Edrwyo, of Ballintobber, Fergananin m'Rob. O Flyne, of
Cloynkwoa, Owen O Flyne, of Keagher, Rorl m'Owen O Flyne,
and Farderogha O Flyne, of same, Rori M'Robert, of Cloynyny-
aklen, Ricoard M'Shane, of Cloynlya, Moris O Crumvaghane, of
Longford in Maglary, Dwaltagh m'Conneghor M'Cahire, of
Lynlaeye, Owen m'Allyne M'Swyne, of Ballintobber, Donald
m'Bryen M'Swyne, Cormock O Fworishe, and Gilleboy
O Flanogan, of same, in co. Roscomon, Shane O Mullany, of
Ballyglasse, Malaghlen O Flanigan, of Rallintobber, Keadagh
O Lavin, of same, Thady M'Grewe, of Ballymullyn, Feagh
m'Donall O Flyn, of Mealaugh, Collo m'Davi m'Cormock O Flyn,
and Comhor more m'Owen M'Brian, of same, Laghlen more
m'Owan M'Bryen, Taige O Taige, of Clonsaliagh. Roel duffe
M'James, of same, Edm. O Lavin, of Ballintobber, Murtagh
reogh M'Kevan, of same, Fergananym m'Tibbot M'Ullick, of
Casteltoghor, Gilleyattrick ogo Sarson, of Ballintobber, and Teig
M'Gillemartin. Security in co. Roscommon; with other provisions
as in 553½.—[   ].

5617 (4497.) Pardon to John M'Costellowe, of Tulrohain, John
    M'Costellowe, Walter duffe M'Costellowe, of same, Wm. M'Lea,
    of Brocklin, Ollan M'Lea, of same, Davy m'Moilre M'Faltymoyle,
    of (same), Ricard in Collin, James m'Moilre m'Hune M'Jordan,
    Hubert M'Sheroin, of same, Hubert roe m'Shean Moilre, of
    Clontariffe, Ullick m'Tibbot reogh M'Jonyn, of Ballenyonomagh,
    Edm. une M'Johnyn, of same, Ullick roe Bourke macMoilre,
    of Cloghan, Rich. macRugh M'Jonyn, of Cloghnela, Onora ny
    Moylre M'Ricard, of Killollynan, Evelin ny M'Moriah, of same,
    Edm. m'Ricard M'Roddary, of Dumkyn, James roe mac Ricard
    M'Roddery, of same, John O Connlgaine, of Castell m'Gerlair,
    Gilla Colcym M'Veha, Davy M'Mariah, of same, Edm. m'Tho.

Y m'Iona, of Kilmean, Conla m'Shean Y Kannan, of same,
Phelym m'Brian boy M'Conell, of Mokarha, Alexander m'Hugh
boy M'Conell, of Moylla, Ullick m'Moilre m'Shane boy, of
Cahir in Ullick, Ricard Bourk, of Ballohacagh, Tho. M'Jonyn, of
Kilkoyr, in co. Mayo, Ricard m'Moylre M'Richard, of Tamnyndan,
Donell m'Hue M'Walter, of Torloghvanin, Rich. Bermigham,
Wm. m'Oonor M'Hue, of same, Tho. O Gilligann, of Lyaleagh,
Tullius O Mulconry, of Gort in vaga, Walter balagh, of Castell
Moyle, Taige O Conksnaln, of Moylagh, Wm. roe M'Hugh, of
Killovoyr, Edm. oge M'Heu, of same, Moylmore ketagh
O Higin, of Illan Ballenynolla, Donell M'Tunolta, Hogho
O Higin, of same, Edm. une M'Jonyn, of Ovultoyr, Henry
m'Moilre M'Ricard, of Tobokeogh, Ricard m'Moilre M'Ricard,
Ricard m'Ricard Ymlona, Taige O Morghowe, of same, Ricard
M'Jonyn, of Fartaglar, co. Galway, Davy mac Hubert M'Jonyn,
of Krigduffe, Redmund m'Gilleduf og M'Jonyn, of Kilkeran,
Davy duf, of Ballindagin, Moylre m'Henry boey, of Donnygege,
in co. Mayo, Edm. M'Morish, of Shroankeogh, Wm. M'Davy,
of Garriduf, John m'Moilre Orone, of Garraduf, and Maurice
O Dally, of Balleboy. Security in cos. Mayo and Galway ;
with other provisions as in 5532.—[   ]

5618 (4504.) Pardon to Wm. M'Quynegan alias Wm. nagenghy,
Rich. m'Shane oge M'Cotter, of Coppingarstown, Teige O Tohy
alias O Tohy, of Graung in Itawne, Donogh m'David I Kive,
of Donbollogh, Teige m'Donogh I Morowghowe, of same, Tho.
O Mulpatrick, of same, John m'David fits James Barry, of
Ballynecorry, Conoghor m'Teige m'Donell I Mahowny, Mori-
hartagh O Mahowny, Conoghor m'Teige O Mahowny, Tho. fits
David oge Barry, of Rathvillak, Conohor O Regane, yeoman,
Conohor O Regane, of Rathclaryne, Fallym O Hogan, of
Doneghell, John and Wm. Hurly, of Glanlarhy, in co. Limerick,
Teige Olary, of Annagh, Tho. O Flyne, of Clonamyne, and
John Powre fits John fits Edm. Security in cos. Cork or
Limerick ; other provisions as in 5531. Also excluding from
pardon any person in prison or on bail.—[   ]

5619 (4508.) Pardon to Nich. fits Michael Blwett, Fynen O Driscoll,
of Rynkule Iaky, MacCon O Driscoll, of same, Dermod m'Conn
M'Fahy, of Driahane, Cahire m'Teige M'Curtie, Donogh m'Teige
O Boughals, Wm. Poore, Maurice Poore, John Dowlagh,
Maurice m'Donell O Healehy, of Fernagh, Menlamus O Mahowny,
Connoghor m'Donell O Mahowny, of Laragh, John Galwan,
Riccard Condon fits Jordau, Wm. Cmdon fits Garret, of
Killokinty, James Condan fits Jordan, Edm. m'Shane oge
M'Cotter, of Coppingarstown, and Edm. duffe fits Nicholas Barry,
of Ballonetyrriagh. Security in cos. Cork or Limerick, other
provisions as in 5618.—8 [   ] xxx [iii.]

5620 (4669.) Pardon to Henry Bagenall, knt., marshal of the
army, Rees ap Hugh, vice marshal or provost marshal of the
army, captain Tho. Henshae, George Thornoton, vice marshal or
provost marshal of Munster, Moyses Hill, provost marshal in
Clandhuboy, Matthew Smith, gent, Lolwick Briskett, gent,
George Eaton, and Tho. Edwardes. Not to include intrusions
into crown lands or debts to the crown.—17 Nov., xxxiv.

1591.   FIANTS.—ELIZABETH.

5621 (4559.) Grant to Cowlo m'Ever M'Mahon; the half town or
   half ballybetagh of Cargagho, containing 8 tates, lying in the
   barony of Crymorn, co. Monaghan.—17 Nov., xxxiv.
   *This and the following fiants to 5673 are grants of lands in the
   county Monaghan, to be held for ever, by the several grantees and
   their heirs according to the course of the common law of England
   and Ireland. To be held as of the castle of Monaghan, by fealty
   only, in free and common socage, and not in capite. The rents to be
   20s. English for each tate. The grants are made pursuant to
   queen's letter of 20 January, xxxiii. (Morrin's Calendar of
   Patent Rolls, vol. ii., p. 315), and in accordance with the allotment
   of the lands, made by the commissioners appointed in No. 6682,
   and printed in Repertory of Inquisitions of the Chancery of
   Ireland, vol. II. Ulster, pp. xxvi.-xxxvi.*

5622 (4599.) Grant to Edm. carragh M'Owen; two tates—Moy, and
   Tullamacka. To Patr. m'Edm. M'Mahon; two tates—Ready,
   and Dromora. To Gilledof m'Ever M'Mahon; two tates—
   Mullaghgarry and Clonchorna. To Patr. M'Mahon m'Ever;
   the tate of Hawlaght. To Ever M'Mahon; the two tates of
   Crommore. To Manus M'Mahon; the tate of Crossebeg. To
   Patr. m'Shane M'Mahon; two tates—Onahall, and Lisnakilty.
   To Hugh M'Mahon; two tates—Tonekillin, and Anehnbe. To
   Patr. m'Hugh M'Mahon; the tate of Moyoghtoragh. To Art
   m'Hugh M'Mahon; the tate of Glasterne. The premises form
   the ballibetagh of Ballcalriaghan in the barony of Crymorne, co.
   Monaghan. See 5621.—17 Nov., xxxiv.

5623 (4604.) Grant to Edm. m'Melaghlen M'Mahon; the four tates
   called Carewe Itra. To Tole m'Melaghlen M'Mahon; two tates,
   viz.: half of the four tates called Carewe towne. To Melaghlin
   m'Melaghlin M'Mahon; two tates being the other half of Carewe
   towne. To Toole boy M'Mahon; two tates, viz.: half of the
   four tates called Carewe Ity. To Edm. m'Owen M'Mahon; two
   tates being the other half of Carewe Ity. To Toole m'Owen
   M'Mahon; the four tates called Carowneoraive. The premises
   form the ballibetagh of Ballenecraive in the barony of Crymorn,
   co. Monaghan. See 5621.—17 Nov., xxxiv.

5624 (4605.) Grant to Owin m'Colla m'Breine M'Mahon, Ardell
   m'Colla m'Breine M'Mahon, Rosse m'Colla m'Breine M'Mahon,
   and Art m'Ever M'Mahon; to each, four of the 16 tates forming
   the ballibetagh of Dollokillawny in the barony of Crymorne, co.
   Monaghan. See 5621.—17 Nov., xxxiv.

5625 (4606.) Grant to Con O Clerian; four tates—Lapan, Lislon-
   doff, Alghill, and Kenard. To Shane O Clerian; the tate of
   Gnowe. To Thorne O Clerian; the tate of Gnoweghtoraght.
   To Patr. boy O Clerian m'Flyn; the tate of Dronacka. To
   Breine boy O Clerian m'Arte; the tate of Nobber. To Toole
   m'Gilduffe M'Mahon; four tates—Cavancrevie, Glasmnollagh,
   Drumeude, and Cornehowa. To Hugh roe M'Mahon; the tate
   of Tullaghoumyakie. To Arte m'Hugh roe M'Mahon; the tate
   of Grenan. To Breine m'Hugh roe M'Mahon; the tate of Fad-
   dan. To Toole m'Phelym roogh; the tate of Dromgolaght.
   The premises form the ballibetagh of Ballaglanka, in the barony
   Crymorne, co. Monaghan. See 5621.—17 Nov., xxxiv.

1591.   FIANTS.—ELIZABETH.

5626 (4607.) Grant to Toole boy m'Hugh oge M'Mahon; two tates
—Lemeyere and Skeagh. To Patr. m'Edm. M'Mahon; the tate
of Dyrrenehollagh. To Art m'Colla M'Mahon; the tate of Inche.
To Owin m'Edm. M'Mahon; two tates called the two Ballaghea.
To Patr. m'Hugh oge M'Mahon; two tates—Tyrem'move, and
Cowleardagh. To Owin moyle O Duffy m'Owen; four tates—
Ologheran, Corenollahe, Aghnasyraghe, and Dromhoe. To Patr.
m'Cormock O Duffy; four tates—Branlitter, Correakeagh, Lis-
tynnie, and Shanmollagh. The premises form the ballibetagh of
Ballevickenally in the barony of Crymorne, co. Monaghan. See
5621.—17 Nov., xxxiv.

5627 (4610.) Grant to Hugh m'Borie m'Breine M'Mahon; the
ballibetagh of Ballemelghan, containing 16 tates, in the barony of
Crymorn, co. Monaghan. See 5621.—17 Nov., xxxiv.

5628 (4611.) Grant to Edm. m'Ever M'Mahon; ten tates parcel
of the ballibetagh of Ballelogblaghin, in the barony of Crymorn,
co. Monaghan. To Hugh m'Ever M'Mahon; six tates, being
the remainder of said ballibetagh. See 5621.—17 Nov., xxxiv.

5629 (4612.) Grant to Hugh m'Cowloe M'Mahon; eight tates parcel
of the ballibetagh of Ballerawer in the barony of Crymorn, co.
Monaghan. To James m'Cowlo M'Mahon; eight tates, being
the remainder of said ballibetagh. See 5021.—17 Nov., xxxiv.

5630 (4614.) Grant to Melaghlin m'Gilpatrick M'Mahon, Con-
siantyn m'Gilpatrick M'Mahon, Agby m'Gilpatrick M'Mahon,
and Redmund m'Gilpatrick M'Mahon; to each, four of 16 tates
forming the ballibetagh of Balladromger, in the barony of Crymorne, co. Monaghan. See 5621.—17 Nov., xxxiv.

5631 (4615.) Grant to Dreine M'Mahon fitz Patr.; two tates—
Cloghan, and Lacoagh. To Gilpatrick m'Hugh M'Mahon; two
tates—Crevemartin, and Anyalla. To Phelym m'Hugh Mac-
Mahon; the tate of Coraleighe. To Breine m'Art M'Manus;
two tates—Corrakyne, and Coriogh dargin. To Gilduff m'Hugh
M'Mahon; the tate of Coreeaple. The premises form the half
ballibetagh of Ballyleck, in the barony of Crymorne, co. Monaghan.
See 5621.—17 Nov., xxxiv.

5632 (4618.) Grant to Patr. m'Rosse M'Mahon, Laghlen m'Breine
oge M'Mahon, Breine oge m'Hugh MacMahon, Toole m'Phelym
duff M'Mahon; to each, four of the 16 tates forming the ballibetagh of Ballytawlaght, in the barony of Crymorn, co. Monaghan. See 5621.—17 Nov., xxxiv.

5633 (4624.) Grant to Rory m'Cowle M'Mahon; eight tates, part
of the ballibetagh of Ballsnenye, in the barony of Crymorn, co.
Monaghan. To Cowle m'Cowle M'Mahon; eight tates, being
the remainder of said ballibetagh. See 5621.—17 Nov., xxxiv.

5634 (4626.) Grant to Con m'Colla m'Breine M'Mahon; the ballibetagh of Bulleveaghan, containing 16 tates, in the barony of
Crymorn, co. Monaghan. See 5621.—17 Nov., xxxiv.

5635 (4663.) Grant to Art mac Rory m'Breine M'Mahon; the ballibetagh of Balleportenawe, containing 14 tates, lying in the
barony of Crymorn, co. Monaghan. See 5621.—17 Nov.,
xxxiv.

5636 (4658.) Grant to Con m'Colla M'Mahowne; eight tates
called Carretobber, Carvyn, Tyreluke, Dromboriahe, Corre-
gare, Tonelampill, Wroskernagh, and Dromegreene, in the

1591.   FIANTS.—ELIZABETH.

barony of Dartrie, co. Monaghan. To Henry m'Philip ; the tate of Tagharegh. To Nele m'Philip ; the tate of Tonaclagh. To Owin m'Philip m'Henry ; the tate of Killenena. To Edm. m'Cochonaght ; the tates of Cornihegagh and Druyme, and the half tate called Dromaddy. To Donell m'Donogh more, the tates of Tatercacka and Corretreyn. To Breine m'Morogh m'Philip, the tate of Maghere Jaffrey. All the premises form the ballibotagh of Balleviddegan, in the barony of Dartrie, co. Monaghan. See 5621.—17 Nov., xxxiv.

5637 (4581.) Grant to Patr. m'Rosse M'Mahon ; four tates— Corensive, Corcowau, Corregar, and Inahcman. To Shane m'Collo ; the tate of Coreglea. To Owin m'Brian m'Donogh M'Mahon ; two tates—Rathksraglit, and Lisnyne. To Brian m'Rory M'Mahon ; the tate of Dromore. To James m'Edm. M'Mahon ; two tates—Dowderana, and Lisnnchegan. To Philip m'Edm. M'Mahon ; the tate of Cremoyle. To Gillespatrick m'Philip M'Mahon ; two tates—Corretobber, and Neuagh. To Edm. m'Edm. M'Mahon ; the tate of Dyrraghenard. To Patr. m'Philip m'Collo M'Mahon ; the tate of Correvacoan. To Arte m'Edm. M'Mahon ; the tate of Corragarve. The premises form the ballibetagh of Ballecomey, in the barony of Dartry, co. Monaghan. See 5621.—17 Nov., xxxiv.

5638 (4582.) Grant to Malaghlin m'Gilpatrick beddy M'Mahon ; two tates—Drombymex, and Dromleyne. To Rosse m'Rory M'Mahon ; the two tates of Skenghe. To Con m'Rory M'Mahon ; the tate of Dromhillesgh. To Rory m'Tole M'Mahon ; the tate of Mallaghnoharne. To Patr. m'Aghy m'Art M'Mahon ; the tate (of) Callagh. The premises are parcel of the ballibetagh of Balleheran, in the barony of Dartrie, co. Monaghan. See 5621.—17 Nov., xxxiv.

5639 (4583.) Grant to Rory mac Hugh oge Mac Mahen ; the four ballibetaghs of Ballealawughkyu, Balleun'garohan, Ballecurren, and Balledrucarrell, in the barony of Dartrie, co. Monaghan. Rent for the first three ballibetaghs £28, and for the fourth £16. See 5621.—17 Nov., xxxiv.

5640 (4584.) Grant to Phalym Skippie M'Mahon ; four tates— Kilmore, Coronyshegagh, Tonie, and Kilhervie. To Hugh bane ; the tate of Dengan. To Patr. m'Collo m'Shane M'Mahon ; the tate of Dromore. To Shane M'Mahon m'Hugh roe ; two tates —Dromcahill, and Tonevickemally. To Breine m'Hugh roe MacMahon ; the tate of Aghowlaght. To Edm. oge m'Hugh roe ; the tate of Anaghewduff. To Malaghlen m'Brian M'Mahon ; the tate of Dromgowla. To Shane m'Hugh m'Manus M'Mahon ; the tate of Kilcrowen. To Brian ballagh m'Hugh m'Manus M'Mahon ; the tate of Moynoes. To Brian boy m'Hugh m'Manus M'Mahon ; the tate of Tenaght. To Hugh m'Gilpatrick m'Hugh m'Manus ; the tate of Dromyntin. To Hugh m'Brian m'Art M'Mahon ; the tate of Corrygreahagh. The premises form the ballibetagh of Balledromgowla, in the barony of Dartrie, co. Monaghan. See 5621.—[17 Nov., xxxiv.]

5641 (4585.) Grant to Arte m'Manus M'Donall and Cormack m'Art M'Donell, in equal parts ; the tate of Dromalowa. To Patr. m'Hugh M'Donell ; the tate of Clonyrsen. To Patr. m'Manus duffe M'Donell ; the tate of Colman. To Breine m'Collo boy M'Donell ; the tate of Anaghoragh. To Cochonaght m'Hugh

1591   FIANTS.—ELIZABETH.

roe M'Mahon ; the tate of Clonafaddy ne cononeuch.   To Patr.
m'Shane M'Donell ; the half tate called Cloneveigh.   To Patr.
m'Hugh M'Donell ; the half tate called Clonahanvoos.   The
premises are parcel of the ballibotagh of Ballaroveuch in the
barony of Dartria, co. Monaghan.   See 5621.—17 Nov., xxxiv.

5642 (4589.) Grant to Breine ne Tantant M'Mahowne ; two tates—
Kilnerunnaght, and Caernoen.   To Patr. m'Art M'Mahon ; two
tates—Corlaigarvell, and Eagalla.   To Tho. m'James M'Mahon ;
the tate of Claghery alias Dromy alias Glastruym.   To Philip
m'Melaghlen M'Mahon ; the tate of Dangan.   To Gillepatrick
m'Melaghlen M'Mahon ; the tate of Trevedegan.   To Gilleduf
m'Edm. M'Mahon ; the tate of Cornevala.   The premises are
parcel of the ballibotagh of Rallehoran, in the barony of Dartrie,
co. Monaghan.   See 5621.—17 Nov., xxxiv.

5643 (4590.) Grant to Rosse m'Breine M'Melaghlin ; two tates—
Dromloghon, and Dromavaddy.   To Hugh M'Donogh ; two tates
—Aghevo, and Cornevala.   To Donogh m'Breine M'Melaghlin ;
the tate of Corraghgowrre.   To Tole m'Breine M'Melaghlin ;
the tate of Kilmore.   To Aghy m'Donogh M'Melaghlin ; the
tate of Dirreloste.   The premises are parcel of the ballibotagh
of Ballevallemore, in the barony of Dartrie, co. Monaghan.   See
5621.—17 Nov., xxxiv.

5644 (4594.) Grant to Edm. oge M'Mahon ; the four tates called
Magbarneharnan.   To Chochonaght m'Phelim M'Mahon ; the
tate of Cowlkill alaight Rory.   To Patr. m'Phelim M'Mahon ; the
tate of Anaghnebana.   To Hugh m'Phalym M'Mahon ; the tate
of Dromroughill.   To Phalym m'Patr. M'Mahon ; the tate of
Dromgonny.   To Philip m'Patr. M'Mahon ; the tate of Drom-
arureivea.   The premises are parcel of the ballibotagh of Ballevallemore, in the barony of Dartrie, co. Monaghan.   See 5621.—
17 Nov., xxxiv.

5645 (4595.) Grant to Owin M'Donell m'Alester ; two tates—
Clonowla, and Correvaighan.   To Hugh en Killy M'Mahon ;
the tate of Clanculan.   To Arte boy M'Donell ; the tate of
Clonkerban.   To Edmond m'Edm. M'Donill ; the tate of Mul-
laghaalahanagh.   To Toole more M'Donall ; the tate of Clon-
kenghan.   To Donogh m'Shane M'Donell ; the tate of Clonlowre.
To Gillegrome M'Donell ; the half tates called Eyrenaght, and
Corragh.   The premises are parcel of the ballibotagh of Balla-
coveuche, in the barony of Dartrie, co. Monaghan.   See 5621—
17 Nov., xxxiv.

5646 (4596.) Grant to Hugh m'Breine oge m'Hugh oge M'Mahon ;
four tates—Edorgole, Agbedrumkyne, Tategare, and Cowlkull
alaight Mahon ; in the barony of Dartrie, co. Monaghan.   See
5621.—17 Nov., xxxiv.

5647 (4592.) Grant to Owin m'Hugh MacMahon ; four tates—
Aghnahola, Dromfreino, Lianala, and Cavan.   To Con m'Hugh
M'Mahon ; two tates—Anny, and Cobragh.   To Rory m'Owen
M'Mahon ; four tates—Kilfarge, Aghneskoe, Latteroroman, and
Corokan.   To Owen m'Gillepatrick M'Mahon ; the two tates of
Cowlearta.   To Patr. m'Philip oge M'Mahon ; two tates—Lis-
heagh, and Dromhior.   To Patr. m'Brian oge M'Mahon ; two
tates—Dromavila, and Dromnygran.   The premises form the bal-
libotagh of Balleneglough alias Ballelogheromana, in the barony
of Dartrie, co. Monaghan.   See 5621.—17 Nov., xxxiv.

1591.   PLANTS.—ELIZABETH.

5648 (4608.) Grant to Rorie M'Melaghlin ; two tates—Racruighan, and Lisbrynyn. To Philip m'Breine M'Melaghlin ; two tates—Maghery, and Ovealeigh. To Rosse m'Donogh M'Melaghlin ; two tates—Aghattadowe, and Dromanny. To Ardell M'Phillip ; two tates—Magherenekilly, and Dromyacke. The premises form the half ballibetagh of Balledyrrenamoyle in the barony of Dartrie, co. Monaghan. See 5621.—17 Nov., xxxiv.

5649 (4622.) Grant to Hugh bane M'Mahon ; four tates—Lissespynan, Aghafadda, Lesedromlona, and Boyagher. To Brian m'Colla M'Mahon ; two tates—Glan, and Coronghyren. To Rosse m'Coole ; the tate of Dromola. To Rory M'Mahon ; the tate of Oromeglough. The premises form the half ballibetagh of Ballalismospynan in the barony of Dartrie, co. Monaghan. See 5621.—17 Nov., xxxiv.

5650 (4562) Grant to captain Humfrey Willics ; the ballibetagh of Ballemorshie in the barony and co. of Maughan. Rent £18. See 5621.—17 Nov., xxxiv.

5651 (4563.) Grant to Arte m'Phelym M'Mahon ; three tates—Killenyle, Aneghgamyn, and Lootrynmore. To Toole boy M'Mahon ; three tates—Killyfe, Towlaght, and Garranowghtenaght. To Art m'Gilpatrick m'Ever M'Mahon ; two tates—Garranoghtenaght, and Aghnashana. To Hugh m'Phelym M'Mahon ; two tates—Genghmore and Genghbegg. To Gilpatrick oge m'Gilpatrick m'Ever M'Mahon ; the tate of Lootrymboge. To Art m'Hugh m'Ever M'Mahon ; the tate of Lissecarowkielle. To Gilpatrick m'Hugh m'Ever M'Mahon ; the tate of Killoorbe. To Colle m'Ever M'Mahon ; the tate of Liskyngorough. To Breine m'Phelym M'Mahon ; the middle tate lying on the east towards Tyrone in the hill called Lissecarrowkilly. To Breine vally M'Mahon ; the other middle tate lying on the south and east from the aforesaid tate towards Tyrone. All the premises form the ballibetagh of Ballem'garran in the barony and co. of Monaghan. See 5621.—17 Nov., xxxiv.

5652 (4564.) Grant to Cowle Hagh M'Ardill ; four tates—Aghnaaydagh (two tates), Nemntony, and Skeoryle. To Tirlogh M'Ardill ; two tates—Dromburke, and Dannalleran. To Gilpatrick M'Ardill ; the tate of Tacollat. To Manus M'Ardill ; the tate of Bellaghnegall. To Gilpatrick oge M'Ardill ; the tate of Ballyvickerban. To Philip M'Ardill m'Gilpatrick m'Cowley ; two tates—Rathkyraght, and Carickenoran. To Cormock M'Ardill ; the tate of Orenghglaste. To Cormocke oge M'Ardill ; two tates—Ramanny, and Oressy. To Henry M'Ardill ; the tate of Liswacorke. To Philip M'Ardill ; the tate of Ardaghcreigh. The premises form the ballibetagh of Ballevickenally in the barony and county of Monaghan. See 5621.—17 Nov., xxxiv. (Cal. P.R. p. 262.)

5653 (4591.) Grant to Brian fitz Rorie M'Mahon ; two tates called Tyrrecanne, and two tates called Shalva. To Tirlogh madder M'Mahon ; the two tates of Syvacke. To Patr. fitz Con M'Mahon ; two tates—Dromeghgalven, and Culkill. To Hugh boy m'Cahill M'Mahon ; two tates called Cornehonan. To Patr. fitz Owan M'Mahon ; two tates—Tyrerawre, and

1691. FIANTS.—ELIZABETH.

Mullaghahillock. To Melaghlin M'Mahon fitz Rory; the two tates of Corevally. To Arte fitz Melaghlin M'Mahon; two tates—Corebycke, and Croyla. The premises form the ballibetagh of Ballenethalvie, in the barony and co. of Monaghan. See 5621.—17 Nov., xxxiv.

5654 (4593.) Grant to Breinc M'Cabe fitz Alexander; five tates—Lismarte, Cremoyle, Shraghamodon, Na loate, and Tyrrehannaly. To Edm. M'Cabe fitz Alexander; the tate of Curlaigh. To Cormock M'Cabe; two tates—Aghneglough, and Dyrremgblin. To Breine Iriagh M'Cabe; two tates—Bonagh, and Cowloassook. To Edm. boy M'Cabe; the tate of Tullaghiste. To Bosse M'Cabe m'Melaghlin; the tate of Dromegryna. To Gilpatrick m'Cowla M'Cabe; the tate of Corevama. To Toolo m'Alexander M'Cabe; the tate of Turgher. To James m'Tirlogh M'Cabe; the tate of Tyrearian. To Arte m'Melaghlin dala M'Mahon; the tate of Clogheran. The premises form the ballibetagh of Balloclonangre, in the barony and co. of Monaghan. See 5621.—[17 Nov., xxxiv.]

5655 (4600.) Grant to Christopher Flemynge, late of the Newrie, merchant; the ballibetagh of Ballevickenrewe, containing 10 tates, in the barony and co. of Monaghan. See 5621.—17 Nov., xxxiv.

5656 (4601.) Grant to James Garlon; four tates—Cornakuly, Correvollan, Coradulea, and Aghevricke. To Laghlin Foxe; four tates—Kilcarnan, Dromore, Fedowe, and Clonlonnan. The premises are parcel of the ballibetagh of Balloblagh, in the barony and co. of Monaghan. See 5621.—17 Nov., xxxiv.

5657 (4602.) Grant to Nich. Davies; three tates—Annaghm'nele, Coradm'nele, and Coralea. To Tho. Kelly; two tates—Cornevally, and Killnamaddy. To Ever m'Breine M'Mahon; two tates called Tonakawy. To David Cartan; two tates—Corenenany, and Lismakerke. The premises are parcel of the ballibetagh of Ballencfaragh in the barony and county of Monaghan. See 5621.—17 Nov., xxxiv.

5658 (4603.) Grant to Barnaby Loockan; four tates—Bradoge, Corradd, Carlongort, and Cossoboy. To Lawrence Dermot; three tates—Tyreragh, Loghnelaphinrie, and Corraghnegowne. The premises are parcel of the ballibetagh of Ballenefaragh, in the barony and county of Monaghan. See 5621.—17 Nov., xxxiv.

5659 (4609.) Grant to Toole boy m'Ardell M'Mahon; four tates—Tonnagh, Dromhnny, Coraleck, and Liscomyakia. To Brian m'Redmond M'Mahon; four tates—Dromhucke, Labmard, Callagh, and Dromsaule. To Colla m'Toole M'Mahon; two tates—Slefeave, and Aghadrumchian. To Rory m'Rosse M'Mahon; two tates—Kilgrack, and Agbolaghe. To Shane duffe M'Mahon; two tates—Faltagh, and Rosseclough. To Brian M'Mahon m'Edm.; two tates—Corevellewe, and Liscgomey. The premises form the ballibetagh of Balladromhucke, in the barony of Dartrie, co. Monaghan. See 5621.—17 Nov., xxxiv.

5660 (4613.) Grant to Manus fitz Philip M'Mahon; the two tates of Cromlen. To Gilduff fitz Patr. M'Mahon; four tates—Dromrottagh (two tates), Cullmultkilly, and Killomerlie; after the death of Gilduff one tate of Dromrottagh shall remain to Philip

1591.   . FIANTS.—ELIZABETH.

his son and heir, the other tate of same, to Collo, his second son,
Calmultkilly, to Rorie, his third son, and Killomerlie, to Edmund,
his fourth son. To James M'Mahon ; two tates—Mullaghmore,
..and Cowledough. To Toole M'Mahon ; two tates—Dyrrye, and
Gobrie. To Braine fitz James M'Mahon ; two tates—Tullanor,
and Kiltedowe. To Art fitz Manus M'Mahon ; the tate of Carne.
To Rorie fitz Owen M'Mahon ; two tates—Cavanroogh, and
. Liscarney. The premises form the ballibetagh of Bulleroogh,
containing 15 tates, in the barony and county of Monaghan.
See 5621.—17 Nov., xxxiv.

5661 (4616.) Grant to Rory m'Arte moyle M'Mahon ; six tates
—Killychoran upper, Garvagh, Dyrentonie, Agharishallowe,
Narte, and Inismmen. To Owin m'Aghy M'Mahon ; two tates,
—Sillowe, and Molliglassan. To Arte m'Breine M'Mahon ;
two tates—Limeynan, and Coremyver. To Ardell M'Mahon ; the
tate of Limenaghan. To Ever M'Mahon ; the tate of Maghery.
To Braine m'Con M'Mahon ; the tate of Dromargellan. To
Redmund m'Breine oge M'Mahon ; the tate of Kincorra. To
Cahill M'Woney ; the tate of Kilkryna. To Rosse m'Rory
M'Mahon ; the tate of Drumamperie. The premises form the
ballibetagh of Balletyrebrayn, in the barony and county of
Monaghan. *See* 5621.—17 Nov., xxxiv.

5662 (4617.) Grant to Owin m'Braine M'Mahon ; four tates—
Ballagh Iland, Toegan, Killnacleigh, and Drumgull. To
Hugh m'Covarie m'Con M'Mahon ; four tates—Gortemore,
Drombanny, Rath, and Gnaghill. To Con m'Gilpatrick
M'Mahon ; the tate of Corretagher. To Hugh m'Ouen m'Breine
M'Mahon ; the tate of Calcorragh. To Patr. m'Hugh roe
M'Mahon ; two tates—Carnebane, and Aghem'brackn. To Rory
m'Hugh roe M'Mahon ; two tates—Cornaaowe, and Cabragh.
To Arte m'Hugh roe M'Mahon ; two tates—Dromgarre, and
Greghan. The premises form the ballibetagh of Ballym'egowne,
in the barony and county of Monaghan. *See* 5621.—17 Nov.,
xxxiv.

5663 (4619.) Grant to Con m'Hugh M'Mahon ; two tates—
Dromucke, and Tollmenarny. To Edm. M'Cabe m'Alexander ;
four tates—Currafuagh, Cartenagh, Dromalon, and Kiltabret.
To Tirlogh M'Cabe ; two tates—Lisemyskie, and Brenedrone.
To. Shane M'Cabe ; the tate of Clonevarne. To Breine
M'Cabe m'Donell ; the tate of Lecke. To Braine M'Cabe
m'Foly oge ; the tate of Tyrem'divan. To Foly M'Cabe ;
· the tate · of Tolligillan. To Rosse M'Cabe ; the tate of
Cavaningarvan. To Owin M'Cabe ; the tate of Limeshinnagh.
To Owin M'Magonall ; the tate of Cromlan. To Alexander
M'Cabe ; the tate of Corenaglare. The premises form the
ballibetagh of Ballileck, in the barony and county of Monaghan.
See 5621.—17 Nov., xxxiv.

5664 (4625.) Grant to Tirlogh O Connole, chief of his name, late
· vice marshal under M'Mahon ; the whole ballibetagh of Balleclenlagh, containing 16 tates, in the barony and county of
Monaghan. *See* 5621.—17 Nov., xxxiv.

5665 (4666.) Grant to Rosse m'Manus M'Mahon ; four tates—
--Drombancher, Liege, Taghledan, and Glanan· To Glassny
m'Manus M'Mahon ; the two tates of Monamurry. To Con
m'Manus M'Mahon ; the two tates of Hilledan. To· Redmund

m'Rosse M'Mahon; the tate of Darchose. To Collo: m'Rosse M'Mahon; the tate of Dromullen. To Gilpatrick M'Con; the tate of Mullaghboy. To Rory M'Breine; the tate of Legey. To Toole M'Breine; the tate of Mullaghmartin. To Hugh M'Ouen; the tate of Kelua. To Patrick M'Glasney; the tate of Knockpoble. To Rory M'Rosse; the tate of Shancogh. The premises form the ballibetagh of Dromhanehor in the barony of Trough, and co. Monaghan. *See* 5621.—17 Nov., xxxiv.

5666 (4580.) Grant to Donslewe M'Kena; the three tates of Mullaghmy henaght, Rathluan, and Dyrreneved. To Nele M'Kena; four tates—Mullaghmore, Clonakyne, Dyrraclone, and Groighvanillagh. To Toole boy M'Kena; the tate of Mullanekaska. To Pholly M'Kena; the tate of Ardegeeny. To James M'Kenna; the two half tates of Neaker and Killeloughvally. To Brian M'Kena; the two tates of Tonaghm. To Gilpatrick Ponny m'Owen carragh; two tates—Killedonoghe, and Dyrrenegurd. To Gilpatrick M'Kena m'Nele; two tates—Drombristie, and Glann. The premises form the ballibotagh of Ballstonia, in the barony of Trough, co. Monaghan. *See* 5621.—17 Nov., xxxiv.

5667 (4586) Grant to Brian roe M'Mahon; four tates—Toneygan, Tonagh, Rathrowteaght, and Derenehalge. To John M'Mahon; two tates—Inystanryn, and Dyrrehalloughe. To Patr. M'Arte; two tates—Craliegh, and Corraghbracke. To Hugh oge; the tate of Clonarte, the half tate called Gortemmy, and the half tate called Annealoot. To Ouin M'Quyn; two tates—Oughteraght, and Corroghduff. The premises are parcel of the ballibetagh of Ballynewmere, in the barony of Trough, co Monaghan. *See* 5621.—17 Nov., xxxiv.

5668 (4587) Grant to Phelym carragh M'Kena; the two tates called Balleviagh and another tate called Cullean. To Brian carragh M'Kana; the tate of Aghdrumcruer. To Patr. Ponny m'Shane m'Patrick; the tate of Skyncherna. To Shane ballagh M'Kena; the tate of Lissmcearie. To Bryen m'Edm. oge M'Kenna; two tates—Kildryns, and Tonlomeake. To Patr. beddy m'Melaghlin M'Kena; the half tates of Mollaghealahenaghe, and Mullaghmore. To Phelym M'Gilduffe; the tate of Mullaghooran. To Edm. M'Kena; the two tates of Killnokie. To Owin M'Kena; the half tates of Knockhitin, and Drumlaster, and the tate of Durrenenvak. To Donslewe oge Makena; the two tates of Aghdirrie. The premises form the ballibetagh of Balleveigh, in the barony of Trough, co. Monaghan. *See* 5621. —17 Nov., xxxiv.

5669 (4588) Grant to Patr. m'Gilgrome M'Kena; the two tates called Kilmurry. To Patr. m'Owen M'Mahon; the tate of Kilmahon. To Cormook M'Kena; the tate of Dongarhrie. To Cochonaght m'James M'Kena; one tate and a half called Ballonehown, and half a tate called Knockyrvan. To Tole M'Kena; the tate of Dromerall. To Gilleduff M'Kana; the tate of Killeran. To Patr. m'Nele M'Kena; the tate of Naerishe. To Cormook m'Patr. M'Kena; the tate of Killallon. To Braine m'Gromyn M'Kena; the tate of Dyrrunehinshia. To Shane M'Kena m'Gilpatrick rue; the tate of Tonaghnan. To Owin M'Gillegrome; the tate of Aghenahanan. To Brian boy m'Owen M'Kena; the tate of Killtubret. To Hugh m'Shane M'Kana;

1591.   FIANTS.—ELIZABETH.

the tate of Dromaddagan. To Tirlogh roe Makana; the tate of
Kilkrenan. The premises form the ballibetagh of Ballakillmurry, in the barony of Trough, co. Monaghan. See 5621.
—17 Nov., xxxiv.

5670 (4597) Grant to John Connolan, rector of Moynaltio; the
ballibetagh of Porteclare, containing 18 tates, in the barony of
Trough, co. Monaghan. Rent £8. See 5621.—17 Nov., xxxiv.

5671 (4620.) Grant to Rosse M'Mahon m'Patr.; two tates—Lar-
gan, and Mullaghsewe. To Patr. M'Cabe; two tates—the half
tate called Ballaghnenany, the half tate called Kiltsbeg, and the
tate of Mullaghhurtan. To Arte boy M'Quoad; two tates—
Califfe, and Killeconogan. To Tege M'Quoad; two tates—Conris
and Mullslary. To Nele oge M'Quoad; two tates—Anagh-
gattin and Anaghminton. To Melaghlin M'Mahon; the two
tates of Glaslaghen alias Clonka. To Patr. m'Gillegrome
M'Quoad; two tates—Clonenyok, and Cavan. To Patr.
M'Quoad m'Phalyn; the tate of Tyrerie. To Arte M'Quoad;
the tate of Anyola. The premises form tho ballibetagh of
Balloglaalagh, in the barony of Trough, co. Monaghan. See
5621.—17 Nov., xxxiv.

5672 (4621.) Grant to Don M'Kenna; three tates—Rathkelly,
Correneigh, and Aghedrammucka. To Owin m'Melaghlin
M'Kenna; the tate of Dyrrelamycka. To Toole M'Nale; the
tate of Dromora. To Monny M'Kana; the tate of Killyhoman.
To Hugh m'Manus roe; the two half tates of Dirredarvy, and
Clan. To James fitz Patrick roe; the tate of Drombyrne. To
Ardell M'Kena; two tates—Kiltlevan, and Tyrewan. To
Money M'Kena m'Gilleduffe; the tate of Mullogndan. To
Melaghlin M'Owen; the tate of Dyrreryuan. To Patr. Penny
m'Gillegrome M'Kenna; three tates—Aghvicluna, Dromcurred,
and Dyrresoen. To Patr. m'Gillegrome M'Kenna; the two
half tates called Killebyrne, and Dirrery. The premises form
the ballibetagh of Ballekiltlevan, in the barony of Trough, co.
Monaghan. See 5621.—17 Nov., xxxiv.

5673 (4623.) Grant to. Arte M'Kena; seven tates—Agheruke,
Killo, Nelva, Balleneakragh, the half tate of Aghesard, the half tate
of Derevoy, Killehrian, and Coreclare. To Toole oge M'Kena;
three tates—Dyrrecrynard, Luendengan, the half tate of Gille-
gullan, and the half tate of Corgerbock. To Tirlogh daff
M'Kena; three tates—Lisseagh, Dirrelossad, and Dromconraght.
To Gillegroma M'Kena; the tate and a half called Killeloraght,
and the half tate called Dirrehelan. The premises form the
ballibetagh of Ballaghereaske, in the barony of Trough, co.
Monaghan. See 5621.—17 Nov., xxxiv.

5674 (4580.) Grant (under queen's letter, 20 Jan., xxxiii.), to
Patrick duffe m'Colla M'Mahon; of 2 ballybetaghs of Balla-
vicklewlis and Ballenecrevis, and half the ballybetagh of Balli-
leckis, in the barony of Crymorn, co. Monaghan, each ballybo-
tagh containing 18 tates, and each tate 60 acres of land of all
kinds, by estimation; also a rent of £25 English out of the
two ballybetaghs of Ballenkeaghan and Ballaglanks, and the
other half of Ballyleckis (granted by patents of 17 Nov.), being
12s. 6d. from each tate, with power to distrain in each tate for
the amount if unpaid. To hold in tail male, remainder to Patr.
m'Hugh m'Cormock M'Mahon in tail male, remainder. to Brian

1591.   FIANTS.—ELIZABETH.

m'Gilpatrick m'Hugh roe M'Mahon. To hold by the service of
a fourth part of a knight's fee. Rent £15. He shall answer
hostings within the county and its confines with his whole power
of horse and foot, and to those more than 20 miles beyond it
shall send one horseman and two footmen sufficiently armed
If the person seised under this grant shall assume the title of
M'Mahon or chief of his nation, or be attainted or convicted of
any treason or rebellion, this grant shall be void.—20 Nov.,
xxxiv.

5675 (4561.) Grant (under queen's letter, 20 Jan., xxxiii.) to Ever
m'Cowlie M'Mahon, esq.; of the five ballybetaghs of Ballen-
logh, Ballereogh, Ballenelurgan, Ballaknocksotliste, and Balleogh-
ill, lying in the barony of Crymorne, co. Monaghan; also a
rent of £119 15s. English out of the ballybetaghs of Ballalogh-
layhin, Ballmeny, Ballerawer, Ballsportnave, Ballemelghan,
Ballenecrelve, Balledrumgor, Ballenveighan, Ballalcillawny,
Ballytowlaght, Ballovickanally, and the half ballybetagh of
Cargagh, in said barony (granted by patents of 17 November).
To hold in tail male, remainders severally in tail male to Rory
and Cowlo m'Cowlo M'Mahon, his reputed brothers. Rent
£30 English. Sending 4 horsemen and 8 footmen to distant
hostings, and with other provisions and service as in 5674.—20
Nov., xxxiv.

5676 (4577.) Grant (under queen's letter, 20 Jan., xxxiii.) to
Brian m'Hugh oge M'Mahon, esq.; the five ballibetaghs of
Ballenorloghroe, Balleblagh, Davallintarra (two ballibetaghs),
and Ballevylan, in the barony of Dartris, co. Monaghan; also
a rent of £105 12s. 6d. English, issuing out of the 13 ballibetaghs of Ballealawughkyn, Ballenaogarchan, Ballenourren, Balle-
drumerrall, Balleviddegan, Balledyrremoyle and Lisenaspynan,
containing one ballibetagh, Ballodrumburke, Ballmaglogh alias
Ballelogh Crossan, Balledramgowla, Ballenorony, Ballehoran,
Ballevallymore, and Ballenovench, and four tates of Edargole,
being £3 out of the ballibetaghs of Ballealawughkyn, Balle-
m'garchan, and Ballenourren; and 12s. 6d. out of each of 161
tates in the remainding 10 ballibetaghs, granted by patents of
17 November. To hold in tail male, remainder to Hugh
m'Brian m'Hugh oge M'Mahon, his reputed son, in tail male,
remainder to Rory m'Hugh oge M'Mahon, his reputed brother,
in tail male. Rent £30 English. Provisions and service as in
5675.—20 Nov., xxxiv.

5677 (4578.) Grant (under queen's letter, 20 Jan., xxxiii.) to
Patr. M'Kenn or M'Kenna, chief of his name; three ballibetaghs
of Ballydavough, Ballynany, and Ballilattin, and the 12 tates of
Tullagh (two tates), Dyrregashall (two tates), Pallice (two tates),
Portenaghy, Disart, Tyrarmove, Killarnowle, Nemove, and
Brackagh, in the barony of Troogh, co. Monaghan; also a rent
of £56 17s. 6d. issuing out of the six ballibetaghs of Ballynea-
mere, Ballekittlevan, Balletonie, Ballevicigh, Balleaghevreake, and
Ballakillmurry, (except the tates of Tolliard, Dirreklegh, and
two tates called the two Cargins), in same barony (granted by
patents of the 17 Nov.) being 12s. 6d. from each of 91 tates. To
hold in tail male, remainders to Owin m'Patrick M'Kenna, and
Shane M'Kenna, his reputed sons, severally, in tail male. Rent

N

1591.   FIANTS.—ELIZABETH.

£22 10s. English. Provisions and service as in 5674. Sending
to distant hostings 2 horsemen and also 4 footmen.—30 Nov.,
xxxiv.

5678 (4579.) Grant (under queen's letter, 30 Jan., xxxiii.) to Patr.
m'Arte moylo M'Mahon, esq.; the three ballibetaghs of Balle-
m'cowloe, Ballencorrely, and Ballalue, in the barony and county
of Monaghan; also a rent of £10 English, issuing out of the four
ballibetaghs of Balleclonsugro, Ballem'enrewe alias Ballevickeu-
rewe, Balleclenlagh, and Halletyrebruyn, in the same barony,
granted by patents of 17 Nov., being 12s. 6d. for each of 64
tates. To hold in tail male, remainders to Arte m'Arte moylo
M'Mahon and Toole m'Arte M'Mahons, severally, in tail male.
Rent £18 English. Provisions and service as in 5677.—20
Nov., xxxiv.

5679 (4593.) Grant (under queen's letter, 10 Nov., xxxiv.) to Brian
oge M'Mahon, gent.; the three ballibetaghs of Rallicliors, Balle-
drumarrall, the twelve tates of Clonaoda, and four tates in the
ballibetagh of Balleonmmere, viz., Tolliard, Derrykiegh, and the
Cargins (two tates), in the barony of Trough, co. Monaghan;
also a rent of £20 English, issuing out of the ballibetaghs of
Drombanchor and Ballegisalagh, in the said barony, granted by
patents of 17 Nov., being 12s. 6d. from each tate. To hold in
tail male, by the service of a sixth part of a knight's fee. Rent
£18 English. Provisions as in 5674.—30 Nov., xxxiv.

5680 (4681.) Grant (under queen's letter, 30 Jan., xxxiii.) to
Rosse Lane m'Brane M'Mahon, esq.; five ballibetaghs—Balle-
tullaghosaholl, Ballaracomyle, Balleskonghan, Balleloertia, and
Ballecorrefenlagh, and the half ballibetagh of Balleblaghe, in the
barony and county of Monaghan; also a rent of £34 7s. 6d.
English, out of the 8 ballibetaghs of Ballylecko, Dallym'egowne,
Ballenashalvia, Ballevicgaran, Ballemorchie, Bellmehragh, and
Ballevickenally, and the other half of the ballibetagh of Balleblagh, in the said barony, granted by patents of 17 Nov., being
12s. 6d. from each of 116 tates. To hold in tail male, remainders to Hugh m'Rosse M'Mahon, and Art m'Rosse M'Mahon,
severally, in tail male. To hold by the service of a fourth part
of a knight's fee. Rent £33 English. Provisions and service
as in 5674. Sending to distant hostings 3 horsemen and 6 footmen.—20 Nov., xxxiv.

5681 (4657.) Grant to Tho. Molinex, esq., (formerly deputy of Edw.
Waterhouse, knt., deceased, late collector of the subsidy on wines);
of the office of customer, collector and receiver of the custom or
impost on wines discharged in the ports of Dublin, Waterford,
Limerick, Cork, Drogheda, Galway, Youghill, Carrickfergus,
Wexford, Rosse in co. Wexford, Kinsale, Dungarvan, Dundalke,
Sligoe, Carlingford, and Dingle Hussey alias Dingine ne queise.
To hold during good behaviour, with the usual allowances. Not
to be removed, as in 4976.—24 Nov., xxxiv.

5682 (4652.) Pardon to Rory O Connor, of Clonmore, co. Roscommon, Dermod m'Con O Connor, of same, Donogh bane
O Heraght, of Carrownsmarty, Malaghlyn M'Shane, of Drom-
nagh, Giles ny Teige O Kellie, of Mullaghmore, co. Galway,
Donell m'Donogh O Layne, of same, Wm. M'Conoghor, of
Carowleyvio, Brian mac Hugh O Kelly, of Clogher, Edm. Coolgh,
of Canownlany, Wm. m'Coolgh O Kelly, of Crohen, Rory

1591.   FIANTS.—ELIZABETH.

m'Donnell O Kelly, of Clonlein, Teig M'Morogh, of Anaghmore, Wm. carragh O Birne, of Portroyn, co. Roscommon, Brian O Birne, Edm. O Birne, of same, Tomoltagh m'Colla O Flin, Cormak O Looby, of Oygully, Brian O Hanny, of Teehhuy, Giles ny Flyn Spincer (*ni.* spinster), of Oregdul, Molmory boy O Teige, of Lackane, Wm. oge m'Wm. M'Edmond, of Garrogh, co. Galway, Gellernow O Danellane, of Lowny, Tiago O Donellane, of same, Shane oge M'Edmond, of Cornemacklagh, Donell O Flyn, of Fynury, co. Roscommon, Teige m'Callogh O Connor, of Clonakilly, Tirlagh oge M'Tirlagh, of Annagh, Shane carragh M'Kenuy, of Killuckeny, Farrall duffe M'Kenny, of same, Shane grana M'Branan, of Kiltrustans, Hubert M'Branane, Conoghor m'Hubert Mac Branane, of same, Dermot mac Oahill O Flanegane, of Montagh O Flanogan, Collas m'Rorie M'Dowill, of Ballymy, Neale M'Gillecoell, of same, Con m'Conoghor boy, of same, Dormot m'Cahill M'Farry, of Clonibirn, Tho. m'Wm. moile M'Currelly, Cormak M'Carrelly, of same, Con boy, of Cogullo, Donell oge O Cahellane, of Ballindirry, Wm. mac Donell duf Mac Enchrochane, Hugh m'Dermot M'Kenny, of Kiltuckin, Fiagh mac Hubert, of Carowneglogh, co. Galway, Donell oge O Margn, of Kilkide, co. Clare, Riccard O Killnane, of the Grange, co. Galway, Teige O Treasy, of Clonecony, Hugh mergagh m'Hugh O Madden, of Corgane, Roris kiltagh lawan M'Moraiue, of Downemacmernine, Moris Keogh m'Melaghlen O Maden, of Bracklone, Donell roe M'Shane, of same, Fiagh O Flyn, in co. Roscoman, Cormack mac Manas Keogh M'Enerihine, Tho. M'Henry, in co. Galway, Brian M'Grevy, in co. Roscoman, Mortagh m'Teig M'Cormook, Tomultagh M'Morlertagh, Beanveen ny Gillegrome, Gillernowe O Calgie, Melaghlen oge m'Laughlen M'Dowill, Donogh m'Gillechlan O Oultacker, Moriah Roche, Flan Mac Enylk, of Killeruy, Tirlagh O Teige, Katherin ny Henry, Tirlagh m'Teige M'Coyn, Hugh O Cohane, Ferdorogh mac Manas O Flanogane, Teige carragh m'Hugh m'Rorie O Connor, Teige mac Shane O Flanegane, Shane M'Branane alias Higgen, Teige M'Dermot roe, Cahill m'Conoghor O Birne, Morogh Mac Elvochra, Cahill O Morane m'Shane, Teige reogh m'Brien Mac Owhnsy, Brian Keogh mac Brian Mac Croughan, Manus O Gary, Shane m'Donell O Morane, Rory grana m'Phelym boy O Connor, Dermot m'Coyne m'Teige oge O Connor, Cahill m'Manus m'Enaryhine alias O Branan, Edm. O Donooluie m'Cahi[ ], Donell m'Arrelly M'Moyntally, Conoghor O Hanly m'Edm., Conoghor m'Gillegrome O Hanly, Shane O Corrogune, Brian O Carrogane, Teige m'Gillegrome O Hanly, Conoghor m'Edm. O Kelly, Conoghor m'Teige Mac Stine, Brian m'Brian O Flanegane, Beavy ny Byrn, Tirlagh m'Dermod O Hanly, Anablo ny Cooill, of Aghloghan, Donell M'Ewarde, of Balligartin, Conor M'Ewarde, Callough M'Donell, of the Neile, co. Mayo, Edm. ballagh M'Donell, of Aghleharde, same co., Hugh O Higen, of Dungunerick, co. Galway, Mallaghlen O Donellane, of Ballydonallane, Wm. roe O Higgen, of the Park, Shane O Clorys, Hugh O Clury, Tomultagh mac Hugh, Katheryn ny Dermot roe, Lasarine ny Dermot roe, Melaghlen M'Rorie, Shane M'Rorie, Teige O Flanohie, Brian M'Teige, of Killinydoda, Comako M'Kegane, Cormack Mac Edmond, Brian M'Edmond, and Shane O Higgan, of Behagh, in co. Galway.

1591.   FIANTS.—ELIZABETH.

Security as in 4943. Excluding from pardon any persons in prison or on bail, or any who are not resident in Connaght, or who have committed offences outside that province. Excluding also intrusion on crown lands or debts to the crown.—26 Nov., xxxiv.

5683 (4686.) Grant (under letter of the English privy council) to Gurald fitz Rich. Fitz Gerald; of the right of redemption of a certain mortgage made by Tho. Fitz Gerald called M'Thomas, of Pallice, co. Limerick, gent., of Illanhobbuck, Kildeglan, Ballivallonie, and Garridaf, co. Waterford, to James Sherlock fitz Tho., for £136. Rich. fitz Thomas alias M'Thomas, son and heir of said Thomas, was slain in rebellion with the earl of Desmond, so forfeiting the right of redemption; but the present grantee claimed as brother and heir of Thomas, alleging Richard to be a bastard.—26 Nov., xxxiv.

5684 (4676.) Commission to sir Rob. Gardener, chief justice, sir Rob. Dillon, chief justice of the Common Pleas, Nich. Walshe, second justice of the Chief Place, John Allen, of S. Wolstanes, esq., George Dormar, justice of the co. Wexford, and Rich. Netterfield, of Killaughau, esq. ; to examine witnesses concerning the title to the possessions of the manor or abbey of Dunbrodye, whereof there is a controversy depending before the privy council in England between John Itchingham and sir Nich. Whitt, knt.—27 Nov., xxxiv.

5685 (4651) Pardon to Conogher O Brien m'Mortagh, of Cahircorkaane, co. Clare, Mortagh O Flanegan, of Ballivohana, Edm. O Rea, of Boghuale, Brian M'Gillenetrick, of Intraght, Dan O Garmully, of Cahircorkoano, Donald roe m'Teige O Hehir, of Clairmore, co. Clare, Hugh m'Tomoltagh M'Dermod roe, in co. Galway, Hugh boy M'Tneargy, Shane O Higen, of the Boagh, Mela ilen O Dmclen, of Ballydonalane, Owen m'Melaghlin O Madden, Tirlagh M'Swyne, of Nonaduff, Hugh oge O Madden, of Killowney, Riccard m'Cahill M'Colleghane, Cahill M'Breamill, of Corelogby, Rory m'Anmghoy O Madden, of Iskir, Feariagh m'Morogh O Madden, Brian m'Colla M'Mclaghlen, Edm. O Doolane, kern, Conogher M'Coochogerie, of Lyaduffe, Daniel m'Wm. O Moylane, of Kilhide, co. Clare, Conogher M'Cormake, of Garanaralh, Tho. m'Brien O Doolane, Finin m'Owen M'Coghlane, Patr. O'Kynnye, Rory O'Corerane, of Cloynowce, co. Galway, Peter Taylor, of Ellphin, Wm. Carre alias Stewarde, Donogh ne Closy G'Connor, of Cloyngarry, Molmury M'Dermod, Con M'Donall, Coochonagh O Carlrane, of Isarnoe, Brian bane M'Gilladuff, Cormack m'Phelim O Mullaglen, Donoghane O Carroll alias M'Guyakine, Shane M'Brannane, Owen boy M'Brannane, Conogher M'Branane, Conogher O Hanly, Brian m'Morogh moyle O Ferrall, Owen O Tyvnane, of Sligo, in co. Sligo, Donogh Leurer, of Balliwemer, co. Clare, Dermod reoghe m'Tirlagh boy, of Clonmurragh, co. Roscommon, Bryan M'Owen, and Hubert M'Brannane, co. Roscommon. Provisions as in 6682.—27 Nov., xxxiv.

5686 (4649) Pardon to Gilleduf m'Tho. M'Shane, of Cloynowyll, Edm. roogh m'Edm. M'Ullyck, of Cloynmmore, Cartry O Menlan, of the Abbert, Brian M'Gillorce, of same, Shane O Conehanon, of Kiltullagh, Tho. Maglyn m'Donill, of the Kappagh, Cooohogerie m'Mahowne M'Oogbalane, of Oghill, Teigroogh M'Faryne, of Faba, Donogh M'Gilleroaill, of Mullaghmore, Shane m'Brien M'Gilleballagh alias Shane Burk, of Killin, Donogh boy M'glyn, of Killm'dongh, Henry O Grady, of Gort Inshiguiry, Gilleduff O Killane, of Bealleghduff, Wm. roogh, ofsame, Wm. O Loghnane, of Downnore, Redmond Burk m'Ullick, of Derym'lagbne, Wm. M'Conoghor, of the Laasiny, Redmond m'Riccard boy, of Carowtallagh, Shane m'Moriertagh M'Gillakolly, of Mulrough, Moriertagh M'Tirrelly, of Olonyne, Una ny Higgen, of Tobberroe, Ferdorogh m'Hugh M'Shane, of Lawally, Donell and Conoghor m'Hugh M'Shane, of same, Connoghor M'Ea, of the Shillihane, Rory O Looba, of Clonfoase, Conoghor M'Hugh, of the Feddane, Conoghor O Killane, of Ranegh, I'helim lish O Loghlen, of Enagh, Moriertagh m'Donogh M'Rasy, of Nallycnalane, Gilbride ogm M'Brodyno, of Lettermalano, Donogh m'Teige O Brien, of Ballym'Conin, John Mellane, of Ballynknoiek, John M'Brodyn, of Kilkylly, Riccard O Conaill, of Annaghmore, Teig m'Donoll O Beolane, of Inahibegg, Donogh m'Teig I Turry, of Ballynakally, John Ne'land, of Ballym'Cahill, Conoghor O Dorrechy, of Killynobranan, Moyler m'Tybbott braak, of Iland Kaak, Teigo O Hanly, of Tuan maak graaill, Con m'Brien M'Melaghlen, of Athy Cnockan, Tho. Burk, of Ra'iyounoghor, Wm. M'Moyler, of same, and Anmobo m'Faurry O Maddeu, of Capp alevane. Security in coa. Galway, Clare, Mayo, or Roscommon, with other provisions as in 5083.—27 Nov., xxxiv.

5687 (4650) Pardon to Tho. O Cahill, of Ballm'lannac, Donogh O Cahill, of same, Ownhie m'Lyseagh O Loghlen, of Turlugh, Rosse m'Ownhie m'Lyseagh, of same, Shane oge M'en Cargie, of Kiltohoroghe, Redmond M'William, of Muckannys, F.dm. Nelland, of Kilnemona, Donall Nelland, Wm. Nelland, of same, Rory O Mollrona, of Clonfish, Teig ne Keartan, of Killearagh, Denys M'Teig, of Clony, and James Nelland, of Eyrymgh, all in coa. Clare. Provisions as in 6682.—28 Nov., xxxiv.

5688 (4645) Pardon to David m'Edmond roo, of Ballinigory, Tho. m'Shane Craake, of Gragemoyesshill, John Barry alias Gilleduff Barry, of Coyleygowirk, Daniel O Bryn, of Tirimurte, Edm. meigaghe m'Mortagh M'Kashine, Teige m'Philip O Shea, of Killaha, Moris O Bryn, of Ballioaorigh, Donigh M'Costaligho, of Cloghitupedig, Donill and Thomas m'Shane ni Teige O Shea, of Cloghran, Wm. m'Wm. O Conoragh, of Kappaeoyne, Tho. m'Shane M'Walter, of Dryngane, Edm. fitz James Fannyn, of Ballintagart, Tho. M'Gibbon, of Ballinlondrie, Conohor O Madden, of Killinenallye, Conohor m'Mahowne I Cormaak, Edm. O Moelin, of Lealoakie, Brian m'Firr M'Swyne, of Castill'mow, Neale M'Donill, of Mashanaglisha, Tho. m'Moriah O Hurly, Morris fitz Edmond alias Morris Deag, of Coillyknoakane, James ballagh Tobyn fitz Wm., Dermot m'Hugh m'Dermot I Douovan, Mary ny Moriertagh, of Garinkaharegh, Dermot roo m'Dermot m'Shane M'Inrightighe, Donigh m'Shane M'Phillipp, of Ballinveogighe, Conohor m'Dermott I Croly, of Carrignicorrie, Donigh m'Conohor O Leary, of same, Owen O Bryn m'Tirlagh, of Longhurt, Donill m'Teige I Callane, of Ashiveaghine, David and John m'Teige I Calane, of the Kaharougarry, Owen roe m'Donigh M'Owen, of the Broghane, Mohowne O Killie, of Meane, Ricard m'Donill Y Kahill, of Ballawliff, Ricard more Tobyn, of

1591.   **FIANTS.—ELIZABETH.**

Shanran, Garrott Tobyn fitz Edm., of Balligoeyrighs, Garrott
Sutzan fitz David, of Cloghinaris, Teigo O Oleary m'Donigh, of
Anmgha, Pheenen m'Dermott Cartie, of Lisalloina, Morihir-
tagh m'Mahowne m'Teige I Hanaghan, Philip m'Shane giahe
I Mulrean, Philip m'Shane M'Ineyrie, of Balilawlif, Morihirtagh
m'Philip m'Shane, of same, Ricaard fitz Tho. Fitz Nicholas, of
Walshestowne, Ricard Ristigog, footman, Donill m'Donigh ros
I Mulrean, John m'Oonohor I Rourdane, Moghowne O Goho-
righe, Cormuck O Oonnell, of Oloncriblue, Donnot O Mulrean,
Donigh m'Shane I Mulyorriu, of Killworrighe, Rory oge O Hif-
ernane, of Sronill, Morris Hibbard, of Kyntre, Wm. Young, of
Carrigmondle, Tho. O Flaghavane, of Cloven, Moroghow M'Ko-
nedie, of Dowghill, Philip M'Donill, of Clancorbario, and David
fitz Redmond Fitz James, of Hassigissalon.   Security in qo. Cork
or Limerick, with other provisions as in 5558.—7 Dec., xxxiv.

5889 (4644.) Pardon to James fitz Riccard Currie, of Balynchlabir,
gent., Edm. Breanhagh, David Breanhagh, Wm. O Quynleano,
and Morris Breanhagh, of same, Rich. Roche, of Ballingarvy, Eliu
ny Melaghlin ny Awly, Owin m'Art oge O Keevo, Malaghlin
m'Teige O Daly, of Killaliahane, Boohallagh m'Brien M'Birehu-
gree, of Srah, Awly m'Hugh moile, of Ballynvoninc, Wm. alias
Don M'Conoghor, of Glan, Donogh oohnagh M'Teige, of Atheam-
vohi, Oohney O Kenedy m'Donogh oge, of Ballyhagh, Donell
m'Hugh M'Shida, of Killcridane, Oonoghor m'Owen M'Keirie, of
Breackcodil, Donell m'Donogh ros M'Teige, of Drommallagh,
Mahowne awre m'Mahowne awre, of Ballivekeogh, Tho. Fitz
Morid, of Rallinvollen, Donell M'Clanechie, of Urlen, Diermot
M'Edmond, of Bleinegaltie, Mahowne m'William M'Conoghor,
of Clonconinee, Teig m'Conoghor oge, of Killinlomohluone,
Diormott M'Shane, of Killnakemppegh, Shano m'Conoghor
m'Donogh duffe, of Ouldeite, Mahowne m'Teige M'Mahowne, of
Clonburno, Wm. m'Olluf alias Dermott M'Donell, of Ourragh-
duff, Donogh m'Donell m'Shane glasso, of Killtenlieb, Oohney
m'Keirie M'Oohney, of Maidde boy, Rich. M'Edmond, of Bally-
neckohi, Onora ny Thomas, of Glan, Philip m'Shane glasse, of
Olandeurgane, Riccard M'Ullck, of Cahir Kenlia, Shano
m'Wm. m'Donogh duff, of Roskyne, Shane m'Mahowne duffo
M'Conoghor, of Ononinc, Donell M'Kenedie, of Liskreagh, and
Rich. Roche, of Kinsale, merchant.   Security in coa. Cork,
Kerry, Limerick, or Tipperary ; other provisions as in 5304.
Excluding any person in prison or on bail, and excepting murder.
—8 Dea, xxxiv.

5890 (4655.) Grant (under queen's letter, 10 Nov., xxxiv.) to captain Tho. Henshaw, esq., who had served a long time in Ulster ;
of the office of seneschal of the county of Monachan.   To hold
during good behaviour ; with the annual pension of £121 13s. 4d.
sterling out of the revenues of the county.   With power to
assemble the inhabitants for defence of the county, for suppression of rebels, and punishment of malefactors ; to punish by all
ways notorious rebels and malefactors, and those who assist them;
to send offenders to prison until delivered by course of law ; to
treat with, and give safe conducts to, traitors.   Not to be removed, as in 4976.—12 Dec., xxxiv.

5891 (4670.) License to George Carewe, knt., one of the privy

1591. FIANTS.—ELIZABETH.

council, and master of the ordinance; to be absent in England for three months.—18 Dec., xxxiv.

5692 (5976.) Surrender by Richard Bacon; of the office of queen's attorney of the province of Munster.—Dated at Rahernam, 20 Dec., xxxiv.

5693 (5926.) Grant to Thomas Cahell, gent.; of the wardship and marriage of Robert, son and heir of Robert George, late of Tecolme, Queen's co., gent., and of Thomas, son and heir of Josias George, of Tawre, same co., gent.; and custody of their lands, during minority. Rents, 26s. 8d. and 6s. 8d., retaining 10s. out of the rents, for support of the minors. Fine £5 English.—21 Dec., xxxiv.

5694 (4926.) Cancelled patent of grant to Nich. Kenney, esq.; of the offices of general escheator and feodary. To hold during good behaviour, as in 4976. With a fee of £5 English, and such other profits as John Crofton had. Surrendered 10 Feb., 1596. —23 Dec., xxxiv.

5695 (4690.) Lease (under queen's letter, 12 May, xxix.) to captain English. Piers Hovenden, of Tankardstown, Queen's co., gent.; of the tithes of corn of Coulbanchar alias Cowlebanger, Queen's co., and Ballicowlen near Ardskoll, co. Kildare, with the advowson of the vicarage of Errye, the tithes of corn of the rectory of Ballinskille alias Ballinrumple, with the advowson of the vicarage, (recites 2208); White's lands in Rathaniore, co. Kildare, (recites 4322); the tithes of corn of the parsonage of Rathregan, co. Meath, gathered in Rathregan, Linnochon, Ribbastone, Woodlands, Parunstone, Belianstone, and Cremore, co. Meath, possessions of S. Peter's of Newton near Trym, (recites 3980); a messuage in Mariborough, lands in Bathelreman, and Kilvinfyn or Killvinoyn or Killvinain, Bealadd, and Clonakeyne, Queen's co. (granted in tail male to Rob. Aire, see 1334); the lands of Magaffo alias Fenlaus, Ballebrayna, Dromelahane, and Dromoleakene, and two ruined weirs upon the Narrowe water, in co. Down, in Oryars country (recites No. 1793); lands in Cloninga, and Rathecowohs, co. Tipperary (recites 5408); lands called Farronemanaghe alias Monokes lands, near the city of Limerick (recites 5472); two cottages and gardens in Mullingar (recites 4980); the rectory of Killenny in M'Gilpatrick's country (recites 2872); the chapel called Mullaghanedoe alias Ballintoluber, in the barony of Ballintobber, with one cartron otherwise called the fourth part of a quarter of land, and the tithes, co. Roscommon (recites 5253). To hold for 50 years from the end of the leases in being. Rent in all £25 13s. 8½d., part in corn. The rent for Coulbeanchare being £4 16s. Irish or 8 fat cows, at the election of the queen. Maintaining 2 mounted archers or shot of English nation. Provisions as in 5811. Five membranes.—24 Dec., xxxiv.

5696 (4681.) Grant to Rich. Langford, gent.; of the place of a soldier or gunner in the castle of Dublin, vacant by the surrender of Nich. Piggott; with a fee of 12d. English a day, i.e., 8d. for himself, and 4d. for a servant, with all other profits that N. Piggott, Rich. Metcalf, or any other had. To hold during good behaviour.—27 Dec., xxxiv.

5697 (4646.) Pardon to Teige M'Mahowne, of Killmasrully, Carbry M'Kegane, of Sheshirecale, Conogher O Regane, of Kilcolmane,

1591.

FIANTS.—ELIZABETH.

Telgn m'Tirlagh duffe, of Oranagh, Donell M'Diermody, of Curraghmore, Shane reogh O Hogane, of Knockane, Teig M'Donell alias Teig ne stiall, of Knockan, Donell m'Teig, of same, Donogh M'Mahon, of Calir raoon, Brien m'Donogh on calhie, of Bally Ea, Donogh roe M'Kenedie, of Fahio, Turrelagh O Brien, of Knockamanyne in Arm, Donogh O Kenedy, of Killoayne, Ogane O Hogan, of Gragnekelly, Hugh fitz Wm. O Kenedy, of Ballyrork, Wm. m'Ea O Kenedy, of Knyghe, Shane O Hurowe, of Enishmackar, James O Ourren, of Nenagh, yeoman, James fitz Wm. O Kenedy, of Ballyrork, Edm. M'Davie, of Ballynccavrigie, Brien M'Morirtagh, of Cloghintaky, husbandman, Donell O Bolane, of Donaghmore, husb., Wm. reogh O Deane, of Bonnochoen, John m'Donnell Y Glisane, of Killonyne, Philip oge M'Crah, of same, Mahowne M'Shide, of Reneanyn, Teig m'Donogh M'Convae, of Ballipallie, Teig M'Donell, of Ballivichinee, Philip M'Thomas ne barnen, husbandman, Owin M'Donell, of Castlanevinanagh, Mahowne M'Gullevoyle, of Balliorly, Anthony oge O Mullryane, of Cragy, Donell O Brien, of Tuogh, Conoghor m'Rorie alias Conoghor ne Kelly, of Cowlrieogh, Moriagh O Brien, of Ballihigane, co. Tipperary, yeoman, and Wm. M'Cashldy, of Geyshall, horseboy. Security in co. Tipperary, Limerick, and Clare, with other provisions as in 5680.— 29 Dec., xxxiv.

5698 (4667.) Lease (under commission, 10 Feb., xxx.) to Edw. Lenton, gent.; of the castle and land of Cabbraghe, co. Meath, and land in Churchetowne near Taurnghe, same co., possessions of Rich. Penteneye, late of Cabbraghe, attainted, as by inquisition, and by a particular under the hand of Nich. Kennye, gent., deputy auditor, may appear. To hold for 21 years. Rent £16 1s. 6d. Provisions as in 5311.—31 Dec., xxxiv.

1591-2.

5699 (5999.) Surrender by John Maplealen, gent; of the office of constable of the castle of Dublin.—Dated 16 Jan., xxxiv.

5700 (4660.) Grant to Michael Kottlewell, gent.; of the office of constable of the castle of Dublin. To hold during good behaviour, with a fee of £36 13s. 4d., as John Maplealon or any other had. Not to be removed, as in 4076.—21 Jan., xxxiv.

5701 (5921.) Grant to John Knowles; of the wardship and marriage of Thomas, son and heir of Richard FitzGarret, late of Morett, Queou's co., and custody of his lands, during minority. Rent, 13s. 4d., retaining out of the rent 3s. 4d. for support of the minor. Fine 40s.—21 Jan., xxxiv.

5702 (4664.) Grant to Nich. Dutton, gent; of the office of usher of the Exchequer. To hold during good behaviour, with all such fees as John Durninge clerk had.— 24 Jan., xxxiv.

5703 (4642.) Pardon to Nyse duff m'Owen reogh, Donogh bane m'Owen reogh, Nale oge M'Eleownane, Henry M'o lattie, Donogh boy M'Eleownane, Owen M'Eleownane, Doole M'Eleownane, Patr. M'Eleownana, Gilleariste M'Eleownane, Owin M'Eleownane m'Gillepatrick, Tho. Walshe, of Portfiry, Donogh m'Donogh m'Doole M'Eleownan, Gillaspick M'Eleownane, Malmury M'Eleownane, Owin m'Colla M'Gorneghane, Nich. m'Collas M'Gorneghane, Donell sallagh M'Gorneghane, Wm. m'Rob. oge M'Gorneghane, Brien oveally m'Rob, oge M'Gorneghane, Doole M'Gillavearnoge, Ever oge M'Gillavearnoge, Dwaltagh m'Owen m'Doole M'Alexander, Alexater m'Colla M'Alexater, Brian M'Mony, Owin M'Mony, Randall m'Nyee M'Sawerly, Colla M'Enookery, Patr. M'Many, Alexater m'Toole m'Gillaspick ooey, Donell boy M'Cressagane, and Colla m'Bowrly M'Alexater. Security in co. Down as in 4945.—3 Feb., xxxiv.

5704 (4645.) Pardon to Con m'Collo M'Mahown, of Ballihaggigan, co. Monaghan, gent., Rory M'Melaghlin, Rosse, Hugh, and Agbe m'Donogh M'Melaghlin, Ardall m'Philip m'Collo M'Mahon, Philip, Rosse, Donogh, and Toole m'Brien M'Mahon, Patr. m'Art M'Mahown, Maha m'Brien M'Inty, and Owin m'Brien M'Melaghlin.　Security in co. Monaghan, as in 4943.　Excluding from the pardon any but those who were born, or who now live in co. Monaghan.　Excepting also intrusion on crown lands or debts to the crown.—13 Feb., xxxiv.

5705 (4666.) Lease (under commission, 16 Feb., xxx.) to capt. as Geh. Tho. Henshawe, esq., seneschal of the co. Monaghan; of the castle, town, and friary of Monaghan, and all the lands called the Loghtie, and the two tates called the Frieres tates adjoining Monaghan, in the whole containing by estimation three ballibetaghs and two tates, parcel of the land escheated by the attainder of Hugh M'Mahon alias Fitz Usley.　To hold for 21 years, if he shall so long continue seneschal.　Rent £40.　He shall twice a year provide her majesty's justices of assize with horsemeat for not above 20 horses each time.　Provisions as in 4939.—12 Feb., xxxiv.

5706 (4668.) Lease (under commission, 16 Feb., xxx.) to Moyses English Hill, of Carickafargus, gent., sheriff of Antrim; of the castle of Olderfleete now ruinous, with the lands belonging, being 3 quarters of land, containing by estimation 180 English acres, bounded by the sea from the castle on the north west to the river Mulgha, and from thence bounded by the said river to the bog next the church of Dumalea, and from the bog to the sea side, wherewith the said land is likewise bounded on the south, east, and west sides; the lands belonging to and adjoining the church of friars called Cloghahnnales adjoining the said lands of Olderfleete on the north and bounded on the other side by the town land of Learne, with the tithes of Olderfleete, Blackeanus, and Grillamhill, appertaining to the said church; all in co. Antrim, long concealed and waste.　To hold for 31 years.　Rent 26s. 8d.　Lessee shall not alien without license under the great seal.　Other provisions as in 6311.　In consideration of having civil and dutiful subjects inhabiting those remote parts of Ulster, and of Hill's charges in rebuilding part of the castle, and in finding an inquisition for the premises.—14 Feb., xxxiv.

5707 (4658.) Grant to John Ashefelde, esq.; of the office of attorney-general in the province of Munster.　To hold during pleasure, with such fees as Rich. Benson had.—15 Feb., xxxiv.

5708 (4641.) Pardon to Nich. Mowre, John Vyn, Walter Power, Donill M'Donogh, and Donill M'Laghlin, of Downemogan, co. Kilkenny, husbandmen; who being watchmen in the queen's service at Downemogan, had at night slain David m'Wm. M'Cody, kern, who would not submit to them.—15 Feb., xxxiv.

5709 (4640.) Pardon to Neal oge m'Hugh M'Phelym, Donell and Shane m'Hugh M'Phelym, Murtagh Mahallon m'Hugh Mahallon, Arte groome Mahallon, Hugh oge Mahallon, Hugh M'Mahallon, Art M'Mahallon, Owin m'Gill m'Rory Owen, James Mahallon m'Hugh, Donell m'Cormack Mahallon, Manus dologh Mahallon m'Cormake, Mortagh Mahallon m'Cormake, Pat. moder Mahallons, Owin oge M'Mahallon, Colloe Mahallon, Colloe m'Brien boy Mahallon, Donell m'James Mahallon, Manus M'Gilleonall, Edm. m'Manus M'Gilleonall, Edm. m'Donell M'Gilconell, Donell m'Nell boy M'Gilleonall, Glasky M'Gilleonall, James O Haghen, Gilledoff O Haghen, Hugh groome Mahallon m'Prior, Cormake Mahallon m'Prior, Donogh O Mullan, Tirlagh O Mallane, Henry boy M'Onoloe, Cormake moder Mahallon, and Brien O Bhn. Security in co. Antrym, as in 4943. Debts to the crown and intrusions on possessions of the crown excepted—16 Feb., xxxiv.

5710 (5918.) Grant to Roger Wilbraham, solicitor-general, and John Fitzwilliam, esq. ; of custody of the lands of Hamond le Strange, son and heir of Nicholas le Strange, knt., during minority, rendering the value to the Exchequer.—16 Feb., xxxiv.

5711 (4681.) Pardon to Gerald m'Donagh O Birn, of Conlevuoy, co. Dublin, gent. Provisions as in 5504. Also excepting murder.—17 Feb., xxxiv.

5712 (4634.) Pardon to Taige O Kellie, of Mullaghmore, gent., John oge m'Shane no Moy, of the Killan, gent., Shane O Mullane, of Mullaghmore, Manus O Raghtoury, Teige Maglin, Brian Maglyn, Morogh M'Gillananeeffe, of same, Tirrellagh M'Rorie, of the Moy, Shordan m'Redmond M'Costy, of Congilte, Mahowne oge O Haragy, of Kealla, Donogh reogh M'Gormayne, of Inahiqnin, Conogher O Dernne, of Bynyn, Hugh oge O Heahir, of Kahir m'Enne, Mahowne M'Fynyn, of Carrowgar, Donall M'Clanechy, of Killolle, Diarmoid O Mulbane, of Inles, Owen M'Donell, of Fynagh, Moriertagh m'Conoghor O Brien, of Glankyn, Carbry M'Egowne, of Kilmacegowne, Donogh O Brien, of Ballisanne, Edm. reogh O Hogane, of same, Cahill boy O Nelane, of Kilnamona, Connogher duff O Hallorane, of Morcan, Loghlyn O Halloran, of same, Don M'Cormaine, of Cahirnorochowe, Brien O Karin, of Moyball, Teige m'Ricoard M'Shane, Shane m'Teige ne Nea, of same, Conoghor duff O Hehir, of Cahireorcrane, Shane M'Conoroe, of Ballym'onoroe, Shane moell O Hogan, of Mahill, Donogh O Orgran, of Corraghkealla, Donogh oge O Griffa, of Moyhell, Shane O Flahiff, of Inshyquin, Rich. Mynstare, of same, Donell og m'Moriertagh O Hehir, (of) Ilaulaghtin, Dormiot O Hahir m'Owly, of Coulsshoangane, Donogh m'Hugh O Hogane, of Ballynelane, Edm. O Hess, of Boughnealle, Donogh O Malane m'Conogher, of Killridy, in the counties Galway and Clare ; Shane O Connor, of Clonkyne, gent., Cormak og m'Cormak, of Skormoe, gent., Tirlagh m'Donall O Connor, of Clonkine, gent., Hugh M'Qnyn, of Boer, Tirlagh og O Connor, gent., Tomultagh more, of Ballikillin, gent., Farryll M'Doy, of Croghan, husb., Cahall M'Gan, of Clongownagh, co. Roscommon, husb., Donogh roe M'Donell, of Lognagowne, Edm. roe O Haher, of Cahir loughey, Laughlen duff O Haher, of same, Teig O Maddigan, of Mahill, Shane echnock O Mulryan, of Drietteneyn, co. Clare, Teige O Conchanon, of Anaghbegg, Hugh O Kelly, of Garually, Morogh

1591-2. FIANTS—ELIZABETH.

O Keny, of Rathaglasse, Donell O Keny, of same, in co. Galway, Hugh O Dorlahie, of Killinobrenan, in co. Mayo, Tho. O Fure, of Remagh, and Laughlan glasse M'Grawlie, of the Killin, co. Galway. Provisions as in 6682.—16 Feb., xxxiv.

5713 (4638.) Pardon to Chr. Fitz Johnes, second son of Tho. Fitz Johnes, of Fianstown, co. Meath, gent. Provisions as in 5504.— 21 Feb., xxxiv.

5714 (4685.) Grant (under queen's letter, 29 June, xxx), to Patr. Graunt, gent.; of Castell M'Awlie in the lordship of Dowally, co. Cork, with four quarters of land lying from the river Awnaary on the east to the river Burroge on the west, and from the Burroge on the south to the bounds of Bromaghe on the north, lands of Dermot M'Awly, alias M'Awly, late of Castall M'Awly, attainted, half a carucate of land in Knocknyheny, same co., parcel of the possessions of the monastery of Gille Abby; the late religious house of Cloggaghe, in the cantred of Carbrye, in said co., containing half a carucate of land, parcel of the possessions of the late religious house of Monastervalle m'Idane in said co.; all which had been concealed. To hold for ever, in free soccage. Rent £8 15s. Provided that the grant shall be inoperative except for such as are concealed lands.—25 Feb., xxxiv.

5715 (4663.) Grant to Wm. Sarsfield, of Lucan, co. Dublin, knt.; of the office of seneschal of the queen's manors of Newcastle by Lyons, Esker, Tassagard, and Cromlinge, co. Dublin. To hold during pleasure, with the accustomed fees. "This agreeth with the patent granted to sir Lucas Dillon, knight, now deceased."—28 Feb., xxxiv.

5716 (4639.) Pardon to Hugh Maguire, knt., chief of his name, Phelym M'Caffra, chief of his name, Tirlagh M'Caffrie, Rory boy M'Caffrie, Teig M'Caffrie alias Person, Philip M'Caffrie, Edmund, Wm., and Nele m'Redmond M'Caffrie, Shane, Cormack, Cormack oge, Teig, and Nele M'Hugh, Nele m'Brian M'Hugh, Brian oge M'Hugh, Owin M'Hugh, Redmond Flanegane, chief of his name, Tirlagh m'Rorie boy O Flanegane, Brian m'Shane m'Phelym duff Maguire, Tirlagh m'Brian, his son, Brian m'Shane m'Phelym duf Nuguire, Farrall M'Corby, chief of his name, Patr. oge M'Manse, chief of his name, Coochonaght M'Manus, Donogh M'Manus, James M'Manus, son of M'Manus, Hugh m'Patrick m'Philip Maguire, of the Cuill, Phelim duf m'Patr. m'Philip, of same, Brian m'Tho. Maguire, Owin m'Edm. m'Hugh Maguire, Art m'Tirlagh voill Maguire, of Clinkelly, Patr. oge m'Tho. boy Maguire, Tirlagh moyll m'Tho. Maguire, MacDonell, of Clinkelly, chief of his name, Patr M'Donell, son of said MacDonell, Eoghy O Honay, Carovy O Honay, Coochogarie O Honay, Meteghlan oge O Honay, Brian O Corcran, Nele O Dornine, Tirlagh M'Elinnan, Hugh M'Elinnan, Owin O Toman, Boohallagh m'Hugh M'Kegan, Garrubly ny Quyn ny Buoirk, and Cahill M'Sharroe. Debts to the crown and intrusions on possessions of the crown excepted.—28 Feb., xxxiv.

5717 (6554.) Grant to William Carter, gent.; of the town, manor, English castle, and lands (611 acres) of Castelton, the lands of [Ardlonan] (400A.), Kilbride (360A.), [Cloughrane] (310A.), Ballilongford, Fubis (12A.) [with 20A. near] the Shanyne almost overflowed with water, the castle and lands of Beagh with an old chapel (254A.), Balvestin (282A.), all in the country called Kenrye and co. Limerick; the town of Kepanghe with an old castle, in

Conniflo (422A.), Ballicogblane (80A.), Lismocky (153A.), Ballingowie (100A.), Ballincurragh, Cloughentred (255A.), in the country called Connolaght in co. Limerick, possessions of Thomas Fitz Gerald, knight of the Valley, attainted, and (with others granted to Edmund fitz Thomas, of the Glanne, and his heirs) demised to the late sir William Drarie, for 21 years ending in 1599 (See 3277), who assigned to Arthur Cartar, esq., deceased, whose brother and administrator the present grantee is. Also the rents following: out of Shanyvalymore, 10s., Killaghe, 10s., Ballynymony, 10s., Rigort, 5s., Ballynegowle, 20s., Ballynoe, 10s., Moys, 10s., Ballyoshane, 10s., Bally Jonickshane, 10s., Boolane, 10s., Bally-vadir near Castlebeagh, 6s. 8d., Killyne, 10s., Ballygaugh, 5s., Dygen, in the tenure of Morieho M'Gerrit, 5s., Irish money, amounting to £4 18s. 0d. sterling, all belonging to the late knight of the Glanne. To hold for ever, in fee farm, by fealty, in common socage. Rent £30 19s. 10d. English, for the lands, from the expiration of the above lease in 1599, and £4 18s. 9d. English for the rents; and ½d. for every acre of common or waste land enclosed. Grantee may impark 150 acres. He must erect houses for 20 families—one for himself, 2 for freeholders, one for a farmer, and 11 for copyholders; with other conditions usual in grants to undertakers in Munster as in 5032. 2 membranes.—2 March, xxxiv. (Cal. P. R., p. 223.)

5718 (4688.) Charter of the college of the Holy and Undivided Trinity by Dublin, at the place called 'Allhallows' by Dublin, for the instruction of youths and students in the arts and faculties. Granted at the request of Henry Uschor, archdeacon of Dublin, in the name of the city of Dublin. Adam Loftus, s.t.d., archbishop of Dublin and chancellor of Ireland, is made the first provost; Henry Usuher, A.M., Luke Challoner, A.M., and Lancellot Monie, A.B., fellows, and Henry Lee, Wm. Daniell, and Stephen White, scholars. Wm. Cecil, baron of Burghley, to be chancellor. The provost, fellows, and scholars to be a body corporate, with power to acquire and hold lands to the annual value of £400.—3 March, xxxiv. (Cal. P. R., p. 345.)

Printed in "Chartae Collegii Sanctae et Individuae Trinitatis juxta Dublin."

5719 (4572.) Grant (under queen's letter, 29 Dec., xxxiv.) to captain Humfrey Willis, esq.; of all lands known as the termon of Kilmore, containing six tates, in co. Monaghan. To hold for ever, as of the castle of Monaghan, by fealty, in common socage. Rent £3 English. Provided that if within five years he shall not build on some part of the premises, a castle with stone walls, for defence of the premises and of the country adjoining, this grant shall be void.—6 March, xxxiv.

5720 (4575.) Grant (under queen's letter, 29 Dec., xxxiv.) to John Connolan, rector of Moynaltia; of all lands called the two parts of the termon of Tediunet known by the names of Ballenacmurrey and Ballekenan, in co. Monaghan, containing 16 tates. To hold for ever, in common socage. Rent £3. Provisions as in 5719.—8 March, xxxiv.

5721 (4574.) Grant (under queen's letter, 30 Dec., xxxiv.) to Tho. M'Donoghan, Enos M'Cartrie, and Donogh O Hulchill; all lands known as the termon of Ballagolane, in co. Monaghan, containing 16 tates. To hold for ever, one half to M'Donoghan and one fourth to each of the others, in common soccage. Rent £8. Provided that each on his own proportion erect a castle as in 5719.—6 March, xxxiv.

5722 (4575.) Grant (under queen's letter, 19 Dec., xxxiv.) to Henry Pagenall, knt, marshal of the army; of the whole country and territory of Mucknoe alias Mucknie, and all lands called the tarmon of Mucknoe alias Mucknie, in co. Monaghan, containing three ballibetaghs. To hold for ever, in common soccage. Rent £20 English. Provisions as in 5710.—6 March, xxxiv.

5723 (4035.) Pardon to Patr. m'Art moyle M'Mahone, Art oge m'Art moyle M'Mahone, Toahall and Rosse m'Art moyle M'Mahone, Brian m'Rorie m'Art moyle M'Mahone, Neile riagh M'I Conoly, Art and Con m'Tho. M'I Connoly, Brein O Connoly m'Tyrlay, Patr. oge O Connoly fitz Patr., Brem m'Wm. I Connoly, Phelim O Connoly, Henry oge O Connoly, Patr. O Connoly fitz Neil roe, and Naoss M'Killbridy fitz Patrick moyle. Provisions as in 5704.—6 March, xxxiv.

5724 (4637.) Pardon to Ever m'Coole M'Mahon, captain of Fearny, Brian, his son and heir, Coola and Edmund, second and third sons of Ever, Rory, Colla, and Hugh m'Coola, brothers of Ever, Patrick and Owin m'Edm. m'Coola M'Mahoune, Patr. m'James m'Coola M'Mahoune, Toole boy and Patr. m'Hugh oge M'Mahoune, Art m'Colla m'Ever M'Mahoune, Redmund m'Toole oge M'Mahoune, Patr. boy m'Art M'Mahoune, Brian duf m'James M'Mahoune, Patr. and Melaghlin m'Colla M'Mahowne, Brian m'Aghy M'Mahowne, Hugh m'Brian m'Eaghy M'Mahoune, Toole m'Brien m'Aghy M'Mahoune, Rosse boy m'Manus m'Aghy M'Mahoune, Ever m'Redmond m'Aghy M'Mahoune, Melaghlin m'Gilpatrick m'Rory M'Mahon, Rory m'Melaghlin M'Mahon, his son, Con and Aghy m'Gilpatrick m'Rorie M'Mahon, Redmund duff m'Gilpatrick m'Rory M'Mahon, Hugh m'Aghy m'Gilpatrick M'Mahon, Brian m'Owen m'Rorie M'Mahon, Art m'Rory boy M'Mahon, Art m'Brian M'Mahon, Redmund m'Rorie boy M'Mahoune, Hugh duf m'Manus M'Mahoura, Con m'Redmond M'Mahoune, Art oge m'Rorie M'Mahone, Ardell m'Rorie M'Mahone, Art boy m'Rory M'Mahone, Patr. m'Brian m'Redmond M'Mahoune, Ardell m'Ardell M'Mahoune, Colla m'Ever M'Mahone, Patr., Con, Rosse, and Edm. m'Colla M'Mahone, Manus oge m'Hugh m'tleive M'Mahon, Hugh roe and Glaisney m'Manus oge M'Mahone, Collo roe m'Hugh intleive M'Mahone, Patr. boady m'Glasny M'Mahone, Brian and Ardell m'Coyn m'Art M'Mahone, Glaisny m'Manus m'Art M'Mahone, Brian m'Rosse m'Donogh reagh M'Mahone, Owin m'Brian m'Rosse M'Mahone, Melaghlin m'Rosse m'Donogh reogh M'Mahone, Edm. M'Mahoune, uncle of said Melaghlin, Ever and James m'Brien m'Ardill M'Mahone, Toole m'Owen M'Mahoune, Glaisny, Art, and Hugh m'Toole m'Owen M'Mahon, Ardell, Manus, and Art m'Brian boy m'Owen M'Mahoune, Brian oge m'Brian M'Mahon, Brian and James m'Rosse m'Owen M'Mahon, Patr. and Brian m'James m'Owen M'Mahon, Melaghlan m'Colla M'Mahone, Patr., Con, and Colla m'Con m'Toole M'Mahone, Ardall roe m'James m'Toole M'Mahoune, Melaghlin m'Gilpatrick m'Ewer M'Mahon, Toole duff and Patr. m'Manus m'Glasny roe M'Mahone, Owin m'Ardell m'Melaghlin M'Mahone, Ardell m'Gilpatrick m'Con

M'Mahon, Melaghlin roe m'Con in'Melaghlin M'Mahon, Me-
.laghlin roe m'Gilpatrick m'Con M'Mahon, Melaghlin and
Manus m'Hugh m'Manus oge M'Mahon, James boy m'Glasny
M'Mahoone, Patr. m'Rosse m'Brien M'Mahoune, Edm., Art,
Owin, and Hugh m'en shbw M'Mahon, Hugh boy m'Hugh
m'Phelym og M'Mahon, Brian m'Rory m'Hugh m'Phelym og
M'Mahon, Brian m'evicenry M'Mahone, Patr. m'Hugh m'evic
oarie M'Mahoune, Manus and Rosse m'Brian m'Henry M'Ma-
hone, Hugh m'Brian bane M'Mahouo, Art reogh m'Rorie
M'Mahone, Brian ahogge m'Rorie M'Mahone, Toole m'Donogh
M'Mahon, Patr. reogh m'Brian m'Donogh M'Mahon, Patr.
m'Hugh m'James M'Mahone, Brian more M'Mahoune, Toole
gare M'Mahon, James m'Brian brookagh M'Mahon, Redmund
m'Melaghlin carragh M'Mahone, Coochenugh more M'Mahon,
Toole m'Phelim reogh M'Mahoune, Art m'Brien oge M'Mahon,
Patr. oge m'Edm. O Kewellane, Patr. moyle M'Ewaird, Awe
M'Ewaird, Patr. m'eviccarie M'Kwaird, Conner m'Flyr
M'Ewaird, Patr. m'Tho. M'Ewaird, Dermot m'Gilpatrick
M'Ewaird, Patr. bane m'Toole M'Ewarde, Morie m'Toole
M'Ewaird, Shane more M'Conine, Patr. m'Manus moyle
Magarvie, James m'Manus Leany Magurvey, Henry Ma-
geogh, Art m'Phillip O Callane, Patr. m'Awe roe O Callane,
Edm. carragh O Calane, Cahir O Calane, Brian and Edm. m'Gil-
patrick bane O Calane, Edm. duff O Calane, Manus moyle
M'Enemy, Owin roe M'Enemy, Owin and Shane in'Edm. O Brine,
Henry duf m'Gilpatrick boy O Brine, Henry m'Dolyne O Brine,
Patr. m'Cormake bane O'Brine, Brian koogh O Brine, Wm.
O Donoghowe, Cormak M'Carbry, Patr. Lalsagh O Doffy, James
m'Owen O Doffy, Hugh boy and Tirlagh m'Owen m'James
O Duffy,Coochonoght roe m'Tho, M'Gillamartin, Patr. roe m'Tho.
M'Gillemartan, Brian roe m'Tho. M'Gillemartin, Melaghlen,
Donogh,and Hugh m'Tho. M'Gillemarten, James m'Art O Calane,
Teig reogh m'James O Calane, Cormake ballagh m'James
O Calane, Brian m'Shane M'Kasa, Malaghlin m'Teige boy M'Glary,
Hugh roe m'Brian m'Donogh M'Mahon, Brian and Art m'Hugh
roe M'Mahone, Patr. m'Phelem reogh M'Mahon, Edm. m'Melagh-
lin Clibostagh M'Mahon, Patr. m'Edm. m'Melaghlin M'Mahone,
Redmund m'Toole m'Melaghlen, Edm. oge m'Edm. O Reylle,
Henry oge m'Cormack M'Ardell, Patr. M'Gormane, and Maurice
Ketten. Provisions as in 6704.—8 March, xxxiv.

5725 (4836.) Pardon to Kenedie m'Tirlagh O Brian and Peter
Buller fitz Rich., of the Glan, co. Waterford. Provisions as in
5504, also excluding treason.—7 March, xxxiv.

5726 (4662.) Grant to Patr. Morgan, gent.; of the office of constable
or gaoler of the gaol at Enyshe, which is by this grant appointed
as the common shire gaol of the co. Clare. To hold during
pleasure. Recites that the county had since its formation been
without a shire gaol; Morgan had offered to build one at Enishe,
if made gaoler, without any charge to the crown, but only such
ordinary allowances of prisoners as have been accustomed.—7
March, xxxiv.

5727 (4675.) License (under a letter from lord Burghley) to Geffraie
Browne, of Galwaie, merchant; to erect on the river of Galwaie,
two corn mills, and one tucking mill. One mill to be situated

1591-2.   FIANTS.—ELIZABETH.

on the river without the walls of the town, between Garriglasse
and the Friars mill; another between the mill of Wm. Martin,
and the church of our lady without the said town, upon the lands
called Ballymanaghe; and the third in a place near Martin's mill.
It having been certified by sir Rich. Bingham, governor of
Connaught, and Ulick Linch, mayor of Galwaie, that the mills
may be erected with benefit to the country.—30 March, xxxiv.

1592.

5728 (5919.) Grant to Josias Belknapp, gent.; of the wardship and
marriage of Henry, son and heir of Edmund Brickly, late of
Ballykahan, co. Limerick, gent., and custody of his lands, during
minority. Rent, £13 6s. 8d., retaining £4 of the rent for support
of the minor. Fine £20.—31 March, xxxiv.

5729 (4673.) Commission (under queen's letter, 20 Jan., 1590) to
English. Wm. Bath, esq., second justice of the Common Pleas, Roger
Wilbraham, solicitor general, Nich. Aylmer, and Gerald Flem-
mynge, gent.; to enquire what castles, lands, and hereditaments,
Philip O Reylie, of Ballynocargie, co. Cavan, gent., hath of right
in that county. He having offered to surrender his possessions,
in order to receive them again by letters patent. Recites that in
former times, by pretence of such surrenders, many subjects had
been wrongfully put out of their inheritances, by the express
insertion of their lands in the surrenders.—March, xxxiv. 1592.

5730 (5343.) Grant to Rob. Newcomen, esq.; of the office of surveyor general of the victuals for the army. To hold during
good behaviour, with a fee of 10s. English a day. Not to be removed, as in 1976. Recites his surrender of his former patent,
5556.—13 April, xxxiv.

5731 (4684.) Grant (under queen's letter, 10 July, xxxiii.) to Dermot
m'Morris Cavanagh, of Knockangarrowe; the lands of Knockangarrowe, half of Clanhenratt or Clonhanry, a fourth part of
Balleduf or Balladuf ne Killmor, Tully, Ballaloakey, and Ballen-
attin; also half of Ruhine Cormickmore, half of Tonne m'Tyre
or Tonnamackdirye, half of Ballim'damore, and half of Knock-
glasmony or Knockglaswony. To hold for ever: the first six
denominations by the service of a twentieth part of a knight's
fee; rent 45s. 10d. English; the remaining four in free socage;
rent 16s. 8d. The last four had belonged to Cryon Cavanaigh
m'Donill, of Rahin Cormockmore, on Wexford, gent., and are to be
reconveyed to him by Dermot. Dermot is to send two horsemen
and four footmen to all hostings. Recites the surrender of the
premises by Dermot and Cryon, dated 8th Dec. last, to Nich.
Maisterson, then sheriff of Wexford, Lodwin Briskett, esq., and
Rob. Codd, gent., commissioners.—20 April, xxxiv.

5732 (4571.) Grant (under queen's letter, 29 Dec., xxxiv.) to
Gerald Dillon, of Artnecoan, co. Meath, gent.; of all lands
known as the termon of Killyvan, containing two tates. To hold
for ever, in common socage. Rent 20s. English. Given free
from the seal at the bishop of Meath's suit.—3 May, xxxiv.

5733 (4687.) Grant (under queen's letter, 3 Feb., xxx.) to Wm.
Browne, of Malrankan, co. Wexford; of the lands of Croaka,
parcel of the preceptory of Oroak, co. Waterford, a free rent of
30s. out of the ferry there, 12d. out of Drumynaghe, and 20d.
out of Ferremolagh, with certain customs there valued at

2s. 11d., in 'co. Waterford (recites 527) (rent 48s. 11d.); a
house in Molingar called a Franke house, co. Westmeath (recites 3323) (3s. 4d.); seventeen tenaments with their gardens
and other appurtenances, in Trym, possessions of the monastery
of the B. V. M. of Tryme (recites No. 1714) (58s. 6d.) (A ruined
water mill in Esker, co. Dublin, of the queen's ancient inheritance, struck out). To hold for ever, in common socage. Rent
as above.—5 May, xxxiv.   (Cal. P. R., p. 218.)

5734 (6289.) Indenture between the crown and John Bancotar, of
Rathmaknoe, co. Wexford, infant. Recites that by an inquisition (Exch. Wexford, Eliz., No. 65) taken on the death of
Thomas Rawesler, the queen's title had been found to the wardship of the lands of Rathmaknoe, Walshestone, and others,
which finding Bancster travered. A lease is made to him (pending the decision of the traverse) of the lands, excepting the
dower of Constance Stafford and Anstace Synnot, and lease of
Knockanegall and [   ]. Signed John Raucater.—Dated
7 May, xxxiv.

5735 (4633.) Pardon to Philip Lamport, of Ballohire, co. Wexford,
esq., Donall O Murchoe m'Art ne Kille, of Kilgowne, Tho.
O Molan, of Balleahclane, Dermot M'Tholim, of Killcotty, Owin
m'Shane M'Sheuine, of Corgreige, Donogh bane M'Edmond, of
Ballyna, Rich. O Molan, of Balleahelane, Wm. Mowron fitz Philip,
of Ballyseakeline, Wm. Power fitz Rich., of Ballekerockmore,
Edm. fitz Henrie Fitz Nicholas, of Cornewall, and Rob. Joyce fitz
Adam, of Roselare. Security as in 4043 (Lamport excepted).
Excluding any in prison or bail (Joyce excepted); other provisions as in 5504; excepting also from pardon any murder, arson,
or coining.—8 May, xxxiv.

5736 (4568.) Grant (under queen's letter, 29 Dec., xxxiv.) to Tho.
Ashe, of Trym, co. Meath, gent.; of all the lands known as the
termon of Barnakmallis containing three tates, the termon of
Donaugh, one tate, the termou of Ereghlan and the Grange, six
tates, and by the information of the said Ashe containing three
other tates, in co. Monaghan; in all, by the estimation of the commissioners 10 tates, and by the information of Ashe 13 tates. To hold
for ever, in common socage. Rent £6 10s. English. Provision as
in 5719.—8 May, xxxiv.

5737 (4569.) Grant (under queen's letter, 29 Dec., xxxiv.) to Wm.
Garvey, gent., son of the lord primate; of all lands known as the
termon of Clontubbed containing six tates, in co. Monaghan. To
hold for ever, in common socage. Rent £3 English. Provision
as in 5719.—9 May, xxxiv.

5738 (4568.) Grant (under queen's letter, 29 Dec., xxxiv.) to Hugh
Strawbridge, of Dublin, gent.; of all the lands known as the
termon of Tullecarbet containing 12 tates, in co. Monaghan. To
hold for ever, in free socage. Rent £6 English. Provision as
in 5719.—13 May, xxxiv.

5739 (5977.) Surrender by John Lye, of Rathbride, co. Kildare,
gent.; of the lands of Rathbride, Moriahtown biller, and Crottans-
town, co. Kildare, held under lease, 1958. (Signed) John Lye,
—Dated 13 May, xxxiv.

5740 (4632.) Pardon to Tiernan O Rwoirk, of Dromaheir, co.
Leitrim, Donall O Rwoirke, of same, Connor M'Glanchis, of

1592.   FIANTS.—ELIZABETH.

Tullagh, co. Sligo, Teig M'Glanchie, of same, John M'Donogh, of Cowles, and Hugh M'Gwire, of same, gentleman, Brian O Hely, of same, horseman, Fergananim M'Donogh, of same, gent., Wm. Feddigan, of Bonnenedane, horseman, Manus O Hurkoy, and Tho. O Loane, of same, husbandmen, Edm. O Hart, of Ballynekarry, and Wm. Teth, of Muchelity, gentlemen, Stephen Lynch, of Tawnagh, Tho. Linch, Rich. Linch, of same, Teig M'Cormacke, of Aghero, Edm. M'Teig, of the Cargin, Lynagh roe M'Paghna, of Moynylagane, Connor M'Gyllarulyne, of Mullaghmore, Gillepatrick O Corkrane, of Two m'Granell, Teig duffe M'Skallie, Cormak O Hanly, of same, Rich. m'Tho. Magogegane, Wm. oge M'Henry, of the Lorgun, co. Mayo, gent., Gilleduff roe M'Henry, Ricard Keogh M'Hanry, of same, Edm. m'Davie M'Costelloe, of Aghelost, Wm. and Callough m'Davie M'Costelloe, of same, Fergananim O Garie, of Kintarke, Owin M'Enille, of the Carn, husbandman, Kodagh O Ferrall, of Castlemore, kern, James Duckett, of Clonboke, Hugh O Bwoirk, of Killandowne, husbandman, Nich. Nugent, of same, horseman, Maurice Helford, and Brian M'Enanny, of same, husbandmen, Andrew Nugent, of Clondabrackan, Edw. Nugent, of Cloanmorey, horseman, Tho. Walsh, of same, bush., Patk. Duignam, of Achchurren, gent., Jordan M'Konse, of Konmorghane, Donogh M'Evelly, of Macknehanny, Edm. Bourk, of Kilbegh, horseman, Laurence M'Gilleboy, of Balliassedare, Hugh M'Donall, of Kilglasse, Rory O Dowde, of Ardneglasse, Wm. ballagh O Doode, Phelim, Teig, Brien, Shane, and Donell O Doode, of same, Tho. O Beolane, Ferdorogh O Beolane, Owin M'Swyne, and Gillecrist O Beolane, of same, Teig and Edm. M'Gilleboy, of Ballyassedary, Edm. O Beolane, of Tonregoe, Owin keogh O Dowgane, of Kearowruissell, Mary ny Donell, of Agheloist, Callogh M'Mile, of Iland m'gillevalle, Ricard m'James M'Jordan, Shane M'Tibbott, of same, Owin grane m'Cahill M'Enylle, of Teaghboyen, Nicoll O Kearne, of Clontough, Melaghlan O Garee, of Kinturk, Donogh roe M'Morogh, Phelim O Hares, of Castlecarragh, Morogh M'Garee, of Ballygartnalaig, Diarmod, Hugh duf, Connor, Cahill, and Carbery M'Garee, of same, Patr. boy M'Carmick, Philip Walsh, of Inshenegarrie, Tho. O Beglsyn, of Gartlanstowne, weaver, Teig O Biglsyn, of Dirrenegarragh, cottier, Cahill m'Diermod M'Granill, of Rousky, Brian and Shane M'Granill, of Tonnaghmore, Yrə M'Granill, of Gortallowre, Donell oge M'Granill, of Dromardie, Tirlagh M'Granill, of Gartenowre, Teig M'Ulaiglon, of same, Ferooragh m'Phelim M'Granill, of Gortnelowre, Donell M'Hugh, of Gartenowr, Edm. M'Granell, of Dromard, Morogh M'Granill, of Eskerigh, Shane m'Gerrott O Farraill, of Connagh, Lynagh O Ferrall, of Monylaggane, Enyas M'Donall, of Aghelshards, Moyler Brenahagh, of same, Walter m'Edm. M'Tibbott, of Carrikhold, David oge m'Davis M'Enerin, of same, Ricard Boork m'Thomas ballev, of Derry m'laughlen, Tho. O Morane, of same, David Prindregast, of Castlekowle, Henry Prindregast, Garrott Prindregast, Moyler Prindregast, and Henry O Collenen, of same, Shane O Manine, of the country of the Kellics, Brian O Kelly, of same, Alexander m'Hugh boy, of Rahleckane, Shane O Higgen, Fariagh M'Donell, and Shane m'Hubbart M'Eperson, of same, Fariagh M'Donell, of the Clonine, Unanyck Morye, Walter M'Donell, Edm. O Donell,

                                                                        O

1592.   FIANTS.—ELIZABETH.

Moylar M'Feary, and Brian O Farrey, of same, Walter m'Davy
bane, of the Karns, Amerus Burk m'Davy bane, of same, Tibbott
Roork fitz Water, of Beallck, Gillepatrick O Dugenane, of Castle-
more, yeoman, Hugh O Raddygan, of Kilbegg, yeoman, Edm.
O Donellan, of Leitheragh, yeoman, Teig m'Brian O Connor,
Hubbert M'Moyler, of Cartone, gent., and Wm. Tuaff, of Bonna-
nedans, gent. ; cos. Clara, Mayo, Leitrim, and Boscommon.
Provisions as in 5682.—21 May, xxxiv.

5741 (4674.) Commission (under queen's letter, 20 Jan., 1590), to
sir Rich. Bingham, knt., chief commissioner of Connaght and
Thomond, Tho. Dillon, chief justice, and Gerald Comerford,
attorney of that province, and to the sheriff of co. Galway, for
the time being; to inquire what castles, lands, and hereditaments
Shane M'Ne marrowe Fyn, chief of his name, of right hath in
co. Clara. Reciting as in 5729.—22 May, xxxiv.

5742 (4672.) Licence to Lodowyke Bryskett, esq. ; to erect and use
a tan house and other requisites for tanning leather at Magh-
mayne, co. Wexford. The statute of 11 Eliz. notwithstanding.
Provided that he shall not take off the bark of any tree before it
be fallen or cut down.—26 May, xxxiv.

5743 (4567.) Grant (under queen's letter, 29 Dec., xxxiv.) to John
Elliott, esq., third baron of the Exchequer ; of all the lands known
as the termon of Ballilovan, containing 8 tates, the termon of
Aghnamollen and Anny, 10 tates, and the termon of Drommatt,
6 tates, in co. Monaghan ; containing in all by the estimation of the
commissioners 24 tates, and by information of said Elliott, 26 tates.
To hold for ever, in common socage. Rent £13 English. Provision as in 5719.—30 May, xxxiv.

5744 (4570.) Grant (under queen's letter, 29 Dec., xxxiv.), to Tho.
Clinton, of Dowderston, co. Louth, gent. ; of all the lands known as
the termon of Thihallen or Tihallan, containing six tates, in co.
Monaghan. To hold for ever, in common socage, Rent £3
English. Provisions as in 5719.—31 May, xxxiv.

5745 (4680.) Lease (under queen's letter, 21 Feb., xxxiv.) to John
Lye, gent. ; of the lands of Rathebride, co. Kildare, containing
60 acres great measure according to the custom of the country,
making 180 acres of standard measure, lying towards the bater
or lane of Bollickestons on the east, leading to the King's way
betwixt the lands of Rathebride and Priortone on the west, and
so from Richard Fitz Gerralde's cross on the west side of Cookes-
land, to the Curraghe of Kildare, and to the river Boure on the
north, and the Curraghe of Kildare on the south, with common
of pasture on the Curraghe, and liberty to cut turf on the moor
near the west side of the Channon's wood ; the lands of Morish
tonhillar, adjoining the lands of Gerald Wealis, of the Deagine,
on the east, Pollardstone on the west, and the lands of Wm.
Ewstace, of Castlemarten, called Cornelscourte, on the north ; the
lands of Crottanestone, lying to the lands of the late abbey of
Connall, on the east, the Curraghe of Kildare, on the west, Gig-
genestone, on the north, and Bolchie, on the south ; co. Kildare,
possessions of David Sutton, attainted. To hold for 60 years.
Rent £10 12s. Maintaining one English horseman, archer, or
arquebusier. Recites the previous lease 4953. The queen's
letter, as above, also recited, authorizes the acceptance of Lye's
surrender of that lease. the lands being rented and surveyed

1592.   FIANTS.—ELIZABETH.

above their true value, the taking of a new survey, the leasing
to him anew of these lands, and such others as will make up the
value of £50 a year, and the regranting, on his surrender, of certain lands granted to Tho. Morishe and Edm. Barrett, gent.,
which had been purchased by Lye. The lands in former lease
were given in lieu of certain left to Lye by his father, and which
were passed to Callongh O Moore. Recites further that a new
survey was taken by Francis Capstock, gent, deputy surveyor to
sir Jeffrie Fenton, knt.; also the surrender of the premises, 5739.
Provisions as in 4939.—1 June, xxxiv.

5746 (5531.) Grant (under queen's letter, 29 April, 1592) to Edie
Regist. or Edward Byrne; of a pension of 12d. ster. a day, for life.—
13 June, xxxiv.

5747 (4630.) Pardon to Sislie Bermingham alias Syslie Kelly, wife
of lord Bermingham, Edm. Burke fitz Hubert, Edm. M'Crobuck,
Riccard M'Gibbon, Jonick M'Gibbon, Donogh M'Fariagh, Edm.
M'Robuck, Donogh M'Cusoge, Wm. O Tressy, Odloballogh
M'Rorie, Rorie boye O Cane, Wm. m'Rich. Dalton, of Knynagh,
Gerrat m'Rich. Dalton, of same, Conoghor m'Dermot O Dolan, of
Killamor, Wm. duf M'Murtaghe, of Ballinacelley, Owin M'Mur-
tagh, of Kyallnobyres, Donogh more m'Shane M'Edmond, of
Toymhally, Dermot m'Brian M'Dous, of Lyenmore, Owin m'Horie
moyle, of Kilm'Shane, Shane M'Braull, of Corologhaghe, Shane
M'Davis, Alexander M'Dowall, and Shane O Fallon; in counties
Galway, Roscommon, and Mayo. Provisions as in 5532, also
excepting murder.—13 June, xxxiv.

5748 (4628.) Pardon to George Vaughan, gent; for the homicide of
Nele O Morrey, slain when resisting Vaughan, who had a warrant of the marshal to recover certain mares stolen from him by
Nele. Given free—Vaughan being a poor soldier.—14 June,
xxxiv.

5749 (4629.) Pardon to Teige mac Shonine M'Gorromane, Tho.
M'Oragh, Conoghor duffe O Carhy, Conoghor m'Loghlen O Mea-
ghane, Doole M'Swyne, Wm. O Conell, Morieriagh m'Teige
M'Shane, Dana O Hassia, Taige M'Conoghor, Mahowne m'Kenly
O Maddigane, Conoghor reogh O Hahir, James m'Edm. O Hally,
David O Gulligane, Diarmot O Dree, Shane mac Owen O Madde-
gane, Edm. O Hogane, James O Cahane, Maris M'Piris, Tirlagh
M'Swyne, Teige mac Brien M'Tsarowky, Donogho meile M'In-
erome, John more M'Bartra, Morogh meall m'Teige M'Shane,
Gillepatrick O Conigan, Conoghor m'Shonine M'Goraman, Diar-
mot m'Philip O Mire, Rory O Cahane, Shane de Wall, Moris
O Hownine, Teige m'Philip O Mire, Shane mac David O Mul-
lony, Moris m'Teige M'Shane, Morieriagh mac Brian M'Tirlagh,
Gilleduff M'Swyne, Teige M'Mahowny, Wm. O Dullane, Rory
M'Conoghor, Morieriagh Mac Brian, Donogh O Benghane, James
reogh M'Garrot, Owen O Hiky, and Shane O Mullony, in co.
Clare. Provisions as in 5582. Excluding murder, or any riot
or offence of which they are accused in the Castle Chamber.—
14 June, xxxiv.

5750 (4654.) Grant (under queen's letter, 15 Jan., xxxiv), to Raphe
Regist. Lane, esq.; of the office of clerk of the cheque of the army, vacant
by the death of sir Tho. Williams, knt, muster master and
clerk of the cheque. To hold for life. With the leading of ten

1592.   PLANTS.—ELIZABETH.

horsemen at 9d. English a day each, and 4s. English a day for
himself. Not to be removed, as in 4976.—19 June, xxxiv.

5751 (4182a.) Receipt by the Lord Chancellor for a fiant to sir Tho.
Parrot, knt., of the office of [master] of the ordnance, to be cancelled by direction of a letter of the English council of 30 April,
1592. Dated 27 June, 1592. (See Cal. P. R., p. 116.)

5752 (5739.) Commission to Hugh Strawbridge, gent; that he
English and his deputies for 3 years may inquire by oath of jurors
or otherwise of concealed wardships, intrusions, and fines
of alienations, with the mesne issues and profits growing
thereby, in Leynster, Meath, Westmeath, Connaght, and
Thomond. He to receive a moiety of all arrears due to the
queen before the fourteenth year of her reign, and discovered
by him.—23 July, xxxiv.

5753 (4669.) Livery to Michael, son and heir of James Waters,
late of Rathjordan, co. Limerick, gent. Fine 40s. English.—
2 Aug., xxxiv. (Cal. P. R. p. 217.)

5754 (4864.) License to Edw. Brabazon, esq., one of the privy
council; to be absent in England for 16 months.—10 Aug., xxxiv.

5755 (4671.) License to Wm. Phillips, esq., clerk of the hanaper
and clerk of the crown, in Chancery; to be absent in England
for three months.—20 Aug., xxxiv.

5756 (4627.) Pardon to John alias Shane O Relie, of Killenhara,
co. Longford, gent. Provisions as in 5504. Excepting also
murder.—28 Aug., xxxiv.

5757 (4659.) Grant to John Danett, gent.; of the office of
second remembrancer of the Exchequer. To hold during good
behaviour. With such fees as John Dongan or any other had.—
9 Oct., xxxiv.

5758 (5978.) Surrender by Sir George Bowrchier, knt.; of the
English office of lieutenant of the fort of Phillipstowne, King's co.,
with the fee of 13s. 4d. sterling a day. In consideration of being
made master of the ordnance and munition under queen's letter,
22 Aug., 1592. (Signed) G. Bowrchier. Dated 16 Oct., xxxiv.

5759 (4665.) Grant (under queen's letter, 22 Aug., 1592) to George
Bowrchier, knt., having surrendered the office of lieutenant of
the King's co.; of the office of master of the ordnance. To
hold for life: with a fee of 6s. 8d. sterling a day, and the leading
of 18 horsemen at 12d. sterling a day each, with a lieutenant or
vice captain, and a standard bearer called a guydon. Recites
the grant of the office to George Carewe, knt. (5372), and his
surrender on being appointed general lieutenant of the ordnance
in England.—16 Oct., xxxiv.

5760 (4576.) Grant (under queen's letter, 29 Dec., xxxiv), to
Roger Garnon alias Garlon, of Stabanon, gent., learned in the
laws; all lands known as the larmon of Downdanaght, containing four tates, in co. Monaghan. To hold for ever, in common
socage. Rent 40s. Provisions as in 5719.—26 Oct., xxxiv.

5761 (4689.) Grant (under queen's letter, 29 March, xxxiv) to Wm.
Eustace, esq.; of the manor and town of Castlemartin, the
lands of Brenogstowne, Carnalvey, Rosstowne, Norestowne,
Cornels Court, Millotstowne, Baltwaney, Coverstowne, Uske,
Brownastowne, Milton, Loghbratoke, Marienstowne, Littlehole,
Kilcullen, 26s. 8d. chief rent out of Tippeman, 40s. out of
Clongoeswood, and one pair of gloves oh of rent out of the Upper

1592   FIANTS.—ELIZABETH.

Born in Harrestowne, land in Sillotehill held of Wm. Sutton at 10s. 4d. a year, and a water mill in Castlemartin, all in co. Kildare; the use or uses of which John Eustace was possessed in Surdalstowne; also Bermynghain's land in Kilcoke, co. Kildare. To hold in tail, remainders to James, Alexander, and Edmund Eustace severally in tail, at the rents and services by which they were previously held. Recites an inquisition, 30 Jan., xxiv, (see Inq. Chy., Kildare, Eliz. No. 16) finding that Maurice Eustace executed for high treason, being son and heir of John Eustace, of Castlemartin, was by two feoffments and by the will of his father seized of the premises. Also a second inquisition, 9 Oct., xxv. (Inq. Chy., Kildare, Eliz. No. 5) finding that John Eustace **had made** his son, William, the present grantee, his heir, **with** remainders, as in the present grant, to his sons, James, Alexander, and Edmund.—8 Nov., xxxiv. (Cal., F. R., p. 339.)

5762 (6233.) Grant to captain Jenkyn Conway, esq.; of the castle ᴵⁿᵍˡⁱˢʰ. and lands of Killorgan, in the counties of Kerry and Desmond, containing 1804 acres of which 476 are arable. To hold for ever, by the name of Castle Conwaie, in fee farm, in common soccage. Rent, £8 18s. 8d. from 1594 (half for preceding three years), and ½d. for each acre of waste ground enclosed. Grantee may impark 80 acres. He shall build houses for 8 families, of which one to be for himself, one for a freeholder of 80 acres, and one for a farmer of 80 acres; other conditions usual in grants to undertakers **in** Munster, as in 5032.—[6 Nov., xxxiv.] (Auditor-General's Patent Book, 23, p. 94.)

5763 (4677.) Commission **to** sir **Henry** Duke, knt., John Elliott, ᴵⁿᵍˡⁱˢʰ. second baron; capt. Chr. Carliall, **Tho.** Henshawe, seneschal of co. Monaghan, Rice ap Hughe, provost marshal, the mayor **of** Carrigfergus for the time being, Charles Egerton, constable of the castle of Carrigfergus, Wm. Pratt, Tho. Danbie, and Moyses Hill, gentlemen. Whereas the queen, by an English patent, dated [9 May,] xviii, granted to Walter, late earl of Essex, the territories called Ferney alias Hilbarne, and Macguyes Island, in the province of Ulster, with all lands and hereditaments in Ferney, Downsmayne, Clanarville, and Macguyes Island, theretofore under the government of any captain **or** chieftain of Ferney, or any captain of Macguies Island. **The** commissioners, at the instance **of** Robert, now earl of Essex, son and heir of said Walter, **are** to survey, search out, and appoint the bounds of the premises, certifying their inquisitions into chancery.—7 Nov., xxxiv.

5764 (5969 and 5970.) Surrender by Henry, earl of Kildare, and William Talbott, of Malaghid, esq., surviving feoffee to the use of the earl; of the White castell, land by the river Barros in Grangewoden, a common of pasture in the bog called Mone Cather lawge, half of Mortalleston, half of Donganston, Ballivorghill, Ballinrahin, half of Ardenhue, Kilfenor, and Ahadd, in co. Carlow, and King's (recte Queen's) co., adjoining the queen's castle of Catherlaughe. The lands are surrendered in exchange for others of the like value (£41 2s. 3d. English, making £54 16s. 4d. Irish) **to** be granted to the earl under queen's **letter**, 8 Jan., xxxiii. (Signed), H. Kildare, W. Talbott, **Dated** 14 Nov., xxxiv. Attached (5969) is power of **attorney**

to Edward Wogan, of Belgard, and Richard Barre, of Kilka, co.
Kildare, gentlemen, to deliver seisin.

5765 (4656.) Grant to Raphe Lane, esq., lately appointed clerk of
English the cheque; of the office of muster master of the army, vacant
by the death of sir Tho. Williams, knt.   To hold during
pleasure, without fee.   *Not dated (of record with fiants of thirty-
fourth year.)*

5766 (4692.) Grant (under queen's letter, 16 July, xxxiv.), to
English. Rich. Grafton, gent. ; of the office of serjeant-at-arms, in the
province of Connaught and Thomond, with all accustomed fees
as John Fitz Henrie had.   To hold for life.   Further, that he
may the better bear his charges in attending the governor in
sessions and hostings, he shall have the charge of all prisoners
bound to appear at any assizes or sessions, with all profits appertaining.—24 Nov., xxxv.

5767 (4739.) Lease (under queen's letter, 0 Sept., xxxi.), to Henry,
English. earl of Kildare ; of the rectories of Downe, Balli, Dunforde,
Ballakehuilter, Rathmullan, and Bright alias Bretten, in Lecaile,
Dromeathe, Rathekehatt, in M'Cartan's country, Dromkholin,
in Evagh alias M'Gennyes country, Lairge, called Kymalaorty in
M'Cartan's country, Sheanekill, in Cloneboy, Ballefonnoraghe,
in Ardee, S. Evod, Killaryne, Rincheon alias Portmakke,
Teamplekenny in Ardes, the Grange in Ardes, Clonetaghe in
the Dufferanes, Dellebe in the isle of Man, and Culmaine in
Cloneboy.   To hold for 50 years from the determination of 4770.
Rent £45 1s. 6d., part in corn, to be delivered at Dondrom, in
Lecaile, according to the measure of Drougheda.   Provisions
as in 5311.—30 Nov., xxxv.

5768 (4697.) Grant (under letter of English privy council, 34
June, xxxiv.), to Wm. Marten, of Galwaie, gent. ; of the office
of gentleman porter in the province of Connaght, with the
accustomed fees.   To hold for life.—2 Dec., xxxv.

5769 (4747.) Lease (under queen's letter, 10 Aug.; xxxiv.) to cap-
English. tain Wm. Pyeros, esq. ; of the site of the priory of the B.V.M.,
of Tristernaghe, co. Westmeath, the lands of Tristernaghe,
Abbotestone, and the Grunnge, co. Westmeath, Templeforan,
Kilbiskie, the Prior's weir in the parish of Kilbiskie on the logh
called the Naviwater, Ballicarge, Milforan, Munckstone, Rath-
corballin, Siffine, and Donnowre, in said county ; the rectories of
Tristernaghe, Kilbiskie, Killenaknovan, Imper, Sonnaghe,
Raisebacke, Staforran, Loon, and Lenkine, co. Westmeath, Killos,
in the Annale, and Balrotharie, co. Dublin ; and a house in the
parish of the B.V.M. in Drohaile alias Tredaghe (recites nos.
1678 and 3658).   To hold for 31 years from the end of the
recited interest.   Rent £80, part in corn.   Maintaining two
English horsemen.   Provisions as in 4299.—0 Dec., xxxv.

5770 (4720.) Pardon to Phelim m'Tirloghe m'Coolie oge O Neile,
Donell oge M'Evage, Teige m'Owen O Mulchallan, Donell
groome m'Owen O Mulchallan, Gillogrome m'Owen O Mulchal-
lan, Manus M'Eviuche, Tirlagh duffe M'Cristian, Cormock and
Brian m'Donogh O Mulchallon, Conlle O Mulchallan, Cormock
oge O Hanrya, Bryan more M'Christiane, Dalken O Brennan,
Ever m'James oge M'Enully, Toole M'Canne, Dalken O Sheile,
Tirlagh m'James O Mellan, Phelim moidire Magie, Ever

1593.   PLANTS.—ELIZABETH.

m'Rorie M'Coolie, Phelemy duff O Neile, Murtagh duff O Neile,
Ristard O Shelle, and Neece roe M'Connell—7 Dec. (?), xxxv.,
1592

5771 (4725.) Commission to sir Peirs fitz James, knt., capt. Tho.
Len, esq., Chr. Flattisburie, esq., learned in the laws, Michael
Kettelwell, and Terence O Dempsie, gentlemen; whereas the
queen desired that Garrett, son to capt. Humfrey Mackworth,
slain in the queen's service in Ireland, should possess the lands
which his father purchased from Tho. Woulf, and which were
forfeited by the attainder of viscount Baltinglas to whom
Woulfe formerly conveyed them; the commissioners are to enquire whether the lands of Beardthe and Newton were so in
possession of capt. Mackworthe at his death. See 5689.—7
Dec., xxxv.

5772 (4736.) Grant (under queen's letters, 9 Sept., xxxi, and 6
Jan., xxxiii.) to Henry, earl of Kildare; of the castle and lands
of Castelrioard, co. Meath (recites leases 842 and 2427); a messuage and land in Blancherstone, co. Dublin (recites 2703); a
moiety of a measuage and land in Rathe by Nall, co. Dublin
(recites 3126 and lease to Wm., son of John Bathe, 7 March,
xxix). To hold for ever, by the service of the hundredth part of
a knight's fee, without rent. Recites the surrender 5764, in
exchange for this grant.—7 Dec., xxxv.

5773 (4736.) Grant (see 5772) to Henry, earl of Kildare, of lands
in Tobbergragan, and Garrston, parcel of the possessions of the
abbey of the B.V.M., by Dublin (recites 2563). To hold for
ever, in common socage, without rent. Recites the surrender
5764 in exchange for this grant.—12 Dec., xxxv.

5774 (4745.) Lease (under queen's letter, 17 Nov., xxv.) to Rob.
Nangle, gent.; of the rectory of Newtown of Lynnan, co. Tipperary, with the advowson (recites 3066, also that Nangle had
surrendered a previous lease, which incorrectly described the rectory as in co. Kilkenny). To hold for 40 years from the determination of 3066. Rent £11, part in corn. Not to charge
coyne or livery.—12 Dec., xxxv.

5775 (4736.) Grant (see 5772) to Henry, earl of Kildare; of the
lands of Balrickard, co. Dublin (recites 1390 and 5252). To
hold for ever, in common socage, without rent. Recites the surrender 5764, made in exchange for this grant.—23 Dec., xxxv.

1592-3.

5776 (4706.) Pardon to Henry Greene, late vice-constable of the
castle of Dongarvan, co. Waterford; indicted and attainted for
having permitted the escape of Tho. Fay, of Dongarvan, yeoman,
committed to the gaol on suspicion of murder.—10 Jan., xxxv.

5777 (4728.) Grant (under queen's letter, 5 July, xxxi,) to Tho.
Morrice, gent.; of the castle of Ballicoen with three carucates
of land appertaining, in the country of O Mulloy, in King's co.,
parcel of the lands of Brian O Mulloy, of Ballicoen, attainted
(rent £4); two carucates in Moyelly, and one cartron of land in
the Park, same co., parcel of the land of Arthur Melaughan and
Keadough O Melaughan, late of Moyelly, attainted (20s.); lands
in Killnegorronagh, same co., parcel of the lands of Shane
m'Donnell M'Coghlan, of Killnegurronaghe escheated (6s. 8d.);
half of Killoghgreagh, and two quarters of land in the parish o

Killuckyne, in the Clonties, in the country of O Connor Roe, co. Roscommon, parcel of the lands of Terence or Tirlangh roe O Connor, of Killuckyne, attainted (90s.); two quarters of land called respectively Lishallinardan, and Balliboige, in the parish of Kiltrustann, in the Clonties, in said co., and in O Connor Roe's country, parcel of the lands of Ouin M'Dowle, late of Kiltrustan, attainted (20s.); one quarter of land called Lessaboye in the parish of Shankill, in said co., parcel of the lands of Shane m'Laughlin bane, of Shankill, attainted (10s.); a fifth part of a quarter of land in Creggan arrowe, co. Mayo, parcel of the lands of Tho. duffe Mallot, of Cregan arrowe, attainted (2s.); half the castle of Adragule with two quarters of land, half of Ballemoynagh with three quarters, half of Balliclogh 2 qr., half of Ballidonaghe 2 qr., half of Ballodreante 2 qr., half of Drommore 2 qr., half of Ballinry 2 qr., half of Ballevilly 1 qr., half of Likenny 1 qr., half of a quarter of land in Boghadowne, half of a quarter of land in Carrodlew, and half a quarter of land in Rainhellan, in co. Mayo, parcel of the lands of Theobald Bourk, of Turlanghe, attainted (£9 15s.); two carucates of land in Kilvolbyne and Kiltsane, co. Limerick, parcel of the lands of Tho. macDavid M'Ruddery, of Kilvolbyne, coming to the queen as escheated (20s.); lands in Ballingowle, and Mornan, in said co., parcel of the lands of Gerald Fitz Morrice, of Mornan, attainted (21s.); the town of Croaghnaburgage (six burgages there of Peter Purcell excepted) and land of Ballicannan, land in Ballivedock, and Balligawge, land called Ferrinegerry in Ardaghe, land in Ballywilliam, and Gralge, two parts of Ballindeganaghe, Ballinwiry with half a carucate of land, parcel of the lands of Tho. fitz John M'Ruddery alias Knight of the Valley, attainted, being in co. Limerick (43s. 0d.); Cappymonts with half a carucate, and land in Garriglas, in said co., parcel of the lands of Nich. M'William, of Garriglas, attainted (9s.); half a carucate in Kilteynan in said co., parcel of the lands of James Vale, of Boberbradaghe, attainted (6s. 8d.); one carucate in Cloaghredagh in said co., parcel of the lands of Wm. M'Kennydy alias Tinaltye, of Cloaghreadagh, attainted (18s. 4d.); Ballinrostye with one carucate, and half a carucate in Killinaghton in said co., parcel of the land of Morongh moyle O Bryene, attainted (16s.); the old castle of Cloughdalton with land appertaining in said co., parcel of the possessions of Connoghor M'Brien, of Cloughdalton, attainted (3s.); the castle of the Shully with one quarter of land, the castle of Donanyhunchell, with one quarter of land, in co. Clare, parcel of the lands of Terence M'Bryane, of Fomer, attainted (5s. 10d.); one quarter of land called Boulevin, Tullaughe 1 qr., Killoncoke 1 qr., Derynooleghan ½ qr., Pollaghtegun ½ qr., in said co., parcel of the lands of Mabound O'Bryen, of Clondoane, attainted (14s.); land called the Smokins and Gortandawk, by Lyons, parcel of the lands of the abbey of S. Thomas the Martyr by Dublin, lying in co. Kildare (20d.); land in Stephenston, and the place for a water mill, called the Rowe of an old mill, parcel of the possessions of the monastery of S. John of Naas, lying in said county (16d.); land in the east part of a parcel of land called the Rowe, on the south part of the old town of Clanoglia, in said co., in the occupation of Henry Davis, of Lyons, parcel of the lands belonging to the parish church of

Oughterard and given to it contrary to the statute of mortmain (2s.); one quarter of land in Lissurrereaghe in the barony and co. of Roscomon, parcel of the lands of Hugh O Flannogan, late of Lissurrereaghe, attainted (9s. 4d.); one quarter of land in Pollynaltye in the barony of Ballintobber, in said co., parcel of the lands of Connor grany O Flynne, attainted (9s. 6d.); one cartron of land in Carobohill, parcel of the lands of Thady m'Donnell M'Briene, attainted (3s.); the castle of Turlaughe with two quarters of land, half of Moyrany with two quarters of land, half of Valley Fraghe containing one quarter of land, in co. Mayo, parcel of the lands of said Theobald Bourk, late of Turloughe, attainted (40s.); half of the castle and the bawn of Creaghe with a cartron of land, half of Bathardo containing two quarters of land, Ballynanne alias Clonycloughan with four quarters of land, half a quarter in Keppaghe duffe with two little islands on the water called Loughkere, parcel of the possessions of Walter M'Tibbot, of Creaghe, called M'Tibbot, attainted, in said co. (£3 8s. 4d.); and land in Carnulf, co. Meath, parcel of the lands of David Sutton, attainted (26s. 8d.) All which having come to the queen's right by attainder or forfeiture, were concealed and detained. To hold for ever, in free and common socage. Rent £33 5s. 9d. as above. If any of the premises have not been concealed and unjustly detained the grant in so far to be void. If any be already passed by the commissioners to undertakers in Munster, the grantee shall surrender such land and receive others for them.—4 Feb., xxxv. (Cal. P. R. p. 271).

5778 (4729.) Grant (see 5772) to Henry, earl of Kildare; of a messuage and land which Walter Colman held in Little Clonsheaghe, co. Dublin, land there formerly in the tenure of Wm. Cooke, six messuages and land, with a pasture called Cowmore, in great Clonsheaghe, formerly in the tenure of Wm. Fowlaine, Rich. Harrole, Tho. Walshe, Wm. Kelly, Rich. Hampton, and Henry Bartholomew, also four cottages in the same, possessions of the monastery of the B.V.M. by Dublin (recites a lease 2616); a castle and lands in Orangeclare, formerly in the tenure of Donald M'Gilledoroughe, and a cottage with appurtenances in Robertaston, co. Kildare, parcel of the possessions of the priory of Connall (recites a lease No. 1216). To hold for ever, in common socage, without rent. Recites a surrender, 5764, in exchange for the lands herein granted. 6 Feb., xxxv.

5779 (4730.) Grant (see 5772) to Henry, earl of Kildare; of the lands of Palmarstm, co. Dublin, parcel of the lands of John Burnell, attainted (recites leases 1390 and 4298); Ladicastell, co. Kildare, parcel of the lands of David Sutton, attainted (recites 4324); a maiety of a messuage and land in Lucan, parcel of the lands of John Burnell (recites 3126, and a lease to Wm. Baths, 7 March, xxix); a piece of land in the parish of S. Andonens alias S. Owen, formerly in the tenure of James Orphis, parcel of the lands of the monastery of S. Thomas the martyr, Dublin (recites 2576 and 3552); the tithes of the rectory of Powerstowne, co. Kilkenny, with the glebe land belonging to it, in the country of O Rian, in said co., parcel of the preceptory of Killargy, parcel of the possessions of the late hospital of S. John of Jerusalem (recites 3982 and 4709); land

1592-3.   FIANTS.—ELIZABETH.

In Maristowne Moynaghe, co. Kildare, parcel of the lands of
David Sutton (recites 4127); a waste piece of land in the suburbs of Dublin, in Thomastreete, by the New gate of the city,
parcel of the possessions of the late hospital of S. John the Baptist, without the New gate. To hold for ever, in common socage,
without rent. Recites the surrender 5764 as in exchange for
this grant.—6 Feb., xxxv.

5780 (4734) Grant (see 5772) to Henry, earl of Kildare; of the
lands of Kilcraghe, co. Dublin, and two water mills there, parcel
of the possessions of the abbey of the B.V.M., by Dublin (recites
No. 1594, and lease to the earl of Ormond, 28 Aug.; 1575); a
tenement with a garden in Thomastreet, formerly in the tenure
of Tho. Stephens, now of Nich. Fotterell, three gardens in S.
Francis street, formerly in the tenure of Dionysius Cororan, in
the suburbs of Dublin, parcel of the possessions of the late hospital of S. John Baptist, without New gate of Dublin (recites a
lease to Rich. Netterfeild, 20 June xi, and 4410). To hold for
ever, in common socage, without rent. Recites the surrender
5764 as in exchange for this grant.—6 Feb., xxxv.

5781 (6532) Grant to Robert Strode, esq.; of Mnakereye Nownan, containing 4½ quarters of land, in the parish of Ballicastilane,
late the lands of Donogho O Nownan, attainted; Lyahecore,
Ardlynan, Ballynobnck alias Ballyrobnoke, 2¼ qrs. in parish of
Clonaltie, late of Robert oge Qwyshen, attainted; Ardrean, 1 qr.
in parish of Granshagho, late of Thomas Wale m'Redmond, attainted; Kyllydeye, Killinbowcher, Clanoghe, Culshonekyn,
Langhmore, Langhbegg, Kilhonrroughe, Ballymakereye, Fyne-
glas, Ballaghoe, Grossan, Kylheylaghe, Clonecknha, and Cappa,
9 quarters, in the parishes of Kyllydeye and Monaghdare, late of
Thomas Came, attainted; Curraghnegale, Kahirlavyleye, Knonk-
monye, Knockandar, Balligewell, Dronstrasmaghe, Cnonkbrak,
Ballycowlethe, Kyllycowleth, Rower, Glannomore, Cloonlagharde,
Shabanoghe, 7½ quarters, in the parishes of Brasmanghe,
Moneaghdare, Kilmeylin, Clonshermore, and Kilshanell, late of
Gerald, earl of Desmond, attainted; Swyterasse, Ardbologhe,
Ballewallane, Cappamuddo, Garran Clomyk, Ferancaharrowre,
Ballyea, Ballynlahaghe, Kylcohman, Ballycohell, Ballyntrowna,
and Allynaghe, 6½ quarters, in the parishes of Kilcolman, Rathe-
kealy and Clonaltie, late of Nicholas Fitz Williams, attainted;
Kilcran, Kyltennanloghe, 2 qrs. in parish of Croghe, late of
Ulighe Walle and Thomas Walle, attainted; Croghnamorego,
Clohecotredboye, Ballygowell, Lynnemukey, Ballyoghowlane,
Ballyduke, Ballydegin, Ballycottired, Cappnaghe, and Kilne-
cappa, 6 quarters, in the parishes of Croghe, Nantynan, and
Cappa, late of Thomas M'Ruddorye, attainted; Clonelara, Ballyn-
rankeye, Kilcomoden, Ballychamon, Rathmacandon, Dowelyahe,
Ballycana, Kilcohan, Ballylonderygg, Tyrwanaghe, and Reyne,
5 quarters, in the parishes of Garrastowne, Clonahaghe, Kill-
akanell, and Killnadran, late of David Encorigg, attainted;
and Ballywolane, ½ qr., in parish of Croghe, late of Patrick
Wolf, attainted; all being part of the 16 toughes in Osmile, co.
Limerick, and amounting to 47½ ploughlands or quarters, or
11,220 English acres. To hold for ever in fee-farm, by the
name of Boxwillowe, by fealty, in common socage. Rent £142
10s. from 1594 (half only for preceding three years). If the

lands are found on survey to contain more than the estimated
number of acres, grantee shall pay 3d. for each English acre
so in excess. Grantee to erect 91 houses, of which 1 for himself, 6 for freeholders of 800A., 6 for farmers of 400A., and 42
for copyholders of 100A.; with other conditions usual in grants
to the undertakers in Munster *as in* 5032. *Three membranes.*—
6 Feb., XXXV.

5762 (6583.) Grant to Henry Ughtred or Oghtred, esq.; of the
English barony, manor, and castle of Meane alias Mahownaghe, and
Treanmeane in the parish of Mahownaghe containing 2
quarters or ploughlands, Ballynaughty, Shanonlosan, and Bally-
gellycrogh, in parish of Brewrye, 3 pl., Ballyoullan alias Ballig-
wallan and Carrogare alias the Short quarter, in parish of
Ballycastellane, 1½ qr.; the house of Mahownaghe and Trean
Tawnaghe, in parish of Mahownagh, late of Thomas or Philip
M'Gibbon, 4 quarters; the castle and town of Graunshaughe
with Lymneselaughe, in parish of Graunshaughe, 4 quarters;
and Ballinwryleye, in parish of Ballincastelane, late of Philip
O Kaell, ½ quarter; all are parcels of the 16 toughes in the
country of Conilo, late in the occupation of Gerald, late earl of
Desmond, Thomas or Philip M'Gibbon and Philip O Kaell,
attainted, containing 15 ploughlands; the town and castle of the
Pallice in the parish of Castelane with the mill and gardens
there, Pubullmynterqwyllane, and Bollymertynet there, Garre-
floyne, Ballintubbrad, Clonefert, and BallynaJamurrey alias
Palmerston, in the parish of Brewris, Ballynolman, par. Cloneltie, and Cawogare, par. Graunshaghe, in all 13 quarters and
26A., late the lands of Richard M'Thomas attainted; the castle
and lands of Gortnstubberde, par. Killnighill alias Killnighan,
Trean meane, Enffhannanghe, Clonfearna, and Trean faltaghe,
par. Mohownagh, 0 quarters, late the lands of Thomas Cam,
lord of the Clenllahe, attainted; the castle and lands of Ballynoe
alias Newtowne, par. Clonelty, Kilgullobon and Kiltyanna,
same parish, Carrowmore, and Balligmoria alias Balligar-
rell, par. Kiloolman, 4½ quarters and 20A., late of Owen
m'Edmond oge M'Shee, and Owen m'Bryan M'Shee, attainted;
Rathfoyle alias Rathphyrle, Lyanyakye, Ballibegg-m'ydeangane,
and Ballibegg m'Thomas, in parish of Cloneltie, 2 ploughlands,
late of Garret duffe, son to David oge Croan, attainted; Cloneskrean, Dromon, Downgebee, and Ballynegowne, in parish of
Graunshaughe, 3½ quarters, late of James Wale, of Cloneskrean,
attainted; Ballymorishen and Bohernabatanghe and Ogallobore,
in parish of Graunsaughe, 1 pl. and 30A., late of Robert oge
Quyshen, attainted; Cloneorawe, in parish of Cloneorawe, late
of Henry Fitz James and Gerald Fitz Thomas, 1 quarter; all
being parcels of the 16 toughes in Conilo, co. Limerick; amounting in the whole to 49 ploughlands and 66 acres, which after the
rate of 50 ploughlands in Conilo to the seignory of 12,000A.
amounts to 11,958 English acres, after the rate of 16½ feet to
the perch. To hold for ever, in fee-farm, by fealty, in common
socage. Rent £148 10s. English from 1594 (half only for the
preceding three years). If the lands are found on survey to
contain more than the estimated number of acres grantee shall
pay 3d. for each English acre so in excess. Grantee shall erect
houses for 91 families, of which one to be for himself, 6 for

freeholders, 6 farmers, and 42 for copyholders; with other conditions usual in grants to the undertakers in Munster as in 5032. *Three membranes*—6 Feb., xxxv.

5783 (4709.) Pardon to Patr. deffe m'Colla M'Mahowne, Art oge m'Rorie m'Brian M'Mahowne, Hugh and Patr. m'Rorie M'Mahown, Con and Owin m'Colla m'Brian M'Mahowne, Ardill m'Colla, Rosse m'Colla m'Brian M'Mahowne, Patr. m'Hugh m'Cormack M'Mahowne, Patr. and Art m'Edm. carragh M'Mahowne, Cormack O Duff m'Neil m'Cormuck, Cormuck m'Neile m'Cormuck O Duffy, Philip m'Cormuck O Duffy, Patr. m'Philip m'Cormuck O Duffy, James and Cahill m'Owen O Duffy, Ever and Manus m'Tuohill M'Mahowne, Patr. and Hugh m'Shane M'Mahowne, Patr. m'Cahill M'Morogh, Patr. oge m'Gilpatrick O Duffy, Brian m'Gilpatrick M'Mahowne, Brian m'Donogh O Duffy, Phelim and Gilleduff m'Hugh M'Mahowne, Owin m'Colla M'Cabe, Owin m'Gilpatrick O Duffy, Gilleduf and Patr. M'Mahowne m'Ever, James m'Henry O Dovine, Rory O Flanagane, Peter O Hollogane, Brian m'Cormuck O Duffy, Patr. O Duffy, Phellym O Duffy, Tirlagh oge O Duffy, Patr. oun O Duffy, Donogh O Duffy, Brian O Duffy, Rosse M'Cabe, Tirlagh M'Ardill, Hugh O Gowne, Ferrall O Roley, Rich. Fitz Johnes, Owin O Roylly, Shane M'Brian, Brian M'Owen, Tuohill boy M'Mahowne, Art m'Manus M'Ardill, Brian O Seeke, Hugh m'Phelim duff, Toohill m'Con m'Colla, Rosse m'Gillepatrick m'Brian oge, Patr. m'Melaghlin m'Brian oge, Hugh m'Brian oge, Brian carragh O Calana, Patr. M'Gawran, Donogh O Callane, Matthew O Carrall, Donell duf O Callan, Shane M'Morlertagh, Toohill duf M'Manus, Redmond m'Rorie boy, Manus Magorman, Convie roo m'Tho. M'Gilmartin, Hugh M'Gilmartin, Patr. m'Phellim duffe, and Patr. M'Gorman. Provizions as in 5704; also excepting any riot or offence of which they are accused in the Castle Chamber.—9 Feb., xxxv.

5784 (4708.) Pardon to James Richffard, of Limerick, merchant, Mahon M'Loghlin, of the Mullick, co. Clare, Loghlin O Nihil, and Telgem Knoghor O Mackan, of same, labourers, Conoghor m'Edm. O Conill, of co. Clare, horseboy, Taige M'Knogbor, of Conyhy, same co., labourer, Owen M'Edmond, of same, horseboy, and Dermod O Cahisaie, of Cahirasaie ; for the robbery of three horses or garrans ; to Rich. Dawten, of Limerick, butcher ; for the robbery of one garran ; and to Donogh m'Morogh M'Wonhy, of Ballifirrin, co. Limerick ; for the robbery of two cows. Security as in 4943. The pardon not to extend to any in prison or on bail.—10 Feb., xxxv.

5785 (4737.) Grant (see 5772) to Henry, earl of Kildare ; of a moiety of a messuage and lands of Balgeth, co. Dublin (recites leases 1390 and 4886) ; a tenement with appurtenances in the parish of S. Katherine, in the street of S. Thomas, in the suburbs of Dublin, parcel of the possessions of the abbey of the B. V. M. by Dublin (recites 1627) ; the rent of a gate with chamber over it, in the West street in Drogheda (recites 4420). To hold for ever, in common socage, without rent. Recites the surrender 5764 in exchange for this grant.—[10 Feb., xxxv.] (*Rolls Office Calendar.*)

5786 (5971.) Surrender by Wm. Cotgrave alias Athlone ; of the office of Athloon pursuivant (held under 3240) ; on condition

1592-3. FIANTS.—ELIZABETH.

that it be granted to William Leverot. (*Signed*) William Cotgrave.—*Dated* 12 Feb., xxxv. (Cal. P. R., p 336.)

5787 (4696.) Grant to Tho. Dillon, esq., chief Justice of the province of Connaught; of the office of third justice of the court of Common Bench. To hold during pleasure.—16 Feb., xxxv.

5788 (4724.) Pardon to Donell Cavanaghe alias Spainagh, of Clonmollen, co. Wexford or Carlow, gent., Teige M'Donoghe, of Kilcarowe, Griffin m'Gerald Cavenaghe, of the Clony, Maurice m'Edm. Cavanaghe, of Clonmollen, Callogh O Nolan, of the Carrickilane, Hugh O Feraile, of Temblasanvaghe, James O Feraile, of same, Edm. M'Petroe, of Carickstone (Ferdinand M'Gilpatrick, of Kilticky, *struck out*), Phelim O Nolan, of Ballykely, Gerald Cavenagh, of Ballynebranaghe, Henry m'Shane eyne, of Clonamollen, Conoghor M'Rorie, of Clonemollen, Malaghlin M'Fier, of same, Shane M'Murtagh, of Toms m'Morishe, Teige M'Murtagh, of Bolynawhorecran, Owin O Doyle, of Ballinrowan, Gerald O Nolane, of Kilmaglishe, Owin roe M'Donoghe, of Bolaghne, Farpananim M'Tirlogh, of the Coleloch, Morogh duff, of Balliteige, Shane O Doyle, of Churchstowns, Donogh duffe O Rian, of Tymeline, Daniel O Nolan, of the Sangarry, James m'Owen O Doyle, of Coleoan, Rorie m'Shane O Clerie, of Ballinlog, James m'Dermot O Curren, of the Borres, Maurice M'Taige, of the Rossard, Tirlagh M'Moroghowe, of the Dorran, Geoffrey m'David O Rian, of Lysalycan, and Moroghowe m'Donogh O Kelly, of the Borres. Provisions *as in* 5504; also excepting murder, perjury, or making of false writings, and any person not born and at this time dwelling in the counties of Catherlogh or Wexford.—21 Feb., xxxv.

5789 (4704.) Pardon (under a letter of the privy council of England, 16 July, xxxi) to James M'Shane alias fitz John, of Powleycurry, co. Cork; he having submitted on the general proclamation in the time of the rebellion of the earl of Desmond. Intrusion in crown lands, crown debts, and murder excepted.—24 Feb., xxxv.

5790 (5975.) Surrender by Paul Greane, of Kilmainhame, gent.; of *English* the office of keeper of the house of Kilmainham, granted by 1156, with the intent that it be regranted to his son-in-law, Thomas Chamers. (*Signed*) Paulle Greane.—*Dated* 29 Feb., xxxv.

5791 (4710.) Pardon to Art oge m'Art moyle, Brian m'Rorie m'Art moyle, Colla liah M'Ardill, Tirlagh M'Ardill, Philip M'Ardill, Cormack oge M'Ardill, Colla carragh M'Ardill, Connor oge M'Ardill, Tirlagh M'Ardill, Philip m'Colla carragh, Philip M'Ardill m'Gillepatrick, Patr. oge M'Ardill, Mulmora O Raylie, Shane evealle M'Craly, Philip M'Elearny, Farrall M'Elearny, Tho. M'Elearney, Morrogh O Linch, Tirlangh M'Tyarnan, Patr. oge M'Ardill m'Gillepatrick m'Ferrall, James M'Ardill m'Henry, Awe M'Ardill, Cormack M'Ardill, James M'Ardill, Donogh oge M'Ardill, Phelim M'Ardill, Rory m'Teige M'Ardill, Brian O Kegly, Patr. m'Philip m'Colla M'Mahowne, Manus M'Ardill, Brian M'Molrony, Patr. M'Molrony, Tho. boy M'Molrony, Donogh M'Molrony, Hugh O Neyll, Phelym oge M'Brian, Henry O Conalane, Philip O Connalane, Patr. O Connally, Art reogh O Connally, Neyle O Connally, Henry O Connally, Henry oge O Connally, Brian cron O Connally, Henry O Connally, Con

1592-3.　FIANTS.—ELIZABETH.

O Connally, Patr. m'Brian cron O Connally, Patr. O Connally m'Tho. bane, Tyrlagh keygh O Connally, Coola more O Connally, Aghy m'Horie O Connally, Tirlagh barnagh O Connally, Aghy m'Gilpatrick O Connally, Cahill O Connally, Patr. m'Edm. boy O Connally, Patr. m'Donogh M'Mahowne, James m'Donogh M'Mahowne, Hugh O Gowne, Melaghlan M'Mahowne, Aghy m'Hugh O Connallye, Patr. m'Aghy O Connally, Aghy roe O Connally, and Donell m'Sallagh M'Coade; co. Monaghan. Provisions as in 5783.—[ ] Feb., xxxv.

5792 (4718.) Pardon to Philip O Reighly, of Ballincarg, esq., Owin O Reighlie, of Downmore, his brother, Evlin ny Reighlie, his sister, Conogbor m'Shane O Reighlis, of Aghmillans, Tirlagh O Relly, of Correcloghane, Hugh O Reylly, of Dromhallagh, Moriartagh O Mullphadrick, of the Crynan, Cormack oge M'Clery, of Aghmillane, Ferdorogh O Daly, of Sarcoick, Conoghor O Daly, of same, Hugh m'Brien bane O Reylly, of Aghondrong, Phelym moyll M'Symon, of Claghvoly, Shane O Reighlie, of Beallaghnee, Brian m'Cahill O Reighly, of Dromcomlan, Mollmorry O Reighly, of Dromadda, Cahill O Reighly, of Keilhacroizzy, Brian O Reylly, of Leare, James O Reighly, of Lizahlie, Farrall O Reighlie, of Donankery, Tho. m'Morogh Brady, of the Cavane, Gillecatrick m'Shane bane Brady, of Bealancearg, Donogh M'Cabbe, of Aghohe, Shane m'Conoghor O Reighlie, of the Orney, Tirrelagh m'Farrall O Reighly, of Orosriogh, Owin O Reighlie, of Drommock, Moriartagh m'Tirlagh M'Eclery, Tirrelagh m'Gillymahoy M'Eclery, Conoghor M'Eclery, Neill O Gowne, of Keilvacknarrane, James roe M'Brady, of Bealancearg, James M'Conyne, of Sarcoick, Phelym m'Tho. m'Shane O Reyly, of Mointerchonaty, Foly m'Tho. O Reylly, of same, Connoghor m'Brian O Reyly, of Aghotegill, Patr. O Gowen, of Lottakroitt, Shane m'Tho. O Reylly, of the Partoe, Henry m'Brian M'Echey, of the Cabberagh, John m'Tirlagh M'Echey, of Edentakey, Niall m'James M'Echey, of the Derry, Tirlagh and Cahill m'Neill M'Echey, of the Carretobber. Brian m'Donell M'Eclery, of the Leare, Tirlagh m'Conyn M'Nicholas, of Dromgloin, Manus O Briody, of Aghe Cryvy, Brian O Molady, of Devvoy, Juan ny Ganchoy, of Agh Cryvy, Brian O Briody, of same, Cahill O Sheridane, of the Derry, Myllagh M'Symon, of Aghollrr, Cahill duf M'Brady, of Boalinecarg, Gilpatrick M'Brady, of Dromshroallagh, Donall O Flyn, of Keillegowne, Conla carragh M'Diermott, of the Derry, James M'Echey, of Dromchalpp, Gilpatrick M'Echey, of Droimchroin, Tirrelagh M'Echey, of Liettry, Felym M'Echey, of Droimchallpp, Ferylym M'Echey, of Correshova, Brian M'Echey, of Dromm, Gerald M'Echey, Cahir M'Echey, of same, James M'Echey, of the Larragh, Henry M'Echey, of same, Tyrlagh M'Echey, of Dromchalpp, Henry M'Echey, of Correveliahe, Cahill M'Echey, of same, Melaghlin modderhin M'Brady, of Dromregres, Redmund M'Cabe, of Keishill, Ever M'Keigh, and Tho. Gallsarrey, tanner; co. Cavan. Provisions as in 5504. Excluding also murder, and any in prison or on bail.—8 March, xxxv.

5793 (4705.) Pardon (under an order of the lord deputy and council, 20 Feb., 1592) to all the queen's subjects and other persons in the county Mayo, except Theobald m'Walter kittaugh Bourk, Rich. Bourk m'Doyll O Coran, Edm. duffe M'Jordaine, and

1592–3.   FIANTS.—ELIZABETH.

Crobar gar, except also any now in prison or on bail to appear.
Provided that within one year they appear at a general session
in the county, and seek the benefit of the pardon, paying only 6d.
English for their appearance, that it may be known to whom the
pardon shall extend. Treasons against the queen's person,
coining, offences committed outside the county, intrusions on crown
lands, and debts to the crown excepted.—6 March, xxxv.

5794 (4719.) Pardon to Wm. Morghooe, of Clowanstown, labourer,
for slaying in self defence Patr. Morane, of same. Security in
co. Meath, as in 4943.—6 March, xxxv.

5795 (4691.) Grant to Tho. Chambers, gent.; of the office of keeper
English of the house of Kilmaynan, as in 1156, surrendered by Paul
Greane (5790). To hold during pleasure, and not to be removed
without special order of the queen.—7 March, xxxv.

5796 (4714.) Pardon to Teige M'Guialae, of Killowrin, Teige
O Clowan, Morisrtagh O Clowan, Cormock O Clowan, of same,
Donogh O Clowan, of Canboe, Shane oge O Hare, of Ballianareogh,
Brien oge O Higen, of Garrignan, Teige M'Manus, of Carow-
nycrive, Wm. duffe M'Manus, of same, Donell O Hare, of the
Clonyn, Mulrony M'Encahe, of Cowlany, Farriall M'Encahe,
Cormock m'Keane m'Erriell O Hare, Shan M'Encahe, Rory
M'Loghlan, Wm. duffe m'Teige reoghe, Taige m'Cormock
O Hare, and Katherine ny Reily, of same, Farriell leigh
m'Connoghor M'Cahill, of Dromnegrangy, Rory m'Shane ne
Backy, of Anthoonrey, Frier O Fynallan, of Carowmcamhell,
Owen O Boolan, of same, Manus O Chary, of Cowlalna, Shane
m'Hugh M'Brien, Rory leigh O Doyn, and Wm. M'Encahe, of
same, Owen M'Donoghe, of Cowlwony, Teige O Sreighan, of
Boynin, Malaghlen m'Gillspatrick O Convan, of Cowlnany,
Dermot m'Donell O Mulkyle, Morisrtagh glasso m'Brien
M'Encahe, of same, Dermot O Comon, of Athconry, and Rory
O Brienan, of Kilvarnad; cos. Sligo and Leitrim. Provided that
they appear and give security before commissioners in their
county, as in 4943. The pardon not to extend to any in prison
or under bail to appear; nor include intrusion into crown lands
or debts to the crown, nor any riot or offence of which any of them
are charged in the Castle Chamber. In consideration of their
poverty they shall not pay more than 12d. English each on
appearance, nor more than 2s. 6d. for pleading the pardon. Fine
5s. each. Crimes committed outside the counties of Sligo and
Leitrim also excepted.—7 March, xxxv.

5797 (4715.) Pardon to Wm keigh Bourke, of Ballenabarra, Rich.
Bourke m'Wm., and Walter Bourk m'Wm., of same, gentlemen,
Sawe Bourk, of same, Shane O Maly, of same, yeoman, Jhonen
Branagh, Moyler Branagh, David Branagh, Wm. duffe
Branagh, Walter Branagh m'Ullick, Rich. Branagh m'Ullyck,
Tho. reagh Branagh, and Tho. O Ryle, of same, Shane crone
m'Walter M'Gerrott, of Killenarraght, Tho. buy m'Shane crone,
Wm. Owny m'Shane crone, and Walter ogo m'Walter M'Gerrott,
of same, husbandmen, Ever roe M'Connell, of Sinottanagh,
galloglas, Hugh m'Teige O Birne, of same, Wm. brugh O Karne,
of Lowny, husbandmen, Wm. Bourke m'Moyler, of Lissetane,
and Tho. kettagh Bourk m'Wm., of same, gentlemen, Hugh
m'James M'Vahey, of the Leyne, chirurgeon, Rich. oge O Byrne,
of Knockelegan husb., Cnore ni Byrne, of same, Walter

1592–3.   FIANTS.—ELIZABETH.

m'Ullick oge, of Kynturke, kern, Edm. m'Tho. M'Gibbon, of the
Clonen, husb., Tho. m'Edm. M'Gibbon, of same, kern, Daniel
O Togher, of Moyice, yeoman, Manny M'Rory, of Loranny, Rory,
Connor, Brene oge, Shane, and Art M'Manny, of same, husbandman, Edm. boy Bourk, of Ballenloube, gent., Rich. m'Ricard
M'Enally, and Hubbert boy m'Ricard M'Enally, of same, hus-
bandmen, Rich. leigh M'Jhonen, of Coole Con, and Shan
Bremegham, of Clonshanoe, kerns, David M'Moriah, of Castle
m'Gerrald, gent., Cartry M'Keigan, of Castle Karron, gent.,
Redmund and Shane m'Tho. M'Gibbon, of the Glan, husbandmen, in co. Mayo. Provisions as in 5796. Excepting crimes
or offences committed outside the counties of Mayo, Galway, Roscommon, or Sligo. Fine 5s. sterling each.—7 March,
XXXV.

5798 (1679.) Pardon to Edm. Bourk m'Richard Eneryne, gent,
Tibott Bourk m'Richard Eneryne, Walter Bourk m'Richard
Eneryne, Marcus m'Enabb M'Connyll, of Togher, Cahaire
M'Connyll, Phealim M'Coenyll, and Enisse M'Connyll, of same,
gentlemen, Honora oge ny Marous, of same, Connyll M'Connyll,
of same, gent, Rich. M'Gibbon, kern, Falliagh M'Murryne,
labourer, Edm. M'Donyll, karn, Teige O Moroghowe, husbandman, Rob. O Nowne, kern, Melaghlin duff O Ryalla, hush,
Shane O Howbane, carpenter, and Tho. bwy Rocha, kern, of
same place, Tyerlagh M'Connyll, of Twoght, gent, Ustion
m'Ranyll M'Coenill, and Callowgh oge M'Coenill, of same, gentlemen, Rich. O Donyll, of the Clonina, Donyll O Nowne, Wm.
O Nowne, and Walter M'Moiller, of same, husbandmen, Enisse
M'Marcus, of Ballyssakesly, and Owen O Cleary, of same,
farmers, Wm. O Foedy, Gillepatrick buy O Harrati, Shane oge
O Cahassy, of same, Cormock O Maylly, of Raharownye, Hugh
m'Cormock O Maylly, of same, and Moriertagh O Lenean, of
Boalyok, husbandmen, Manus O Flanill, of Rossirk, priest, Tho.
Feale, of Moyne, hush, Edm. Bourk, of Balliglannae, gent,
Owen oge M'Mahae, of the Rosse, husb., Gilleduff O Clary, of
Gurtaitogher, Edm. ballagh M'Androwe, of Brenane, Teige
O Clary, of Gortmilogher, Twobill O Clary, Donayll and Ferdo-
rogh m'Twohill O Clary, of same, and Rich. O Cannovane, of
Oryvagh, husbandmen, David Enry Burke, of Inishcowe, Rich.
m'Davy Burk, of Raharwoe, Tho. reogh m'Teige Eneryne, of
Cnocanshane, Gilleduff M'Edmund, of same, Mahae M'Edmund,
of Corrane M'Moyllar, Walter m'Moyller M'Phillpine, of Ropagh,
and Walter Burke m'Edm., of same, gentleman, Shane bwy
M'Mayle, of same, husb., Annerus Burk, of Garrane, Edm. bwy
m'Tho. Burk, of Cloghana, and Tibbott Burke m'Tho, of same,
gentleman, Hubbert oge Merryok, of Raharegh, and Art
Merryck, of same, kerns, Edm. bwy m'Rich. Burk, of Castell
Reogh, gent., Wm. Joye, of Farrowe, husb., Farregh m'Enisse
M'Coenill, of Ballincaahill, Farregh m'Rory M'Coenill, of same,
Rory oge M'Sawerly, of Clonenase, Naghten M'Ranyle, of
same, Enisse m'Keadagh M'Coenill, of Ballinglan, and Phelim
m'Edmund ballagh, of Ballincaahill, gentlemen, Shearane M'Heali,
Melaghlin oge m'Philip O Monylla, Tho. M'Downchy, Edm.
m'Wm. O Monylla, Cormock O Monillae, Edm. m'Ricard
O Monillae, Shan m'Edm. O Coony, Donnill O Greghane, Shan
oge O Monyllae, and Oveny O Monyllae, of same, husbandmen,

1592-3.   FIANTS—ELIZABETH.

Mary croane ny Dowde, of same, widow, Rich. O Monyllae, and
Wm. m'Rickard buy, of same, husbandmen, Moriartagh O Fyegh,
of Downoyny, priest, Donogh m'Davy bwy O Clery, of Garte-
togher, Brien m'Davy buy O Clery, of same, Rich. O Twohell,
of Downeynye, Gilleduff, David, and Hubert O Twohell, of same,
and Gillegrome Lynod, of Kyncann, husbandmen, Art O Cnoray,
of Ballincashall, chirurgeon, Callowgh m'Rory oge, of Ballin-
glanna, Shane m'Davy duffe, of Carrigmashe, Edm. m'Shane
leigh, of same, Wm. m'Henry, of Castell Reogh, David oge
m'Davy duffe, of same, and Rich. m'Richard oge, of Ballintober,
gentlemen, Hugh O Donowghowe, and Teige O Donowghowe,
of same, husbandmen, Wm. m'Davy duffe, of Moallae, Donyll
M'Bryane, of Gortneberry, Ferdorogh M'Gorhae, of Kilbride,
and Walter M'Gorhae, of same, gentlemen, Tirlagh M'Gorrhae,
of same, priest, Farregh m'Enisse oge, of Ballykinlatragh, gent.,
Donogh Magwire, Donill reogh Magwire, and Neil buy
M'Moyller, of same, Tho. O Sheredane, of Ballincashill, Dyermod
Cohiegh O Mullowane, of Ballyvickhie, Walter buy O Mollownae,
of same, and Edm. Croane m'Wm. buy, of Ballinlatrogh, hus-
bandmen, Teige M'Kyevony, of Castell Reogh, horseman, Shan
O Higon, of Trinagh, husbandman, Diarmod M'Rickard, of
Castellreogh, kern, Walter Lynod, of Kinconn, husb., Rob. ne
hoally Barrett, of Balliphillip, Edm. m'Rickard Barrett, of same,
Wm. Burke m'Shane m'Phrusty, David duff m'Rickard M'Hub-
bert, and Rich. oge m'Rickard M'Hubert, gentlemen, Sawe ny
Phillipina, of Castell Reogh, widow, Jonyne Wale, of Castell
lacoan, kern, Walter M'Ullick, of Garran Annack, husb., Rich.
M'Phillip, of Portnehaylla, gent, Tho. O Higgen, of Tryenagh,
Rich. O Molownae, of Ravrane, and Wm. Granae m'Richard, of
same, husbandmen, Rich. Burk m'Tho., of Carrowmure, gent.,
Morogh M'Bryene, of Gortneberry, and Mahowne m'Morogh, of
same, husbandmen, Rory O Dowde, of Killglasse, Farriogh
O Dowde, Donill O Dowde, Shane glasse O Dowde, and Dahie
m'Rory O Dowde, of same, gentlemen, Farriell O Keavane, of
Carrowenruddye, Molmory M'Keavany, of Iskrowne, yeoman,
Wm. O Tynine, of Bonneny, and Gillechrist O Beollaine alias
M'Enillowe, of same, kerns, Briene Kriogh m'Rory O Dowde, of
Killglasse, gent., Mellaghlan m'Shane O Farry, of Lonngford,
kern, Wm. O Kelly, of Ballmonk, yeoman, Farriogh O Dowde,
of Iskerowne, and Edm. M'Farriall, of same, gentlemen, in cos.
Mayo and Sligo. Provisions as in 5797. Fine 5s. sterling
each.—8 March, XXXV.

5799 (4731.) Pardon to Tharlegh ro m'Marcus M'Donnell, of
Keologelaighe, gallogias, Phelim m'Marcus M'Donnell, of same,
galloglas, Ellan ny vic Morishe, of same, Garry m'Farrieghe
m'Eneas, of Moynallis, galloglas, Brien boy and Alastrum
m'Tharlegh m'Eneas M'Donnell, Connoghor reogh m'Owen nic
Grewe, of same, Rory oge M'Soarly, of Keologeliaghe, and Marcus
roo m'Phelim m'Marcus M'Donnell, of Lisgowre, galloglasses,
Onora ni vic Morishe, of same, Tho. m'Moylar M'Thomas, of
Grelaghebeg, kern, Moylar M'Thomas, Rich. boy m'Moyler
M'Thomas, of same, Donell eveaoky m'Moroghe M'Gillarnewe, of
Glanveghe, and Wm. m'Donnall M'Gillarnewe, of same, kerns,
Hugh roe M'Gillarnewe, and Morogh M'Gillarnewe, of same,
husbandmen, Cormock O Cleary, of same, kern, Rory

P

O Mulaleighe, of Lishgowre, Cormock Mowrnagh, of same, hush., Edm. M'Stephen, of the Corran,.and Shane m'Moylar m'Walter M'Stephen, of same, gentlemen, Edm. boy and David m'Wm. M'Moyler, of same, kerns, Moylar ro M'Stephen, of Belavarie, and Walter m'Moiler M'Stephen, of same, gentlemen, Teige boy M'Gillallan, of Keologeliaghe, Cahill M'Gillallan, Walter duffe M'Cahill, Wm. crone M'Keale, Shan sallagh M'Keale, Rich. m'Farrieghe O Kenevan, Rich. m'Owen keogh O Kenevan, Owen duffe O Flin, and Rory O Flin, husbandmen, Shane M'Gillallim, kern, Gilleduff O Kearney, hush., Moilmurry m Tirlagh M'Artor, galloglas, Eneas O Higen, hush., Moylerry bane M'Keale, Edm. boy Breinagh, Tho. reogh m'Gilleduffe bane, kerns, and Hugh O Howley, hush., of same place, Onora ni vic Morishe, of Moynully, Hugh O Mullany, of Ardanary, kern, Donogh ro m'Therlagh m'Eneas M'Donell, of Moynully, galloglas, Moyler Bourk, of Ballieregh, gent., Manus M'Enilly, of Belacolly, hush., Manus M'Multolloey, of the Togher, hush., Collo M'Donnell, of the Clonin, Donogh grana M'Donnell, and Eneas M'Donnell, of same, galloglasses, Rich. Stanton m'Shane boys, and Rich. O Mollawney, of same, husbandmen, Owney ni vic Moriah, of same, Hubert oge m'Shane M'Enarreny, of Dunnamona, gent., Theobald m'Shane M'Jonyn, of Kilooire, gent., Tho. O Laghan, Tho. O Moelly, of same, husbandmen, Cisely duff ny Connell, of Aghelahard, widow, Roris oge M'Kanlaghe, Neile M'Kaulagh, of same, Tho. oge M'Ewaddy, of Curry, husbandmen, Ulick boy M'Ullardyne, Teige boy M'Evaddye, kern, Theobald m'Red M'Gibon, of Kellinaboyan, gent., Edm. Bourk m'Davy, of Clonokery, Shan and Tho. Bourk m'Davy, of same, gentlemen, Rich. m'Rich. more M'Enallye, of same, Wm. owny m'Edmond boye, of Cregmore, Tho. boy M'Grevain, of Robyn, kerns, Walter oge m'Walter m'Finghe, of Clonegalo, gent., Mary ni Ricard ny Garrott, of same. Hugh M'Genin, of Ballilloghmaake, hush., Moyler Browne, labourer, Jonack m'Walter M'Theobod, gent., Shane O Hanerieraghe, Edm. Browne, Dermot O Fyny, and Hugh O Fyny, labourers, Walter Sourlock, hush., Dowdurra oge O Connill, Donogh ro O Brien, and Allan M'Grevan, labourers, Gilleduffe m'Walter M'Murry, hush., Wm. m'Henry M'Theobod, Moyler m'Riccard M'Theobod, and Ricard oge m'Ricard M'Theobod, gentlemen, of same place, David m'Wm. M'Jonack, of Litirbrock, Wm oge m'Wm. M'Richard, of Knocktalene, Edm. m'Wm., Rich m'Wm., of same, and Walter Bourk m'Hubert, of Ballivighan, gentlemen, Donell grana O Maran, of Boreshowle, Shane O Cleary, of Ballintoler, husbandmen, Wm. Bourk, of Newton, gent., Katherin Bourk, of same, Rickard Bourk, of same, gent., and Farrieghe m'Therleghe ro M'Donell, of Carrignedy, in co. Mayo. Provisions as in 5797.—10 March, XXXV.

5800 (4707.) Pardon to Brian E Cowily O Flaherty, of Ballyoane, Moyler oge m'Moyler duff Joy, of Glantraige, Tho. boy m'Ewer Joy, Ricard m'Ed. dnf Joy, Ricard oge m'Ricard m'Moyler Joy, Shane sallagh m'Ricard m'Moyler Joy, Gilleduf O Kaneran, Ricard m'Theobald m'Collo Joy, Edm. m'Collo Joy, Henry oge m'Henry boy Joy, Shane m'Henry boy Joy, and Fiagh Joy, of same place, Redmund oge m'Redmund m'Davy Joy, of Kalmylcon, Walter Vale, of Droeght, Edm. and Rory m'Ewer Joy, of

1592–3. FIANTS—ELIZABETH.

Rosse, Davy owney m'Redmund m'Theobald Joy, of Oahergall, Tho. m'Gilleduf m'Redmond Joy, of Tomanavy, Ricaard m'Henry more Joy, David m'Gilleduf Joy, and Walter crune m'Ewer Joy, of same, Morartegh M'Enawe, of Ballynone, Donell O Lye, of Noaskerry, Rory m'Shane sallagh, of Cowlin, Tho. M'Gibon, of Tyovenishe, Henry m'Tho. Joy, of Carrick, Shane m'Redmund Joy, of same, Moyler m'Allen Joy, of the Cowre, Fingh and Shane oge m'Tho. cam Joy, of Cowlin, Margaret iyne Jonyn, of same, widow, Rich. m'Rorie m'Shane sallagh Joy, of same, Moriartagh more m'Conoghor M'Donogh, of the Creg, Theobald reogh m'Ricard m'Moyler Joy, of Glankraige, Ullick m'Donogh Joy, of Rosse, Moyler oge m'Moyler m'Allen Joy, of same, Riccard m'Hubert reogh, of the Syeve, Ullick m'Edm. M'Hubert, Henry m'Edm. M'Shane, and Moyler m'Edm. M'Hubert, of same, Edm. hoy m'Theobald M'Donogh, of Rosse, Walter Bramigham, of Bohagh, Walter fits Moyler Bramigham, of Milton, Walter oge M'Costy, of Rosnomeran, Wm. Dramigham m'Shane hallowe, of Turleghvoghan, Farriell O Higen, of Bohagh, Donogh M'Ewarowly, of Kyllynecoscowrley, Edm. M'Mallaghlen, of Barnedarrig, Shane and Collo m'Edm. M'Malaghlen, of same, Teig M'Mallaghlen, of Tiagbogrinan, Owin grana M'Enilly, of Ballindirry, Shane m'William carragh, of Tisquin, Downough O Manyn, of Ballaghe ne crossyny, Donell O Kelly, of Clonshrock, Therlegh M'Swyny, of Kailskeighe, Gilleduf M'Crahnell, of Eskernoooile, Wm. Bowrck m'Walter, of Rosoam, Farrieghe O Heimie, of Kinturley, Hugh oge m'Hugh M'Edmund, of the Oladaghe, Owin M'Hugh, of Glanfousse, Hugh m'Shane M'William, of Drasdrinagh, Sily ny Higon ny Hue ro, of Ballindusf, Morogh no mare O Flaherty, of Bonowan, Onora ny Flaherty, daughter (of) Donell a coggy O Flaherty, Edm. O Toighall, of Anaghe, Teig M'Rory, of Rallynakilly, Rich. oge m'Conoghor E Conneghe, of Bonowen, Nich. Owett, of Killynecappy Farriell, Shane reoghe O Fynallan, of Killynedymy, Tho. m'Moriartagh M'Conoghor, of Kelny lagg, Redmund m'Ullyck oge, of Kellyvogher, Melaghlin O Manyn, of Mynlagh, Hugh m'Dermot O Manyn, of Crosse, and Farriegh duff m'Teig m'Brasall O Kelly, of Kerownyfrsis. Provisions as in 5798. Excluding murder, and any crimes committed outside the counties of Mayo and Galway. Fine 5s. each.—[10 March,] XXXV. (*Record Commissioners' Catalogue.*)

5801 (4717.) Pardon to Owen howy m'Donall m'Donogho O Sowlivane, of Bantry, Awlife m'Donell m'Donogho O Sowlivane, of same, Morrice O Downy, of Boarehaven, Connoghor oge O Harmady, of Droumdaliege, Owen kittagh O Morogho, of Bearehaven, John m'Donnogho O Howligane, John m'Donall O Heagerdell, Awlife geanchaghe m'Donall geancha, of same, John oge m'Shane M'Owen, of Bantry, M'Con m'Diarmody O Driscoll, of Bally Ilande, John Carvartan, of Kilcowrane, Donogho m'Fynen M'Carty, of Baroshan, John rowe Deasaghe, of Mokerin, John m'Teige beg, of same, Awlife O Cullenan, of same, and Diarmod O Downy, of Boarehaven, in co. Cork. Security as in 4943. Excepting intrusion in crown lands or debts to the crown.—14 March, XXXV.

5802 (4712) Pardon to Teige M'Donogh, of Clonkine, Donogh duff O Hanly, of Gallagh, Kedagh M'Cormack, of Annagh, David O Flin, of Mylacke, Gillarnowe O Flin, Deirmot M'Fearraill, of same, Mullmory M'Owen, of Clonashawe, Tirlagh M'Owen, Manus reogh M'Owen, and Ferdorogh M'Owen, of same, Con O Molloy, of Atskirane, Brian roe M'Cahill, of Torman, Brian M'Hogh, of Cnockglasse, Teige O Mulkyeran, Shane M'Diermott roe, of same, Oonnoghor O Fenilane, of Cashillmighane, Cahill duffe m'Brian M'Delrmott roe, Dwaltagh M'Teige, of Carneshenagh, Dwaltagh m'Brian O Conor, of Clonakellah, Oonoghor O Flanegane, of Clonkyne, Donell O Flin, of Mongahe, Teige m'Donogh O Kelly, of Athleage, Donogh m'Wm. O Kelly, of same, Donell m'Brian O Kelly, Owen m'Shane O Kelly, Rorie O Oonor, of Gagill, Rorie M'Diarmott roe, of Newtowne, Callough m'Allen M'Dowill, Teige m'Gillegrome O Hanly, Hubert Burk, Feargananyn Burk, Wm. m'Tho. Burk, Shane m'Edm. Burk, Theobald Burk, of co. Roscommon, Honora Burk, Mellaghlen O Looba, Darmot carragh, Donogh O Birn, of Dengenyvim, Dwaltagh m'Tuohill O Connor, Evlin ny Kelly, his wife, Carbery O Connor, Phelim O Connor, Donell m'Owen moyle O Connor, Mary nyne Rorie, Donogh m'Hubert oge, Brian m'Shane O Kelly, Rorie moyle O Mullivichill, Mortagh reogh O Kovan, of Ballintober, Wm. reogh, of Ratyfrynge, Rorie M'Swyna, of Gortegobbane, Una reogh ny Gillarneve, of Solallage, Teige m'Rorie ballogh O Conor, Una nye Dwyle, Donogh M'Dwyle, of Carrownwney, Gilledufffe m'Allen M'Dwyle, in co. Galway, Rich. Brimigham, of Turlagh voggane, Tho. oge Brimigham, Redmund Brimigham, Tho. duff Brimigham, of same, Redmund M'Roback, of Cladagh, Moyler M'Roback, of same, Onora Brimigham, Evelin Burk, Carbry O Skosby, Moren ny Hallorane, Chr. Brian, of Newtowne, Owen duff M'Hegan, of Clonyn, Redmund Kittagh, Laughlen oge O Callon, of the Gullwalley in Iaber Connaght, parcel of co. Galway, Rich. m'Shane M'Walter, of Tullaghmore, Moyler M'Tibbott, of Rimillin, Rich. M'Tibbott, of same, Ulick oge, of Lettergaish, Walter oge, of Tullagh, Moyler duff, of Riagh, Henry en Gwoly, of Lenane, Shane and Moyler M'Richard, of Tullagh, Rich. M'Alexander, of Ardagh, Wm. M'Richard, of same, Redmund reogh and Feogh M'Thomas, of Tworinders, Tibbott m'Wm. oge, of Tullaghmore, Edm. M'Henry, of Bonduglaish, Edm. boy M'Tibbott, of Kilbride, Rorie oge M'Richard, Edm. boy M'Tibbott, Moyler oge M'Tibbott, Tho. oge m'Tho. M'Davy, of Aghenenywre, David m'Tho. M'Davy, Gillepatrick O Fewer, of Aghain, Wm. M'Walter, of Gransheagh, Tho. O Ternane, Morogh O Flaherty, of Sallermay, Onora Burk, Moyler oge m'Moyler M'Morogh, and Hugh boy, of same, Oonnoghor oge, of Killeillen, Rich. renghe, of same, Edm. groome m'Donogh M'Oonoghor, Donogh M'Moyler, Shane m'Edm. groome, of same, Teige ne bully O Flaherty, Shile ny Philbine, Owen O Flaherty, of the Ard, Owen M'Henry, of Tyrre, Wm. M'Richard, of Ducholgh, Shane and Colla M'Richard, of same, co. Clare, Donogh m'Mortagh O Brien, of Dromline, Teige m'Donall M'Shida, Brian boy m'Donall duffe, Donogh m'Kenedy Y Vadegaine, Mahowne m'Shane en chally, Donogho moell O Oonnoghor, of Leotrym, Wm. oge M'Bruodyne, of Kylkey, Oonoghor Lyahe O Dea, of Disart, Shane O Dea, of same, Teige O Kerina, of Inchyvollagh, Oonoghor duff O Hehir, of Cahir Crokane, Hugh m'Teige e loggan, of Ballygerredane, Owen O Lynahy, of Domelicky, Mahowne O Tyerna, of Inhy-

1592-3.   FIANTS—ELIZABETH.

nagalne, Deirmott m'Edm. O Dee, of Disart, Donell O Cahell, of
Kylvakeragh, Donogh boy M'Clanchy, Mortagh O Connellane,
of Ballihearraghane, Shane ballagh m'Roeris O'Donell, of
Derryewen, Brian O Donell, of same, in co. Galway, Hugh
O Maddin m'Donell, of Feobegge, Donogh M'Awlye, of Mack-
nehanney, Conoghor O Kenny, of Feebegge, Donell reogh and
Wm. m'Edm. M'Mallaghlen, of Bearnedeargg, Edm. M'Mellaghlen, of Tewry, Donell O Mosny, of Darns, Dermott O Ley,
of Onock, Brian and Teige m'Edmond reogh, of Corre, in co.
Roscommon, Mullrony M'Dermott roe, Cormuck roe, Cahill
m'Teige M'Deirmoda gall, and Cahill M'Kyrrelly, of Ardmollan
in said co. Provisions as in 5796. Excluding crimes committed
outside the counties named. . Fine 5s. English each. Mr. James
Fullarton gave his bond for the fine.—15 March, xxxv.

1593.

5803 (4743.) Lease (under queen's letter, 21 Feb., xxxiii., and letter
English of English privy council, 22 March, 1592) to John Lye, esq. ; of
the lands, mill, and salmon weir of Castelknock and Irishton,
and the customs of the moiety of the manor, chief rents (as in
1223) out of Diswelston, Kellartowne, Clonshillagh, Finnagbes
lands, Janugs lands alias Chorche lands near Clonshillaghs, the
grange of Cloneshil'aghe, out of the lands of the dean and
chapter of Christchurch, and Tho. Hackett, in Stagobb, out of
lands of James Fitz Lionea in Portarston, out of Blanchards-
towne, Pace, Powerston, Kilmartene, Ormoerathe, and Ashtowne ;
the lands of Hartestowne alias Stabenny, Onrraghe alias Castel-
curraghe, Barbleston, Balledowde, and Rikenheads, co. Dublin,
possessions of John Burnell, attainted, (recites 1223 and 2590.) ;
also the eight several quarters of land of Karowkipp, Knock-
tane, Dromeen, Lyneache, Clonaghcarra, Banye, Skoe, and Sharra,
in the country of Leyne, co. Sligo, parcel of the lands of Donagh
O Harrye, attainted ; the chapel and town of Ballintoher with
four quarters of land and the tithes, in the barony of Ballintobber, co. Roscommon, (recites 5256.) To hold for 60 years
from the end of the interests in being. Rents £39 1s. 3d. and
£3 14s. Also the lands of Ballianie, co. Limerick, and the moiety
of one small carew or plowe land, parcel of the lands of Wm. Fitz
Phillipp, late of Balhianie, attainted ; two carewemeeres of land
called Ellanavanie, in the country of Pnblebrene, said co., parcel
of the lands of Morgh moyle m'Donnogh m'Morchoe boye
O Breene, attainted ; land in Greane, parcel of the lands of
Donagh Netoytane, late of Grean, attainted ; one carowemeere
of land in Dronilare, parcel of the lands of Donagh moyle, of
Dronilare, attainted ; one carewemeere of land in Grean, parcel
of the lands of Conlaghe m'Wm. M'Tirrelagh, attainted ; Balle-
imona and the half of a small carew or plow land, parcel of the
lands of John M'Edmond, of Ballymona, attainted, lying in co.
Limerick, the ruined castle of Ballygroffa with four small quarters of land, co. Clare, parcel of the lands of Donagh m'Morghe
O Briens, attainted ; three half cartrons of land—Cornegie,
Carowmeroghe, and Carowkeale, co. Roscommon, parcel of the
lands of Rory boye O Naughtan, attainted, the fourth part of a
quarter of land in Leckan and Ardan, parcel of the lands of John
or Shane m'Egnaghan O Kellye, late in Leckan, co. Roscommon,

1593. FIANTS—ELIZABETH.

attainted and slain in rebellion ; two gardens and 10 acres great measure of the country making 40 acres standard measure, in Rollickestone alias Ballenrellocke, in the barony of Aphaly, co. Kildare, parcel of the possessions of David Sutton, attainted ; a castle and lands in Barretston, co. Tipperary, parcel of the lands of Tho. m'Donaghe roe O Carran, of Barretston, attainted. To hold for 60 years. Rent 34s. 4d. Not to charge coyne or livery. —26 March, xxxv.

5804 (4726.) Grant (under queen's letter, 18 Sept., xxxiv.) to Donagh, earl of Thomond ; of the site of the manor of Ard-mulghane, co. Meath, not containing any remains of buildings, a waste close where was an orchard and the haggard place, an old mill on the river Boigne, a tucking mill ruined, an eel weir on the Boigne, and lands, also the place where was the old haggard, and lands in Carnulphe, a chief rent of 27s. from cottages in Ardmulohane, a chief rent of 38s. from certain lands in Car-nulphe, viz. : 20s. from lands of Simon Porter, called Bathes lands, 4s. from lands of said Simon called Lames lands, 10s. from lands of Mich. Cusack, 4s. from lands called Moores lands, all which premises are in the tenure of Walter Porter, of Kinge-stone, gent., a chief rent of 6s. 8d. out of Kingestone, a chief rent of £7 16s. 8d. out of Oldston and Haiston, viz. > from the lands of James Aílmer called formerly Taffe and Birford's lands (besides the suit of court) £3, from Nugent's lands in Haiston (besides suit of court) 52s., from certain lands called Oldstowne, in the parish of Killcarne, now in the tenure of Patr. Breminghan 44s. 8d., from each house in Ardmulchan a hookday in autumn and a hen at the feast of the nativity of our Lord, valued in common years at 6s., also from each messuage or cottage in Ardmulghane, after the death of any tenant, a heriot, which is valued at 3s. 4d. a year, also the profits of the court of the manor, and the stipend and expense of the seneschal, by the year 6s. ; also land in Har-ristonbarrett, parcel of his demesne of the manor of Harreston-barrett, co. Meath, parcel of the lands of David Sutton, attainted. To hold to him and the heirs of his body to the use of him and the heirs male of his body for ever. To hold by the service of one knight's fee. Rent for the manor of Ardmulghan, £50, and for the lands in Harestone barrett, 58s.—26 March, xxxv.

5805 (4715.) Pardon to Shane oge O Dooda, of Castle Connor, gent, Gillernowe M'Firbishee, of Lackans, Cormuck O Boolaine, of Ballynchowne, Molrony O Doode, of same, Cormuck O Hartt, of Fearran y barpe, Manus O Boolaine, of Carrowen Cashell, Edm. m'Gillochrist O Bool[aine], of Arleneglasse, Mulrony O Kimin, of Killmolaishy, Donnogh O Connellaine, of Lishvony, Dwaltagh roe M'Swine, of Longford, Brian O Flanneragh, of Doonkintrean, Owen M'Gillerewagh, of Rosselye, Connoghor roo M'Evrehoose, of Arde[ne]gi[asse], Bryan O Connor, of Fassagh Coylly, Owen O Connor, of same, Mullmurry roe M'Swyne, of Ardeneglasse, Chaill O Healy, of Iskerowen, Shane O Tarpy, of same, Diermot Crone of (rects O) Flannylla, of Killmolash, Edm. Owen M'Brady, of same, James O Kywaine, of Lishwony, Gillsbride M'Ocnyllan, of Rosly, Teige O Hartt, of Doonlynn, Melaghlen O Flanuragh, of Lequarrowe, Donogho og M'Swyne, of Ardneglasse, Donogh O Canana, of Ballynahowen, Dyermott O Kivelegban, of Balliasse-darre, Diermott M'Mahowne, of Aghris, Connor O Fearryne, of

1598.   FIANTS—ELIZABETH.

Donkeantreanl, Edm. kittiagh M'Jonin, of same, Wm. ne broky
O Hara, of Boalchlair, Manns O Hara, of same, Alexander
M'Swyne, of Dromnegrainshegh, Mulrony O Flin, of same,
Diarmod grana m'Manus M'Donogh, of Bricklyewa, Cahill roe
and Hugh boy m'Manus M'Donogh, of same, Hugh boy m'Con
M'Donogh, of same, Cormack m'Gilladuffe O Beolaine, of Ardne-
glasse, Wm. grane O Harte, of Doonell, Nyall O Higgan, of
Clononghill, Moriartagh og O Conilan, of Coolvony, Hugh
O Hargedaine, of Killmolaish, Moriertagh duff O Fearey, of
Fynyd, Edm. m Tibbott Albonagh O (o/f) Raddlyewe, Donogh
M'Donell, of Killmolaishe, Cormuck O Comain, of Liebrony,
Diermot O Duygenain, of Killmolaisho, Connor O Hargedaine,
Teige M'Crycuhy, of same, Hugh O Hely, of Raddlyewe, Cahill
O Hargedaine, Hugh O Carhy, of same, Wm. O Teige, of Pollakiny,
Donogh O Corraine, of same, Teige O Beolalno, of Tonregoe,
Owen m'Gillechrist O Beolaine, of Ardneglas, Donalcive O Fearry,
of Doonloon, Edm. sallagh M'Gillegallingee, of Rathlio, Hugh
O Doonnegaine, of Castle Connor, Cormuck M'Gillecharry,
Diarmot Magoreighta, of sama, Hugh O Conowginaima, of Roaly,
Rory O Doodegam, of same, carpenter, Donogh M'Firbishy, of
Lockan, carpenter, Fiall O Dalganain, of Ballindein, Shane
O Higgan, of same, Mullmory and Rory M'Donell, of Roaly,
Morogh M'Swyne, of Ardneglasse, Oyn M'Swyne, of Quarrown-
chaahill, Teige boy O Dooda, of Tonregoe, Lawrence M'Gilhoy, of
Ballyassadarry, Mullmorry and Fynnegony M'Firbisse, of Loc-
kana, Tomultagh O Kiarrgaine, of Castle Connor, Gillasbuleke
M'Donnell, of Roalie, Rouse ny Conny, of Collynae, Fennolla ny
Art, of Doon m'trealne, Cormuck O Doogaine, of Ardneglame,
Walter M'Philbin, of Killmolaish, Cahill O Kywaine, of Kear-
rownrode, Fearryll O Kywaine, of sama, Tho. oge O Tarpy, of
Iskerowne, Connor O Hart m'Gilleduff, of Doonell, Edm. M'ne
roy, of Ardneglasse, Mullmory more M'Swyne, of Doonkintrealn,
Tirrellagh roe M'Caggaine, of Kilmolaish, Grany ny Higgen, of
Granugenore, widow, Cahill oge M'Donnell, of Roamely, Looder
and Cahire M'Donnell, of same, Brian m'Teige O Dooda, of
Liebvony, Fearregher O Fearyea, of Ballychostall, Mulmury
M'Camy, of Rathliewe, Donell O Dooda, of same, gent., Dahie
O Dooda, of Castle Connor, and Phelim O Dooda, of Donnell,
gentleman, Wm. O Kiarregain, of Roasely, David boy O Fimilain,
of Loquarrowe, Rory M'Donnell, of Roasely, Rich. duff M'Jonin,
of Doonloomie, Moriertagh M'Gillaghny, Shane keogh M'Gillaghny, of same, Connor O Dooda, of Domychohy, gent., Owen
and Diarmot O Dooda, of same, gentlemen, Manns O Nary, of
Tonregoe, Cormuck O Comaine, of Killmolaish, Nich. O Flanne-
gaine, of same, Connor O Fynnghty, of Corkagh, James O Flanylla,
of Castle Connor, Donell O Doonegaine, Wm. O Doonegaine,
Brian M'Gillecharry, of same, Donall M'Analy, of Rathliewe,
Hugh O Flanylla, of Killmolaishe, Gilleduff O Flanylla, Bryan
O Mullanny, of same, Owen M'Gillamarten, of Ardneglasse, Wm.
grana O Beolane, Edm. O Boyll, Brian O Boylle, of same, and
Shane oge M'Coinny, of Rathliewe, in co. Sligo. Provisions as
in 5796. Excluding any crime committed outside said county.
Fine 6s. sterling each.—5 April, xxxv.

5806 (4701.) Pardon to James Gowo alias Smith, of Finter, King's
co.; for the robbery of a brass pan in the market at Mollngar,

1593.   FIANTS—ELIZABETH.

. .   belonging to Rob. Pantinge, of Dublin. Security as in 1913.—
10 April, xxxv.

5807 (5632.) Grant (under queen's letter, 10 March, xxix.) to John
Benyon ; of a pension of 2l. English a day, till he be rewarded
in some other way.— 13 April, xxxv. (Cal. P. R., p. 270.)
A note mentions that he had already been in receipt of the
pension under the Queen's letter.

5808 (4682.) Pardon to Dwaltagh M'Dyermod roe, of Killyconnor,
gent., Brian and Owen m'Dwaltagh M'Deirmod roe, Teige keogh
m'Dermod grany, Donnell crone O Dogherty, Manus roe M'Ferdorogh, and Gillachriste O Conellane, of same place, Mulrony
M'Enanny, of Kyllm'Enanry, Melaghlen m'Cobney M'Brien, of
Clonfroy, Cormock M'Benny, of Clonella, Margaret ny Gillegooly,
of Clonyragh, Donnell M'Gillochlogny, of Killm'nanny, Edm.
m'Teige M'Brenan, of Granshaghe, Mellaghlen O Byrn, of Balli-
connell, Brian m'Rory O Connor, of Oogahnore, Rory m'Edm.
M'Deirmod, of Bellanemoylly, Meowe ny Connor, of Neadd ne
viagh, Donell M'Morogh, of Cugalmore, Hugh M'Eally, of Clon-
faddy, Onora ny Brien O Flanegan, of Ballahuoghter, Wm.
O Gibbullan, of Skyrvog, Shan O Birn, of Dangen, Hugh
M'Shane, of Tryen volagains, Peirce O Donowre, of Cashillenoyda,
Rory m'Phelim boy, of Annagh, Una reogh ny Gillernowe
O Farrall, Donnell garrowe m'Donogh M'Teige, of Balligortanelly,
Brien m'Donogh M'Teige, Phelim m'Cormuck M'Teige, of same,
Rory O Connor, of Cloynyvirm, gent., Farryle M'Carrylle, of
Clonkahs, Sawe ny Kegane, of Limonniff, widow, Cormuck
m'Wm. M'Brien, of Nyrrowe, gent., Ferdorogh m'Shane carragh,
of Triancrevy, Shane O Flin, of Cleynonone, gent., Colla O Flin,
of same, gent., Moriartagh O Cowane, of Baslik, Hugh O Skanlane,
and Carbry M'Gawny, of same, husbandmen, Onora ayn Lysagh
O Farrall, of Cloyncarran, widow, Donogh ne Clinsy O Connor,
of Clongarry, and Hugh O Connor, of Balanahefadde, gentlemen, Terrelagh m'Phelim M'Teige, of Clonamorrey, Manus
O Cowan, of Clonooysh, husb., Owen m'Tirlagh keogh M'Bwyne,
of Onokelaghty, Tirlagh oge m'Tirlagh keogh M'Bwyne,
of same, Gilleboy O Flanegan, of Ballantober, Kadagh
O Lavine, of same, Florence O Dowilly, of Killynane, Wm. begg
O Lurkane, of Haggard, Donnell O Flahartie, of Raibally, Shane
M'William, of same, Rob. m'Faoghrn O Flin, of Ballanlaghy,
Mellaghlen m'Donogh duffe O Carne, of same, Donogh O Carnahn,
of Clonamorrey, Cormuck O Fyny, of same, husb., Wm. reogh
m'Morogh O Phylly, husb., Shane m'Riccard Barke, of Gorte-
vickory, in co. Galway, Wm. M'Kegan, of Clinake, Tho.
M'Hubert, of Balyfoyle, Tho. M'Moriartagh, of Keranane, in co.
Clare, Morogh O Misakell, of Dyrrychrossane, Donnell m'Morogh
O'Misakell, Shane m'Morogh, More ny Moroghe, of same, in co.
Roscommon, Tho. carragh O Collman, of Limodyn, Teige oge
O Birn, of Dangen, gent., Wm. Curragh M'Gillegowly, Hary oge
M'Branan, of Clonfynlagh, Hugh boy O Conor, of Ballentobber,
gent., Moriartagh M'Gillecomau, of Boyagh, James M'Geoghe-
gaine, of Fewnagh, Una ayn Teayn oge, of Tulleyre, widow,
Mary.nyn Riccard Burk, of Dromore, James Ultagh, of Kilkyda,
Riccard m'Tho. Durk, of Downesandell, Connoghor M'Gilleroyn,
of Mynlagh. Moyler m'Rich. M'Jonine, of Cnockenemalbanagh,
Donogh M'Donell, of Tulleyre, Ullyuk m'Edm. Bourk, of Aghe-

1593.   FIANTS—ELIZABETH.

nayore, Ullick m Tho. M'Edmund, of same, Moroghoe roe M'Mahowne, of Derricroman, Colla m Wm. O Kelly, of Slyew-shannakuogh, Moriartagh O Cahan, of Haggart, Hugh mergeagh O Flin, of Isarisclerane, Donogh oge and Morogh m Donogh M'Mahowne, of Kilchide, Moriartagh m Hugh O Donoghoe, of Killm'onogh, Connogher more M'Marrowy, of Orattelagh, Wm. grane m'Connor more, Morogh m'Connor more, and Tibbot M'Hubert, of same, Rosse m'Mellaghlen O Loghlen, of Ballyhiobane, Donall O Mongevaine, of Rynanny, Donnell m'Mahowne M'Teige, of Clonglasaan, Donogh oge O Cowony, of Quyn, husb., Morogh M'Clone, of Lixduffe, Donogh M'Loghlen, of same, Shane M'Moyler, of Clonsabansraghe, Diarmott O Lyddy, of Shandangan, Shida M'Teige, of Carnvally, Connogher oge M'Connor, of Kiltreckan, Convea M'Shane, of Coolafadde, Donogh m'Donall M'Tyrrely, of Cnappook, Wm. Boark m Walter, of Rosscam, Brian and Tirlagh m Tirlagh gankagh O Loghlen, of Cappoghe, Edm. oohny m'Riccard boy, of Castle-kyall, Wm. m'Hubert M'Jonine, of Kilkirane, Donogh M'Ever-rolly, of Ballandarry, Shane oge O Tywnan, of Killor, Shane O Daly, of Quyn, Shane M'Awly, of Clonshangane, Donall M'Duarnll, of same, Diarmott M'Donall, of Downogoyre, Teige O Downavane, of same, Teige M'Diarmott roe, of Rath, Teige O Hywar, of Coolshangane, Donogh oge O Gryffa, of Moehill, Connor O Brien, of Ballachorick, Shane boy M'Donall, of same, More ny Eyllereogh, Diarmot oge O Hehir, of Lyasmelia, Donogh M'Clansy, of Belachorick, Brian m'Gillaglasse O Coman, of Coolany, in co. Sligo, Edm. O Harane, of Fahy, Conogher m'Con-nogher M'Donogh, of same, Rory m'Hugh O Hiky, of Tullagh, Connogher O Shisnan, of Knappook, Andrew O Griffa, of Kilne-mona, Nich. Nolan, of Ballyally, Morogh Mynaragh, of Killno-mona, Edm. duffe m'Deirmott O Conell, Teige M'Corrosan, of Tullyahim, Teige oge Mackenst, of Cloghane, Shane oge O Hiky, of Tullagh, Tho. m'Conogher M'Mahon, of Urbb, Loghlen O Grady, of Kynaldoony, Donall moell m'Con M'ne marre, of Carroononer, Donogh m'Connor M'Shane, of Ballynegdym, Teige m'Mahowne O Gerane, of Ballimolahai, Connogher M'Loghlen, of Boylagh, Mellaghlen duff O Quyn, of Roscanon, Teige oge O Kelly, of Dangendricke, Hugh O Conohanon, of Feddane, Hugh m'Shane m'Wm., of Trasternagh, Donall O Hutrrlly, of Killmack-dowanny, Tho. O Hurrelly, of same, Donogho Lynchy, of Rea-luirragh, Connogher oge Ballagh, of Hihan, Brien O Hanyne, of Taghboy, Donall O Birna, of Dengan, Brian anohogga M'Glyn, of Moyntagh, Brian O Carrowyll, of Quarrowemore, Melaghlen O Flanegan, of Ballintobber, Anable oge ny Brian M'Swyna, of Gortgoban, Oyne M'Swyne m'Brian, of Quarrokeale, and Cahill M'Errelly, of Ardmollane, in cos. Roscommon, Galway, and Clare. Provisions as in 5796. Excepting crimes committed out-side the counties of Roscommon, Galway, and Clare. Fine 5s. English each.—18(?) April, xxxv.

5809 (4733.) Grant (under queen's letter, 28 June, xxv.) to Terence or Tirlagh O Brene, knt.; of the castle of Lemeneaghe, co. Clare, with three quarters of land adjoining, the castle of Balli-griffa, with one quarter of land adjoining, co. Clare, parcel of the lands of Donatus son of Manrise alias Donogh m'Murogh O Brene, of Dromolane, attainted. To hold for ever, by the service of a twentieth part of a knight's fee. Rent 20s. Maintaining one English horseman, and answering all hostings.—26 April, xxxv.

5810 (4746.) Lease (under queen's letter, 31 Feb., xxxiv., and letter of English privy council, 22 March, 1591) to John Lye, esq.; of the rectory of Crovaghe in Harroldes country, co. Dublin (recites a lease No. 1591, for 21 years from the end of a lease, 8 July, xxx. Hen. VIII., from the prior of Kilmainham, to John Wyrall, of Dublin, shoemaker, for 61 years). To hold for 60 years from the end of the recited interest. Rent 20s. — 26 April, xxxv.

5811 (4742.) Lease (see 5810) to John Lye; of the lands of Mai-deso, Monymuck, and Cowlogarrie, co. Roscommon (reciting 5255), Ballimore, Macmehanis, Enesherick, and Killorans, co. Galway (reciting 5256), a messuage and garden in Athboye (recites a lease to Arthur Brierton, 25 June, xix.), the tithes of the rectory of Beakin, co. Westmeath (reciting 5158). To hold for 60 years from the end of the interests in being. Rent £4 10s. 11½d. Also the following lands which had been concealed and detained from the crown: two quarters of land, parcel of the possessions of the abbey of Ballyraggadan in Barrett's country, co. Cork, late in the tenure of Cormuck M'Diarmod, the church of Agherie with the tithes of two quarters of land in Agharie, parcel of the possessions of the abbey of Shroyll, co. Longford, one cartron of land in Taghshinat alias Taghsanny, co. Longford, parcel of the lands of the abbey of Loghsaudy, one cartron of land called Syan, near Pairstowne, co. Westmeath, parcel of the lands of Oliver Fitz Gerald, attainted, the ruined castle of Dromfingles with two quarters of land, co. Clare, parcel of the lands of Donogh O Brien, attainted, the ruined castle of Clonark, with three parts called cartrons of a quarter of land in the barony of Athloane, co. Roscommon, parcel of the lands of Rorie boy O Naghten, attainted, Little Morishtowne, co. Kildare, containing three places for messuages with three little crofts or gardens and land, parcel of the possessions of the monastery of Oonall. To hold for 60 years. Rent 30s. 11½d. Not to charge coyne or livery.—26 April, xxxv.

5812 (5534.) Grant (under queen's letter, 22 Aug., xxxiv.) to Gerald O'Furrall; of a pension of 2s. (Irish) a day, for life.—26 April, xxxv.

5813 (4693.) Grant to Zachary Pears, of Dublin, gent.; of the office of clerk of the crown, peace, and sessions, and keeper of the records in the counties Meath, Westmeath, co. of town of Drogheda, Louth, and Longford. To hold during good behaviour, with such fees as Tho. Dillon had. Not to be removed, as in 4976. Given free from the seal in respect he is the lord deputy's secretary.—30 April, xxxv.

5814 (4698.) Grant to Zachary Pears, of Dublin, gent.; of the office of chief chamberlain of the Exchequer, in succession to Tho. Dillon. To hold during good behaviour, with a fee of £13 6s. 8d. Not to be removed, as in 4976. Given free from the seal in respect he is the lord deputy's secretary.—30 April, xxxv.

5815 (4723.) Pardon to Tho. M'Tomoltagh, of Daghclowne, Owen M'Tomoltagh, of same, Cahill M'Donogh, of Kyltefadde, Donell

FIANTS—ELIZABETH.

O Flyn, of same, Hugh M'Swyne, of Bonyn, Teige O Shragane, of same, Loghlen O Beolayne, of Behie, Mallaghlen M'Calery, of Clonymahin, Molrony M'Donell, of Brickllswe, Fergananyn M'Donell, Dermot O Larkans, Teige boy M'Melaghlan, of same, Callough O Connor, of Clonderroe, Dunell and Rorie m'Brien boy O Hart, of Clonyne, Connor oge O Hart, of Ardtermon, Mulrony m'Owen O Hart, of same, Dwaltagh O Connor, of Lehvally, Donogh grane O Harte, of Ballionnell, Patr. O Hart, Brian O Fnery, and Shane O Harte, of same, Owen O Tomane, of Sligoe, Roris O Hart m'Rorie ballagh, of Bradcallyna, Melaghlen O Gealane, of Downarona, Donogh O Gealane, of same, Delrmot reogh O Roynian, of the Court, Donell O Hart, of same, Connor O Hart, of Ballyneoarre, Owen m'Tirrelagh M'Swine, of Ardneglasse, Cormuck O Beolaine, Teige O Kevan, Donoghan O Hughe, of same, Owen duff M'Eward, of Ballineglogh, Rory O Hannaghan, of Killasser, Edm. buy O Davan, of the Courte, Teige m'Cormuck M'Elearre, of Balliarrereegh, Melaghlen m'Gillepatrick O Comain, of Coolany, Farrall M'Enchae, Mulrony M'Enchae, of same, Melaghlen O Serkett, of Ballyndowne, Carbry m'Melaghlen oge, of same, Dwalagh m'Carbry M'Donogh, of Coolany, Teige O Boyle, of Ballyassedarre, Gilleoomyn M'Gwyne, of Aghris, Hugh O Connor, of same, Brian O Hardagane, of Killglasse, Dermott M'Greave, of Tunycarragh, Hian O Higgen, of Sligoe, Tho. Davies, of same, Dermot m'Rory M'Carbry, of Tullinemoylla, Edm. M'Gillemarten, of Kilorane, Connor roe m'Brebowne, of Ardeneglasse, Rory M'Dyer, of Cleaveragh, Loghlen M'Dyer, Mortagh M'Dyer, of same, Farrall oge M'Cahill, of Roscribe, Tomultagh keogh M'Thomas, Edm. boy m'Teige M'Ferrall, of same, Tho. Crome O Oullany, of Moyntagh, Ullick Burke, of Ardnary, Roris O Casye, of Kiltofadde, Shane O Higgen, of Ballyndowne, Donogh O Doolegana, of Coolvony, Tomultagh O Coyniiske, Donogh O Carre, of same, Gillepatrick modder M'Calery, of Ballineshian, Wm. O Shaghnes, Connor O Cloan, of Kyllorane, Don M'Gilleryewe, Manus O Kenryne, of Ballicddordaowen, Brian M'Carr, of same, Hugh O Healy, of Ballyndowne, Connor O Flanery, of Downcontrahe, Farfassy O Doogenan, of Roscribbe, Owen O Beanaghana, of Balliahian, Mary ny Swyne, of Longeforde, Cormuck O Kesvane, of Killorane, Patr. M'[   ], of Killmorogh, Soroghe ny Fianilla, of Iskrowne, Patr. M'Enylly, of Bonyne, Brian m'Hugh M'Kevane, of Ballemost, Ferdoragh O Beolane, of Ardneglasse, Mulrony oge m'Mullrony buy, of Aghris, Brian M'Garve, of Tonregoe, Brian O Raghteruna, of Ballydavnowne, Diermott M'Dyer, of Ewlaghfadde, Edw. Baker, of Ballymoate, Nich. Lovet, of Ardneglasse, Gilleglasse O Beolaine, of same, Flan O Cloane, of Killorane, Manus m'Connor oge, of Ballyndowne, Connor m'Meleghlen oge, of same, Tho. O Cleary, of Tawnagh, Henrias O Cleary, of same, Hugh boy O Connor, of Teotemple, Shano M'Donnogh, of Ballyneclogh, James M'Owen, of Larrans, James m'Teige M'Farrall, Owen Keogh, of Larrass, Brian O Dowde, of Iskrowne, Margaret ny Swyne, Connor O Healy, Dermott roe O Beolane, Dairmott M'Carhee, of same, Roris O Connor, of Skardane, Owen O Connor, of same, Donell M'Gillechallyn, Conoghor oge O Benaghan, of Tyrerall, Kyrrhus M'Nyca, of Ooola, Wm. keogh O Doode, of Emlaghyshall, Owen O Hart, of

Grannge, Diarmott O Flaghny, of Ballineglogh, Owen buy
M'Carre, of Kyllagowne, Mahy M'Carre, Phelim O Mullnoghe-
rie, of same, Philip O Garmuly, of Kyllorry, Tyrrelagh Marre
M'Donogh, of Boscribbe, Teige M'Nemarre, Tomultagh M'Conell, of Boneneddans, Wm. M'Elearne, of Tallaneglogge, Honora
reogh ny Doode, of Ardenaglasse, Rory M'Swyne, of same, Fear-
feasy O Doogenan, of Behy, Cahill M'Tomultagh, of Lymmowe,
Teige m'Tirlagh carragh O Conor, of Annagh, Sourly m'Cormuck O Hart, of Sligoe, Edm. m'Brian oge O Hart, of Balline-
carre, Phelim M'Collrick, of Eadden, Hugh and Brian m'Brian
oge O Hart, of same, Brian m'Tho. backagh O Hart, of Sligoe,
Rich. O Creayn, of same, Patr. O Gaallane, of Bradcxyllyn, Brian
oge O Hart, Fellm m'Hugh O Hart, Owen O Fein, of same, Shane
. O Fallane, of Ballynecarre, Hugh O Currane, of Courte, and Wm.
O Tef Jnane, in co. Sligo.   Provisions as in 5805.   Fine &c.
English each.—[April 1] xxxv.

5816 (5533.) Grant (under queen's letter, 16 March, xxix.) to Ra-
dolph Bruerton, gent. ; of a pension of 4s. (Irish) a day, till he
be rewarded otherwise.   In consideration of his services in Ireland and at Newhaven.—13 May, xxxv.

5817 (6198.) Commission (under privy signet, 20 Jan., 1590) to sir
Richard Bingham, knt, chief commissioner of the province of
Connaught, Thomas Dillon, esq., chief justice, and Garrett Comber-
ford, esq., attorney of the province ; to enquire of the title of Edmund Barrett, of the barony of Orrum, co. Mayo, and Edmund,
his son, to the following lands claimed by them :—Innewer, Toran,
Leam, Corraghry, Twiscart, Inniskey, Ballencarne, Balleglangho,
Dukeghan, Ballighrohy, Ballevonnell, and Dukceghan, supposed
to be in their possession, and Crosmolyna, Bellike, Inniskoo, Cah-
lanlaccan, Ballaglanna, and Kilbrid, supposed not to be in their
possession, all in the baronies of Laris and Tirauly, co. Mayo.
With the intent they may be surrendered and regranted by
English tenure.—[30 May, xxxv.]   Date taken from the Commission attached to Inquisition Chy. Mayo, Eliz. No. 2.

5818 (4718.) Pardon to Cormac O Doyne, of Balleakeanagh, gent.,
Joan ny Carroll, his wife, Donogh M'Brien, Malaghlan m'Connor
O Skully, and Rorie M'Cahir, his servants, Carroll M'Gilpetrick,
Donell oge M'Rorie, Cogherie M'Gilphoile, Hugh M'Thomas,
Conn M'Rorie, Hugh m'Conogher O Coffie, Nich. Parsons,
Daniel Rawlis, Tho. Galserie, of Phillipstown, in King's co.,
tanner, and Teige m'Murtagh m'Nellis O Moore, of Stradballie,
in Queen's co.   Provisions as in 5504.—10 June, xxxv.

5819 (4741.) Lease (under commission, 17 Feb., xxx.) to Tho.
Chambers, of Kilmaynham, gent. ; of messuages and parcels of
land in the town and fields of Kilmainham, co. Dublin, &c., as
in 5418 (the name O Donelaus is here written O Dowlan ; the
west gate of the town of Kylmaynam is here the west side of the
town).   Also 70 acres arable and 10 pasture from the little river
Camock towards the south side to the bound called the black
hedge and broad meer, which lands are between the limits of the
demesne lands and the lands of the church of Kilmainham, and
6 acres meadow by the Camock ; 140 acres arable and 30 pasture
on the west side of the manor of Kilmainham from the river
Liffie unto a small river called the Camock, and from the way
called the mill bater unto the west side of the parcel of land

called the Druggs, parcel of the lands of the late hospital of
S. John of Jerusalem in Ireland, in co. Dublin. To hold for
21 years. Rent £22 4s. 11d. Provisions as in 4299.—28
June, xxxv.

5820 (4694.) Grant (under queen's letter, 10 April, xxxv.) to Anthony Sentleger, knt.; of the office of clerk or master of the
rolls, books, writs, and records of chancery. To hold during
pleasure, as fully as the master of the rolls in England, with a
fee of £50 out of the customs of Dublin and Drogheda and such
other fees as Nich. Whyte, knt., or any other had. With power
to keep the rolls and records; to hear and, in the absence of the
chancellor, to determine causes, and grant injunctions; to take
recognizances, examine witnesses, admit attorneys and other
officers, and remove or punish them. Whereas Rich., bishop of
Laighlin and dean of S. Patrick's, had by deed dated 24 March,
xxxv., granted to the queen a rent of 300 marks English, for 10
years, out of the deanery of S. Patrick's, in consideration of the
release of a fine of £2,000 English imposed on him by the court
of Star Chamber in England; 100 marks a year of the said rent
is hereby granted to Sentleger.—29 June, xxxv. (Cal. P. R.
p. 268.)

5821 (4695.) Grant (under queen's letter, 10 April, xxxv.) to Rob.
Napper, knt.; of the office of chief baron of the Exchequer.
To hold during pleasure, with a fee of £67 10s., as fully as
Lucas Dillon or any other had. Also 100 marks sterling a year
out of the rent payable from the deanery of S. Patrick's, as in
5820.—29 June, xxxv. (Cal. P. R., p. 270.)

5822 (4700.) Grant (under queen's letter, 10 April, xxxv.) to Wm.
Weston, knt.; of the office of chief justice of the Common Bench.
To hold during pleasure, with the usual fees. Also 100 marks
sterling a year out of the rent payable from the deanery of
S. Patrick's, as in 5820.—29 June, xxxv.

5823 (4711.) Pardon to Brian m'Sawny M'Mahon, Patr. M'Cabe,
son of said Brian, Owin O Cassets, Roris M'Granell, Doke
O Lowan, Rory O Lowan, Laleinge bane O Lowan, Tirlagh
O Lowan, Owin O Brene, James oge O Brene, Granie ny Brian,
and Nele M'Quoada. Provisions as in 5704. Excepting also
any riot or offence of which they are accused in Castle Chamber.
M'Quoad excepted from the clause excluding persons not born
in co. Monaghan. Given free from the seal by the direction of
the lord deputy, and for that one of the parties named in this
fiant was once hanged, the lord deputy and council thought good
to grant him his pardon, and not to hang him again, and so it
was granted him in forma pauperis.—26 July, xxxv.

5824 (4722.) Grant (under queen's letter, 14 June, xxxv.) to Alex.
Cosbie, of Stradbally, Queen's co.; of a messuage and garden in
Marlboroughe, late in the tenure of Edw. Fitz Henry, the lands
of Cayrshell, Cassinloghe, and Kilbolan alias Ballehalan, Cloughe-
powke and Balleonilan, Balleknookan, Ballakeroke alias Balle-
keroun, Kilcolmanbane, Kepowle alias Kilpowly, Clonebriake, and
Cowlkhre, also the rectory of Hilcolmanbane, with the tithes
extending to Kilcolmanbane, Balleknookan, Ballakeroke alias
Ballakerans, Kepowle, Rathbege, and Ballequill, the rectory of
Ballequillan with the tithes extending to Balleqnillan, Cloghpowle,
Townleven, Nenaghe, Ballickbullan, and Ourragh, three

messages with a little garden in Mariborough in the tenure of
John Tomkyns, Wm. Goode, and John Painter, lands of Clonyne
and Clonruske in the tenure of same, Moynrath, Cloneneynagh,
Rossakelton alias Rossequillan, and Tromro, Cloncadoran,
Kilbride, and Kildonam, another messuage and garden in the
tenure of Tho. Lamham, in Mariborough, and a messuage and
garden outside the east gate, in the tenure of Wm. Vicars,
land in the wood of Clonebarna, Rayland in the tenure of Wm.
Vicars, Clonekyne in the tenure of same, another messuage and
garden in Mariborough, lands of Rativine, Bealard, and Clonkyne,
a messuage and garden in the tenure of Anthony Rogers in
Mariborough, lands of Baylard, and Clankene, all in Queen's co.
To hold in tail male, by the service of a twentieth part of a
knight's fee. Rent, £27 3s. 5d. Maintaining six English
horsemen and two footmen. Provisions as in 174 substituting Maryborough and Queen's co. for Philipstown and King's
co. (The liability to attend hostings not deferred; and instead of
the clause referring to alienation is one forbidding alienation
without license under the great seal).—6 Aug., xxxv.

5825 (4731.) Grant (under queen's letter, 14 June, xxxv.) to
Alexander Cosbie, gent., and Dorcas Sidney, his wife; of the
lands of Lisboyne or Lisbigne, Monedars and Doghell, Kilnsuan
and Ballonekyll, Kilnrounane, Kilruyshe alias Kilruiske, Ballane-
bane, Desert Gallins, Knockard Khorre, Graignahowen, Eolebogg,
Liscoman, Graignnemohan, Rockeshell, Aghulabber or Aghus-
lubber, Clogboge, Moyade, Ballekesheland and Graige, Balle-
ritas or Ballyvicas, and Tulmore alias Clonetikho, Queen's co.
To hold in tail male, by the service of a twentieth part of a
knight's fee. Rent, £17 5s. 0d. Maintaining four English
horsemen. Provisions as in 174 substituting Maryborough and
Queen's co., for Philipstown and King's co. (The liability to
attend hostings is not deferred).—6 Aug., xxxv. (Cal., P. R.,
p. 265.)

5826 (4737) Grant (under queen's letter, 4 July, xxx.) to Terence
or Tirlagh O Byrne; of land in Killmakenock which James
M'Phelim now has in mortgage, lands there of Farragh M'Tirelagh,
of Kilmakenock, attainted (rent 13s. 4½d.); land between Naas
and the Maddlin, co. Kildare, called the Blackediches land,
parcel of the lands of Tho. Ewstace, of Cardistowne, attainted
(4s.); land at the Clonings in same co., parcel of the possessions
of David Sutton, attainted (7s.); land called Ballidalowge, same
co., parcel of the possessions of the priory of Connall (4s.); land
in Leixlipp, formerly belonging to the parish church of Leixlipp,
and granted to the church contrary to the statute of mortmain
(17s.); a place for a messuage upon the green of the Naas, with
land called Farrenearraghe in said co., parcel of the possessions
of Tho. Ewstace, [of Cardiatowne], attainted (3s.); Mongan alias
Mongananehona in the Rowrye, co. Kilkenny, parcel of the lands
of Donagh m'Arte Cavenagh, attainted of felony (5s.); Knockyne,
Ballioleghis, and Inchnafowkie, co. Carlow, parcel of the possessions of Moriartagh m'Cahir m'Arte Cavenagh, late of
Knockyne, attainted (4s.); half of Lyssalican, parcel of the lands
of Maurice m'Dermot m'Cahir Cavennaghe, late of Pollemonta,
attainted (2s.); Ballileighe, Ballinecowleighe, Balligoblan, Rahinmore, Ballinveighis, Clanmacurry, Cromepane, Pellrathbegge, and

Ballinakill, in said co., parcel of the lands of Maurice [m'Moroghe
M'Moriahe, and Moriartagh m'Moroghe], late of .Ballileighe,
attainted (4s.); a messuage and garden in Old Laughlin in said
co., parcel of the lands of James Ewstace, viscount Baltinglas,
attainted (12d.); half of Gowlin, and Ballibrack, in said co.,
parcel of the lands of Edm. M'Tirelaugh, Dermot M'Tyrelaugh,
and Donagh M'Tirelaugh, attainted (2s.); land in Ballindary
with a castle (9s.), Killeighe (3s. 8d.), Tullaghbane (2s. 8d.),
Killehinoe (2s. 8d.), Clonelan (16d.), parcel of the lands of Arte
O Melaghlin, attainted, in co. Westmeath; land in Clonamore,
same co., parcel of the lands of Arte m'Phelim O Melaughlin,
attainted (16d.); four tenements with gardens in Ballimore with
land called Bogganmore, in the fields of Ballimore, land called
Pallace mone, and Cloneonrre, in said co., parcel of the possessions
of the abbey of Loughsewdie (6s. 7½d.); land in Clonlonan (16d.)
and Clonemore (16d.) in said co., parcel of the lands of Kedagh
oge O Melaghlin, attainted; half a carucate of land in Donamonlo
called Cloghananaghe, parcel of the lands of Gerald m'Gerald
Dillon, of Ballinooloye, attainted (4s. 6½d.); land in Donamone,
in said co., parcel of the lands of the priory of Kilkenny (8½d.);
land in Ballihigin, Knockaoaquer, Dirringoolay, Aghboye,
Rahinmore, and Loghanlonoght, in said co., parcel of the lands
of Callogh m'Keadaghs M'Geoghegan, attainted (13s. 8d.); the
lands of Painstowne alias Ballifegine, in said co., parcel of the
lands of Theobald Dalton, attainted (15s. 6d.); Holliwood's acre
in Ballimoore, in said co., parcel of the lands belonging to the
church of Ballimoore (4d.); Balligannaghe alias Channanstone,
in said co., parcel of the possessions of the abbey of the B. V. M.
by Trym (10s.); half a quarter of land called Loghnamuck, in
the barony of Ath'lone, co. Roscommon, parcel of the lands of
Egnaghan m'Edm. oge O Kelly, late of Knockynconoghor,
attainted (5s.); a lake and island called Ardkillin in the country
called the Clountyes in said co., and three quarters of land by
the said lake, in the town and lands of Ardkillen, another quarter
of land called Carrownrowne, parcel of said Ardkillan (10s.), a
quarter of land called Lasaephoocke in said country (10s.), two
quarters called Killeraghe by Clonamurry in said country (20s.),
a little stone fortress called Ballinemullin in said country, and a
third part of a quarter of land adjoining (3s. 4d.), and the half
town called Leighbally Ardmanasran in Shanlios country (3s.),
all which are in co. Roscommon, and are parcel of the lands of
Teige oge O Connor Roe, attainted; the toll of the Saturday
market held beside the church of S. Nogan called the church of
Issertnowne in co. Roscommon (6s. 8d.), and a fourth part of a
cartron in Ardkynan, in said co. (6d.), parcel of the lands of Conoghor O Nanghten, of Ardkynan, attainted; half a cartron in
Ballidaker in co. Galway, parcel of the lands of Melaughlen
m'Teige oge, late of Ballidaker, attainted (6d.); half a quarter
of land in Ballyroddes, co. Roscommon, parcel of the lands of
Onin gran O Flannegan, attainted (5s.); half a burgage containing three messuages in the town of Wexford, parcel of the
lands of Isabella Wale, attainted (2s.); land in Rosard, co.
Wexford, parcel of the lands of Hugh duffe O Ferrall, of
Rosard, attainted (9d.); the church of Rossdroyte (5s. 4d.),

and the church of Sacro Bosco called Templescobe (18s. 4d.), in co. Wexford, parcel of the possessions of the house of nuns of Tymolinbegg, co. Kildare; lands in Lorgins in King's co. (11d.), and Moyhownoghe in same co. (18d.), parcel of the lands of Arte m'Phelim O Melaughlin, of Ballindirry, &c. Westmeath, attainted; land in Tullymourath or Tullymoyrath, King's co., parcel of the lands of Teige m'Cahir O Mulloy, of that place, attainted (6d.); and half a quarter of land in Carrownetobber in the barony of Taquin, co. Galwny, parcel of the lands of Cornelius [Oreggan] of that place, attainted (6s.) All which promises had been concealed from the queen. To hold for ever, in common soccage. Also one quarter of land called Rarce in the country called Clonechahill alias Flanegans country, in co. Roscommon (10s.), and half a quarter of land called Rantinclan in said country (5s.), parcel of the lands of Eugene son of Dowalagh or Owen m'Dowaltagh O Flanegan, of Rarce, attainted; the house of nuns of Ardcarna, co. Roscommon, the land on which it stands called Fernanne Callinghe (2s.), a parcel of land near Ardcarna called Crene Callisghe (20d.), a parcel of land called Clonacalliagh, in the parish of Lisertrowne (3s.), the rectory of Ardcarna, viz., all tithes belonging to it except those of Loghporte, which amount to three copies (13s. 4d.), the rectory, viz. half the tithes belonging to the chapel of Ellinaghbrocho alias Clonecum, in the barony of Ballintobber (5s.), in co. Roscommon, possessions of said house of nuns; half a quarter of land in Killismogan or Killismongan, in the barony of Taquin, co. Galway (6s.), and a third of a quarter in Kilbegg, co. Galway (4s. 6d.), parcel of the lands of Cornelius Cregan, of Carrowntobber, attainted; the site of the priory of canons of Moghill, co. Leitrim, and three quarters of land adjoining (40s.), the rectory, viz. the third part of the tithes of two towns called Ballym'how and Ballyngare or Cowlensgare, co. Leitrim (13s. 4d.), possessions of said priory; one quarter of land called Killnedwan or Killedowan, with the tithes (13s. 4d.), another quarter called Carne, with the tithes (13s. 4d.), in co. Roscommon, possessions of the house of friars of Tulske; three quarters of land by the water called Lorgbella, viz., two carucates beyond the water towards the north, and another quarter on this side the water towards the west, co. Roscommon, possessions of the religious house of Killarights, in said co. (30s.) All which were concealed from the queen. To hold for ever, by the service of a twentieth part of a knight's fee. Rent £21 6s. 7d., as above. If any of the parcels had not been concealed the grant to be in so far void.—[3 Sept., XXXV.]   (Cal. P. R., p. 286).

5827. (4732.) Grant (under queen's letter, 14 June, XXXV.), to Alexander Cosbie, of Stradbally, Queen's co., gent.; of the site of the house of friars of Stradbally, a water mill there, the lands of Stradbally, Ballenowlane, Kilrowry, Ballaredder and Loghill parke, Ballecolman, Ballemadoke, Kilmarten, the Grange, Garrymadoke, Clonevcock, Ballepevicar and Kilmoho, Moyannagh, Corriell, Racrehin, Cloduff, Nogbemole, Ballaghmore, Shanemollan, Ballym'mairus, and the castle of Baribroke, Queen's co. (certain land in Shanemollan, granted to Edw. Brereton excepted). To hold in tail male, by the service of a twentieth part of a

knight's fee. Rent £17 6s. 8d. Maintaining nine English
horsemen. Provisions as in 5824.—18 Sept., xxxv. (Cal. P. R.
p. 268.)

5828 (5972.) Surrender by Robert Dillon, knt.; of the office of
chief justice of the Common Bench, which he held for life, "a
matter not allowable in any such office." William Weston, knt.,
having been appointed by queen's letter, 10 Ap., xxxv. (*Signed*)
Robert Dillon. *Dated* 5 Oct., xxxv. (Cal P. R. p. 261.)

5829 (4699.) Grant (under queen's letter, [10 Ap.,] xxxv.), to Wm.
Weston, knt.; of the office of chief justice of the [Common
Bench], surrendered by Rob. Dillon, knt. To hold during pleasure, with the usual fees. Also 100 marks sterling a year out
of the rent payable from the deanery of St. Patrick's, as in 5830.
—10 Oct., xxxv. (Cal. P. R. p. 270.)

English ⌐ **5830** (4744.) Lease (under queen's letter, 29 Nov., xxxv.) to Piers
Butler 6ts Edm., of Roscrea, co. Tipperary, gent.; of the castle
and lands of Ballisax, co. Kildare (recites a lease of 13 Dec.,
xxvii. to Rob. Nangle, see 4348); the rectories of Galmole and
Glashare, co. Kilkenny; (recites 5368). To hold for 40 years
from the end of the recited interests. Rent £33 0s. 0d. Maintaining at Ballisax three English horsemen. Provisions as in
5811.—14 Oct., xxxv. (Cal. P. R. p. 270.)

English **5831** (6644.) Commission to Adam, archbishop of Dublin, chancellor;
to administer publicly the oath of supremacy under the statute of
2 Eliz., to the officers of the court of Chancery.—4 Nov., xxxv.
(Cal. P. R. p. 252.)

Like to sir Robert Gardiner, for the officers of the Queen's
Bench.

Like to sir William Weston, for those of the Common Pleas.

Like to sir Robert Napper, for those of the Exchequer.

English **5832** (4776.) Lease (under queen's letter, 25 Aug., xxxv.), to
Francis Shane, [of Killare, co. Westmeath], esq.; of the site of the
abbey of Loughsewdie, lands in Callaughton, Ferrencrois alias the
Crosse lands in Bravin Vrin's country, land in Icoynes country,
and Sare, the rectories of Srure, Hillockanooke, Clonglishe,
Kilsy, Ballymacurmycke, Moygowe, Tanynert, Tanany, Kilglasse, S. Michael's Rabutts, and S. Patrick's of Moymore, co.
Westmeath, and Moyagher, co. Meath, (recites 3154, and 2806);
rent £35 14s. 4d.; and maintaining one English archer. The
site of the manor of Granard in the Annally, co. Longford, and the
lands, rents, six score beeves, and customs belonging, (recites
4904); rent £36; and maintaining two English horsemen. The
tithes of certain lands which the heirs of Morogh O Farrell held
in co. Longford, the tithes of Maghery granard, in said co., and
the tithes of the rectory of Strade with land belonging thereto
in co. Westmeath, (recites 5499), rent £17. To hold for 45
years from the end of the interests in being. Provisions as in
4939.—20 Nov., xxxvi. (Cal. P. R. p. 271.)

English **5833** (4760.) Grant to Francis Capstoke, gent.; of the office of
clerk general of the works of all the queen's castles, manors and
other works in Ireland, with the usual fees. To hold during
good behaviour. Not to be removed, as in 4976.—27 Nov.,
xxxvi. (Cal. P. R. p. 260.)

1593.   FIANTS.—ELIZABETH.

5884 (4758.) Commission to Adam, archbishop of Dublin, lord chancellor, John, archbishop of Armagh, Tho. earl of Ormond and Ossory, treasurer, Tho., bishop of Meath, sir H. Wallop, knt., vice treasurer, sir H. Bagenall, knt., marshal, chief justices Gardener and Weston, chief baron Napper, sir A. St. Leger, master of the rolls, sir G. Bourchier, master of the ordnance, sir R. Bingham, chief commissioner of the province of Connaught and Thomond, sir T. Norreis, vice-president of Munster, sir R. Dillon, one of the privy council, sir G. Fenton, secretary of state, N. Walshe, second justice of the Chief Bench, the mayor of Dublin for the time being, Charles Calthroppe, attorney general, R. Wilbraham, solicitor general, Rob. Conway, doctor of laws, Henry Usher, archdeacon of S. Patrick's; to execute the acts of Supremacy and Uniformity, with power to enquire judicially of all offences against these acts, and also all heretical opinions, seditious books, conspiracies, false rumours, seditious libels, tales, evil education of children by schoolmasters, scandalous words and sayings against the laws or proceedings ecclesiastical; to visit and correct all heresies, schisms, and offences which by any ecclesiastical authority may be redressed; to correct all unlawful marriages, adulteries and fornications, usuries, sacrileges, simonies, and other ecclesiastical crimes; to use and devise all politic ways for trial, by confession of the parties, lawful witness, or by due means and conviction, and thereupon to order such punishment by all or any ways of correction as to their wisdoms appear meet; with power to summon and examine witnesses, and to punish those who disobey by imprisonment and fine; and to take recognizances from persons for their appearing and obedience to orders. As divers perverse persons refuse to acknowledge the queen's prerogative and preeminence, and the order of service as established by law, the commissioners are to administer the oath of Supremacy to all bishops, parsons, or other ecclesiastical ministers, to every judge, mayor, or other lay officer. They shall put in force as far as concerns the clergy the act of xxviii. Henry VIII., for the English order, habit and language. They may delegate their powers as to taking examinations and recognizances of persons in remote parts. They may proceed against persons who refuse to appear, after affixing their precept to the door of the offender's house, and proclamation at fair or market, or in church. Whereas merchants and others keep copes, vestments, chalices, idols, crosses, and other superstitious relics, to the maintenance of popery, and and daily bring over books and writings repugnant to the ecclesiastical laws, seditious to the crown, and pernicious to the subjects, whereby conspiracies and rebellious practices are raised and maintained, the commissioners are to search ships, shops, and houses, seize such articles, and ballads, songs, sonnets, or other writings, and punish the offenders by fine and imprisonment. Lists of names of persons to be proceeded against to be kept, and care taken that they are not tampered with by the officials. The commissioners shall oblige impropriators to repair the chancels of the churches and to find curates to serve in them, and also require incumbents to repair their chancels, and parishioners to maintain the churches, with power to sequester the benefices of those who do not comply.—[27 Nov., xxxvi.] (*The latter part of this*

1593. FIANTS—ELIZABETH.

fiant is wanting. It is given at great length in Cal. Patent Rolls,
pp. 291–5.)

5835 (5596.) License to Alexander Cosbie and Dorcas his wife; to
English demise to any faithful subjects, for one, two or three lives or 21
years, their lands in the Queen's co., held under several grants.
Recites that the land is waste from the recent rebellions and the
difficulty of obtaining occupiers.—28 Nov., xxxvi. (Cal. P. R.
p. 281.)

5836 (4770.) Commission to Adam, archbishop of Dublin, and
English. chancellor, chief justices Gardiner and Weston, chief baron
Napper, and sir A. St. Leger, master of the rolls; to hear and
determine a controversy long pending before the privy council in
England, between John Itchingham, gent., and sir Nich. White,
knt., and since his death, Andrew White, esq., his son and heir,
for the recovery of the barony of Donbrodie and other lands.
This commission is issued on the recommendation of sir John
Popham, chief justice of England and the attorney and solicitor
general there, to whom the matter had been referred by the council.
—3 Dec., xxxvi.

5837 (6624.) Presentation of Meredius Hanmer, clerk, s. t. p.; to
the treasurership of the cathedral of Waterford, vacant by the
deprivation of Thomas Granger.—4 Dec., xxxvi.

5838 (6647.) Pardon to Alexander Cosbie, of Stradbally, Queen's
co., esq.—6 Dec., xxxvi. (Cal. P. R., p. 277.)

5839 (4764.) Grant (under queen's letter, 30 July, xxv.) to Garret
English. Maskworth, son and heir to Humfrey Maskworth, slain in the
queen's service; of the lands of Beardth and Newton, co. Kildare. To hold for ever, in common socage. Rent 13s. 4d.
Recites that Humfrey had purchased the lands from Tho. Wolf,
who held them of the earl of Kildare, but who had only a life
estate, having previously mortgaged them to the viscount of Baltinglas, by whose attainder they had passed into the queen's
hands as appeared by inquisitions in the xxvi. year (Inq. Chy.
Kildare, Eliz. No. 6.), and 12 July last.—6 Dec., xxxvi. (Cal.
P. R., p. 272.)

5840 (4761.) Lease (under queen's letter, 29 Nov., xxxv.) to Piers
English. Butller Sts Edm., of Rosoren, co. Tipperary, gent.; of the tithes
of corn of the rectory of Moymed, co. Meath, extending to
Moymed, Kilbride, Fillaeston, Clonefan, Skroan alias Eskeroan,
and Robartstowne, containing 16 copies of grain, price 13s. 4d.
each, and a portion of the altarages valued at 13s. 4d., parcel of
the possessions of the priory of Molinger (recites 6003); land in
Little Raths, co. Kildare, late in the tenure of John Hasquine,
parcel of the lands of Tho. Eustace, of Kardiston, attainted
(recites 4322); five messuages in the High street of Trym, late
waste, one messuage with a small orchard in the Skinner's street,
one messuage with a small close without the walls on the west,
late in the tenure of John Smythe, three other messuages in the
Skinner street, a small messuage and orchard in Scarlet street, a
small orchard in the same late in the tenure of John Monaghan,
another messuage in said street late in the occupation of John
Gwerrine, a messuage in the Wyne street, a waste messuage called
the Blacke hall in the Fayre street, a garden on the north side of
the town in the occupation of Wm. Ruddy, five messuages there, a
garden without the south gate, and six messuages there, parcel of the

1593.   FIANTS—ELIZABETH.

possessions of the abbey of S. Peter of the Newton near Trym; land near the town of Trym, including the Saffie park, Mandelans lands, and Claneberry, parcel of the lands of the monastery of S. Mary near Trym. To hold for 40 years, from the end of the recited interests so far as they concern the premises. Rent £20 6s. He shall not charge coyne or livery. He shall enroll with Auditor general, within three months.—25 Dec., xxxvi. (Cal. P. R. p. 276.)

1593–4.

5841 (4775.) Lease (under queen's letter, 6 July, xxxi.), to Rob.
English. Bostoke, gent. ; of the tithes of Sherlokeston, co. Kildare, parcel of the possessions of the late hospital of S. John of Jerusalem in Ireland (recites a lease from the prior, sir John Rawson, in 1535, to David Sutton for 60 years); the tithes of corn of the rectory of Killaghe, co. Kilkenny (recites 6056); a messuage in Drogheda, parcel of the possessions of the house of nuns of the Grace of God alias Gracedine (recites 4420); the parsonages and vicarages of Ardfynan, Rathoronan, and Mortellston, and the parsonage of Kilmologe, co. Tipperary, parcel of the preceptory of Ausy, parcel of the late hospital of S. John of Jerusalem in Ireland (recites 2206); lands of Ballinrody, co. Waterford (recites 3193); divers shops in the Bridge-street, of Drogheda (recites 4420); also a messuage in the city of Waterford in the occupation of Patr. Maddan parcel of the possessions of the abbey of Tinterne. To hold for 31 years from the end of the interests in being. Rent £12 18s. 2d. [Provisions as in 4939.]—19 Jan., xxxvi. (Cal. P. R., p. 284.)

5842 (4780.) Lease (as in 5610), to John Lye, esq. ; of a messuage
English. and garden in Athboye, co. Meath, late in the tenure of Marian Blake, gent. To hold for 50 years, from the determination of 842. Rent 13s. 4d.—20 Jan., xxxvi. (Cal. P. R., p. 272.)

5843 (4787.) Commission (under queen's letter, 20 Jan., 1590), to
English. sir Wm. Weston, chief justice of the Common Pleas, Wm. Bath, second justice of same, Roger Wilbraham, solicitor general, Nich. Aylmer, and Gerald Flemynge, gent. ; to enquire by the oaths of jurors what castles lands and other hereditaments, Philip O Reylle, of Ballincargie, co. Cavan, gent, hath in that county, either contained in the indentures between the queen and him, passed in the time of the late lords justices, or since purchased by him. Recites that Philip had offered to surrender his possessions in order to receive them again by patent; and that formerly subjects had been put out of possession of their inheritance by their lands being wrongfully inserted in such surrenders.—20 Jan., xxxvi.

5844 (4750.) Grant to Wm. Jones ; of the office of janitor of the castle of Dublin with a fee 12d. a day as Wm. Rilands had. To hold during good behaviour. Not to be removed, as in 4976. —31 Jan., xxxvi. (Cal. P. R., p. 280.)

5845 (4785.) Lease (under queen's letter, 30 June, xxxv.), to
English. Lodowick Briskett, gent. ; of the castle of Palleyes, Queen's co., the lands of Palleyes, Clonedergarmoyle, Clonisgawnaghe, Garrismore, Cappanghe, Coulesnemore, and Clonecarragh. To hold for 50 years from the death of Anthony Hungerforde, without heirs male (recites 2778.) Rent £7 2s. 6d. Maintaining four

English horseman. With conditions usual in grants of land in this county (see 474), excepting the clauses relating to jointures, alienations, residence, and marriage. Also provisions as in 4989.—31 Jan., xxxvi. (Cal. P. R., p. 272.)

5846 (6646.) Pardon (under queen's letter, 6 Dec., xxxvi.) to Robert Johnes, Garrett Birne, Thomas Correll, David Burke, William M'Edmond, Tirlogh M'Keyne, Tibbot Bourke, Ennes O Neale, Patrick Morohoe, William Jordain, and Griffin Cavanohe ; of all treasons committed with William Stanley, knt., from the time when he delivered the town of Deventry to the king of Spain. Not to extend to treasons against the royal person, nor to any person who may afterwards have dealings with rebels or enemies. Provisions for security as in 4943.—8 Feb., xxxvi. (Cal. P. R., p. 277.)

5847 (6649.) Pardon to Conoghor O Camhell, late messenger to Maguire, Katharine Kannane, his wife, Sawe ny Camhell, his sister, Katherine ny Camhell, his daughter, Patrick m'Rorie Maguire, his son-in-law, Moriah O Camhell and Melaghlin O Camhell, his brothers, Owen O Tewan, and Melaghlen O Toole, his tenants, in co. Fermanagh. Provision for security as in 4948. Pardon not to include intrusion into crown lands, or debts to the crown. " Free, for service done upon Maguira."— 19 Feb., xxxvi. (Cal. P. R., p. 278.)

5848 (6652.) Pardon to Tarman m'Owen O Rowrke, of Sligo, Bryan m'Owen O Rowrke, of same, Phalim m'Owen m'Laghlan m'Farall buye O Rwrke, of same, Donell m'Murtagh m'Owen buye O Gillegan, of same, Owen m'Hughe O Harte, of Bradcullen, Donogh oge O Harte m'Oweny ne Harte, Teige and Patrick m'William roe O Harte, Phelim m'Phelim O Harte, Bryan oge m'Wm. roe O Harte, and Wm. O Mullegan m'Tha. roe O Bronan, of same, Nolan boy O Harte m'Connor oge O Harte, of Artarman, Shan roe Lewlasse, of Courte, Phelim m'Teige oge O Harte, of Dunfore, Shan m'Teige oge O Harte m'Hugh m'Teige O Harte, of Granndge, Bryan m'Teige O Harte m'Hughe m'Gillodufie, of Lishadilli, Teige m'Donnagh O Harte, of Annagh, Owen m'Shane keogh O Harte, of same, Shan m'Fargynanhaim O Connor, of Scarden, Cormucke Omullagh m'Fardaroe O Harte, of Graundge, Donnell oge O Connor, of Larris, Honora ny Burke, of Kyllanullye, Bryan O Hargidan, of Kyllinlasye, Honora oge ne Swyne, of Ardnyglasse, Brean O Connell m'Thomas Lovett, of same, Owen O Flannelly, of Killglasse, M'O Mullawne, of Kyllinlasey, Dermot crone O Flannelly, of Lyevonye, Shane O Flannelly m'James Albonagh, of same, Teige buye O Dowde, of Ballinehowan, Philip Albonagh, of Rathlewe, Allen Albonagh m'Turlogh m'Sharrye, of Dunlon, Cahell O Flannellia, of Nyakreowen, Dermot O Tarpe m'Cormucke O Dowde, Tege reoghe O Flannelly m'Dermot O Flannally, Cormuck keogh M'Ervisse, Wm. duffe m'Collat m'Sele grana ne Flannellia, Owen grome O Logher m'Manas duffe O Tolan, Con O Farris m'Wm. duffe O Logher, and Farrell O Flannelly m'Hugh O Flannelly, of same, Edmund fore m'Farel m'Brian O Harte, of Dower, Rory O Harte, of Downeshoye, M'John Flore, of Belake, Hugh O Syredan, of Ardnarie, M'Anus O Kirran, of Lencmagh, Thomas oan M'Combayne, of Lencerowe, James duffe M'Donnell, of Costalye, Donnagh O Harte, of Dunneale, M'Teige O Harte, of same, Hugh

1593-4.   FIANTS—ELIZABETH.

O Harte m'Gillapatricke O Harte, of same, Bryan duffe M'Gean, of Eaike, Bryan M'Eward, of Screnanarte, M'Manus, of Courte, Gerald Dyrlun, of Mannyn, Wm. oge m'Hubert baye, of Cerran, Kuchonnaght M'Nemye, of Ballechotale, Kayer m'Kedo m'Donnell, of Terraghlye, Ennis m'Donnell m'Donnell O Cleare, of same, Fardaro O Clare m'Sela ne Mughan, of Kilcoman, Wm. O Mughan m'Morris in'Coumye, of Kyll, Farrall M'Rorie, of Bonnanedan, Wm. taells m'Mullrouy O Harte, of Turnegloge, Tege O Carvill m'Cahall M'Brabon, of Rosse, Dualtagh and Rorie m'Shane glasse O Garye, of Belassallagh, Owen grome m'Shane glasse O Garye, of same, Shan O Murragh, of Ballemote, Thomas m'Cogh m'Owen M'Dannagh, of Colmonye, Bryan na kills M'Donnagh, of Cola, Rory m'Donnagh m'Kayer M'Donnagh, of same, Donnagh oge m'Donnagh m'Iryll O Gary, of Moygh, Tege O Gary m'Fargynanham O Gary, of same, Dualtagh m'Shane oge O Gary m'Brian 'm'Dermot, of Dirremore, Kedo M'Dermotie roe, of same, Donnell m'Murriertagh O Healy, of Longford, in coo. Sligo and Mayo, Hibbert baye m'Redmon m'Shane m'Ulyke Burke, of Killemugher, Richard Bryningham, of Turloghvaghan, Thomas oge Bryningham m'Redmond Dryningham, of same, Thomas duffe Bryningham m'Carburye Oscobe, Owen grane M'Enree, of Terre, Donnell M'Enree m'Richard m'Tybbott, of Raye, Henry m'Tibbotz m'Moyler duffe, of same, Malaghlin roe m'Wm. O Kelly, of Gallaghe, Bryan m'Connor O Kelly, of Abyett, Bryan O Hamim, of Teghboy, M'Hugh O Kelly, of Myllegh, Radmond M'Crobacke, of Cladagh, Moyler M'Crobacke m'Morae ne Holleran, Bryan O Connall, of Innyamaghan, Hubbert M'Rickard, of Kilcolye, Flan M'Carrolla, of Galway, Ulick Bourke, of Hallemanan, Shane karro O Kelly, of Garrill, Ulicks m'Connell Burke, of Lebynch, co. Galway, Tege m'Redmond M'Dermott roe, Shane m'Ulyck m'Shane O Conygay, of Ogloe, Murtagh baye m'Wm. M'Thomas, of Killoran, Redmund reogh M' an Orygon, of Tomonagh, Tege m'Bryan bnckagh, of Clontois, Brazell m'Donnell m'Owen O Flannelly, of Graundge, Owen M'Donnell, of Korkipnetege, M'Mulrony, of Mullurge, Wm. Wene m'Dermott reogh O Naughten, of Loghan, Murtagh baye O Naughten m'Owen Grorke, of Lymgar, Tege m'ekallo O Connor, of Ragharrowe, Turlogh m'ekallo O Connor m'Toghall m'Kado O Connor, of Clonykyll, and Alexander M'Doell, of Kyllciogh, in co. Roscommon, Dualtagh myle O Knogher, of Lettram, Wm. oge O Browodyn, of Kyllehye, Knogher lych O Daey, of Dryncrett, Dermot m'Redmond O Daey, of same, Shane O Daey m'Duffe daro m'Redmon, of Ballenebynah, Tege O Kyrine, of Inysbykologhe, Knogher duffe O Herrere, of Eaberkroken, Hugh m'Teige Ioggayne, of Ballegurelayne, Owen Lytoye, of Donleky, M'Loghlin O Therin, of Lyamagham, Donnell O Kahill, of Killiocrich, m'Miell O Moelan, of Kelkedo, and Maghan moell m'Rorye O Hygan, of Balletample, co. Clara. Provisions as in 5798. Fine 1d. Irish each.—22 Feb., XLVI. (Cal. P. R., p. 279.)

5849 (4782.) Lease (as in 5810) to John Lee, of Rathbride, co. Kildare, genl.; of two pooles of land in Tullebricke, parcel of the lands of Shane reogh M'Cabill of that place, attainted; two gallons of land in Rathmlckfortie and Aghgalcharkie, parcel of the lands of Brian and Edm. m'Mulmore O Relie, of Rathmick-

1593–4.   PLANTS—ELIZABETH.

fortie, attainted; one gallon of land in Cowlemonia, parcel of the
lands of Mulmore O Relie, attainted; a half pottle of land in
Croakenghe, parcel of the lands of Brian m'Cormack M'Brady,
of Oroakeagh, attainted; one pull of land in Sonnine, one pull
called Snavonkill, and two pulls called the half quarter of
Carnesere, parcel of the lands of Cahir m'Prior O Relis, late of
Sonnine, escheated by common escheat; one pottle of land in
Dravile, parcel of the lands of Brian roe O Ferrall, of Dromlean,
attainted; 1½ pottles in Drumalaighe, parcel of the lands of Shane
m'Philip O Relis, of Dromlean, attainted; one pull in Correcharra, and one gallon in Downe, parcel of the lands of Brian
m'Cahir O Relie, of Correcharra, attainted, one pull called the
Nether Conett, parcel of the lands of Farrell m'Donell m'Tirlogh
O Relie, of Conett, attainted; 3 pulls of land known as the town
of Ballym'carroll, parcel of the lands of Gillekaaghhe M'Carroll,
of Ballimackoarroll, escheated by common escheat, all in co.
Cavan; one cartron of land in Walterstown, co. Westmeath,
parcel of the lands of Edm. Dillon, of Walterstown, attainted.
To hold for 60 years. Rent £3 4s. 6d. To be enrolled in the
Auditor General's Office within three months.—1 March, xxxvi.
(Cal. P. R. p. 274.)

5850 (4769.) Commission to sir Wm. Weston, chief justice of the
Common Pleas, and sir Rob. Napper, chief baron; reciting that on
examination of the records of the court of Common Pleas by the
justices of the court it was found that many were wanting; and that
they had been in the private custody of Bartholomew Talbott,
late prothonotary, until removed to safe custody in Birmyngham's
tower in the castle of Dublin. The present commissioners are
empowered to search out on oath where the missing records may
be, and to restore them if found; also to make an inventory of
the rolls and bundles of records, according to reigns, to prevent
embezzlement thereafter.—2 March, xxxvi.

5851 (4766.) Commission to Adam, archbishop of Dublin, chancellor,
sir Rob. Gardener, chief justice, and sir Anthony St. Leger,
master of the rolls; to repair towards Dondalke, or other part of
the county of Louth or province of Ulster, and to treat with
Hugh, earl of Tyrone, Hugh roe O Donell, or any other within
that province; with power to grant safe conducts. The forces
in the province to be at their command.—7 March, xxxvi.

5852 (4748.) Grant to Stephen Jenninges; of the office of clerk
controller or surveyor general of the ordnance and munitions.
To hold during good behaviour, with such fees as Michael
Kettallwell had. Not to be removed, as in 4976.—9 March,
xxxvi. (Cal. P. R. p. 281.)

5853 (4759.) Grant to Wm. Usher, of Dublin, esq.; of the office of
general and principal clerk of the council or clerk of the council
general, with such fees as Roland Cowick, Lodovic Briskett, or
Nathanial Dillon, had. To hold during good behaviour. Not to
be removed, as in 4976.—22 March, xxxvi. (Cal. P. R. p. 264.)

1594.

5854 (4774.) Grant (under queen's letter, 29 June, xxx.) to Patr.
Grante; of Plebardstane, co. Kilkenny, and the tithes of grain
and hay of Plebardstowne, Brownstowns, Foamm'Coddie, and
Disartbegg, same co., parcel of the possessions of the priory of

1594.   . FIANTS—ELIZABETH.

Kenlis, same co. (rent 16s.); a messuage and garden in Kilkenny,
between the land of John Sweeteman on the west and the way
called Boyshis lane on the east, a bake house in the same town
between the cemetery of the church of St. Mary on the west, and
the way called Loslane on the east, a toft or vacant place between
the said bakehouse on the south and the messuage of Rob. Forstale
on the north, half of a messuage with a garden lying in length
between the high street near the market cross on the east and
the land of Rich. Shea, knt., on the west, and in breadth between
the land of Rob. Roothe on the north, and the land of the said
Robert on the south, a rent of 2s. out of a messuage and garden
in which John Routhe fitz Peirs dwelt, in the town of Kilkenny,
parcel of the possessions of the abbey of Docske, in said co.; a
messuage in Kilkenny with a garden in the tenure of Rich.
Ragged near the mill of the Earl of Ormond called Genkyns
mill, parcel of the lands of the abbey of Jeriponte (6s. 4d.); the
fourth part of Kylrobyn, parcel of the land of Daniel or Donill
ballogh O Brenan, of that place, attainted; Rathcally, parcel of
the lands of James O Brenan m'Donnogh more, of that place,
attainted, the fourth part of Croghtynohlye, parcel of the lands of
Geoffrey O Brenan, late of Croghtinchlis in Idoughe, attainted,
Killderogan in Idoughe, parcel of the lands of Farr M'Molaghlin,
of that place, slain in rebellion, Clonyns in Idoughe, parcel of
the land of Hugh alias Eae O Brenan m'Shire, attainted of felony,
Kyllina, in Farrin O Ryan, parcel of the lands of Ouin O Ryan
m'Henry, slain in rebellion, Ballymhanboye, Barnawaddan,
Burris, and Killyns, parcel of the lands of Terence or Tirlagh
m'Donill m'Edm. Ryan, of Ballemahanboy, in Farrin O Ryan,
attainted, Ollard and the sixth part of Knockwarrowe, parcel of
the lands of Ferginanim O Ryan, of Ollard in Farrin O Ryan,
attainted of felony, Barnenycoll, parcel of the land of James
Brenaghe fitz Edm., of that place, attainted (12s. 1d.); Ballyn-
wale alias Walestowne, parcel of the lands of Peter Grace, of
Brenahaughe, attainted, the tithes of Farrinbrock and Chappell,
parcel of the possessions of the monastery of Blackstriers (5s.),
all in co. Kilkenny; Cullaghs, co. Tipperary, in Ony Mulryan,
parcel of the lands of Daniel m'Knoghor Edbllie O Mulryan, of
that place, slain in rebellion, Inchofogarde in the barony of
Poblanfogertie, in said co., parcel of the lands of Molaghlin
m'Shane E Carr O Fogertie, of that place, slain in rebellion,
Towryn, in Muskriquirk, in said co., parcel of the lands of John
m'Ulick Bourke, of that place, slain in rebellion, Rathgowls, in
said co., parcel of the lands of the priory of St. John Baptist
without Newgate of Dublin, Cowlegorte, in Muskriquirck, in said
co., parcel of the lands of Mahowne ne Bowlye O Quirke, of that
place, attainted, Lymine by Ballinlogan, in the country of Clon-
william in said co., parcel of the lands of Tho. Bourke, of Cowle,
same co., attainted (9s. 7½d.); Knockskillie, in said co., parcel
of the lands of Peter Butler, of that place, attainted of felony
(16s. 8d.); Killmoonage in O MulRyan, same co., parcel of the
lands of Donill giwe O Mulryan, of that place, slain in rebellion,
Castlegarr, in Arra, in said co., parcel of the lands of Morughe
m'Knoghor O Brien, of that place, attainted, Ourraghnawony in
said co., parcel of the lands of Knoghor m'Doyne M'Ivannye, and
Mahowne m'Doyne M'Ivannye, of that place, attainted, a third

1594.   FIANTS—ELIZABETH.

part of Boghir in Kilvalloughegertis in said co., attainted, Crosseayle in Kilnovannaghe in said co., parcel of the lands of Donell m'Donough O Doyre and Donogh Dullhenrie O Doyre, of that place, attainted, Garranmore in Ormonde in said co., parcel of the lands of Dermot m'Shane O Glynne, of that place, attainted, Kilkersaher in said co., containing half a cartron of land making three acres of the small measure, parcel of the lands of Owin m'Maloghlin roe O Dowdye, of Ballycurrye, in said co., attainted, a messuage and garden in Carrigmagriffin in said co., lying in length between the house of the earl of Ormond on the west and the river Showre on the east, and in breadth between the said house of the earl on the north and the land of Patr. Dobyn on the south, parcel of the possessions of the priory of S. John of Jerusalem in Ireland, Ballinegillevile in said co., parcel of the land of Rob. duffe Bourke, of Ballinegillevile, attainted (13s. 4d.) All the premises were concealed and detained from the crown. To hold for ever, in common socage. Rent £4 9s. ¾d.—25 March, xxxvi. (Cal. P. R., p. 264.)

5855 (5998.) Release by Robert Harrison, of Dublin; of the sum
English. of £411 17s., due to him for victuals supplied when the late earl of Essex served in Ireland. In consideration of grants of land to be made to him to the value of £20 English. (*Signed*) Robert Harrison.—*Dated* 29 March, xxxvi. (Cal. P. R., p. 369.)

5856 (4768.) Grant (under queen's letter, 3 Feb., xxx.) to Wm. Browne, of Mulranckan, co. Wexford, gent.; of land in the west part of Kilmainham wood, co. Dublin (rent 12s.), a house called a frankhouse in Skrine, co. Meath (18d.), parcel of the possessions of the monastery of S. John of Jerusalem in Ireland; half a carucate of land in Mologholoo (13s. 4d.), one quarter of land in Clonmikgillerowe (3s. 4d.), one quarter in Kilcrawe (6s. 8d.), one quarter in Jordianston (6s. 8d.), parcel of the lands of Oliver FitzGerald, in co. Westmeath, attainted; the tithes of Tebehin, in said co., received by the executors of Tho. Oumcke, knt., parcel of the possessions of the monastery of Clonard (13s. 4d.); and the site of the priory of Flare alias Loghsewdic in said co. (12d.) To hold for ever, in free socage. Rent 57s. 10d.—22 April, xxxvi. (Cal. P. R. p. 285.)

5857 (5535.) Grant (under queen's letter, 18 July, xxxiv.) to Dowlin
English. m'Brian Cavenagh; of a pension of 2s. 6d. (Irish) a day, during good behaviour. In consideration of his services in Ireland and the Low Countries.—23 Ap. xxxvi. (Cal. P. R. p. 375.)

5858 (4772.) Grant (under queen's letter, 15 April, xxvi.) to Nich. Meagh, sovereign of Kilmallock, co. Limerick, and the brethren and commonalty of that town; of the site of the monastery of friars preachers of Kilmallock, land in the town and a water mill adjoining it. (Recites *No.* 1484.) To hold for ever, in common socage. Rent, 53s. 3d. Maintaining two English archers.— 24 April, xxxvi. (Cal. P. R. p. 275.)

5859 (6645.) Pardon to Thomas M'Morrishe, of Clanmorrishe, co. Mayo, gent. Provision for security as in 4943. Pardon not to extend to intrusions into crown lands, or debts to the crown.— 30 Ap., xxxvi. (Cal. P. R. p. 275.)

5860 (6742.) Patent of grant (under queen's letter, 5 July, xxxi.) to Rob. Harrison, of Dublin; of 40 messuages, a water mill, and five carucates of land in the lordship of Muybrecko alias Moy-

breckre, co. Westmeath, a ruined weir on the river Clonelaghe,
a wood called Derfadd, with the sixth part of the red bog beginning at the entry of the said wood and the water course of
Rehinye, and extending in length between Cloghran and Derfadd,
and the tithes of grain and hay and other profits in Ballilagoran,
in said co., parcel of the possessions of the priory of Tristernagh
(rent £8 6s. 2d.) ; one carucate in Ballom'gilleboy, in the barony
of Moculleu, co. Galway, parcel of the land of Thade or Teig
M'Morroghe, late of Ballem'gilleboy, attainted ; Ballinriodall,
co. Limerick, the land of John or Shane O Riadiall, of Ballinri-
diall, attainted, (12s.). To hold for ever, by fealty, in common
socage. Rent £8 18s. 2d. as above. If any of the lands be
recovered at law by undertakers, or be found not to have been
concealed, he shall surrender. In consideration of £411 17s. 0d.
due to him for victuals in the time of the service of the late earl
of Essex in Ireland. See 5877.—2 May, xxxvi. (Cal. P. R.
p. 275.)

5861 (4751.) Grant to Arthur Corys, esq.; of the office of serjeant
    at laws. To hold during pleasure, with such fees as Rich. Finglas,
    John Bathe, or Patr. Barnewall, or Edw. Fitzsimons had.—9 May,
    xxxvi. (Cal. P. R. p. 255.)

5862 (4773.) Grant (under queen's letter, 10 July, xxxiii.), to Der-
    mot m'Morishe Cavonaghe, of Knockangarrowe, co. Wexford ;
    of the lands of Cownelyne, Cronearcmlaghte, Clonlnemannaghe
    alias Clonynymannaghbegge, and Kilchime, co. Wexford, lands of
    Griffin m'Murrogh Cavenaugh, of Cownaline, attainted ; Kilmi-
    hilie, parcel of the lands of Dermot O Nittin, of Kilmichile,
    attainted. To hold for ever, in common socage. Rent, 24s. 7d.
    —15 May, xxxvi.

5863 (4815.) Commission to Thomas, earl of Ormond and Ossory,
    high treasurer, sir Tho. Norreis, knt., vice president of Mounster,
    John, bishop of Lymericke, Wm., bishop of Corke, the mayor of
    Lymericke, George Thornenton, provost marshal of Mounster,
    Francis Barkeley, esq., and John Crosbie, preacher ; to put in
    execution the acts of Supremacy and Uniformity, in the dioceses
    of Lymericke, Corke, Clone, and Rossarbery, as in 5834.—
    [23 May], xxxvi.

5864 (6648.) Pardon to Oliver Eustace, of Kilcowell, co. Carlow,
    gent. Recites that he was convicted of the robbery of 2 horses
    of Dermot M'Shane, of Kilknock, same co., husbandman, and
    sought benefit of clergy, and had further pleaded guilty to an
    indictment for escaping from prison. Security as in 4943.—
    31 May, xxxvi. (Cal. P. R. p. 277.)

5865 (4778.) Lease (under commission, 16 Feb., xxx.) to John
    Hawarn and Henry Deane, gent. ; the third part of Rosaribbe, co.
    Sligo containing one triane of land, six quarters of land in Cororyn
    Sleight Morishe, viz. : Carowe Dromearnyuke, Carowe Owmygyn,
    Carrowe carrynnyllin, Carrowe Grany more, Carrowe ne Crove,
    and Carrowe Lisdowgan, and two quarters of free land in Clone-
    gashell in said co., parcel of the land of Gallechrista ny Donaghe,
    late of Rosaribbe, and in the queen's hands by escheat ; two
    quarters of land in the territory of Sleighte Shane boy mac Owen
    O Hary, in the barony of Offiyny, in said co., parcel of the land of
    Rory knaghe O Hary, of Balnesinoge, in said co., attainted of
    felony ; three quarters of free land lying nigh the lands of Cowlas,

in said co., the lands of Ferdorogh MacDonnogh, late of Cowlae, attainted; land at Cashilcormycke, in said co., parcel of the lands of Tumoltagh m'Wm. O Hary, of Carrowe-Carraghe, attainted; lands adjacent to Cashilcormick, parcel of the lands of Edm. O Hary, of Cashilcormycke, Arthur O Harry, Donald O Hary, and Brian macPhelim O Harye, attainted; a quarter of land in said co. called Leighe Carrowe Tullaughe and Leighe Carrowe Knappae, late the lands of Donell macShane Eglyn O Connor, of Forosage, attainted; the rectory called the rectory between two Bridges, in the barony of Carbry in said co., parcel of the possessions of S. John's without Newgate, Dublin; the site of the house of friars of Knockmor, with one quarter of land and the tithes, in the country of O Garye in said co.; the fifth part of the castle of Caherenemarte, and of a quarter of land adjoining, the lands of Thady roe O Maly, of that place, traitor; half a quarter of land called Leighe Carrwe neoladdy, co. Mayo, the lands of Sherowyn M'Gibbon, late of Ballinknocke, traitor; the moiety of the castle of Ballinknock and land in Ballinknocke, and one quarter called Kilterbrocke, in said co., the lands of Wm. ni'Jonycke MacGibbon, of Ballinknock, traitor; land in Knappagh, Cossyn, and Bahane, in said co., parcel of the lands of Wm. oge M'Gibbon, in the barony of Muricke, in said co., traitor; half a quarter of land called Leighe Carrowe Correvegan, and land in Carrownerahine in said co., the lands of Charles MacAndrew and Shane M'Andrew, of Barcae, in the barony of Tirowly, in said co., attainted; the castle of Ballicke with 8 quarters of free land, in the barony of Tirawly, viz.: one quarter adjoining Ballicke, Carrowne Collyn, Carrowe Farrenakollaige, Leighe Carrowe Clondekilly Boalick, Leighe Carrowe ne Enoigyn, Leighe Carrowe Farrenaleighte-Moyle in Beslicke, Leighe Carrowe Cowensyle, Carrowe Kidleaghe leige, Leighe Carrowe Bracklowne, Aghleigh Carrowe garrowe Crummoliene, Ackeighe Carrowe Carowclongh, in said co., and one carew of land in the barony of Kilpeane, in said co., called Ballykinlaghe, the lands of Theobald Bourke, of Boalicke, attainted; one quarter of land called Carrowekilurone, in said co., the lands of Ricard beg Malodd, of Kiltrone, attainted; Carrowaksile Ralackan, and Carrowkinlana, Carrowmoare, Downapatrick, Cartrone Knockan, and Cartrone Killeneatryenoad, in the barony of Tirawly in said co., parcel of the lands of Hugh boy M'Coanyll, of Balackan, attainted; Tullagiagan, in same barony and co., parcel of the lands of Gilleduffe O Cleary, of that place, attainted; Rathcarryn, in the barony of Kilmaine, in said co., parcel of the lands of Ricard macEdmonde Roggie and Shane mac Eddy Reoggy, traitors; Cairrowe Leighsballymacke, in the barony of Tirawlie, in said co., parcel of the lands of Edm. Eecraghe, of Keirnan, traitor; half a quarter of land in and adjacent to Garrannamacke, in said co., parcel of the lands of Rich. M'Ricard, of same, traitor; Carrowe Gortzillig, in said co., parcel of the lands of Ulick Mac Athony and Walter Mac Anthony, of Glanedaghe, traitors; Leighe Carrowe Moynteroyn, Carrowe Ballydowlaghe, Carrowballyvoan, and Carrowe Cappi-Cowmbe, in the barony of Rosse in said co., parcel of the lands of Thomas Cham Joy, of Ballydowlagh, attainted; Ballisbemon or Ballybemon, in the barony of Carra in said co., with the tithes, parcel of the possessions of the monastery of Ballyntobber,

in said co. ; Mocare, in said co., parcel of the lands of Rory oge
m'Brien boy, of Mocare, attainted ; the tenth part of the castle
of Killelenan, and lands in Killelenan, and Cloghleghe in Bally-
necarraghe in said co., parcel of the lands of Edm. Owny mac Davy
oge, of Killelenan, attainted ; Ballydnff alias Balligowghie, in the
barony of Tirawlie, in said co., parcel of the lands of Edm. buy and
Maller m'Henry Crone, of Ballyeduffe, slain in rebellion ; a ruined
castle called Clonyn, and half a quarter of land adjacent called
Cleykille, half a quarter called Eunyniall, two quarters called
Leighballynecloy, three quarters in and adjoining Lyssenyue,
and half a quarter called Leigh Carowe Rowghane, in the
barony of Carras in said co., parcel of the lands of Farragh
M'Connill, of Clonyn, attainted ; the rectory of Ballingaria, co.
Mayo, parcel of the possessions of the abbey of Mayo ; three
parts of a ruined castle of Clankorry, and three quarters of land,
that is to say three cartrons of land in Carrowe Clonekurria,
three cartrons in Knockglasse, half a quarter in Rathedmond,
and one quarter called Knockmegulshe, co. Mayo, parcel of the
lands of Moyler m'Tibbott Reoghe, Wm. Bourke mac Shane
Etermyn, Davy Bourke, Walter ne Moilye Bourke, and others,
traitors ; a ruined castle and 8 quarters of land called Carrowe
Killecownane, Carrowe Kilcurryn, Carrowe Tubbere Wraighe
durshie, Carrowe Balmonie, Carrowe Killenedeona, Carrowe
Ardnegiaghe, Carrowe Brknadrum, Gurtecurryn, Carrowe
Knockglasse, and Knockmarte, in the barony of Rosse in said
co., parcel of the lands of Thady or Teige Mac Morroghe, of
Ballanonoighe, in said co., slain in rebellion ; the ruined castle
called Leume, and one quarter of land, the ruined castle called
Barrauaghe, with half a quarter of land, and one quarter called
Ellagh in said co., parcel of the lands of John Bourke mac
Moyler, John boy M'Phillipp, and Shane Bourke m'Hubbert, of
Ellaghe, slain in rebellion ; a small island called Dromereagh,
and one quarter and a half of land round it, one quarter called
Knockliteragh, one quarter of land of the Carne called Carrowe
ne Clonen, and one quarter called Imlsvegger in said co., parcel
of the lands of Ullick Bourke, of Drumreaghe, Edm. Bourke
mac Ulick, and Fargan Acgill mac William Croane, of Emle-
vegger, slain in rebellion ; ½ quarter in Clonkeane, in the barony
of Croshohin, in said co., parcel of the lands of Allen Mac Connel,
of Clomin, in said co., attainted ; the ruined castle of Inver, and
one quarter of land adjacent, and half a cartron in Glanturke, in
said co., parcel of the lands of Edm. boy m'William duff, Rich.
oge M'Dowdall, and Evaran M'Ricard, of Inver, slain in rebellion ;
three quarters of land in the territories of Slught Rowry roe
O Flartie, in the barony of Moycullen, co. Galway, parcel of the
lands of Teige oge O Flartie, of Ahinure, killed in rebellion ;
seven quarters of stony land called. Carrowelewshell Knockin
Oshiloge, and Innishbarkan, Carrowe Killanaloirhis, Carrowe
tkrina in Garinnae, Carrowelstermoyn, Edirtra Auncie, Leter-
mackoe and Mukenaghe Ederdahalle, and Carrowe Nagevannaghe
in Killinkelly, in the barony of Moycullen, co. Galway, parcel
of the lands of the abbey of Annaghmoyne alias Annaghdowne.
All the premises were concealed and detained from the queen's
hands, until by the industry and at the cost of the lessees they
were found to belong to her. To hold for 21 years. Total rent,

1594.   PLANTS—ELIZABETH.

£26 13s. 8d. Provisions *as in* 4939. Recites a letter of the English Privy Council, 26 May, 1592, for Rawson, for a grant which he had not received; and his surrender of the toll of Athlone.—5 June, xxxvi. (Cal. P. R. p. 278.)

5866 (4784.) Lease (under queen's letter, 4 Aug., xxxv.) to Rich. Brett, of Tullocke, co. Meath, gent.; of the lands of Colronan, co. Meath, the rectory of Rathmolian, with the tithes extending to Rathmolian, Focoarton, Molinaghe, Cloncurrie, Colintraughe, Bolin, Tiptynan, Troman, Corballie, Castleton, Rath, and Colder, co. Meath, lands of Killeononcon alias Killeconogon, co. Meath, the rectory of Killeononogon alias Killeononogon, with the tithes extending to Killeononogon, Keranston, Cloghreny, Clonkman, Keylenalyner, Colronan, Kilbarghe, Crossanyston, Mouchewood, Derchewa, Ballyuar, Cloghmorrye, Moystagher, Parktone, Portclaster, Balrobin, and Partan, co. Meath. To hold for 21 years from the determination of 5680. Rent, £42, part in corn. Provisions *as in* 4939. Recites 3680, and assignment from Aylmer to Brett, 14 March, 1590.—8 June, xxxvi.

5867 (4783.) Lease (under queen's letter, 25 Jan., xxxiii.) to Rice ap Hughe, gent., provost marshal of the army; of the tithes of fishing of the river of Carlingeforde, parcel of the rectory of Carlingeford, co. Louth (recites 3142), (rent 40s.); the tithes of Castleringe, Knocksmyll, the grange near Allordeston, and the grange near Mylton, co. Louth (recites 3981) (£7); the tithes of Holmagrange, parcel of the rectory of Holmagrange, the tithes of Balliturkegan and Corballye, parcel of the rectory of Ballylurkegan, the tithes of Clonnyffe, Ballylagkyn, and Ballylstyn, over and above the third part belonging to the vicarage, parcel of the rectory of Clonnyfin Evaghe, co. Down (recites 4788) (£5 5s. 10d.); the tithes of Tullaghes, Dronleake, Milton, Stephanston, Gibbeston Palmer, Nynelyrathe, Ryaghston, Clintonrathe, Gardenston, Tullaghekaillie and Mareton, Tullaghards, Milton beside Tarmonfeighin, and Galrotheston, Kerreston, Priorton, and Newhouse, (recites 5416) (£25 13s. 4d.). To hold for 30 years from the end of the recited leases. Rent as above. Provisions *as in* 4939.—19 June, xxxvi. (Cal. P. R. p. 273.)

5868 (6210.) License to Bartholomew Talbott, gent., prothonotary of the Common Bench; to be absent in England for three months. *No date, (but earlier than succeeding).*

5869 (4749.) Grant to George Robinson, esq.; of the office of prothonotary and keeper of the writs and records of the Common Bench. To hold during good behaviour, with the usual fees.— 2 July, xxxvi. (Cal. P. R. p. 260.)

5870 (4752.) Grant to John Slade, gent.; of the office of chirographer of the Common Bench. To hold during good behaviour, with the usual fees.—2 July, xxxvi. (Cal. P. R. p. 278.)

5871 (4786.) Lease (under queen's letter, 20 March, xxxv.) to capt. John Newton, gent.; of the lands of Killahenie, Ballahenry, Charowyerbagh, Glan, and Kilurecan, co. Kerry, the lands of Tho. mc Rich. mc Riccard Coursey, of Ballenoluher in said co., attainted, containing 4½ quarters or ploughlands. To hold for 31 years. Rent 12s. 10d. He shall not charge coyne or livery. —3 July, xxxvi. (Cal. P. R. p. 278.)

1594.   FIANTS—ELIZABETH.

'5872 (4761.) License to Wm. Fitzwilliam, principal registrar of the
commissioners for ecclesiastical causes, Zachary Pierce, gent.,
chief chamberlain of the Exchequer, and clerk of the crown in
Meath, &c., and Rich. Chichester, controller of the customs in
Drogheda; to be absent in England for 12 months.—6 July,
xxxvi. (Cal. P. R. p. 261.)

5873 (4777.) Lease (under queen's letter, 18 July, xxxiv) to Rich.
Poore, of Poorestowne, co. Tipperary; of the lands of Asantowne,
co. Dublin, Almonston, co. Louth, a messuage in Navan, co.
Meath, and a house and close in Grallaghe, co. Dublin, possessions
of the late hospital of S. John the Baptist, Dublin (recites 5408);
the lands of Beggarye, co. Wexford (recites 3206), lands in Luske,
co. Dublin, the tithes of Byglas, and all customs of Luske, chief
rent of 6s. 8d. by Patr. Finglas for lands in Dulloghe, and 13s. 4d.
by Chr. Capron and Wm. Spencer in Lomolanghe, and a stang of
land in Gremocke, in counties of Meath and Dublin (recites 2694);
lands of Kennaghan, co. Meath (recites 3207), the tithes of
Walterston, Branganston, Ferrans, Dromlargan, Donganston,
Balfeighan, Pierstowne, Ballynoowle, Kilgline, and Padenston,
co. Meath (recites No. 1663), the tithes of lambs and fish of the
rectory of Portraven, co. Dublin (recites 2332); also the lands of
Wotton with 8s. 4d. of custom, and the lands of Moffoarston, co.
Meath, parcel of the possessions of the monastery of Thomascourt,
the lands of Tobber, with common of pasture called the Wards
of Tobber, in the tenure of Ralph Manwaringe, and an old mill,
parcel of the possessions of James viscount Baltinglas, attainted.
To hold for 31 years from the end of the interests in being.
Rent £50 6s. 10d.   Provisions as in 4299.—16 July, xxxvi.
(Cal. P. R. p. 278.)

5874 (6651.) Pardon to John Hardinge, of Barkinge in England.—
30 July, xxxvi.

5875 (6650.) Pardon to Garrott fitz Lewes, of Whitewall, co.
Kilkenny, John Shortall fitz Rice, of Pollistowne, Nele m'Shane
O Brenan in Idoghe, Donogh O Brenan m'Shane, of same, Arlont
Gramt, of Ballyneboly, Robert Shortall, late of Balletrennagh,
Teige O Meagher m'Donell moale, of Roscon, Alexander Grace
fitz Philip, of Glasmare, Walter Barron, late of Goolingston, all
in the co. Kilkenny, Chonor M'Echroe, of Tore in Kilne-
managhe, co. Tipperary, Molaghlin m'Knochor M'Echroe, of
same, Keadagh O Meagher, of Aghnamneare, same co., Wm.
Daton, of Kepaghe, co. Waterford, Peter Grace fitz James, of
Whytewall, co. Kilkenny, James O Quyne, of Kilmanagh, Wm.
Phelan, of the Newe garden, co. Kilkenny, Johanne ny Worren,
of Kilkenny, and More ny Vraddan, of Mollingare.   Provision
for security in co. Kilkenny or Tipperary, and other provisions
as in 5504.   The pardon not to include treasons, coining,
murder, arson, robbery, or rape.—6 Aug., xxxvi.   (Cal. P. R.
p. 278.)

5876 (5968.) Surrender by Robert Harrison, of Dublin; of lands
in the lordship of Moybreeko alias Moybreakre, co. Westmeath,
and others, held under 5860.   (Signed) Robert Harrison.
Dated 9 Aug., xxxvi.   (Cal. P. R. p. 282.)

5877 (4771.) Grant (under queen's letter, 5 July, xxxi.) to Rob.
Harrison, of Dublin; of one ruined messuage built in the Irish

1594.   FIANTS—ELIZABETH.

manner, and land between the wood of Kilmartyn and Belgre,
co. Dublin (rent 6s. 8d.), a cartron of land in Ballynamoylane
by Peirston, co. Westmeath (8s. 10½d.), parcel of the lands of
the house of nuns of the Holy Trinity of Lexmollen; messuages,
a mill, and five carucates of land in Kinard in the lordship
or barony of Moybracko alias Moybreckro, co. Westmeath, a
ruined place where was a weir on the river of Clonaleagh, a
wood called Derfadd, with a sixth part of the red bog beginning at the entrance of the said wood and the water of Ethaye,
and extending between Cloghran and Derfadd, co. Westmeath,
parcel of the possessions of the priory of Tristarnagbe, in said
co. (£8 3s. 8d.); one quarter of land in Ardmoyle, parcel of
the lands of Melaughlen m'Cormock M'Dermott, of Ardmoyle,
in the country called Moylarge, co. Roscommon, attainted
(8s. 10½d.); a cartron or fourth part of a quarter of land in the
country of Threowne alias O Byrne's country, called Coryalyan,
parcel of the lands of Teige roe O Birne, of Clonrealyan, in
said co., attainted (2s. 1½d.); 1½ cartrons in Moyletrangh, in
said co., parcel of the lands of Hugh m'Wm. O Kelly, late of
same, attainted (2s. 1½d.); the site of the ruined cell or chapel
of Killstrynade, co. Mayo, and one small quarter of land adjoining, parcel of the possessions of the late house of canons of the
Holy Trinity in Loghkey, in Moylurge (6s. 8d.); two ruined
castles and nine quarters of land in the islands of Innisheskre,
Innishebofin, and Innishekeaa, in the barony of Irris, co. Mayo,
parcel of the ancient inheritance of the crown of long time
concealed (59s. 6½d.); lands in Drangan in the country of
Mowakery, co. Tipperary, parcel of the lands of John Bourk
fitz Walter, late of Drangan, attainted (20s.); the ruined chapel
or cell called Killamoye, between the mountains called the Cur-
lewe and the Mralewe, in the barony of Tirenagh, with a carucate of land and the tithes appertaining (13s. 4d.), a ruined
church called Kilvegond in same country, with the globe, and
three parts of the tithes extending ordinarily to 1½ coples of
grain when the land is cultivated (7s. 8d.), another ruined
church called Killrasse with the island of Innisheskilleghan,
with lands belonging, and a third part of the tithes which
extend to 1½ coples when the land is cultivated (30s.), the
ruined church of Gewagh alias Shencbo, with the globe and
three parts of the tithes, extending when the land is cultivated
to one cople of grain beyond the stipend of the curate and
other charges (7s.), a third part of Tryem Roebirne, in the
barony of Carbry, co. Sligo (10s.), parcel of the possessions of
the monastery of canons of the Holy Trinity of Loghkee, in
Moylurge; the tithes of corn and hay of Killeighe alias Kilgher
and Almanston, co. Louth, the tithes of Balligander and
Glaspirtoll, Baltra, Newton and Rathe, parish of Termonfeighan,
same co., the tithes of Waltenton, in the parish of Dromynkyn,
co. Louth, parcel of the possessions of the abbey of Lowthe, co.
Louth (£9 15s. 9½d.) To hold for ever, in common socage.
Rent £36 13s. 8d., as above. Recites a previous grant, 5860,
which he had surrendered owing to some inaccuracies and
omissions in the patent. In consideration of his having released a debt of £411 17s., owing to him for victuals supplied

1594.   FIANTS—ELIZABETH.

in the time of the earl of Essex.—10 Aug., xxxvi. (Cal. P. R., p. 288.)

5878 (4779.) Lease (see 5810) to John Lye, of Rathbride, co. Kildare, gent.; of lands of Killelet, and Donarde, co. Dublin, parcel of the lands of James FitzGeralde, attainted; the eighth part of a quarter called the half cartron of Ballynoryewghter, in the barony of Tesquin, co. Galway, parcel of the land of the monastery of Clonkeane; lands of Garrewe, in said barony and co., parcel of the lands of Shane boy m'William m'Shane buy, of Garrewe, attainted; lands of Addergowlbeg, the Rathe, and Growrsleg, in the barony of Downmore, in said co., parcel of the lands of Peirs M'Ferrick, of Adergoulebeg, attainted; one town of land called Ballym'gillsboye, in the barony of Mocullen in said co., parcel of the lands of Thady or Teige m'Moroghe O Flaherde, slain in rebellion; Ballemollen alias Miltowne, Queen's co., parcel of the lands evicted out of the hands of the O Moores, traitors; three carews of land called the Morgans alias the Morergans, co. Limerick, parcel of the lands of John Fitz Geralde alias Desmonde, knt., attainted; a ruined castle and two carews of land in Rath Jordan in said co., parcel of the lands of James m'Garrott duffe Marshall, attainted; three carowmeers of land in Dromlarye, and two called Knockroe and Kilduffe, in said co., parcel of the lands of Donoghe moyle, of Dromlarye, attainted; a ruined castle and land of Kilvehinne in said co., parcel of the lands of Mahowne m'Morogh O Breen, attainted; land in Cloghean and Whitertown, in said co., parcel of the lands of Kenedy M'Brian, attainted; land in the barony of Karkinliahe in said co., which were given to the church of S. Michael, in said barony, contrary to the statute of mortmain; the rectory of Rathreoughe, co. Longford, parcel of the possessions of the priory of Flaris alias Loghanwdle; lands of Ballyoollynae, co. Clare, parcel of the lands of Thadys O Connor alias Teige ne gall, attainted; Knockebealanaforuys and Cradockeneshenaghe in said co., parcel of the lands of Donald m'Henry duff, attainted; Coolworts in said co., parcel of the lands of Brien boy oge, of Cooleworts, attainted; Kilcayte and Moydawe, Skryne, and Kilmedime, co. Roscommon, parcel of the lands of Edm. m'Thomas oge, of Skryne, attainted of felony; land between Lisduller and Clonarcke, in said co., and in Lisduller, in O Naughton's country, parcel of the lands of John or Shane m'Melaughlen moyle O Naughton, of Lisduller, attainted. To hold for 60 years. Rent, £7 5s. 8¼d. Not to charge coyne or livery.—10 Aug., xxxvi.

5879 (5749.) Fragment of commission for ecclesiastical causes containing the names of [Tho.] Norreis, knt., vice president of [Munster], Nich. bishop of Ardath, sir Warham [Sentleger], Jeam Smithes, chief justice of Munster, [Rich.] Beacon, esq., attorney of the province, John Fitz Edmunds, Arthur Hide, Phane Beacher, esq., the dean of Roscarbry, Mr. Patr. Gallw[ay], Stephen Waters, and James Trant. Recites a former commission including the names of John, archbishop of Armagh, [T. earl of Ormond] high treasurer, [   ] Fearnes, John, bishop of Kilmore, sir Rob. Dill[on], [sir E] Waterhouse, sir Tho. [   ] [   ] Brabazon, esq., Geoffrey

1594.   FIANTS—ELIZABETH.

Fen[ton], [A.] Forth doctor of laws, [   ] of S.
Patricks, Henry [   ] Kilkenny for the
time being.—[   ]*

5880 (5831.) Commission to Ambrose Forth, LL.D., and Edward
Edgworth, preacher of the word of God ; to be additional delegates for the purpose stated in 5278. In consequence of delay in
the execution of the former commission.—[   ]

5881 (6190). Commission to Henry Moyle, sheriff of the county
Cork ; to execute martial law in that county, as in 219.—No date.

5882 (6200.) Commission to Henry Duke, gent., sheriff of the
King's county ; to execute martial law in that county, as in
219.—No date.

5883 (6357.) Commission to the sheriff of the county of Wexford ;
to execute martial law in that county, as in 218. Torn.—Date
destroyed.

5884 (6211.) Commission to John Forster, mayor of Dublin, Edward
Fitz Symons, serjeant at laws, Charles Calthrop, attorney general,
George Delves, esq., George Taylor, recorder of Dublin, and
Robert Fowle, esq. ; to make inquisition of all felonies and
robberies committed by Thomas Wollies, of Dublin, yeoman,
within the county of the city of Dublin.—No date.

5885 (6180.) Pardon to Robert Harpoole, gent., constable of the
castle of Catherlagh, and Thady M'ne Mye, horseman.—No date.

5886 (6183.) Pardon to Laurence Hamonde, of Trym, gent., James
Walshe, of Clonard, co. Meath, gent., George Lull, of Ballensvany,
co. Meath, and Rory Eynos, of Dallestowne, co. Meath, gent.—
No date.

5887 (6202.) Pardon to Laughlen O Hanlye, of Tyn Iber, Brian
O Hanlie, of the same, Edmund dorroghe m'Teige balaghe, of
Clanmore, Connor arann O Hanlie, of Killnerton, Teige oge
m'Teige ballaghs O Hanlie, Donnogh reogh O Hanlie, of Aghe
Irim, Fargananim O Hanlie, of same, Ownye m'Mortaghe
O Hanlie, of Coultobarre, Hugh m'Mortagh, of same, Mortaghe
M'Teige, of Cloencassill, Wm. carraghe O Hanlye, of Caro-
renghe, Rcrye renghe, of same, Malaughlen glass, of same, Hugh
M'Gillegroome, of Lavalmim, Cormock reogh M'Hughe, of
Killegroome, Wm. Makgarrohan, of Anghu Irim, Bowrio Bob,
of Cowlaughten, Donnell ballaugh O Hanlie, of Aughutrins,
Ferdorraugh O Hanlie, of same, Malaughlen duff O Hanlie, of
Cloennalglas, Connor ballagh O Hanlie, of same, Malaughlen
M'Laughlen, of Loualanan, Melaughlen madder O Hanlie, of
Logobben, Edmund reogh O Hanlie, of Karrowban, Shane ge
O Hanlie, of Clonshaare, Teige m'Rorie balloghe O Hanlie,
Melaughlen m'Donnough duff, of Galliggha, Rorie oge m'Rorie
grane, of Carroward, Rory M'Teige, of Clonkin, Hugh m'Rorie
grane, of Cloenreddowne, Edmund m'Hugh carraghe, of Clonin-
aulglas, Donnogh grane O Hanlie, of Carrokrin, Owan boy
O Hanlie, of Carrobans, Donnogh O Mortin, of Balladuff, Shane
m'Gillegroome O Hanleie, Dultaghe m'Brian M'Branon, Connor
grane m'Brian, Teige duff M'Branan, Alstrina ny Brannan, of
Caroard, Rorie O Howins, of Cloenrebrackin, Dervorgill ny

---

* This and 10 following fiants, without dates, are signed by Sir William Fitz Wylliam
as lord deputy, and are therefore not later than 11 August, 1594, when his successor,
Sir William Russell, was sworn in.

s

Conela, of Trien reade, Shane Vin, of Carruward, Owen O Dowan, of Clonrehracken, Filagh O Fillo, of Clouulrian, Brian O Gibbelan, of same, Cormuck m'Dumulto M'Gannlele, Rorie karraghe M'Ganleie, Uah reaghis ny Dumultaghe, of Clonfree, Dualtaghe O Narie, of Killeniakist, Hugh M'Gerrott, of Clonivurman, Donnell m'William M'Brenan, and Cateline ny Carleie, of Skrevoge, co. Roscommon; for offences committed before 24 June, 1590. Provision for submission as 4943. Excluding from pardon, intrusion into crown lands or debts to the crown.—*No date.*

5888 (6203.) Pardon to Hugh Magulro, knt., Conner m'Cahill O Farrell, of Duffolenny, horseman, Thomas, Teige, and Hugh m'Cahill O Farrall, of the same, horsemen, Melaghlin m'Donill O Farrall, Edmund m'Convucke O Farrall, and Hugh m'Geralte O Farrall, of the same, Phelim m'Donell O Farrall, Forderaughe moyle m'Convuck O Farrall, of same, Gerald m'Shan O Farrall, of Cully, Thomas Balfe O Cowlinn, Shane bane O Courlanne and Gillernowe O Conolans, of same, Hobbert m'James M'Cormooke, of Ballicowe, and Thomas O Burder, of Teaghsim, karns, Donnowgh m'Hobert oge O Ferrall, horseman, Tirlagh m'Kedoghe O Furrall, of Shellyane, gent., Thomas O Cassie, of Clondarra, scholar, Donnogh O Donolan, of Raothage, kern, Gerald O Farrall, of Curtownanboggan, gent., Dermott m'Owan knighte M'Cormoucks, of Mortin, kern, Padrykins O Coyn, Connor m'Wm. O Farrall, Rossi and Shane m'Connor O Farrall, Shane m'Thomas O Farrall, Convacke O Coyne, of Carne, Hobert m'Edmond O Farrall, of Brenowne, gent, Connor m'Hughe M'Gaffry, of Palyst, Dermot m'Ferdorraghe M'Brownan, of Clonfinlag, freeholder, Conn m'Hughe oge M'Bronan, of same, kern, Shane m'Donowgh M'Brownan, of Cloynerany, stockagh, Thady m'Ferrall M'Brownan, of Palishclonfrey, kern, Cormack m'Wm. M'Brownan, of Portnern, kern, Melaghlin M'Anloghie, of Clonoony, stokaghe, Cormack M'Andowalty, of same, kern, Conn M'Andowalty, of Cloynfinglagh, kern, Cormack O Downever, of Cloynfinglaghe, scholar, Mullmory O Mulconary, of same, Moyllyns O Mulonary, of Killreagho, Loghtney O Mulconary, of the same, Arrhally m'Caoh M'Multolly of Oldins, Mathe Riane, of Clonealdy, co. Tipperary, husbandman, Rori O Mulriany, of Oughterisinan, Donald O Tuogher, husbandman, Thady O Tuogher, Sayeffe wife of O Toughor, Donowgh fitz Cormack, of Ballynaclaythe, James fytz (   ), of Killcorgan, Hugh M'Shana, Owen M'Sheane, and Malaghlin M'Shane, of same, Owen Duffi fytz Owen, of Clonny, Donald roe fytz Teige, of Cloinleyne, Malaghlin O Durry, of Corry, husbandman, Patrick Winterford, of Killkindon, husbandman, and Brian m'Edmonde O Farrall, of Lisduffe, gent.; for offences committed before 26 June, xxxii. Provision for submission as in 4948.—*No date.*

5889 (6363.) Pardon to Donell m'Donogh Y Swllivane, of Barehaven, Teig m'Donell ny killy, Edmund m'Dierby Cartie, and John Hill, of same, Donell m'Teig M'Kenealis, of Caribrie, Donogh m'Donell M'Owen, Gwiloisie oni Cantie alias Oni Cantre, of same, Morris Sippell, of Roche's country, Redmund bwy Roch, of same, Philip bwy O Coghlane, of Kenale, Thomas Fitz Edmond, of Cloine, husbandman, Done m'Owen Y Cassidigh, of Muskrie,

1594.   FIANTS—ELIZABETH.

Nicholas Stanton, of Imokellie, Katharine Rivans, of same, Edmund fitz John Barrie, of Corrabie, Conoghor m'Teige Y Hologhane, of Berehaven, John fitz David fitz James Barrie, of Barries country, James fitz Gerald fitz Richard, of the same, Wm. fitz Nicholas Stanke, of Carrabie, and John oge O'Tliallihia, of Imokellio. Provision for security as in 4943. The pardon shall not include any murder, burglary, arson, or intrusion into crown lands; and shall not extinguish any forfeiture of their lands. Crimes committed before 16 Nov., xxxii. only, pardoned. —*Not dated.*

5890 (4756.) Grant (under queen's letter, 29 March, xxxvi.) to Wm. Saxei, esq.; of the office of chief justice in the province of Munster. To hold during pleasure, with such fees as Jesse Smithes had.—13 Aug., xxxvi. (Cal. P. R., p. 281.)

5891 (4766.) Commission to Tho., earl of Ormond and Ossory, high English. treasurer; to be general and chief leader of the forces in the counties Wexford, Kilkenny, Queen's, Catharlagh, Kildare, and Dublin, and elsewhere in the province of Leinster, during the absence of the deputy from the county Dublin. With power to pursue with fire and sword any who openly rebel; to raise and command the inhabitants; to treat with rebels and grant protections; to execute martial law; to command any subjects to remain in their several counties with such forces as he shall direct for their defence at their own charges; to take man's meat and horse meat without oppression, paying ready money at the queen's prices; to impress horses, cart, and drivers; and do all other things for the furtherance of the queen's service; also to wage espials and messengers. Recites that the deputy sir Wm. Russell had resolved to repair into Ulster with such of the army as were needful; and that the evil disposed persons bordering on the said counties—Faagh m'Hugh and his sons, Walter reogh alias Fitz Gerrat, and the sons of the late traitor Rory oge, and of Peirs Grace—might be emboldened by his absence to rise. —15 Aug., xxxvi. (Cal. P. R., p. 281.)

5892 (4765.) Commission to Adam, archbishop of Dublin and English. chancellor, Tho., bishop of Meath, sir Wm. Weston, knt., chief justice of the Common Pleas, sir Rob. Napper, knt., chief baron, and sir Anthony St. Leger, knt., master of the rolls; to hear and determine all such causes as may arise in the province of Leinster, and give such directions for civil government as is usually done by the deputy and council at the council table, during the absence of the deputy out of the county Dublin. Not to abridge the authority of martial government granted to the earl of Ormond by 5891.—18 Aug., xxxvi. (Cal. P. R., p. 282.)

5893 (4757.) Grant (under queen's letter, 15 June, xxxvi.) to captain Henry Dockwray; of the office of constable of the castle of Dongarvan, co. Waterford. To hold for life so long as it is thought expedient to retain a ward there; with a fee of 4s. a day for himself, 6d. a day for each of three archers, and 8d. a day for each of fifteen footmen; with such other profits and authorities as Anthony Hungerford had. He shall maintain the castle by the fines levied within the liberty. Not to be removed, as in 4976.—20 Sept., xxxvi. (Cal. P. R., p. 280.)

5894 (4762.) Livery to William, son and hair of Donald Ryan, of Solloghod, in the co. of the cross of Tipperary. Saving the

R 2

benefit of a recognizance for payment of £25 by said William and Dermot Rian. Fine £12.—2 Oct., xxxvi.

5895 (5597.) License to Robert Harpoole, of Catherlogh gent.; to English. alien to Walter Harpoole, dean of Leighlen, Robert Bowen, of Ballinslam, gent., and John Hovenden, of Ballefile, the grange of Kilmagobocke alias the Monkes graunge, Queen's co., with the tithe, held under 3164. To be held to the use of Grane, wife of Robert Harpoole, remainder to his heirs. Fine 16s.— 2 Oct., xxxvi. (Cal. P. R., p. 283.)

5896 (4787.) Lease (under commission, 10 May, xxxvi.) to John English. Mealings, of Drogheda, gent.; of the customs of the port of Drogheda (the import of wines excepted). To hold for 21 years. Rent £104 2s. 1½d. He shall not alien without license except to persons of English nation. He shall enroll the lease in the Auditor General's office within 4 months.—16 Oct., xxxvi (Cal. P. R., p. 290.)

5897 (4755.) Grant to Wm. Harpoole, gent.; of the office of constable of the castle of Catherloghe, co. Carlow; with ten footmen for its defence, also a fee of £20 a year, and 8d. a day for each of the footman. To hold during good behaviour, with all other profits which his father Rob. Harpoole had in the same office. Not to be removed, as in 4976.—21 Oct., xxxvi. (Cal. P. R., p. 283.)

5898 (4753.) Grant to John Williams, gent.; of the office of marshal English. or gaoler of the High Court Ecclesiastical and to the high commissioners in those causes. To hold during good behaviour, with the usual fees. "Given free for that the patentee is my lord chancellor's man."—23 Oct., xxxvi. (Cal. P. R., p. 290.)

5899 (4754.) Grant to Wm. Synnot, of Ballynra, in the Morres, co. Wexford, esq.; of the office of justice of the liberty of Wexford. To hold during good behaviour, with such fees as George Dormer had.—8 Nov., xxxvi. (Cal. P. R., p. 283.)

5900 (4758.) Grant to Wm. Clercke, knt.; of a pension of 10s. English a day, vacant by death of Brian Fitzwilliams, esq. To hold for life, as B. Fitzwilliams or Wm. Collier, knt., enjoyed it. In consideration of his having come to Ireland with the lord deputy Russell at his own expense and maintained 10 horses and many servants prepared to subjugate the Irish enemies.—14 Nov., xxxvi. (Cal. P. R., p. 283.)

5901 (4834.) Livery to Ullic de Burgoe alias Rourke, earl of Clanrickard, son and heir of Rich. de Burgoe, knt., late earl of Clanrickard and baron of Dunkyllen. Fine £81 5s. 2d. English.— 26 Nov., xxxvii. (Cal. P. R., p. 304.)

Attached is an extent of his lands as appeared by an office taken xxvi. Eliz., viz.:

The manors of Loghrioghe, Dunkilline, Leotrim, Clare, and Cloncastle, the castles of Clandagowe with two quarters of land, Portamna with two, Ballynailo 1, Kilmacray 1, Leckaghfine 2, Balladugaine 3, Ballatarry 3, Kilcolgan 5, Bealanehowly 1, Rathgurgine 4, Twolobane 2, Moyne 6, Lisharvaflane 2, two quarters called Quillaghnedotoske, the castles of Monydufe with two quarters, Feartamore 4, Ardraghen 3, Corrofynny 7, Oranmore 4, the lands of the Beaghe containing four quarters, Layragh 4, Loghoutra 4, Ballyurname and Kilratcruo 4, Ballaahrue 2, Tuanentanan ½, Stradbally and Twoyne 4, Culynie 3, Ducastle ¼, the lands of Moyntarduwilla 1, Monymore 1, Lismeckanan 2, Oregnementa 2; all these are valued at £61 5s. 2d. Irish; a chief rent of 20 marks sterling out of the country of Montermoruho, 12 marks out of the country of Clonconway, 6 marks out of the territory of Gnowbeg in the country of the O Flartis, 7 marks out of the territory of Oreaghmoyle alias M'Tibbotts land. The whole country of Clanrickard beyond the other usual services in cows and money, when well cultivated and inhabited (which it was not at the time of the inquisition) is valued at £300 sterling.

5902 (4805.) Grant to Lodowicke Briskett, esq.; of the office of English clerk of the casualties, with power to levy estreats, fines, forfeitures, and recognizances, accruing in the courts of Star Chamber, Chancery, Chief Place, Common Pleas, and Exchequer, or before any justices of Assize, or in anyway happening in the provinces of Munster, Connaght, and Ulster, and all other casualties. To hold during good behaviour, with an allowance of 12d. in the pound for the sums recovered by him. Recites 3578.—28 Nov., xxxvii. (Cal. P. R. p. 304).

5903 (5953.) Surrender by Conoghor O Kallaghan, alias O Kallaghan, of Dromynyne, co. Cork, gent.; of the castle and land of Clomyne, co. Cork, containing 4½ carucates, viz., Gortmoore, Dromrahye, Kylewoy, Koolekiltyh, Nymonane; the castle and lands of Dromynyne 2 carucates, viz., Kilstany, Kilsvellen, Kilonowe, Dowkile, Kiltylane, Itallord, Knocknymonye, Kilebeg, and Kilecolman; the castle and lands of Dromare, Kilepatricke, Carrygklynye, Knockycairg, Knockaney, Narroure, Shanyvyaloid, Byalahabwy, and Curwillane, 2 car.; the lands of Kilecougtoragh, Dromhane, Coarryneyvesye, 3 car.; Kilevyaladae 1 car.; 3 carucates in Scarrough with appurtenances, viz., the quarter of Scarrowe, Kileknocke Igownay, Brittas, Cameraure, and Kileverehurte; 3 car. in Gortvelier, Linyvogboly, Lackygarragh, Kilitraugh, Kiloutraugh, and Cappengyrryu; 1 car. in the Rantyer; 3 car. in Kilecascane, Dromecurnyre, Lirmohilis, Kilerusse, and Gurtinarda; ½ car. in Rathebeg and Rathmoore; 8 car. in Nikippagbe, Gortinilurahalye, Kudllynaghane manye; ½ car. in Clonytinybeg, and Clonitynymoore; ½ car in Roskyne; ¼ car. in Knockyveraghane; ½ car. in Geithrynissagh; 1 car. in Kilegobanet; Gartzrowe containing 3 carucates, viz., Dromfise, Kilegortroe, Kilachobanet, Gortnygadderye and Knolaryaye; the Pallace containing 2 car. viz., Gortenydowny and Farredorisse; 1 car. in Gortboffynny, and Geyry-Inskahag; Rathcomane containing 3 car. viz., Trelair Tynytonyh, Gornynagh, Kileaskyth, and Kilecuranade; 2 car. in Gortnygrusse; 1 car. in Kilcolman; 2 car. in Bantier Ieraghe, Formule, and Knockynanytadyry; 1 car. in Kilepeadir; ½ car. in Drome Hastall, Tyhyngyaryh, and Kilerowe; 3 car. in Ballym'marrougho; 1 car. in Rullyhier; 1½ car. in Gortnychonolye, Garrym'owny, Kilemihill, and Rallynyfehye; and Kilecrany, 1 car.; all in Poble I Callaghan, co. Cork, extending from Glanda Ieyghe and Molyne Intrynnane, on the west, to the water of Clyeslagh, Bearnynymohir, Bearny Inolynowe on the east, and from Porlddiih and Bear Icanhin, on the south, to the foss of Ballynowe on the north. *Signed*

1594.   FIANTS—ELIZABETH.

Conogho' o Kallaghan.—*Dated* 2 Dec., xxxvii. (Cal. P. R.
p. 835.)

5904 (4806) Livery to Isaac, son and heir of Nich. White, late of
Rathleige, Queen's co. Fine 88s. 9d.—6 Dec., xxxvii.

5905 (4885) Livery to Thomas, son and heir of Jophiphus or
Jophesus George, late of Togher, Queen's co., gent. Fine £3.
—6 Dec., xxxvii. (Cal. P. R. p. 886.)
Attached is an extent of lands of Tower alias Togher.

5906 (4836) Livery to Donald, son and heir of Morragh M'Eboy,
late of Balladin, Queen's co., gent. Fine 40s.—6 Dec., xxxvii.
(Cal. P. R. p. 804.)
Attached is an extent of the lands of Ballyfynn.

5907 (4829) Grant (under queen's letter, 9 Aug., xxxvii.) to Edm.
fitz John oge Gibbon de Garraldin, called the White Knight; of
half a carucate of land in Garrynchonie, half a carucate in Ballin-
wilye, half a carucate in Rathenswhitaghe, half a carucate in
Cleighaghe, half a carucate in Ballincarrowne, the seventh of a
carucate in Rathphillipp, one carucate in Killenam, and one
carucate in Ballingoosighe, co. Limerick; which were possessions
of John Fitz Gibbon de Gerrald alias John og fitz John Gibbon,
late of Michelston, co. Cork, alias the White Knight, father of
said Edmond, attainted. To hold in tail male, by the service of
a fortieth part of a knight's fee. Rent 34s. ¼d.—6 Dec., xxxvii.
(Cal. P. R. p. 886.)

5908 (4825.) Grant (under queen's letter, 4 March, xxxiv.) to
Conoghor O Callaghan, alias O Callaghan, of Drominine, co. Cork,
gent.; of all the castles, lands and tenements in co. Cork which
have come to the queen's hands by his charter of surrender
(5903). To hold for ever, by the service of a twentieth part of
a knight's fee. Rent 40s. Reserving any composition imposed
or to be imposed by the council of Ireland. Provided that the
grant shall not prejudice the rights of other persons as found by
an inquisition taken at Moallo, co. Cork, 25th October, 1594. In
consideration of the reserved rent and composition, O Callaghan
is discharged from liability to Irish exactions, cesses, bonaght or
other demands of the crown.—7 Dec., xxxvii. (Cal. P. R., p. 886.)

5909 (5979.) Surrender by John Linche alias Turcke; of the office
of one of the pursuivants at arms (granted by 4412). The reversion of which belongs to Egidius (Gyles) Standley.—Dated 8 Dec.,
xxxvii. (Cal. P. R., p. 336.)

5910 (4798.) Grant to Gyles Stanley, gent.; of the office of one of
the pursuivants at arms. To hold during good behaviour, with
a fee of 12d. a day, and all profits as John Lynch had. Recites
4412 and its surrender (5909) in pursuance of an agreement with
the present grantee; Lynch having become incapacitated by ill-
health.—11 Dec., xxxvii. (Cal. P. R., p. 336.)

5911 (4845.) Lease (under queen's letter, 30 June, xxxv.) to Lodovick
Briskett, esq.; of the site and possessions of the abbey of Ballen-
droghod alias Ballendrett, *as in* 3028 (recites 3028); the premises
in the castle ditch, Dublin, leased in 5175 (recites 5175); the
site of the house of friars of Kilconell with Twohall O Donellan's
chapel, and land belonging to the house, co. Galway, 65 ash trees
reserved for the repair of the houses (recites 4878); the castle of
Castallbarrie in the barony of Carra with 10 quarters of land,

1594.   FIANTS—ELIZABETH.

viz. : six quarters of land lying near the castle, one quarter
called Cleggar, and three quarters in Sleowynmy, possessions of
Edm. Bourke, of Castellbarrie, co. Mayo, attainted (recites 5256);
a castle or gate on the north side of Athlone, with 80 feet of
foundation or loft adjoining, part of the queen's ancient inheritance (recites 4220); the castle and town of Beallicke with eight
free quarters of land in the barony of Tireawly, viz. : one quarter
adjoining Beallick, Carrowneoollin, Carrowferren[oakelangby],
Leigh Carrow Clonde Ellis Beallick, Leigh Carrow Knoigin, Leigh
Carrow ferrenalighto Moiliui Beallick, Leigh Carrow Cowneils,
Carrow Kidliagbe, Liagh Carrow Breoklone, Aghleighe Carrow
garrowe Crossmullen, Acloighe Carrow Carrowaloughe, one
quarter in the barony of Kilmean called Ballikinlaghe, possessions of Theobald Bourke, attainted; the ruined castle called
Clonyn with half a quarter of land adjoining the castle called
Clonekill, half a quarter called Bunymell, two quarters called
Leighbaellinecloughe, three quarters in and adjoining Limonine,
half a quarter called Leigh Carrowroughan, in the barony of
Carra, possessions of Ferreigh M'Conell, of Clouyn, attainted, in
co. Mayo; one quarter of land with the tithes called Ballohimon,
parcel of the possessions of the monastery of Ballintobber,
co. Mayo; one quarter in Rathcarrin in the barony of Kilmean,
parcel of the possessions of Richard and John m'Edmond Faoggie,
attainted; half a quarter called Leigh Carrow Carrovagan, two-
fifth parts of a cartron in Carronerahin, possessions of Charles
and John M'Androw, of Barco, in the barony of Tireawly,
attainted; one cartron in Tullaghbegan, parcel of the possessions of
Gilleduffe O Clerie, attainted (recites 5865); Leigh Carrowbe-
goughall and other lands in 5610 (recites 5610); one quarter of land
in Ballyviltin alias Ballevickensuny, parcel of the lands of Gerald
m'Hubert boy O Ferall, attainted, in co. Longford (recites 3439);
the tithes of the rectory of Palmerston, co. Dublin (recites
4012); the ruinous castle and lands of Loggtreyny alias Lough-
treiney, parcel of the possessions of James viscount Baltinglas,
attainted, co. Dublin (recites 4122); three messuages with gardens and lands in Kilcullen, parcel of the possessions of David
Sutton, attainted, in co. Kildare (leased to Gerrot Sutton, esq.,
deceased, and Dermot O Birne, clerk, by indenture dated
18 May, 1574, for 31 years). To hold for 50 years from
the end of existing interests. Rent £47 10s. 3¼d. He shall
not charge coyne or livery. He shall enroll the lease in
the Auditor-General's office within 4 months. Much obliterated.
—13 Dec., xxxvii. (Cal. P. R., p. 303.)

5912 (4819.) Grant (under the queen's letter, 1 July, xxxi.) to Edm.
Barret, gent.; of the town of Ballaloghran owghter and Balli-
loghran Eaghter, one carucate, parcel of the lands of Maurice
fitz Gerald oge Stacke, of Ballilogbran, co. Kerry, attainted (rent
2s. 6d.); Killebeny and Gortreshanahe, 1 carucate, parcel of the
lands of Wm. oge Bonan alias Bonanaghe, of Killebeny, attainted
(2s. 6d.); Derico and Knockmenan ¼ carucate, parcel of the
lands of John Fitz Morice, of Derico, attainted (10d.); Balli-
hawregan, Banegaran, Mynemore, and Gortcardo, 2 carucates,
and three messuages with gardens in Ratowe, parcel of the lands
of Edm. M'Kierrie, alias M'Kierrie, of Rallihawregan, attainted
(5s. 6d.); Craignagihe, ¼ carucate, the land of Rob. Fitz Gerrot

1594.   FIANTS—ELIZABETH.

of Graignegihe, attainted (10d.); Galie, Carowknock, Cowikeraghe, Ballidmoughe, Cowlard, the Inses, Kilkerevan, Dromore, Tully-more, Gloris, Carowbloughe, Dyrryumloght, and Kiltean, 9 carucates, lands of Tho. M'Kilgod, chief of his nation, of Galie in said co., slain in rebellion (22s. 6d.); Cloghanshenan, ½ carucate, lands of Gerald M'Morice and Nich. M'Morice, of Cloghanshenan, attainted (16d.); Downalins Ballinrealighe, Trisnieraghe, Kilvena, Moate, Illananen, Inshehanrie, Fowran, and Ballim'gerrot, 6 carucates, lands of Edm. M'James, of Confeali, attainted (15s.); Mynechmen ½ carucate, land of Rob. Fits Morice, of Mynecho-nan, attainted (10d.); Balligoddran, Oreggan, and Ballim'Jordan, 5 carucates, lands of Shane m'Thomas ne Manowe, of Balligoddran, attainted (12s. 6d.); Gortsvaher, Gortnegaraghe, Cowle, Farinsts, and Kilmolean, ¼ carucate, and three messuages in Ratowe, lands of Teige oge O Downy, Morice m'Hugh O Downy, and Rory O Downy, of Gortevohur, in said co., attainted (20d.); Rathkeny, Ballylahive, Darinabe, Robertston, and Ballicvin, 7 carucates, lands of Shane oge m'Shane M'Thomas, of Kilfynorighe, in said co., attainted (17s. 6d.); Ballinorig and Garigankighe, 2½ caru-cates, lands of John fits Edm. Fitz Ullick, of Ballinorig, in said co., attainted (5s. 8d.); Dromarien and Knockmaghe, 1¼ carucate, lands of Nich. m'Shane Piers, of those places, attainted (3s. 9d.); Fynallymore, Ballyncrahe, Ballynylancnssere, and Ballihumickin, 3 carucates, lands of Tho. Browne, of Kilkellan, attainted (10s.); Kilgolbin, 1½ carucates, lands of John e tarmyn, of Kilgolbin, attainted (3s. 9d.); Ballilongan 1 carucate, lands of Wm. kisgte Stacke, of Ballilongan, in said co., attainted (2s. 8d.); Cowlam-lygher 1 carucate, lands of Eneas m'Moroughe M'Oraghe, of Cowlamligher, attainted (2s. 6d.); Killarid or Killaridie 1 caru-cate, a third part of Fynowick called Iphan, ½ carucate, lands of James M'Morice, of Killaridi, attainted (3s. 4d.); Knockaniheige 2 carucates, lands of Edm. M'Morice, of Knockaniheige, in said co., attainted (5s.); Dromorrowne 2 carucates, lands of James M'Edmond, of Ballinccart, attainted (3s.); 2 carucates in Irry-more, lands of John M'Thomas, of Irrymore, said co., attainted (5s.); also Ballikuff (10s.), Downe (16s.), Closcollan (7s. 6d.), in the queen's hands by a statute of 3 and 4 Ph. and Mary. To hold for ever, in free socage. Rent £8 2s. 6d., distributed as above. Conditions similar to 474 are added for the lands in Queen's co., (tenure and alienation omitted).—16 [Dec.], xxxvii. (Cal. P. R. p. 333.) ·

1594–5.

5913 (4798.) Grant to Stephen Jennings, gent.; of the office of **English** clerk general of the works. To hold during good behaviour, with the usual fees. Not to be removed, as in 4976.—10 Jan., xxxvii. (Cal. P. R. p. 337.)

5914 (4608) Pardon to Dermott Ower, of Clanmore, co. Carlow, condemned at the sessions at the Nass, for the theft of a garran, of the goods of Donill O Heverin, of Moone, co. Kildare. It having soon after been proved that the horse belonged to Dermott himself.—1 Feb., xxxvii. (Cal. P. R. p. 311.)

5915 (4851.) Commission to Tho., earl of Ormonde and Ossory, high **English** treasurer, Donell, earl of Clancar, sir Tho. Norris, knt., vice-president of Mounster, John, bishop of Limerick, Wm., bishop

1594–5.   FIANTS—ELIZABETH.

of Corke, Nich., bishop of Arderth, tho chief and second justices of the said province for the time being, Rich. Beacon, esq., Geo. Thornston, provost marshal of Mounster, Edw. Gray, Francis Berkelie, Charles Herbert, esquires, the mayor of Limerick, James Trant fitz Morrice, of the Dingan, the archdeacon of Arderth now being, Henry Glover, M.A., and John Orosbie, preacher; to be commissioners for ecclesiastical causes in the dioceses of Limericke, Corke, Cloana, Roscarbery, Arderth, and Achadew, with powers as in 5834. "This fiant is according to the late fiant made for the diocese of Limerick and Cork, saving that there is added thereunto the diocese of Arderth in Kerry, and the bishop thereof, and other commissioners."—11 Feb., xxxvii.

5916 (4791.) Grant (under queen's letter, 4 Feb., xxxvii,) to Rob. Dillon, knt., one of the privy council; of the office of chief justice of the Common Bench. To hold during pleasure, with such fees as Wm. Weston, deceased, had. Recites that he had formerly held the office.—15 March, xxxvii. (Cal. P. R. p. 332.)

5917 (4797.) Grant to Charles Huett, of Dublin, gent.; of the office of general controller of the custom on wines in the ports of Dublin, Waterford, Limerick, Cork, Drogheda, Galway, Yoghill, Wexford, Rosse in co. Wexford, Kinsale, Carrickfergus, Dungarvan, Dundalk, Carlingford, Sligo, and Dingle alias Dingleneqria. To hold during good behaviour, with such fees as Lodovic Briskett had. Not to be removed, as in 4976. Recites 4333, and its surrender.—30 March, xxxvii. (Cal. P. R., p. 338.)

1595.

5918 (4796.) Grant to Wm. Leverst, gent.; of the office of one of the pursuivants and the name Athloon. To hold during good behaviour, with a fee of £10 English a year. Recites 3240, and its surrender 5786 for the purpose of this grant.—28 March, xxxvii. (Cal. P. R., p. 338.)

5919 (4805 a.) Grant to Chr. Berfords, long time a clark in the English court of Chancery; of the office of clerk and engrosser unto the seal, of all original writs whereby any courts shall be authorised to hold plea. To hold during good behaviour, with the accustomed fees. Not to be removed, as in 4976. Recites 3306, and its surrender.—1 April, xxxvii. (Cal. P. R., p. 31L.)

5920 (4837.) Livery to James Dillon, of Moymet, co. Meath, esq., son and heir of Lucas Dillon, knt., late chief baron. Fine, £100 sterling, and £15 for pardon of alienation and intrusions.—8 April, xxxvii. (Cal. P. R., p. 337.)

5921 (4794.) Grant to Wm. Robinson, esq.; of the office of attorney general of the province of Munster. To hold during pleasure, with such fees as Rich. Beacon or John Ashfield had.—9 April, xxxvii. (Cal. P. R., p. 337.)

5922 (5880.) Memorandum of the surrender by Wm. Colgrave at Curraghboy, co. Roscommon, of the office of one of the pursuivants commonly called Athlone.—Dated 15 April, xxxvii.

Attached is a commission, dated 22 March, xxxvii, to Tho. Dillon, chief justice of Connaught, and Gerald Commerford, queen's attorney of that province, to accept the surrender. (Cal. P. R., p. 337–8.)

1595.   PLANTS—ELIZABETH.

5923 (4838.) Livery to Maurice, son and heir of Patr. Browne, late of Huristowne, co. Waterford, gent. Fine, 50s. sterling. "The intrusion whereof was granted unto Steven Smyth, gent. as appeareth by a custodiam under the Exchequer seal."—8 May, xxxvii. (Cal. P. R., p. 841.)

5924 (4795.) License to Wm. Englande, of Kilcocks, co. Kildare; to erect and use a tan house in Kilcock, under the statute 11 Eliz.; also to make and sell aqua vitae there; during his life. Recites that he had a license for a tan house in the time of sir H. Sydney's government, which license was burned.—21 May, xxxvii. (Cal. P. R., p. 837.)

5925 (4827.) License to Wm. Phillippa, esq., clerk of the hanaper, and clerk of the crown in Chancery; to be absent in England for two years.—22 May, xxxvii. (Cal. P. R., p. 332.)

5926 (4839.) Livery to Robert, son and heir of John Whitney, of the Sheane, Queen's co., gent. Fine, £5 sterling.—24 May, xxxvii. (Cal. P. R., p. 841.)

5927 (4844.) Livery to George Hetherington, of Tullye, Queen's co., son and heir of Patrick Hetherington, late of same, gent. Fine, 20s.—24 May, xxxvii. (Cal. P. R., p. 311.)

5928 (4811.) Commission to sir Warham St. Leger, knt., the mayor of Corke, Philip Goulde, archdeacon of Corke, the mayor of Youghall, the sovereign of Kinsalle, and Henry Goldfinch, esq.; to be commissioners associate and adjoined to the high commission of 11 Feb. last (5915), for the dioceses of Cork, Cloane, and Rossonbria.—28 May, xxxvii.

5929 (4792.) Grant to Rob. Bowan, gent.; of the office of provost marshal of the province of Leynster, and the counties of East-meath and Westmeath. To hold during pleasure, with a fee of 2s. 3d. sterling a day. With the leading of six horsemen, at 9d. a day each.—3 June, xxxvii. (Cal. P. R., p. 332.)

5930 (4832.) Livery to Agnes Salsbury alias Stanley, one of the sisters and co-heirs of Henry Stanley, late of Crosshall, co. Lancaster, esq.; of a moiety of his lands. Recites an inquisition, 16 March, xxxiv., finding that he was seised of the lands of Glaskearne, co. Westmeath, and that Thomas, son and heir of Rob. Hesketh, who married one of the sisters of Henry, and Agnes Salsbury the other sister, were his co-heirs. Fine £13. —3 June, xxxvii.

5931 (4822.) Grant (under queen's letter, 3 Feb., xxx.), to Wm. Browne, of Malrankan, co. Wexford, esq.; of the castle of Pallsys, and the lands of Pallsys, Cloudstgarmoyle, Clonsgawnaghe, Garrymore, Cappoughe, Clonemore, and Cloncarraghe, Queen's co., as fully as John Newton, Anthony Hungerforde, or Lodovicus Brisket, held them. Recites 5845. To hold for ever by the service of a twentieth part of a knight's fee. Rent £7 2s. 6d. Maintaining four English horsemen. Provisions as in 474, substituting Queen's for King's co., and Maryborough for Philipstown. The clause referring to hostings immediately operative.—3 June, xxxvii. (Cal. P. R., p. 332.)

5932 (4814.) Commission to sir John Norries, knt., president of Mounster; to be general and chief leader of the army, especially in the province of Ulster, in the absence of the deputy. With power to punish rebels with fire and sword, to assemble and

lead the forces, and to arm the queen's subjects in Ulster, and
erect or complete the fortifications in the province; to execute
martial law, to treat, grant protections, and promise pardons,
which shall be made good by the lord deputy; to take man's meat
and horsemeat at the usual rates, and do all other things for the
advancement of the service. Recites that the people of Ulster
had rebelled and were murdering and spoiling the queen's subjects.—5 June, xxxvii.

5933 (4820.) Grant (under queen's letter, 1 July, xxxi.) to Edm.
Barrett; of the lands of Charowlougharts, Bodevismeane alias
Farren negate, and Tenemartia, containing two cartrons of land
(rent 5s.), 1 cartron in Charowbeg (2s. 6d.), 1 in Ardenore and
Ardenegienghe (2s. 6d.), 1 in Banealoone (2s. 6d.), 2 in Shane-
raghe (5s.), 1 in Ardlaghes (2s. 6d.), 1 in Lecaknoghor (2s. 6d.),
in the barony of Charowlougharts of Kilsallaghe, 1 cartron of
Kissapirashe (2s. 6d.), Megawhin 1 (2s. 6d.), Charowmeareyeagh-
ter 1 (2s. 6d.), Bragheraghe 1 (2s. 6d.), Chaherdonnellyearaghe 2
(5s.), Charowmeareyeaghter-Glanaloghe 1 (2s. 6d.), Monafalaghe
1 (2s. 6d.), and Derilacraghwaghe 1 (2s. 6d.), co. Kerry, lands of
Donald Geraldaghe M'Gillacudd, of Bodevismeane, slain in
rebellion, and attainted; ½ carucate of land in Kilgobnet (7½d.)
and ½ carucate called Kieppaghe (15d.), in said co., lands of
Donnoghe M'Diermott, of Kilgobnet, slain in rebellion and
attainted; one carucate in Killieaghterqno (2s. 6d.), and ½ of 2
carucates in Termonemeanaghe (3s. 4d.), land of Donald m'Owen
Skootaghe, of Killieaghterqno, in said co., slain and attainted; ½
carucate of Killieaghterqno (15d.), and ½ carucate in Dortkierrye
alias Dromekeere alias Corevanan (15d.), in said co., lands of
Diermot rivas M'Fynnin, of Killieaghterqno, slain in rebellion
and attainted; 1½ carucates in Silxena (3s. 4d.), and 2 carucates
in Cabirmaire (5s.), same co., lands of Teige M'Dermott, of
Silxena, attainted; one carucate in Kilknokaghte, in said co.,
(2s. 6d.), lands of Mortagh Sallogho, of Kilknokaght, attainted;
three parts of a carucate in Faynevisealodig, in said co. (20s.),
lands of Margaret Belade, of same, attainted; one carucate in
Clainelcood, in said co. (2s. 6d.), lands of Diermot Yreaghe, of
Clainelcood, attainted; the site of the monastery of S. Francis,
called Moyne, in the country of Tyrawlye, co. Mayo, with appurtenances (5s.); the ruined castle of Clonelaghan, co. Galway,
and ½ quarter of land, ½ quarter in Corballye, and ½ cartron in
Corballybeg, in said co., parcel of the lands of Malaughlyn
m'Awlye oge O Madden, of Clonolaghan, attainted (6s.); the
third part of Garrydaffe, containing the 18th part of a quarter
of land in Killeboggye, ½ cartron in Charowemore, ½ of ½ quarter
in Ballynorewoaghter and Kilmaiode, near Killowan, in said
co., parcel of the lands of Tho. oge m'Brien M'Teige, of Killeboggye, attainted of felony (20d.); ½ quarter in Lenereaghe, one
cartron each in Gurtyn, Orearhan, Charowmore, and Charowene-
chrranniaghte, lands of Edm. Kyltaghe m'Donnell, attainted, son
and hair of Donnell M'Edmond, of Kyllleboggye, deceased (10s.);
½ of ½ quarter in Templelenan and ½ of Trismocany containing
the ninth part of a quarter of land in Kilkmeyode, in said co.,
lands of Wm. M'Brien, of Tamplelenan, attainted (12d.); a cartron in Cromelen (15d.), a ruined castle called Abbert, and a
cartron adjoining the castle (2s. 6d.), in pledge for £8 with

Oliver oge Frenche, of Galway, merchant, a fourth part of the
castle of Monemeane and ½ of 2 quarters of land in Garbally,
in said co. (2s. 6d.), lands of Brian m'Connor m'Shane Fname,
of Abbert, attainted ; the waste rectory of Charureaghe, co.
Sligo, parcel of the abbey of Conge (5s.) ; lying in co. Mayo
and Sligo ; the carucate of Ballymoyhannala adjoining Drome
Iriell, in the barony of Cargallen, co. Leytrim, parcel of the lands
of Brian O Rworck, attainted (3s. 4d.) ; the castle of Glansleyed
and a quarter of stony land in Glansleyde, co. Clare, of the lands
of Tirrelaugh O Loghlin, of same, attainted (2s. 6d.) ; the rectory
of Killocoan alias Killuckall, in the country of Olontes, co.
Roscommon, parcel of the possessions of the abbey of Elphin
(5s.) ; four quarters of land in Ballym'guearle (20s.), one quarter
in Lisaedufie in Clonecahah (5s.), ⅓ of a quarter in Clonegarrie,
in the country of O Connor Roe, in said co. (3s. 4d.), of the
'and of Hugh m'Tirlaugh roe O Connor, of Clonebryne,
attainted ; the tithes of grain and hay of two quarters of land
in co. Mayo, belonging to the abbey of Rosirks, co. Mayo, and
the tithes of two other quarters in said co., belonging to the
abbey of Strade, in said co. (2s. 4½d.) ; one quarter of land in
Dowereighan, co. Mayo, of the land of Theobald or Tibbot
m'Thomas dufe, attainted (6s. 8d.) ; one quarter in Glanoeaghe,
in said co., of the land of Tho. M'Edmond, of Clontakille, in
said co., attainted (5s.) ; three quarters in Ballyvonell and Tow-
skeart, in said co., of the land of Edm. boye, and Tho. duff, and
Moyler Rourcke m'Ullck, attainted (15s.) ; two polls of land
belonging to the termon or hospital of Kyldallon, co. Cavan, called
hospital lands (6s. 8d.) To hold for ever, in fee farm, by fealty,
in free and common socage. Rent £9 as above. In consideration of injuries sustained in the queen's service.—8 June, xxxvii.
(Cal. P. R., p. 312.)

5934 (4842.) Livery to Mark, son and heir of Edw. Barnewall, of
    Dromnaghe, co. Dublin. Fine £50. Recites inquisitions taken
    9 July and 5 June, xxxii., finding that Edward died seised of
    the manors of Dromnaghe, Balrotherye, Belriade, Ballybrigane,
    co. Dublin, and Ardye, co. Louth.—11 June, xxxvii.

5935 (4818.) Grant (under queen's letter, 1 July, xxxi.) to Edm.
    Barrett, gent. ; of the termon or hospital of Casheltorra, con-
    taining 3½ polls of land, with the tithes, co. Cavan (rent, 18s.),
    the termon of Urrney 3 polls (15s.), the termon of Ballimac-
    chinche alias Ballim'hugh (4d.), the termon of Larras 3 polls
    (15s.), the termon of Annaghgalley ½ poll (2s. 6d.), the termon
    of Larganboy ½ poll (2s. 6d.), with the tithes of all these lands,
    co. Cavan, devolved to the crown by act of parliament ; the
    island of Innishmaine and all lands and islands in Logh Maske,
    and the lands of Ballinechalla lying on the west side of said
    island, containing 4 quarters of land with the tithes, and a
    ruined castle in said island, co. Mayo, parcel of the possessions
    of the house of nuns of Kilcreaght alias Kilcrevania (20s.) ; the
    rectory of Borrakarroe and Ballihean, co. Mayo (5s.), the half
    town of land called Okmark, co. Mayo (5s.), one quarter of land
    called Kilteyne (5s.), a ruined castle and a quarter of land of the
    Twoght (5s.), co. Mayo, with their tithes, possessions of the
    abbey of Ballintober, co. Mayo ; one quarter of land called Kar-
    rownevanle in the town of Coolreaghe (5s.), and one quarter called

1595.   FIANTS—ELIZABETH.

Carrownacloggs in the town of Knocknamannaghe (5s.), co.
Galway, possessions of the abbey of Knockmoye; the church or
chapel of Tamplamoil kiltullaghe, of the third order of Franciscan
friars, two parcels of land called Farrenbridden and Gortna-
gireneasgarde, with the tithes and appurtenances to the said
chapel belonging, in co. Galway, in the queen's hands by its dis-
solution (7½d.); ½ cartron of land in Crevaghe and Adamston,
co. Westmeath, parcel of the lands of Rory O Brenan, of Adamston, attainted (6d.); the rectories of Srure (7s. 1d.), Killocamock
(7s. 1d.), Clonagiss (24s.), Kilmesue (12s. 8d.), Moygowe
(14s. 2d.), Tanenart (9s. 4d.), Tananny (9s. 4d.), Kilglasse (7s.),
and S. Michael of Rabuck (8s. 4d.), co. Longford, possessions of
the priory of the B. V. M., of Loughsewdin. To hold for ever.
Rent £10 4s. 5½d. as above. In consideration of the injuries he
sustained in the queen's service.—16 June, xxxvii. (Cal. P. R.,
p. 318.)

5936 (4821.) Grant (under queen's letter, 3 Feb., xxx.) to Wm.
Browne, of Mahrankan, co. Wexford, esq.; of a tenement and
garden and land in Grenocke (rent 8s.), and land in little Bow-
linton (26s. 4d.), co. Meath, possessions of the monastery of the
B. V. M., Dublin (recites the lease 2060); the glebe land of
Knockmarke, co. Meath (6s.), parcel of the possessions of the
monastery of Thomascourt (recites 3198); lands in Baltrasna,
Bailihiggan, Killaloryn, Moyldrom, Swirins, Grange of Kiltobar,
Ballisowder, and Cowlas, co. Westmeath (36s. 2d.), lands of the
abbey of the B. V. M., of Kilbegan (recites 5539). To hold for
ever, by fealty, in free socage. Rent £8 18s. 6d., as above.—
17 June, xxxvii. (Cal. P. R., p. 341.)

5937 (6559.) Grant to sir Warhams St. Leger, knt.; of the castle
and lands of Cariglyn alias Beaver, containing 4½ ploughlands,
the fishing of Croahaven and Awneldie, the lands of Ballyngarry
7 pl., Ballyrisye 80 acres, and the castle and lands of Carrig-
roghan 4 pl., with appurtenances in co. Cork, containing by estimation 6,000 acres. Saving to the crown the services and
rents belonging to the castle of Carigroghan. To hold the premises except the castle of Carigroghan for ever, in fee-farm, by
fealty, in common socage; and to hold the castle for 999 years.
Rent £33 6s. 8d. Grantee to erect houses for 46 families, of
which, 1 for himself, 3 for freeholders, 3 for farmers, and 31
for copyholders. Other conditions usual in grants to undertakers
in Munster as in 5032. 2 membranes.—17 June, xxxvii. (Cal.
P. R., p. 314.)

5938 (4813.) Commission to Adam, archbishop of Dublin, lord
chancellor, Tho., earl of Ormond and Ossory, lord treasurer, Tho.,
bishop of Meath, Henry Wallop, knt., vicetreasurer, chief justices
Gardener and Dillon, chief baron Napper, Anthony St. Leger,
master of the rolls, N. Walshe, second justice of the Chief Place,
George Burchier, knt., Edward Moore, knt., members of the
privy council, Geoffrey Fenton, knt., principal secretary, Edw.
Brabazon, one of the privy council; to be justices, commissioners,
and keepers of the peace, in the counties of Dublin, Meath,
Westmeath, Kildare, Wexford, Kilkenny, Louth, Queen's co.,
King's co., and Catherlogh, during the absence of the deputy,
Wm. Russell, knt., in Ulster and the northern parts. With
powers as in 2445; the lord chancellor may grant protections.

They may also hear and determine causes in as ample manner as if the lord deputy were present.—18 June, xxxvii.

5939 (4810.) Commission to Arthur Cory, serjeant at laws, and Charles Calthrop, attorney general; to receive of Gerald or Gerard Dillon, clerk of the crown in the Queen's Bench, and John Moore, clerk of the crown in the province of Connaght, the oath of Supremacy.—19 June, xxxvii.

5940 (4824.) License to John Slade, gent, chirographer of the Common Bench; to be absent in England for four months.—21 June, xxxvii. (Cal. P. R., p. 321.)

5941 (4840.) Livery to Alison and Margaret, sisters and heirs of Lucas Tirrell. Fine £7 11s. 4d. Recites an inquisition taken on the morrow of Holy Trinity xx., on the death of Lucas, son and heir of Nich. Tirrell, late of Dublin, finding that he was seised of lands in Eaker, Ballydowde, Balvenston, Tobberboyne, and Loughton, co. Dublin.—23 June, xxxvii. (Cal. P. R., p. 345.)

5942 (4818.) Grant (under queen's letter, 29 March, xxxiv.) to Wm. Ewriace, esq.; of the reversion and remainder after the interest granted to him by 5761 in the town and manor of Castlemarten, co. Kildare. To hold for ever; by the like services and rents by which it was held before the attainder of Maurice Ewriace. - 25 June, xxxvii. (Cal. P. R., p. 339.)

5943 (4828.) License to Wm. Haidon, clerk, treasurer of the cathedral of the Holy Trinity, Dublin; to be absent in England for one year.—29 June, xxxvii. (Cal. P. R., p. 849.)

5944 (4849.) Livery to Philip, son and heir of Patr. Lamporde, late of Ballohure, co. Wexford, gent. Fine £6 13s. 8d.—8 July, xxxvii.

5945 (4825.) License to John Klyot, esq., third baron of the Exchequer; to be absent in England for three months.—23 July, xxxvii. (Cal. P. R., p. 349.)

5946 (5922.) Grant to John Hoy, gent.; of the wardship and marriage of Patrick, son and heir of Robert Barnewall, late of Senkill, co. Dublin, gent.; and custody of his lands during minority. Rent 30s., retaining out of the rent 10s. for support of the minor. Fine £5. Recites Exchequer inquisitions, Carlow No. 6 Eliz., and Dublin No. 227 Eliz.—4 Aug., xxxvii. (Cal. P. R., p. 348.)

5947 (6548.) Grant to captain Robert Collum, esq.; of the lands of
English. Ballynnokemor and Ballymuckebeg, in the parish of Kylloollman in Conallo, in the great county of Limerick, parcel of the toghe of Olehan, late in the tenure of John Suple, attainted, containing 1 quarter; land in Ballyferrais lying in the Grannaghe on the mountain of Slalogher, par. Castellroow alias Newcastle, parcel of the toghe of Meaghan, same co., late of Terlagh and Owen m'Edmond oge M'Shihis, attainted, ½ quarter; land in Glannegowne in the Grannaghe, same parish, late of the said Terlagh and Owen, ½ quarter; the lands of Rathronan and Carrowblloye, par. Rathronan, upon Slalogher in Yeaghtrewgh, called the lowest part of the towghe of Meaghan, late of Richard M'Thomas, of the Pallace, attainted, 1 quarter, same co.; also the patronage of Rathronan, late in the gift of M'Thomas, of the Pallace; land in Ballyferria, par. Ballingarrye, parcel of the toghe of Gortacallagan, late of John Suple and Gibbon roe M'Shane, attainted, 20 acres, same co.; land in

Ballyne, same par. and co., late of Donell backagh Fitz Phillip, attainted, 20 acres; land in Rathnegar and Dromturk, par. Kyllvradane, late of Donogh m'Connogher M'Shihie, attainted, parcel of the half toghe of Drynan, same co., 53 acres; land in Cloneaherryn alias Cloneaherryk, par. Mohownaghe, in the country called Tre[n]lawnaghe, parcel of the toghe of Tawnaghe, late of Thomas m'Phillip M'Gibbon, attainted, 30 acres; land in Monalanaghe, same parish and proprietor, 30 acres; lands in Lyakyllin, Gortakeighe, Gortinlinaghe, Ballynakyllye, two Curraghes, and Bally[w]artaghe, same parish, late of Thomas m'Shane M'Gibbon, attainted, 100 acres; lands in Clonedyne and Clonefarte, same parish and proprietor, 20 acres; land in Ballibranagh, same parish and proprietor, 15 acres; the patronage of Mahowna, late in the gift of the earl of Desmond; a castle and land in Morragan, parcel of the toghe of Donmullin, late of Edmund M'Phillip, attainted, 3 quarters; the lands of Carrowbeg alias Carowbeg Rydall, par. Rakeylle, parcel of the toghe of Farranaheaheraghe, late of Richard Rydall, attainted, 20 acres; burgages in Crogh called Russell's burgages, par. Croghe, late of Patrick Wolf, attainted, 10 acres; the patronage of Croghe, late in the gift of the earl of Desmond; the lands of Croghnemallagh and Cooroglasse, par. Castellnow, parcel of the toghe of Menghan, late of Morrogh m'Brien M'Tirlagh, attainted, 1 quarter; lands called Farrinvollaghe with the site of a water mill, late of the earl of Desmond; 35 acres in the parish or burgage of Ardagh, parcel of the toghe of Ardaghe, one of the eight toghes of Callowghe called church toghes in said county, lands called Berage Ruddery, Minitern, and the Spitill, containing 33 burgage acres, making 18 Irish acres, in the same parish and toghs, Burges land in the same parish and toghe, late of Moriah m'Edmond M'Shane and Gerald M'Davye, of Ardaghe, attainted, 35 acres; land called Dromranaghe alias Dromcananaghe, same parish, 10 acres, parcel of the priory of Rathkeylle; lands called Athis and Moymore, par. Temple Cloe, late of Tirlagh m'Edmond oge M'Shiehie, attainted, 3 quarters; Ballirobbin and Lywaduff, par. Ballingarry, of the lands of John Suple, late of Kyllmoka, attainted, 20 acres; a tenement with appurtenances, in the town of Adare, and land in Clonesherbegg called Peck and Clonecurry, of the lands of Redmund Wale, attainted, 7 acres; lands in Balleolachan and Kennelowre, par. Kyllferris, parcel of the Tarmon lands or church lands of long time concealed, 30 acres; lands in Kyllaconnell and Skahannaghe, parcel of the toghe of Kyllaconnall, one of the eight toghes of Calloghe called church toghes, late of [Richard] Lyaton, 1½ quarter; two messuages in the town of Kyllmallck, of James Fant and Robert Fant, attainted; lands in Balljollan, 1 quarter, and 24 acres in Dallym'kerye, late in the possession of Richard M'Thomas, of the Pallas, and now of Conogher oge M'Shehie; land in Glanstale, late of Donogh m'William oge, attainted, 20 acres; the patronage of Teclogin, late in the gift of the earl of Desmond; land in Adare called Tonnegye and Cappapecood, late of John Suple, attainted, 30 acres, in the said county; also the custom and profit of two fairs or marts in the town of Rakeyle; the abbey of Irrelaghe, co. Kerry, with appurtenances, containing 4 acres of land, 3 orchards, and a garden;

the abbey of Inishfallen, co. Kerry, with appurtenances containing 3 ploughlands or 120 acres arable, whereof one ploughland is called Mauleigh, another Aghachurryn, and another Dennis and Bo[wnerure], with the advowson of the churches of Kyllettle and Kennye morra, same co. ; also the parsonage of Teclagin with the presentation of the vicar, co. Limerick, parcel of the possessions of the late abbey of Donbrodie ; the half ploughland in Rathjordan, co. Limerick, called Cowleahe[ini]e, of the possessions of James Marisca[ll], late of Rathjordan, attainted ; lands of Rath[o]lowen, 30 acres of small measure, and 80 acres of the same measure in Cowrt vecowghe, making in all of Irish measure 20 acres, of the lands of Gerald Fitz Morice, late of Rallingowle, attainted ; the parsonage of Kyllcorpan ; 32 acres in Ballynadoke, 15 acres in Ballingowge, 4 acres in Graig with the the site of a mill there, amounting to 51 acres of small measure making 17 of Irish measure, of the possessions of Thomas Fitz Gerrald, called the Knight of the Valley, attainted ; lands in Garreduffe, in Monaghare, late in the occupation of Tirlaghe m'Edmond oge M'Sheehe, 1 quarter, parcel of the toghe of Gortenughe ; 24 acres of land late of Geoffroy Fitz Tibbot, attainted, in Wellshestowne ; lands in Gortgalboye, Graganmallen, Graganportell, and Shanclogh bane, late of Edmund Bower and William beg m'William oge Ba[ne], attainted, ¼ quarter ; lands in Kylbeg, late of John Suple, 20 acres ; lands in Ballymullen, late of Mulhnory roe, and Thomas m'Phillip M'Gibbon, attainted, 15 acres ; lands in Ballylimy, Clonemolta, Kyllahine, and Illanemore, par. Rakeyle, late of Davyd en Coorik, attainted, 1 quarter ; and land in Digganmore and Digganbegg, par. Mohownaghe, of the lands of Thomas m'Phillip M'Gibbon, attainted, 20 acres, in the said county of Limerick ; all the premises contain 22½ ploughlands and 45 acres.   To hold for ever, by the name of Oullams vale, in fee-farm, by fealty, in common socage.   Rent, £72 3s. English, viz. : for Irrelaghe abbey, 13s. 4d. Irish, for the profit of the fairs, 40s. Irish, for Innishfallen abbey, 53s. 4d. Irish, for the rectory of Teclagyn, 13d. Irish, for the land in Rathjordan, 4s. Irish, and for the rest £66 1s. 3d. starling. Grantee shall erect houses for 32 English families, one to be for himself, 2 for freeholders, 2 for farmers, and 14 for copyholders. Other conditions usual in grants for planting the undertakers in Munster, as in 5032.   3 membranes.—18 Aug., xxxvii.   (Cal. P. R. p. 315.)

5943 (4812.) Commission (under queen's letter, 20 Jan., xxxiii., and letter of the lords of the council in England, 1 June, xxxvii.) to sir Rich. Bingham, knt., chief commissioner of Connaught and Thomond, Tho. Dillon, chief justice of the province, Garrett Commerforde, attorney of the province, Anthony Brabhason, esq., Rob. Fowle, provost marshal of the province, John Crofton, esq., and Francis Shane, esq. ; to enquire by the oaths of jurors what title sir Rich. Bourke, knt., late chieftain alias M'William of Nether Connaght, had, or his son and heir, Theobald Bourke, has to any manors, lands, and hereditaments in the Lower Owles called the barony of Boresmoule, co. Mayo, in the province of Connaght ; similarly Miles Stanton fitz Miles, of Castle Karrye, in the barony of Karry, co. Mayo ; Morogh O Flahertie, and Donall in coggie O Flahertie, sons to Grana ny Mally, in the

1593.   FIANTS—ELIZABETH.

barony of Ballnehenny, co. Galway; Owen O Mally, Dermod
O Mally, and Donall O Mally, in the manors, lands, islands, and
hereditaments of Owil O Mallis called the Uppermost Owle
O Mallis, on Mayo With the intention of the queen accepting
their surrender of the premises, and regranting them by letters
patent.—20 Aug., xxxvii.

5949 (4809.) Livery to Alexander, son and heir of John Barrington,
of Callanaghs, Queen's co., gent Fine, £10. Recites an inquisition in the Exchequer, 20 Jan., xxxvii, finding that John,
who died 15 Sept., 1593, was seised of the lands of Callenagh,
Ballyhillane, Rahinduffe and Capceke, Corcagh, Kylvane and
Dromloo, Queen's co.; that Alexander was his son and heir,
of full age, and married, and that Johanna Barrington was his
widow.—38 Aug.; xxxvii.

5950 (4811.) Grant to George Sherlock; of a fourth part of
a moiety of the lands of Kilrushe, co. Limerick, containing ½
a carucate (rent, 1s.), parcel of the lands of James Nugent, late
of Kilrush, yeoman, attainted; Kilmelagie, Dromellaghe,
Kyappendick, and Mongfoyne, 1½ carucates, lands of Donnogh
roe M'Teige, of Kivalahie, slain in rebellion, (12s.); a third part
of a moiety of one carucate in Cwige, same co., the lands of
[Iwraem'ShaneO Hee, Donel] m'Edmond [O Hee], and Malaghlin
Skinnoghe m'Conogher O Hee, yeomen, late of Liskanmill, slain
in rebellion, (3s.); land in Rathduffe, parcel of the lands of
Donald m'Edm. O Riordan, of Rathcluffe, slain in rebellion,
(10d.); ½ of half a carucate in Rakivintane, same co., parcel of
the lands of Mahon and Murrogh [O] Brien fitz Miriartagh, of
Rakinvintan, attainted, (3s.); ¼ of a carucate in Oshirdavin,
same co., parcel of the lands of Moriartagh m'Donnogh m'Knogher
Cnowaghe, slain in rebellion, (2s.); ½ of a carucate in Ballifarren,
(2s.); ¼ of a quarter of land in Cloghfionde, (16⅓d.); land in
Cloghy or Cloghin (4s.), same co.; lands of Kennedy M'Brian.
of Whiteston, attainted, which Wm. M'Nicholas mortgaged to
said Kennedy O Brien for 1½ cows; 8 acres in Boggotston, same
co., parcel of the lands of Maurice and John Boggott, of Boggoda-
ton, attainted, mortgaged to them by Edm. Baggat, of same
place, for 8 cows (16d.); 8 acres in Boggodston, parcel of the
lands of Dermod O Flannor, of same, attainted, mortgaged to him
by said Edm. Baggott for 16 cows (16d.); ½ of a carucate in
Killdonnell, parcel of the lands of Donnogh Obegg and Owru
O Haleran, of same, attainted, which Laughlan reagh O Halran
mortgaged to [ ]ver O Brien for 8 cows, on whose death the
land descended to the said Donnogh and Owin, sons of Laughlin,
according to the custom there, (2s.); certain land granted in
mortmain to the church of S. Michael in the barony of
Carginglishe, occupied by persons called Canverbini, in same co.,
(8s.); land in Grainegonaghe, same co., parcel of the land of Wm.
(son) of Terence M'Brien alias Wm. m'Tirlaughe O Brien, late
of Grainegonaghe, attainted, (12d.); certain land in Cloghin and
Whiteston, same co., mortgaged by Nich. O Riordan, gent, to
Kennedy M'Brien, of Whiteston, attainted, (8d.); land in
Glancallie or Glanstalie, same co., parcel of the lands of Donnogh
oge, of same, attainted, (20d.); a ruined house near the castle of
Holy Trinity in Youghall, co. Cork, parcel of the lands of Gerald,
earl of Desmond, attainted, and for a time allotted as part of the

                                                                    s

jointure of Katherine, countess of Desmond, (12d.); two other waste messuages in Youghell, parcel of the lands of the said earl, put in pledge to Rob. Tobin for £4, (6d.); ½ a carucate of land called Minaighter, in the barony of Imokelly, co. Cork, parcel of the lands of the said earl, (3s.); an old ruined castle in the city of Cork, on the south part, in a place called the key of Cork, near the wall of the city, parcel of the queen's ancient inheritance, (3s.); lands of Athmickmange near Ballimarten, in Imokelly, co. Cork, parcel of the lands of John fitz Jeamis Fitz Geralde, of Geraldine, attainted, (2s. 8d.); land called Owlye lying by Castellishine, co. Cork, parcel of the lands of Euginius alias Owin m'Edm. oge M'Shihie, attainted, (12d.); lands in Ballyanandrohid, co. Cork, parcel of the lands of John Fitzgerald, of Geraldine, attainted, (5s. 2d.); one carucate in the barony of Imokellie called Rathcowrry, co. Cork, parcel of the lands of Maurice fitz Edmond, of the Geraldines, attainted, (5s.); the tithes of Loughdowan, co. Waterford, parcel of the lands of the late hospital of S. John of Jerusalem in Ireland, (6d.); land in Newton, co. Waterford, parcel of the lands of the late house of S. Katherine by Waterford, (2s.); one quarter of land called Chyarowntobber, being a fourth part of a ploughland, co. of Cross Tipperary, parcel of the lands of S. John of Jerusalem in Ireland, (6s.); Croilard containing one acre of great measure of the country making four acres of the standard measure of Ireland, same co., parcel of the lands of the priory of Fethard, co. Tipperary, (12d.); ¼ acre great measure in Gortogowne, co. Cross Tipperary, (6d.), land called Donnogh m'Thomas M'Donnall's great acre, by the lands of Cahire, co. Tipperary (12d.), 9 acres of said measure adjoining Lyma on the south, Slevegroth on the west, the river Shower on the north, and Beladrohed on the north (sic), in co. Tipperary, (9s.), 2½ acres of said measure, adjoining the Great Grange and Ballin'adam on the east, the river Shower on the south and west, and the lands of Cahire on the north, (2s. 6d.), 3½ acres of great measure in Killmelagh, co. Tipperary, adjoining Kiedaghe on the east and north, the lands of the lord (?) of Cahire on the south, and Cloghbredi on the west, (3s. 6d.), land in Litlegrange, same co., between the lands of Cahire on the south and west, Herrois on the north, Morreis's land on the east (2s.), 1½ acre of like measure in Loghnamorraghe, same co., (18d.), parcels of the lands of the priory of Cahir, same co.; the lands of Liskillin, Gorteaka, Gortyna, Lanaheaghe, Ballowortamvyc, Rollanekiliye, and Corrughe, co. Limerick, lands of Tho. m'Shane M'Gibbon, of Liskillin, attainted, (30s. 3d.); lands in Ballipiers, same co., parcel of the lands of Gibbon roe m'Shane oge, late of Kilmore, same co., attainted, which Roris M'Shea hold in mortgage, (5s.); land in Balliroe, same co., parcel of the lands of David Backagh Fitz Philip, of same, attainted, (5s.); Rathroan, and Charowbloos, same co., parcel of the lands of Rich. M'Thomas, of Pallaice, same co., attainted, (5s.); lands in Ardanghe, same co., parcel of the lands of Maurice M'Edmond, of same, attainted (7s. 6d.); ¼ of a carucate in Dromlarie, Garimorie, and Grainea, same co., lands of Donald m'Conlo O Brien, of Grainegonnoghe, same co., attainted (2s.); lands in Clonescroghan, same co., parcel of the lands of James

1595.	FIANTS—ELIZABETH.

and Stephen Wuale, of Clonsoroghan aforesaid, attainted (10s.);
all tithes of the late house of friars preachers of Rosbrekan
co. Kilkenny (3s. 4d.); 12 carucates of Mowskerrylowgher in
[the lordship] of Desmond, in co. Cork and Kerry, parcel of the
lands of Donnell m'Fynin M'Owin, of same, attainted (37s. 4d.);
the rectory of Corioghlan in the barony of Roscommon, extending in the parishes of Kiltrcakan, Clonfealaghe or Clonfan-
lagh, and Templeroaghs, co. Roscommon, parcel of the possessions
of the late house of nuns of Ardkearne, in same co. (40s.); lands
of Agbonaghe and Droninsahie, on Longford, parcel of the
lands of Tirlough m'Donoghie M'Gerald, attainted of felony
(3s 11½d.); ½ of a cartron called Aghlistowill in Knoakbwy, same
co., containing 3 acres, lands of Murrogh duff M'Qwin, attainted
of felony (14d.); the tolls of the market held weekly in Kill-
mayod or Kilneiodie, same co., parcel of the queen's ancient
inheritance (2s. 6d.); ½ of a cartron in Loghill, same co., parcel
of the lands of Teige m'James O Farrall, attainted (1s. 9d.); all
the premises were for long time concealed from the crown. To
hold for ever, in free socage. Rent £13 10s. 8½d., distributed
as above.—31 Aug., xxxvii. (Cal. P. R., p. 341.)

5851 (5974.) Surrender by Richard Chechster, gent. ; of the office
English. of controller of the customs of Tredatho, held under 5406. Signed
Richard Chechester.—Dated 31 Aug., xxxvii.
    Attached (5973) is commission dated 16 Aug., xxxvii., to Tho.
Sherley, knt., Rich. Wilbraham, Nich. Syllyarde, Rich. Vandraye,
esquires, George Lacester and Tho. Dod, merchants ; to accept the
surrender.

5852 (4790) Grant to Gerald Moore, esq.; of the office of principal
registrar and writer of the acts of the high commissioners for
ecclesiastical causes and clerk of recognisances taken before them.
To hold during good behaviour, with such fees as Wm. FitzWilliams or any other had. Not to be removed, as is 4976.—8 Sept.,
xxxvii. (Cal. P. R., p. 350.)

5853 (4793.) Grant to James Ware, gent. ; of the office of clerk of
the pleas of the Exchequer. To hold during good behaviour, with
such fees as John Kernon had. Not to be removed, as in 4976.—
9 Sept., xxxvii. (Cal. P. R., p. 344.)

5854 (6294.) Surrender by Wm. James ; of the offices of controller
English. of the customs, and searcher and ganger of Dublin and
Drogheda, held under 5154.—Dated 1 June, xxxvii. Signed
W. James. Executed 16 Sept., xxxvii.
    Attached is commission dated 15 Aug., xxxvii., to Tho.
Sherley, knt., Rich. Wilbraham, Nich. Syllyarde, Rich. Van-
draye, esquires, George Lecester and Tho. Dod, merchants, to
accept the surrender. (Cal. P. R., p. 320.)

5855 (4801.) Grant to Philip Hore, gent. ; of the office of treasurer,
general receiver, and bailiff of the lordship and county of Wexford. To hold during good behaviour, with a fee of £20 from
the death of Walter Jerbard, deceased, and all other fees that
James Sherlock, Henry Drasott, or Wm. and Walter Jerbard had.
Not to be removed, as in 4976.—24 Sept., xxxvii.

5856 (4853.) Lease (under queen's letter, 10 Aug., xxxvi.) to Henry
English. Broncard, esq.; of the impost on wines imported, and the rents
due on any lease previously made of them. To hold for 12 years
from Michaelmas 1593. Rent £2,000 English. He shall not

alien to any of the Irishry. If any breach occur between the
queen and the countries of the kings of Spain or France, whereby
the import of wines is impaired, the rent to be discharged, and the
lessee only to pay on a true account made on oath by him,
and subject to the oversight of the queen's collectors. The queen
may revoke the lease at pleasure. Lessee to give security
annually for the rent.—5 Oct., xxxvii.

5957 (4800) Grant to Wm. Daniport alias Wm. Smythe; of the
office of controller of the customs of Dublin. To hold during
good behaviour, with such fees as Wm. James or Tho. Plunckot
had. Recites 5154 and 5954. Not to be removed, as in 4976.
—10 Oct., xxxvii. (Cal. P. R. p. 321.)

5958 (4802) Grant to Edw. Manwaringe, gent.; of the offices of
searcher and ganger in the town and port of Drogheda. To hold
during good behaviour, with such fees as Wm. James had.
Recites 5154 and 5954. Not to be removed, as in 4976.—10
Oct., xxxvii. (Cal. P. R. p. 830.)

5959 (4803) Grant to Edw. Manwaringe, gent.; of the offices of
searcher and ganger in the city and port of Dublin. To hold
during good behaviour, with such fees as Wm. James had.
Recites 5154 and 5954. Not to be removed, as in 4976.—10 Oct.,
xxxvii. (Cal. P. R. p. 820.)

5960 (4804) Grant to Rob. Leceater, gent.; of the office of con-
traller of the customs of Drogheda. To hold during good
behaviour, with such fees as Wm. James had. Recites 5154 and
5954. Not to be removed, as in 4976. Given free from the
great seal to Rob. Leceater for that he is the Right Ho.
the L. Chancellor's servant, and one of the attorneys of the
court of Chancery.—10 Oct., xxxvii. (Cal. P. R. p. 821.)

5961 (4841) Livery to Theobald, son and heir of Henry Walshe,
late of Killencarge, co. Dublin, gent. Fine £6 10s.—24 Oct.,
xxxvii.

5962 (4836) License to sir Henry Bagnaall, knt., marshal of the
Lagan army; to be absent in England for two months, for recovery of his
health, and to take with him 15 horsemen in the queen's pay.—
31 Oct., xxxvii. (Cal. P. R. p. 349.)

5963 (4817) Grant (under queen's letter, 22 May, xxxvii.) to Henry
Wallop, knt., treasurer at wars; of the site of the house of friars
of Eneworthy, a mill by the site, an orchard there, land on the
east side of the said house, co. Wexford; the manor, ruined
castle, and lands of Eneworthie, an old weir there, lands of
Garran, Kilkenan, Loughwarty, Barrykrow and Ballynsparke,
the customs of boards, laths, timber, and boats carrying victuals,
the customs of lodges during the fairs, and of things bought and
sold, and fishings and all other appurtenances of the manor and
house of friars. Recites lease to Edm. Spenser, 3785, conveyance
from Spenser to Rich. Synot, 9 Dec., 1681, and lease to Synot,
4002. To hold for ever, by the service of a twentieth part of a
knight's fee. Rent £18 6s. 4d. He shall not alienate to
any of Irish nation, without license.—4 Nov. xxxvii. (Cal. P.
R. p. 819.)

5964 (4830) Grant (under queen's letter, 22 May, xxxvii.) to Henry
Wallop, knt., treasurer at wars; of the site of the house of
friars of the Trinity, of Adare, co. Limerick, called the house of
friars of the redemption of captives, seven cottages, certain

gardens in or near the burgage of Adare, and other lands in the fields of Adare among the lands of the burgesses, by estimation one carucate of land, half a carucate in Castelrobart, half a carucate in Kylcoille alias Kilkrile with a mill, the tithes of the rectory of Adare, collected in Adare, Ballyfinter, Choro, Cloghran, Twothe Ourragh, Kilhiag, Roer, Killoryll, Ballyrobart, Bally-faning, and half Ballypall, (the altarages and two coples of grain for the curate excepted), also a wair or fishery for salmon in the river May, possessions of the said house, co. Limerick. The site of the house of friars of S. Augustin of Adare, with all houses and lands belonging to it in Adare, half a carucate in said parish called Moddultie alias Modollaghie and its tithes, and the tithes of certain other land, and a wair or fishery for salmon on the said river May, possessions of said house, in co. Limerick. The site of the abbey of Newnagh, co. Limerick, with its appurtenances. The monastery of S. Katherine alias the monastery of Kaylagh alias Negaylagh, co. Limerick, with its appurtenances. The site of the house of friars minor of the order of S. Francis in Adare, co. Limerick, containing, besides the buildings, a great park on the west of the house surrounded by stone walls, and two other parks with mud walls and ditches, in which parks trees are growing, a water mill, a wair or fishing place for eels and salmon in the said river May, and all other possessions of the said house in co. Limerick. To hold for ever, by fealty, in free and common socage. Rent, for the house of friars minor £4, and for the remainder £32 17s. 8d. Maintaining two horsemen. He shall not alien to any Irish on pain of forfeiture; he shall fulfil the covenants in other patents for inhabiting with Englishmen. He shall build 15 houses, one to be for granies and his assigns with 300 acres, 2 for free tenants with 300A. each, a fourth for a farmer with 300A., and the remainder for copyholders, cottiers, and tenants at will, to whom he is to allot 25 or 50 acres each, with conditions of re-entry as in 5032. The principal house may be aliened only to English persons for ever. He shall have power of exporting victual, imparking 120 acres, and freedom from charges and customs, as in 5032. Recites 5116. In consideration of his great expense in building on the premises for the defence of those parts.—4 Nov., xxxvii.

5965 (4769.) Grant to Rowland Delahide, gent.; of the office of constable of the gaol lately erected in the town of Inish, co. Clare. To hold during good behaviour, with such fees as Patr. Morgan, deceased, had. Not to be removed, as in 4976.—5 Nov., xxxvii.

5966 (5923.) Grant to Peter Barnewall, of Lexpopell, gent.; of the wardship and marriage of Richard, son and heir of Theobald Walsh, late of Carrickmayne, co. Dublin, gent.; and custody of his lands, during minority. Rent £7 Irish. Fine £15 English. —8 Nov., xxxvii. (Cal. P. R., p 322.)

5967 (6257.) License to Alexander Cosbye; to alienate to any English person his lands as granted by 5825. Fine 20 marks sterling.—10 Nov., xxxvii.

5968 (6258.) License to Alexander Cosbye; to alienate to Thomas Corkelie, knt., his lands as in 5825. Granted without fine to supply legal defects in the preceding fiant. Torn.—10 Nov., xxxvii.

1595.   FIANTS—ELIZABETH.

5969 (4849.) Grant to Henry Jolly, of Dublin, gent ; of the office *English* of master gunner. To hold during good behaviour in as ample manner as Rob. Paynter held it, with the stipend of 20d. sterling a day, that is, 12d. for himself, and 8d. for a man to attend him. Not to be removed, as in 4070.—23 Dec., xxxviii. (Cal. P. R., p. 377.)

5970 (4880.) Lease (under commission, 16 May, xxxvi.) to John *English* Eustace, gent. ; of the tithes of the rectory of Newton, co. Meath, the tithes of Rathnallia, the tithes of the town of Galtrym, parcel of the rectory of Galtrym, same co., and two parts of the tithe turf there, possessions of the monastery of S. Peter of the New-towne by Trym ; the tithes of Artealande, the tithes of Surdwal-leston, parcel of the rectory of Kill, co. Kildare, half the tithes of the rectory of Lucan and Waspaylerton, co. Kildare, possessions of the monastery of Thomascourt ; Gibbonston, parcel of the lands of the late viscount Baltinglas, attainted ; lands in Knockmarcke, co. Meath, parcel of the possessions of the late hospital of S. John of Jerusalem. To hold for 21 years. Rent £25 0s. 8d. Provisions as in 4939.—31 Dec., xxxviii. (Cal. P. R., p. 370.)

1595–6.

5971 (4850.) Grant to Rich. Cooke, gent. ; of the office of clerk of court, prothonotary, and keeper of the writs and records before the commissioners, and clerk of the crown and peace, and clerk of the peace and of assizes, in the province of Connaught and Thomond. To hold during good behaviour, with the usual fees, as Roger Waffer or John More had. Not to be removed, as in 4975.—7 Jan., xxxviii. (Cal. P. R., p. 388.)

5972 (4882.) Commission to sir Henry Wallop, knt., vice-treasurer, *English* and sir Rob. Gardener, knt., chief justice ; to repair towards Drohedagth or Dundalk, or other part of Lowth or Ulster, and treat with Hugh earl of Tirone, and O'Donell, and conclude articles or compositions for a peace, and promise them and their followers the queen's pardon. The Commissioners may grant safe conducts. The lord deputy had appointed to treat with them on the 8th of January at Drogheda or Dundalk, but O'Donell being not likely to come there, the present commission is issued.—8 Jan., xxxviii.

5973 (4871.) Pardon to Alexander Barnewall, of Luxton, Chr. Barnewall, of Arrotixston, and Peter, son and heir of John Barne-wall, of Lespople, gent., and of Janet his wife ; of alienations of the lands of Lespople and Dromynesfelde, co. Dublin, and Derver, co. Louth. Recites inquisitions finding that these lands had been alienated, without license, by George Kenton, of Bothiston, gent., to said Alexander and Christopher, to the use of John and Janet, with remainder to Peter. Fine £66 1s. 8d., as well for the alienation as for the profits of the lands since the taking of of the inquisitions.—10 Jan., xxxviii. (Cal. P. R., p. 357.)

APPENDIX III.

CHANGES in PLACES of DEPOSIT of PAROCHIAL RECORDS.

I.—Parishes, the Records of which have been transferred to the Public Record Office in the years 1882–3.

Parish, Church, or Chapel.	County.	Vols.	Baptisms.	Marriages.	Burials.	Date of Removal.
Aghanloo,	Londonderry,	2	1827–1851	1829–1849	1828–1851	1882
Ahamplish,	Sligo,	2	1811–1843	—	1815–1840	1882
Assey,	Limerick,	1	1780–1841	1781–1843	1719–1843	1882
Ardbraccan,	Meath,	2	1792–1845	1791–1845	1791–1845	1882
Ardmayle,	Tipperary,	1	1818–1875	1820–1840	1815–1874	1882
Athassell, or Hollamurry,	Tipperary,	3	1804–1880	1805–1844	1855–1877	1882
Altmagh,	Queen's,	2	1820–1882	1816–1874	1820–1844	1882
Ballinaboy,	Cork,	4	1816–1872	1820–1840	1816–1840	1882
Ballycahane,	Limerick,	1	1824–	1875–	—	1882
Ballynakill,	Waterford,	5	1822–1841	1815–1840	1793–1841	1882
Ballyroan,	Cork,	2	1843–1857	—	1816–1875	1882
Ballyvourney,	Cork,	1	1818–1843	1843–1844	1843–1849	1882
Bally,	Antrim,	5	1806–1843	1804–1845	1824–1843	1882
Burrishoole,	Tipperary,	1	1787–1841	1787–1844	1779–1843	1882
Camus (Bann),	Londonderry,	3	1816–1877	1834–1844	1807–1877	1882
Celbridge, or Kildrought,	Kildare,	1	1777–1841	1779–1840	1787–1877	1882
Clonmeen,	Cork,	2	1766–1841	—	1784–1840	1882
Clonmore,	Carlow,	2	1826–1841	1826–1877	1827–1841	1882
Cork—St. Anne, Shandon. Foundling Hospital Chapel,	Cork,	13	1772–1842	1772–1844	1776–1842	1882
Drehidferain,	Limerick,	4	1810–1844	1811–1841	—	1882
Dunmore,	Galway,	5	1815–1875	1814–1840	1854–1874	1882
Dunshaughlin,	Meath,	5	1678–1882	1777–1841	1717–1882	1882
Enrigh Portelan,	Tyrone,	2	1814–1882	1816–1845	1814–1879	1882
Faughart,	Louth,	1	1840–1842	—	1840–1842	1882
Fenagh,	Leitrim,	1	1829–1857	1834–1849	1840–1844	1882
Garrane Mausoleum (also for Rostellan).	Cork,	1	1840–1857	—	1840–1878	1882
Girley,	Meath,	2	1848–1840	1841–1844	1840–1842	1882
Green,	Limerick,	5	1779–1840	1780–1840	1779–1841	1882
Hollymount,	Down,	1	1810–1842	—	—	1882
Moretown,	Wexford,	2	1809–1842	1805–1843	1804–1843	1882
Reedy,	Armagh,	2	1740–1871	1740–1844	1812–1841	1882
Kilardan,	Cork,	2	1809–1842	1809–1847	1809–1841	1882
Kilcully,	Cork,	1	1844–1849	—	—	1882
Moyrus,	Kerry,	2	1803–1841	1804–1879	1804–1879	1882
Killeagan,	Antrim,	1	1843–1843	—	—	1882
Killeshandra,	Cork,	2	1840–1875	1840–1841	1843–1842	1882
Killeedy,	Cork,	2	1740–1840	1774–1847	1770–1877	1882
Kilmurry,	Galway,	1	1873–1843	1825–1844	1822–1841	1882
Kilcoursey,	Tipperary,	2	1840–1843	1841–1843	1843–1843	1882
Kilvakydn,	Leitrim,	1	1824–1843	1823–1841	1823–1843	1882
Kilwaughter and Cormastle,	Antrim,	1	1871–1843	1820–1844	1834–1843	1882
Laskagh,	Kildare,	4	1830–1843	1830–1843	1879–1879	1882
Lavey,	Cavan,	1	1824–1843	1830–1843	1830–1843	1882
Lismalin,	Tipperary,	5	1801–1842	1806–1844	1809–1843	1882
Listellin,	Kilkenny,	1	1824–1879	1830–1840	1827–1829	1882

I.—Parishes, the Records of which have been transferred to the Public Record Office in the years 1882-3—continued.

Parish, Church, or Chapel.	County.	Vols.	Baptisms.	Marriages.	Burials.	Date of Removal.
Louth.	Louth.	4	1720–1871	1771–1840	1787–1883	1882
Middleton.	Cork.	4	1689–1843	1685–9–1844	1695–1843	1884
Mothel.	Waterford.	1	1798–1879	1797–1879	1794–1879	1882
Nobber.	Cork.	1	1812–1870	1812–1868	1820–1870	1882
Newbliss.	Monaghan.	9	1841–1878	—	1837–1877	1882
Ossuath.	Louth.	3	1636–1883	1639–1844	1689–1883	1883
Oran.	Roscommon.	1	1833–1841	1839–1815	1833–1871	1882
Rouvin.	Galway.	1	1843–1861	—	—	1842
Rowe.	Kilkenny.	9	1762–1880	1819–1871	1826–1882	1841
St. Luppan's, Cork.	Cork.	1	1666–1887	—	—	1881
Streete.	Longford.	4	1799–1849	3772–1816	1793–1849	1842
Timoleague.	Cork.	3	1680–1879	1839–1843	1839–1843	1883
Slavin.	Fermanagh.	9	1824–1875	1824–1843	1889–3872	1883
Stabannon.	Louth.	8	1844–1883	1763–1844	1879–1883	1883
Taghmon.	Westmeath.	1	1806–1849	1802–1843	1800–1844	1880
Trecton.	Cork.	9	1765–1874	1763–1845	1765–1875	1843
Tulloh.	Clare.	9	1806–1882	1836–1844	1805–1842	1879
Whitechurch.	Cork.	1	1874–1874	1847–1844	1831–1873	1883

II.—Parishes, the Records of which have been returned from the Public Record Office of Ireland to the former custody of the respective Incumbents under Retention Orders, during the years 1882-3.

Ballymore Eustace.
Castlecomer and Castlecomer Colliery.
Clones.
Dundalk.
Finnagh.
Kenly.

Kilfergus.
Kilmilin.
Kilmood.
Minemagh.
Kiltarara.
Maaroon.

Muff.
Newblies.
Oregus.
Molando Chapel, Dublin.
Shrule.
Whitechurch, Dublin.

III.—Parishes in which the Parochial Records have been retained under Retention Orders in the years 1882-3.

Abbeyleix.
Aghadowney.
Aghaturcher.
Ardamine.
Ballyadams.
Ballyeglish.
Ballyhacourty.
Bumlin.
Clonmel (Cloyne).
Camber, Upper.
Delvin.

Derg.
Desertmartyn.
Drumkelagun.
Dromore (Dromore).
Drumakena.
Drumkeeran.
Ferragh.
Glyns.
Inishmacaan.
Kilrootenna.
Kildare.

Kilmakelear.
Kilmanagh.
Kilmaghdin.
Listowel.
Magairasbridge.
Quivy.
Roscrea.
St. George, Belfast.
Swanlinbar.
Tipperary.

DUBLIN: Printed by ALEX. THOM & Co. (Limited), 87, 88, & 89, Abbey-street,
The Queen's Printing Office,
For Her Majesty's Stationery Office.

STATE OF BAYS

ON

EAST AND WEST SIDES OF RECORD TREASURY,

31st DECEMBER, 1841.

www.ingramcontent.com/pod-product-compliance
Lightning Source LLC
Chambersburg PA
CBHW030629030726
47497CB00006B/1704